She HULK
LAWS
of Attraction

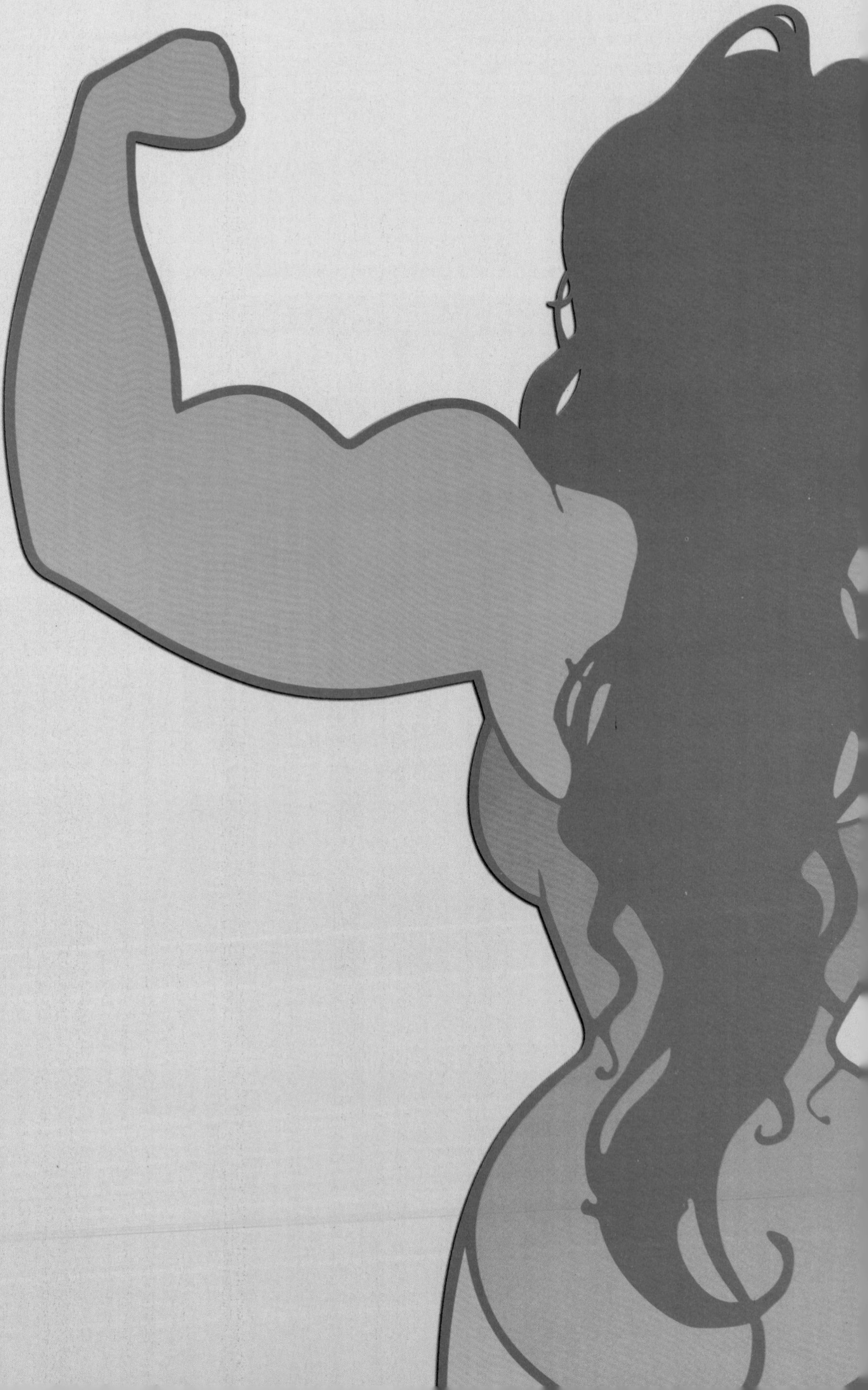

She-HULK

LAWS of Attraction

WRITER: Dan Slott

ISSUE #6-7
ARTIST: Will Conrad

ISSUE #8
ARTIST: Paul Smith

ISSUE #9
PENCILS: Paul Smith
INKER: Joe Rubinstein

I MARRIED A MAN-WOLF
BREAKDOWNS: Ron Frenz
FINISHES: Sal Buscema

ISSUES #10-13
PENCILS: Rick Burchett
INKS: Nelson (Issue #10) &
Cliff Rathburn (Issue #11-13)

COLORS: Avalon's Dave Kemp
LETTERS: Dave Sharpe
COVER ART: Greg Horn
ASSISTANT EDITORS: Molly Lazer & Aubrey Sitterson
ASSOCIATE EDITOR: Andy Schmidt
EDITOR: Tom Brevoort

COLLECTION EDITOR: Jennifer Grünwald
ASSISTANT EDITOR: Michael Short
ASSOCIATE EDITOR: Mark D. Beazley
SENIOR EDITOR, SPECIAL PROJECTS: Jeff Youngquist
SENIOR VICE PRESIDENT OF SALES: David Gabriel
BOOK DESIGNER: Patrick McGrath
VICE PRESIDENT OF CREATIVE: Tom Marvelli

EDITOR IN CHIEF: Joe Quesada
PUBLISHER: Dan Buckley

6

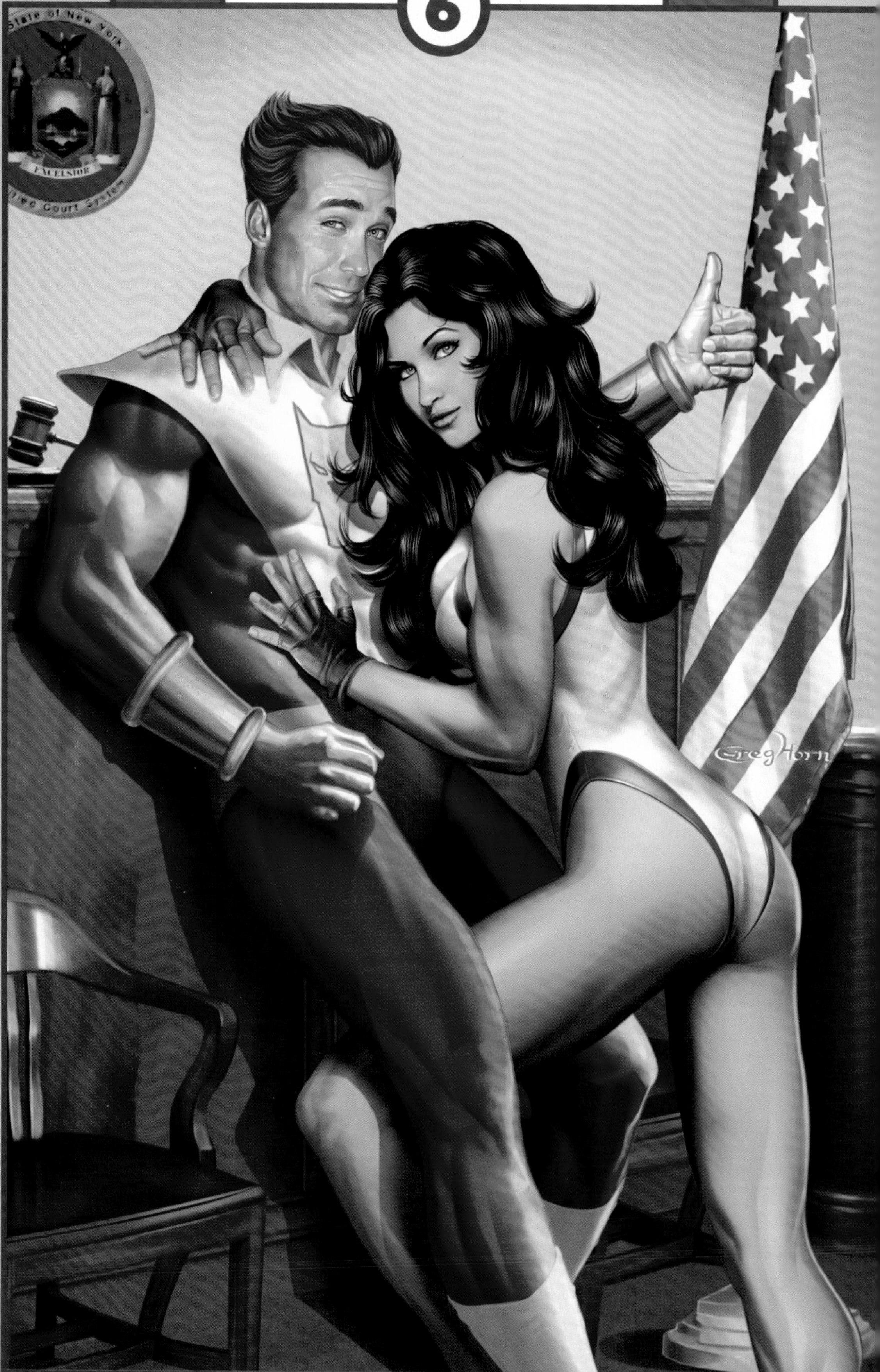
State of New York
EXCELSIOR
Greg Horn

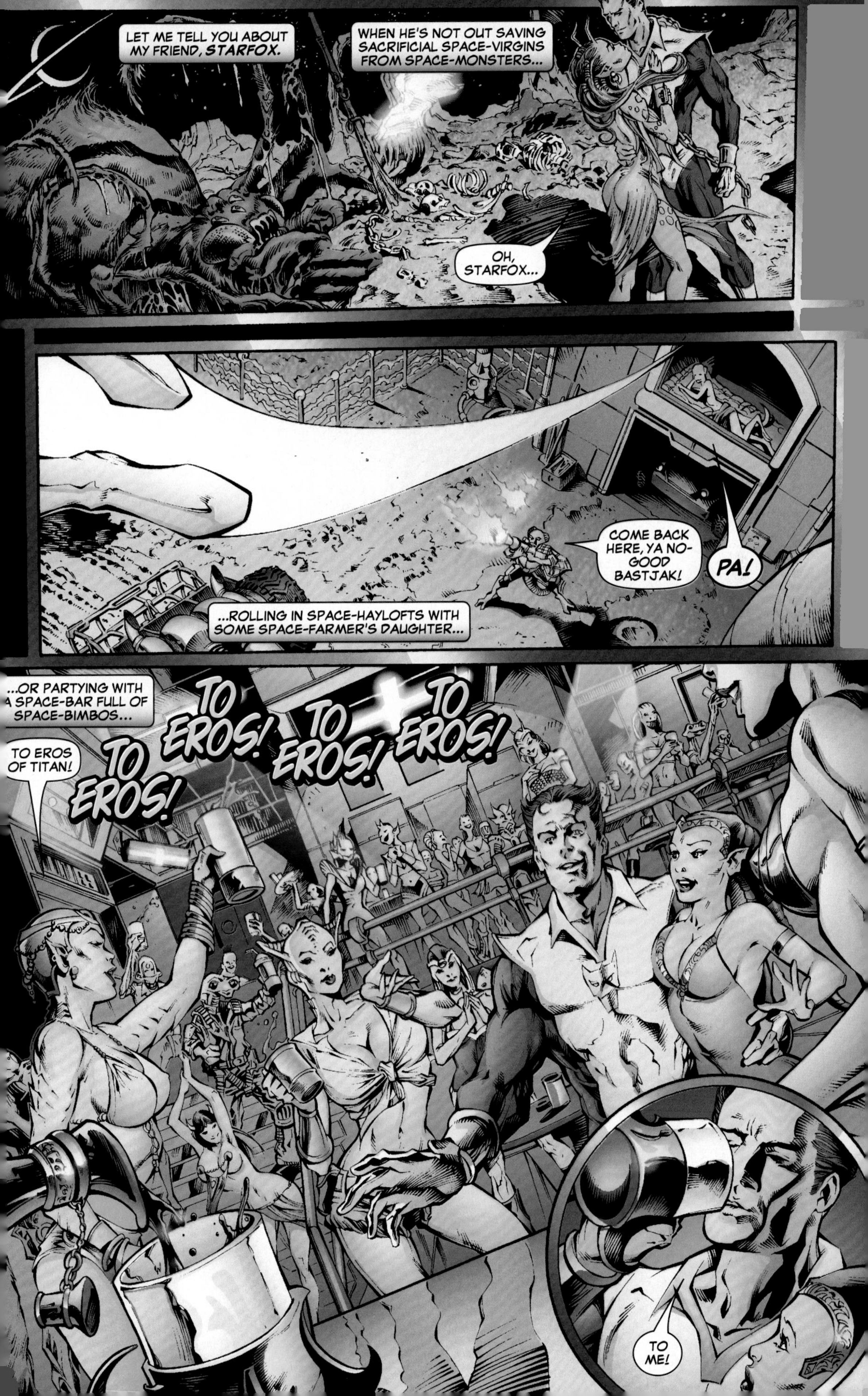
LET ME TELL YOU ABOUT MY FRIEND, STARFOX.
WHEN HE'S NOT OUT SAVING SACRIFICIAL SPACE-VIRGINS FROM SPACE-MONSTERS...
OH, STARFOX...
COME BACK HERE, YA NO-GOOD BASTJAK!
PA!
...ROLLING IN SPACE-HAYLOFTS WITH SOME SPACE-FARMER'S DAUGHTER...
...OR PARTYING WITH A SPACE-BAR FULL OF SPACE-BIMBOS...
TO EROS OF TITAN!
TO EROS!
TO EROS!
TO EROS!
TO EROS!
TO ME!

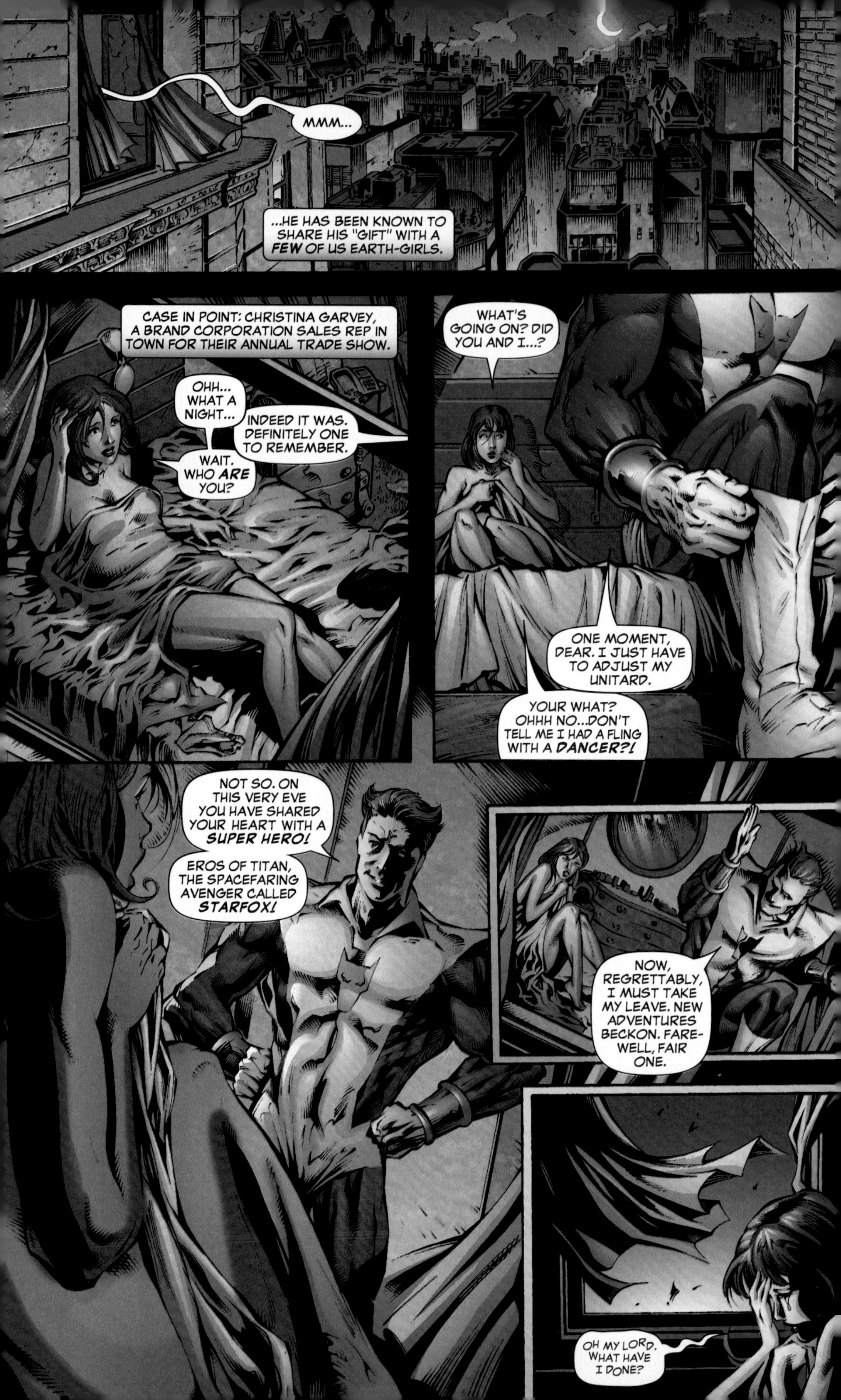
MMM...
...HE HAS BEEN KNOWN TO SHARE HIS "GIFT" WITH A FEW OF US EARTH-GIRLS.
CASE IN POINT: CHRISTINA GARVEY, A BRAND CORPORATION SALES REP IN TOWN FOR THEIR ANNUAL TRADE SHOW.
OHH... WHAT A NIGHT...
INDEED IT WAS. DEFINITELY ONE TO REMEMBER.
WAIT. WHO ARE YOU?
WHAT'S GOING ON? DID YOU AND I...?
ONE MOMENT, DEAR. I JUST HAVE TO ADJUST MY UNITARD.
YOUR WHAT? OHHH NO...DON'T TELL ME I HAD A FLING WITH A DANCER?!
NOT SO. ON THIS VERY EVE YOU HAVE SHARED YOUR HEART WITH A SUPER HERO!
EROS OF TITAN, THE SPACEFARING AVENGER CALLED STARFOX!
NOW, REGRETTABLY, I MUST TAKE MY LEAVE. NEW ADVENTURES BECKON. FARE-WELL, FAIR ONE.
OH MY LORD. WHAT HAVE I DONE?

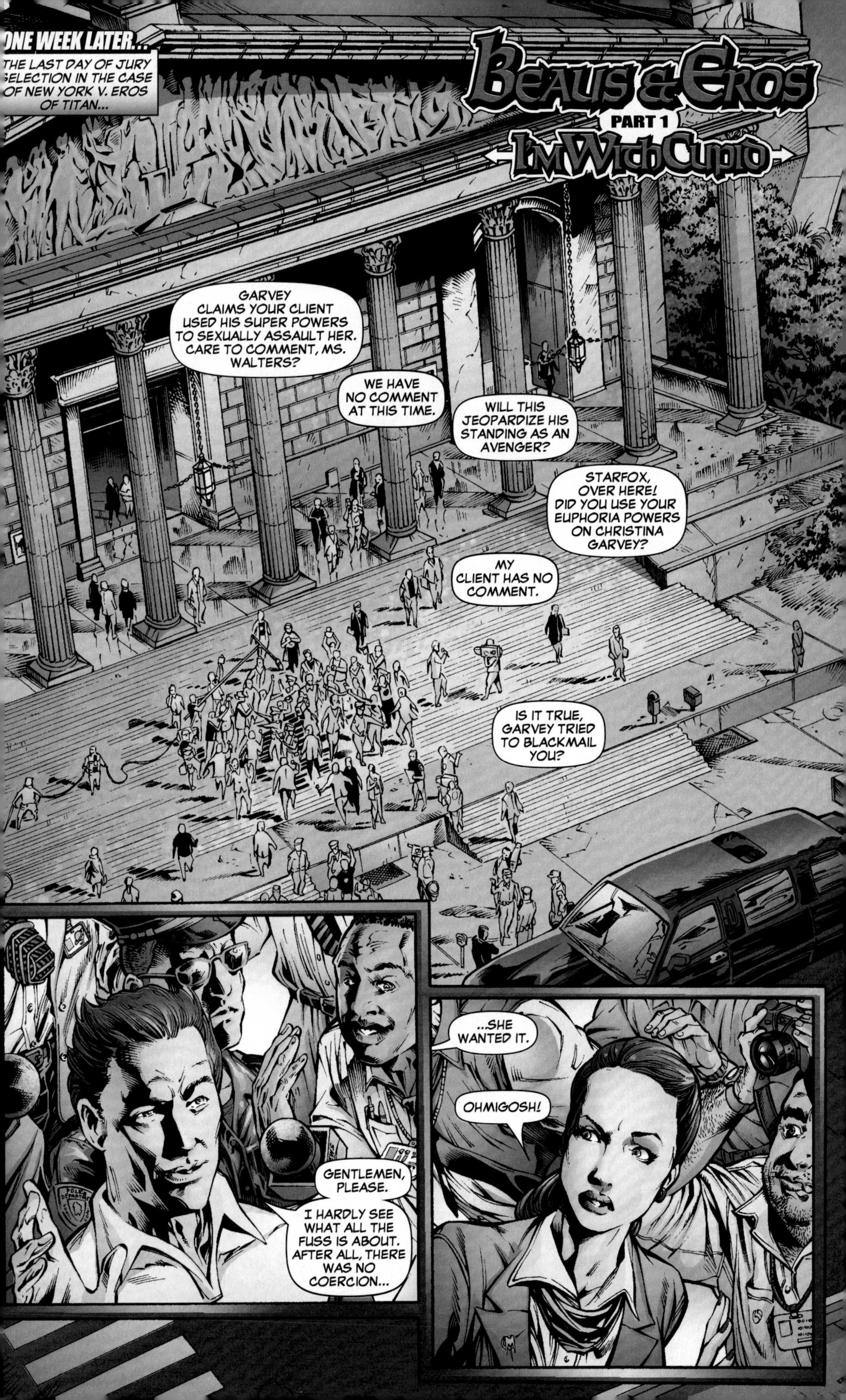
ONE WEEK LATER...
THE LAST DAY OF JURY SELECTION IN THE CASE OF NEW YORK V. EROS OF TITAN...
BEAUS & EROS
PART 1
I'M WITH CUPID
GARVEY CLAIMS YOUR CLIENT USED HIS SUPER POWERS TO SEXUALLY ASSAULT HER. CARE TO COMMENT, MS. WALTERS?
WE HAVE NO COMMENT AT THIS TIME.
WILL THIS JEOPARDIZE HIS STANDING AS AN AVENGER?
STARFOX, OVER HERE! DID YOU USE YOUR EUPHORIA POWERS ON CHRISTINA GARVEY?
MY CLIENT HAS NO COMMENT.
IS IT TRUE, GARVEY TRIED TO BLACKMAIL YOU?
GENTLEMEN, PLEASE.
I HARDLY SEE WHAT ALL THE FUSS IS ABOUT. AFTER ALL, THERE WAS NO COERCION...
...SHE WANTED IT.
OHMIGOSH!

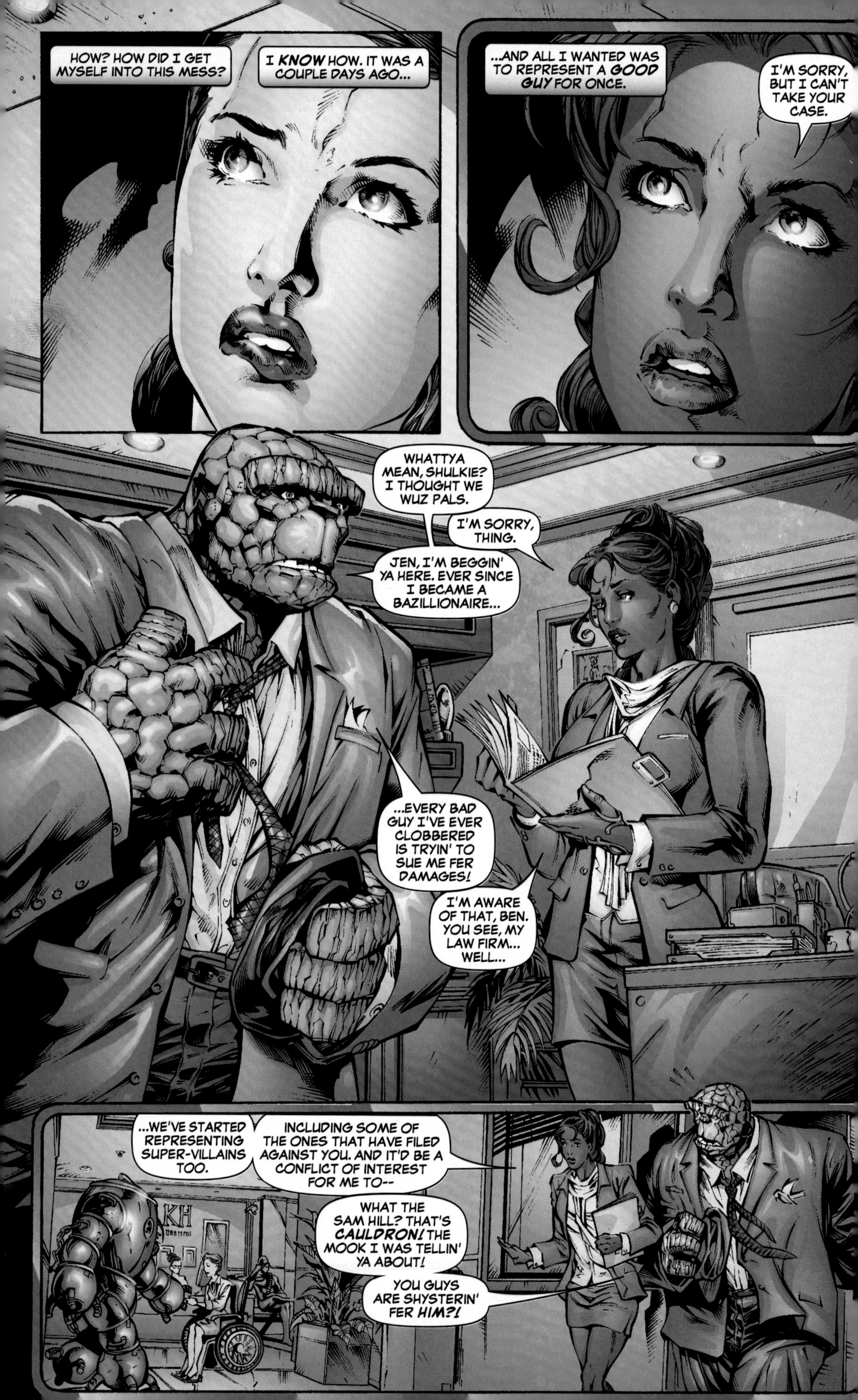
HOW? HOW DID I GET MYSELF INTO THIS MESS?
I KNOW HOW. IT WAS A COUPLE DAYS AGO...
...AND ALL I WANTED WAS TO REPRESENT A GOOD GUY FOR ONCE.
I'M SORRY, BUT I CAN'T TAKE YOUR CASE.
WHATTYA MEAN, SHULKIE? I THOUGHT WE WUZ PALS.
I'M SORRY, THING.
JEN, I'M BEGGIN' YA HERE. EVER SINCE I BECAME A BAZILLIONAIRE...
...EVERY BAD GUY I'VE EVER CLOBBERED IS TRYIN' TO SUE ME FER DAMAGES!
I'M AWARE OF THAT, BEN. YOU SEE, MY LAW FIRM... WELL...
...WE'VE STARTED REPRESENTING SUPER-VILLAINS TOO.
INCLUDING SOME OF THE ONES THAT HAVE FILED AGAINST YOU. AND IT'D BE A CONFLICT OF INTEREST FOR ME TO--
WHAT THE SAM HILL? THAT'S CAULDRON! THE MOOK I WAS TELLIN' YA ABOUT!
YOU GUYS ARE SHYSTERIN' FER HIM?!

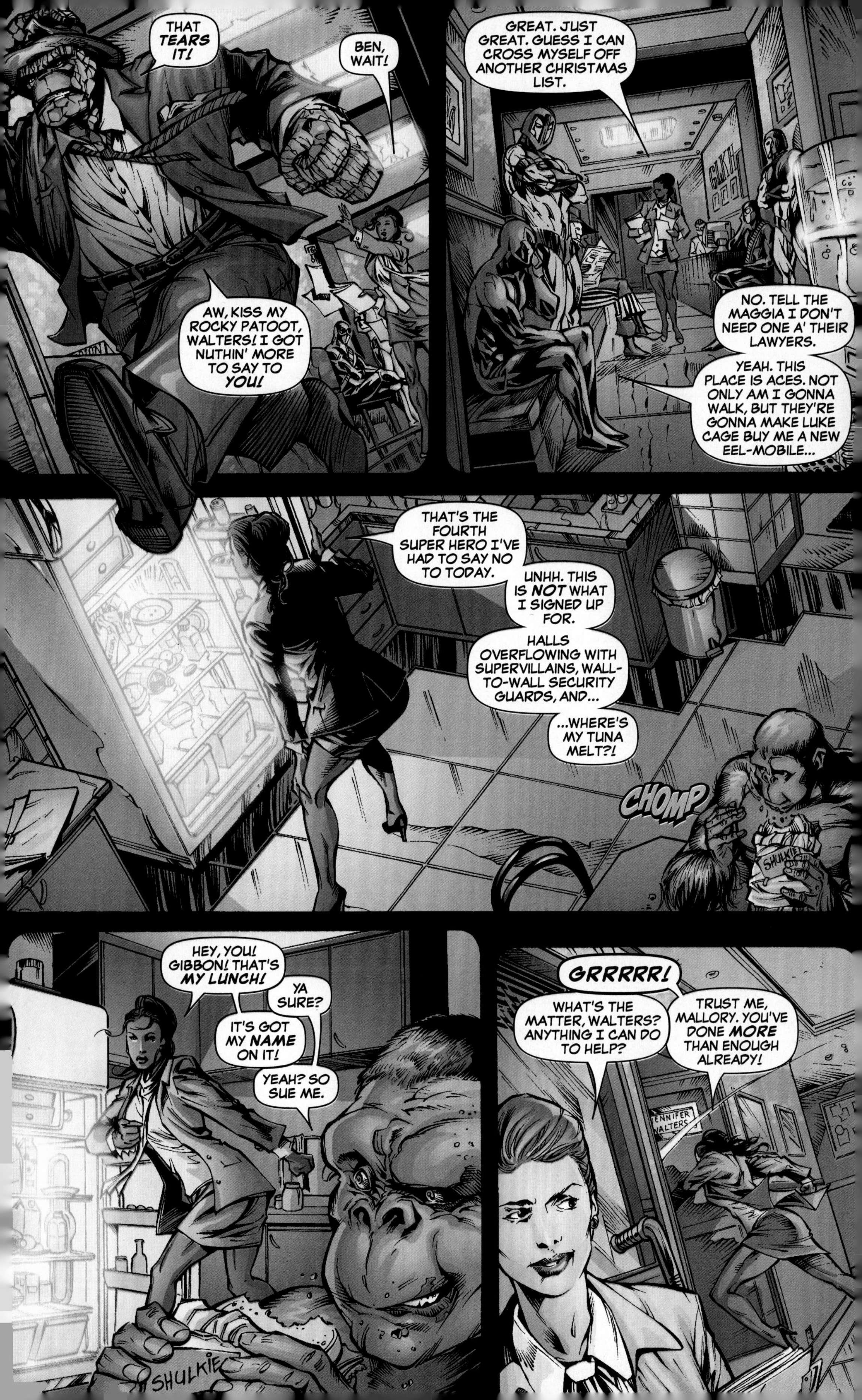
THAT TEARS IT!
BEN, WAIT!
AW, KISS MY ROCKY PATOOT, WALTERS! I GOT NUTHIN' MORE TO SAY TO YOU!
GREAT. JUST GREAT. GUESS I CAN CROSS MYSELF OFF ANOTHER CHRISTMAS LIST.
NO. TELL THE MAGGIA I DON'T NEED ONE A' THEIR LAWYERS.
YEAH. THIS PLACE IS ACES. NOT ONLY AM I GONNA WALK, BUT THEY'RE GONNA MAKE LUKE CAGE BUY ME A NEW EEL-MOBILE...
THAT'S THE FOURTH SUPER HERO I'VE HAD TO SAY NO TO TODAY.
UNHH. THIS IS NOT WHAT I SIGNED UP FOR.
HALLS OVERFLOWING WITH SUPERVILLAINS, WALL-TO-WALL SECURITY GUARDS, AND...
...WHERE'S MY TUNA MELT?!
CHOMP
SHULKIE
HEY, YOU! GIBBON! THAT'S MY LUNCH!
YA SURE?
IT'S GOT MY NAME ON IT!
YEAH? SO SUE ME.
SHULKIE
GRRRRR!
WHAT'S THE MATTER, WALTERS? ANYTHING I CAN DO TO HELP?
TRUST ME, MALLORY. YOU'VE DONE MORE THAN ENOUGH ALREADY!
JENNIFER WALTERS

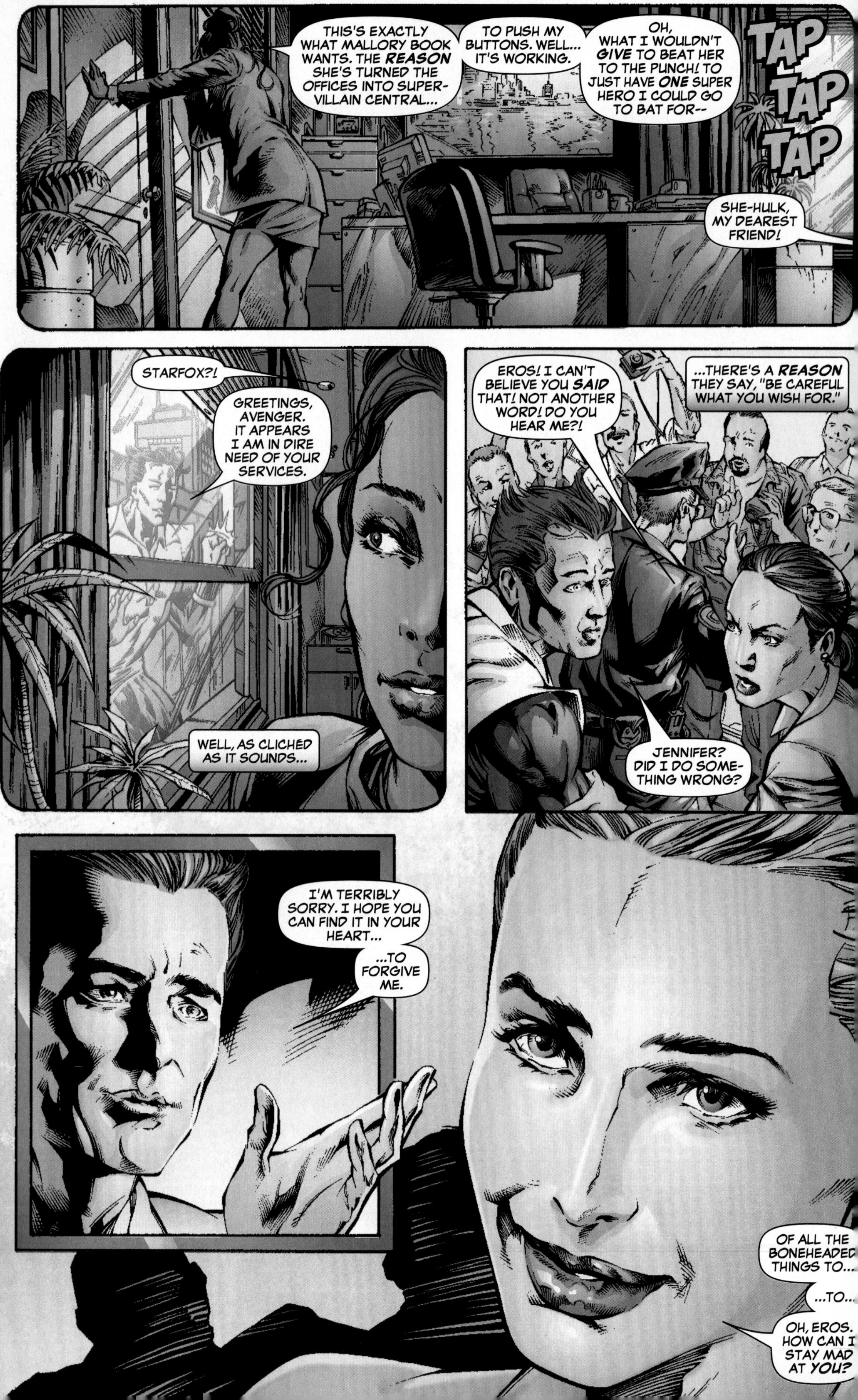
THIS'S EXACTLY WHAT MALLORY BOOK WANTS. THE REASON SHE'S TURNED THE OFFICES INTO SUPER-VILLAIN CENTRAL...
TO PUSH MY BUTTONS. WELL... IT'S WORKING.
OH, WHAT I WOULDN'T GIVE TO BEAT HER TO THE PUNCH! TO JUST HAVE ONE SUPER HERO I COULD GO TO BAT FOR--
TAP TAP TAP
SHE-HULK, MY DEAREST FRIEND!
STARFOX?!
GREETINGS, AVENGER. IT APPEARS I AM IN DIRE NEED OF YOUR SERVICES.
WELL, AS CLICHED AS IT SOUNDS...
...THERE'S A REASON THEY SAY, "BE CAREFUL WHAT YOU WISH FOR."
EROS! I CAN'T BELIEVE YOU SAID THAT! NOT ANOTHER WORD! DO YOU HEAR ME?!
JENNIFER? DID I DO SOME-THING WRONG?
I'M TERRIBLY SORRY. I HOPE YOU CAN FIND IT IN YOUR HEART...
...TO FORGIVE ME.
OF ALL THE BONEHEADED THINGS TO...
...TO...
OH, EROS. HOW CAN I STAY MAD AT YOU?

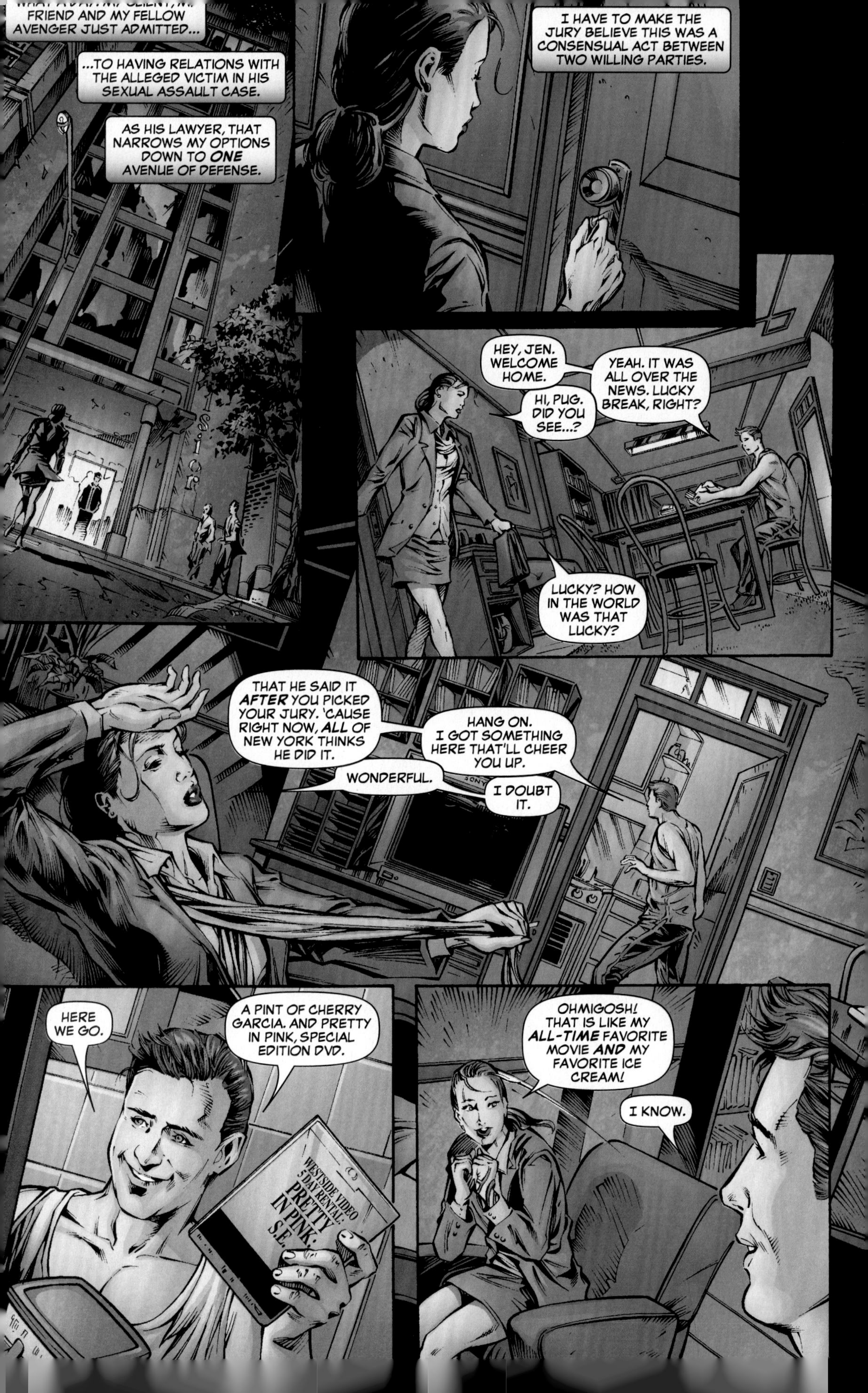
FRIEND AND MY FELLOW AVENGER JUST ADMITTED...
...TO HAVING RELATIONS WITH THE ALLEGED VICTIM IN HIS SEXUAL ASSAULT CASE.
AS HIS LAWYER, THAT NARROWS MY OPTIONS DOWN TO ONE AVENUE OF DEFENSE.
I HAVE TO MAKE THE JURY BELIEVE THIS WAS A CONSENSUAL ACT BETWEEN TWO WILLING PARTIES.
HEY, JEN. WELCOME HOME.
HI, PUG. DID YOU SEE...?
YEAH. IT WAS ALL OVER THE NEWS. LUCKY BREAK, RIGHT?
LUCKY? HOW IN THE WORLD WAS THAT LUCKY?
THAT HE SAID IT AFTER YOU PICKED YOUR JURY. 'CAUSE RIGHT NOW, ALL OF NEW YORK THINKS HE DID IT.
WONDERFUL.
HANG ON. I GOT SOMETHING HERE THAT'LL CHEER YOU UP.
I DOUBT IT.
HERE WE GO.
A PINT OF CHERRY GARCIA. AND PRETTY IN PINK, SPECIAL EDITION DVD.
WESTSIDE VIDEO 5 DAY RENTAL: PRETTY IN PINK S.E.
OHMIGOSH! THAT IS LIKE MY ALL-TIME FAVORITE MOVIE AND MY FAVORITE ICE CREAM!
I KNOW.

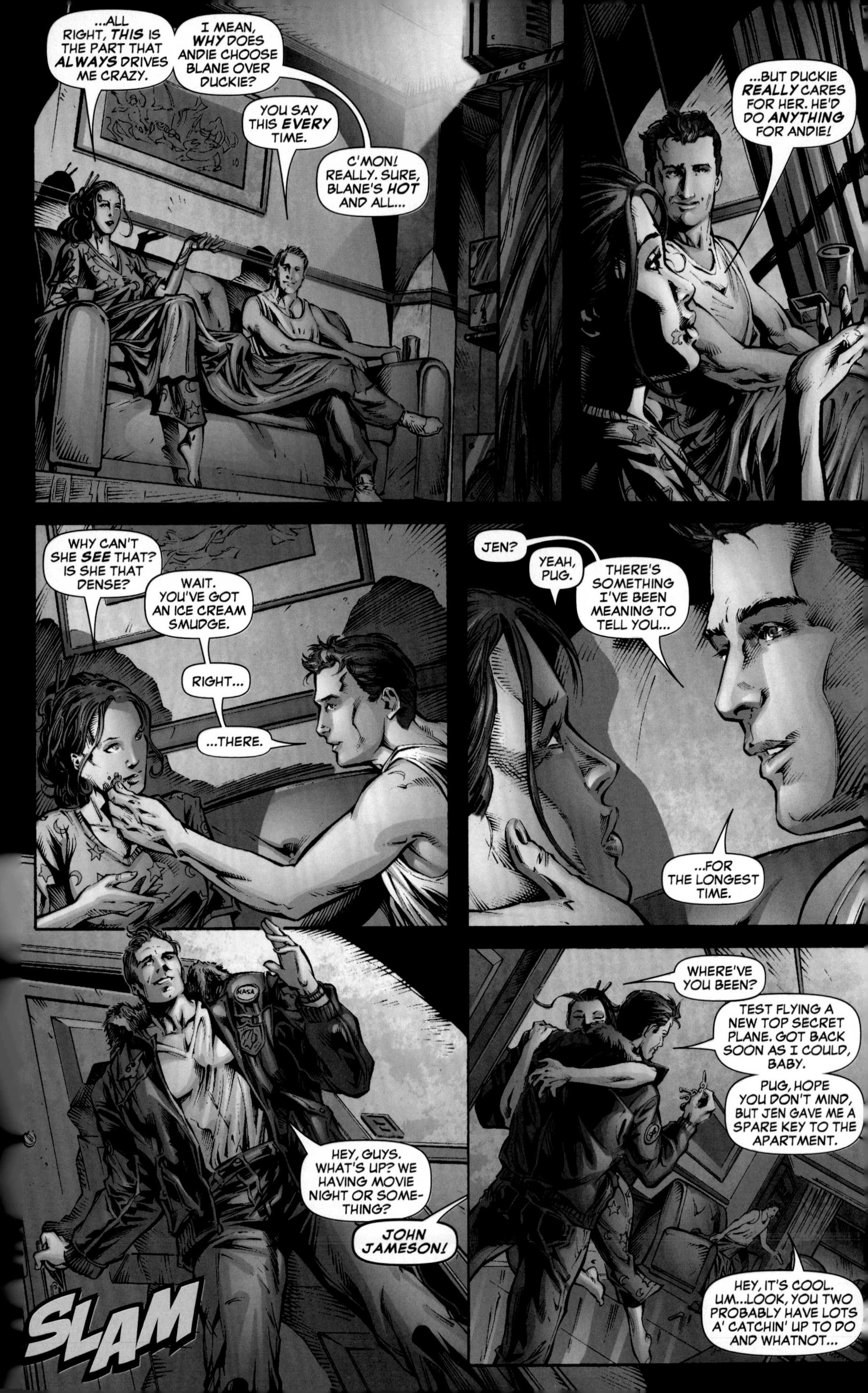
...ALL RIGHT, THIS IS THE PART THAT ALWAYS DRIVES ME CRAZY.
I MEAN, WHY DOES ANDIE CHOOSE BLANE OVER DUCKIE?
YOU SAY THIS EVERY TIME.
C'MON! REALLY. SURE, BLANE'S HOT AND ALL...
...BUT DUCKIE REALLY CARES FOR HER. HE'D DO ANYTHING FOR ANDIE!
WHY CAN'T SHE SEE THAT? IS SHE THAT DENSE?
WAIT. YOU'VE GOT AN ICE CREAM SMUDGE.
RIGHT...
...THERE.
JEN?
YEAH, PUG.
THERE'S SOMETHING I'VE BEEN MEANING TO TELL YOU...
...FOR THE LONGEST TIME.
SLAM
HEY, GUYS. WHAT'S UP? WE HAVING MOVIE NIGHT OR SOME-THING?
JOHN JAMESON!
WHERE'VE YOU BEEN?
TEST FLYING A NEW TOP SECRET PLANE. GOT BACK SOON AS I COULD, BABY.
PUG, HOPE YOU DON'T MIND, BUT JEN GAVE ME A SPARE KEY TO THE APARTMENT.
HEY, IT'S COOL. UM...LOOK, YOU TWO PROBABLY HAVE LOTS A' CATCHIN' UP TO DO AND WHATNOT...

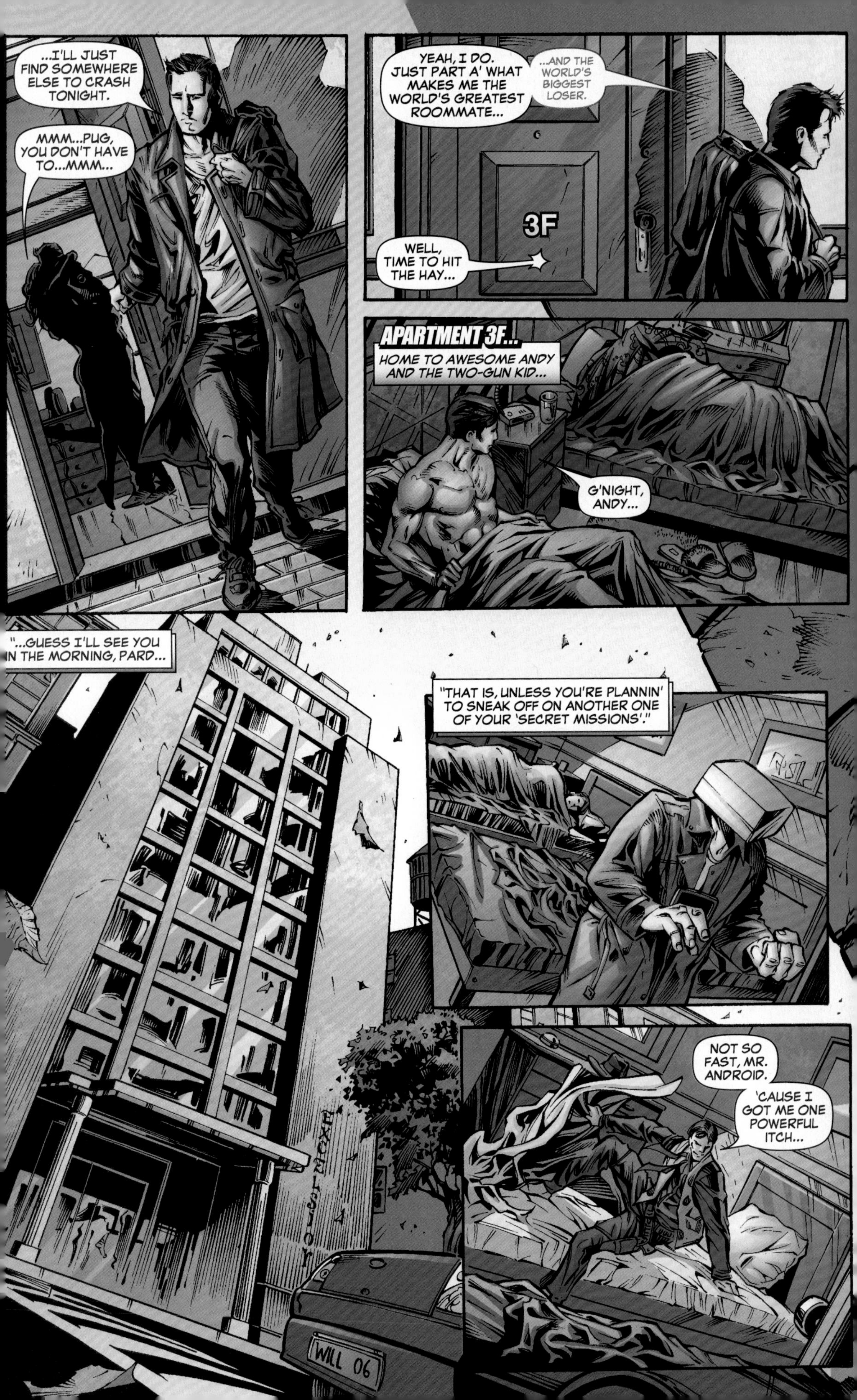
...I'LL JUST FIND SOMEWHERE ELSE TO CRASH TONIGHT.
MMM...PUG, YOU DON'T HAVE TO...MMM...
YEAH, I DO. JUST PART A' WHAT MAKES ME THE WORLD'S GREATEST ROOMMATE...
...AND THE WORLD'S BIGGEST LOSER.
3F
WELL, TIME TO HIT THE HAY...
APARTMENT 3F...
HOME TO AWESOME ANDY AND THE TWO-GUN KID...
G'NIGHT, ANDY...
"...GUESS I'LL SEE YOU IN THE MORNING, PARD...
"THAT IS, UNLESS YOU'RE PLANNIN' TO SNEAK OFF ON ANOTHER ONE OF YOUR 'SECRET MISSIONS'."
NOT SO FAST, MR. ANDROID.
'CAUSE I GOT ME ONE POWERFUL ITCH...
WILL 06

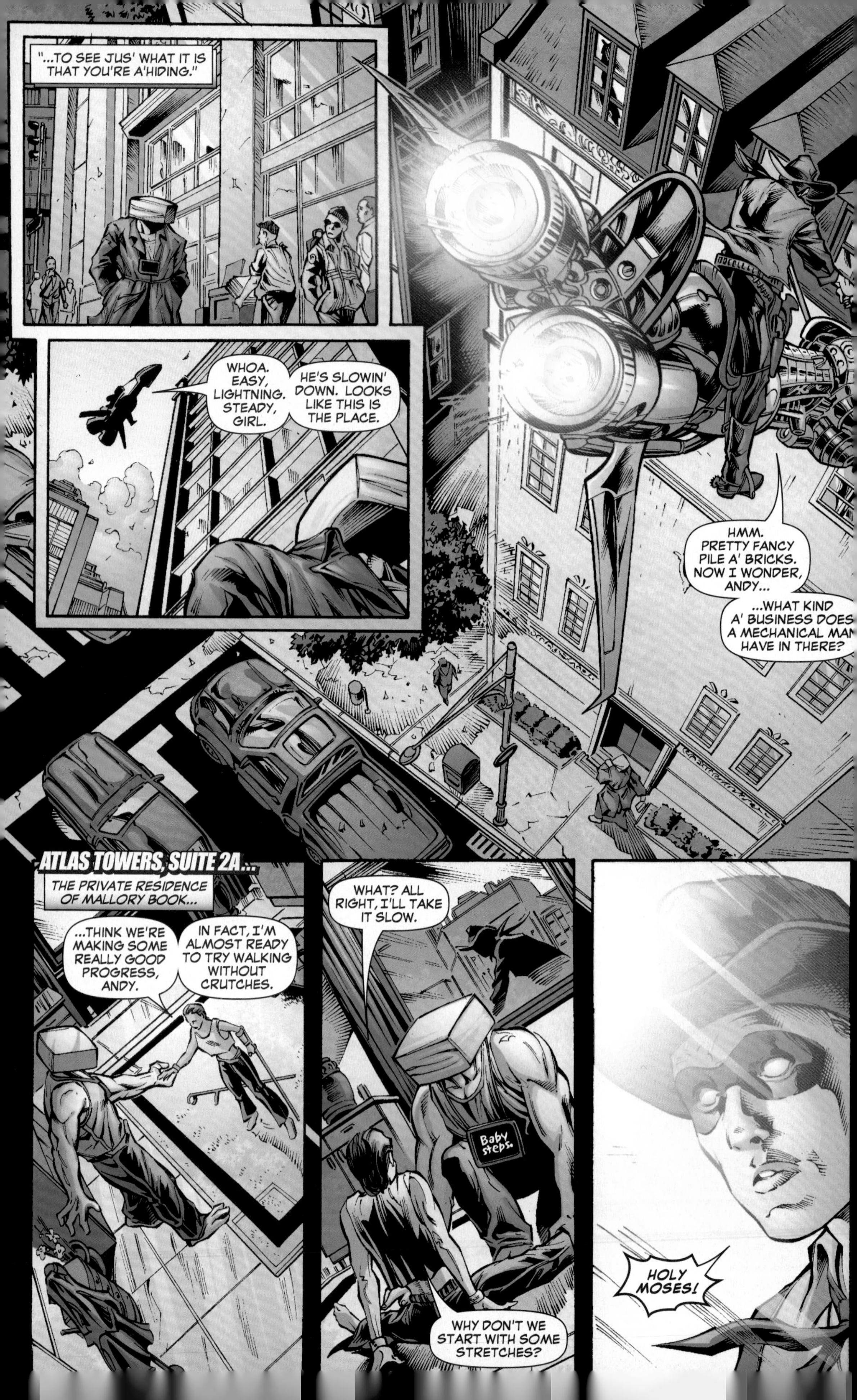
"...TO SEE JUS' WHAT IT IS THAT YOU'RE A'HIDING."
WHOA. EASY, LIGHTNING. STEADY, GIRL.
HE'S SLOWIN' DOWN. LOOKS LIKE THIS IS THE PLACE.
HMM. PRETTY FANCY PILE A' BRICKS. NOW I WONDER, ANDY...
...WHAT KIND A' BUSINESS DOES A MECHANICAL MAN HAVE IN THERE?
ATLAS TOWERS, SUITE 2A...
THE PRIVATE RESIDENCE OF MALLORY BOOK...
...THINK WE'RE MAKING SOME REALLY GOOD PROGRESS, ANDY.
IN FACT, I'M ALMOST READY TO TRY WALKING WITHOUT CRUTCHES.
WHAT? ALL RIGHT, I'LL TAKE IT SLOW.
Baby steps.
WHY DON'T WE START WITH SOME STRETCHES?
HOLY MOSES!

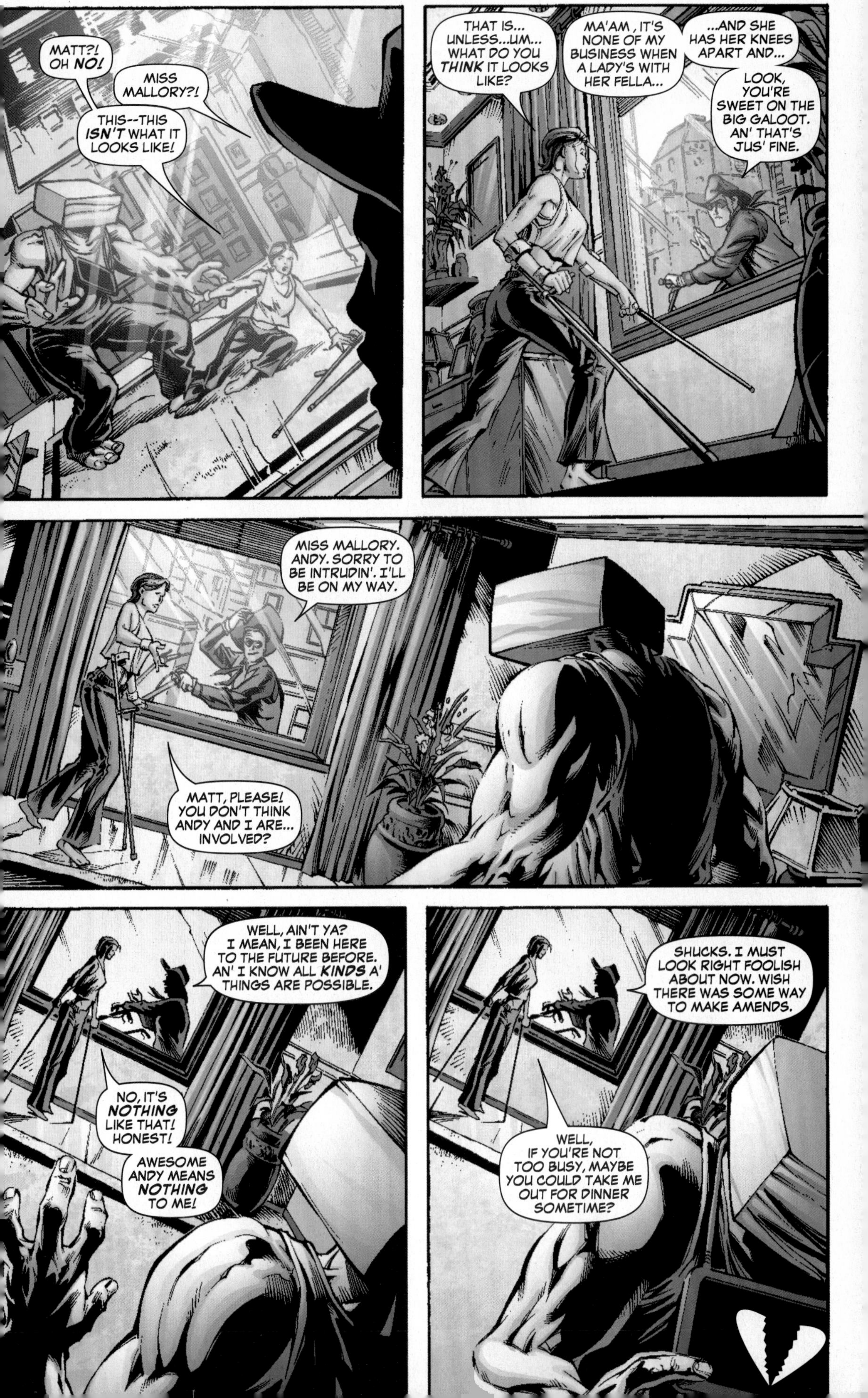
MATT?! OH **NO!**
MISS MALLORY?!
THIS--THIS ***ISN'T*** WHAT IT LOOKS LIKE!
THAT IS... UNLESS...UM... WHAT DO YOU ***THINK*** IT LOOKS LIKE?
MA'AM, IT'S NONE OF MY BUSINESS WHEN A LADY'S WITH HER FELLA...
...AND SHE HAS HER KNEES APART AND...
LOOK, YOU'RE SWEET ON THE BIG GALOOT. AN' THAT'S JUS' FINE.
MISS MALLORY. ANDY. SORRY TO BE INTRUDIN'. I'LL BE ON MY WAY.
MATT, PLEASE! YOU DON'T THINK ANDY AND I ARE... INVOLVED?
WELL, AIN'T YA? I MEAN, I BEEN HERE TO THE FUTURE BEFORE. AN' I KNOW ALL **KINDS** A' THINGS ARE POSSIBLE.
NO, IT'S **NOTHING** LIKE THAT! HONEST!
AWESOME ANDY MEANS **NOTHING** TO ME!
SHUCKS. I MUST LOOK RIGHT FOOLISH ABOUT NOW. WISH THERE WAS SOME WAY TO MAKE AMENDS.
WELL, IF YOU'RE NOT TOO BUSY, MAYBE YOU COULD TAKE ME OUT FOR DINNER SOMETIME?

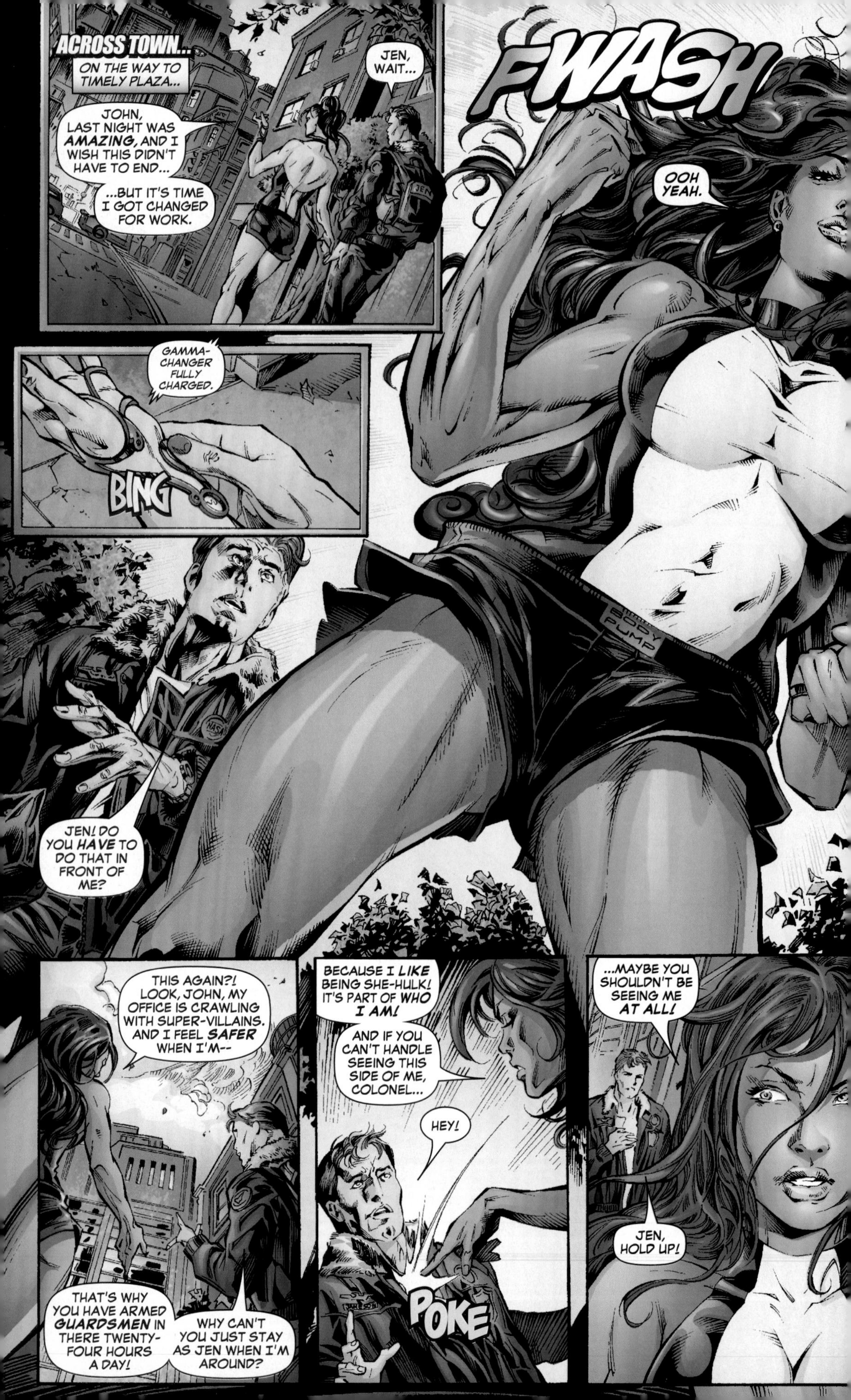
ACROSS TOWN...
ON THE WAY TO TIMELY PLAZA...
JOHN, LAST NIGHT WAS AMAZING, AND I WISH THIS DIDN'T HAVE TO END...
...BUT IT'S TIME I GOT CHANGED FOR WORK.
JEN, WAIT...
GAMMA-CHANGER FULLY CHARGED.
BING
FWASH
OOH YEAH.
JEN! DO YOU HAVE TO DO THAT IN FRONT OF ME?
BODY PUMP
THIS AGAIN?! LOOK, JOHN, MY OFFICE IS CRAWLING WITH SUPER-VILLAINS. AND I FEEL SAFER WHEN I'M--
THAT'S WHY YOU HAVE ARMED GUARDSMEN IN THERE TWENTY-FOUR HOURS A DAY!
WHY CAN'T YOU JUST STAY AS JEN WHEN I'M AROUND?
BECAUSE I LIKE BEING SHE-HULK! IT'S PART OF WHO I AM!
AND IF YOU CAN'T HANDLE SEEING THIS SIDE OF ME, COLONEL...
HEY!
POKE
...MAYBE YOU SHOULDN'T BE SEEING ME AT ALL!
JEN, HOLD UP!

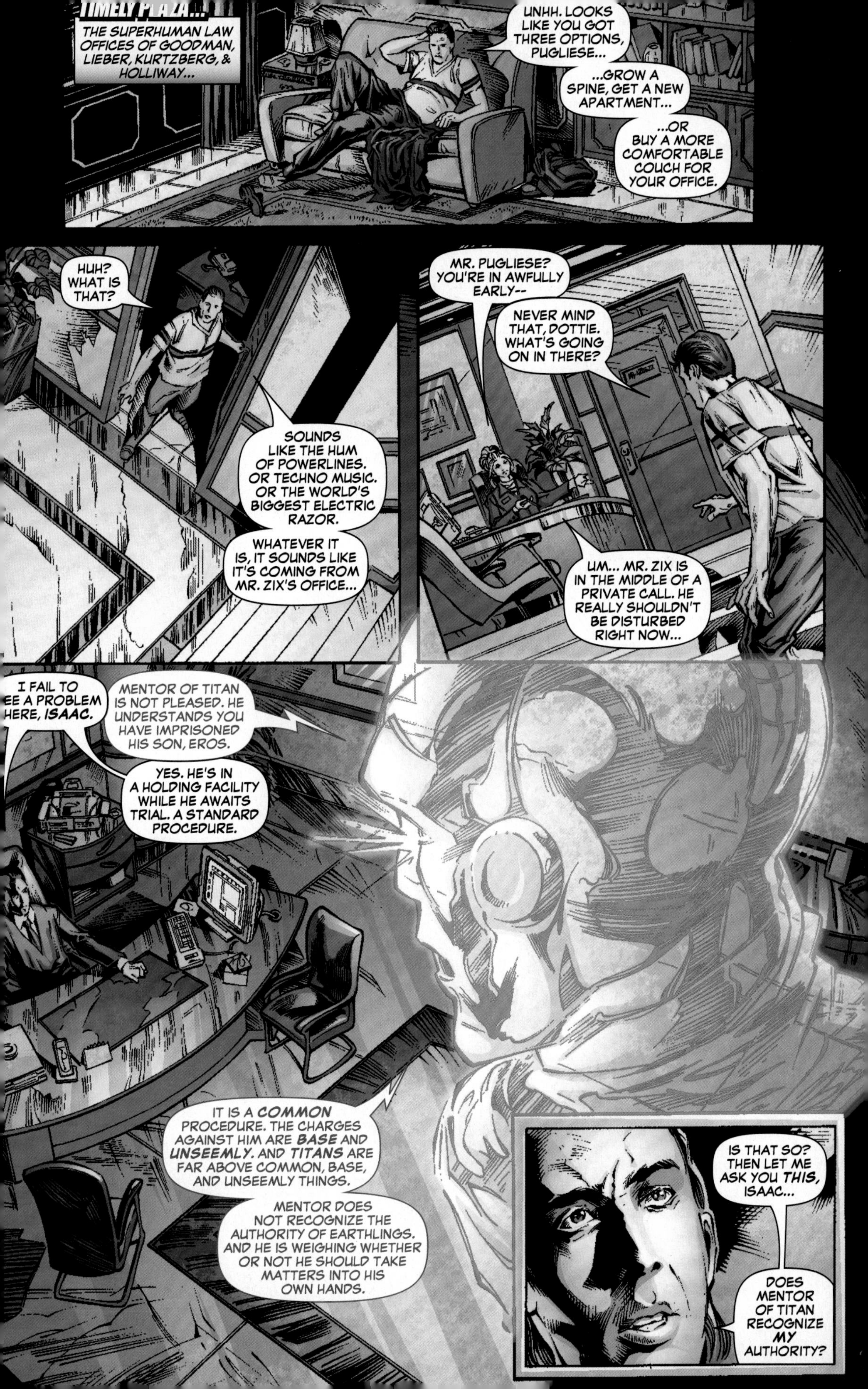
TIMELY PLAZA...
THE SUPERHUMAN LAW OFFICES OF GOODMAN, LIEBER, KURTZBERG, & HOLLIWAY...
UNHH. LOOKS LIKE YOU GOT THREE OPTIONS, PUGLIESE...
...GROW A SPINE, GET A NEW APARTMENT...
...OR BUY A MORE COMFORTABLE COUCH FOR YOUR OFFICE.
HUH? WHAT IS THAT?
SOUNDS LIKE THE HUM OF POWERLINES. OR TECHNO MUSIC. OR THE WORLD'S BIGGEST ELECTRIC RAZOR.
WHATEVER IT IS, IT SOUNDS LIKE IT'S COMING FROM MR. ZIX'S OFFICE...
MR. PUGLIESE? YOU'RE IN AWFULLY EARLY--
NEVER MIND THAT, DOTTIE. WHAT'S GOING ON IN THERE?
UM... MR. ZIX IS IN THE MIDDLE OF A PRIVATE CALL. HE REALLY SHOULDN'T BE DISTURBED RIGHT NOW...
MENTOR OF TITAN IS NOT PLEASED. HE UNDERSTANDS YOU HAVE IMPRISONED HIS SON, EROS.
I FAIL TO SEE A PROBLEM HERE, ISAAC.
YES. HE'S IN A HOLDING FACILITY WHILE HE AWAITS TRIAL. A STANDARD PROCEDURE.
IT IS A COMMON PROCEDURE. THE CHARGES AGAINST HIM ARE BASE AND UNSEEMLY. AND TITANS ARE FAR ABOVE COMMON, BASE, AND UNSEEMLY THINGS.
MENTOR DOES NOT RECOGNIZE THE AUTHORITY OF EARTHLINGS. AND HE IS WEIGHING WHETHER OR NOT HE SHOULD TAKE MATTERS INTO HIS OWN HANDS.
IS THAT SO? THEN LET ME ASK YOU THIS, ISAAC...
DOES MENTOR OF TITAN RECOGNIZE MY AUTHORITY?

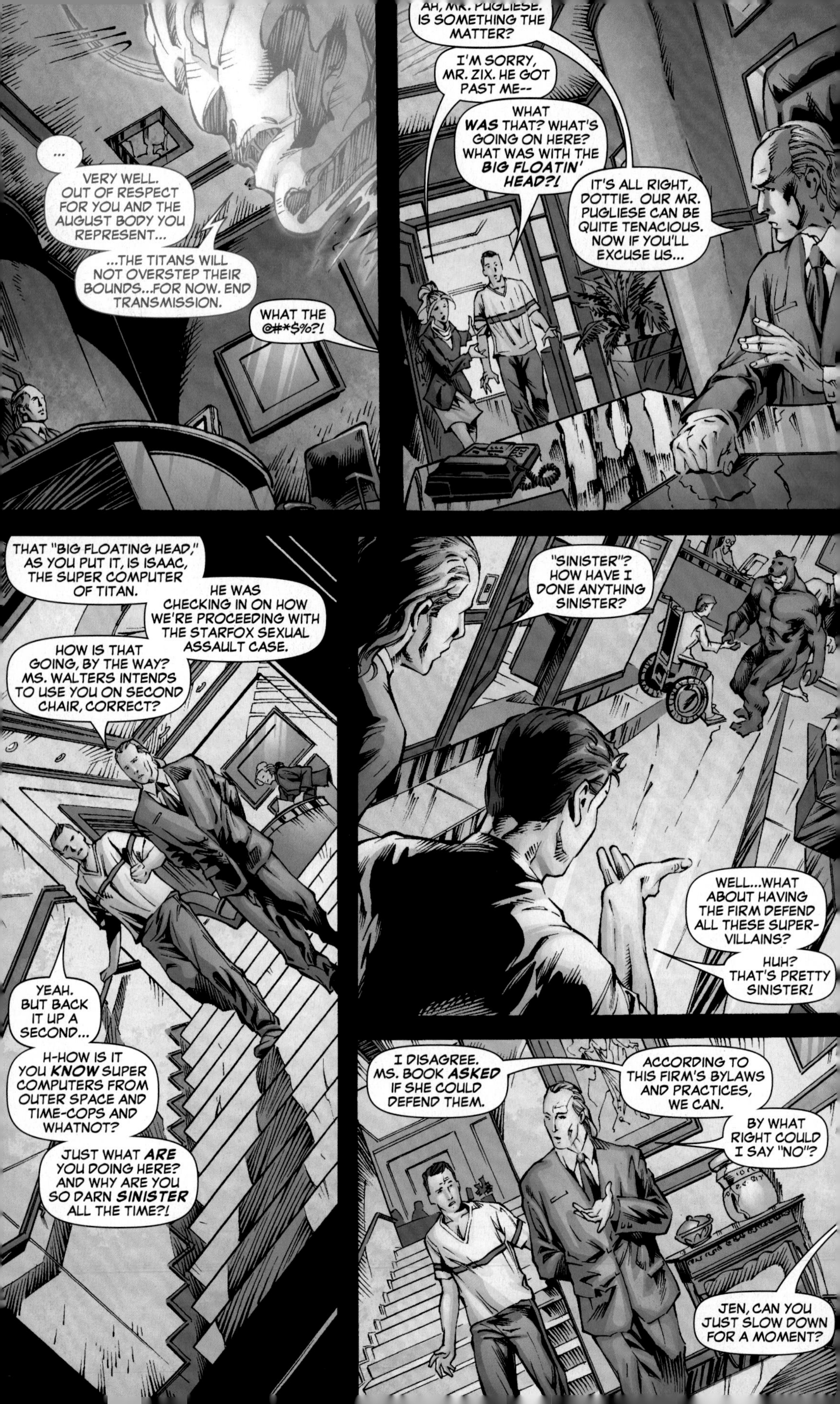
...
VERY WELL. OUT OF RESPECT FOR YOU AND THE AUGUST BODY YOU REPRESENT...
...THE TITANS WILL NOT OVERSTEP THEIR BOUNDS...FOR NOW. END TRANSMISSION.
WHAT THE @#*$%?!
AH, MR. PUGLIESE. IS SOMETHING THE MATTER?
I'M SORRY, MR. ZIX. HE GOT PAST ME--
WHAT WAS THAT? WHAT'S GOING ON HERE? WHAT WAS WITH THE BIG FLOATIN' HEAD?!
IT'S ALL RIGHT, DOTTIE. OUR MR. PUGLIESE CAN BE QUITE TENACIOUS. NOW IF YOU'LL EXCUSE US...
THAT "BIG FLOATING HEAD," AS YOU PUT IT, IS ISAAC, THE SUPER COMPUTER OF TITAN.
HE WAS CHECKING IN ON HOW WE'RE PROCEEDING WITH THE STARFOX SEXUAL ASSAULT CASE.
HOW IS THAT GOING, BY THE WAY? MS. WALTERS INTENDS TO USE YOU ON SECOND CHAIR, CORRECT?
YEAH. BUT BACK IT UP A SECOND...
H-HOW IS IT YOU KNOW SUPER COMPUTERS FROM OUTER SPACE AND TIME-COPS AND WHATNOT?
JUST WHAT ARE YOU DOING HERE? AND WHY ARE YOU SO DARN SINISTER ALL THE TIME?!
"SINISTER"? HOW HAVE I DONE ANYTHING SINISTER?
WELL...WHAT ABOUT HAVING THE FIRM DEFEND ALL THESE SUPER-VILLAINS?
HUH? THAT'S PRETTY SINISTER!
I DISAGREE. MS. BOOK ASKED IF SHE COULD DEFEND THEM.
ACCORDING TO THIS FIRM'S BYLAWS AND PRACTICES, WE CAN.
BY WHAT RIGHT COULD I SAY "NO"?
JEN, CAN YOU JUST SLOW DOWN FOR A MOMENT?

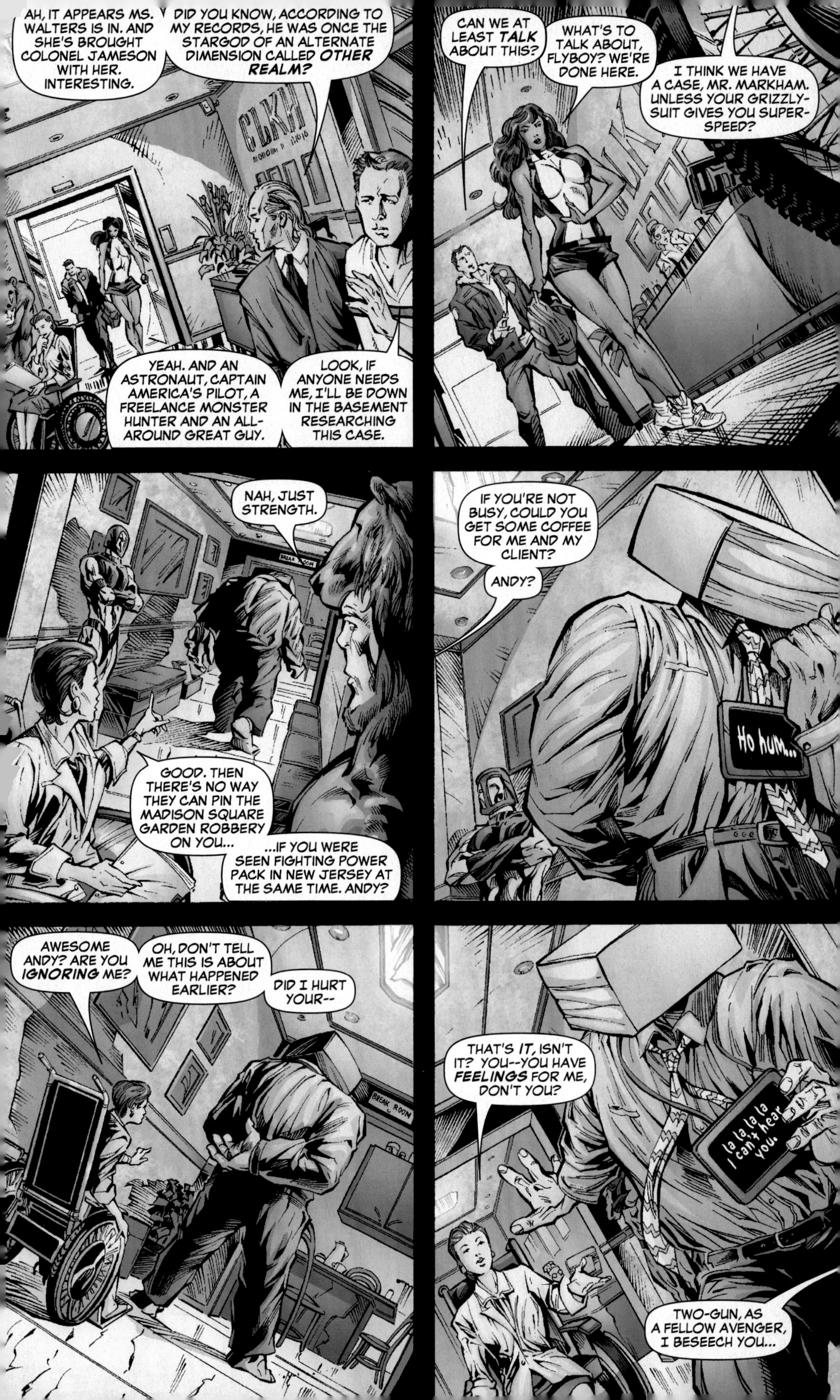
AH, IT APPEARS MS. WALTERS IS IN. AND SHE'S BROUGHT COLONEL JAMESON WITH HER. INTERESTING.
DID YOU KNOW, ACCORDING TO MY RECORDS, HE WAS ONCE THE STARGOD OF AN ALTERNATE DIMENSION CALLED OTHER REALM?
YEAH. AND AN ASTRONAUT, CAPTAIN AMERICA'S PILOT, A FREELANCE MONSTER HUNTER AND AN ALL-AROUND GREAT GUY.
LOOK, IF ANYONE NEEDS ME, I'LL BE DOWN IN THE BASEMENT RESEARCHING THIS CASE.
CAN WE AT LEAST TALK ABOUT THIS?
WHAT'S TO TALK ABOUT, FLYBOY? WE'RE DONE HERE.
I THINK WE HAVE A CASE, MR. MARKHAM. UNLESS YOUR GRIZZLY-SUIT GIVES YOU SUPER-SPEED?
NAH, JUST STRENGTH.
GOOD. THEN THERE'S NO WAY THEY CAN PIN THE MADISON SQUARE GARDEN ROBBERY ON YOU...
...IF YOU WERE SEEN FIGHTING POWER PACK IN NEW JERSEY AT THE SAME TIME. ANDY?
IF YOU'RE NOT BUSY, COULD YOU GET SOME COFFEE FOR ME AND MY CLIENT?
ANDY?
Ho hum...
AWESOME ANDY? ARE YOU IGNORING ME?
OH, DON'T TELL ME THIS IS ABOUT WHAT HAPPENED EARLIER?
DID I HURT YOUR--
BREAK ROOM
THAT'S IT, ISN'T IT? YOU--YOU HAVE FEELINGS FOR ME, DON'T YOU?
la la la la I can't hear you.
TWO-GUN, AS A FELLOW AVENGER, I BESEECH YOU...

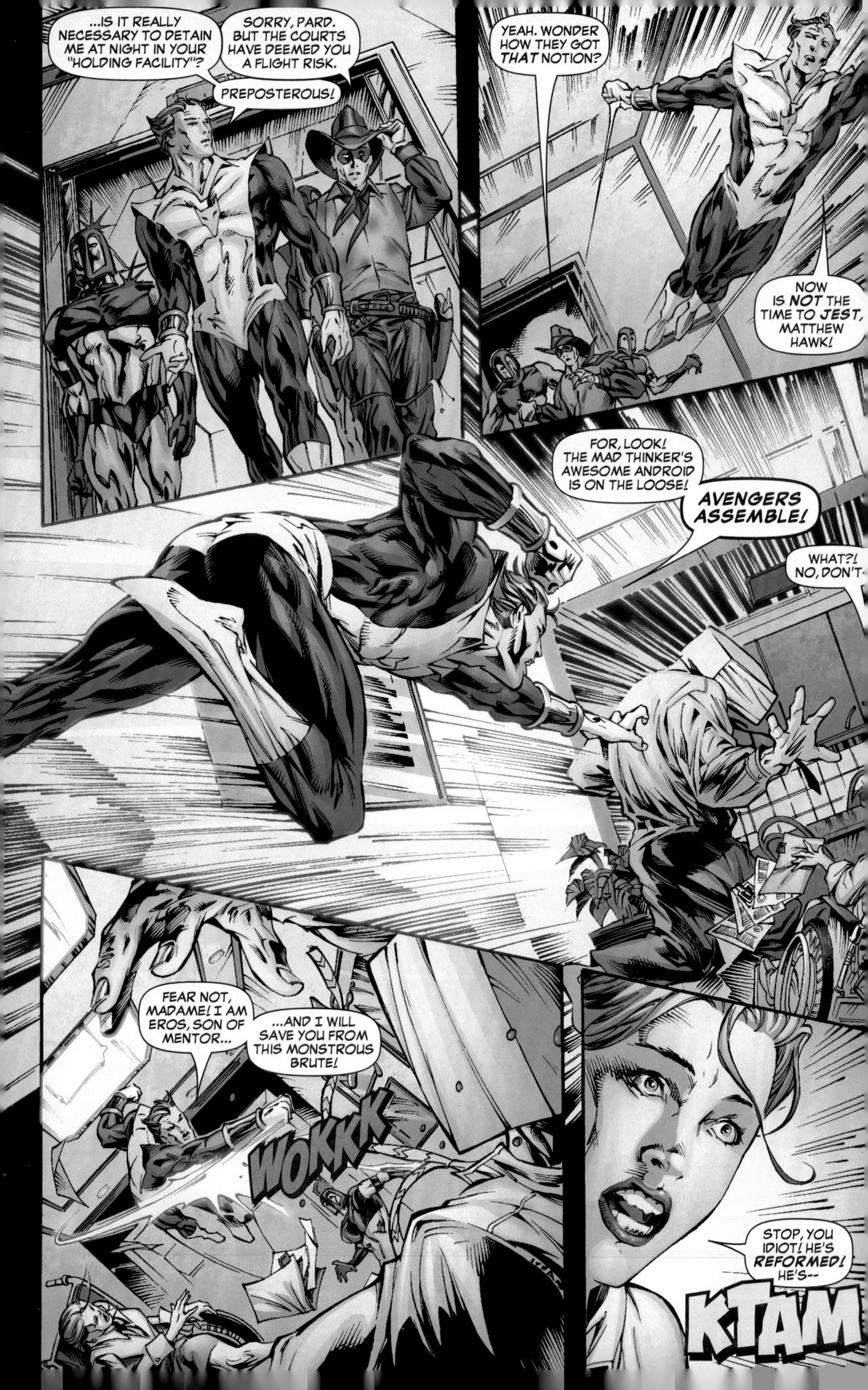
...IS IT REALLY NECESSARY TO DETAIN ME AT NIGHT IN YOUR "HOLDING FACILITY"?
SORRY, PARD. BUT THE COURTS HAVE DEEMED YOU A FLIGHT RISK.
PREPOSTEROUS!
YEAH. WONDER HOW THEY GOT THAT NOTION?
NOW IS NOT THE TIME TO JEST, MATTHEW HAWK!
FOR, LOOK! THE MAD THINKER'S AWESOME ANDROID IS ON THE LOOSE!
AVENGERS ASSEMBLE!
WHAT?! NO, DON'T-
FEAR NOT, MADAME! I AM EROS, SON OF MENTOR...
...AND I WILL SAVE YOU FROM THIS MONSTROUS BRUTE!
WOKKK
STOP, YOU IDIOT! HE'S REFORMED! HE'S--
KTAM

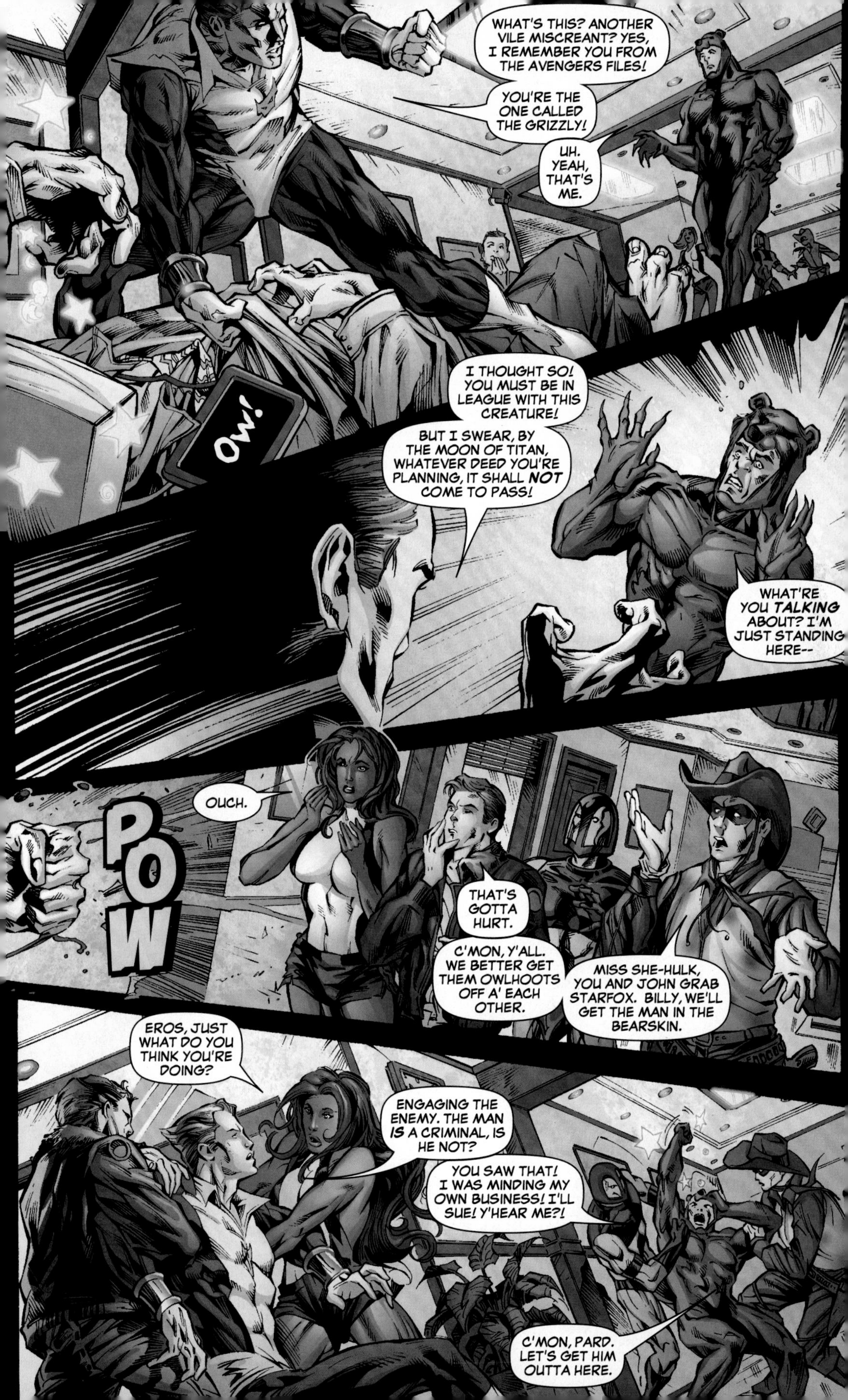
WHAT'S THIS? ANOTHER VILE MISCREANT? YES, I REMEMBER YOU FROM THE AVENGERS FILES!
YOU'RE THE ONE CALLED THE GRIZZLY!
UH. YEAH, THAT'S ME.
OW!
I THOUGHT SO! YOU MUST BE IN LEAGUE WITH THIS CREATURE!
BUT I SWEAR, BY THE MOON OF TITAN, WHATEVER DEED YOU'RE PLANNING, IT SHALL NOT COME TO PASS!
WHAT'RE YOU TALKING ABOUT? I'M JUST STANDING HERE--
POW
OUCH.
THAT'S GOTTA HURT.
C'MON, Y'ALL. WE BETTER GET THEM OWLHOOTS OFF A' EACH OTHER.
MISS SHE-HULK, YOU AND JOHN GRAB STARFOX. BILLY, WE'LL GET THE MAN IN THE BEARSKIN.
EROS, JUST WHAT DO YOU THINK YOU'RE DOING?
ENGAGING THE ENEMY. THE MAN IS A CRIMINAL, IS HE NOT?
YOU SAW THAT! I WAS MINDING MY OWN BUSINESS! I'LL SUE! Y'HEAR ME?!
C'MON, PARD. LET'S GET HIM OUTTA HERE.

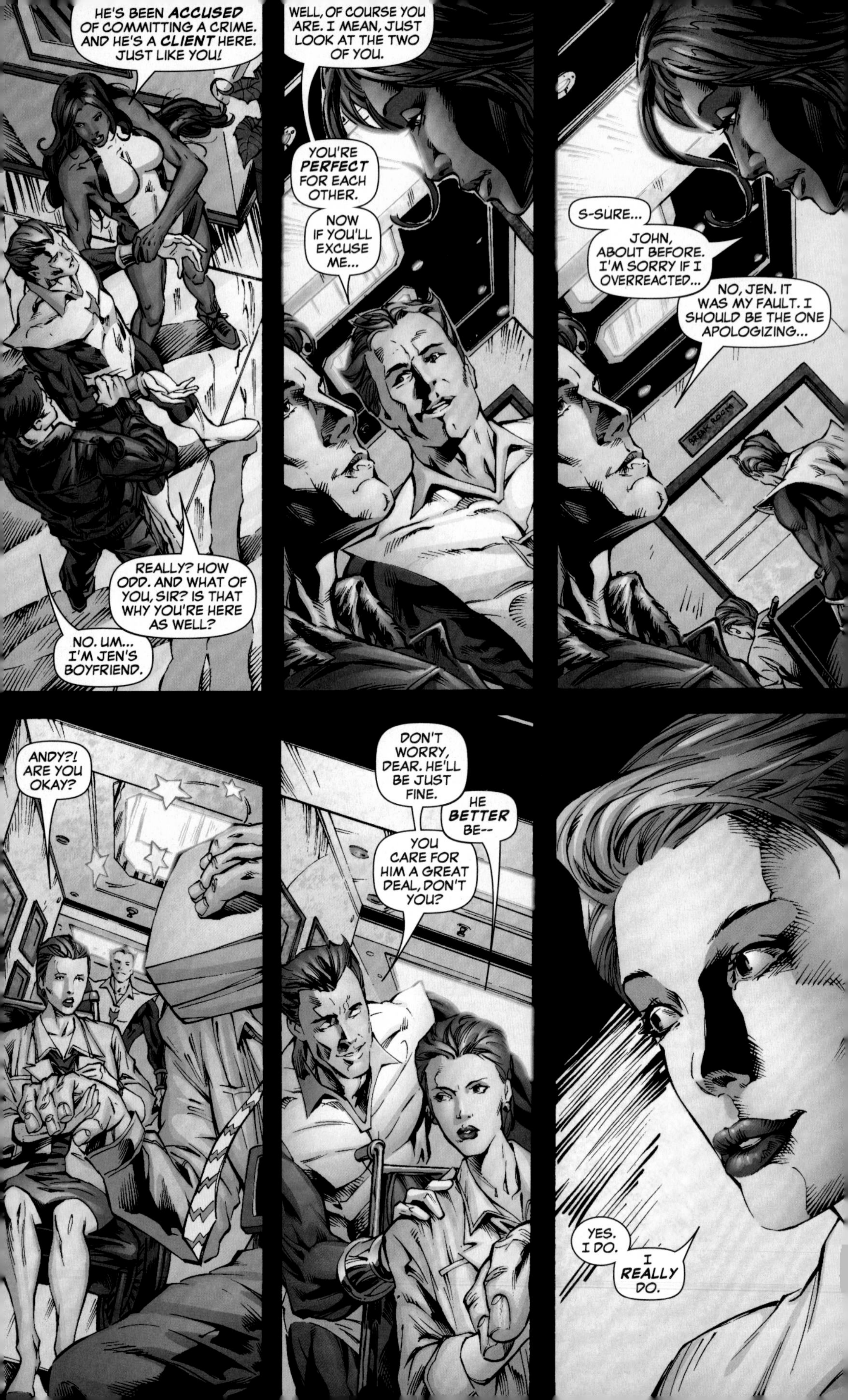
HE'S BEEN ACCUSED OF COMMITTING A CRIME. AND HE'S A CLIENT HERE. JUST LIKE YOU!
REALLY? HOW ODD. AND WHAT OF YOU, SIR? IS THAT WHY YOU'RE HERE AS WELL?
NO. UM... I'M JEN'S BOYFRIEND.
WELL, OF COURSE YOU ARE. I MEAN, JUST LOOK AT THE TWO OF YOU.
YOU'RE PERFECT FOR EACH OTHER.
NOW IF YOU'LL EXCUSE ME...
S-SURE...
JOHN, ABOUT BEFORE. I'M SORRY IF I OVERREACTED...
NO, JEN. IT WAS MY FAULT. I SHOULD BE THE ONE APOLOGIZING...
ANDY?! ARE YOU OKAY?
DON'T WORRY, DEAR. HE'LL BE JUST FINE.
HE BETTER BE--
YOU CARE FOR HIM A GREAT DEAL, DON'T YOU?
YES. I DO.
I REALLY DO.

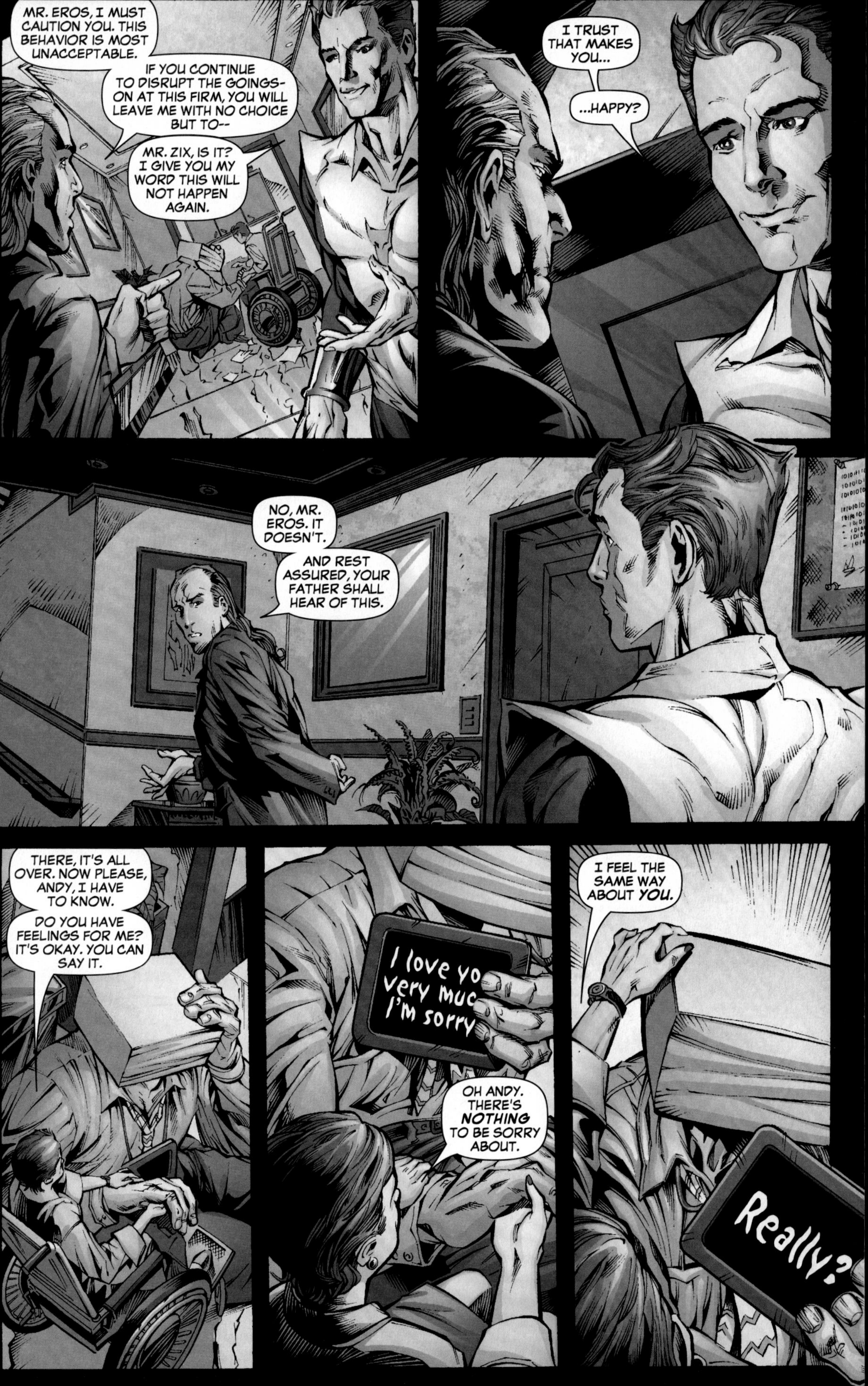
MR. EROS, I MUST CAUTION YOU. THIS BEHAVIOR IS MOST UNACCEPTABLE.
IF YOU CONTINUE TO DISRUPT THE GOINGS-ON AT THIS FIRM, YOU WILL LEAVE ME WITH NO CHOICE BUT TO--
MR. ZIX, IS IT? I GIVE YOU MY WORD THIS WILL NOT HAPPEN AGAIN.
I TRUST THAT MAKES YOU...
...HAPPY?
NO, MR. EROS. IT DOESN'T.
AND REST ASSURED, YOUR FATHER SHALL HEAR OF THIS.
THERE, IT'S ALL OVER. NOW PLEASE, ANDY, I HAVE TO KNOW.
DO YOU HAVE FEELINGS FOR ME? IT'S OKAY. YOU CAN SAY IT.
I love yo
very muc
I'm sorry
OH ANDY. THERE'S *NOTHING* TO BE SORRY ABOUT.
I FEEL THE SAME WAY ABOUT *YOU*.
Really?

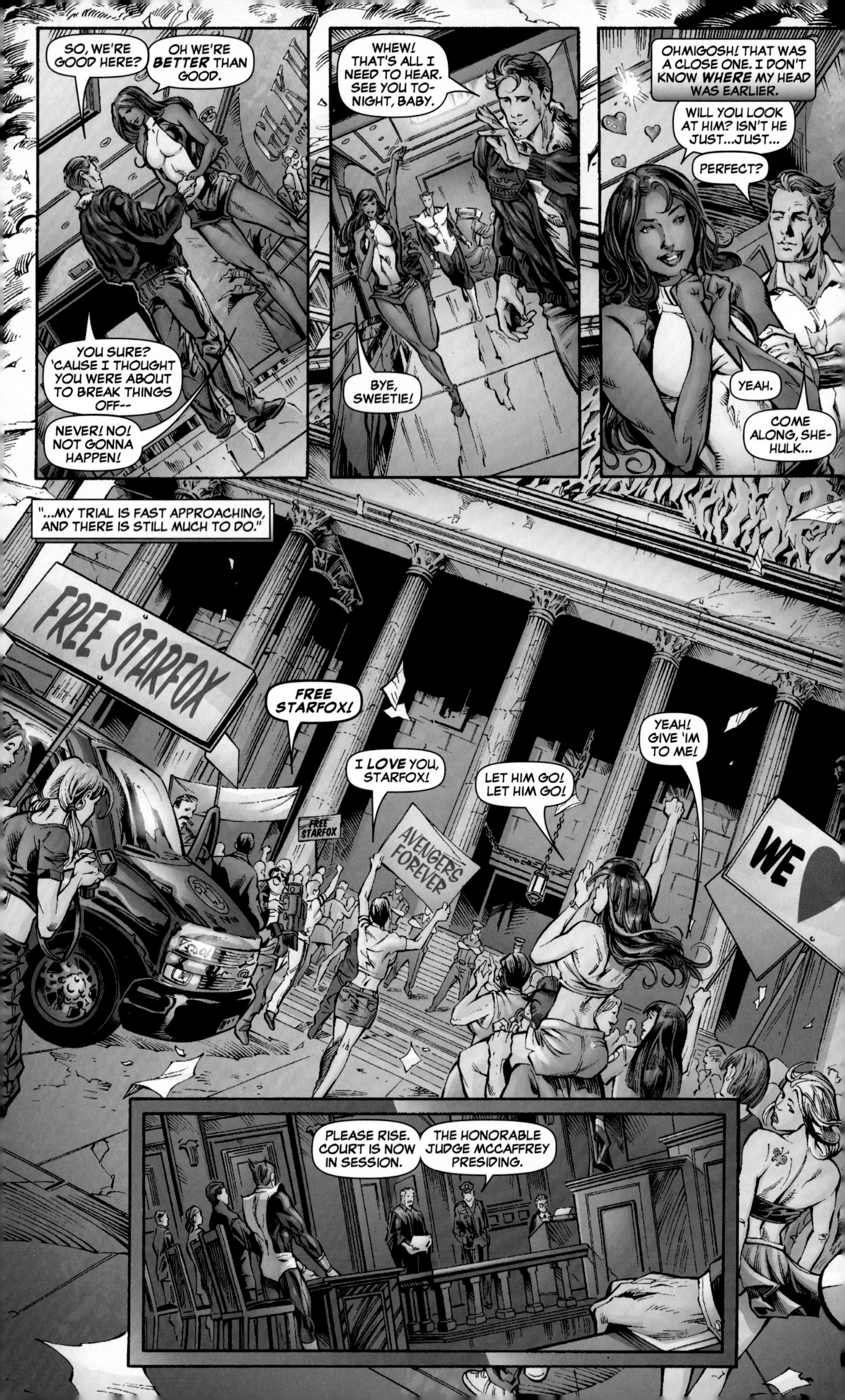
SO, WE'RE GOOD HERE?
OH WE'RE BETTER THAN GOOD.
YOU SURE? 'CAUSE I THOUGHT YOU WERE ABOUT TO BREAK THINGS OFF--
NEVER! NO! NOT GONNA HAPPEN!
WHEW! THAT'S ALL I NEED TO HEAR. SEE YOU TO-NIGHT, BABY.
BYE, SWEETIE!
OHMIGOSH! THAT WAS A CLOSE ONE. I DON'T KNOW WHERE MY HEAD WAS EARLIER.
WILL YOU LOOK AT HIM? ISN'T HE JUST...JUST...
PERFECT?
YEAH.
COME ALONG, SHE-HULK...
"...MY TRIAL IS FAST APPROACHING, AND THERE IS STILL MUCH TO DO."
FREE STARFOX
FREE STARFOX!
I LOVE YOU, STARFOX!
FREE STARFOX
AVENGERS FOREVER
LET HIM GO! LET HIM GO!
YEAH! GIVE 'IM TO ME!
WE
PLEASE RISE. COURT IS NOW IN SESSION.
THE HONORABLE JUDGE MCCAFFREY PRESIDING.

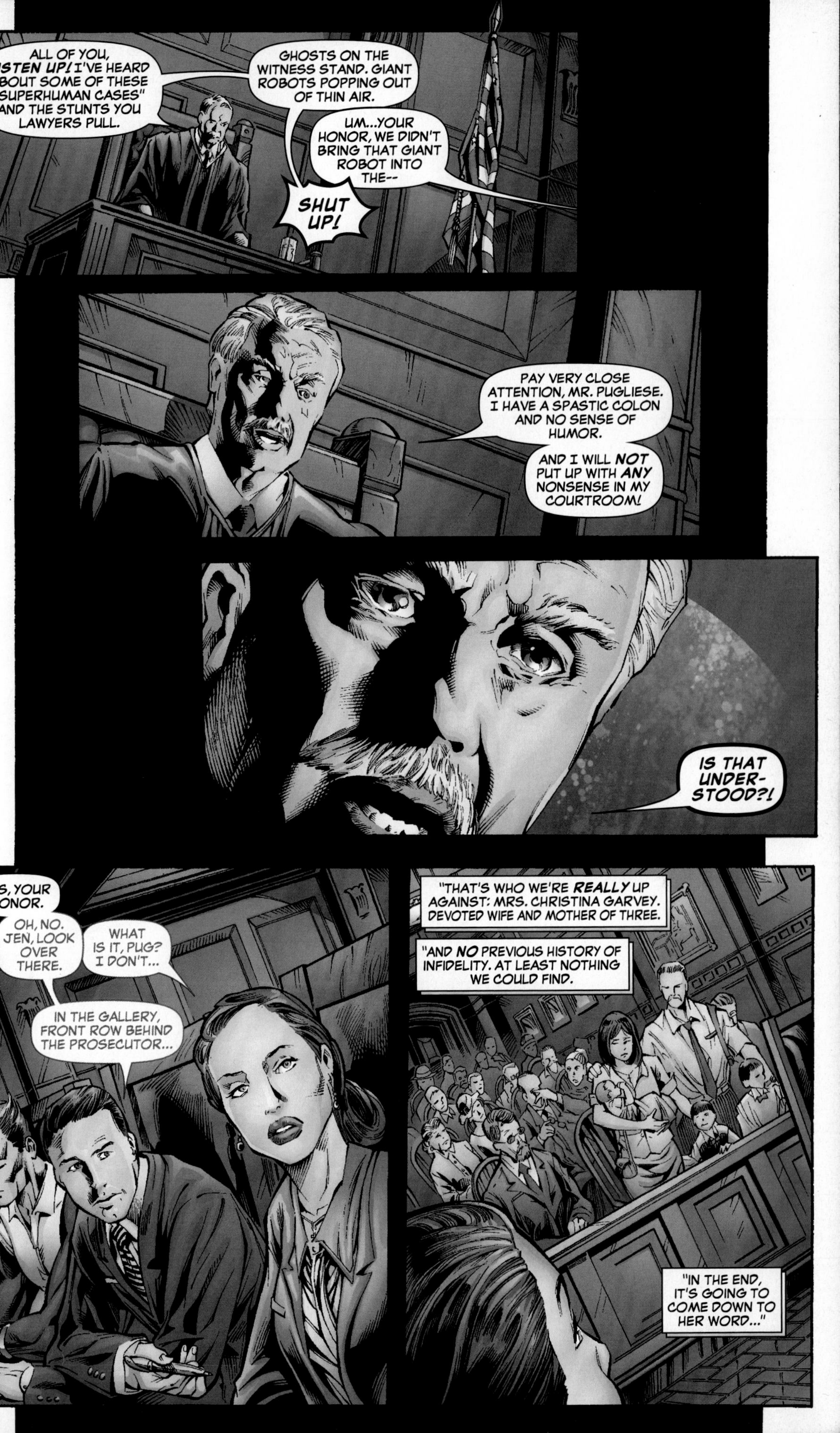

ALL OF YOU, *STEN UP!* I'VE HEARD BOUT SOME OF THESE SUPERHUMAN CASES" AND THE STUNTS YOU LAWYERS PULL.
GHOSTS ON THE WITNESS STAND. GIANT ROBOTS POPPING OUT OF THIN AIR.
UM...YOUR HONOR, WE DIDN'T BRING THAT GIANT ROBOT INTO THE--
SHUT UP!
PAY VERY CLOSE ATTENTION, MR. PUGLIESE. I HAVE A SPASTIC COLON AND NO SENSE OF HUMOR.
AND I WILL *NOT* PUT UP WITH *ANY* NONSENSE IN MY COURTROOM!
IS THAT UNDER-STOOD?!
S, YOUR ONOR.
OH, NO. JEN, LOOK OVER THERE.
WHAT IS IT, PUG? I DON'T...
IN THE GALLERY, FRONT ROW BEHIND THE PROSECUTOR...
"THAT'S WHO WE'RE *REALLY* UP AGAINST: MRS. CHRISTINA GARVEY. DEVOTED WIFE AND MOTHER OF THREE.
"AND *NO* PREVIOUS HISTORY OF INFIDELITY. AT LEAST NOTHING WE COULD FIND.
"IN THE END, IT'S GOING TO COME DOWN TO HER WORD..."

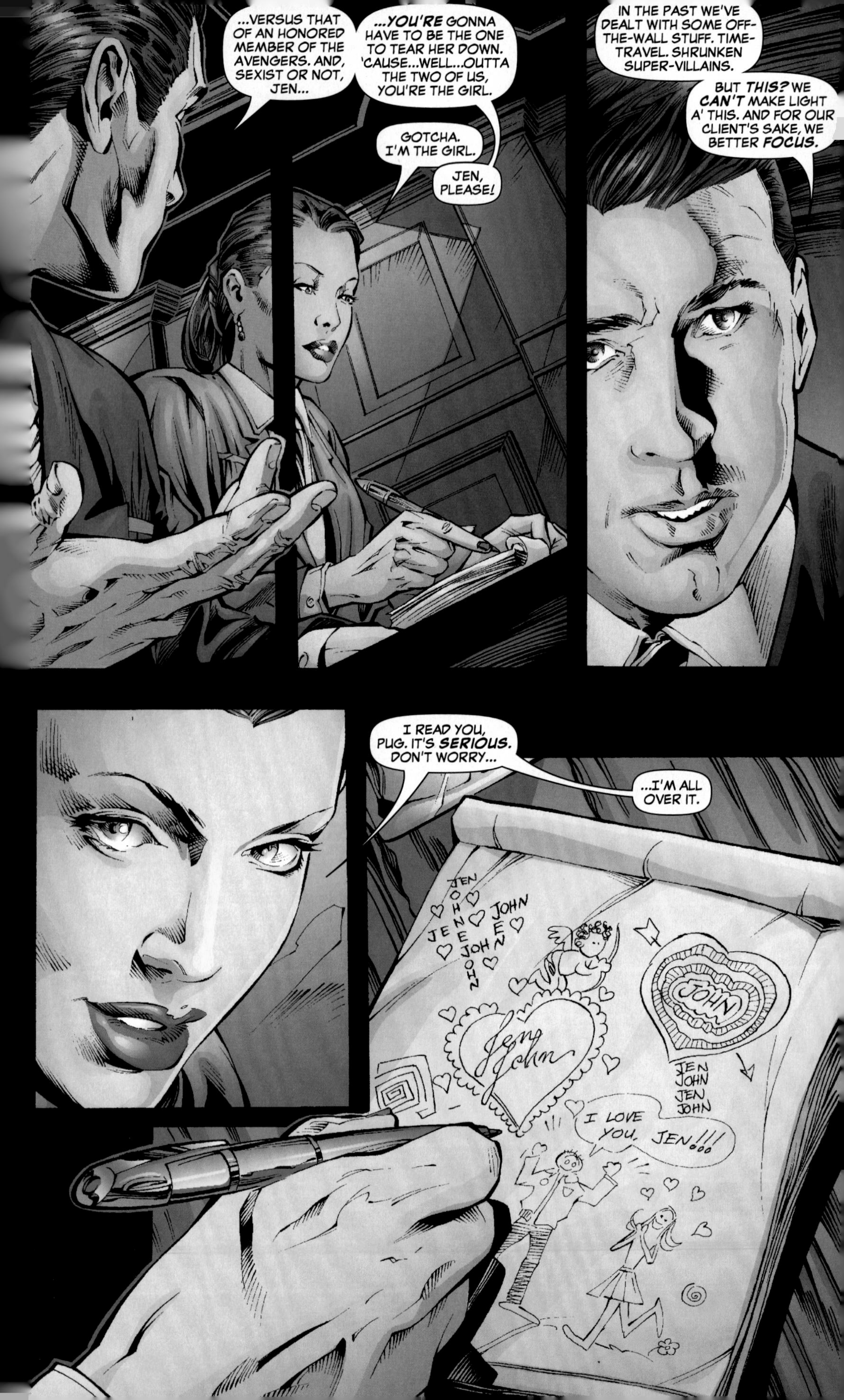

...VERSUS THAT OF AN HONORED MEMBER OF THE AVENGERS. AND, SEXIST OR NOT, JEN...
...YOU'RE GONNA HAVE TO BE THE ONE TO TEAR HER DOWN. 'CAUSE...WELL...OUTTA THE TWO OF US, YOU'RE THE GIRL.
GOTCHA. I'M THE GIRL.
JEN, PLEASE!
IN THE PAST WE'VE DEALT WITH SOME OFF-THE-WALL STUFF. TIME-TRAVEL. SHRUNKEN SUPER-VILLAINS.
BUT THIS? WE CAN'T MAKE LIGHT A' THIS. AND FOR OUR CLIENT'S SAKE, WE BETTER FOCUS.
I READ YOU, PUG. IT'S SERIOUS. DON'T WORRY...
...I'M ALL OVER IT.
JEN
JOHN
JEN
JOHN
JOHN
JEN
Jen
John
JOHN
JEN
JOHN
JEN
JOHN
I LOVE YOU, JEN!!!

7

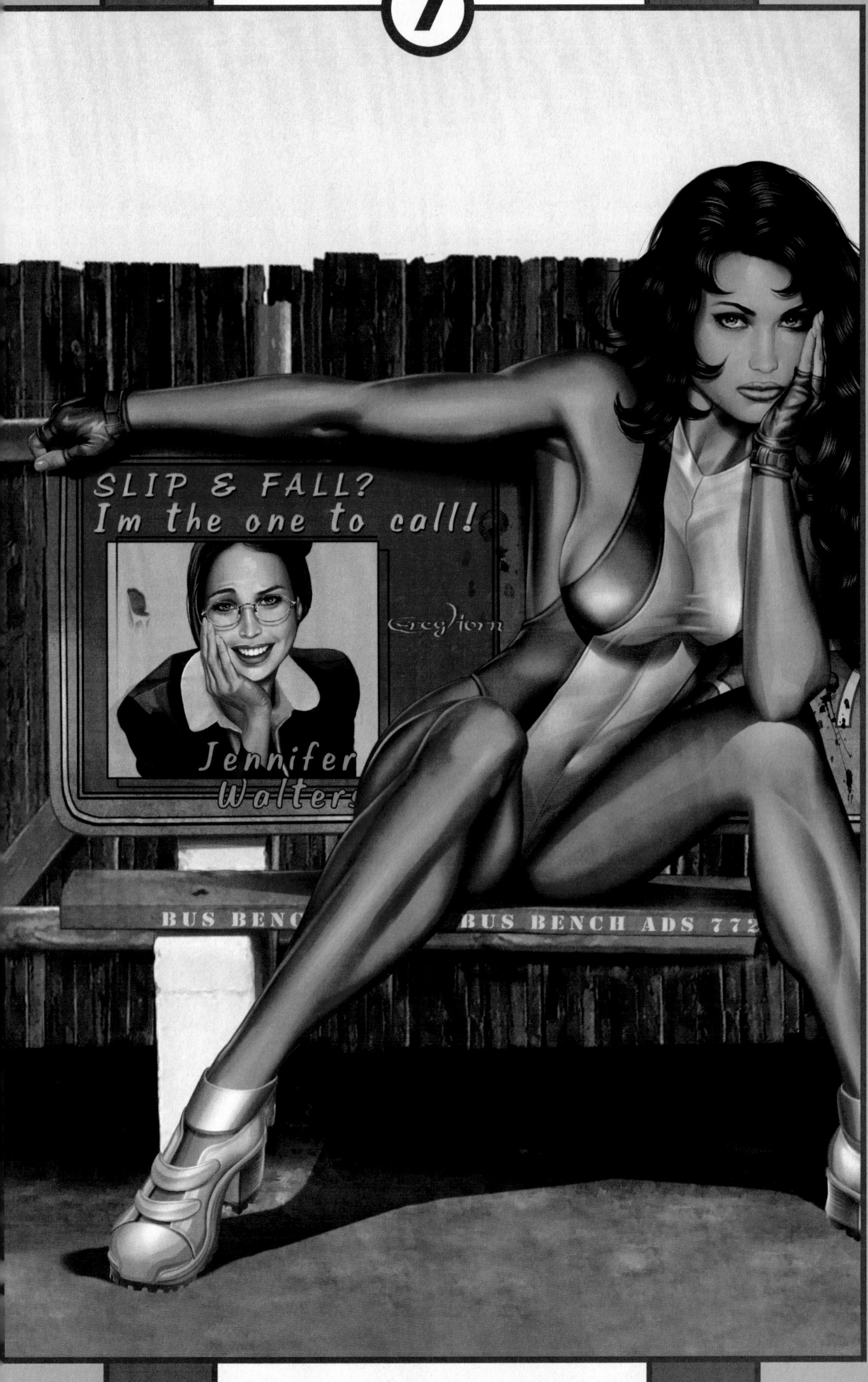
SLIP & FALL?
Im the one to call!
Jennifer
Walter
BUS BENC
BUS BENCH ADS 772

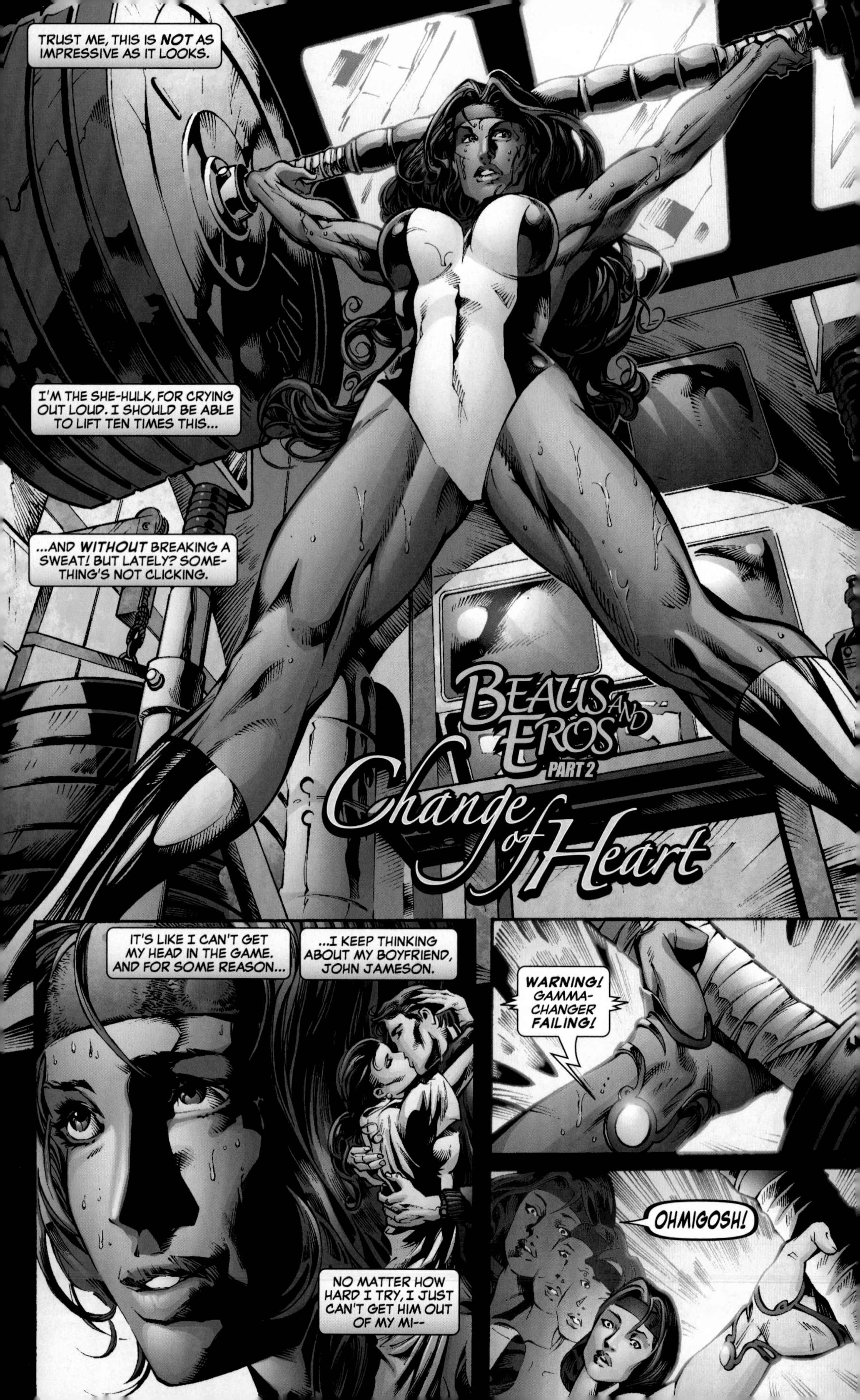
TRUST ME, THIS IS NOT AS IMPRESSIVE AS IT LOOKS.
I'M THE SHE-HULK, FOR CRYING OUT LOUD. I SHOULD BE ABLE TO LIFT TEN TIMES THIS...
...AND WITHOUT BREAKING A SWEAT! BUT LATELY? SOME-THING'S NOT CLICKING.
BEAUS AND EROS
PART 2
Change of Heart
IT'S LIKE I CAN'T GET MY HEAD IN THE GAME. AND FOR SOME REASON...
...I KEEP THINKING ABOUT MY BOYFRIEND, JOHN JAMESON.
NO MATTER HOW HARD I TRY, I JUST CAN'T GET HIM OUT OF MY MI--
WARNING! GAMMA-CHANGER FAILING!
OHMIGOSH!

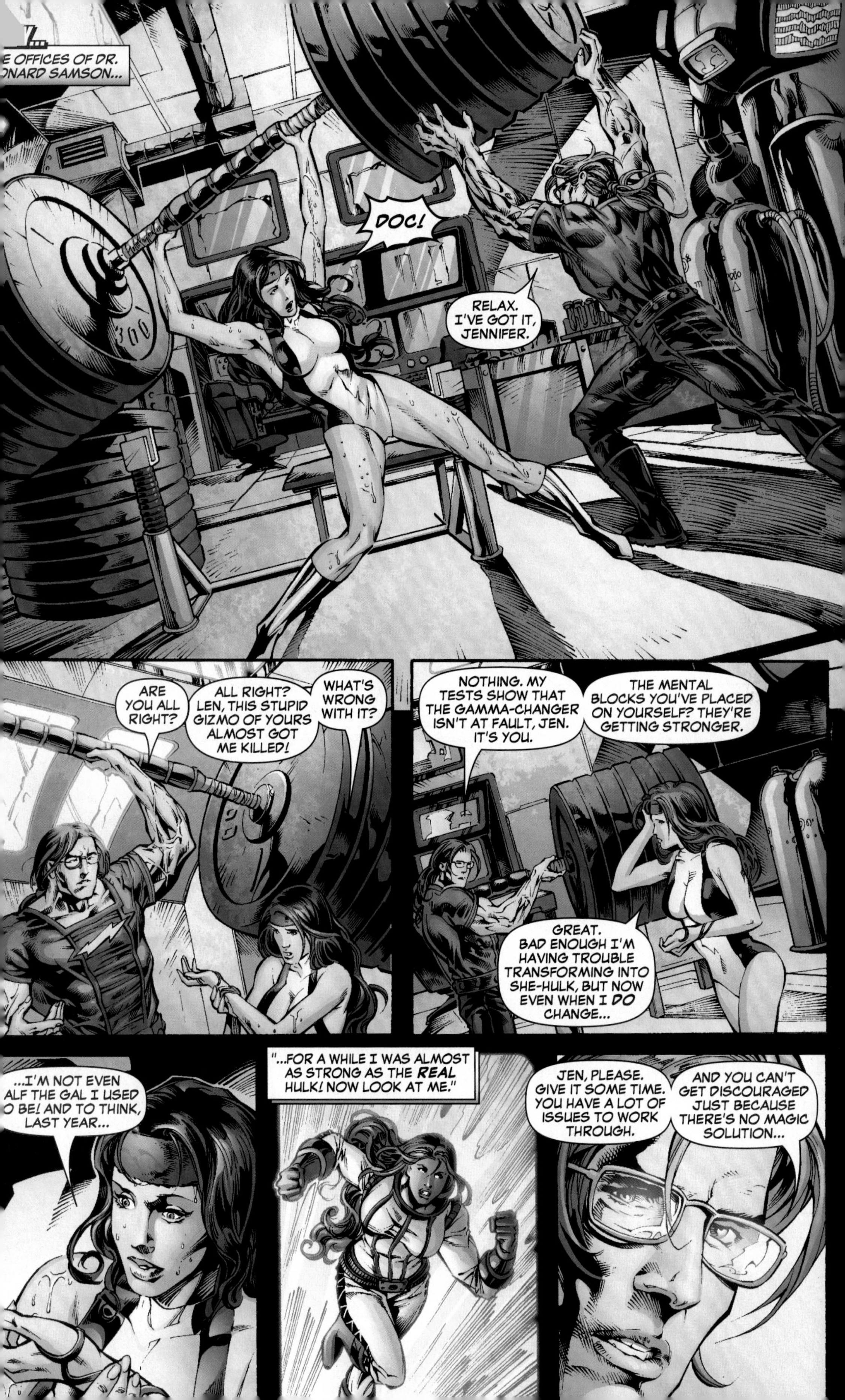

E OFFICES OF DR. ONARD SAMSON...
DOC!
RELAX. I'VE GOT IT, JENNIFER.
ARE YOU ALL RIGHT?
ALL RIGHT? LEN, THIS STUPID GIZMO OF YOURS ALMOST GOT ME KILLED!
WHAT'S WRONG WITH IT?
NOTHING. MY TESTS SHOW THAT THE GAMMA-CHANGER ISN'T AT FAULT, JEN. IT'S YOU.
THE MENTAL BLOCKS YOU'VE PLACED ON YOURSELF? THEY'RE GETTING STRONGER.
GREAT. BAD ENOUGH I'M HAVING TROUBLE TRANSFORMING INTO SHE-HULK, BUT NOW EVEN WHEN I DO CHANGE...
...I'M NOT EVEN ALF THE GAL I USED O BE! AND TO THINK, LAST YEAR...
"...FOR A WHILE I WAS ALMOST AS STRONG AS THE REAL HULK! NOW LOOK AT ME."
JEN, PLEASE. GIVE IT SOME TIME. YOU HAVE A LOT OF ISSUES TO WORK THROUGH.
AND YOU CAN'T GET DISCOURAGED JUST BECAUSE THERE'S NO MAGIC SOLUTION...

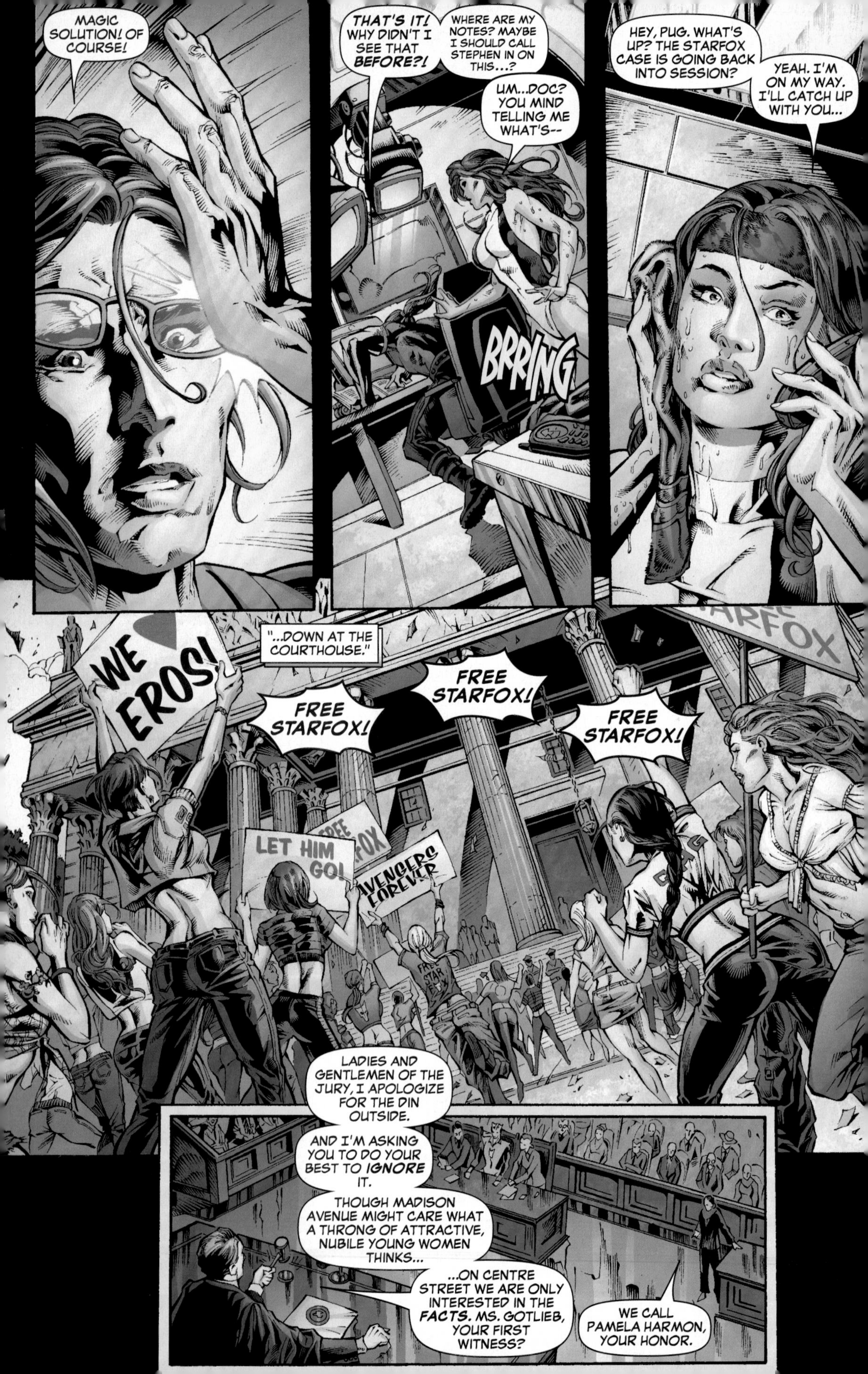
MAGIC SOLUTION! OF COURSE!
THAT'S IT! WHY DIDN'T I SEE THAT BEFORE?!
WHERE ARE MY NOTES? MAYBE I SHOULD CALL STEPHEN IN ON THIS...?
UM...DOC? YOU MIND TELLING ME WHAT'S--
BRRING
HEY, PUG. WHAT'S UP? THE STARFOX CASE IS GOING BACK INTO SESSION?
YEAH. I'M ON MY WAY. I'LL CATCH UP WITH YOU...
"...DOWN AT THE COURTHOUSE."
WE EROS!
FREE STARFOX!
FREE STARFOX!
FREE STARFOX!
STARFOX
LET HIM GO!
AVENGERS FOREVER
LADIES AND GENTLEMEN OF THE JURY, I APOLOGIZE FOR THE DIN OUTSIDE.
AND I'M ASKING YOU TO DO YOUR BEST TO IGNORE IT.
THOUGH MADISON AVENUE MIGHT CARE WHAT A THRONG OF ATTRACTIVE, NUBILE YOUNG WOMEN THINKS...
...ON CENTRE STREET WE ARE ONLY INTERESTED IN THE FACTS. MS. GOTLIEB, YOUR FIRST WITNESS?
WE CALL PAMELA HARMON, YOUR HONOR.

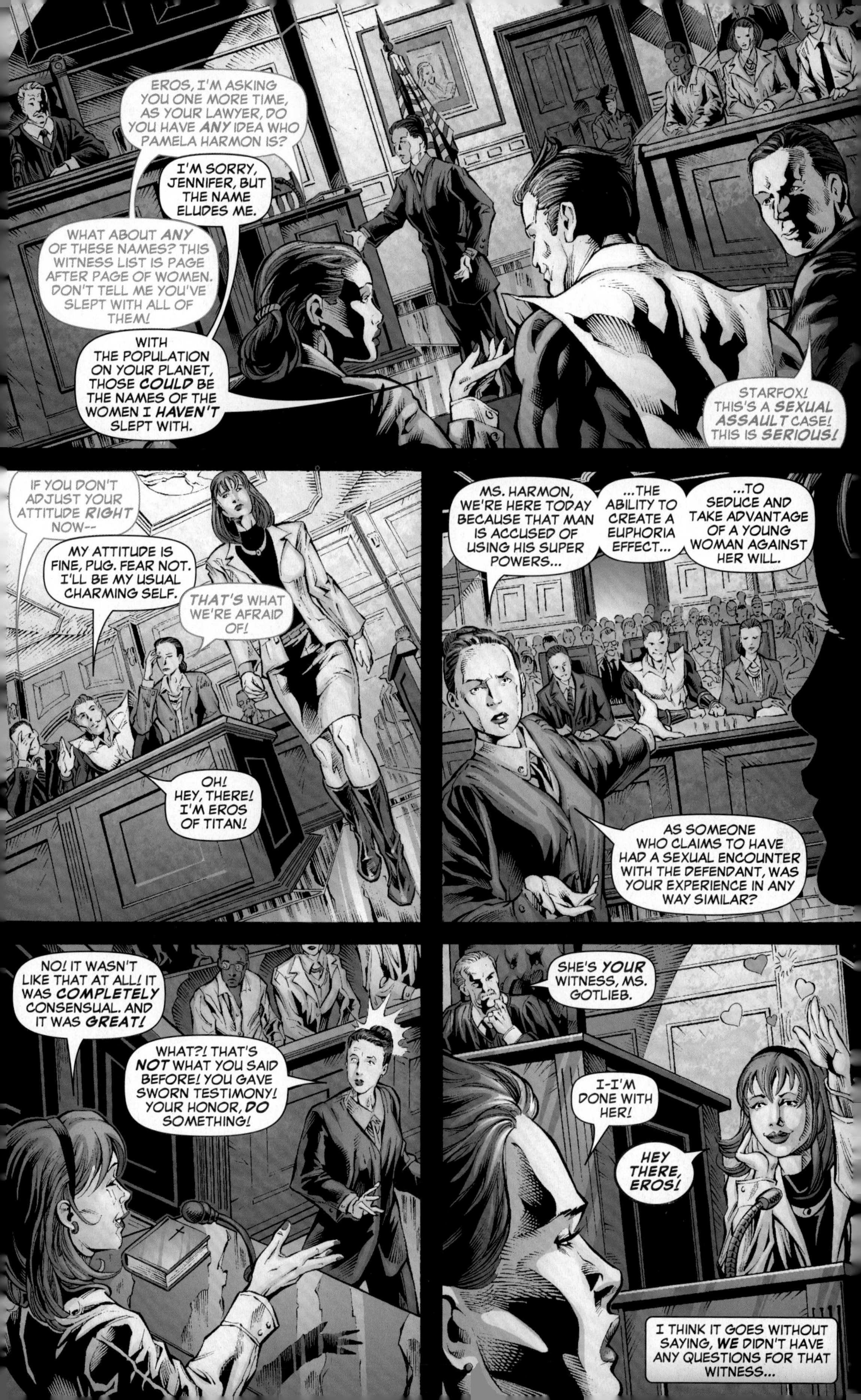
EROS, I'M ASKING YOU ONE MORE TIME, AS YOUR LAWYER, DO YOU HAVE ANY IDEA WHO PAMELA HARMON IS?
I'M SORRY, JENNIFER, BUT THE NAME ELUDES ME.
WHAT ABOUT ANY OF THESE NAMES? THIS WITNESS LIST IS PAGE AFTER PAGE OF WOMEN. DON'T TELL ME YOU'VE SLEPT WITH ALL OF THEM!
WITH THE POPULATION ON YOUR PLANET, THOSE COULD BE THE NAMES OF THE WOMEN I HAVEN'T SLEPT WITH.
STARFOX! THIS'S A SEXUAL ASSAULT CASE! THIS IS SERIOUS!
IF YOU DON'T ADJUST YOUR ATTITUDE RIGHT NOW--
MY ATTITUDE IS FINE, PUG. FEAR NOT. I'LL BE MY USUAL CHARMING SELF.
THAT'S WHAT WE'RE AFRAID OF!
OH! HEY, THERE! I'M EROS OF TITAN!
MS. HARMON, WE'RE HERE TODAY BECAUSE THAT MAN IS ACCUSED OF USING HIS SUPER POWERS...
...THE ABILITY TO CREATE A EUPHORIA EFFECT...
...TO SEDUCE AND TAKE ADVANTAGE OF A YOUNG WOMAN AGAINST HER WILL.
AS SOMEONE WHO CLAIMS TO HAVE HAD A SEXUAL ENCOUNTER WITH THE DEFENDANT, WAS YOUR EXPERIENCE IN ANY WAY SIMILAR?
NO! IT WASN'T LIKE THAT AT ALL! IT WAS COMPLETELY CONSENSUAL. AND IT WAS GREAT!
WHAT?! THAT'S NOT WHAT YOU SAID BEFORE! YOU GAVE SWORN TESTIMONY! YOUR HONOR, DO SOMETHING!
SHE'S YOUR WITNESS, MS. GOTLIEB.
I-I'M DONE WITH HER!
HEY THERE, EROS!
I THINK IT GOES WITHOUT SAYING, WE DIDN'T HAVE ANY QUESTIONS FOR THAT WITNESS...

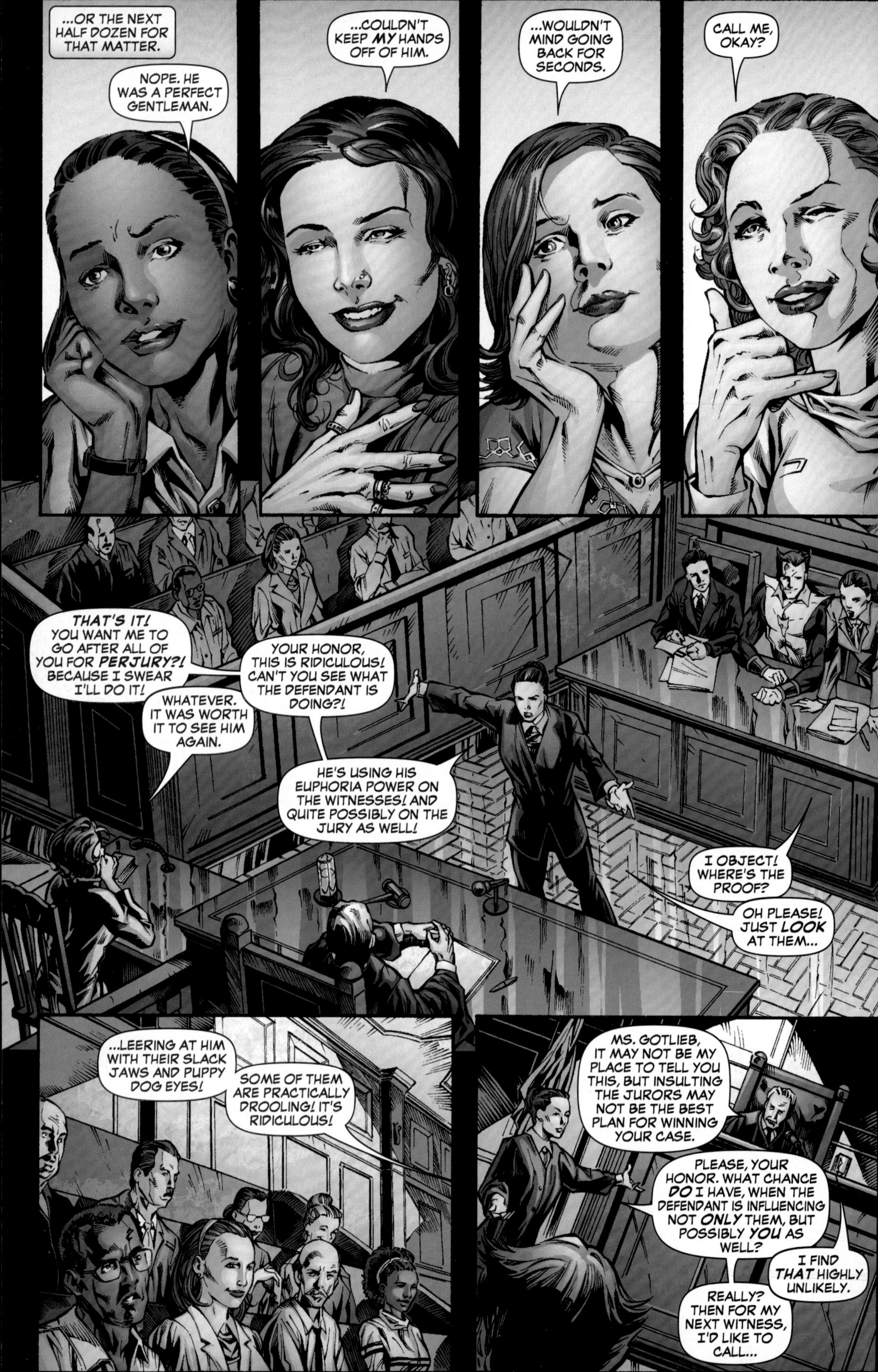
...OR THE NEXT HALF DOZEN FOR THAT MATTER.
NOPE. HE WAS A PERFECT GENTLEMAN.
...COULDN'T KEEP MY HANDS OFF OF HIM.
...WOULDN'T MIND GOING BACK FOR SECONDS.
CALL ME, OKAY?
THAT'S IT! YOU WANT ME TO GO AFTER ALL OF YOU FOR PERJURY?! BECAUSE I SWEAR I'LL DO IT!
WHATEVER. IT WAS WORTH IT TO SEE HIM AGAIN.
YOUR HONOR, THIS IS RIDICULOUS! CAN'T YOU SEE WHAT THE DEFENDANT IS DOING?!
HE'S USING HIS EUPHORIA POWER ON THE WITNESSES! AND QUITE POSSIBLY ON THE JURY AS WELL!
I OBJECT! WHERE'S THE PROOF?
OH PLEASE! JUST LOOK AT THEM...
...LEERING AT HIM WITH THEIR SLACK JAWS AND PUPPY DOG EYES!
SOME OF THEM ARE PRACTICALLY DROOLING! IT'S RIDICULOUS!
MS. GOTLIEB, IT MAY NOT BE MY PLACE TO TELL YOU THIS, BUT INSULTING THE JURORS MAY NOT BE THE BEST PLAN FOR WINNING YOUR CASE.
PLEASE, YOUR HONOR. WHAT CHANCE DO I HAVE, WHEN THE DEFENDANT IS INFLUENCING NOT ONLY THEM, BUT POSSIBLY YOU AS WELL?
I FIND THAT HIGHLY UNLIKELY.
REALLY? THEN FOR MY NEXT WITNESS, I'D LIKE TO CALL...

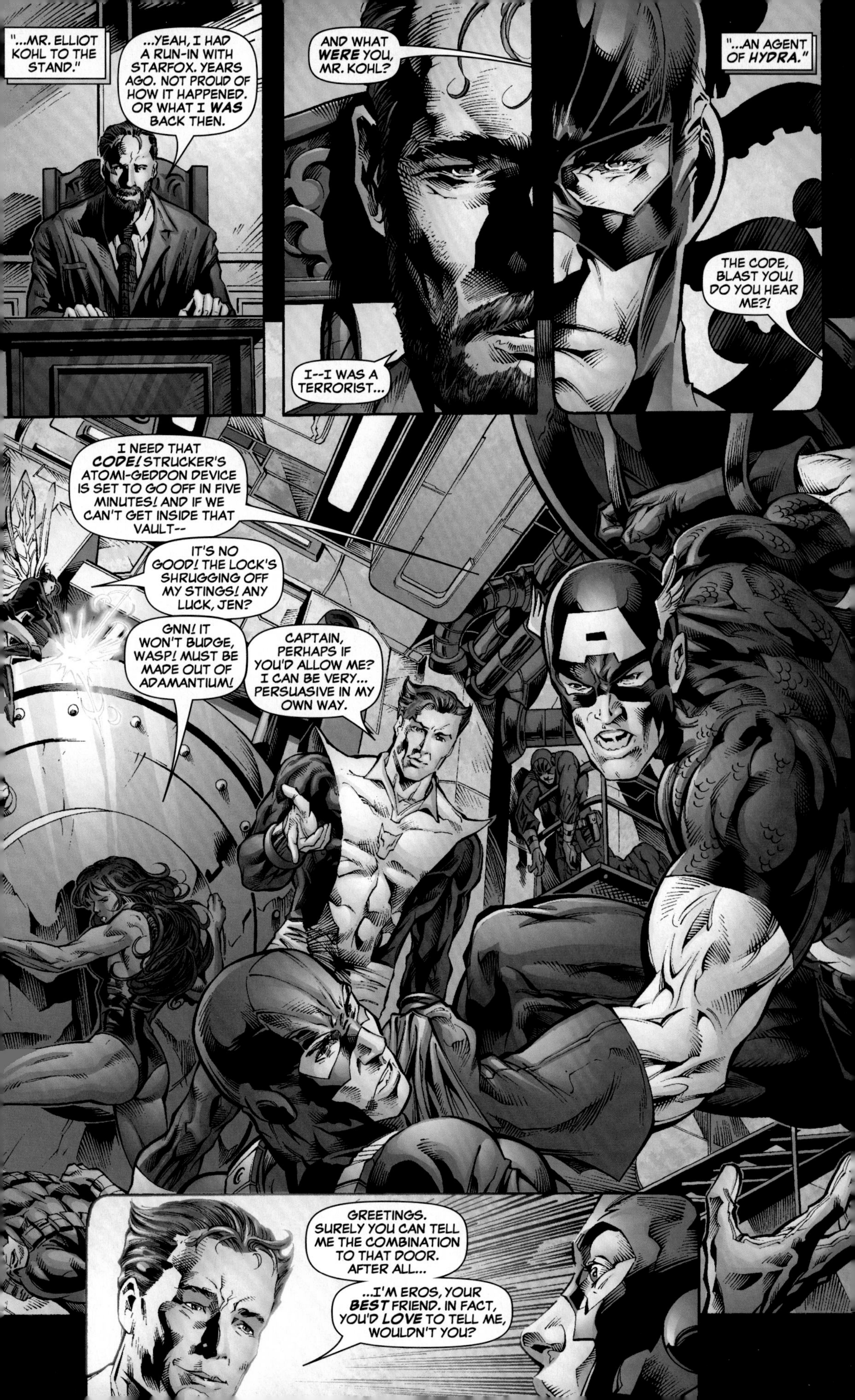
"...MR. ELLIOT KOHL TO THE STAND."
...YEAH, I HAD A RUN-IN WITH STARFOX. YEARS AGO. NOT PROUD OF HOW IT HAPPENED. OR WHAT I WAS BACK THEN.
AND WHAT WERE YOU, MR. KOHL?
I--I WAS A TERRORIST...
"...AN AGENT OF HYDRA."
THE CODE, BLAST YOU! DO YOU HEAR ME?!
I NEED THAT CODE! STRUCKER'S ATOMI-GEDDON DEVICE IS SET TO GO OFF IN FIVE MINUTES! AND IF WE CAN'T GET INSIDE THAT VAULT--
IT'S NO GOOD! THE LOCK'S SHRUGGING OFF MY STINGS! ANY LUCK, JEN?
GNN! IT WON'T BUDGE, WASP! MUST BE MADE OUT OF ADAMANTIUM!
CAPTAIN, PERHAPS IF YOU'D ALLOW ME? I CAN BE VERY... PERSUASIVE IN MY OWN WAY.
GREETINGS. SURELY YOU CAN TELL ME THE COMBINATION TO THAT DOOR. AFTER ALL...
...I'M EROS, YOUR BEST FRIEND. IN FACT, YOU'D LOVE TO TELL ME, WOULDN'T YOU?

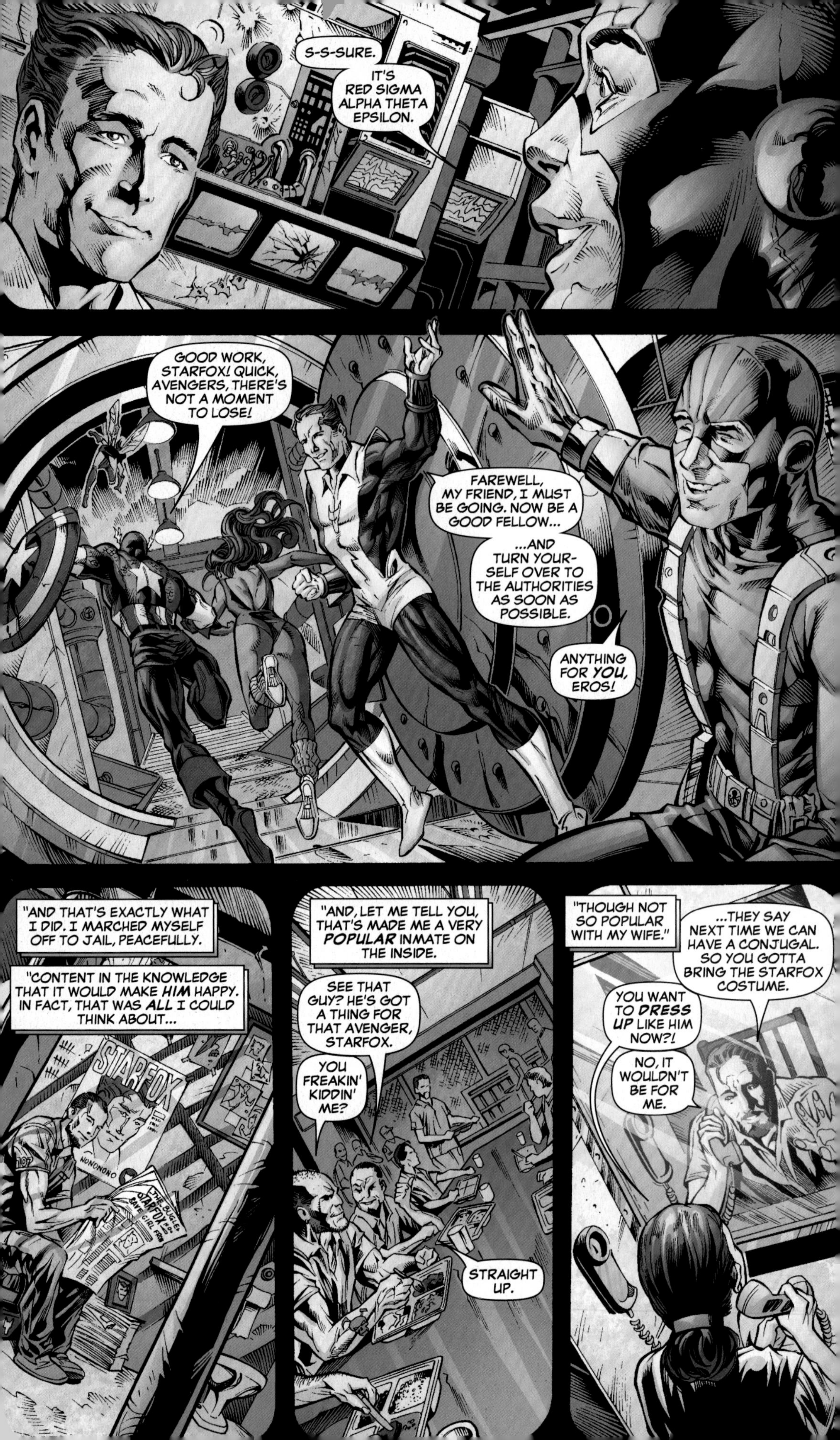
S-S-SURE.
IT'S RED SIGMA ALPHA THETA EPSILON.
GOOD WORK, STARFOX! QUICK, AVENGERS, THERE'S NOT A MOMENT TO LOSE!
FAREWELL, MY FRIEND, I MUST BE GOING. NOW BE A GOOD FELLOW...
...AND TURN YOURSELF OVER TO THE AUTHORITIES AS SOON AS POSSIBLE.
ANYTHING FOR YOU, EROS!
"AND THAT'S EXACTLY WHAT I DID. I MARCHED MYSELF OFF TO JAIL, PEACEFULLY.
"CONTENT IN THE KNOWLEDGE THAT IT WOULD MAKE HIM HAPPY. IN FACT, THAT WAS ALL I COULD THINK ABOUT...
STARFOX
"AND, LET ME TELL YOU, THAT'S MADE ME A VERY POPULAR INMATE ON THE INSIDE.
SEE THAT GUY? HE'S GOT A THING FOR THAT AVENGER, STARFOX.
YOU FREAKIN' KIDDIN' ME?
STRAIGHT UP.
"THOUGH NOT SO POPULAR WITH MY WIFE."
...THEY SAY NEXT TIME WE CAN HAVE A CONJUGAL. SO YOU GOTTA BRING THE STARFOX COSTUME.
YOU WANT TO DRESS UP LIKE HIM NOW?!
NO, IT WOULDN'T BE FOR ME.

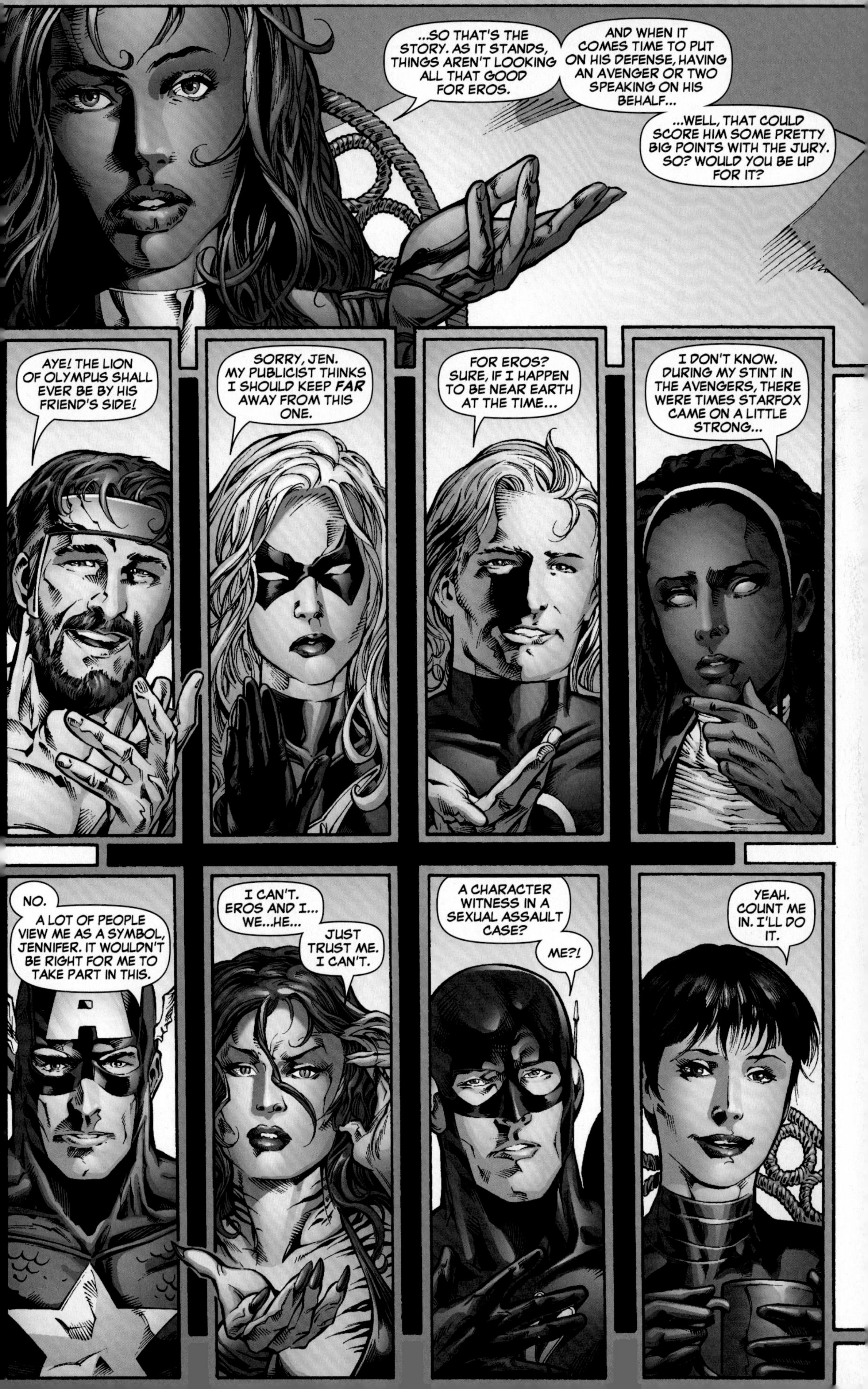
...SO THAT'S THE STORY. AS IT STANDS, THINGS AREN'T LOOKING ALL THAT GOOD FOR EROS.
AND WHEN IT COMES TIME TO PUT ON HIS DEFENSE, HAVING AN AVENGER OR TWO SPEAKING ON HIS BEHALF...
...WELL, THAT COULD SCORE HIM SOME PRETTY BIG POINTS WITH THE JURY. SO? WOULD YOU BE UP FOR IT?
AYE! THE LION OF OLYMPUS SHALL EVER BE BY HIS FRIEND'S SIDE!
SORRY, JEN. MY PUBLICIST THINKS I SHOULD KEEP FAR AWAY FROM THIS ONE.
FOR EROS? SURE, IF I HAPPEN TO BE NEAR EARTH AT THE TIME...
I DON'T KNOW. DURING MY STINT IN THE AVENGERS, THERE WERE TIMES STARFOX CAME ON A LITTLE STRONG...
NO.
A LOT OF PEOPLE VIEW ME AS A SYMBOL, JENNIFER. IT WOULDN'T BE RIGHT FOR ME TO TAKE PART IN THIS.
I CAN'T. EROS AND I... WE...HE...
JUST TRUST ME. I CAN'T.
A CHARACTER WITNESS IN A SEXUAL ASSAULT CASE?
ME?!
YEAH. COUNT ME IN. I'LL DO IT.

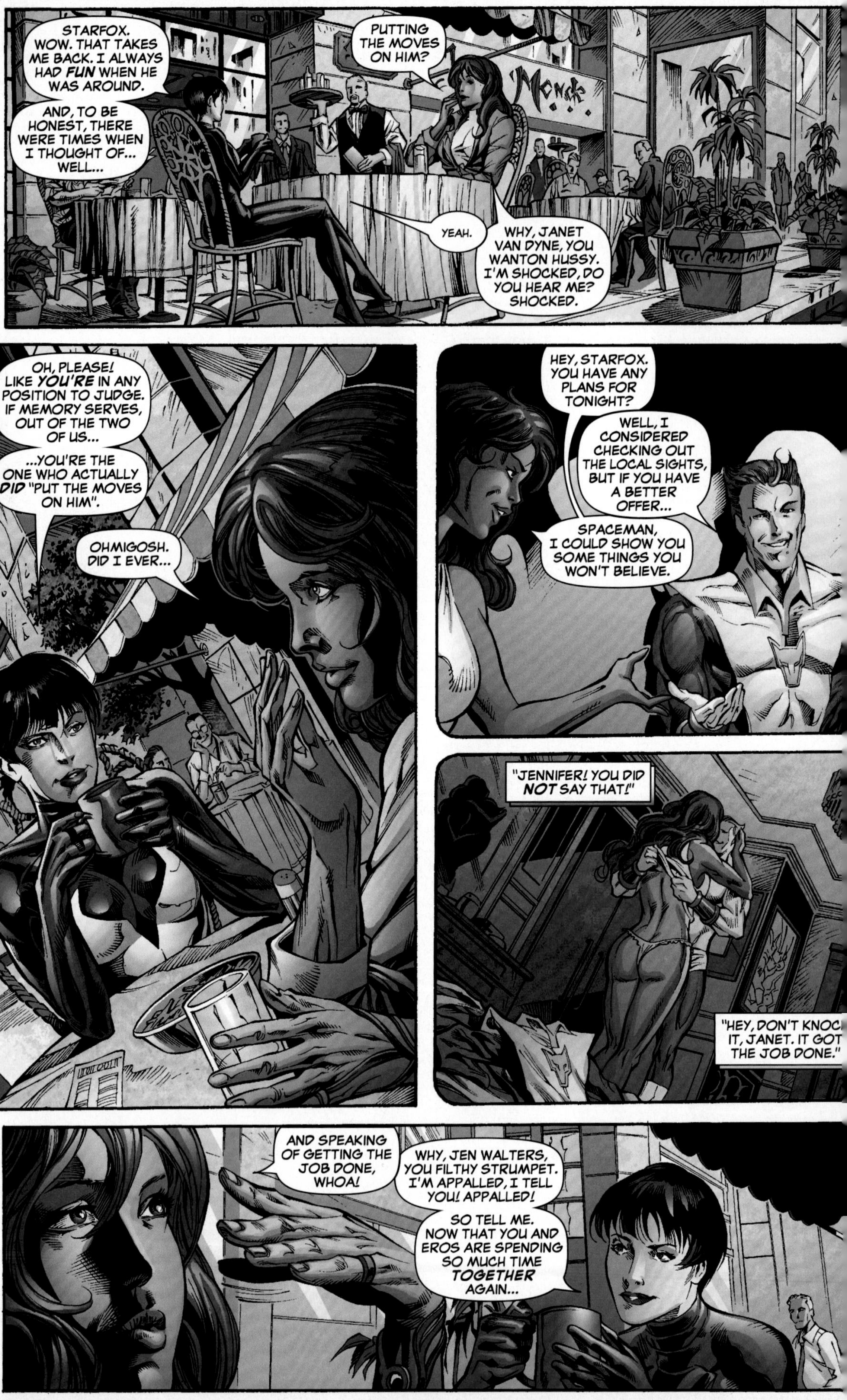

STARFOX. WOW. THAT TAKES ME BACK. I ALWAYS HAD FUN WHEN HE WAS AROUND.
AND, TO BE HONEST, THERE WERE TIMES WHEN I THOUGHT OF... WELL...
PUTTING THE MOVES ON HIM?
'MONCK
YEAH.
WHY, JANET VAN DYNE, YOU WANTON HUSSY. I'M SHOCKED, DO YOU HEAR ME? SHOCKED.
OH, PLEASE! LIKE YOU'RE IN ANY POSITION TO JUDGE. IF MEMORY SERVES, OUT OF THE TWO OF US...
...YOU'RE THE ONE WHO ACTUALLY DID "PUT THE MOVES ON HIM".
OHMIGOSH. DID I EVER...
HEY, STARFOX. YOU HAVE ANY PLANS FOR TONIGHT?
WELL, I CONSIDERED CHECKING OUT THE LOCAL SIGHTS, BUT IF YOU HAVE A BETTER OFFER...
SPACEMAN, I COULD SHOW YOU SOME THINGS YOU WON'T BELIEVE.
"JENNIFER! YOU DID NOT SAY THAT!"
"HEY, DON'T KNOC IT, JANET. IT GOT THE JOB DONE."
AND SPEAKING OF GETTING THE JOB DONE, WHOA!
WHY, JEN WALTERS, YOU FILTHY STRUMPET. I'M APPALLED, I TELL YOU! APPALLED!
SO TELL ME. NOW THAT YOU AND EROS ARE SPENDING SO MUCH TIME TOGETHER AGAIN...

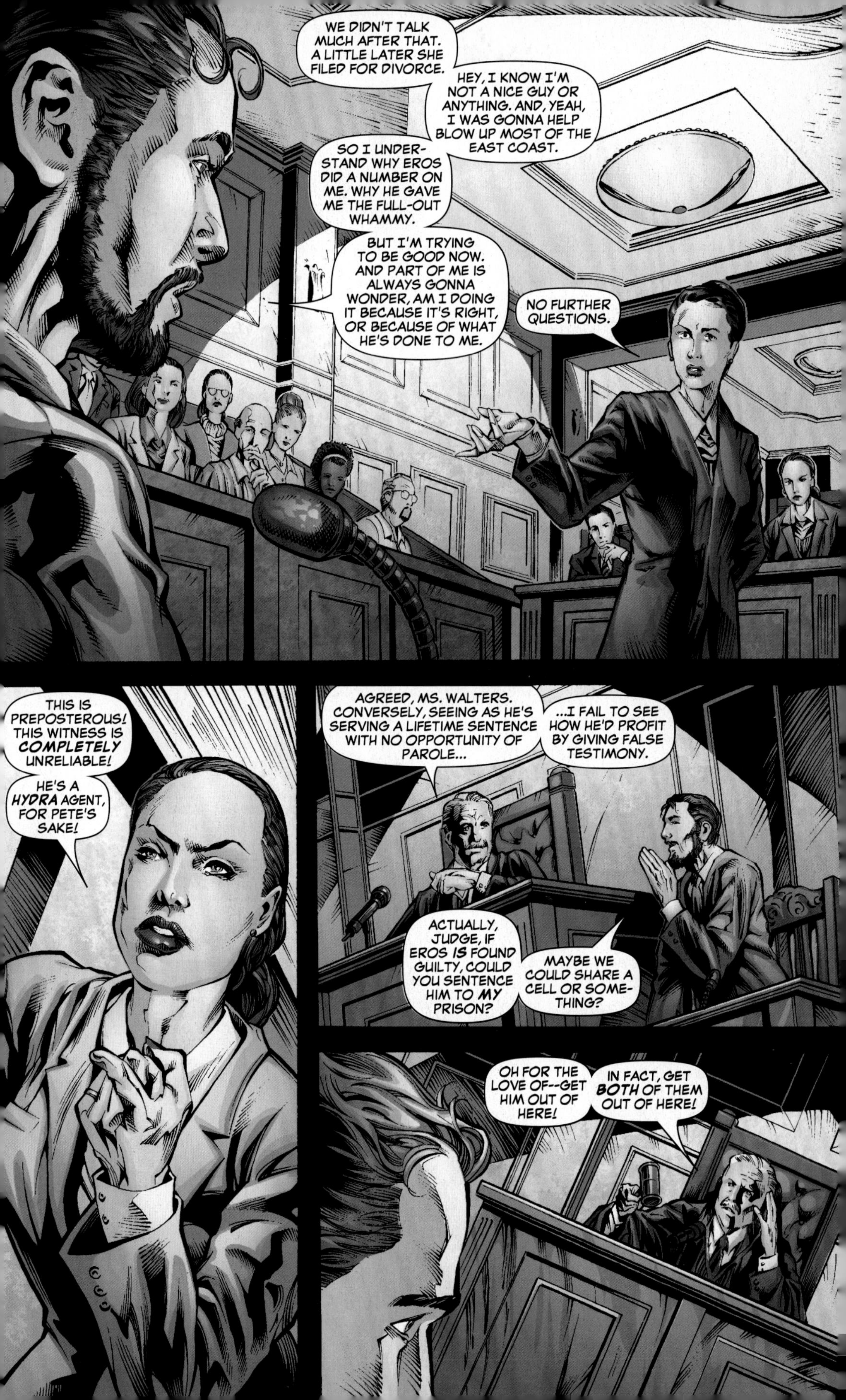
WE DIDN'T TALK MUCH AFTER THAT. A LITTLE LATER SHE FILED FOR DIVORCE.
HEY, I KNOW I'M NOT A NICE GUY OR ANYTHING. AND, YEAH, I WAS GONNA HELP BLOW UP MOST OF THE EAST COAST.
SO I UNDER-STAND WHY EROS DID A NUMBER ON ME. WHY HE GAVE ME THE FULL-OUT WHAMMY.
BUT I'M TRYING TO BE GOOD NOW. AND PART OF ME IS ALWAYS GONNA WONDER, AM I DOING IT BECAUSE IT'S RIGHT, OR BECAUSE OF WHAT HE'S DONE TO ME.
NO FURTHER QUESTIONS.
THIS IS PREPOSTEROUS! THIS WITNESS IS COMPLETELY UNRELIABLE!
HE'S A HYDRA AGENT, FOR PETE'S SAKE!
AGREED, MS. WALTERS. CONVERSELY, SEEING AS HE'S SERVING A LIFETIME SENTENCE WITH NO OPPORTUNITY OF PAROLE...
...I FAIL TO SEE HOW HE'D PROFIT BY GIVING FALSE TESTIMONY.
ACTUALLY, JUDGE, IF EROS IS FOUND GUILTY, COULD YOU SENTENCE HIM TO MY PRISON?
MAYBE WE COULD SHARE A CELL OR SOME-THING?
OH FOR THE LOVE OF--GET HIM OUT OF HERE!
IN FACT, GET BOTH OF THEM OUT OF HERE!

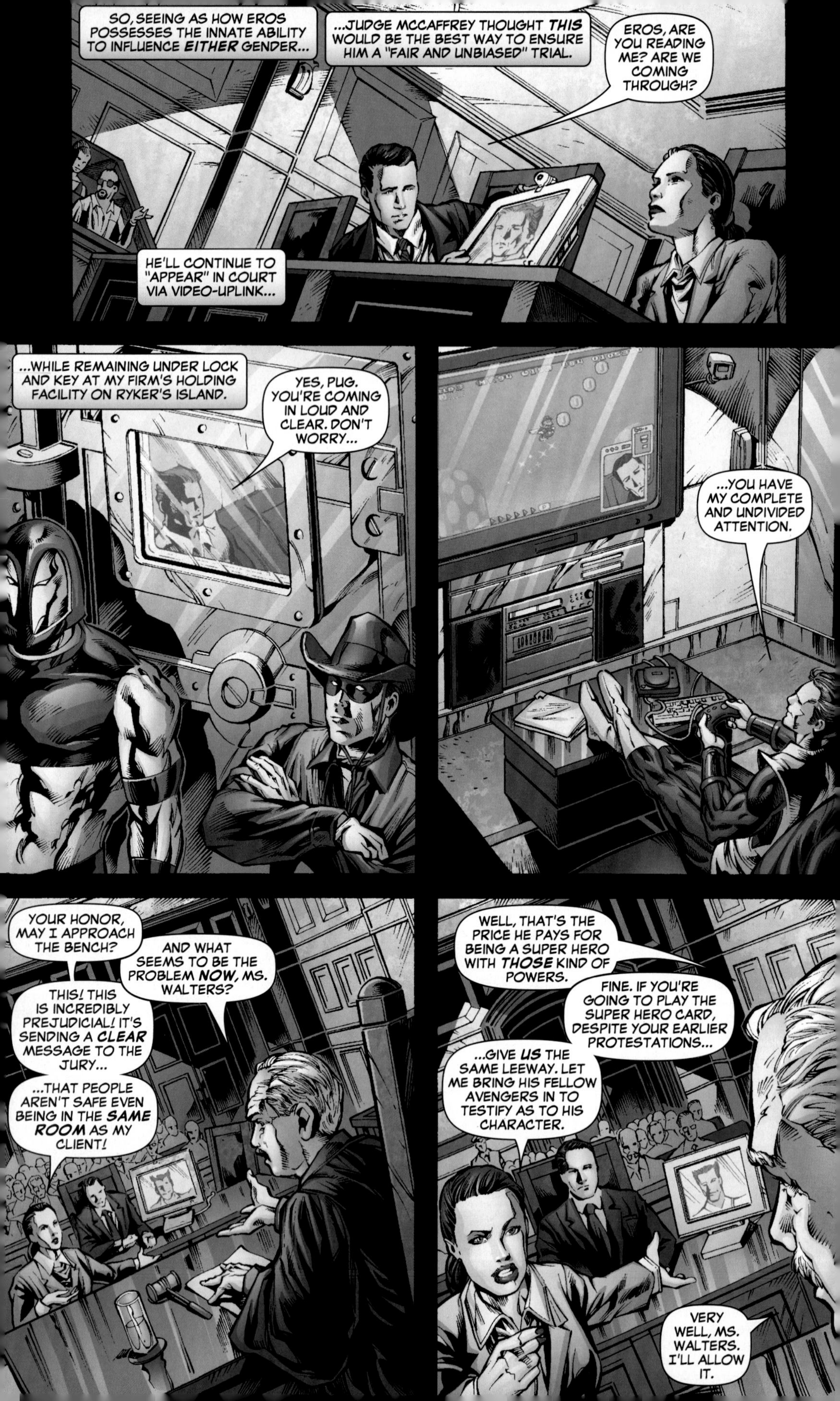

SO, SEEING AS HOW EROS POSSESSES THE INNATE ABILITY TO INFLUENCE *EITHER* GENDER...
...JUDGE MCCAFFREY THOUGHT *THIS* WOULD BE THE BEST WAY TO ENSURE HIM A "FAIR AND UNBIASED" TRIAL.
EROS, ARE YOU READING ME? ARE WE COMING THROUGH?
HE'LL CONTINUE TO "APPEAR" IN COURT VIA VIDEO-UPLINK...
...WHILE REMAINING UNDER LOCK AND KEY AT MY FIRM'S HOLDING FACILITY ON RYKER'S ISLAND.
YES, PUG. YOU'RE COMING IN LOUD AND CLEAR. DON'T WORRY...
...YOU HAVE MY COMPLETE AND UNDIVIDED ATTENTION.
YOUR HONOR, MAY I APPROACH THE BENCH?
AND WHAT SEEMS TO BE THE PROBLEM *NOW*, MS. WALTERS?
THIS! THIS IS INCREDIBLY PREJUDICIAL! IT'S SENDING A *CLEAR* MESSAGE TO THE JURY...
...THAT PEOPLE AREN'T SAFE EVEN BEING IN THE *SAME ROOM* AS MY CLIENT!
WELL, THAT'S THE PRICE HE PAYS FOR BEING A SUPER HERO WITH *THOSE* KIND OF POWERS.
FINE. IF YOU'RE GOING TO PLAY THE SUPER HERO CARD, DESPITE YOUR EARLIER PROTESTATIONS...
...GIVE *US* THE SAME LEEWAY. LET ME BRING HIS FELLOW AVENGERS IN TO TESTIFY AS TO HIS CHARACTER.
VERY WELL, MS. WALTERS. I'LL ALLOW IT.

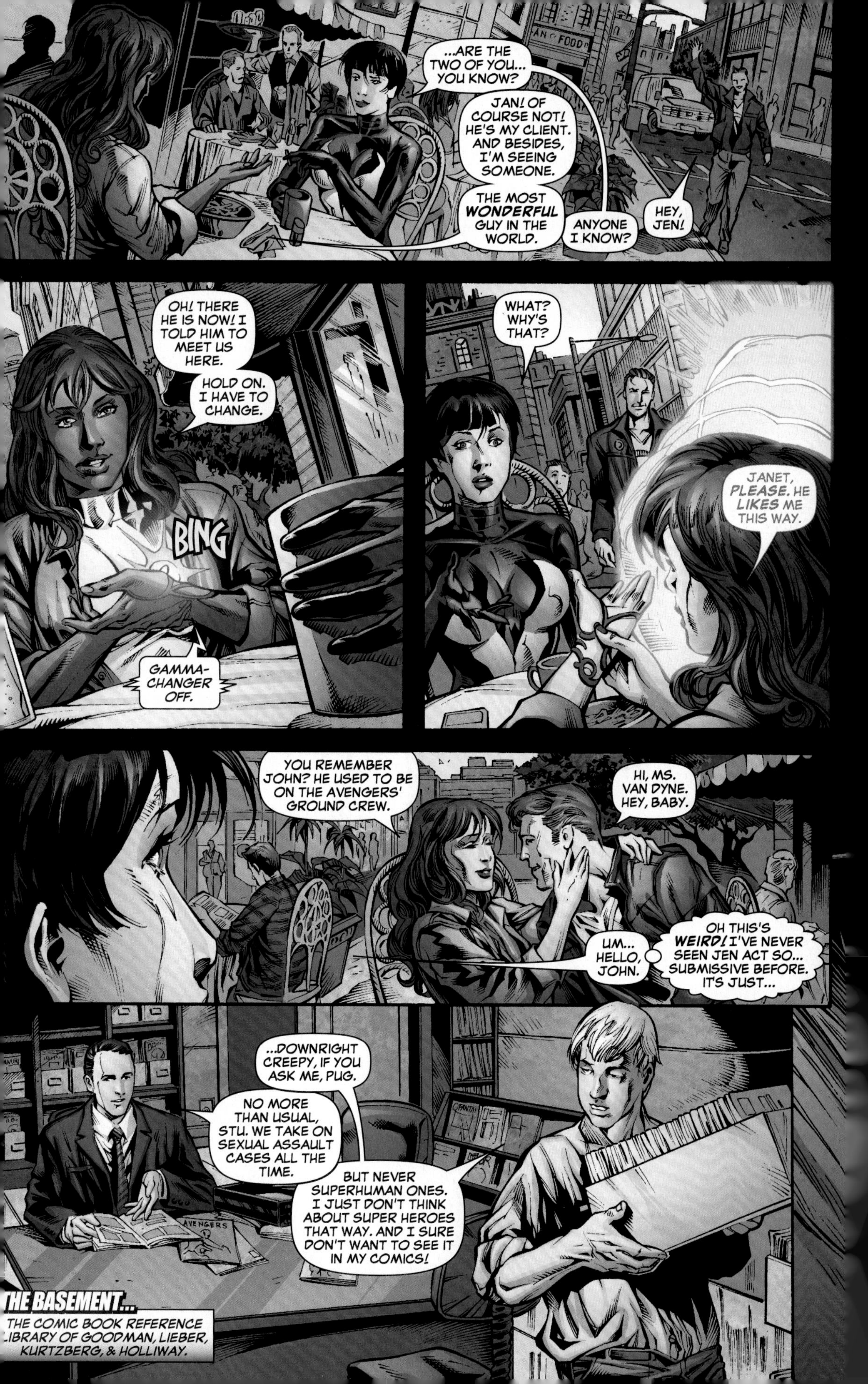
...ARE THE TWO OF YOU... YOU KNOW?
JAN! OF COURSE NOT! HE'S MY CLIENT. AND BESIDES, I'M SEEING SOMEONE.
THE MOST WONDERFUL GUY IN THE WORLD.
ANYONE I KNOW?
HEY, JEN!
OH! THERE HE IS NOW! I TOLD HIM TO MEET US HERE.
HOLD ON. I HAVE TO CHANGE.
BING
GAMMA-CHANGER OFF.
WHAT? WHY'S THAT?
JANET, PLEASE. HE LIKES ME THIS WAY.
YOU REMEMBER JOHN? HE USED TO BE ON THE AVENGERS' GROUND CREW.
HI, MS. VAN DYNE. HEY, BABY.
UM... HELLO, JOHN.
OH THIS'S WEIRD! I'VE NEVER SEEN JEN ACT SO... SUBMISSIVE BEFORE. IT'S JUST...
...DOWNRIGHT CREEPY, IF YOU ASK ME, PUG.
NO MORE THAN USUAL, STU. WE TAKE ON SEXUAL ASSAULT CASES ALL THE TIME.
BUT NEVER SUPERHUMAN ONES. I JUST DON'T THINK ABOUT SUPER HEROES THAT WAY. AND I SURE DON'T WANT TO SEE IT IN MY COMICS!
THE BASEMENT...
THE COMIC BOOK REFERENCE LIBRARY OF GOODMAN, LIEBER, KURTZBERG, & HOLLIWAY.

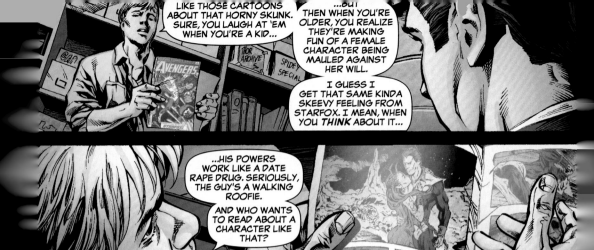

LIKE THOSE CARTOONS ABOUT THAT HORNY SKUNK. SURE, YOU LAUGH AT 'EM WHEN YOU'RE A KID...
...BUT THEN WHEN YOU'RE OLDER, YOU REALIZE THEY'RE MAKING FUN OF A FEMALE CHARACTER BEING MAULED AGAINST HER WILL.
I GUESS I GET THAT SAME KINDA SKEEVY FEELING FROM STARFOX. I MEAN, WHEN YOU *THINK* ABOUT IT...
AVENGERS
THOR ARCHIVE
SPIDEY SPECIAL
...HIS POWERS WORK LIKE A DATE RAPE DRUG. SERIOUSLY, THE GUY'S A WALKING ROOFIE.
AND WHO WANTS TO READ ABOUT A CHARACTER LIKE THAT?
GEEZ, STU. HE'S NOT A "CHARACTER." THIS'S A ***REAL GUY*** WE'RE TALKING ABOUT. A ***HERO,*** AN ***AVENGER,*** AND OUR ***CLIENT.***
LOOK, THANKS FOR DIGGING THIS UP FOR ME, BUT I SHOULD BE HEADING BACK TO COURT...
HEY, THIS AIN'T MY BRIEFCASE...
WALTERS
MUST'VE GRABBED JEN'S BY MIS--
WHAT THE?!--
John loves Jen
John
JOHN & JEN
JEN
UPSTAIRS...
ut enough
space to say
how much
I love yo

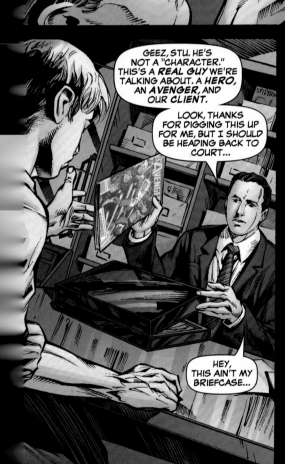

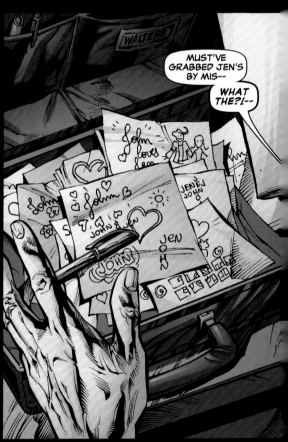

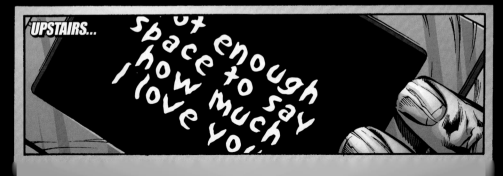

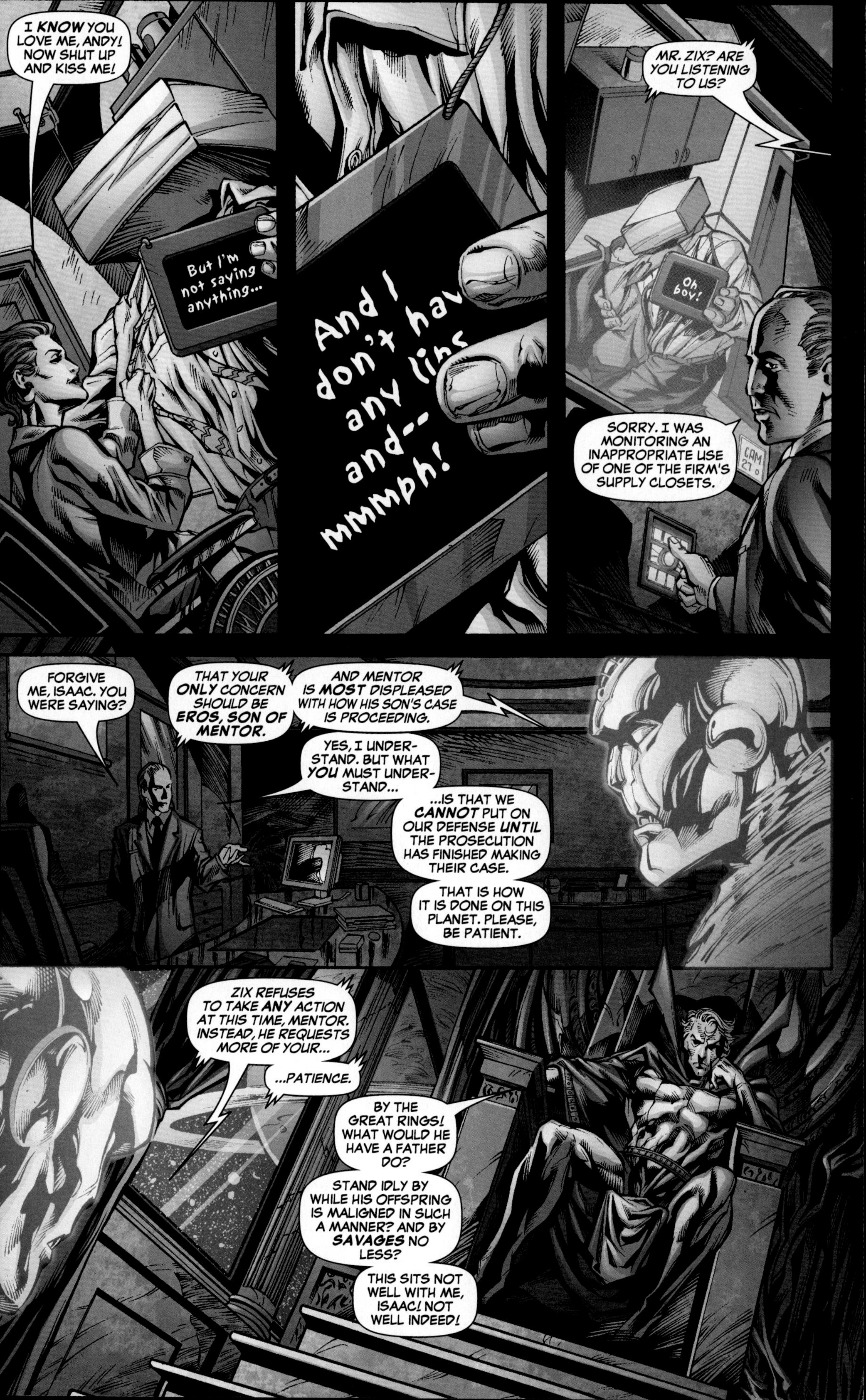
I KNOW YOU LOVE ME, ANDY! NOW SHUT UP AND KISS ME!
But I'm not saying anything...
And I don't hav any lips and-- mmmph!
MR. ZIX? ARE YOU LISTENING TO US?
Oh boy!
SORRY. I WAS MONITORING AN INAPPROPRIATE USE OF ONE OF THE FIRM'S SUPPLY CLOSETS.
CAM 27
FORGIVE ME, ISAAC. YOU WERE SAYING?
THAT YOUR ONLY CONCERN SHOULD BE EROS, SON OF MENTOR.
AND MENTOR IS MOST DISPLEASED WITH HOW HIS SON'S CASE IS PROCEEDING.
YES, I UNDER-STAND. BUT WHAT YOU MUST UNDER-STAND...
...IS THAT WE CANNOT PUT ON OUR DEFENSE UNTIL THE PROSECUTION HAS FINISHED MAKING THEIR CASE.
THAT IS HOW IT IS DONE ON THIS PLANET. PLEASE, BE PATIENT.
ZIX REFUSES TO TAKE ANY ACTION AT THIS TIME, MENTOR. INSTEAD, HE REQUESTS MORE OF YOUR...
...PATIENCE.
BY THE GREAT RINGS! WHAT WOULD HE HAVE A FATHER DO?
STAND IDLY BY WHILE HIS OFFSPRING IS MALIGNED IN SUCH A MANNER? AND BY SAVAGES NO LESS?
THIS SITS NOT WELL WITH ME, ISAAC! NOT WELL INDEED!

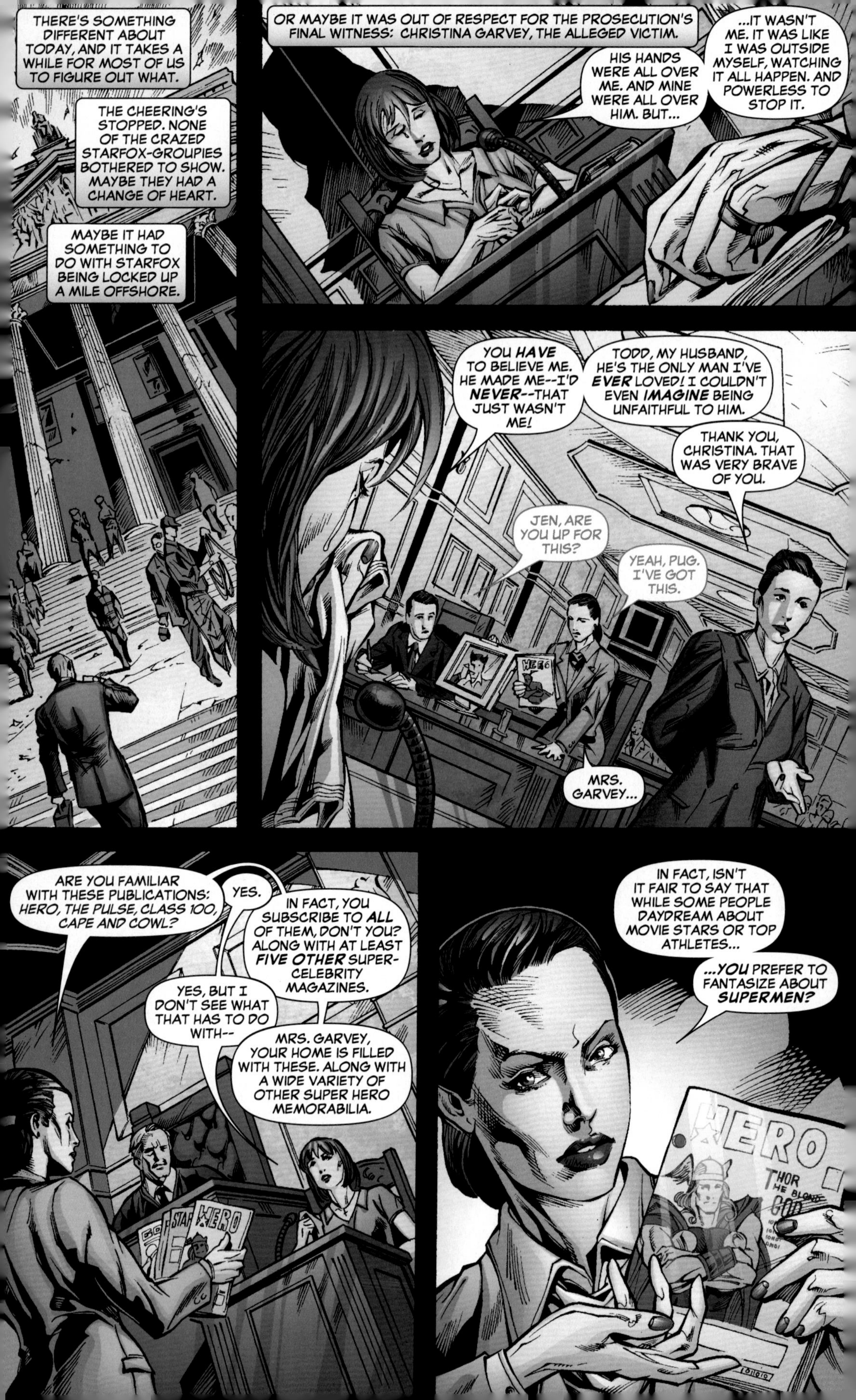
THERE'S SOMETHING DIFFERENT ABOUT TODAY, AND IT TAKES A WHILE FOR MOST OF US TO FIGURE OUT WHAT.
THE CHEERING'S STOPPED. NONE OF THE CRAZED STARFOX-GROUPIES BOTHERED TO SHOW. MAYBE THEY HAD A CHANGE OF HEART.
MAYBE IT HAD SOMETHING TO DO WITH STARFOX BEING LOCKED UP A MILE OFFSHORE.
OR MAYBE IT WAS OUT OF RESPECT FOR THE PROSECUTION'S FINAL WITNESS: CHRISTINA GARVEY, THE ALLEGED VICTIM.
HIS HANDS WERE ALL OVER ME. AND MINE WERE ALL OVER HIM. BUT...
...IT WASN'T ME. IT WAS LIKE I WAS OUTSIDE MYSELF, WATCHING IT ALL HAPPEN. AND POWERLESS TO STOP IT.
YOU HAVE TO BELIEVE ME. HE MADE ME--I'D NEVER--THAT JUST WASN'T ME!
TODD, MY HUSBAND, HE'S THE ONLY MAN I'VE EVER LOVED! I COULDN'T EVEN IMAGINE BEING UNFAITHFUL TO HIM.
THANK YOU, CHRISTINA. THAT WAS VERY BRAVE OF YOU.
JEN, ARE YOU UP FOR THIS?
YEAH, PUG. I'VE GOT THIS.
MRS. GARVEY...
ARE YOU FAMILIAR WITH THESE PUBLICATIONS: HERO, THE PULSE, CLASS 100, CAPE AND COWL?
YES.
IN FACT, YOU SUBSCRIBE TO ALL OF THEM, DON'T YOU? ALONG WITH AT LEAST FIVE OTHER SUPER-CELEBRITY MAGAZINES.
YES, BUT I DON'T SEE WHAT THAT HAS TO DO WITH--
MRS. GARVEY, YOUR HOME IS FILLED WITH THESE. ALONG WITH A WIDE VARIETY OF OTHER SUPER HERO MEMORABILIA.
IN FACT, ISN'T IT FAIR TO SAY THAT WHILE SOME PEOPLE DAYDREAM ABOUT MOVIE STARS OR TOP ATHLETES...
...YOU PREFER TO FANTASIZE ABOUT SUPERMEN?
HERO
THOR THE BLOND GOD

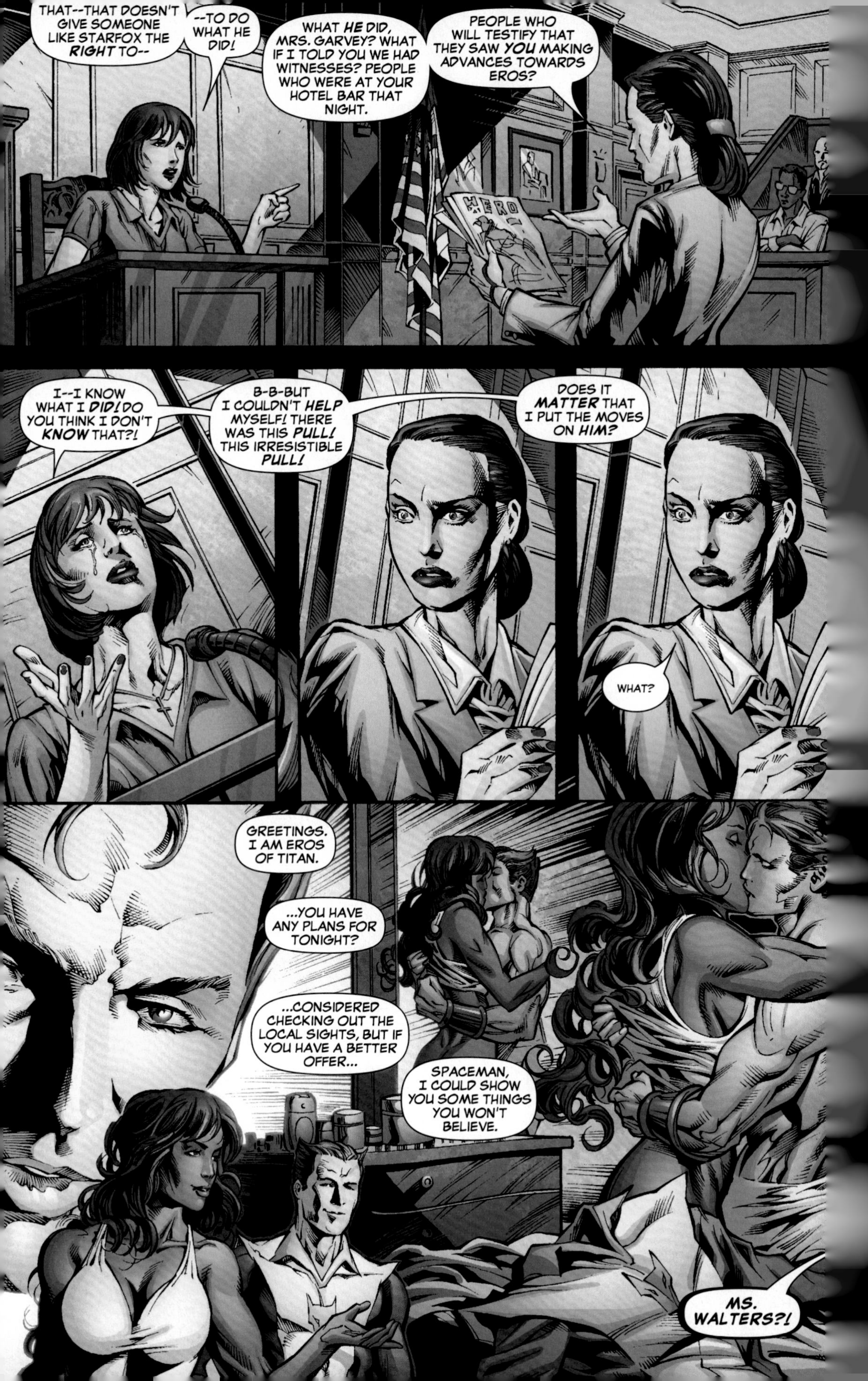
THAT--THAT DOESN'T GIVE SOMEONE LIKE STARFOX THE RIGHT TO--
--TO DO WHAT HE DID!
WHAT HE DID, MRS. GARVEY? WHAT IF I TOLD YOU WE HAD WITNESSES? PEOPLE WHO WERE AT YOUR HOTEL BAR THAT NIGHT.
PEOPLE WHO WILL TESTIFY THAT THEY SAW YOU MAKING ADVANCES TOWARDS EROS?
HERO
I--I KNOW WHAT I DID! DO YOU THINK I DON'T KNOW THAT?!
B-B-BUT I COULDN'T HELP MYSELF! THERE WAS THIS PULL! THIS IRRESISTIBLE PULL!
DOES IT MATTER THAT I PUT THE MOVES ON HIM?
WHAT?
GREETINGS. I AM EROS OF TITAN.
...YOU HAVE ANY PLANS FOR TONIGHT?
...CONSIDERED CHECKING OUT THE LOCAL SIGHTS, BUT IF YOU HAVE A BETTER OFFER...
SPACEMAN, I COULD SHOW YOU SOME THINGS YOU WON'T BELIEVE.
MS. WALTERS?!

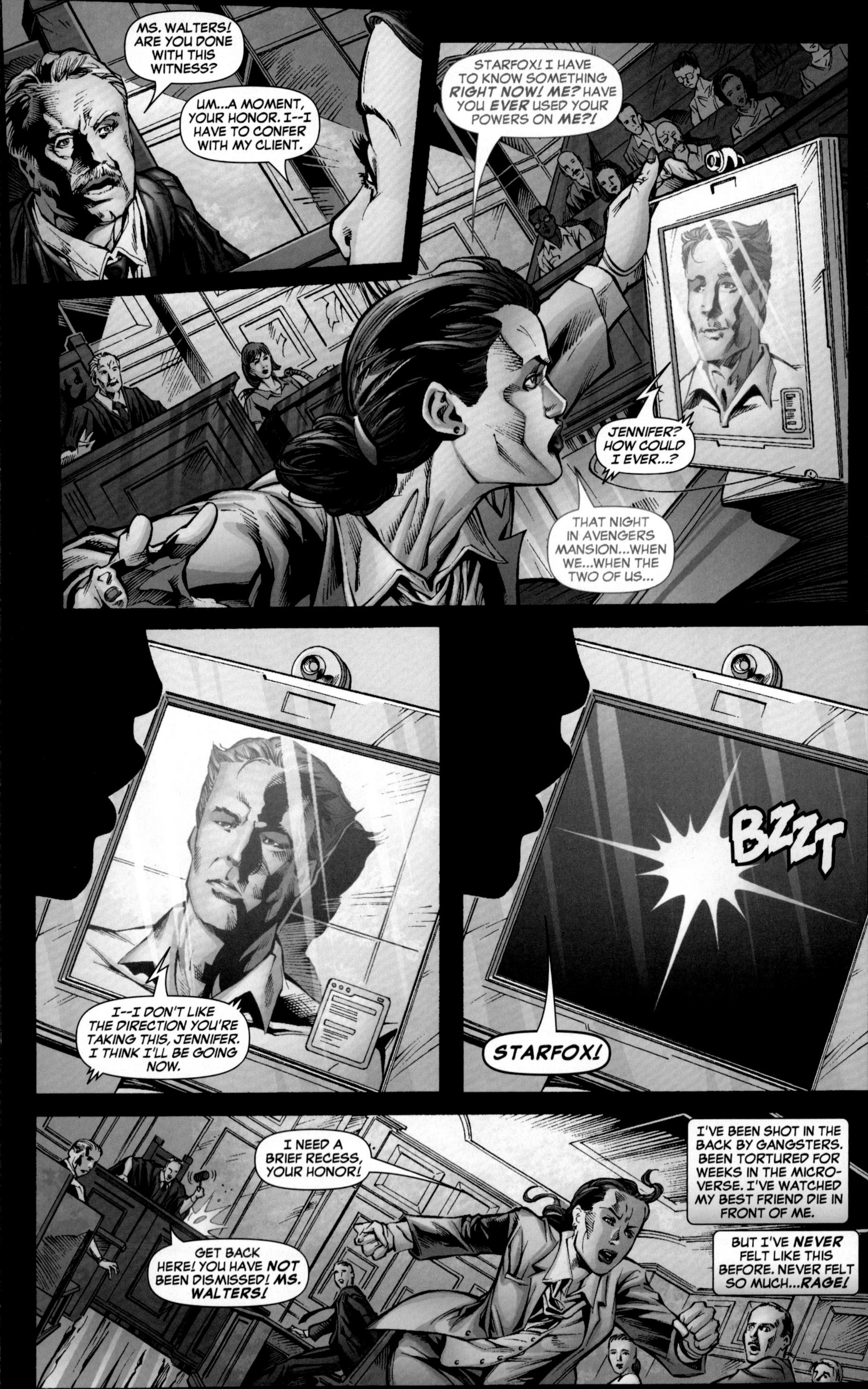
MS. WALTERS! ARE YOU DONE WITH THIS WITNESS?
UM...A MOMENT, YOUR HONOR. I--I HAVE TO CONFER WITH MY CLIENT.
STARFOX! I HAVE TO KNOW SOMETHING RIGHT NOW! ME? HAVE YOU EVER USED YOUR POWERS ON ME?!
JENNIFER? HOW COULD I EVER...?
THAT NIGHT IN AVENGERS MANSION...WHEN WE...WHEN THE TWO OF US...
I--I DON'T LIKE THE DIRECTION YOU'RE TAKING THIS, JENNIFER. I THINK I'LL BE GOING NOW.
BZZT
STARFOX!
I NEED A BRIEF RECESS, YOUR HONOR!
I'VE BEEN SHOT IN THE BACK BY GANGSTERS. BEEN TORTURED FOR WEEKS IN THE MICRO-VERSE. I'VE WATCHED MY BEST FRIEND DIE IN FRONT OF ME.
GET BACK HERE! YOU HAVE NOT BEEN DISMISSED! MS. WALTERS!
BUT I'VE NEVER FELT LIKE THIS BEFORE. NEVER FELT SO MUCH...RAGE!

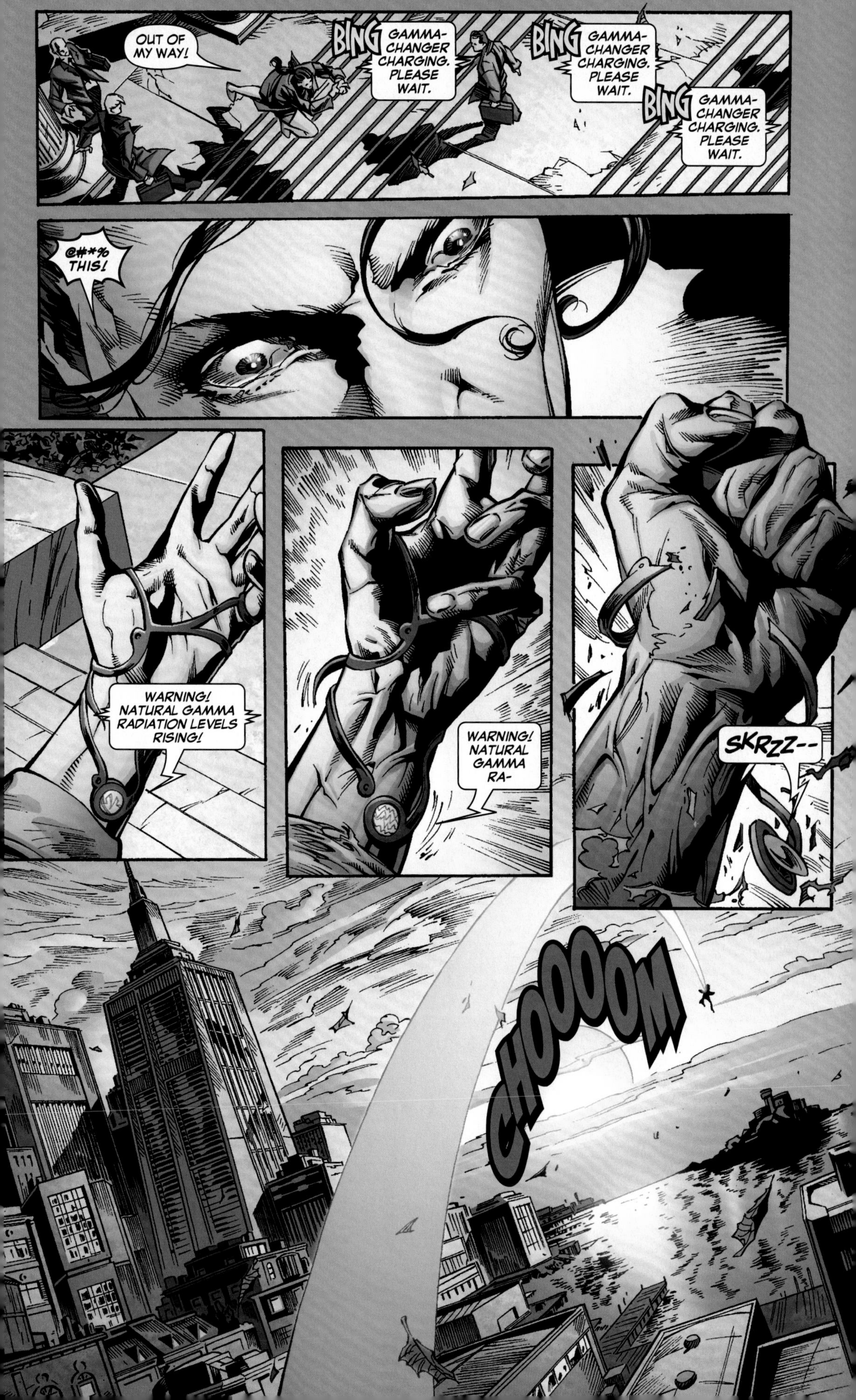
OUT OF MY WAY!
BING
GAMMA-CHANGER CHARGING. PLEASE WAIT.
BING
GAMMA-CHANGER CHARGING. PLEASE WAIT.
BING
GAMMA-CHANGER CHARGING. PLEASE WAIT.
@#*% THIS!
WARNING! NATURAL GAMMA RADIATION LEVELS RISING!
WARNING! NATURAL GAMMA RA-
SKRZZ--
CHOOOOM

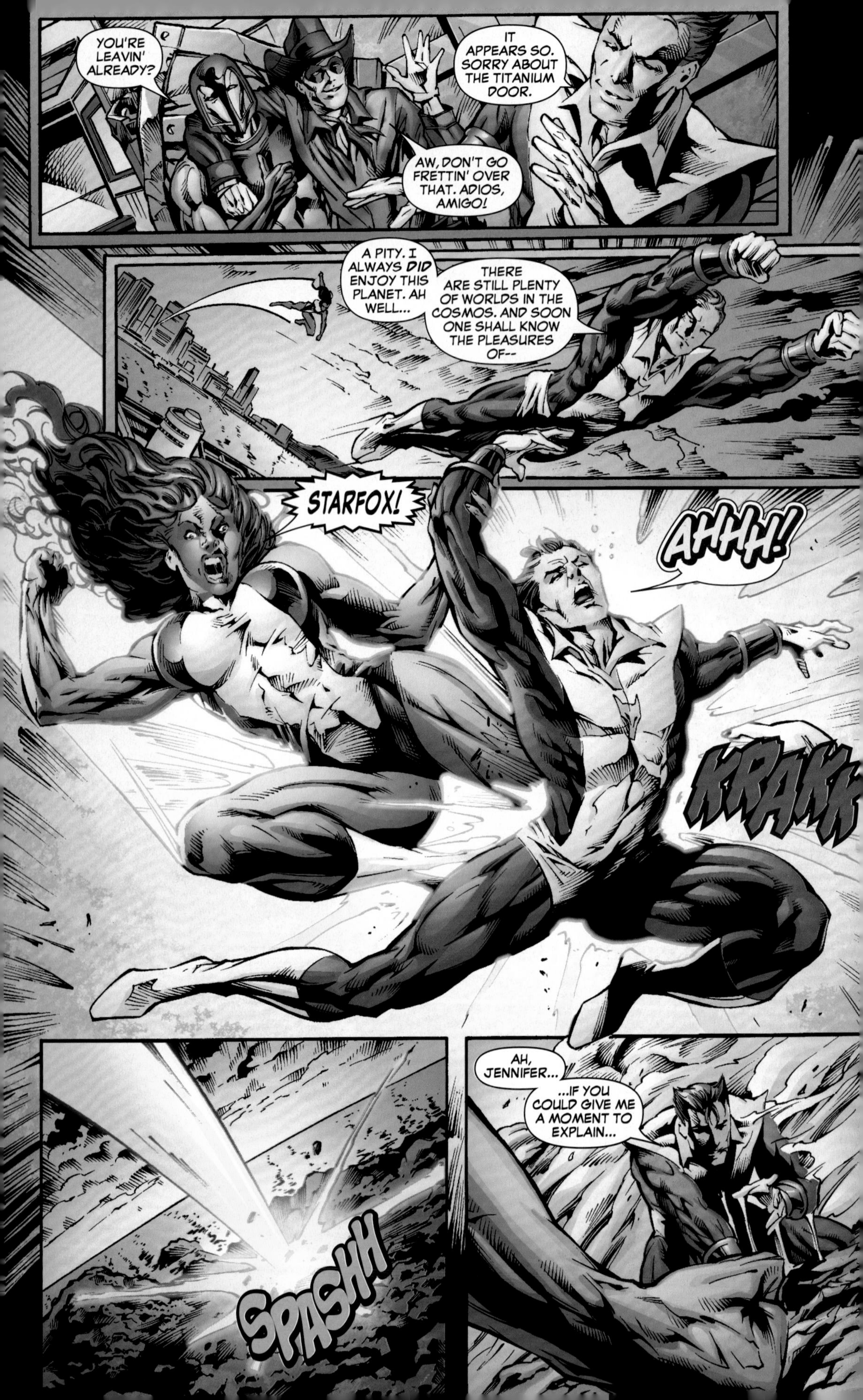

YOU'RE LEAVIN' ALREADY?
IT APPEARS SO. SORRY ABOUT THE TITANIUM DOOR.
AW, DON'T GO FRETTIN' OVER THAT. ADIOS, AMIGO!
A PITY. I ALWAYS DID ENJOY THIS PLANET. AH WELL...
THERE ARE STILL PLENTY OF WORLDS IN THE COSMOS. AND SOON ONE SHALL KNOW THE PLEASURES OF--
STARFOX!
AHHH!
KRAKK
SPASHH
AH, JENNIFER...
...IF YOU COULD GIVE ME A MOMENT TO EXPLAIN...

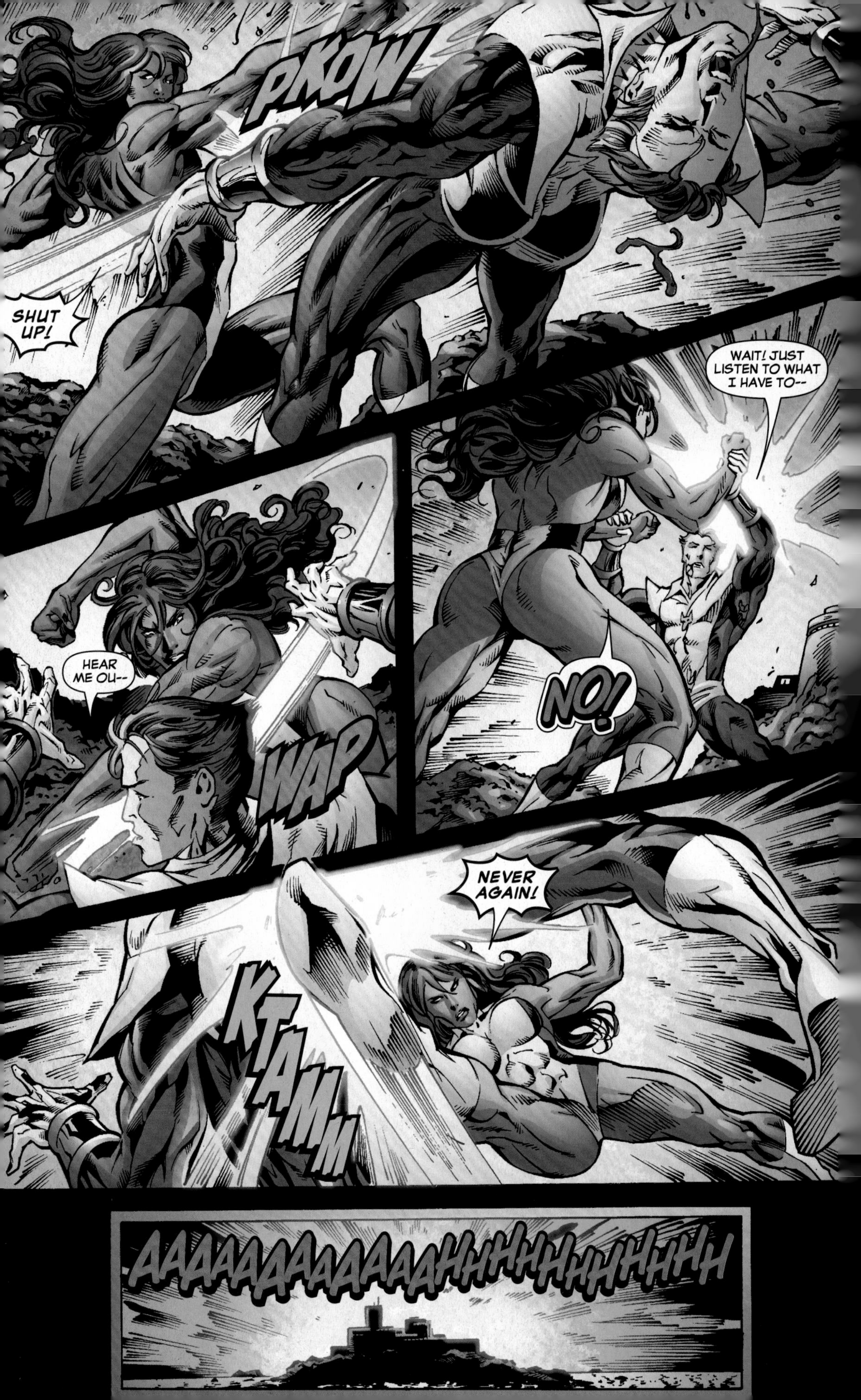
PKOW
SHUT UP!
WAIT! JUST LISTEN TO WHAT I HAVE TO--
NO!
HEAR ME OU--
WAP
NEVER AGAIN!
KTAMM
AAAAAAAAAAAAAHHHHHHHHHHHH

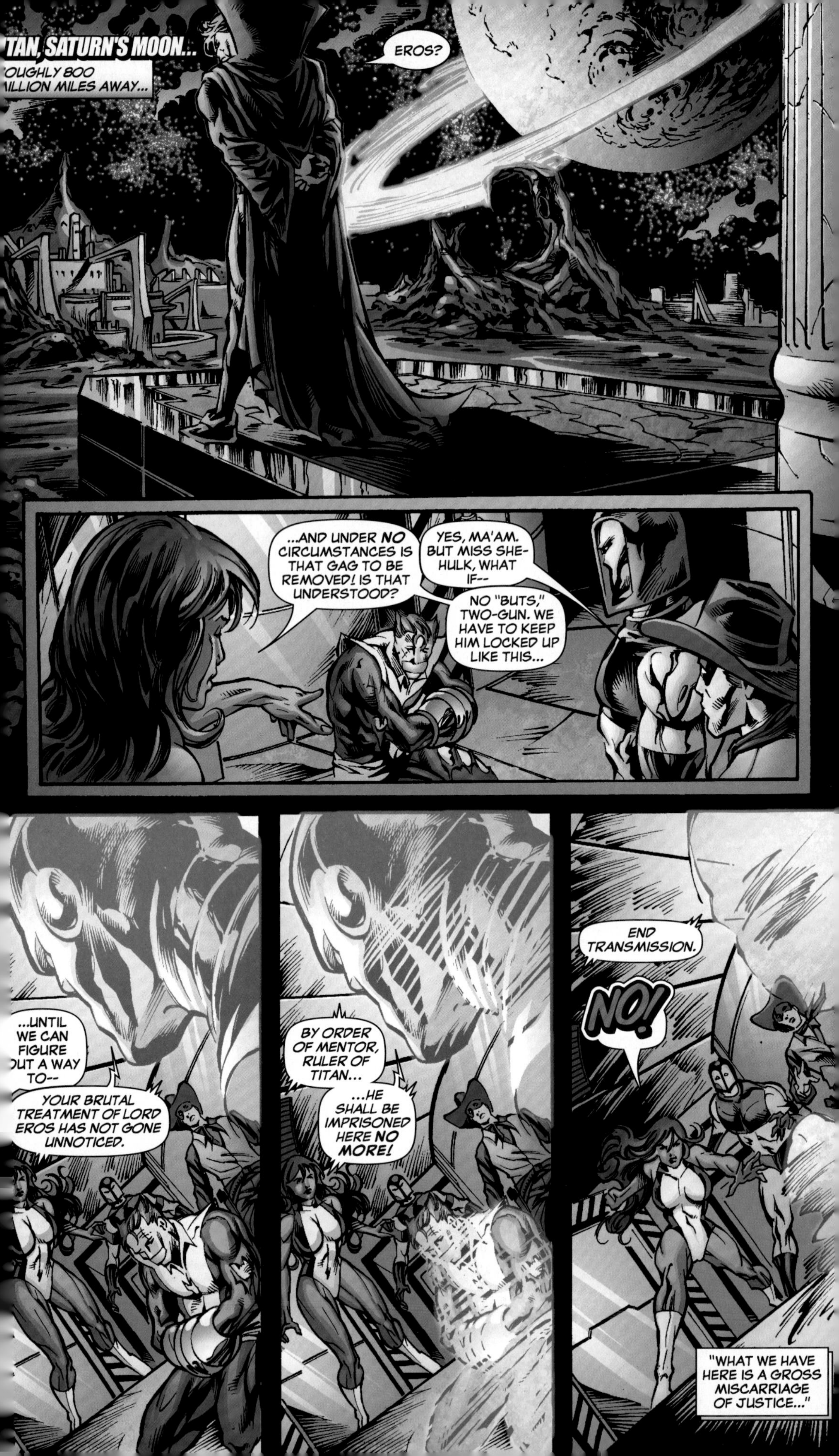
TAN, SATURN'S MOON...
OUGHLY 800
MILLION MILES AWAY...
EROS?
...AND UNDER NO CIRCUMSTANCES IS THAT GAG TO BE REMOVED! IS THAT UNDERSTOOD?
YES, MA'AM. BUT MISS SHE-HULK, WHAT IF--
NO "BUTS," TWO-GUN. WE HAVE TO KEEP HIM LOCKED UP LIKE THIS...
...UNTIL WE CAN FIGURE OUT A WAY TO--
YOUR BRUTAL TREATMENT OF LORD EROS HAS NOT GONE UNNOTICED.
BY ORDER OF MENTOR, RULER OF TITAN...
...HE SHALL BE IMPRISONED HERE NO MORE!
END TRANSMISSION.
NO!
"WHAT WE HAVE HERE IS A GROSS MISCARRIAGE OF JUSTICE..."

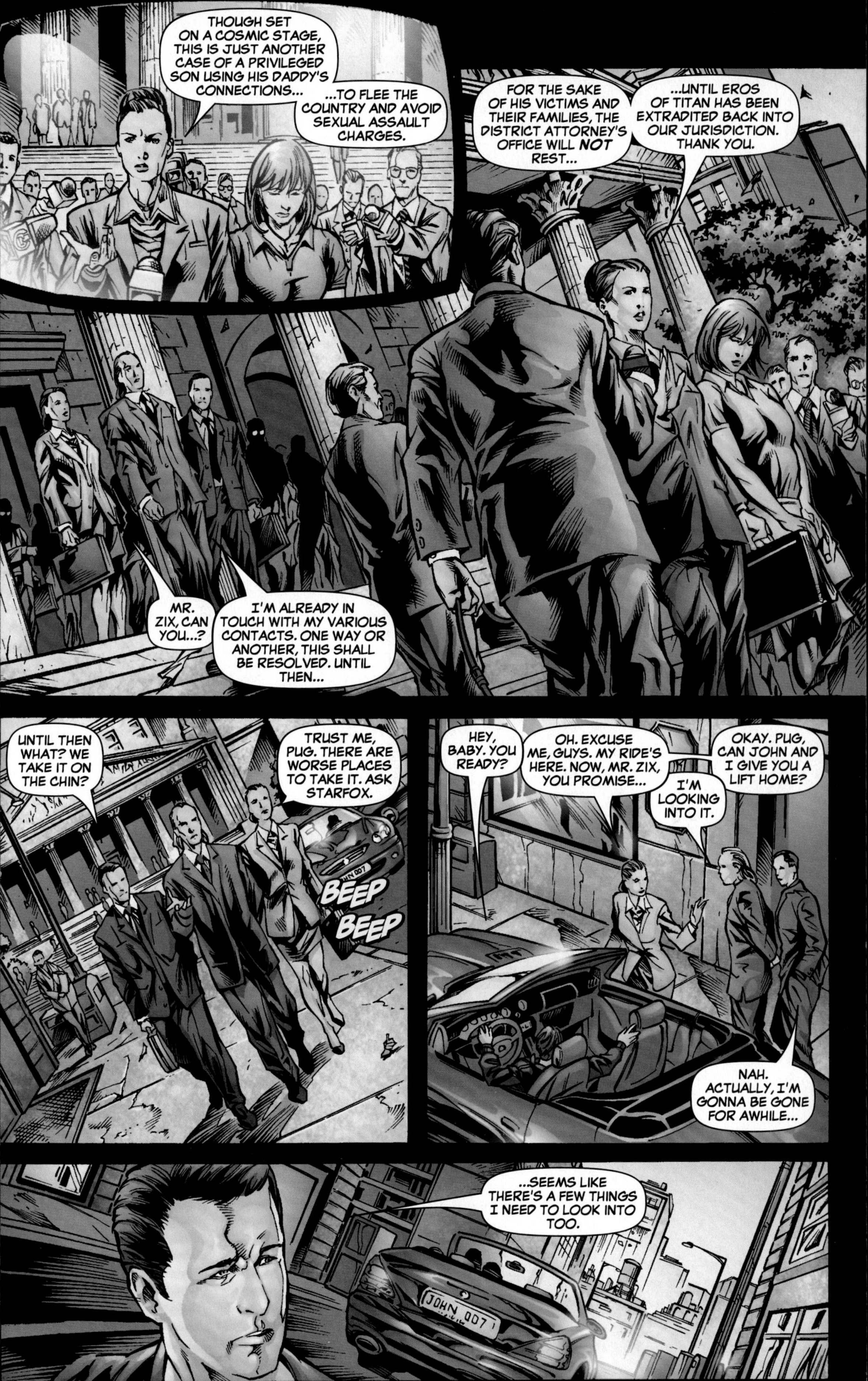
THOUGH SET ON A COSMIC STAGE, THIS IS JUST ANOTHER CASE OF A PRIVILEGED SON USING HIS DADDY'S CONNECTIONS...
...TO FLEE THE COUNTRY AND AVOID SEXUAL ASSAULT CHARGES.
FOR THE SAKE OF HIS VICTIMS AND THEIR FAMILIES, THE DISTRICT ATTORNEY'S OFFICE WILL NOT REST...
...UNTIL EROS OF TITAN HAS BEEN EXTRADITED BACK INTO OUR JURISDICTION. THANK YOU.
MR. ZIX, CAN YOU...?
I'M ALREADY IN TOUCH WITH MY VARIOUS CONTACTS. ONE WAY OR ANOTHER, THIS SHALL BE RESOLVED. UNTIL THEN...
UNTIL THEN WHAT? WE TAKE IT ON THE CHIN?
TRUST ME, PUG. THERE ARE WORSE PLACES TO TAKE IT. ASK STARFOX.
BEEP
BEEP
HEY, BABY. YOU READY?
OH. EXCUSE ME, GUYS. MY RIDE'S HERE. NOW, MR. ZIX, YOU PROMISE...
I'M LOOKING INTO IT.
OKAY. PUG, CAN JOHN AND I GIVE YOU A LIFT HOME?
NAH. ACTUALLY, I'M GONNA BE GONE FOR AWHILE...
...SEEMS LIKE THERE'S A FEW THINGS I NEED TO LOOK INTO TOO.
JOHN 007

SHE-HULK

A MARVEL COMICS EVENT

CIVIL
WAR

8

#8 SECOND PRINTING VARIANT BY JUAN BOBILLO

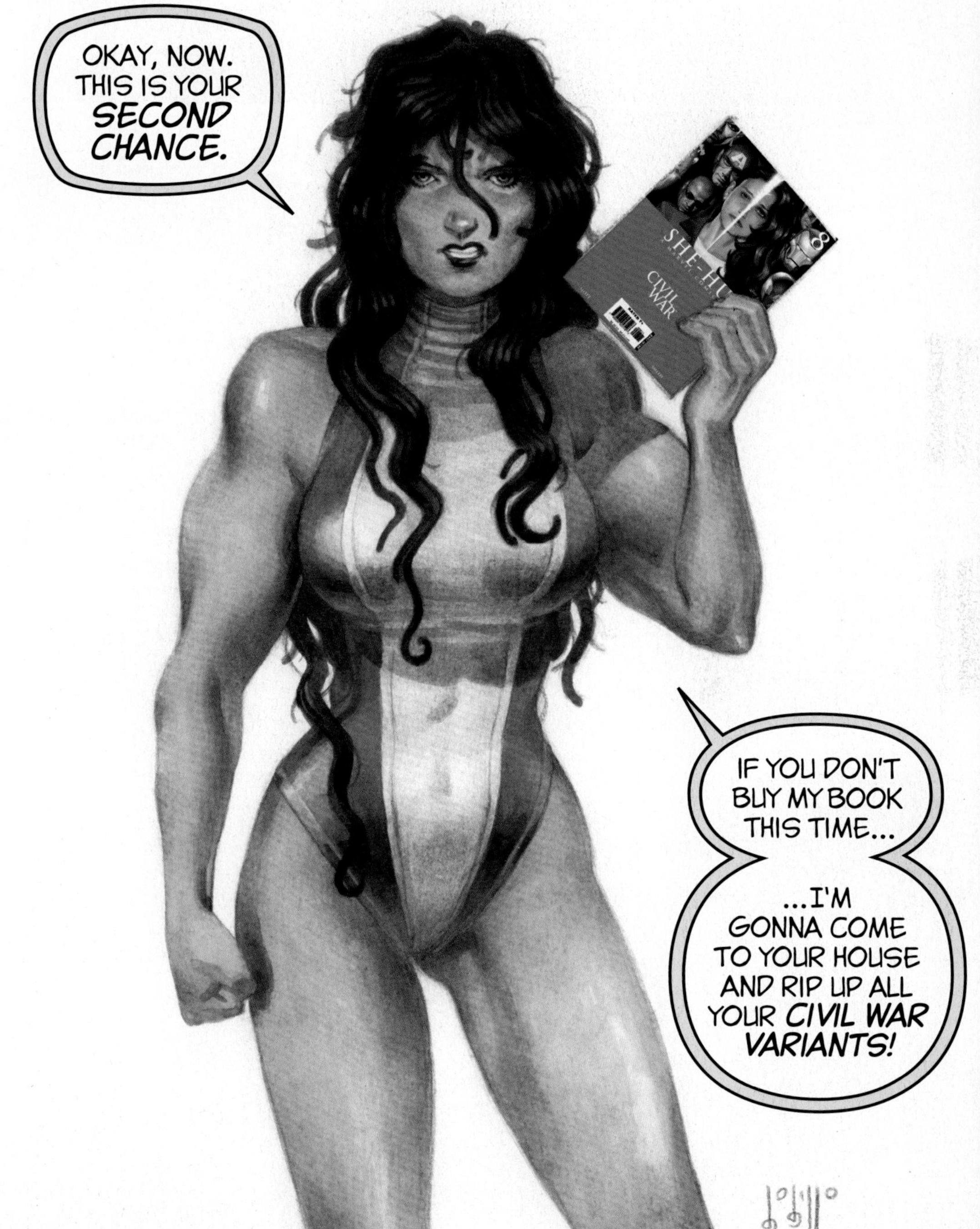
OKAY, NOW. THIS IS YOUR *SECOND CHANCE.*
CIVIL WAR
IF YOU DON'T BUY MY BOOK THIS TIME...
...I'M GONNA COME TO YOUR HOUSE AND RIP UP ALL YOUR *CIVIL WAR VARIANTS!*

JENNIFER WALTERS HAD ALWAYS THOUGHT THAT BEING A LAWYER WAS IN HER BLOOD... UNTIL A GAMMA-IRRADIATED BLOOD TRANSFUSION GAVE HER THE ABILITY TO CHANGE INTO THE WORLD'S SEXIEST, SASSIEST, AND STRONGEST SUPER HEROINE:

PREVIOUSLY IN CIVIL WAR

Hoping to boost their ratings, four New Warriors, young super heroes and reality television stars, attempted to apprehend a quartet of villains holed up in Stamford, Connecticut. Unfortunately, when confronted, the explosive Nitro employed his self-detonation ability, blowing the New Warriors and a large chunk of Stamford to oblivion. The entire incident was caught on tape.

Casualties number in the hundreds.

As a reaction to this tragedy, public outcry calls for reform in the way super heroes conduct their affairs. On Capitol Hill, a Superhuman Registration Act is debated which would require all those possessing paranormal abilities to register with the government, divulging their true identities to the authorities and submitting to training and sanctioning in the manner of federal agents.

Some heroes, such as Iron Man, see this as a natural evolution of the role of super heroes in society, and a reasonable request. Others, embodied by Captain America, take umbrage at this assault on their civil liberties.

When Captain America is called upon to hunt down his fellow heroes who are in defiance of the Registration Act, he chooses to go AWOL, becoming a public enemy in the process.

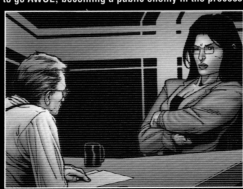

In the wake of the tragedy in Stamford, She-Hulk appears on CNN advocating the training and licensing of super heroes...

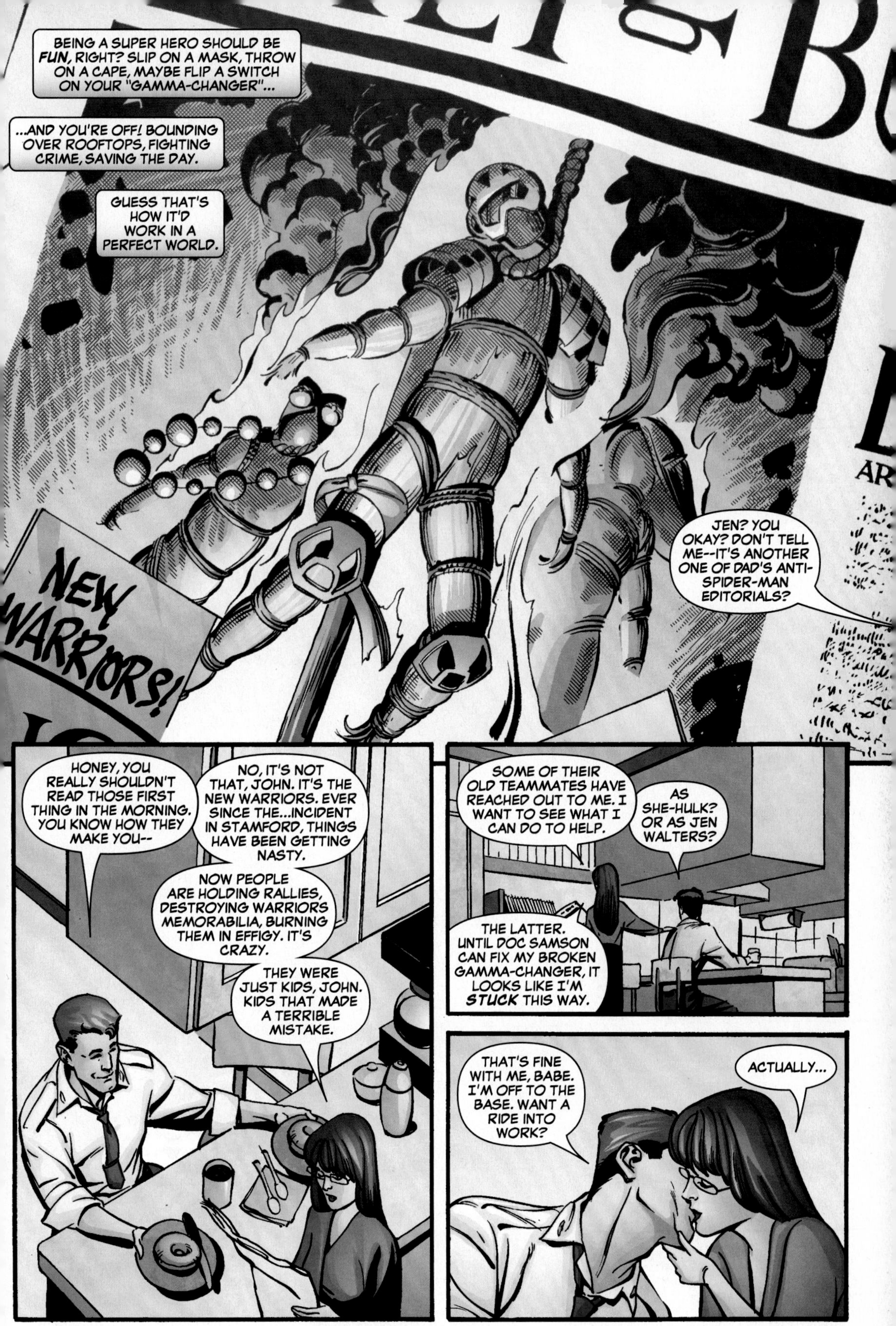

BEING A SUPER HERO SHOULD BE FUN, RIGHT? SLIP ON A MASK, THROW ON A CAPE, MAYBE FLIP A SWITCH ON YOUR "GAMMA-CHANGER"...
...AND YOU'RE OFF! BOUNDING OVER ROOFTOPS, FIGHTING CRIME, SAVING THE DAY.
GUESS THAT'S HOW IT'D WORK IN A PERFECT WORLD.
NEW WARRIORS!
JEN? YOU OKAY? DON'T TELL ME--IT'S ANOTHER ONE OF DAD'S ANTI-SPIDER-MAN EDITORIALS?
HONEY, YOU REALLY SHOULDN'T READ THOSE FIRST THING IN THE MORNING. YOU KNOW HOW THEY MAKE YOU--
NO, IT'S NOT THAT, JOHN. IT'S THE NEW WARRIORS. EVER SINCE THE...INCIDENT IN STAMFORD, THINGS HAVE BEEN GETTING NASTY.
NOW PEOPLE ARE HOLDING RALLIES, DESTROYING WARRIORS MEMORABILIA, BURNING THEM IN EFFIGY. IT'S CRAZY.
THEY WERE JUST KIDS, JOHN. KIDS THAT MADE A TERRIBLE MISTAKE.
SOME OF THEIR OLD TEAMMATES HAVE REACHED OUT TO ME. I WANT TO SEE WHAT I CAN DO TO HELP.
AS SHE-HULK? OR AS JEN WALTERS?
THE LATTER. UNTIL DOC SAMSON CAN FIX MY BROKEN GAMMA-CHANGER, IT LOOKS LIKE I'M STUCK THIS WAY.
THAT'S FINE WITH ME, BABE. I'M OFF TO THE BASE. WANT A RIDE INTO WORK?
ACTUALLY...

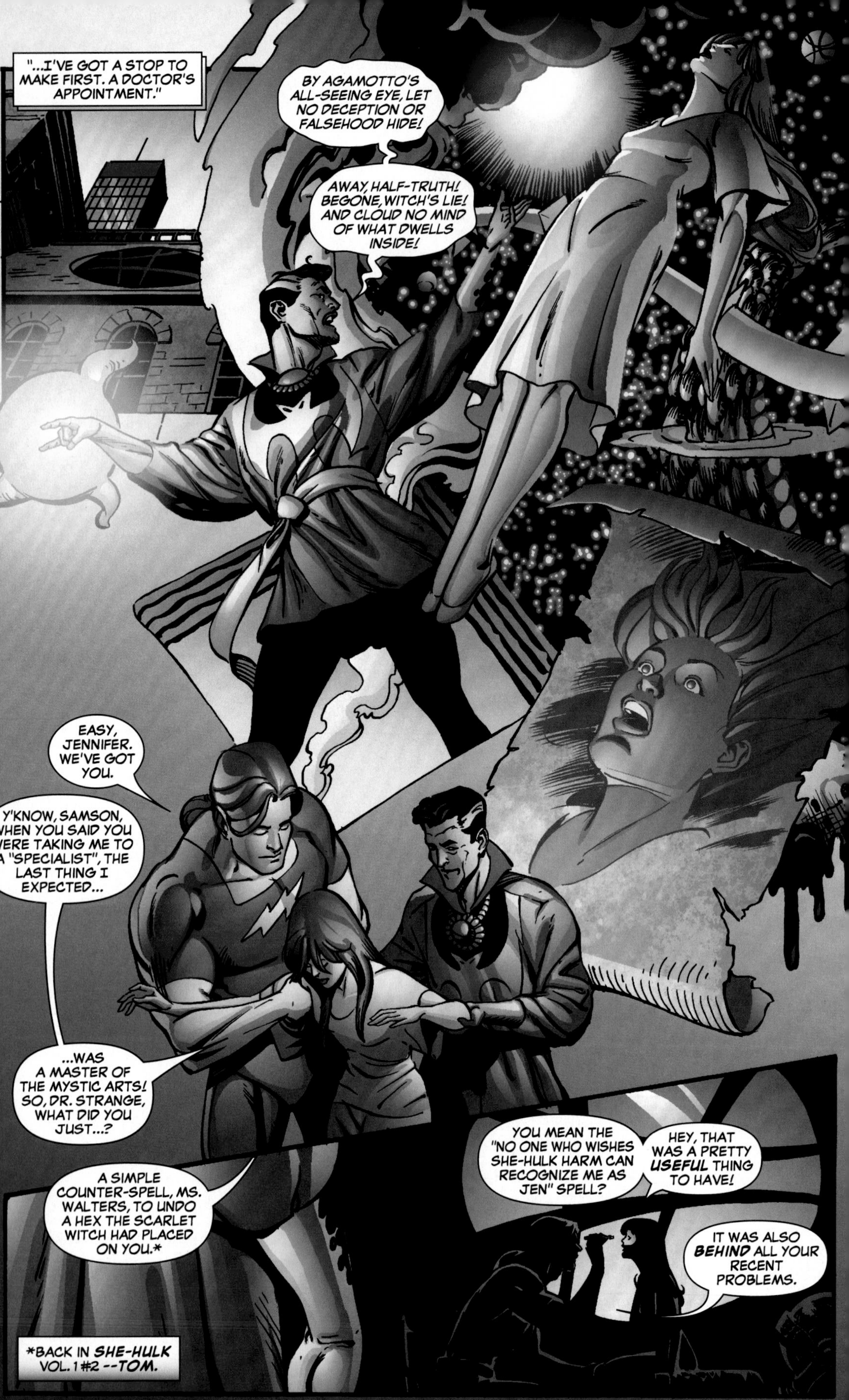
"...I'VE GOT A STOP TO MAKE FIRST. A DOCTOR'S APPOINTMENT."
BY AGAMOTTO'S ALL-SEEING EYE, LET NO DECEPTION OR FALSEHOOD HIDE!
AWAY, HALF-TRUTH! BEGONE, WITCH'S LIE! AND CLOUD NO MIND OF WHAT DWELLS INSIDE!
EASY, JENNIFER. WE'VE GOT YOU.
Y'KNOW, SAMSON, WHEN YOU SAID YOU WERE TAKING ME TO A "SPECIALIST", THE LAST THING I EXPECTED...
...WAS A MASTER OF THE MYSTIC ARTS! SO, DR. STRANGE, WHAT DID YOU JUST...?
A SIMPLE COUNTER-SPELL, MS. WALTERS, TO UNDO A HEX THE SCARLET WITCH HAD PLACED ON YOU.*
YOU MEAN THE "NO ONE WHO WISHES SHE-HULK HARM CAN RECOGNIZE ME AS JEN" SPELL?
HEY, THAT WAS A PRETTY USEFUL THING TO HAVE!
IT WAS ALSO BEHIND ALL YOUR RECENT PROBLEMS.
*BACK IN SHE-HULK VOL. 1 #2 --TOM.

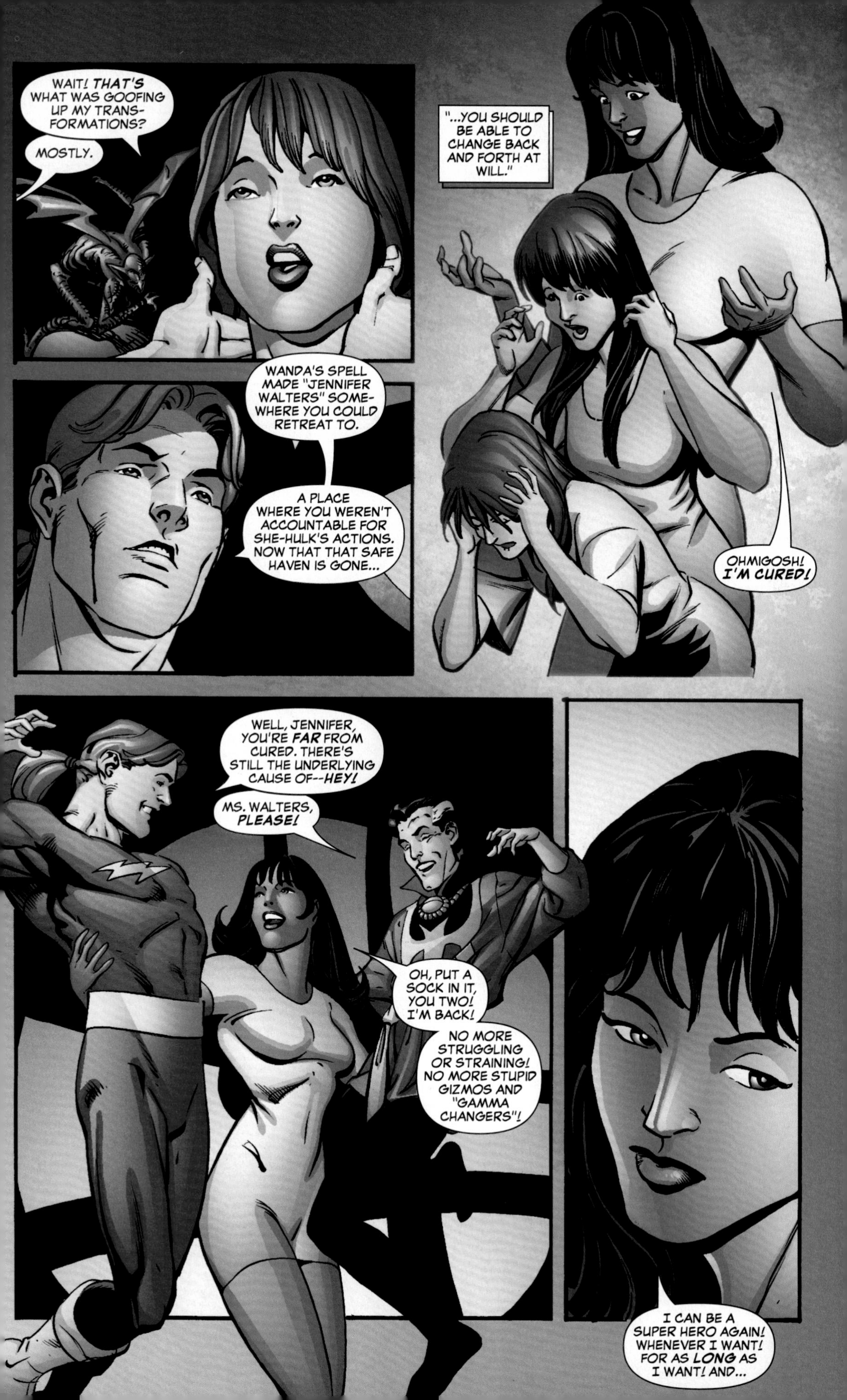
WAIT! THAT'S WHAT WAS GOOFING UP MY TRANS-FORMATIONS?
MOSTLY.
WANDA'S SPELL MADE "JENNIFER WALTERS" SOME-WHERE YOU COULD RETREAT TO.
A PLACE WHERE YOU WEREN'T ACCOUNTABLE FOR SHE-HULK'S ACTIONS. NOW THAT THAT SAFE HAVEN IS GONE...
"...YOU SHOULD BE ABLE TO CHANGE BACK AND FORTH AT WILL."
OHMIGOSH! I'M CURED!
WELL, JENNIFER, YOU'RE FAR FROM CURED. THERE'S STILL THE UNDERLYING CAUSE OF--HEY!
MS. WALTERS, PLEASE!
OH, PUT A SOCK IN IT, YOU TWO! I'M BACK!
NO MORE STRUGGLING OR STRAINING! NO MORE STUPID GIZMOS AND "GAMMA CHANGERS"!
I CAN BE A SUPER HERO AGAIN! WHENEVER I WANT! FOR AS LONG AS I WANT! AND...

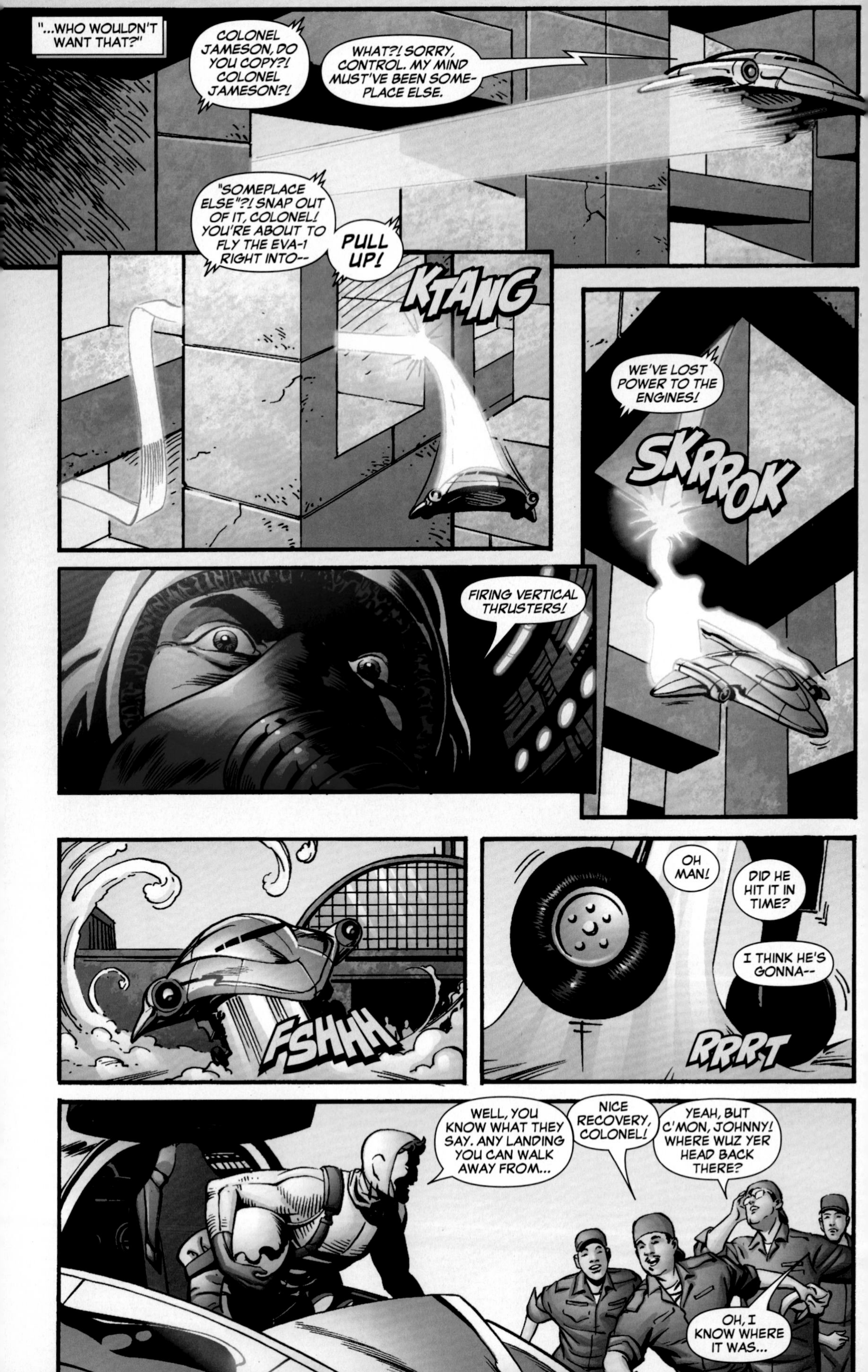
"...WHO WOULDN'T WANT THAT?"
COLONEL JAMESON, DO YOU COPY?! COLONEL JAMESON?!
WHAT?! SORRY, CONTROL. MY MIND MUST'VE BEEN SOMEPLACE ELSE.
"SOMEPLACE ELSE"?! SNAP OUT OF IT, COLONEL! YOU'RE ABOUT TO FLY THE EVA-1 RIGHT INTO--
PULL UP!
KTANG
WE'VE LOST POWER TO THE ENGINES!
SKRROK
FIRING VERTICAL THRUSTERS!
FSHHH
OH MAN!
DID HE HIT IT IN TIME?
I THINK HE'S GONNA--
RRRT
WELL, YOU KNOW WHAT THEY SAY. ANY LANDING YOU CAN WALK AWAY FROM...
NICE RECOVERY, COLONEL!
YEAH, BUT C'MON, JOHNNY! WHERE WUZ YER HEAD BACK THERE?
OH, I KNOW WHERE IT WAS...

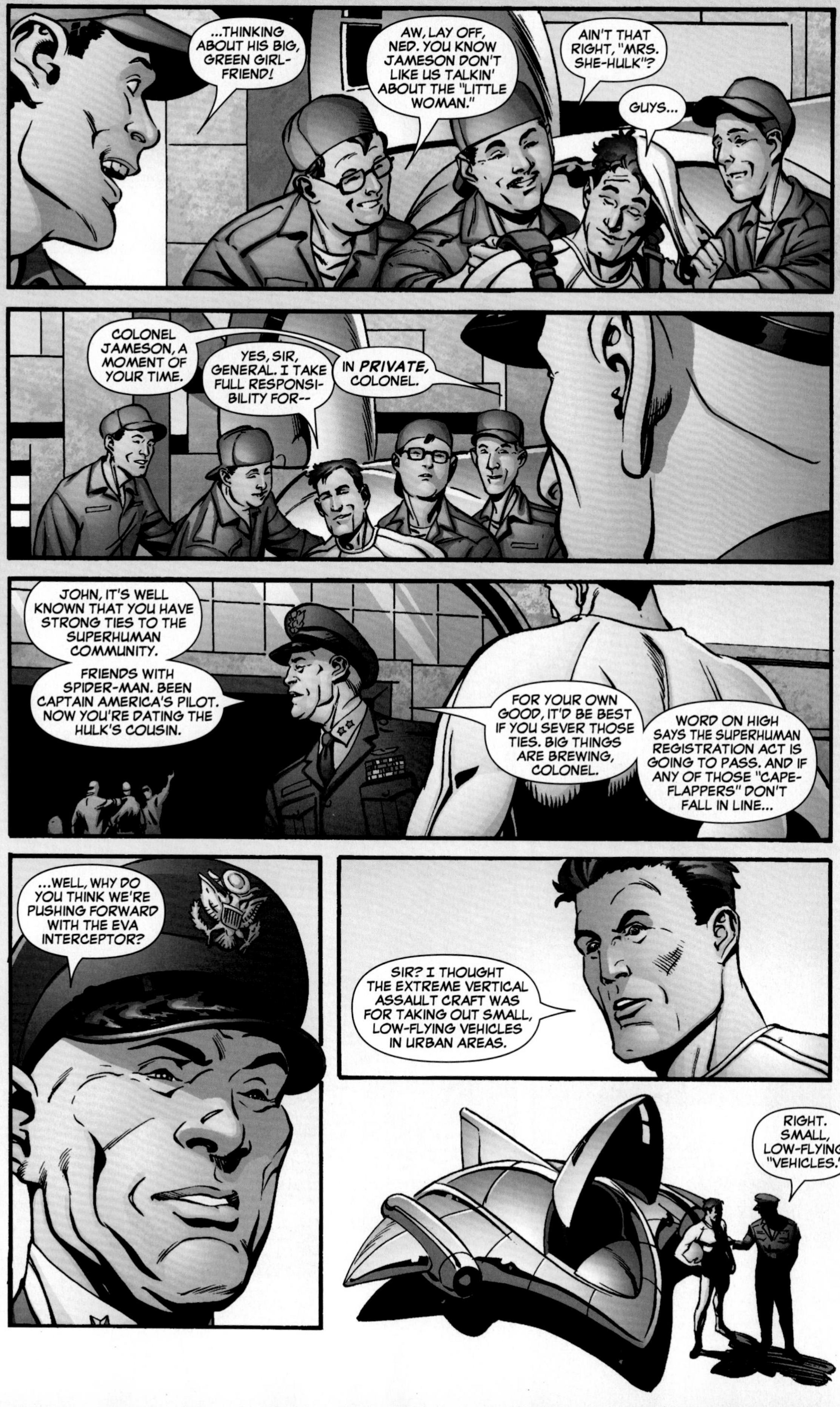
...THINKING ABOUT HIS BIG, GREEN GIRL-FRIEND!
AW, LAY OFF, NED. YOU KNOW JAMESON DON'T LIKE US TALKIN' ABOUT THE "LITTLE WOMAN."
AIN'T THAT RIGHT, "MRS. SHE-HULK"?
GUYS...
COLONEL JAMESON, A MOMENT OF YOUR TIME.
YES, SIR, GENERAL. I TAKE FULL RESPONSIBILITY FOR--
IN PRIVATE, COLONEL.
JOHN, IT'S WELL KNOWN THAT YOU HAVE STRONG TIES TO THE SUPERHUMAN COMMUNITY.
FRIENDS WITH SPIDER-MAN. BEEN CAPTAIN AMERICA'S PILOT. NOW YOU'RE DATING THE HULK'S COUSIN.
FOR YOUR OWN GOOD, IT'D BE BEST IF YOU SEVER THOSE TIES. BIG THINGS ARE BREWING, COLONEL.
WORD ON HIGH SAYS THE SUPERHUMAN REGISTRATION ACT IS GOING TO PASS. AND IF ANY OF THOSE "CAPE-FLAPPERS" DON'T FALL IN LINE...
...WELL, WHY DO YOU THINK WE'RE PUSHING FORWARD WITH THE EVA INTERCEPTOR?
SIR? I THOUGHT THE EXTREME VERTICAL ASSAULT CRAFT WAS FOR TAKING OUT SMALL, LOW-FLYING VEHICLES IN URBAN AREAS.
RIGHT. SMALL, LOW-FLYING "VEHICLES."

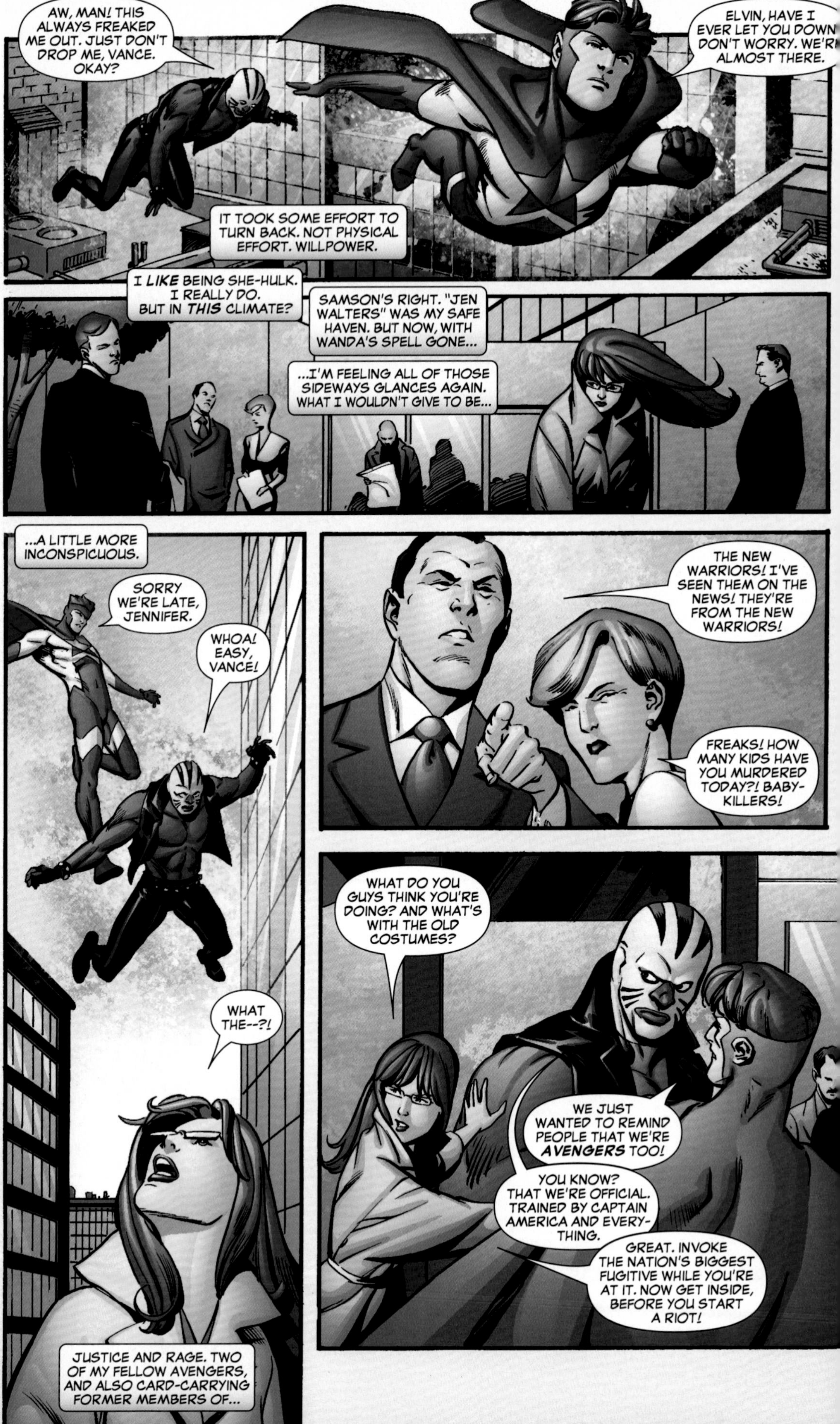
AW, MAN! THIS ALWAYS FREAKED ME OUT. JUST DON'T DROP ME, VANCE. OKAY?
ELVIN, HAVE I EVER LET YOU DOWN? DON'T WORRY. WE'RE ALMOST THERE.
IT TOOK SOME EFFORT TO TURN BACK. NOT PHYSICAL EFFORT. WILLPOWER.
I LIKE BEING SHE-HULK. I REALLY DO. BUT IN THIS CLIMATE?
SAMSON'S RIGHT. "JEN WALTERS" WAS MY SAFE HAVEN. BUT NOW, WITH WANDA'S SPELL GONE...
...I'M FEELING ALL OF THOSE SIDEWAYS GLANCES AGAIN. WHAT I WOULDN'T GIVE TO BE...
...A LITTLE MORE INCONSPICUOUS.
SORRY WE'RE LATE, JENNIFER.
WHOA! EASY, VANCE!
WHAT THE--?!
JUSTICE AND RAGE. TWO OF MY FELLOW AVENGERS, AND ALSO CARD-CARRYING FORMER MEMBERS OF...
THE NEW WARRIORS! I'VE SEEN THEM ON THE NEWS! THEY'RE FROM THE NEW WARRIORS!
FREAKS! HOW MANY KIDS HAVE YOU MURDERED TODAY?! BABY-KILLERS!
WHAT DO YOU GUYS THINK YOU'RE DOING? AND WHAT'S WITH THE OLD COSTUMES?
WE JUST WANTED TO REMIND PEOPLE THAT WE'RE AVENGERS TOO!
YOU KNOW? THAT WE'RE OFFICIAL. TRAINED BY CAPTAIN AMERICA AND EVERY-THING.
GREAT. INVOKE THE NATION'S BIGGEST FUGITIVE WHILE YOU'RE AT IT. NOW GET INSIDE, BEFORE YOU START A RIOT!

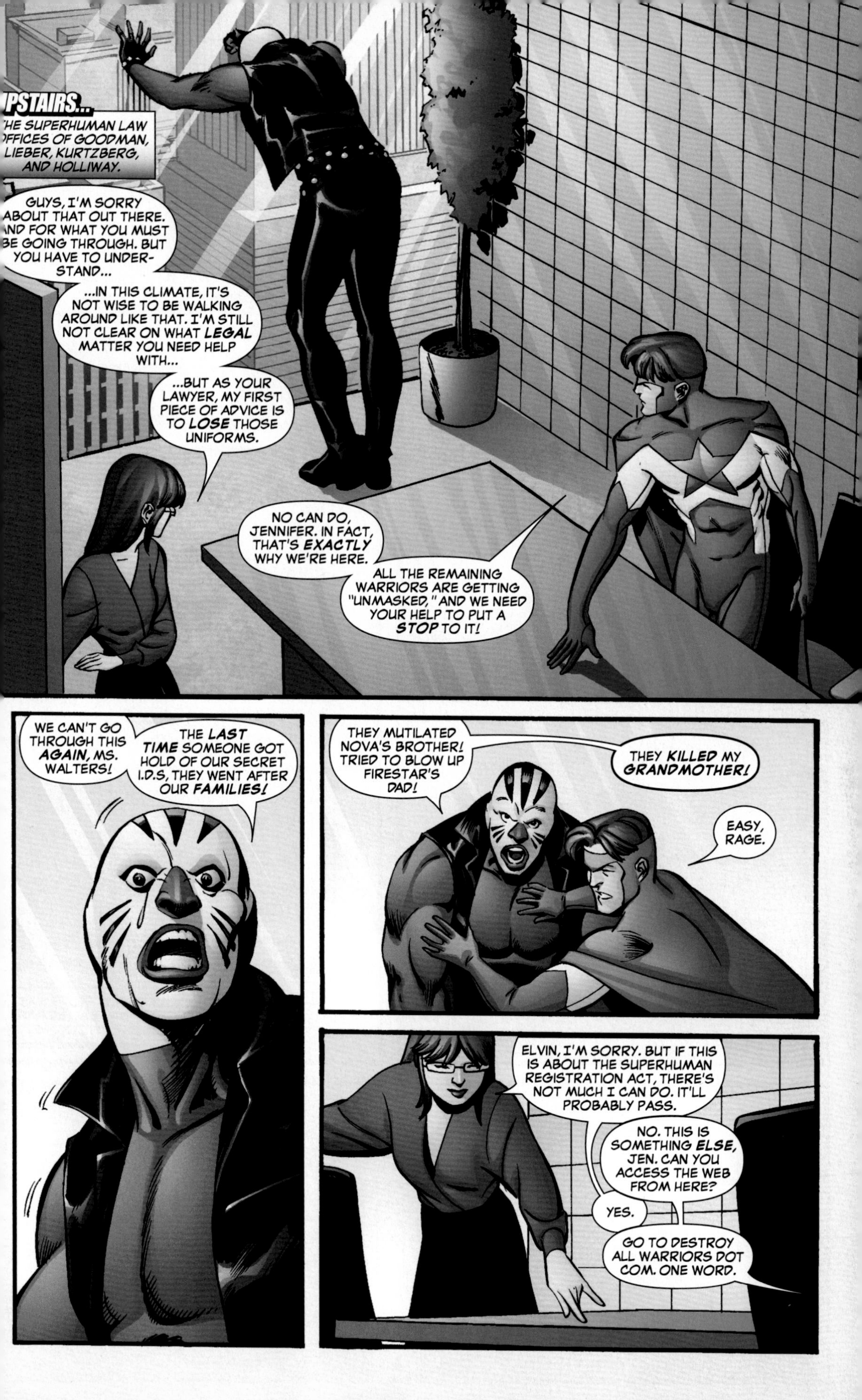
UPSTAIRS...
THE SUPERHUMAN LAW OFFICES OF GOODMAN, LIEBER, KURTZBERG, AND HOLLIWAY.
GUYS, I'M SORRY ABOUT THAT OUT THERE. AND FOR WHAT YOU MUST BE GOING THROUGH. BUT YOU HAVE TO UNDER-STAND...
...IN THIS CLIMATE, IT'S NOT WISE TO BE WALKING AROUND LIKE THAT. I'M STILL NOT CLEAR ON WHAT LEGAL MATTER YOU NEED HELP WITH...
...BUT AS YOUR LAWYER, MY FIRST PIECE OF ADVICE IS TO LOSE THOSE UNIFORMS.
NO CAN DO, JENNIFER. IN FACT, THAT'S EXACTLY WHY WE'RE HERE.
ALL THE REMAINING WARRIORS ARE GETTING "UNMASKED," AND WE NEED YOUR HELP TO PUT A STOP TO IT!
WE CAN'T GO THROUGH THIS AGAIN, MS. WALTERS!
THE LAST TIME SOMEONE GOT HOLD OF OUR SECRET I.D.S, THEY WENT AFTER OUR FAMILIES!
THEY MUTILATED NOVA'S BROTHER! TRIED TO BLOW UP FIRESTAR'S DAD!
THEY KILLED MY GRANDMOTHER!
EASY, RAGE.
ELVIN, I'M SORRY. BUT IF THIS IS ABOUT THE SUPERHUMAN REGISTRATION ACT, THERE'S NOT MUCH I CAN DO. IT'LL PROBABLY PASS.
NO. THIS IS SOMETHING ELSE, JEN. CAN YOU ACCESS THE WEB FROM HERE?
YES.
GO TO DESTROY ALL WARRIORS DOT COM. ONE WORD.

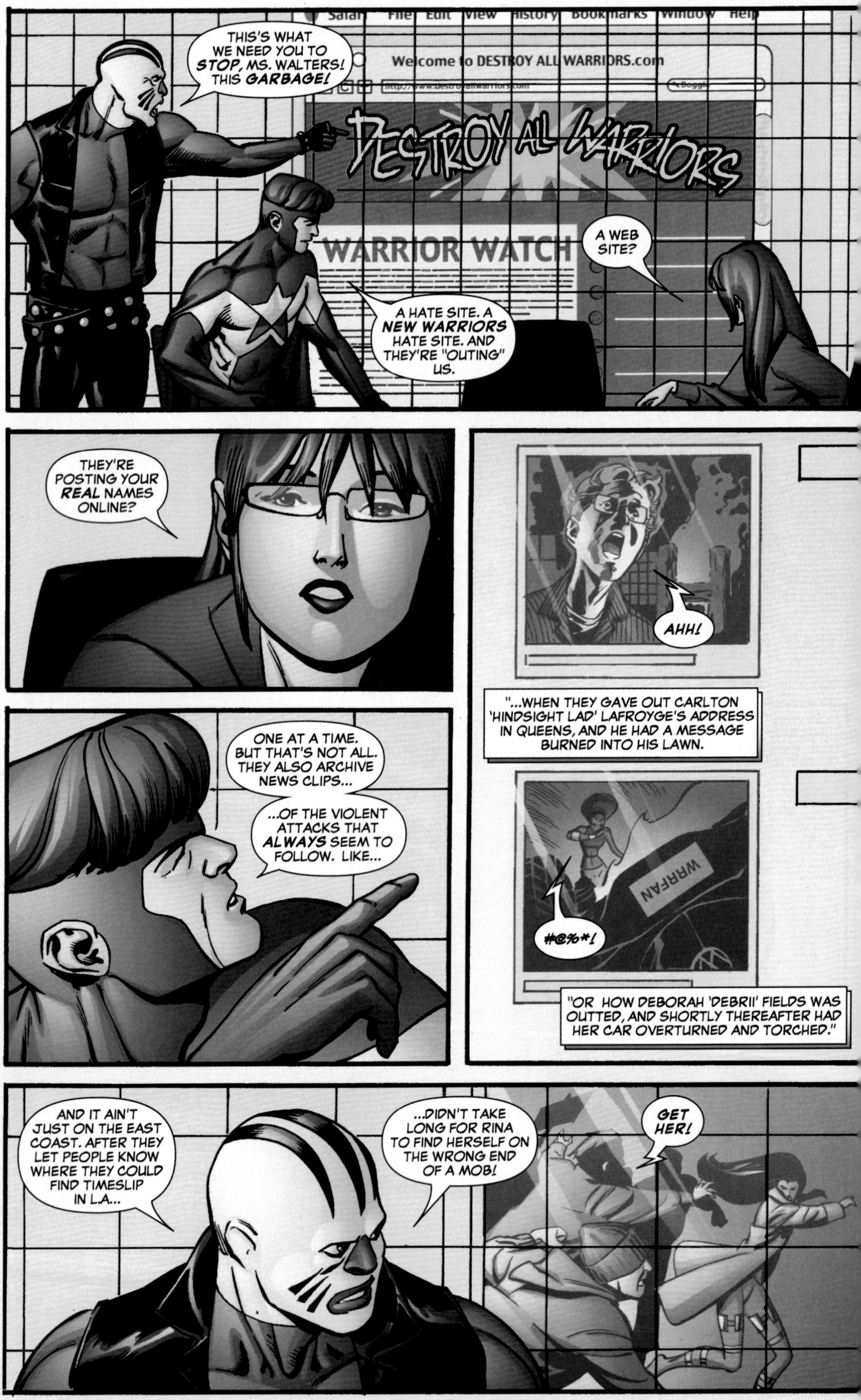
Safari File Edit View History Bookmarks Window Help
Welcome to DESTROY ALL WARRIORS.com
THIS'S WHAT WE NEED YOU TO STOP, MS. WALTERS! THIS GARBAGE!
DESTROY ALL WARRIORS
WARRIOR WATCH
A WEB SITE?
A HATE SITE. A NEW WARRIORS HATE SITE. AND THEY'RE "OUTING" US.
THEY'RE POSTING YOUR REAL NAMES ONLINE?
ONE AT A TIME. BUT THAT'S NOT ALL. THEY ALSO ARCHIVE NEWS CLIPS...
...OF THE VIOLENT ATTACKS THAT ALWAYS SEEM TO FOLLOW. LIKE...
AHH!
"...WHEN THEY GAVE OUT CARLTON 'HINDSIGHT LAD' LAFROYGE'S ADDRESS IN QUEENS, AND HE HAD A MESSAGE BURNED INTO HIS LAWN.
WARFAN
#@%*!
"OR HOW DEBORAH 'DEBRII' FIELDS WAS OUTTED, AND SHORTLY THEREAFTER HAD HER CAR OVERTURNED AND TORCHED."
AND IT AIN'T JUST ON THE EAST COAST. AFTER THEY LET PEOPLE KNOW WHERE THEY COULD FIND TIMESLIP IN L.A...
...DIDN'T TAKE LONG FOR RINA TO FIND HERSELF ON THE WRONG END OF A MOB!
GET HER!

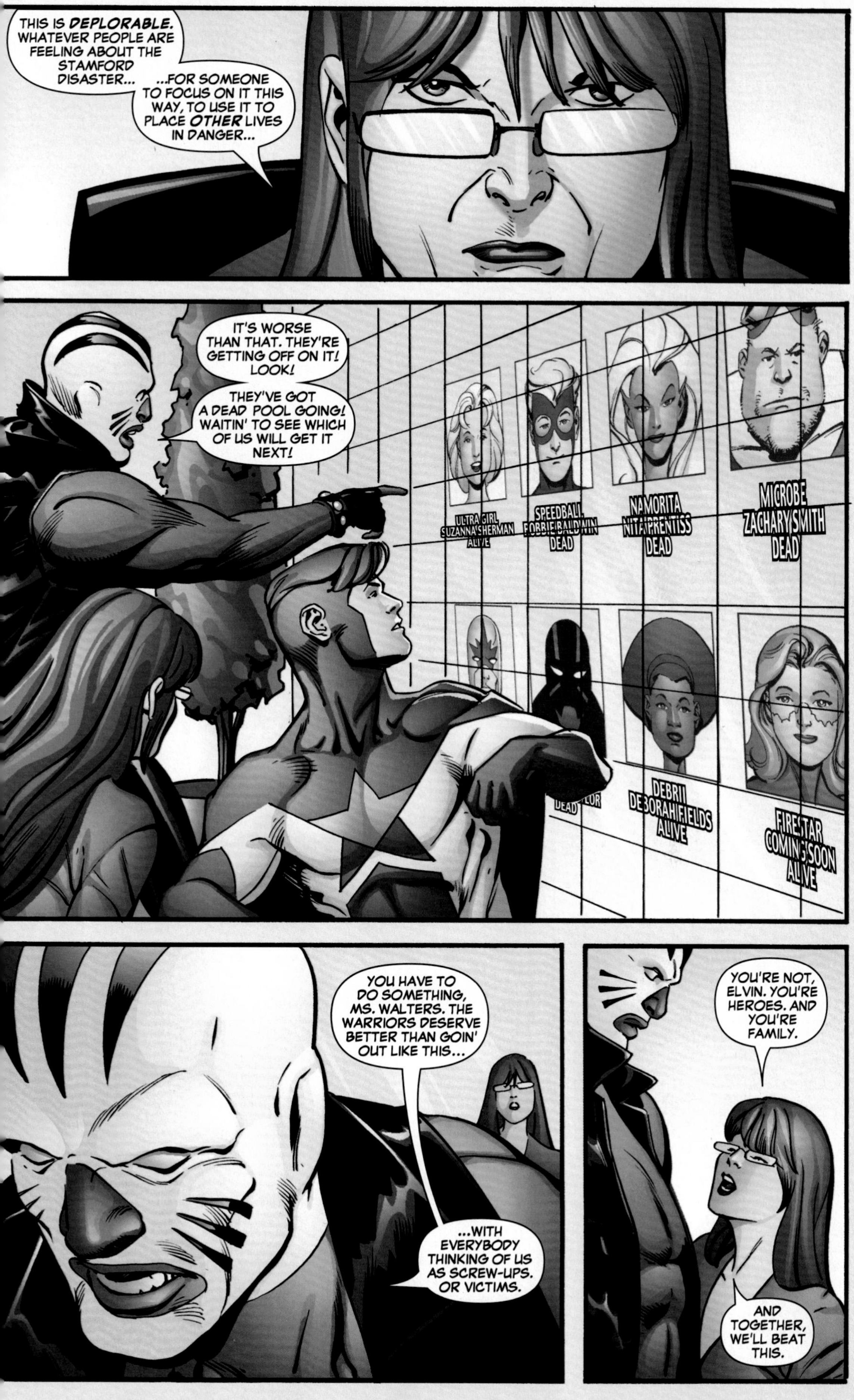
THIS IS **DEPLORABLE.** WHATEVER PEOPLE ARE FEELING ABOUT THE STAMFORD DISASTER...
...FOR SOMEONE TO FOCUS ON IT THIS WAY, TO USE IT TO PLACE **OTHER** LIVES IN DANGER...
IT'S WORSE THAN THAT. THEY'RE GETTING OFF ON IT! LOOK!
THEY'VE GOT A DEAD POOL GOING! WAITIN' TO SEE WHICH OF US WILL GET IT NEXT!
ULTRA GIRL SUZANNA SHERMAN ALIVE
SPEEDBALL ROBBIE BALDWIN DEAD
NAMORITA NITA PRENTISS DEAD
MICROBE ZACHARY SMITH DEAD
DEAD
DEBRII DEBORAH FIELDS ALIVE
FIRESTAR COMING SOON ALIVE
YOU HAVE TO DO SOMETHING, MS. WALTERS. THE WARRIORS DESERVE BETTER THAN GOIN' OUT LIKE THIS...
...WITH EVERYBODY THINKING OF US AS SCREW-UPS. OR VICTIMS.
YOU'RE NOT, ELVIN. YOU'RE HEROES. AND YOU'RE FAMILY.
AND TOGETHER, WE'LL BEAT THIS.

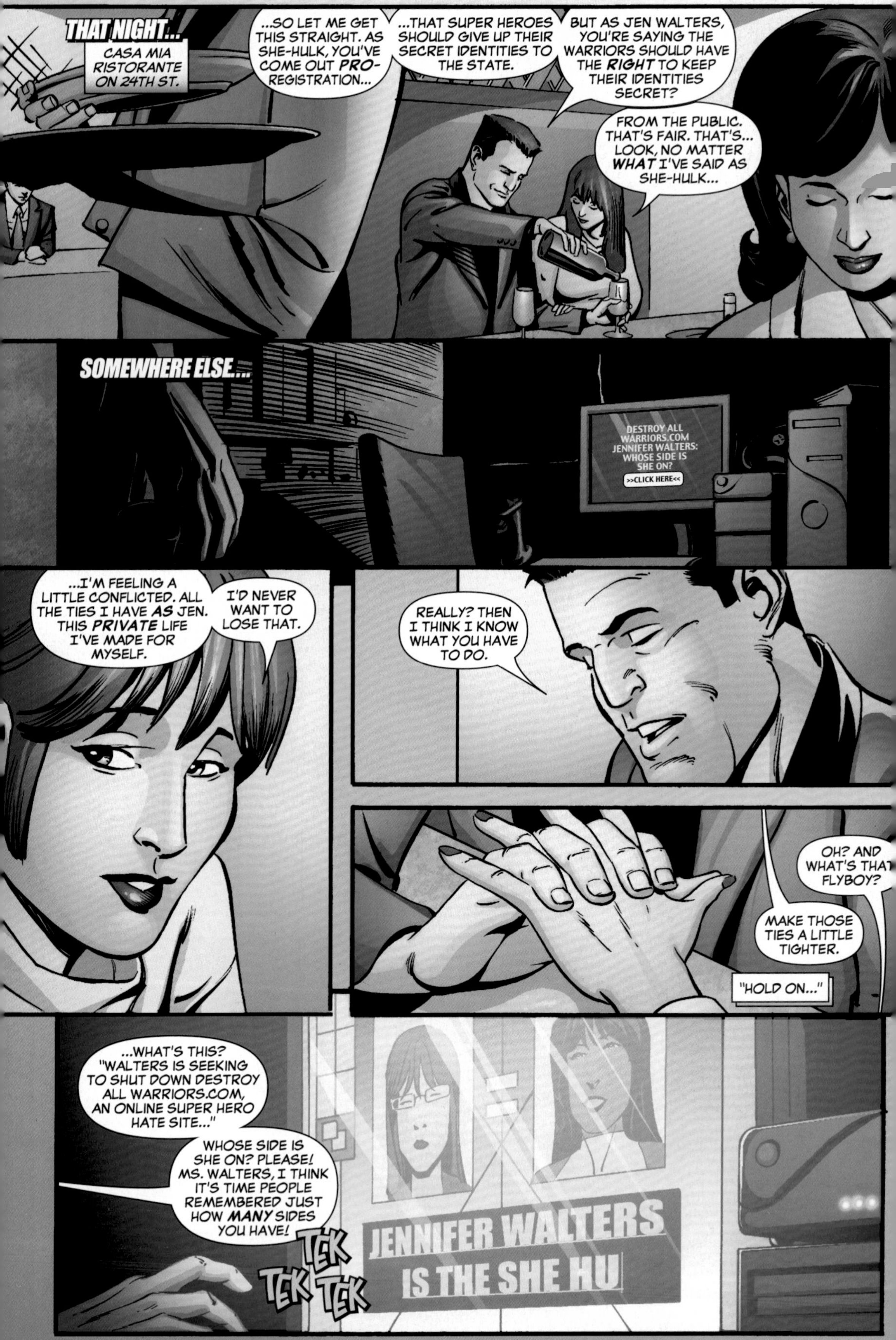
THAT NIGHT...
CASA MIA RISTORANTE ON 24TH ST.
...SO LET ME GET THIS STRAIGHT. AS SHE-HULK, YOU'VE COME OUT PRO-REGISTRATION...
...THAT SUPER HEROES SHOULD GIVE UP THEIR SECRET IDENTITIES TO THE STATE.
BUT AS JEN WALTERS, YOU'RE SAYING THE WARRIORS SHOULD HAVE THE RIGHT TO KEEP THEIR IDENTITIES SECRET?
FROM THE PUBLIC. THAT'S FAIR. THAT'S... LOOK, NO MATTER WHAT I'VE SAID AS SHE-HULK...
SOMEWHERE ELSE...
DESTROY ALL WARRIORS.COM
JENNIFER WALTERS: WHOSE SIDE IS SHE ON?
>>CLICK HERE<<
...I'M FEELING A LITTLE CONFLICTED. ALL THE TIES I HAVE AS JEN. THIS PRIVATE LIFE I'VE MADE FOR MYSELF.
I'D NEVER WANT TO LOSE THAT.
REALLY? THEN I THINK I KNOW WHAT YOU HAVE TO DO.
OH? AND WHAT'S THAT FLYBOY?
MAKE THOSE TIES A LITTLE TIGHTER.
"HOLD ON..."
...WHAT'S THIS? "WALTERS IS SEEKING TO SHUT DOWN DESTROY ALL WARRIORS.COM, AN ONLINE SUPER HERO HATE SITE..."
WHOSE SIDE IS SHE ON? PLEASE! MS. WALTERS, I THINK IT'S TIME PEOPLE REMEMBERED JUST HOW MANY SIDES YOU HAVE!
TEK TEK TEK
JENNIFER WALTERS IS THE SHE HU

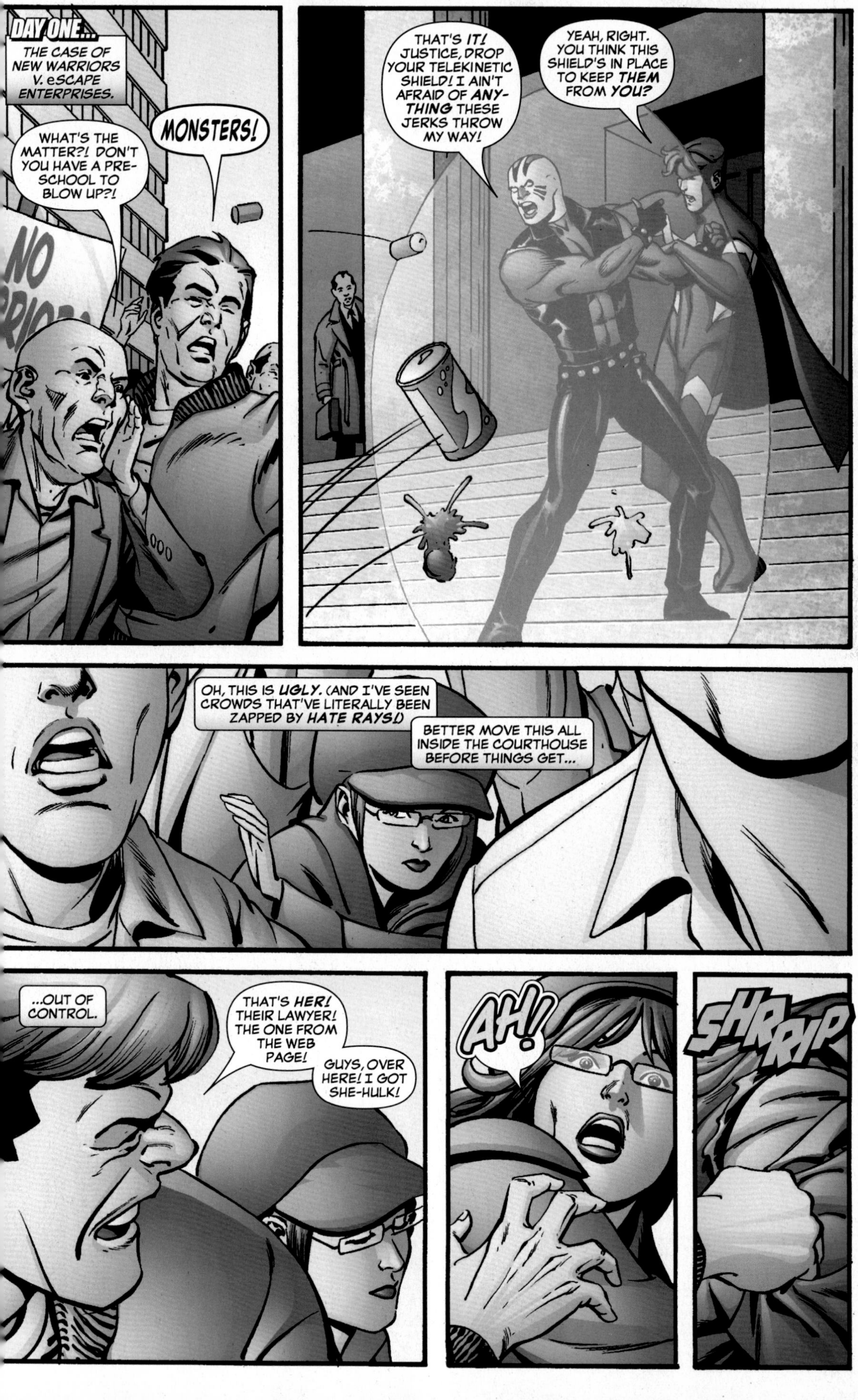
DAY ONE...
THE CASE OF NEW WARRIORS V. eSCAPE ENTERPRISES.
WHAT'S THE MATTER?! DON'T YOU HAVE A PRE-SCHOOL TO BLOW UP?!
MONSTERS!
NO
THAT'S IT! JUSTICE, DROP YOUR TELEKINETIC SHIELD! I AIN'T AFRAID OF ANY-THING THESE JERKS THROW MY WAY!
YEAH, RIGHT. YOU THINK THIS SHIELD'S IN PLACE TO KEEP THEM FROM YOU?
OH, THIS IS UGLY. (AND I'VE SEEN CROWDS THAT'VE LITERALLY BEEN ZAPPED BY HATE RAYS!)
BETTER MOVE THIS ALL INSIDE THE COURTHOUSE BEFORE THINGS GET...
...OUT OF CONTROL.
THAT'S HER! THEIR LAWYER! THE ONE FROM THE WEB PAGE!
GUYS, OVER HERE! I GOT SHE-HULK!
AH!!
SHRRIP

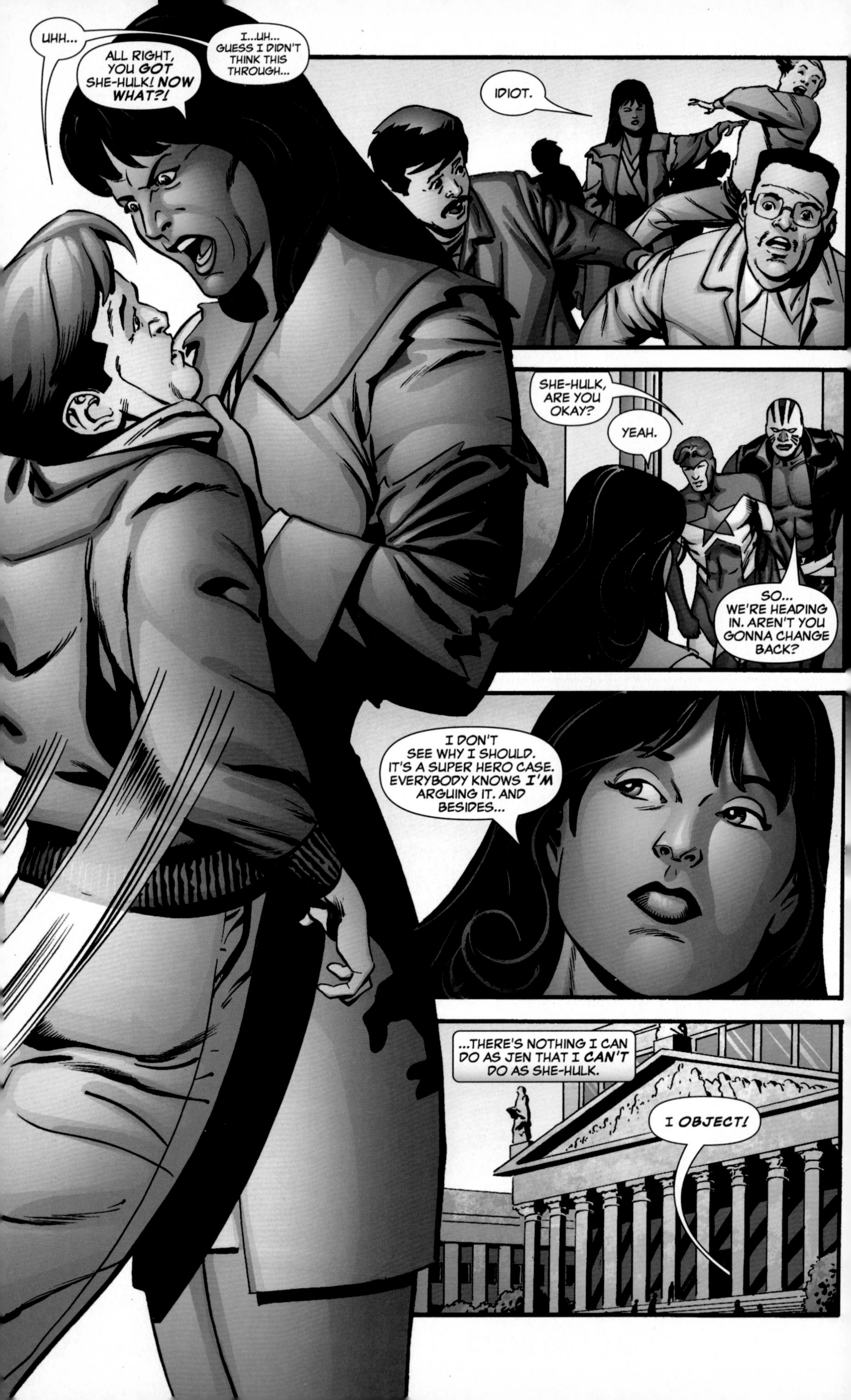
UHH...
ALL RIGHT, YOU GOT SHE-HULK! NOW WHAT?!
I...UH... GUESS I DIDN'T THINK THIS THROUGH...
IDIOT.
SHE-HULK, ARE YOU OKAY?
YEAH.
SO... WE'RE HEADING IN. AREN'T YOU GONNA CHANGE BACK?
I DON'T SEE WHY I SHOULD. IT'S A SUPER HERO CASE. EVERYBODY KNOWS I'M ARGUING IT. AND BESIDES...
...THERE'S NOTHING I CAN DO AS JEN THAT I CAN'T DO AS SHE-HULK.
I OBJECT!

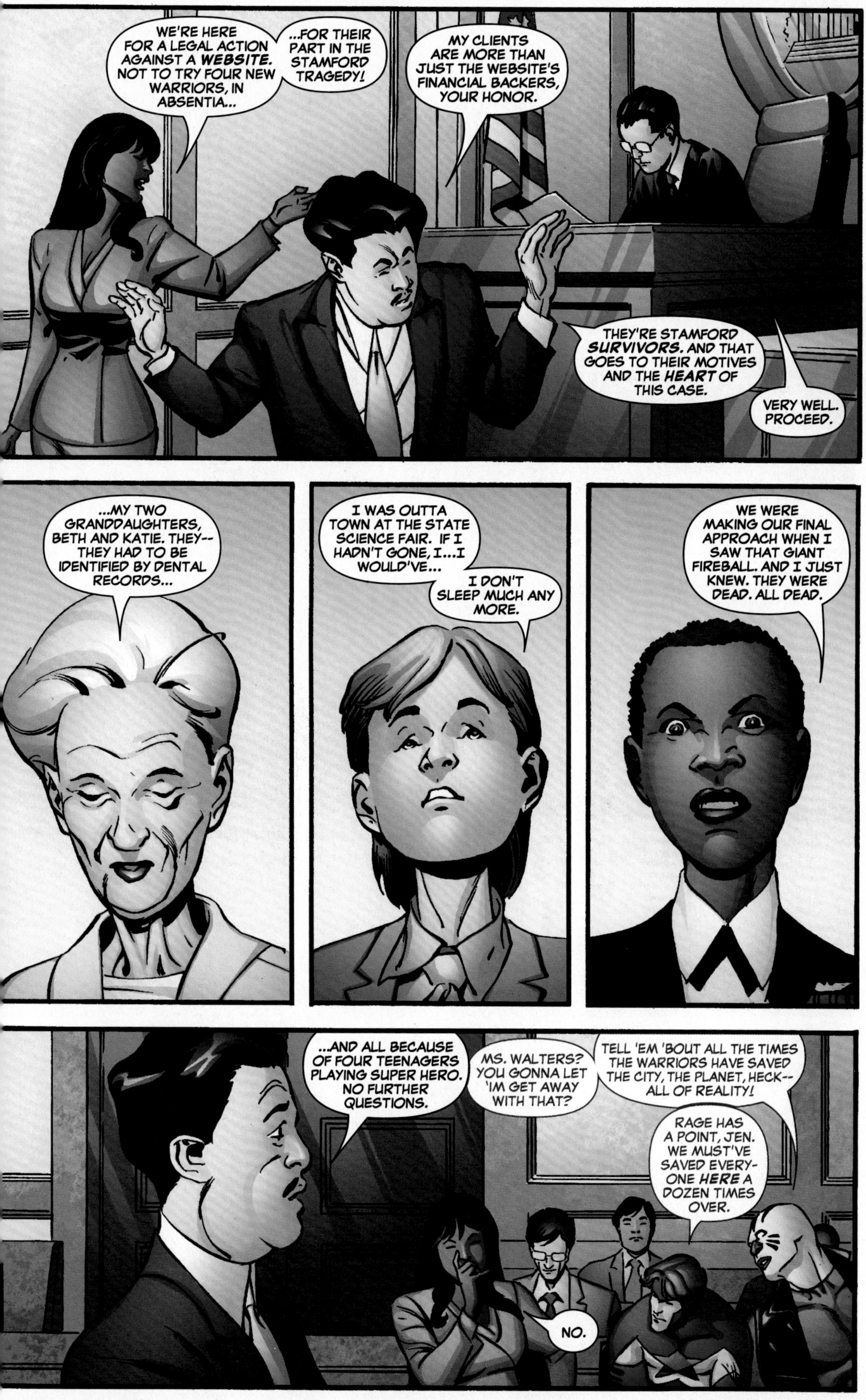
WE'RE HERE FOR A LEGAL ACTION AGAINST A WEBSITE. NOT TO TRY FOUR NEW WARRIORS, IN ABSENTIA...
...FOR THEIR PART IN THE STAMFORD TRAGEDY!
MY CLIENTS ARE MORE THAN JUST THE WEBSITE'S FINANCIAL BACKERS, YOUR HONOR.
THEY'RE STAMFORD SURVIVORS. AND THAT GOES TO THEIR MOTIVES AND THE HEART OF THIS CASE.
VERY WELL. PROCEED.
...MY TWO GRANDDAUGHTERS, BETH AND KATIE. THEY-- THEY HAD TO BE IDENTIFIED BY DENTAL RECORDS...
I WAS OUTTA TOWN AT THE STATE SCIENCE FAIR. IF I HADN'T GONE, I...I WOULD'VE...
I DON'T SLEEP MUCH ANY MORE.
WE WERE MAKING OUR FINAL APPROACH WHEN I SAW THAT GIANT FIREBALL. AND I JUST KNEW. THEY WERE DEAD. ALL DEAD.
...AND ALL BECAUSE OF FOUR TEENAGERS PLAYING SUPER HERO. NO FURTHER QUESTIONS.
MS. WALTERS? YOU GONNA LET 'IM GET AWAY WITH THAT?
TELL 'EM 'BOUT ALL THE TIMES THE WARRIORS HAVE SAVED THE CITY, THE PLANET, HECK-- ALL OF REALITY!
RAGE HAS A POINT, JEN. WE MUST'VE SAVED EVERY-ONE HERE A DOZEN TIMES OVER.
NO.

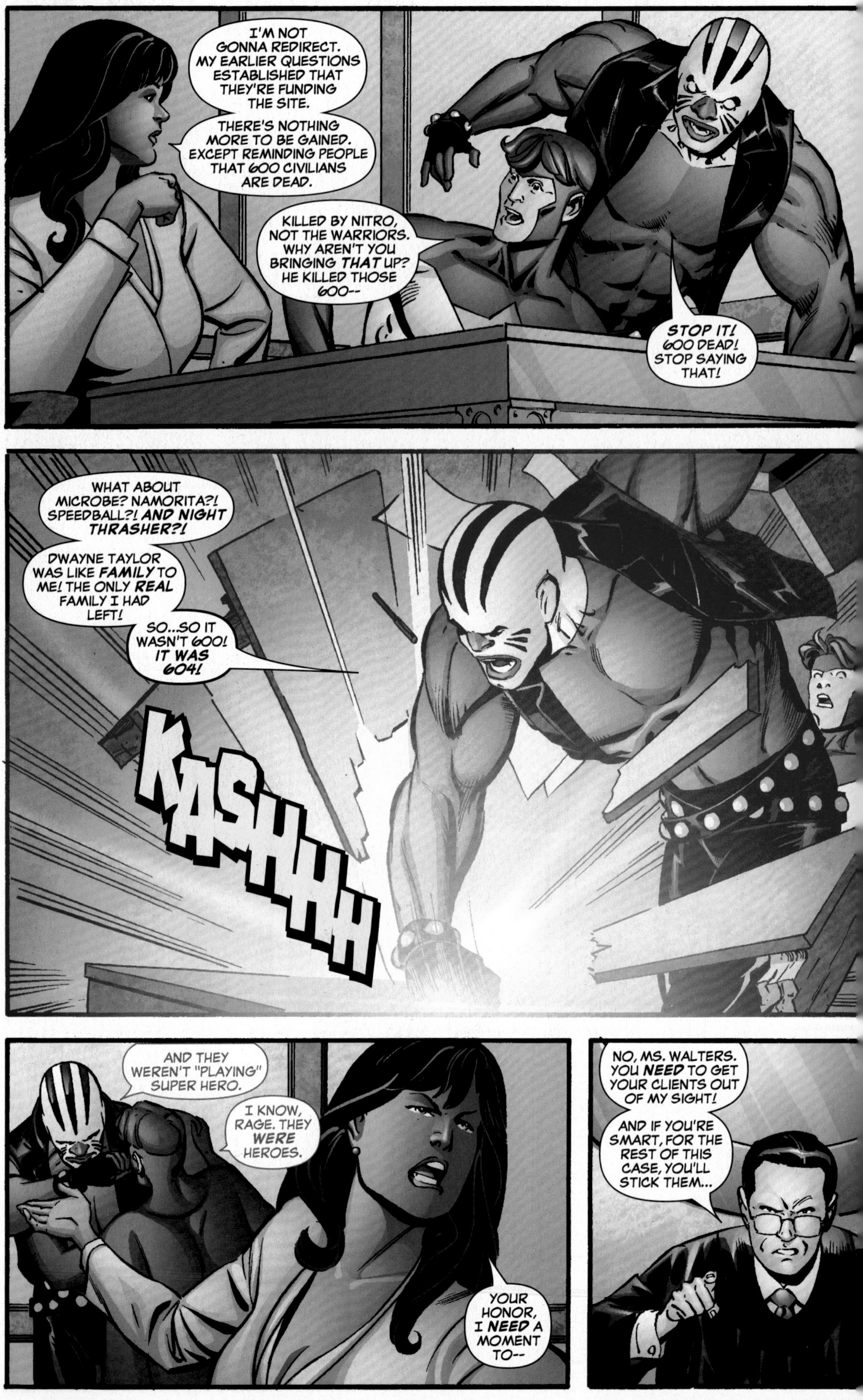
I'M NOT GONNA REDIRECT. MY EARLIER QUESTIONS ESTABLISHED THAT THEY'RE FUNDING THE SITE.
THERE'S NOTHING MORE TO BE GAINED. EXCEPT REMINDING PEOPLE THAT 600 CIVILIANS ARE DEAD.
KILLED BY NITRO, NOT THE WARRIORS. WHY AREN'T YOU BRINGING **THAT** UP? HE KILLED THOSE 600--
STOP IT! 600 DEAD! STOP SAYING THAT!
WHAT ABOUT MICROBE? NAMORITA?! SPEEDBALL?! **AND NIGHT THRASHER?!**
DWAYNE TAYLOR WAS LIKE **FAMILY** TO ME! THE ONLY **REAL** FAMILY I HAD LEFT!
SO...SO IT WASN'T 600! **IT WAS 604!**
KASHHHH
AND THEY WEREN'T "PLAYING" SUPER HERO.
I KNOW, RAGE. THEY **WERE** HEROES.
YOUR HONOR, I **NEED** A MOMENT TO--
NO, MS. WALTERS. YOU **NEED** TO GET YOUR CLIENTS OUT OF MY SIGHT!
AND IF YOU'RE SMART, FOR THE REST OF THIS CASE, YOU'LL STICK THEM...

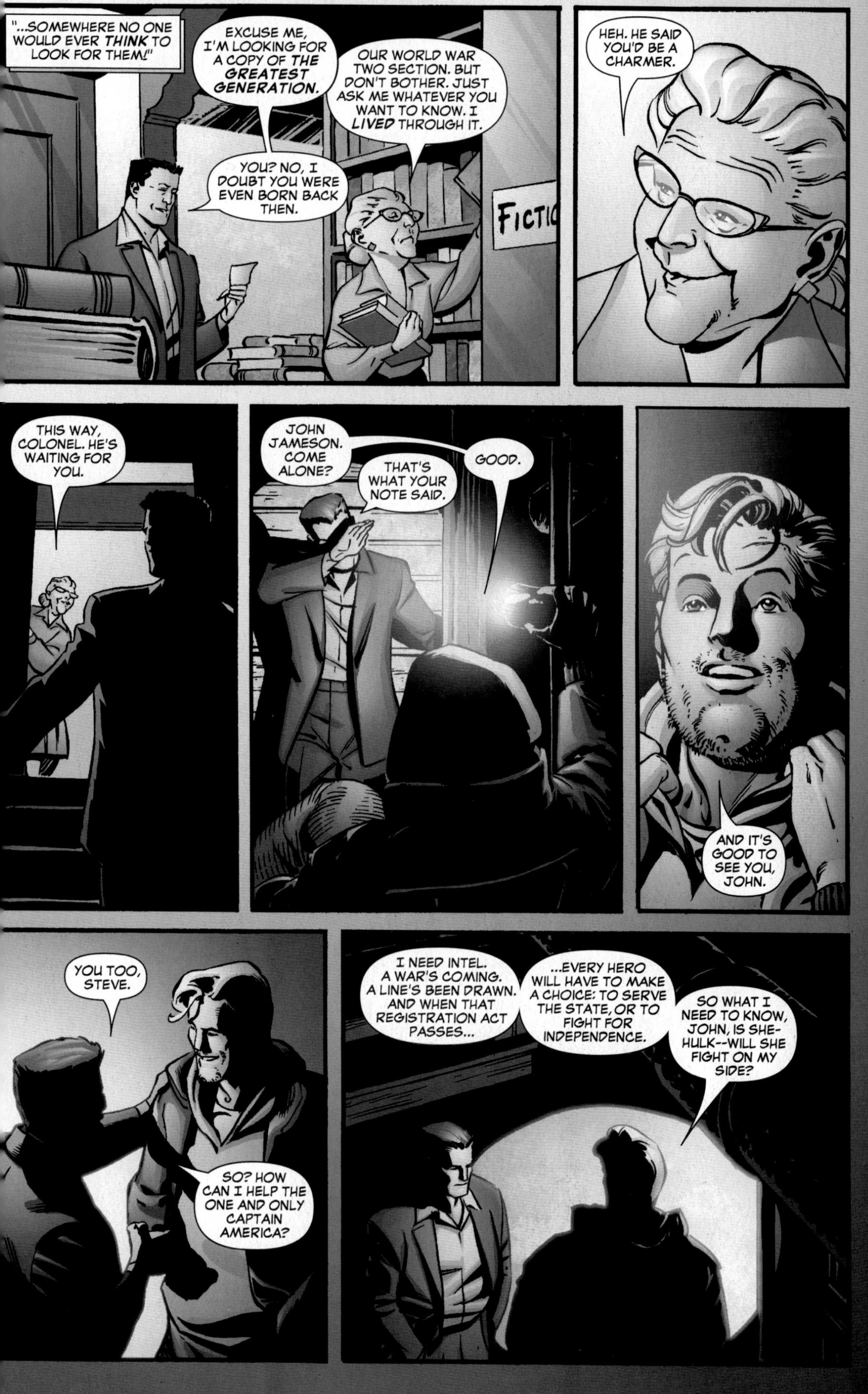
"...SOMEWHERE NO ONE WOULD EVER THINK TO LOOK FOR THEM!"
EXCUSE ME, I'M LOOKING FOR A COPY OF THE GREATEST GENERATION.
OUR WORLD WAR TWO SECTION. BUT DON'T BOTHER. JUST ASK ME WHATEVER YOU WANT TO KNOW. I LIVED THROUGH IT.
YOU? NO, I DOUBT YOU WERE EVEN BORN BACK THEN.
FICTIO
HEH. HE SAID YOU'D BE A CHARMER.
THIS WAY, COLONEL. HE'S WAITING FOR YOU.
JOHN JAMESON. COME ALONE?
THAT'S WHAT YOUR NOTE SAID.
GOOD.
AND IT'S GOOD TO SEE YOU, JOHN.
YOU TOO, STEVE.
SO? HOW CAN I HELP THE ONE AND ONLY CAPTAIN AMERICA?
I NEED INTEL. A WAR'S COMING. A LINE'S BEEN DRAWN. AND WHEN THAT REGISTRATION ACT PASSES...
...EVERY HERO WILL HAVE TO MAKE A CHOICE: TO SERVE THE STATE, OR TO FIGHT FOR INDEPENDENCE.
SO WHAT I NEED TO KNOW, JOHN, IS SHE-HULK--WILL SHE FIGHT ON MY SIDE?

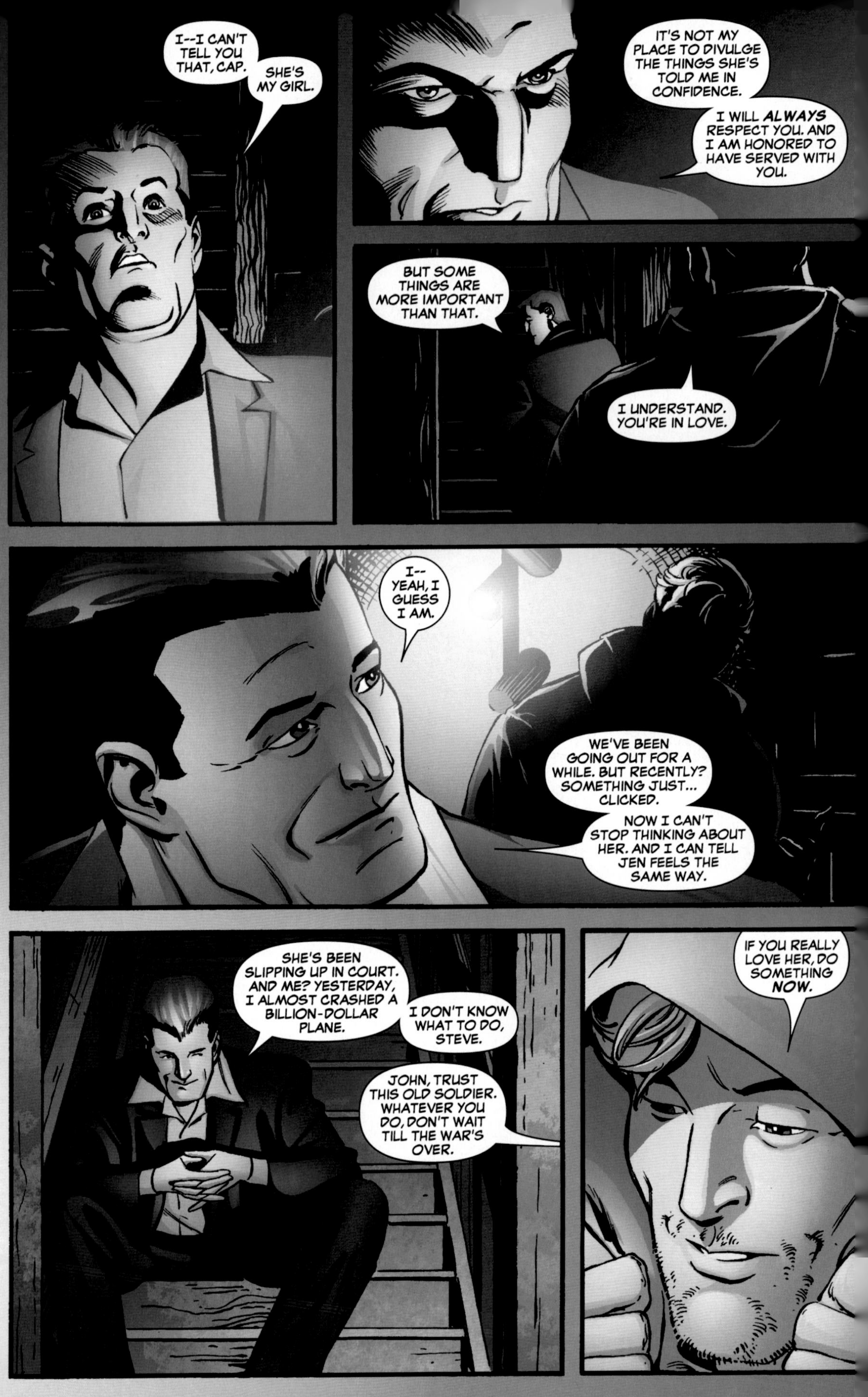
I--I CAN'T TELL YOU THAT, CAP.
SHE'S MY GIRL.
IT'S NOT MY PLACE TO DIVULGE THE THINGS SHE'S TOLD ME IN CONFIDENCE.
I WILL ALWAYS RESPECT YOU. AND I AM HONORED TO HAVE SERVED WITH YOU.
BUT SOME THINGS ARE MORE IMPORTANT THAN THAT.
I UNDERSTAND. YOU'RE IN LOVE.
I-- YEAH, I GUESS I AM.
WE'VE BEEN GOING OUT FOR A WHILE. BUT RECENTLY? SOMETHING JUST... CLICKED.
NOW I CAN'T STOP THINKING ABOUT HER. AND I CAN TELL JEN FEELS THE SAME WAY.
SHE'S BEEN SLIPPING UP IN COURT. AND ME? YESTERDAY, I ALMOST CRASHED A BILLION-DOLLAR PLANE.
I DON'T KNOW WHAT TO DO, STEVE.
JOHN, TRUST THIS OLD SOLDIER. WHATEVER YOU DO, DON'T WAIT TILL THE WAR'S OVER.
IF YOU REALLY LOVE HER, DO SOMETHING NOW.

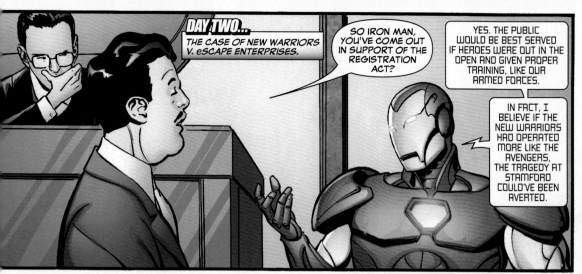

DAY TWO...
THE CASE OF NEW WARRIORS V. eSCAPE ENTERPRISES.

SO IRON MAN, YOU'VE COME OUT IN SUPPORT OF THE REGISTRATION ACT?

YES. THE PUBLIC WOULD BE BEST SERVED IF HEROES WERE OUT IN THE OPEN AND GIVEN PROPER TRAINING, LIKE OUR ARMED FORCES.

IN FACT, I BELIEVE IF THE NEW WARRIORS HAD OPERATED MORE LIKE THE AVENGERS, THE TRAGEDY AT STAMFORD COULD'VE BEEN AVERTED.

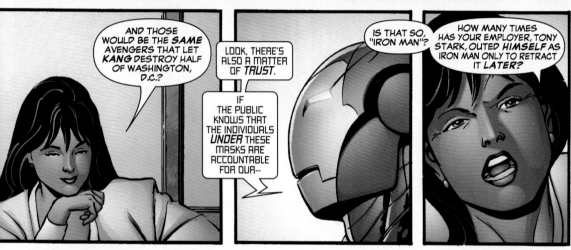

AND THOSE WOULD BE THE *SAME* AVENGERS THAT LET *KANG* DESTROY HALF OF WASHINGTON, D.C.?

LOOK, THERE'S ALSO A MATTER OF *TRUST*.

IF THE PUBLIC KNOWS THAT THE INDIVIDUALS *UNDER* THESE MASKS ARE ACCOUNTABLE FOR OUR--

IS THAT SO, "IRON MAN"?

HOW MANY TIMES HAS YOUR EMPLOYER, TONY STARK, OUTED *HIMSELF* AS IRON MAN ONLY TO RETRACT IT *LATER*?

IN FACT, I RECALL HE ONCE USED AN *ILLEGAL* SATELLITE TO BRAINWASH *ALL* OF EARTH INTO FORGETTING HIS SECRET!

DOES HE PLAN TO DO SOMETHING LIKE THAT *AGAIN* IF ALL OF THIS BLOWS UP IN HIS FACE?!

THAT'S ENOUGH! WE'RE TAKING A RECESS TILL YOU ALL SIMMER DOWN!

JENNIFER!

SMAK

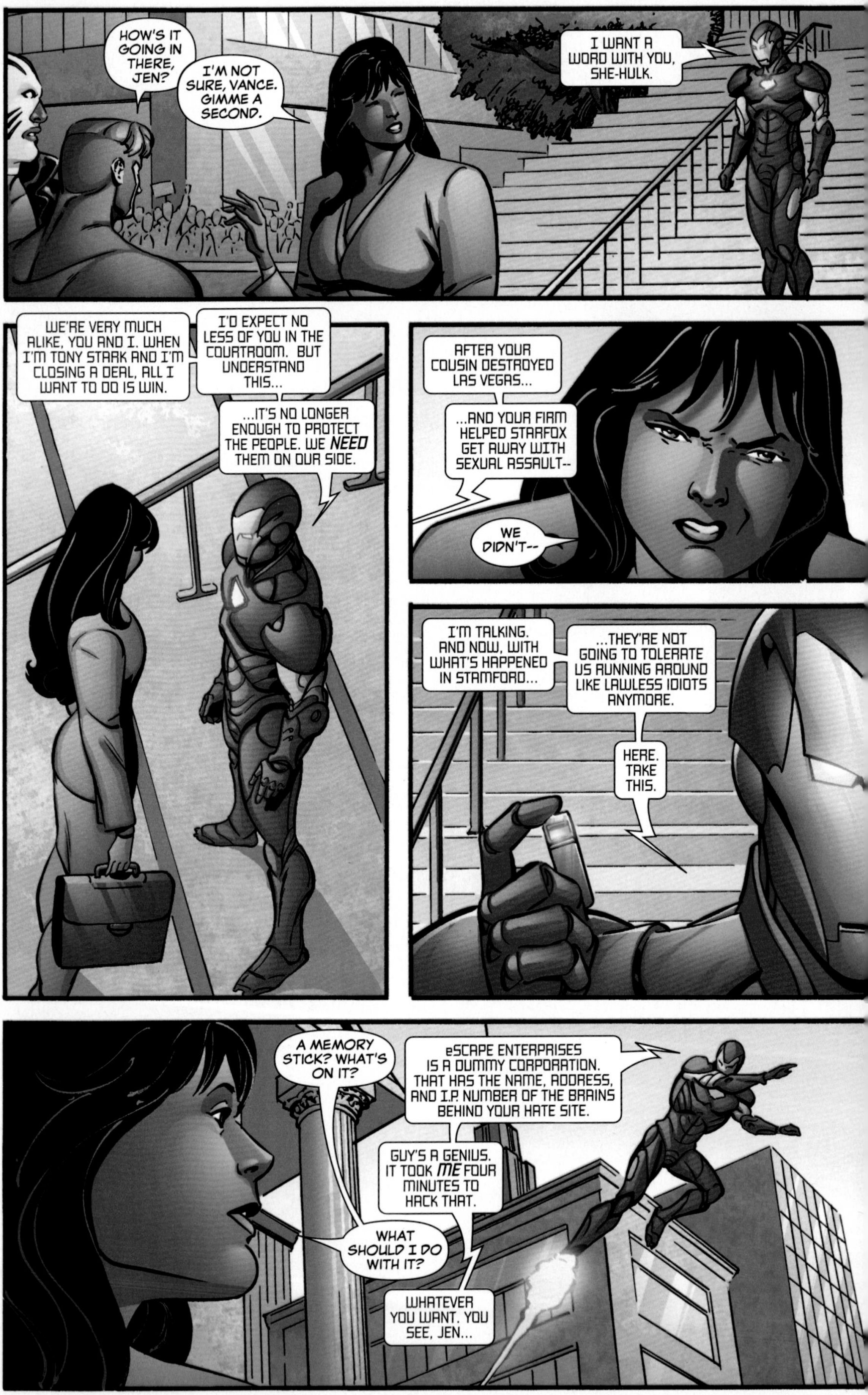
HOW'S IT GOING IN THERE, JEN?
I'M NOT SURE, VANCE. GIMME A SECOND.
I WANT A WORD WITH YOU, SHE-HULK.
WE'RE VERY MUCH ALIKE, YOU AND I. WHEN I'M TONY STARK AND I'M CLOSING A DEAL, ALL I WANT TO DO IS WIN.
I'D EXPECT NO LESS OF YOU IN THE COURTROOM. BUT UNDERSTAND THIS...
...IT'S NO LONGER ENOUGH TO PROTECT THE PEOPLE. WE NEED THEM ON OUR SIDE.
AFTER YOUR COUSIN DESTROYED LAS VEGAS...
...AND YOUR FIRM HELPED STARFOX GET AWAY WITH SEXUAL ASSAULT--
WE DIDN'T--
I'M TALKING. AND NOW, WITH WHAT'S HAPPENED IN STAMFORD...
...THEY'RE NOT GOING TO TOLERATE US RUNNING AROUND LIKE LAWLESS IDIOTS ANYMORE.
HERE. TAKE THIS.
A MEMORY STICK? WHAT'S ON IT?
eSCAPE ENTERPRISES IS A DUMMY CORPORATION. THAT HAS THE NAME, ADDRESS, AND I.P. NUMBER OF THE BRAINS BEHIND YOUR HATE SITE.
GUY'S A GENIUS. IT TOOK ME FOUR MINUTES TO HACK THAT.
WHAT SHOULD I DO WITH IT?
WHATEVER YOU WANT. YOU SEE, JEN...

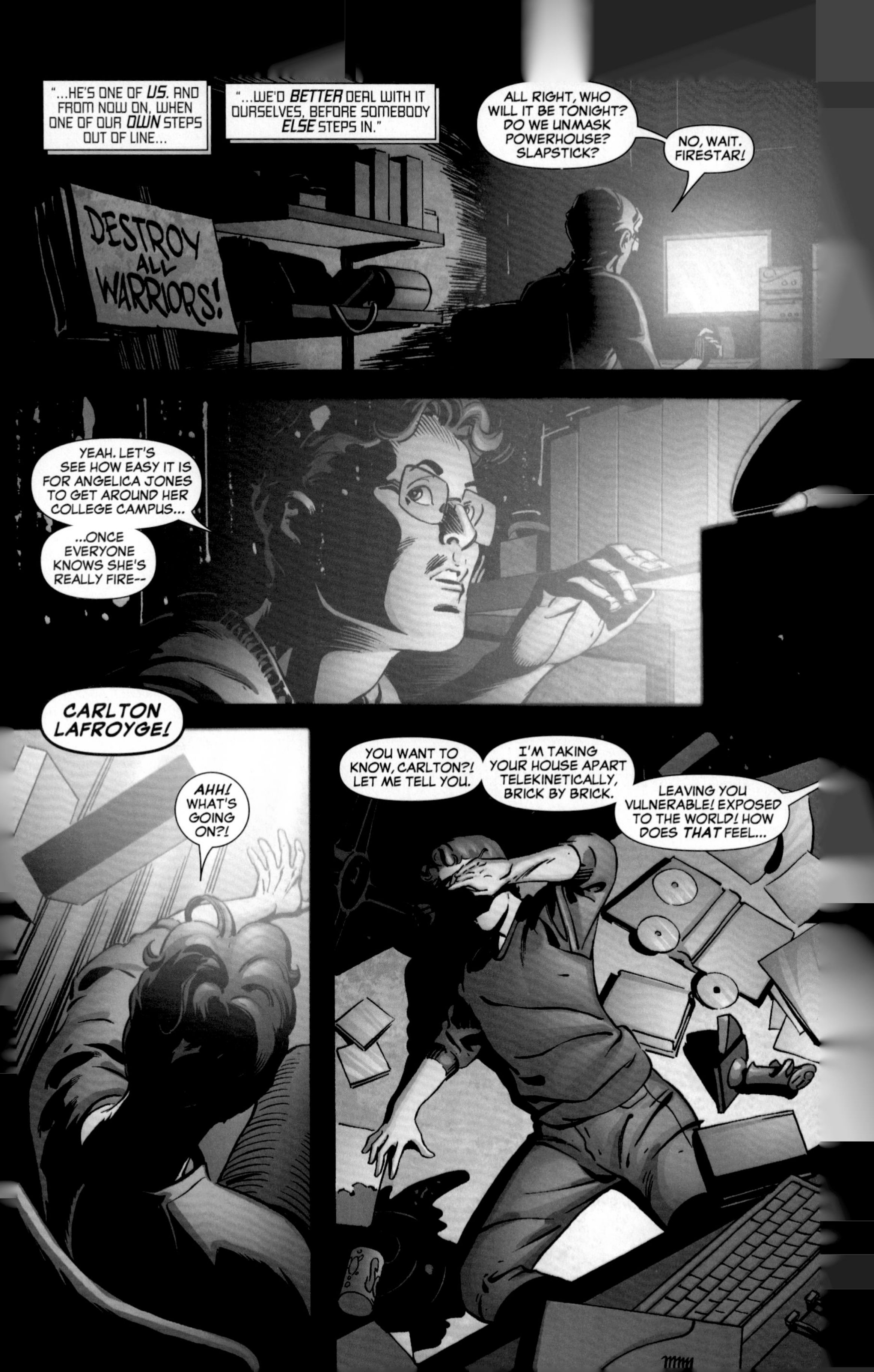
"...HE'S ONE OF US. AND FROM NOW ON, WHEN ONE OF OUR OWN STEPS OUT OF LINE...
"...WE'D BETTER DEAL WITH IT OURSELVES, BEFORE SOMEBODY ELSE STEPS IN."
ALL RIGHT, WHO WILL IT BE TONIGHT? DO WE UNMASK POWERHOUSE? SLAPSTICK?
NO, WAIT. FIRESTAR!
DESTROY ALL WARRIORS!
YEAH. LET'S SEE HOW EASY IT IS FOR ANGELICA JONES TO GET AROUND HER COLLEGE CAMPUS...
...ONCE EVERYONE KNOWS SHE'S REALLY FIRE--
CARLTON LAFROYGE!
AHH! WHAT'S GOING ON?!
YOU WANT TO KNOW, CARLTON?! LET ME TELL YOU.
I'M TAKING YOUR HOUSE APART TELEKINETICALLY, BRICK BY BRICK.
LEAVING YOU VULNERABLE! EXPOSED TO THE WORLD! HOW DOES THAT FEEL...

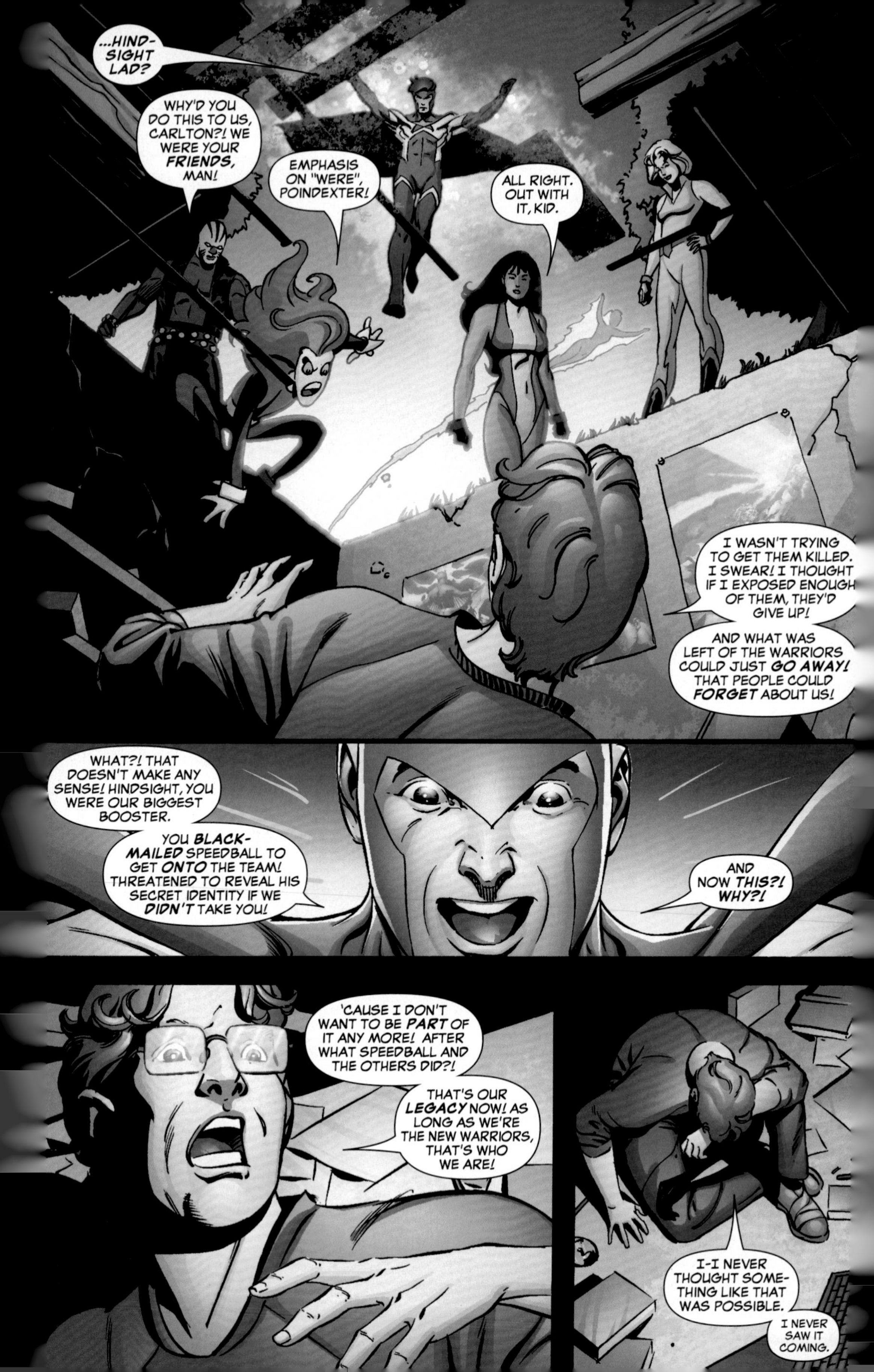
...HIND-SIGHT LAD?
WHY'D YOU DO THIS TO US, CARLTON?! WE WERE YOUR FRIENDS, MAN!
EMPHASIS ON "WERE", POINDEXTER!
ALL RIGHT. OUT WITH IT, KID.
I WASN'T TRYING TO GET THEM KILLED. I SWEAR! I THOUGHT IF I EXPOSED ENOUGH OF THEM, THEY'D GIVE UP!
AND WHAT WAS LEFT OF THE WARRIORS COULD JUST GO AWAY! THAT PEOPLE COULD FORGET ABOUT US!
WHAT?! THAT DOESN'T MAKE ANY SENSE! HINDSIGHT, YOU WERE OUR BIGGEST BOOSTER.
YOU BLACK-MAILED SPEEDBALL TO GET ONTO THE TEAM! THREATENED TO REVEAL HIS SECRET IDENTITY IF WE DIDN'T TAKE YOU!
AND NOW THIS?! WHY?!
'CAUSE I DON'T WANT TO BE PART OF IT ANY MORE! AFTER WHAT SPEEDBALL AND THE OTHERS DID?!
THAT'S OUR LEGACY NOW! AS LONG AS WE'RE THE NEW WARRIORS, THAT'S WHO WE ARE!
I-I NEVER THOUGHT SOME-THING LIKE THAT WAS POSSIBLE.
I NEVER SAW IT COMING.

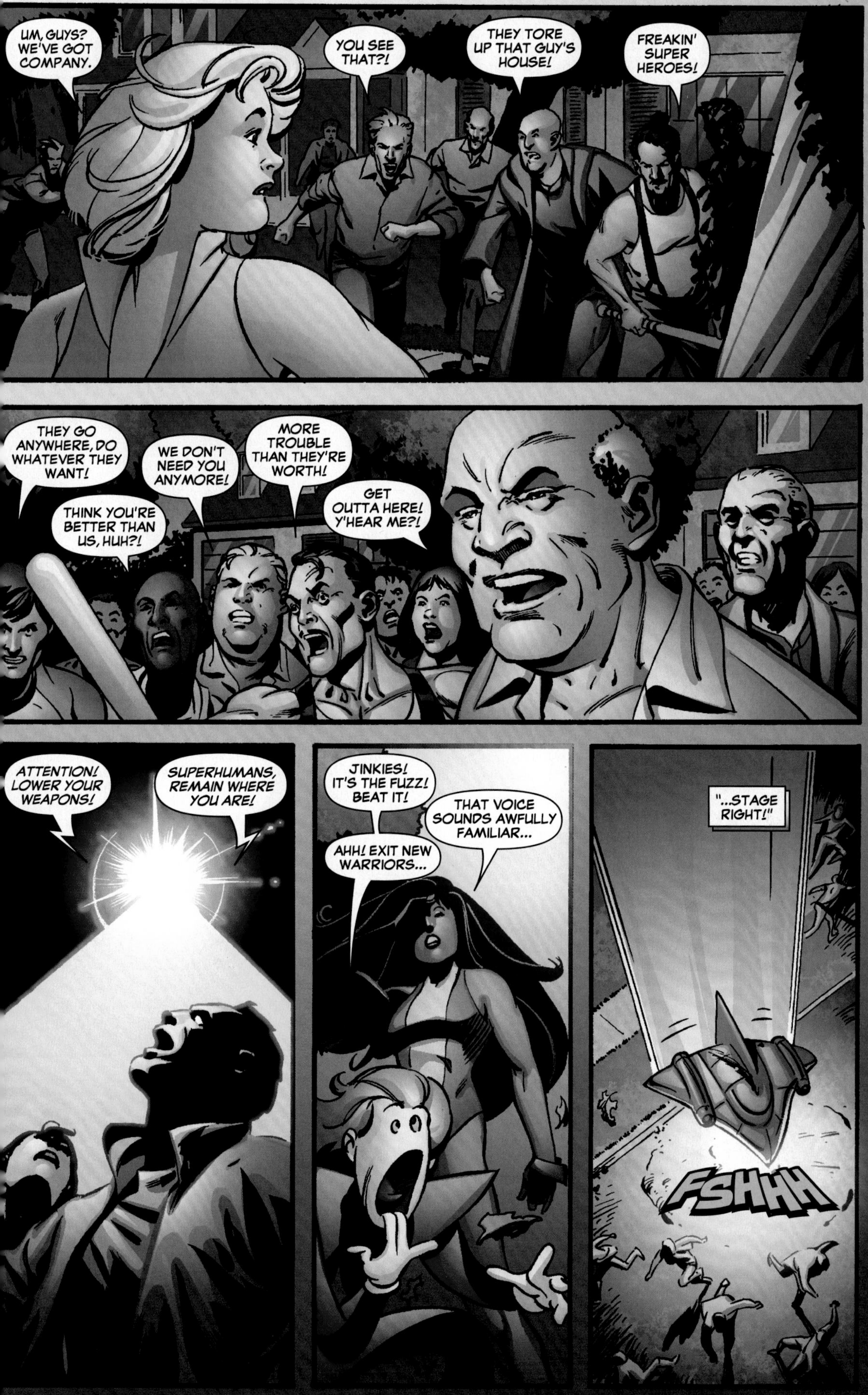
UM, GUYS? WE'VE GOT COMPANY.
YOU SEE THAT?!
THEY TORE UP THAT GUY'S HOUSE!
FREAKIN' SUPER HEROES!
THEY GO ANYWHERE, DO WHATEVER THEY WANT!
THINK YOU'RE BETTER THAN US, HUH?!
WE DON'T NEED YOU ANYMORE!
MORE TROUBLE THAN THEY'RE WORTH!
GET OUTTA HERE! Y'HEAR ME?!
ATTENTION! LOWER YOUR WEAPONS!
SUPERHUMANS, REMAIN WHERE YOU ARE!
JINKIES! IT'S THE FUZZ! BEAT IT!
AHH! EXIT NEW WARRIORS...
THAT VOICE SOUNDS AWFULLY FAMILIAR...
"...STAGE RIGHT!"
FSHHH

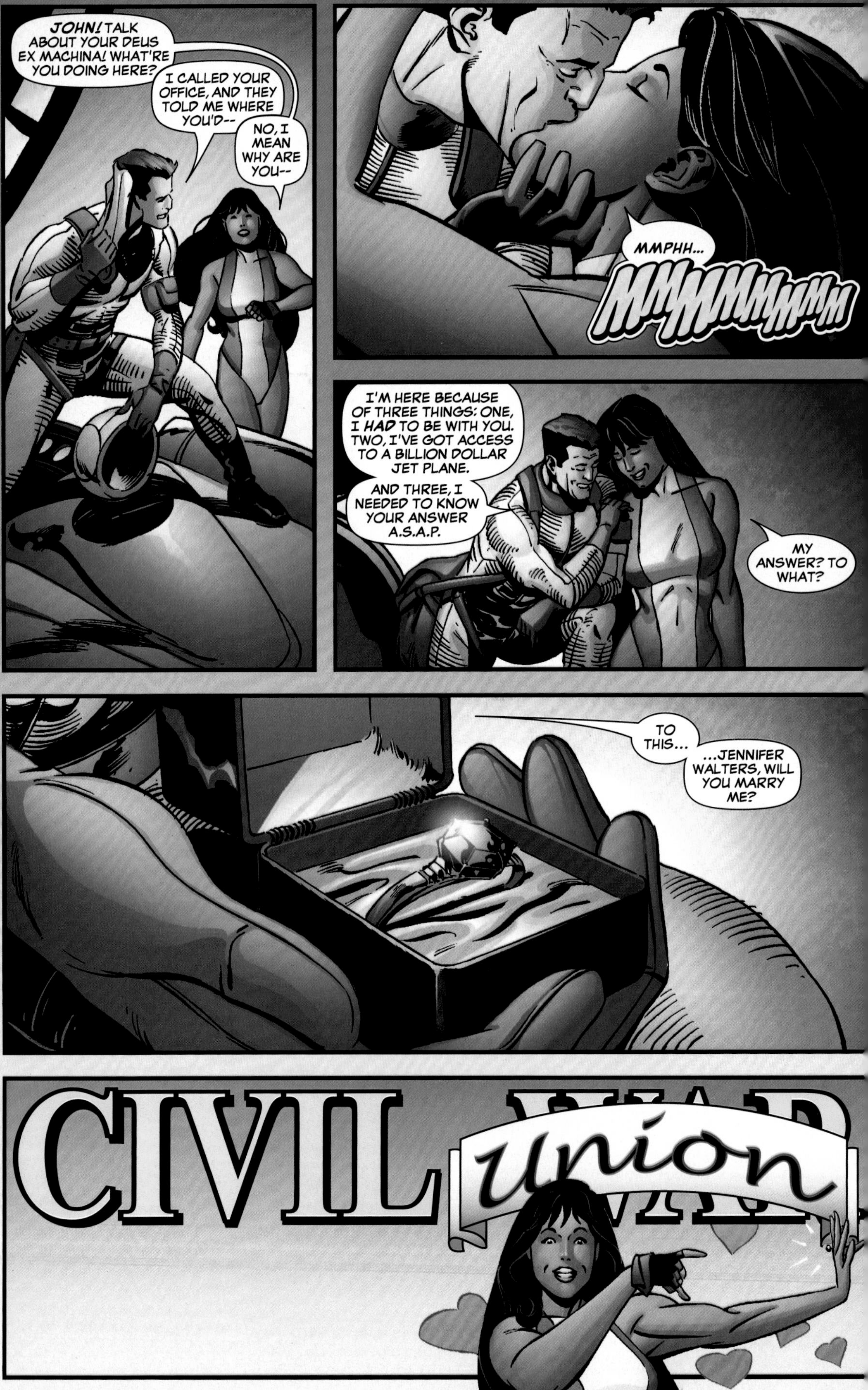
JOHN! TALK ABOUT YOUR DEUS EX MACHINA! WHAT'RE YOU DOING HERE?
I CALLED YOUR OFFICE, AND THEY TOLD ME WHERE YOU'D--
NO, I MEAN WHY ARE YOU--
MMPHH...
MMMMMMMMMM
I'M HERE BECAUSE OF THREE THINGS: ONE, I HAD TO BE WITH YOU. TWO, I'VE GOT ACCESS TO A BILLION DOLLAR JET PLANE.
AND THREE, I NEEDED TO KNOW YOUR ANSWER A.S.A.P.
MY ANSWER? TO WHAT?
TO THIS...
...JENNIFER WALTERS, WILL YOU MARRY ME?
CIVIL
union

ORIGINALLY PRINTED IN THE DAILY BUGLE CIVIL WAR NEWSPAPER SPECIAL

DAILY BUGLE *Editorials*

Super Powers Do Not Equal Super Privileges

By Jennifer Walters-Jameson
SPECIAL TO THE *BUGLE*

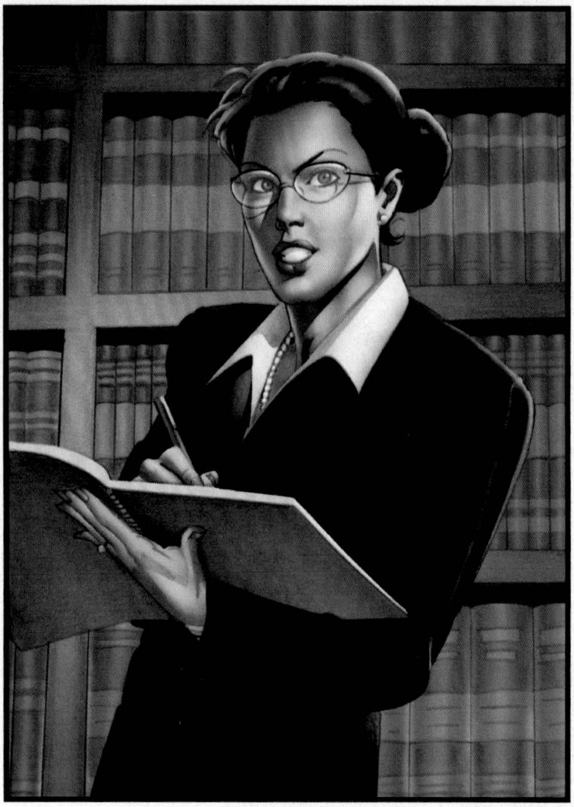

Photo by Mike Mayhew

Recently, I appeared on a cable news show and came out on behalf of the Superhuman Registration Act. Shortly thereafter, my office was inundated with letters, emails, and faxes, many of which called me out as a "flip-flopper" (and a few other choice terms as well). Now, I'm sure that anyone with a good memory or access to a search engine can see where this is coming from.

A few years ago, I was a very loud detractor of the original Mutant Registration Act. In fact, when a young woman, Theresa Handel, refused to register, I acted as her lawyer and argued her case all the way to the Supreme Court. So how is it I supported Terry in her efforts, and yet I'm not standing behind someone like Moon Knight in his? It all comes down to this:

Terry *is* homo superior. She was born that way. Though she has super powers that *could* enable her to become a super hero, she had no say in that matter. To pass legislation against her *as a mutant*, as part of a race, is unconstitutional.

A super hero, on the other hand, *chooses* to adopt a new identity and take on the role of a first responder (policeman, fireman, paramedic, etc.). Let's examine that for a second. Licensed first responders have undergone years of training, they work through agencies with government-controlled oversight, and are held accountable for their actions. A non-registered super hero fits none of those criteria.

If, heaven forbid, you found yourself in a serious accident, would you want a stranger with no medical certification moving your body? If you were held at gunpoint, would you want a stranger with no hostage-negotiating skills injecting himself into such an already tense situation? If you were trapped in a burning building, would you want a stranger with no fire fighting experience to start knocking down walls?

Now in *all* of those scenarios, imagine if that stranger's only credentials were a garish costume and a cape. While these costumed individuals may exhibit great initiative and dedication, none of those attributes endow them with special privileges or place them above the law. What the recently passed Superhuman Registration Act proposes is that if these individuals are that driven, they should continue their good works, but through proper channels.

Imagine how many more lives could be saved if we had trained super-powered firefighters. Imagine the number of convictions a super-powered policeman could make—as opposed to someone with a secret identity, who can't even leave their name on a citizen's arrest form. And, most of all, imagine the acceptance that would exist between the human and superhuman communities if heroes were out in the open, and acting as public servants.

In the wake of one disaster after another, the nation has come to realize that first responders are our *real* heroes. And with some effort and personal sacrifices, our super heroes could graduate to that status as well.

Jennifer Walters-Jameson is an attorney for Goodman, Lieber, Kurtzberg, and Holliway in their Superhuman Law division. As She-Hulk, she is also an accredited and trained member of both the Avengers and the Fantastic Four.

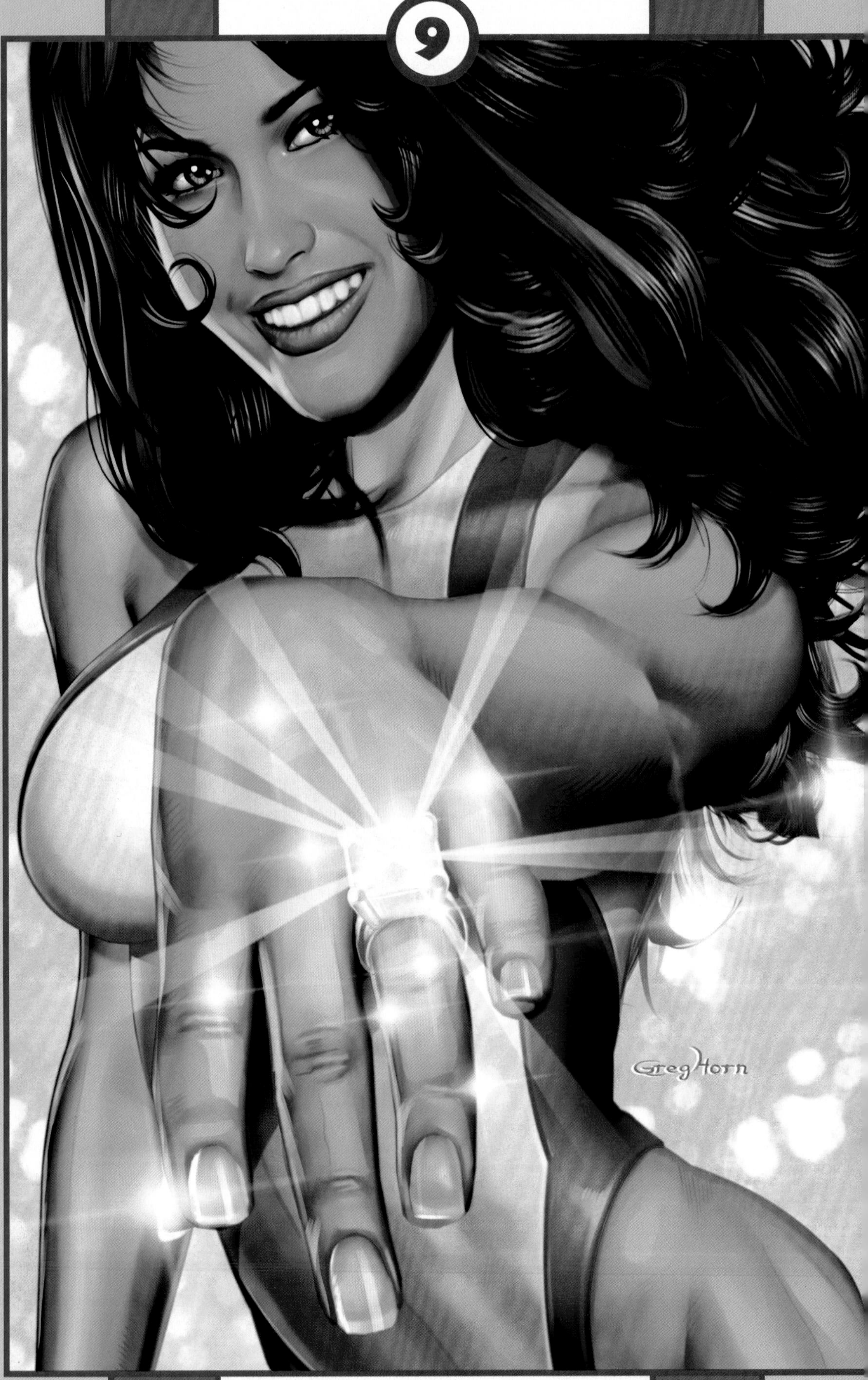
9
Greg Horn

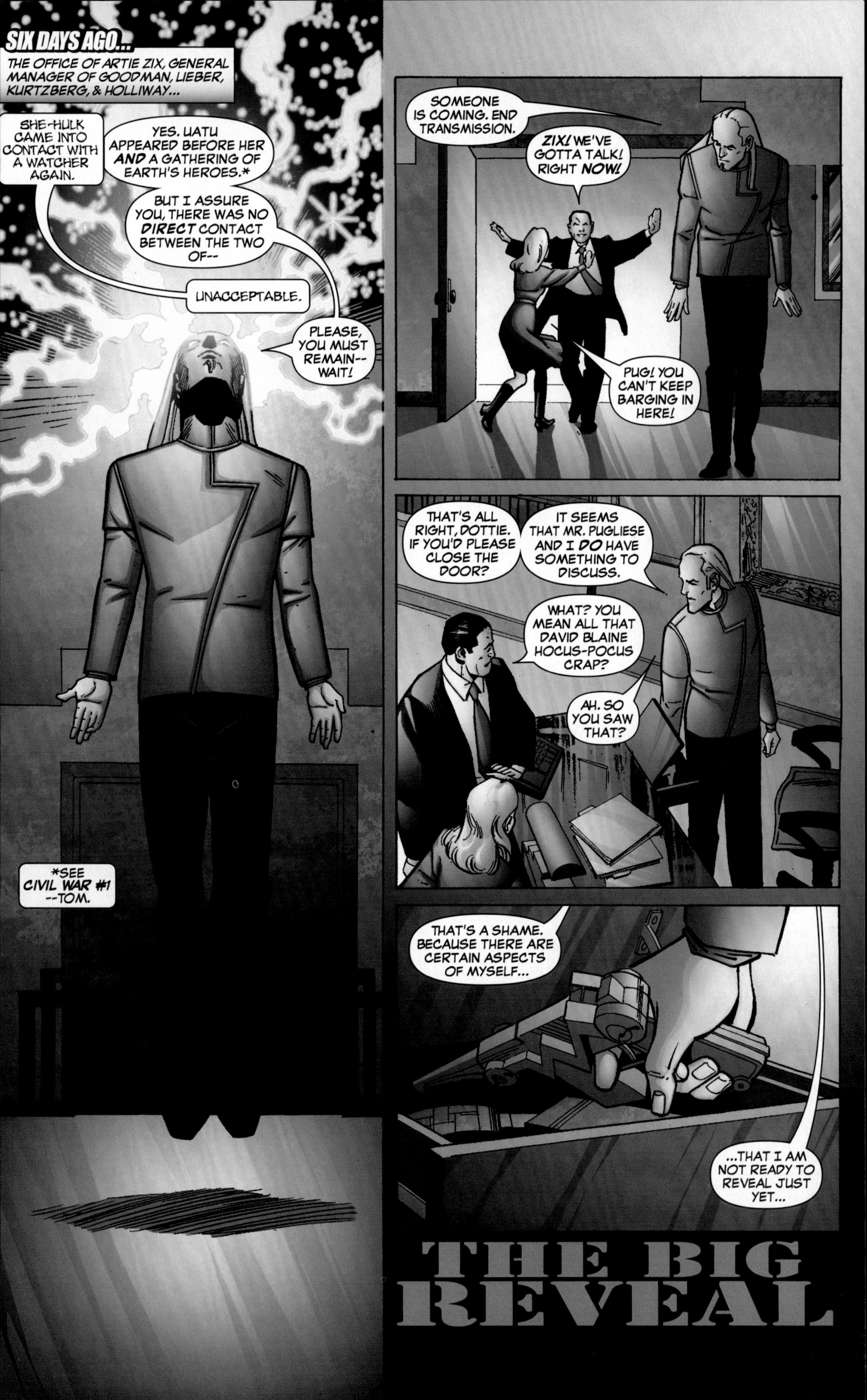
SIX DAYS AGO...
THE OFFICE OF ARTIE ZIX, GENERAL MANAGER OF GOODMAN, LIEBER, KURTZBERG, & HOLLIWAY...
SHE-HULK CAME INTO CONTACT WITH A WATCHER AGAIN.
YES. UATU APPEARED BEFORE HER AND A GATHERING OF EARTH'S HEROES.*
BUT I ASSURE YOU, THERE WAS NO DIRECT CONTACT BETWEEN THE TWO OF--
UNACCEPTABLE.
PLEASE, YOU MUST REMAIN-- WAIT!
*SEE CIVIL WAR #1 --TOM.
SOMEONE IS COMING. END TRANSMISSION.
ZIX! WE'VE GOTTA TALK! RIGHT NOW!
PUG! YOU CAN'T KEEP BARGING IN HERE!
THAT'S ALL RIGHT, DOTTIE. IF YOU'D PLEASE CLOSE THE DOOR?
IT SEEMS THAT MR. PUGLIESE AND I DO HAVE SOMETHING TO DISCUSS.
WHAT? YOU MEAN ALL THAT DAVID BLAINE HOCUS-POCUS CRAP?
AH. SO YOU SAW THAT?
THAT'S A SHAME. BECAUSE THERE ARE CERTAIN ASPECTS OF MYSELF...
...THAT I AM NOT READY TO REVEAL JUST YET...
THE BIG REVEAL

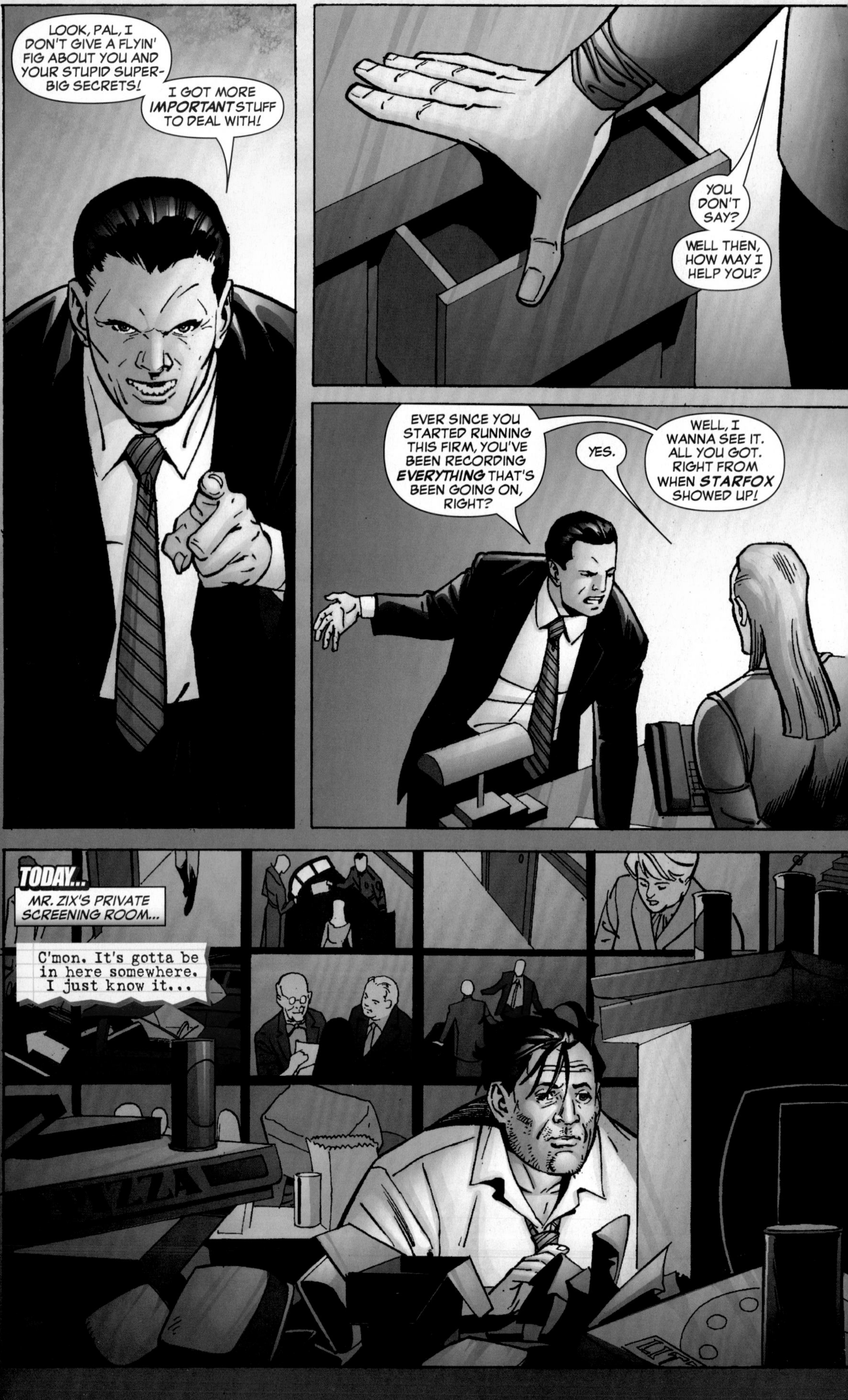
LOOK, PAL, I DON'T GIVE A FLYIN' FIG ABOUT YOU AND YOUR STUPID SUPER-BIG SECRETS!
I GOT MORE IMPORTANT STUFF TO DEAL WITH!
YOU DON'T SAY?
WELL THEN, HOW MAY I HELP YOU?
EVER SINCE YOU STARTED RUNNING THIS FIRM, YOU'VE BEEN RECORDING EVERYTHING THAT'S BEEN GOING ON, RIGHT?
YES.
WELL, I WANNA SEE IT. ALL YOU GOT. RIGHT FROM WHEN STARFOX SHOWED UP!
TODAY...
MR. ZIX'S PRIVATE SCREENING ROOM...
C'mon. It's gotta be in here somewhere. I just know it...
PIZZA

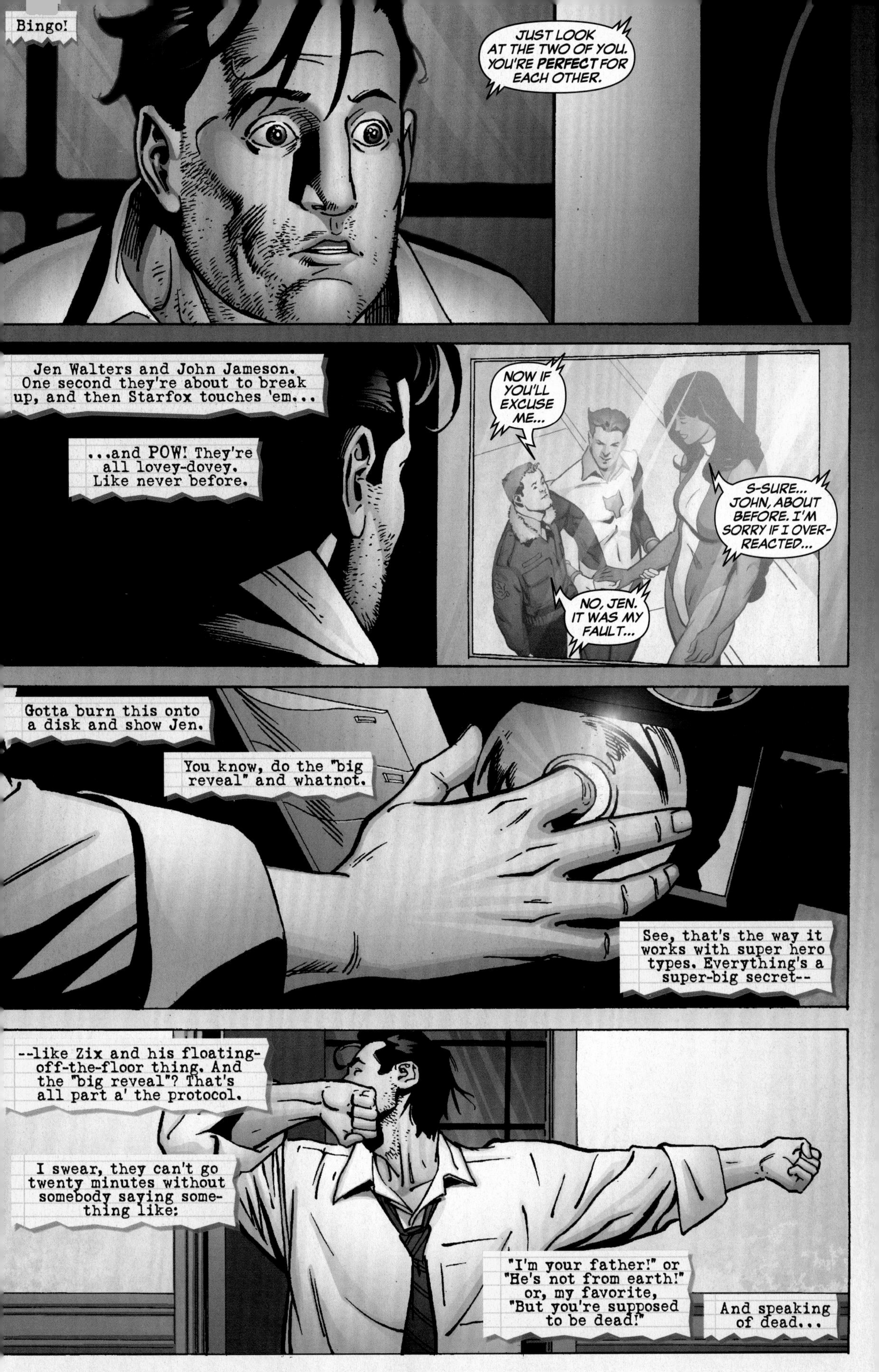
Bingo!
JUST LOOK AT THE TWO OF YOU. YOU'RE PERFECT FOR EACH OTHER.
Jen Walters and John Jameson. One second they're about to break up, and then Starfox touches 'em...
...and POW! They're all lovey-dovey. Like never before.
NOW IF YOU'LL EXCUSE ME...
S-SURE... JOHN, ABOUT BEFORE. I'M SORRY IF I OVER-REACTED...
NO, JEN. IT WAS MY FAULT...
Gotta burn this onto a disk and show Jen.
You know, do the "big reveal" and whatnot.
See, that's the way it works with super hero types. Everything's a super-big secret--
--like Zix and his floating-off-the-floor thing. And the "big reveal"? That's all part a' the protocol.
I swear, they can't go twenty minutes without somebody saying some-thing like:
"I'm your father!" or "He's not from earth!" or, my favorite, "But you're supposed to be dead!"
And speaking of dead...

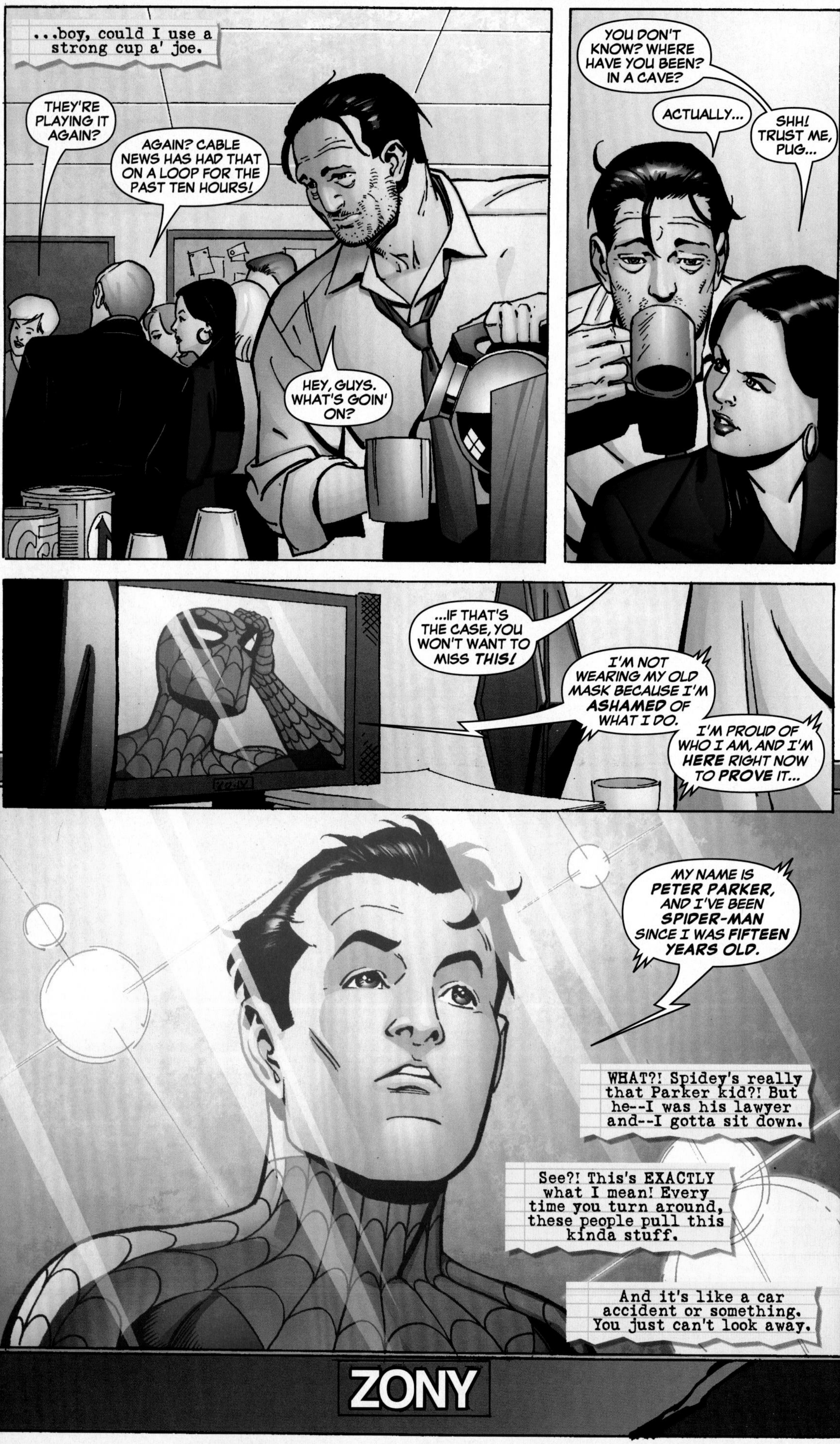
...boy, could I use a strong cup a' joe.
THEY'RE PLAYING IT AGAIN?
AGAIN? CABLE NEWS HAS HAD THAT ON A LOOP FOR THE PAST TEN HOURS!
HEY, GUYS. WHAT'S GOIN' ON?
YOU DON'T KNOW? WHERE HAVE YOU BEEN? IN A CAVE?
ACTUALLY...
SHH! TRUST ME, PUG...
...IF THAT'S THE CASE, YOU WON'T WANT TO MISS THIS!
I'M NOT WEARING MY OLD MASK BECAUSE I'M ASHAMED OF WHAT I DO.
I'M PROUD OF WHO I AM, AND I'M HERE RIGHT NOW TO PROVE IT...
MY NAME IS PETER PARKER, AND I'VE BEEN SPIDER-MAN SINCE I WAS FIFTEEN YEARS OLD.
WHAT?! Spidey's really that Parker kid?! But he--I was his lawyer and--I gotta sit down.
See?! This's EXACTLY what I mean! Every time you turn around, these people pull this kinda stuff.
And it's like a car accident or something. You just can't look away.
ZONY

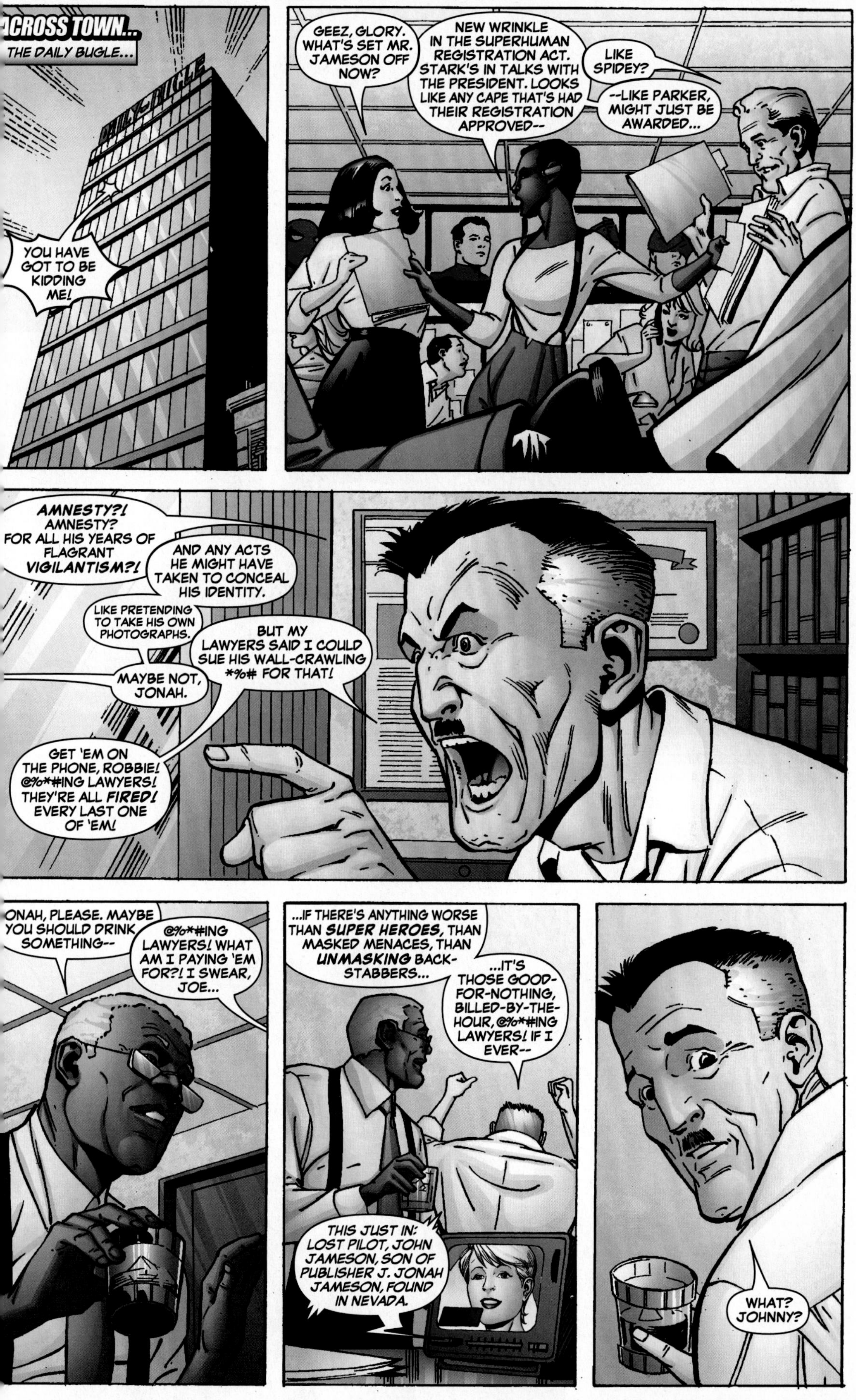
ACROSS TOWN...
THE DAILY BUGLE...
DAILY BUGLE
YOU HAVE GOT TO BE KIDDING ME!
GEEZ, GLORY. WHAT'S SET MR. JAMESON OFF NOW?
NEW WRINKLE IN THE SUPERHUMAN REGISTRATION ACT. STARK'S IN TALKS WITH THE PRESIDENT. LOOKS LIKE ANY CAPE THAT'S HAD THEIR REGISTRATION APPROVED--
LIKE SPIDEY?
--LIKE PARKER, MIGHT JUST BE AWARDED...
AMNESTY?! AMNESTY? FOR ALL HIS YEARS OF FLAGRANT VIGILANTISM?!
AND ANY ACTS HE MIGHT HAVE TAKEN TO CONCEAL HIS IDENTITY.
LIKE PRETENDING TO TAKE HIS OWN PHOTOGRAPHS.
BUT MY LAWYERS SAID I COULD SUE HIS WALL-CRAWLING *%# FOR THAT!
MAYBE NOT, JONAH.
GET 'EM ON THE PHONE, ROBBIE! @%*#ING LAWYERS! THEY'RE ALL FIRED! EVERY LAST ONE OF 'EM!
ONAH, PLEASE. MAYBE YOU SHOULD DRINK SOMETHING--
@%*#ING LAWYERS! WHAT AM I PAYING 'EM FOR?! I SWEAR, JOE...
...IF THERE'S ANYTHING WORSE THAN SUPER HEROES, THAN MASKED MENACES, THAN UNMASKING BACK-STABBERS...
...IT'S THOSE GOOD-FOR-NOTHING, BILLED-BY-THE-HOUR, @%*#ING LAWYERS! IF I EVER--
THIS JUST IN: LOST PILOT, JOHN JAMESON, SON OF PUBLISHER J. JONAH JAMESON, FOUND IN NEVADA.
WHAT? JOHNNY?

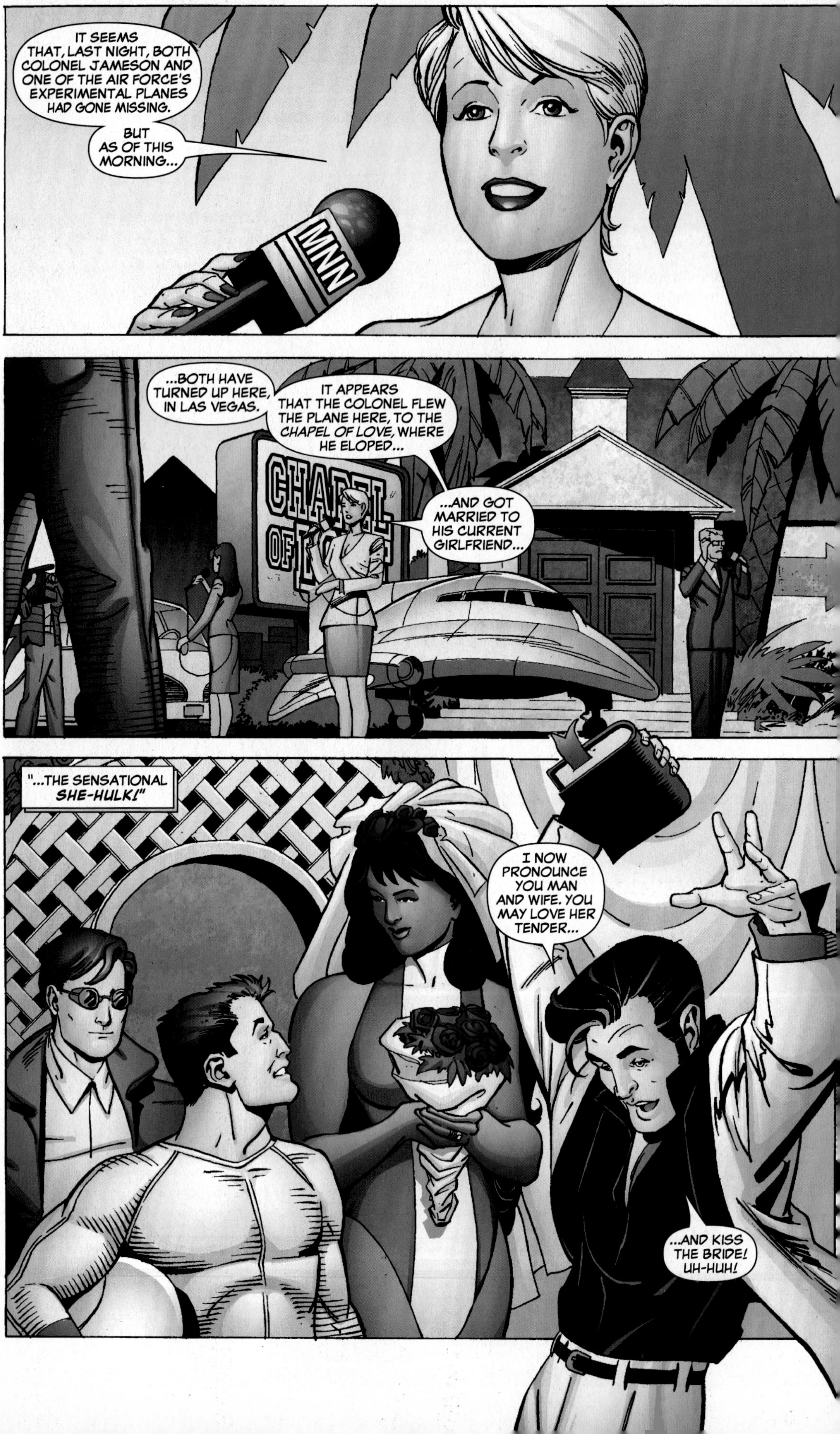
IT SEEMS THAT, LAST NIGHT, BOTH COLONEL JAMESON AND ONE OF THE AIR FORCE'S EXPERIMENTAL PLANES HAD GONE MISSING.
BUT AS OF THIS MORNING...
MNN
...BOTH HAVE TURNED UP HERE, IN LAS VEGAS.
IT APPEARS THAT THE COLONEL FLEW THE PLANE HERE, TO THE *CHAPEL OF LOVE*, WHERE HE ELOPED...
...AND GOT MARRIED TO HIS CURRENT GIRLFRIEND...
"...THE SENSATIONAL *SHE-HULK!*"
I NOW PRONOUNCE YOU MAN AND WIFE. YOU MAY LOVE HER TENDER...
...AND KISS THE BRIDE! UH-HUH!

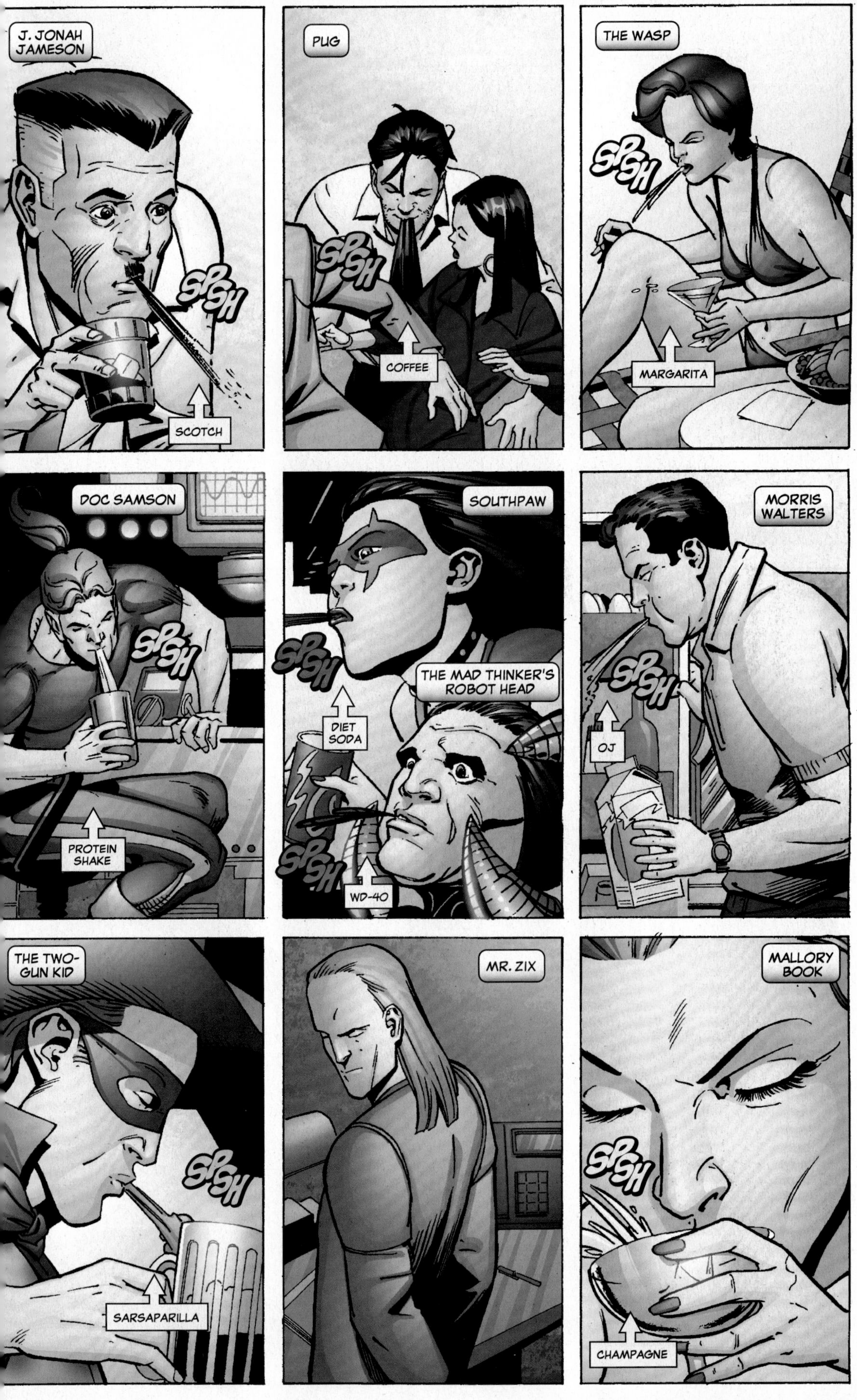
J. JONAH JAMESON
SPSH
SCOTCH
PUG
SPSH
COFFEE
THE WASP
SPSH
MARGARITA
DOC SAMSON
SPSH
PROTEIN SHAKE
SOUTHPAW
SPSH
DIET SODA
THE MAD THINKER'S ROBOT HEAD
SPSH
WD-40
MORRIS WALTERS
SPSH
OJ
THE TWO-GUN KID
SPSH
SARSAPARILLA
MR. ZIX
MALLORY BOOK
SPSH
CHAMPAGNE

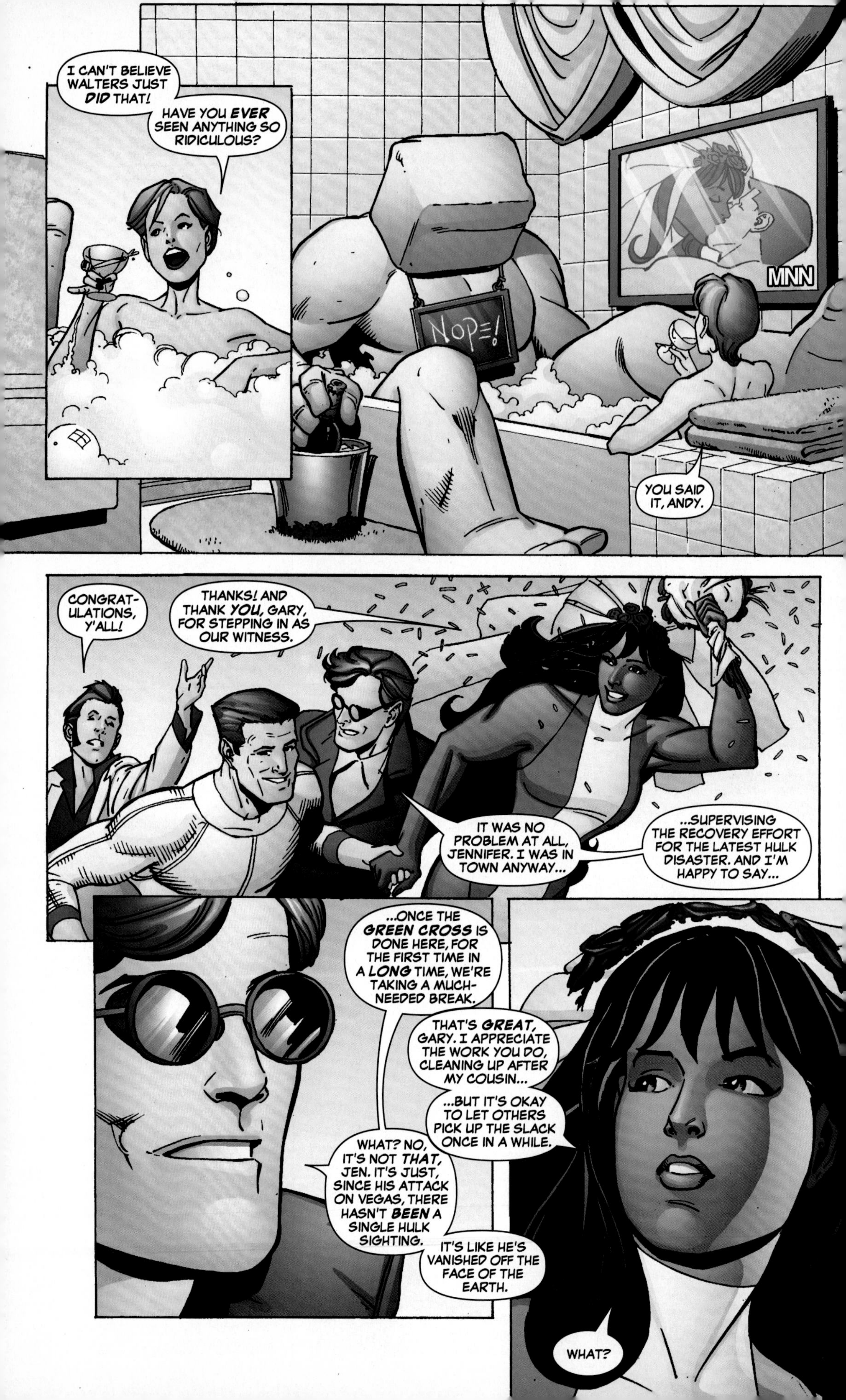
I CAN'T BELIEVE WALTERS JUST *DID* THAT!
HAVE YOU *EVER* SEEN ANYTHING SO RIDICULOUS?
MNN
NOPE!
YOU SAID IT, ANDY.
CONGRAT-ULATIONS, Y'ALL!
THANKS! AND THANK *YOU*, GARY, FOR STEPPING IN AS OUR WITNESS.
IT WAS NO PROBLEM AT ALL, JENNIFER. I WAS IN TOWN ANYWAY...
...SUPERVISING THE RECOVERY EFFORT FOR THE LATEST HULK DISASTER. AND I'M HAPPY TO SAY...
...ONCE THE *GREEN CROSS* IS DONE HERE, FOR THE FIRST TIME IN A *LONG* TIME, WE'RE TAKING A MUCH-NEEDED BREAK.
THAT'S *GREAT*, GARY. I APPRECIATE THE WORK YOU DO, CLEANING UP AFTER MY COUSIN...
...BUT IT'S OKAY TO LET OTHERS PICK UP THE SLACK ONCE IN A WHILE.
WHAT? NO, IT'S NOT *THAT*, JEN. IT'S JUST, SINCE HIS ATTACK ON VEGAS, THERE HASN'T *BEEN* A SINGLE HULK SIGHTING.
IT'S LIKE HE'S VANISHED OFF THE FACE OF THE EARTH.
WHAT?

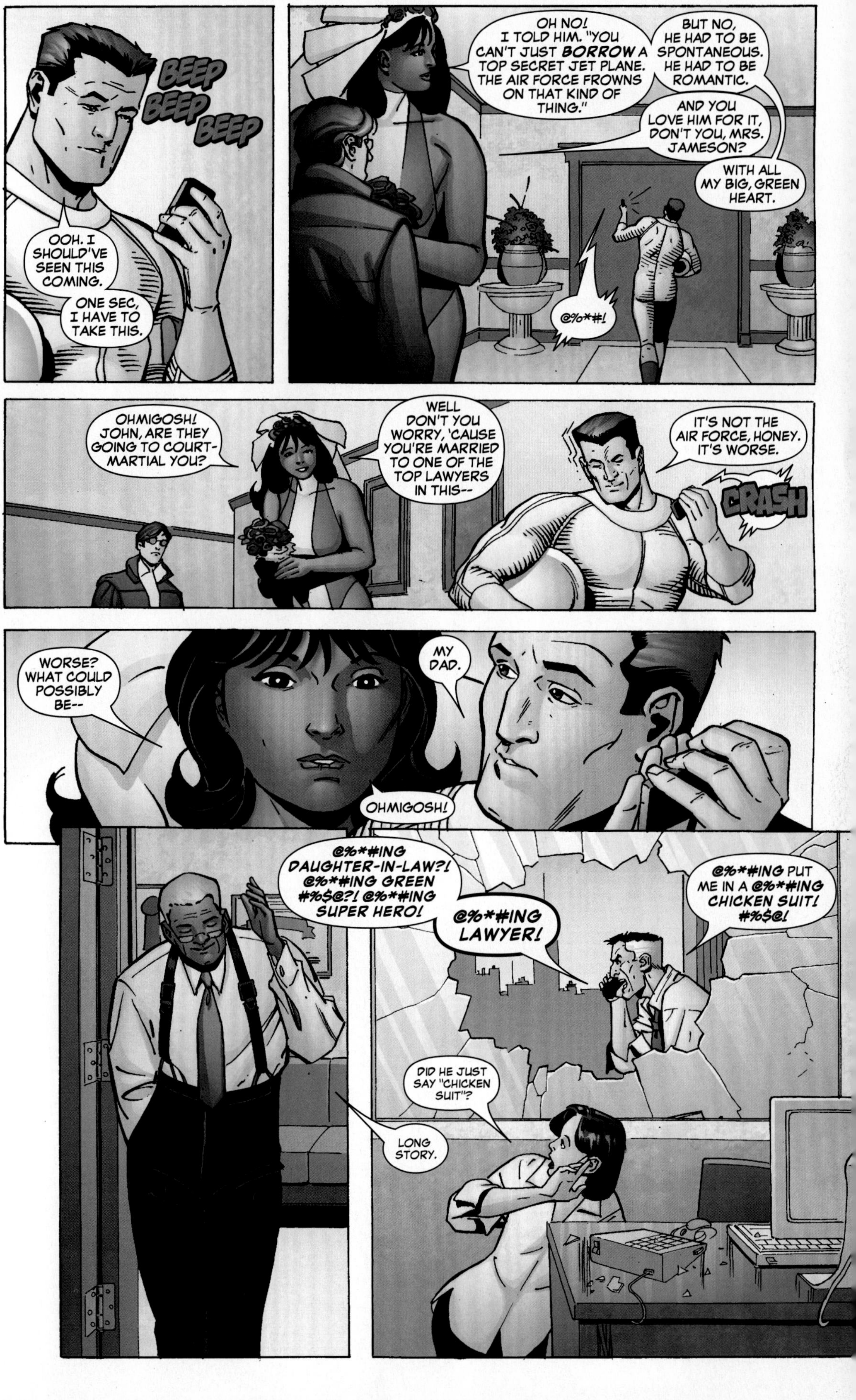
BEEP BEEP BEEP
OOH. I SHOULD'VE SEEN THIS COMING.
ONE SEC, I HAVE TO TAKE THIS.
OH NO! I TOLD HIM. "YOU CAN'T JUST BORROW A TOP SECRET JET PLANE. THE AIR FORCE FROWNS ON THAT KIND OF THING."
BUT NO, HE HAD TO BE SPONTANEOUS. HE HAD TO BE ROMANTIC.
AND YOU LOVE HIM FOR IT, DON'T YOU, MRS. JAMESON?
WITH ALL MY BIG, GREEN HEART.
@%*#!
OHMIGOSH! JOHN, ARE THEY GOING TO COURT-MARTIAL YOU?
WELL DON'T YOU WORRY, 'CAUSE YOU'RE MARRIED TO ONE OF THE TOP LAWYERS IN THIS--
IT'S NOT THE AIR FORCE, HONEY. IT'S WORSE.
CRASH
WORSE? WHAT COULD POSSIBLY BE--
MY DAD.
OHMIGOSH!
@%*#ING DAUGHTER-IN-LAW?! @%*#ING GREEN #%$@?! @%*#ING SUPER HERO!
@%*#ING LAWYER!
@%*#ING PUT ME IN A @%*#ING CHICKEN SUIT! #%$@!
DID HE JUST SAY "CHICKEN SUIT"?
LONG STORY.

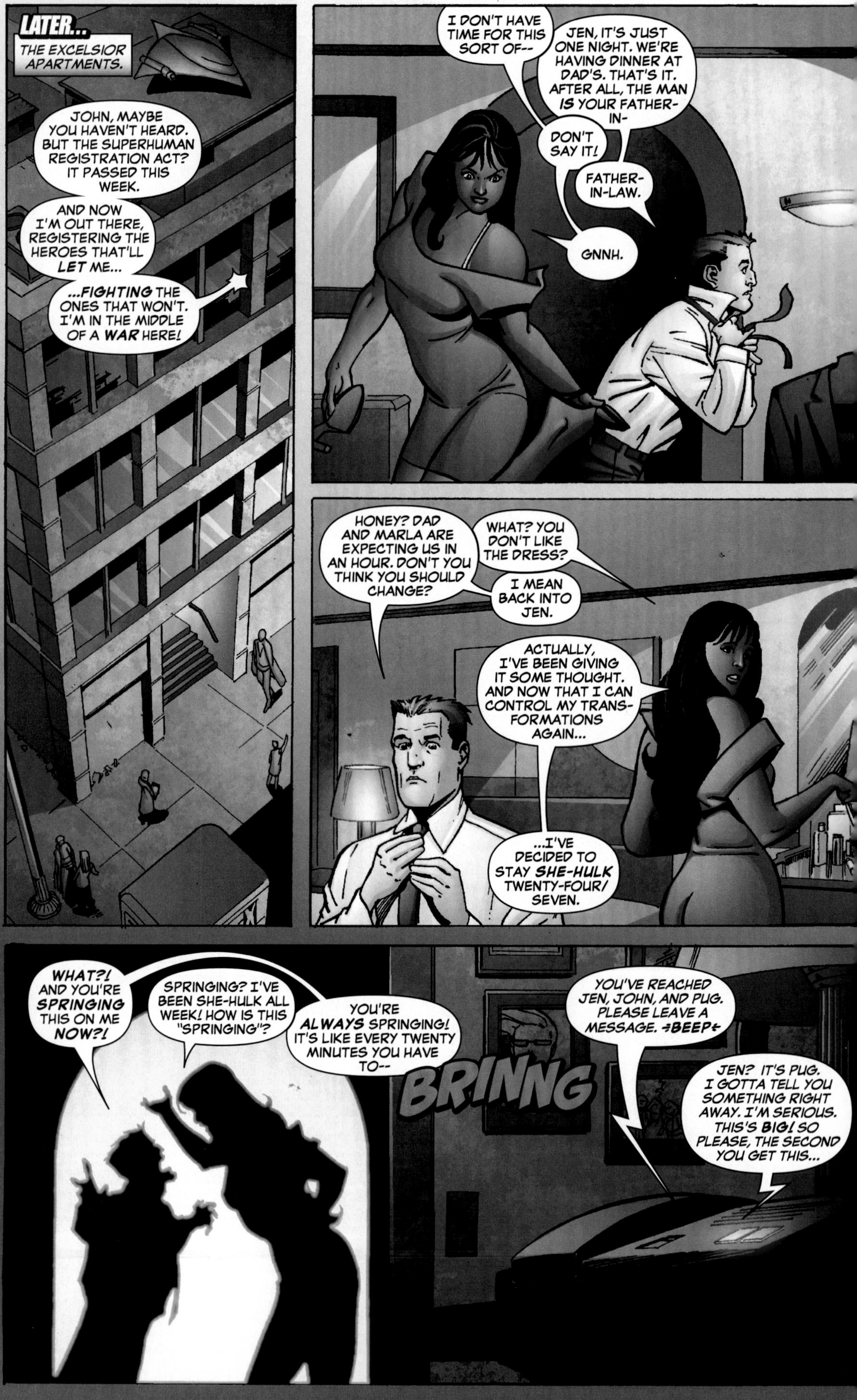
LATER...
THE EXCELSIOR APARTMENTS.
JOHN, MAYBE YOU HAVEN'T HEARD. BUT THE SUPERHUMAN REGISTRATION ACT? IT PASSED THIS WEEK.
AND NOW I'M OUT THERE, REGISTERING THE HEROES THAT'LL LET ME...
...FIGHTING THE ONES THAT WON'T. I'M IN THE MIDDLE OF A WAR HERE!
I DON'T HAVE TIME FOR THIS SORT OF--
JEN, IT'S JUST ONE NIGHT. WE'RE HAVING DINNER AT DAD'S. THAT'S IT. AFTER ALL, THE MAN IS YOUR FATHER-IN-
DON'T SAY IT!
FATHER-IN-LAW.
GNNH.
HONEY? DAD AND MARLA ARE EXPECTING US IN AN HOUR. DON'T YOU THINK YOU SHOULD CHANGE?
WHAT? YOU DON'T LIKE THE DRESS?
I MEAN BACK INTO JEN.
ACTUALLY, I'VE BEEN GIVING IT SOME THOUGHT. AND NOW THAT I CAN CONTROL MY TRANS-FORMATIONS AGAIN...
...I'VE DECIDED TO STAY SHE-HULK TWENTY-FOUR/SEVEN.
WHAT?! AND YOU'RE SPRINGING THIS ON ME NOW?!
SPRINGING? I'VE BEEN SHE-HULK ALL WEEK! HOW IS THIS "SPRINGING"?
YOU'RE ALWAYS SPRINGING! IT'S LIKE EVERY TWENTY MINUTES YOU HAVE TO--
BRINNG
YOU'VE REACHED JEN, JOHN, AND PUG. PLEASE LEAVE A MESSAGE. =BEEP=
JEN? IT'S PUG. I GOTTA TELL YOU SOMETHING RIGHT AWAY. I'M SERIOUS. THIS'S BIG! SO PLEASE, THE SECOND YOU GET THIS...

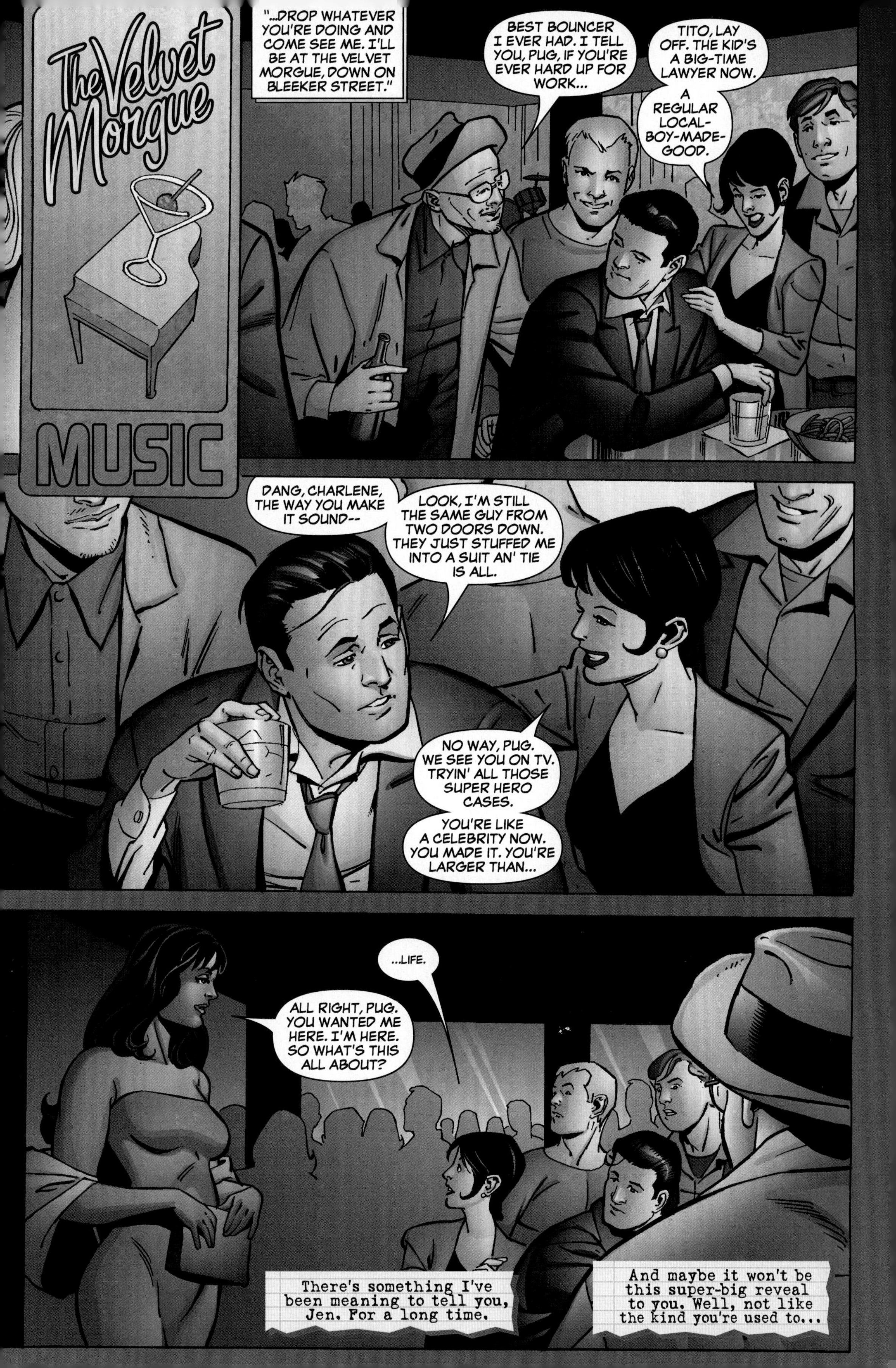
The Velvet Morgue
MUSIC
"...DROP WHATEVER YOU'RE DOING AND COME SEE ME. I'LL BE AT THE VELVET MORGUE, DOWN ON BLEEKER STREET."
BEST BOUNCER I EVER HAD. I TELL YOU, PUG, IF YOU'RE EVER HARD UP FOR WORK...
TITO, LAY OFF. THE KID'S A BIG-TIME LAWYER NOW.
A REGULAR LOCAL-BOY-MADE-GOOD.
DANG, CHARLENE, THE WAY YOU MAKE IT SOUND--
LOOK, I'M STILL THE SAME GUY FROM TWO DOORS DOWN. THEY JUST STUFFED ME INTO A SUIT AN' TIE IS ALL.
NO WAY, PUG. WE SEE YOU ON TV. TRYIN' ALL THOSE SUPER HERO CASES.
YOU'RE LIKE A CELEBRITY NOW. YOU MADE IT. YOU'RE LARGER THAN...
...LIFE.
ALL RIGHT, PUG. YOU WANTED ME HERE. I'M HERE. SO WHAT'S THIS ALL ABOUT?
There's something I've been meaning to tell you, Jen. For a long time.
And maybe it won't be this super-big reveal to you. Well, not like the kind you're used to...

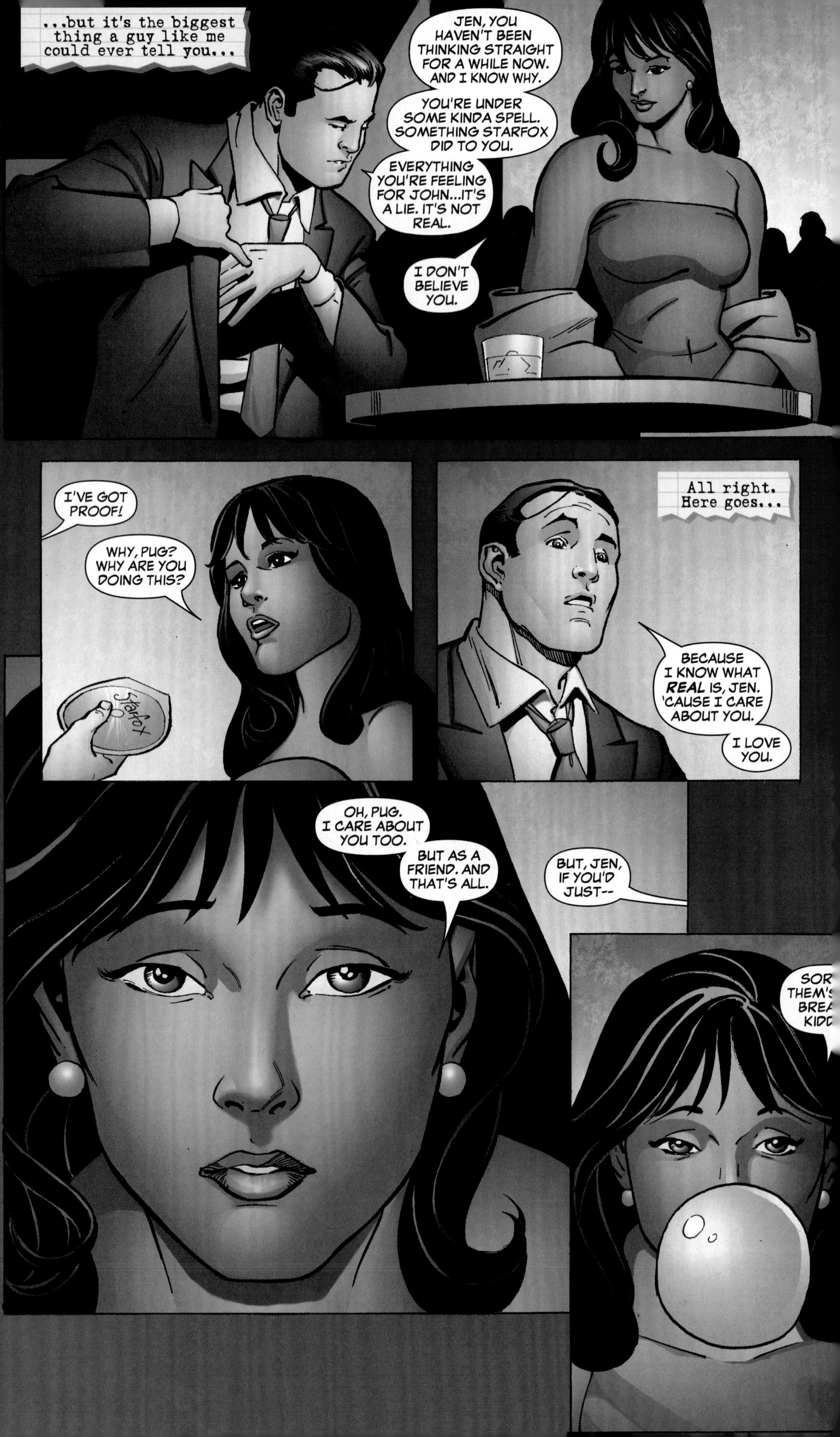
...but it's the biggest thing a guy like me could ever tell you...
JEN, YOU HAVEN'T BEEN THINKING STRAIGHT FOR A WHILE NOW. AND I KNOW WHY.
YOU'RE UNDER SOME KINDA SPELL. SOMETHING STARFOX DID TO YOU.
EVERYTHING YOU'RE FEELING FOR JOHN...IT'S A LIE. IT'S NOT REAL.
I DON'T BELIEVE YOU.
I'VE GOT PROOF!
Starfox
WHY, PUG? WHY ARE YOU DOING THIS?
All right. Here goes...
BECAUSE I KNOW WHAT REAL IS, JEN. 'CAUSE I CARE ABOUT YOU.
I LOVE YOU.
OH, PUG. I CARE ABOUT YOU TOO.
BUT AS A FRIEND. AND THAT'S ALL.
BUT, JEN, IF YOU'D JUST--

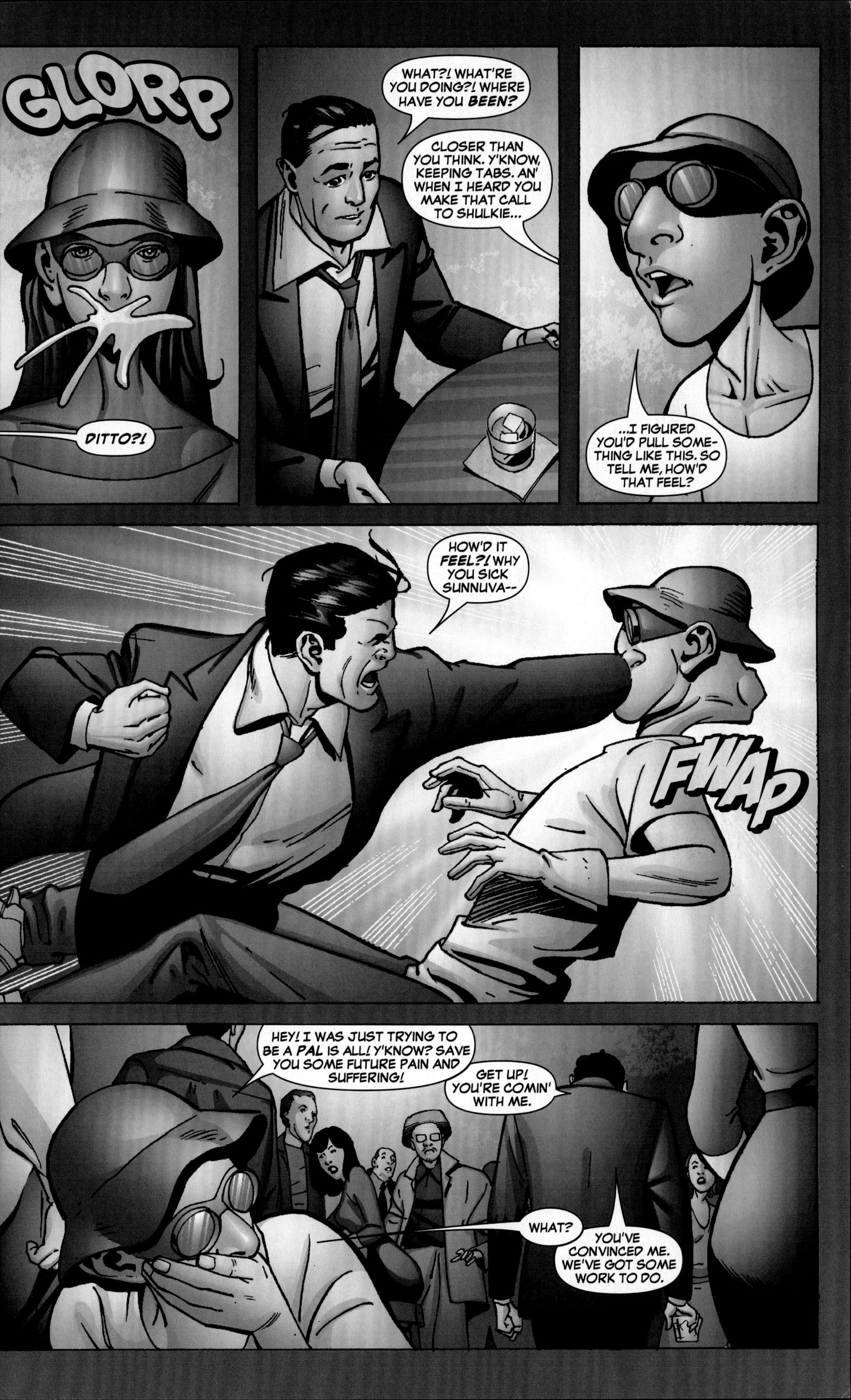

GLORP
DITTO?!
WHAT?! WHAT'RE YOU DOING?! WHERE HAVE YOU BEEN?
CLOSER THAN YOU THINK. Y'KNOW, KEEPING TABS. AN' WHEN I HEARD YOU MAKE THAT CALL TO SHULKIE...
...I FIGURED YOU'D PULL SOMETHING LIKE THIS. SO TELL ME, HOW'D THAT FEEL?
HOW'D IT FEEL?! WHY YOU SICK SUNNUVA--
FWAP
HEY! I WAS JUST TRYING TO BE A PAL IS ALL! Y'KNOW? SAVE YOU SOME FUTURE PAIN AND SUFFERING!
GET UP! YOU'RE COMIN' WITH ME.
WHAT?
YOU'VE CONVINCED ME. WE'VE GOT SOME WORK TO DO.

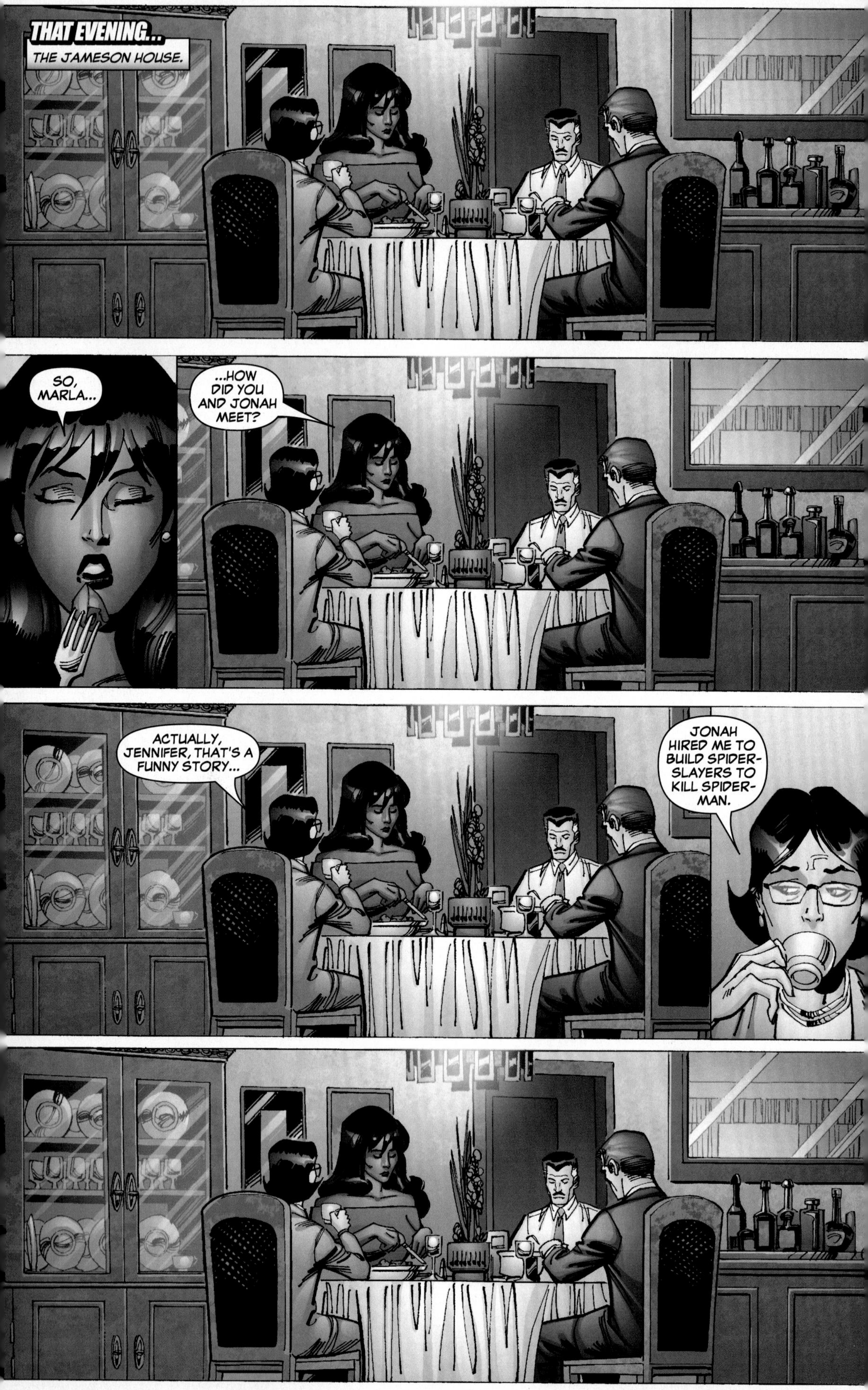
THAT EVENING...
THE JAMESON HOUSE.
SO, MARLA...
...HOW DID YOU AND JONAH MEET?
ACTUALLY, JENNIFER, THAT'S A FUNNY STORY...
JONAH HIRED ME TO BUILD SPIDER-SLAYERS TO KILL SPIDER-MAN.

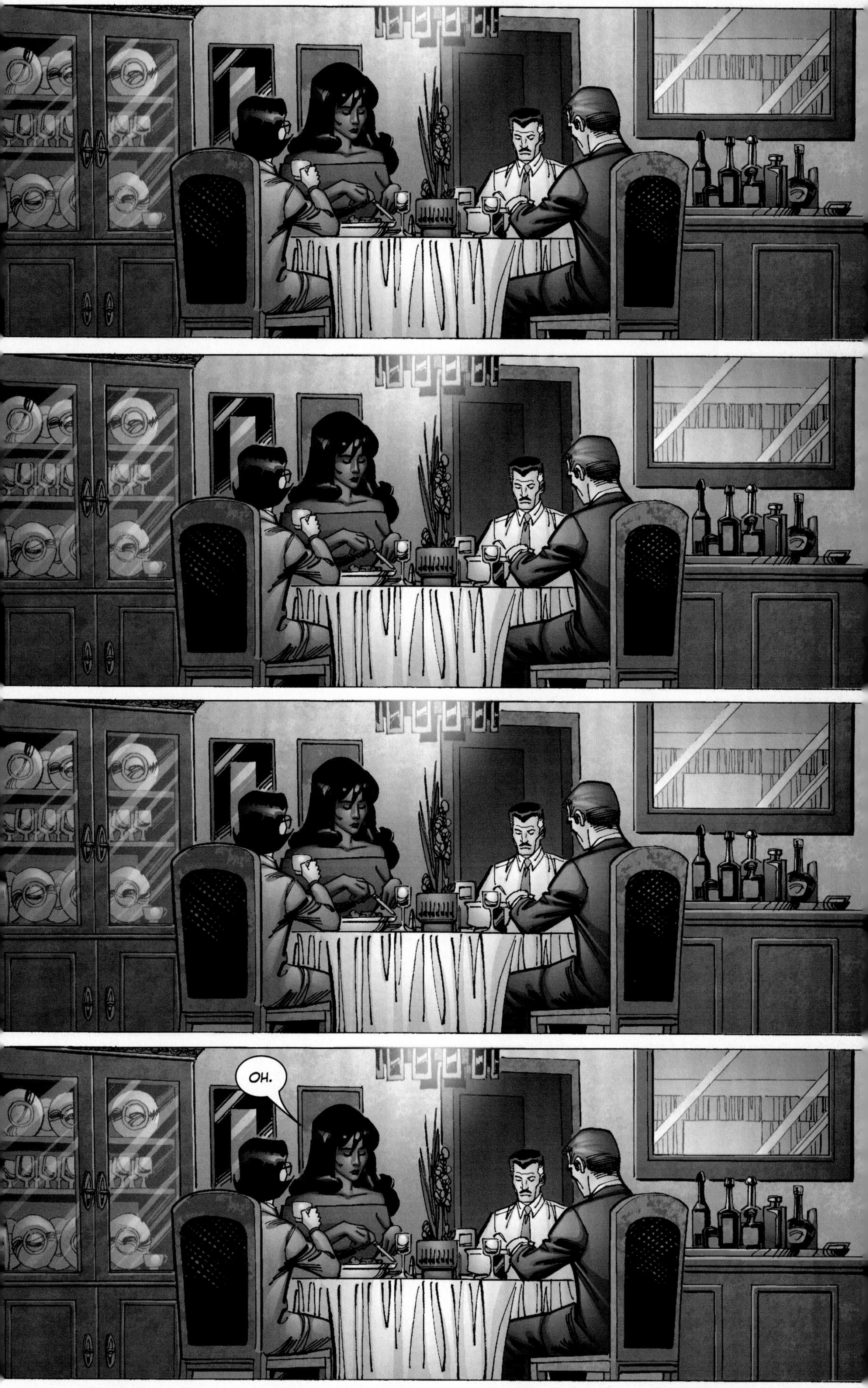
OH.

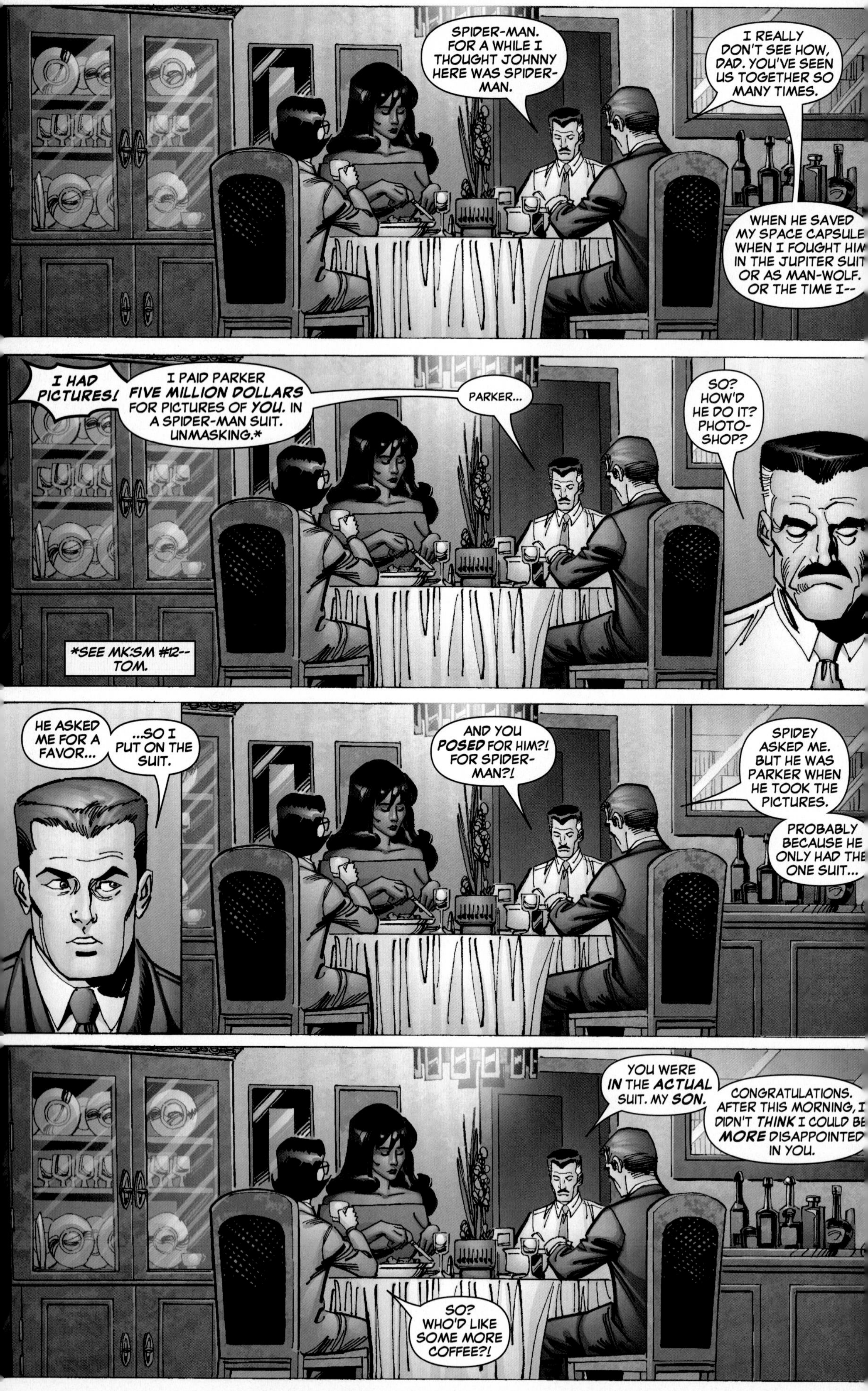
SPIDER-MAN. FOR A WHILE I THOUGHT JOHNNY HERE WAS SPIDER-MAN.
I REALLY DON'T SEE HOW, DAD. YOU'VE SEEN US TOGETHER SO MANY TIMES.
WHEN HE SAVED MY SPACE CAPSULE. WHEN I FOUGHT HIM IN THE JUPITER SUIT OR AS MAN-WOLF. OR THE TIME I--
I HAD PICTURES!
I PAID PARKER FIVE MILLION DOLLARS FOR PICTURES OF YOU. IN A SPIDER-MAN SUIT. UNMASKING.*
PARKER...
SO? HOW'D HE DO IT? PHOTO-SHOP?
*SEE MK:SM #12-- TOM.
HE ASKED ME FOR A FAVOR...
...SO I PUT ON THE SUIT.
AND YOU POSED FOR HIM?! FOR SPIDER-MAN?!
SPIDEY ASKED ME. BUT HE WAS PARKER WHEN HE TOOK THE PICTURES.
PROBABLY BECAUSE HE ONLY HAD THE ONE SUIT...
YOU WERE IN THE ACTUAL SUIT. MY SON.
CONGRATULATIONS. AFTER THIS MORNING, I DIDN'T THINK I COULD BE MORE DISAPPOINTED IN YOU.
SO? WHO'D LIKE SOME MORE COFFEE?!

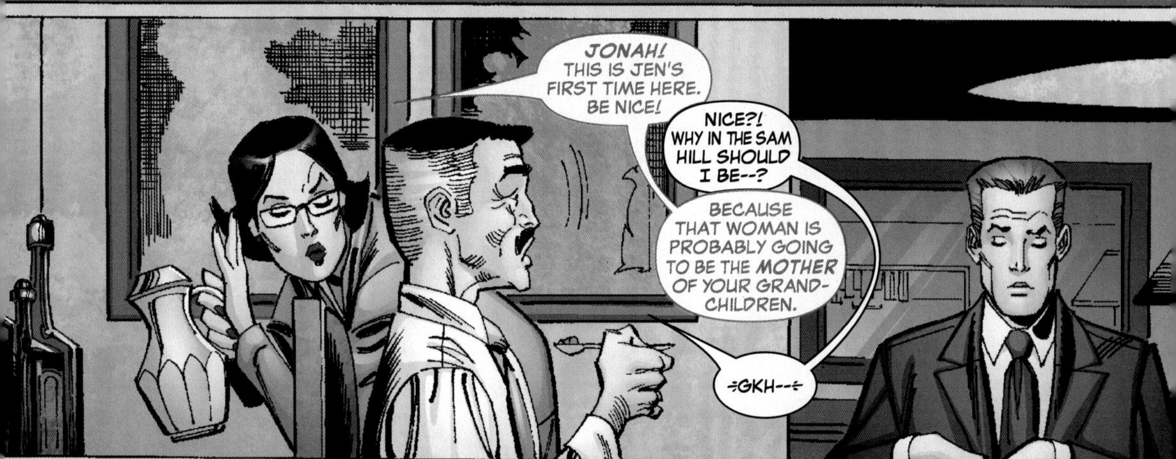
JONAH! THIS IS JEN'S FIRST TIME HERE. BE NICE!
NICE?! WHY IN THE SAM HILL SHOULD I BE--?
BECAUSE THAT WOMAN IS PROBABLY GOING TO BE THE MOTHER OF YOUR GRAND-CHILDREN.
-GKH--

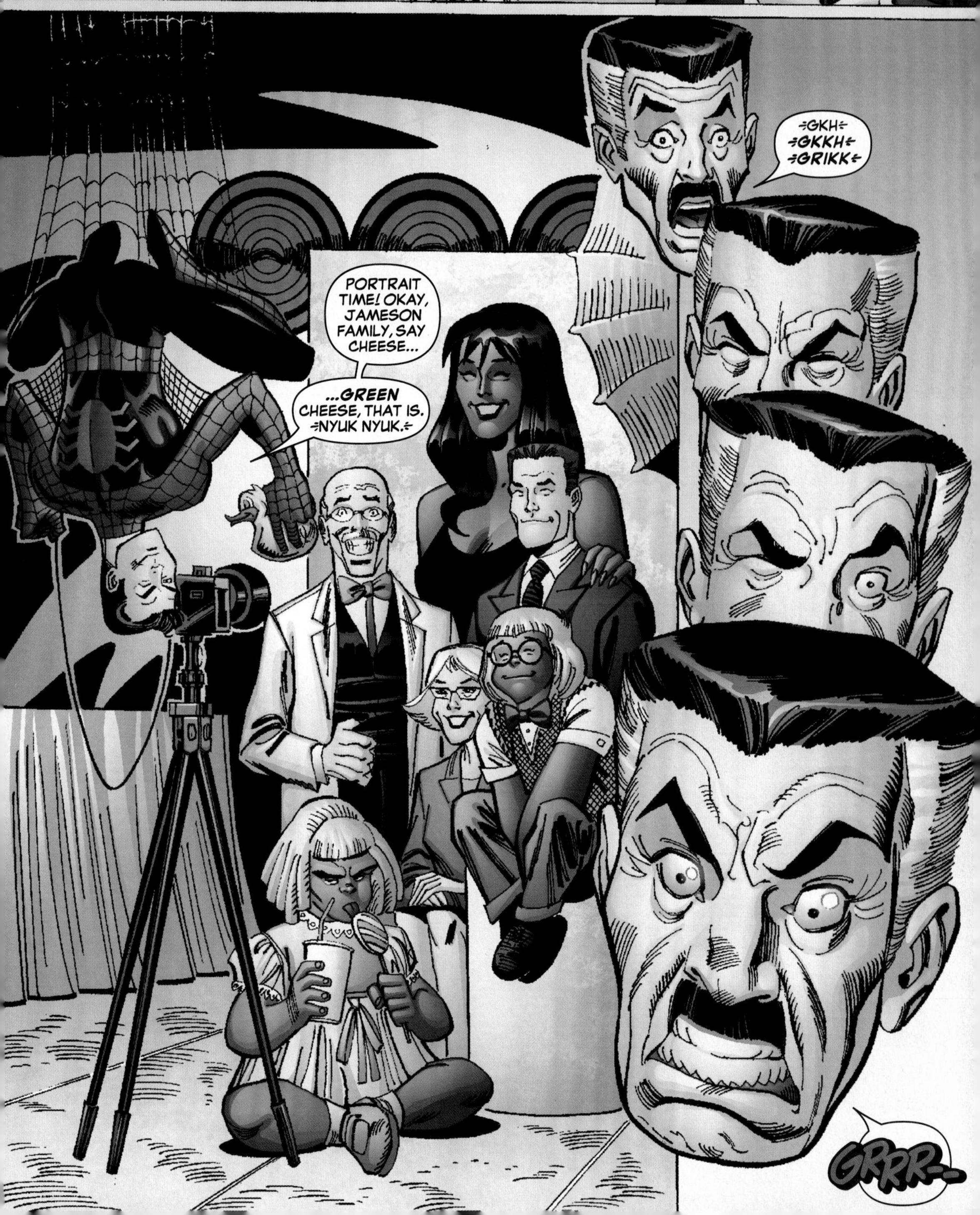
-GKH- -GKKH- -GRIKK-
PORTRAIT TIME! OKAY, JAMESON FAMILY, SAY CHEESE...
...GREEN CHEESE, THAT IS. -NYUK NYUK.-
GRRR--

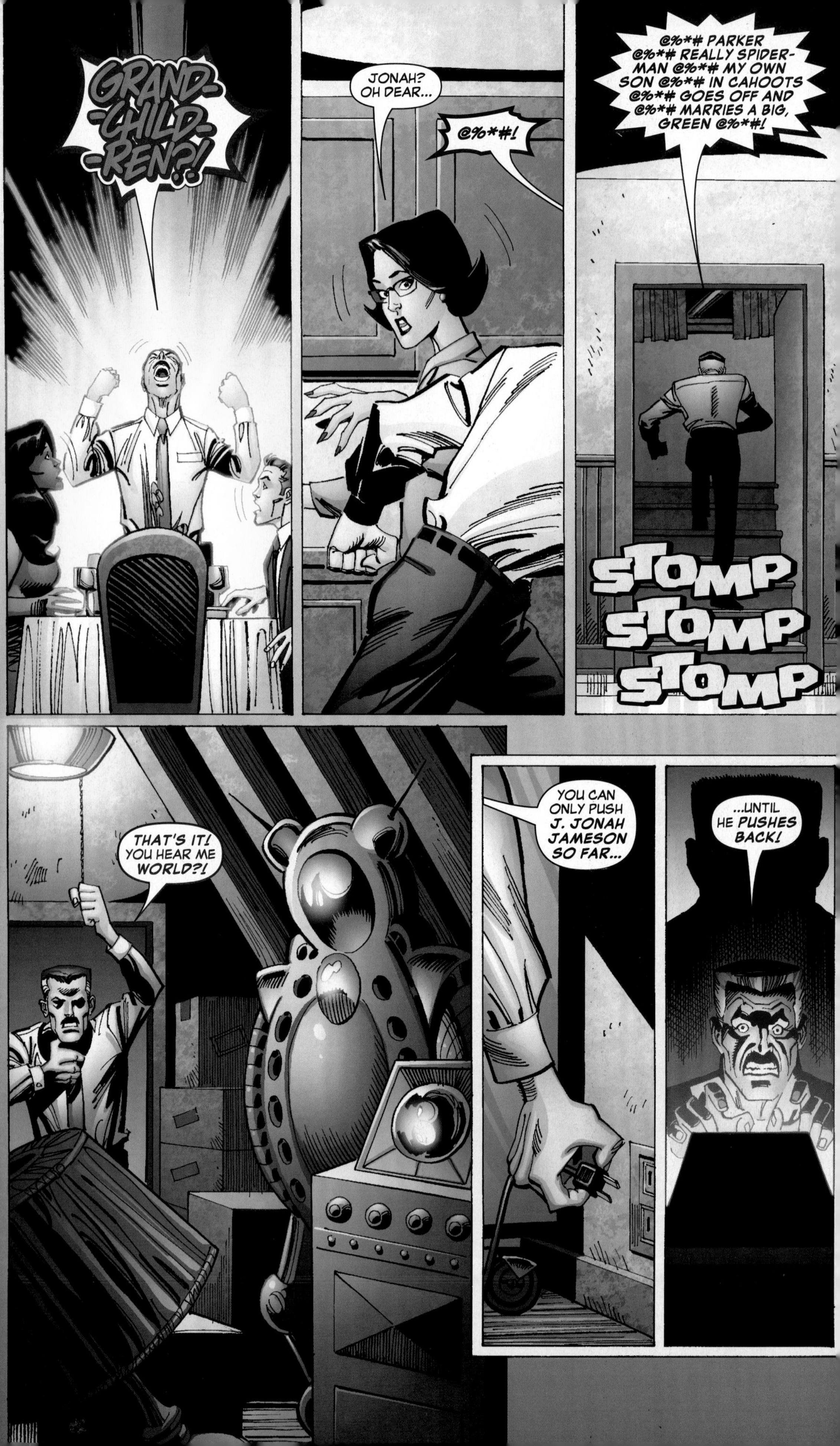
GRAND- -CHILD- -REN?!
JONAH? OH DEAR...
@%*#!
@%*# PARKER @%*# REALLY SPIDER-MAN @%*# MY OWN SON @%*# IN CAHOOTS @%*# GOES OFF AND @%*# MARRIES A BIG, GREEN @%*#!
STOMP STOMP STOMP
THAT'S IT! YOU HEAR ME WORLD?!
YOU CAN ONLY PUSH J. JONAH JAMESON SO FAR...
...UNTIL HE PUSHES BACK!

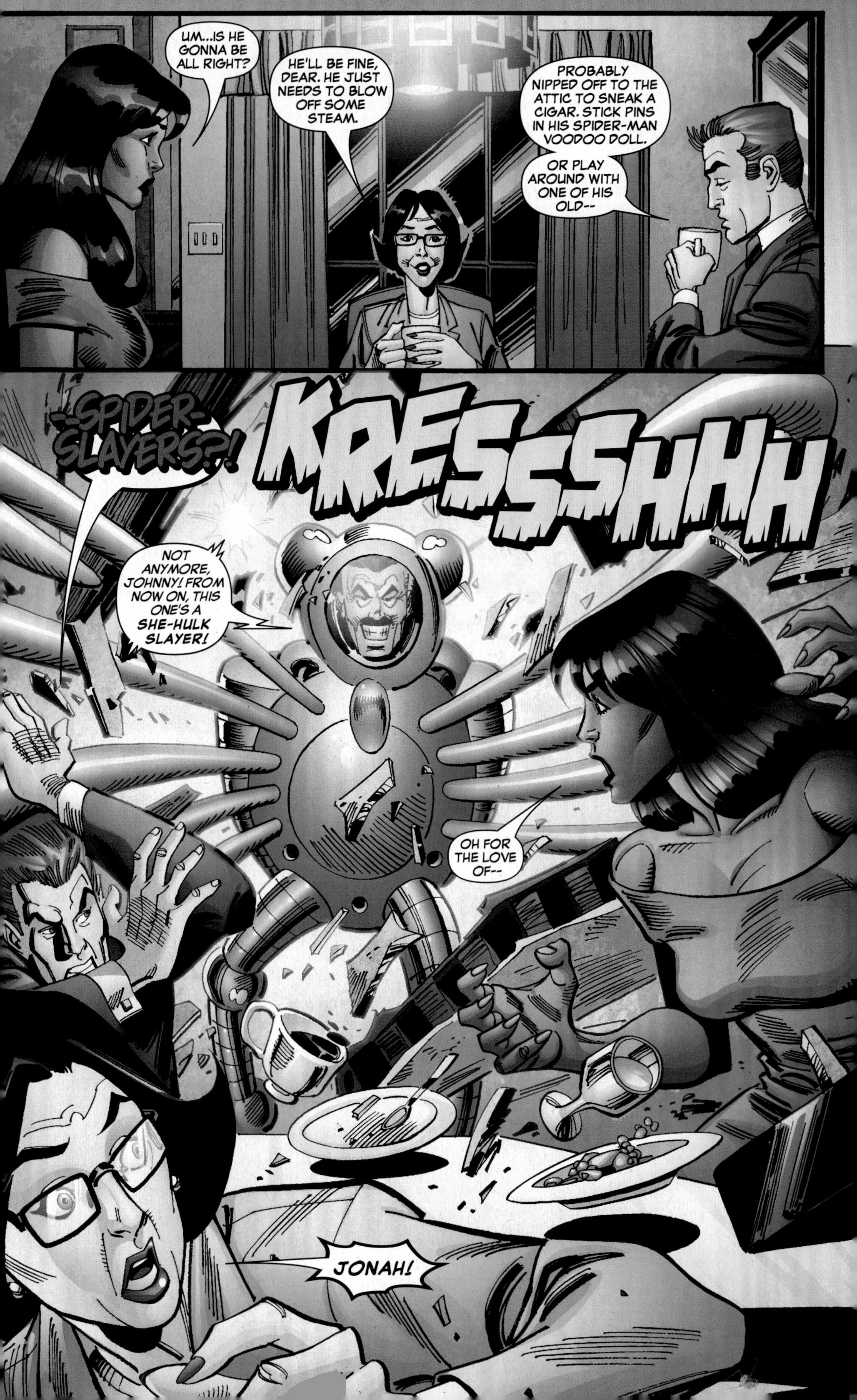
UM...IS HE GONNA BE ALL RIGHT?
HE'LL BE FINE, DEAR. HE JUST NEEDS TO BLOW OFF SOME STEAM.
PROBABLY NIPPED OFF TO THE ATTIC TO SNEAK A CIGAR. STICK PINS IN HIS SPIDER-MAN VOODOO DOLL.
OR PLAY AROUND WITH ONE OF HIS OLD--
--SPIDER-SLAYERS?!
KRESSSHHH
NOT ANYMORE, JOHNNY! FROM NOW ON, THIS ONE'S A SHE-HULK SLAYER!
OH FOR THE LOVE OF--
JONAH!

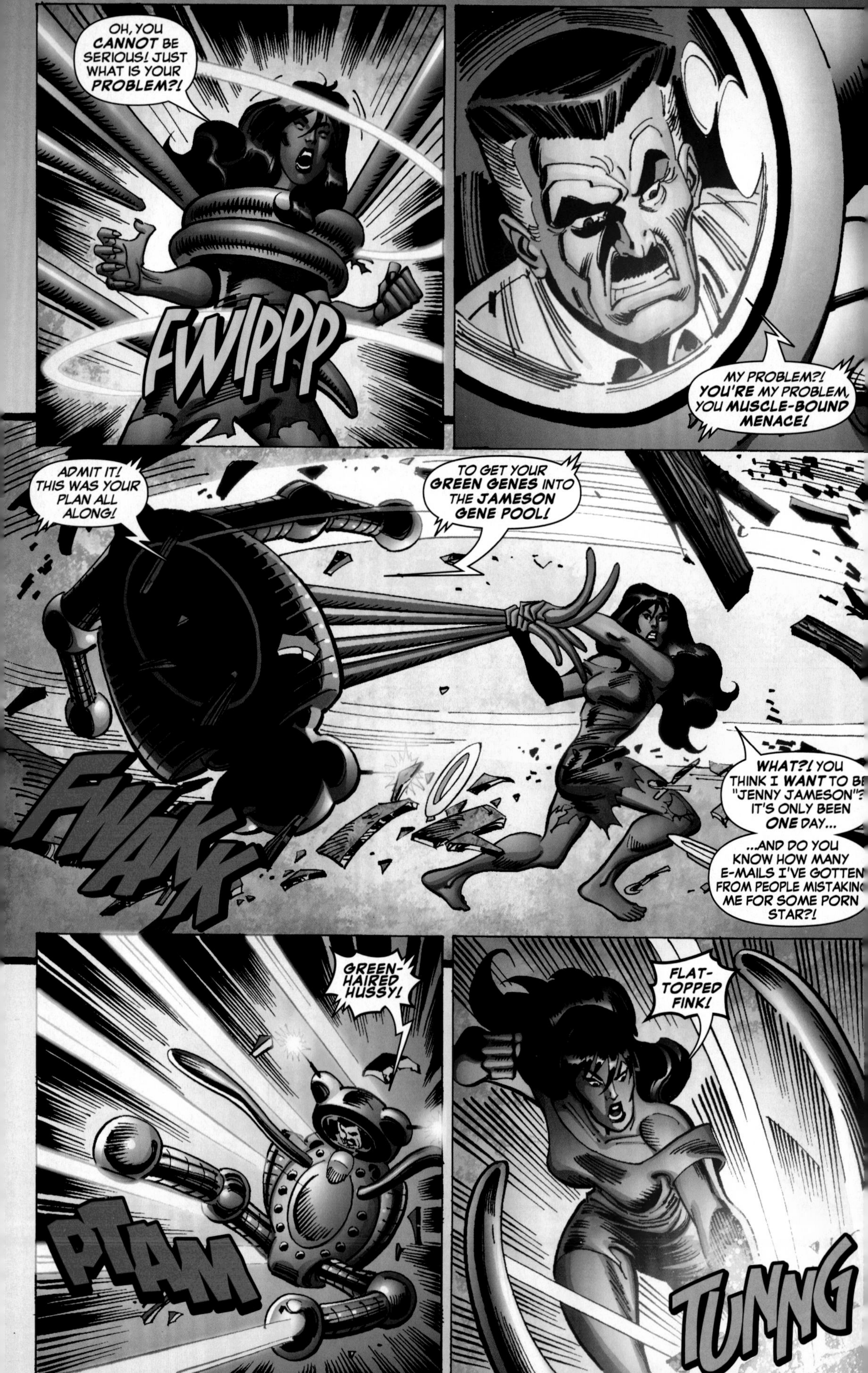
OH, YOU CANNOT BE SERIOUS! JUST WHAT IS YOUR PROBLEM?!
FWIPPP
MY PROBLEM?! YOU'RE MY PROBLEM, YOU MUSCLE-BOUND MENACE!
ADMIT IT! THIS WAS YOUR PLAN ALL ALONG!
TO GET YOUR GREEN GENES INTO THE JAMESON GENE POOL!
FWAKK
WHAT?! YOU THINK I WANT TO BE "JENNY JAMESON"? IT'S ONLY BEEN ONE DAY...
...AND DO YOU KNOW HOW MANY E-MAILS I'VE GOTTEN FROM PEOPLE MISTAKING ME FOR SOME PORN STAR?!
GREEN-HAIRED HUSSY!
PTAM
FLAT-TOPPED FINK!
TUNNG

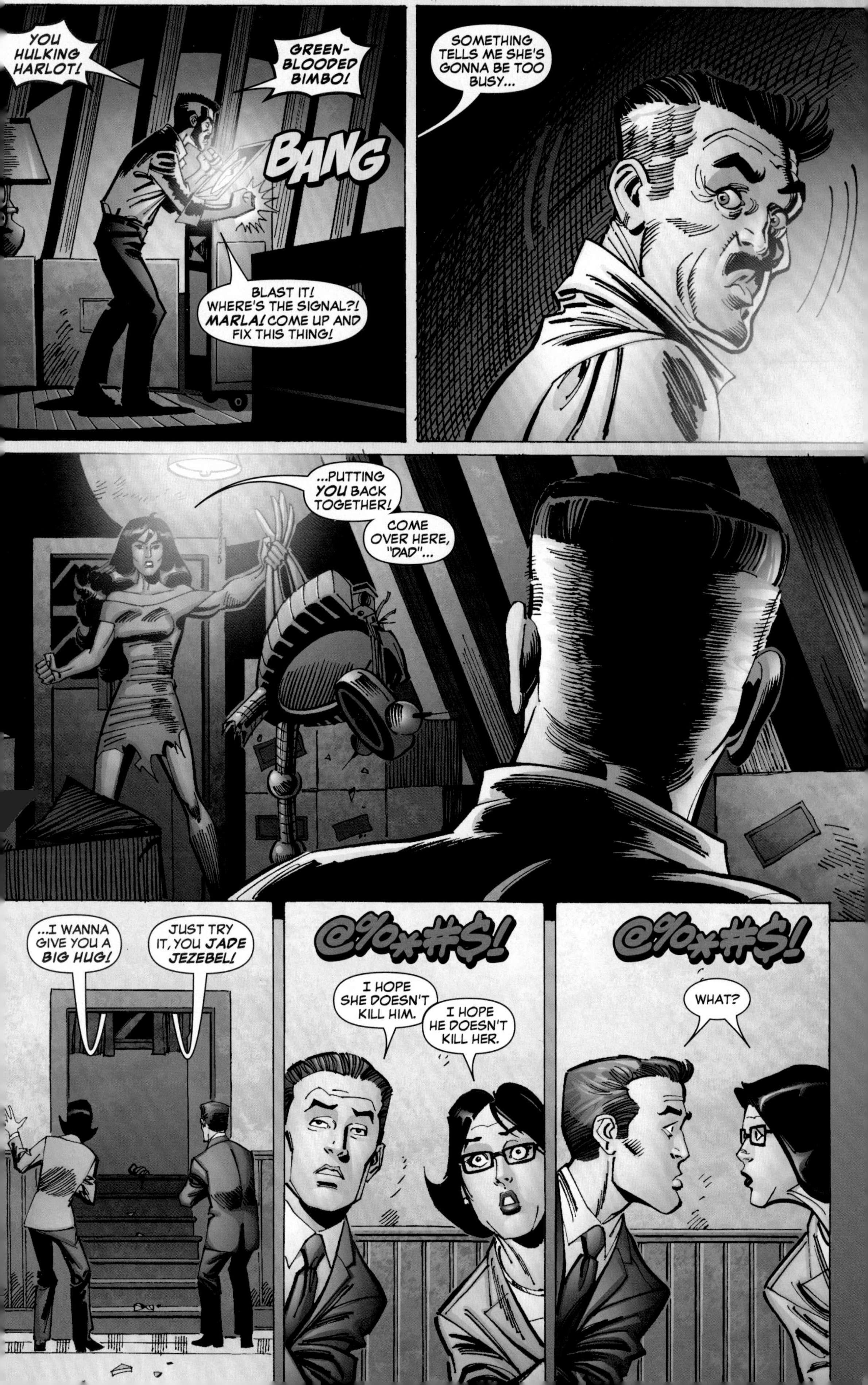
YOU HULKING HARLOT!
GREEN-BLOODED BIMBO!
BANG
BLAST IT! WHERE'S THE SIGNAL?! MARLA! COME UP AND FIX THIS THING!
SOMETHING TELLS ME SHE'S GONNA BE TOO BUSY...
...PUTTING YOU BACK TOGETHER!
COME OVER HERE, "DAD"...
...I WANNA GIVE YOU A BIG HUG!
JUST TRY IT, YOU JADE JEZEBEL!
@%*#$!
I HOPE SHE DOESN'T KILL HIM.
I HOPE HE DOESN'T KILL HER.
@%*#$!
WHAT?

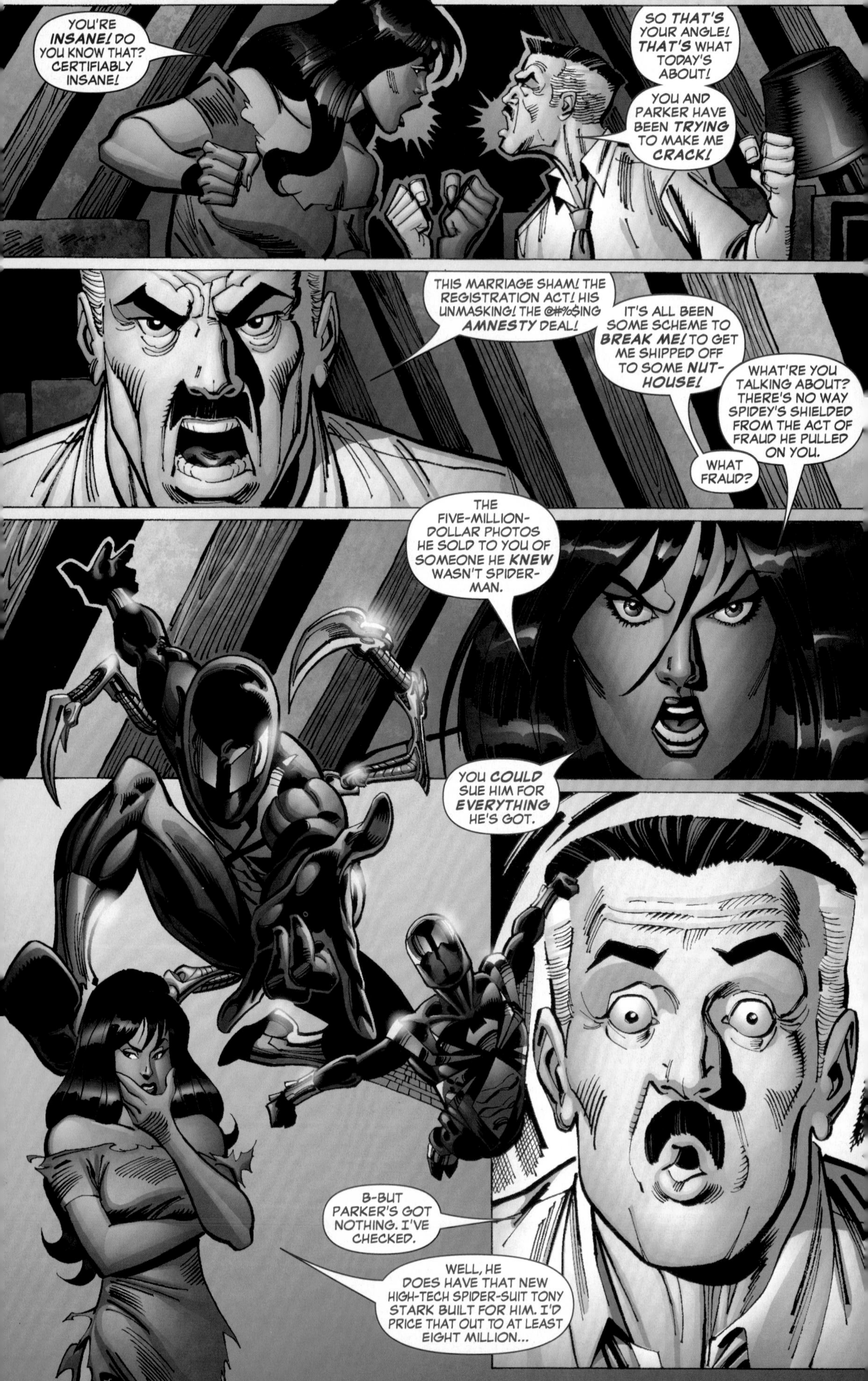
YOU'RE INSANE! DO YOU KNOW THAT? CERTIFIABLY INSANE!
SO THAT'S YOUR ANGLE! THAT'S WHAT TODAY'S ABOUT!
YOU AND PARKER HAVE BEEN TRYING TO MAKE ME CRACK!
THIS MARRIAGE SHAM! THE REGISTRATION ACT! HIS UNMASKING! THE @#%$ING AMNESTY DEAL!
IT'S ALL BEEN SOME SCHEME TO BREAK ME! TO GET ME SHIPPED OFF TO SOME NUT-HOUSE!
WHAT'RE YOU TALKING ABOUT? THERE'S NO WAY SPIDEY'S SHIELDED FROM THE ACT OF FRAUD HE PULLED ON YOU.
WHAT FRAUD?
THE FIVE-MILLION-DOLLAR PHOTOS HE SOLD TO YOU OF SOMEONE HE KNEW WASN'T SPIDER-MAN.
YOU COULD SUE HIM FOR EVERYTHING HE'S GOT.
B-BUT PARKER'S GOT NOTHING. I'VE CHECKED.
WELL, HE DOES HAVE THAT NEW HIGH-TECH SPIDER-SUIT TONY STARK BUILT FOR HIM. I'D PRICE THAT OUT TO AT LEAST EIGHT MILLION...

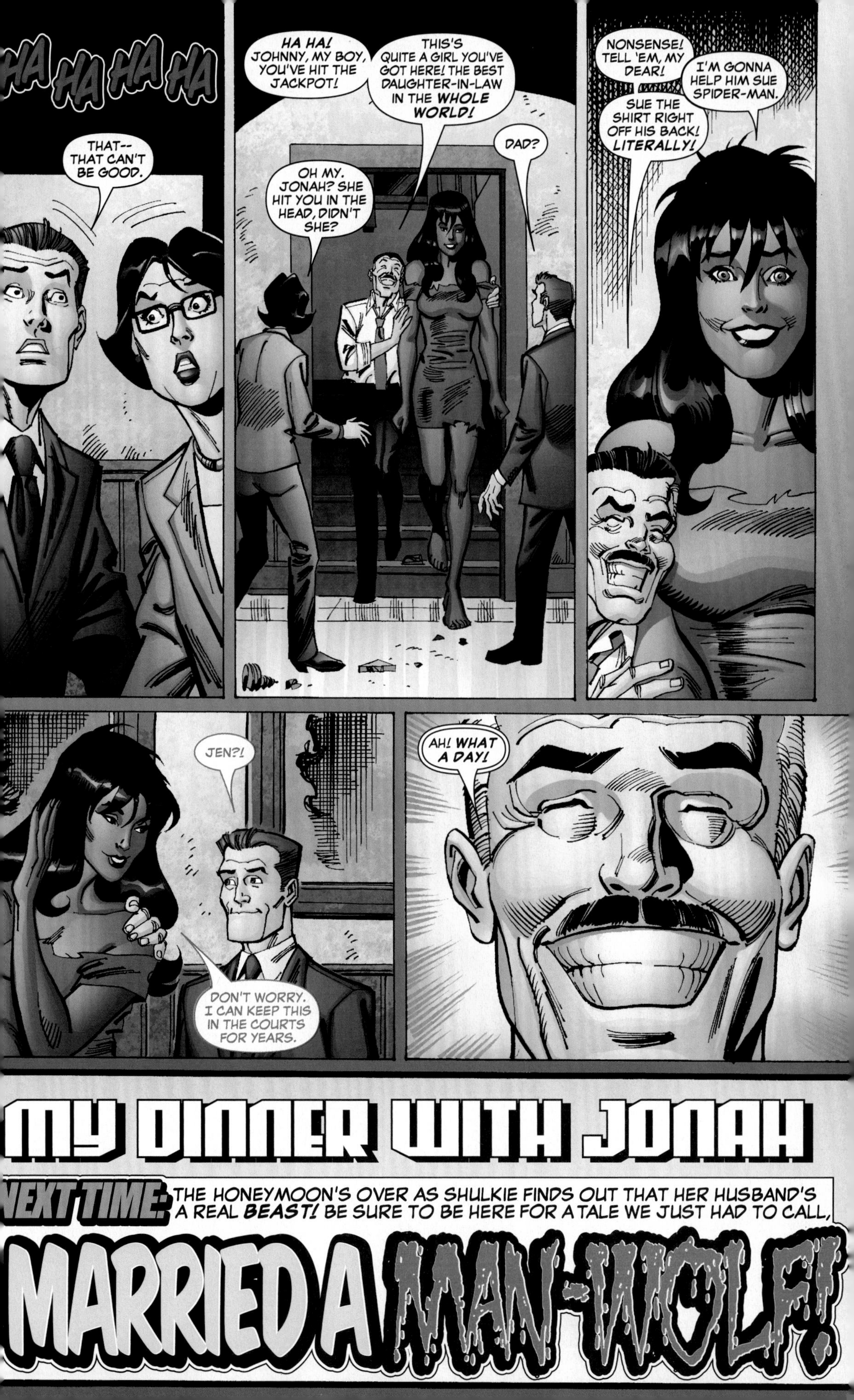
HA HA HA HA
THAT-- THAT CAN'T BE GOOD.
HA HA! JOHNNY, MY BOY, YOU'VE HIT THE JACKPOT!
THIS'S QUITE A GIRL YOU'VE GOT HERE! THE BEST DAUGHTER-IN-LAW IN THE WHOLE WORLD!
OH MY. JONAH? SHE HIT YOU IN THE HEAD, DIDN'T SHE?
DAD?
NONSENSE! TELL 'EM, MY DEAR!
I'M GONNA HELP HIM SUE SPIDER-MAN.
SUE THE SHIRT RIGHT OFF HIS BACK! LITERALLY!
JEN?!
DON'T WORRY. I CAN KEEP THIS IN THE COURTS FOR YEARS.
AH! WHAT A DAY!
MY DINNER WITH JONAH
NEXT TIME: THE HONEYMOON'S OVER AS SHULKIE FINDS OUT THAT HER HUSBAND'S A REAL BEAST! BE SURE TO BE HERE FOR A TALE WE JUST HAD TO CALL,
MARRIED A MAN-WOLF!

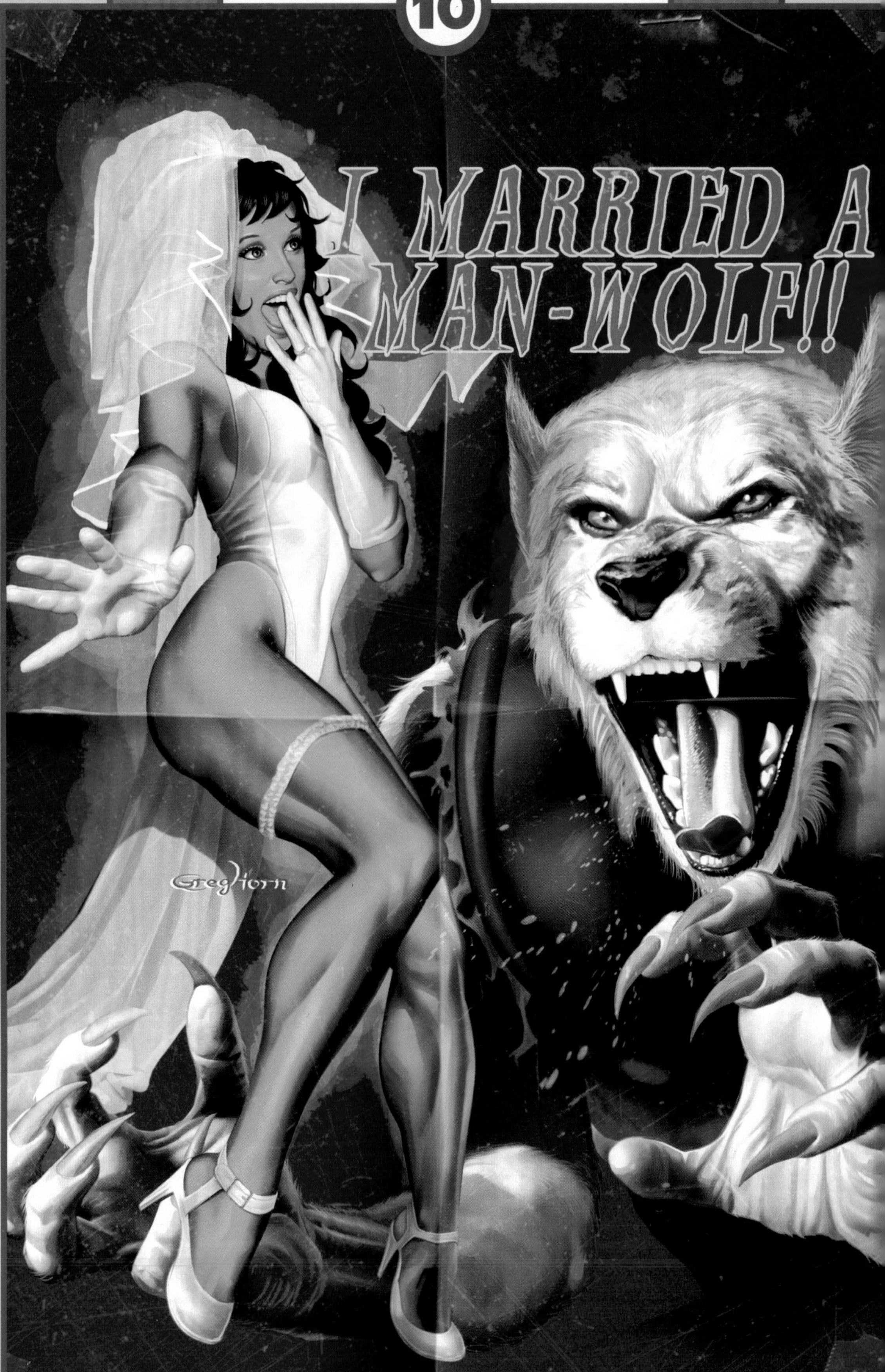
I MARRIED A MAN-WOLF!!
Greg Horn

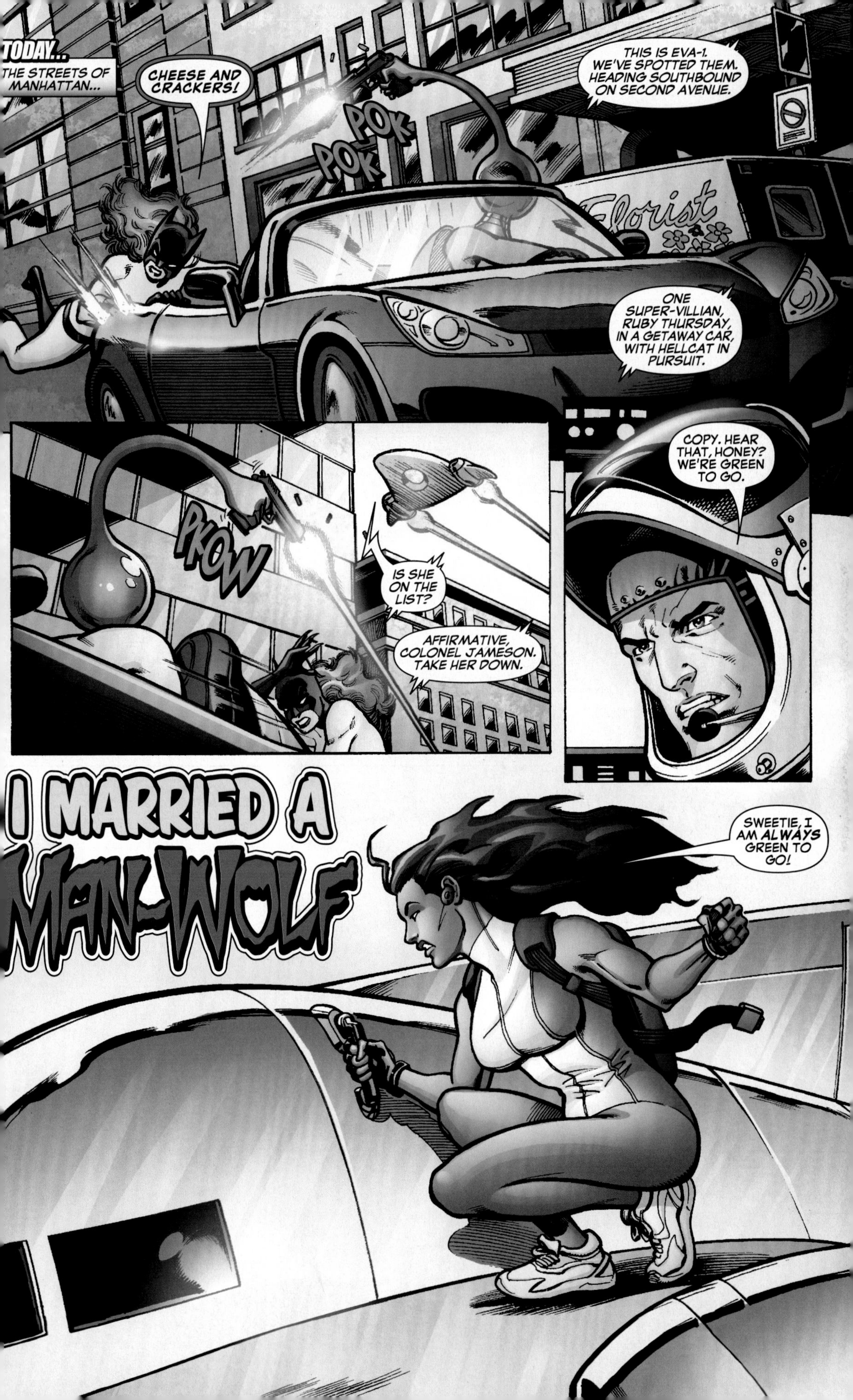
TODAY...
THE STREETS OF MANHATTAN...
CHEESE AND CRACKERS!
POK
POK
THIS IS EVA-1. WE'VE SPOTTED THEM. HEADING SOUTHBOUND ON SECOND AVENUE.
Florist
ONE SUPER-VILLIAN, RUBY THURSDAY, IN A GETAWAY CAR, WITH HELLCAT IN PURSUIT.
PKOW
IS SHE ON THE LIST?
AFFIRMATIVE, COLONEL JAMESON. TAKE HER DOWN.
COPY. HEAR THAT, HONEY? WE'RE GREEN TO GO.
I MARRIED A MAN-WOLF
SWEETIE, I AM ALWAYS GREEN TO GO!

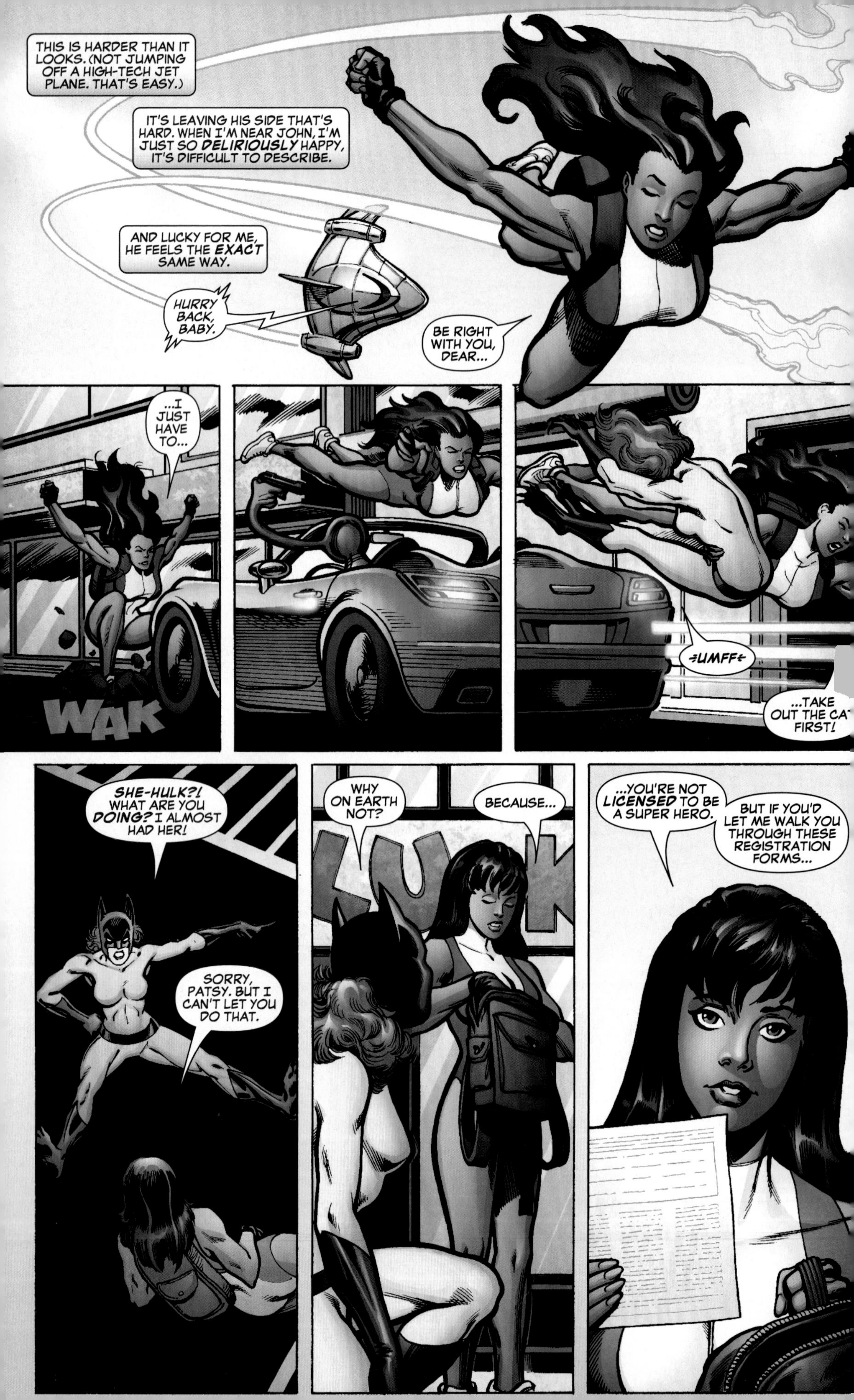
THIS IS HARDER THAN IT LOOKS. (NOT JUMPING OFF A HIGH-TECH JET PLANE. THAT'S EASY.)
IT'S LEAVING HIS SIDE THAT'S HARD. WHEN I'M NEAR JOHN, I'M JUST SO DELIRIOUSLY HAPPY, IT'S DIFFICULT TO DESCRIBE.
AND LUCKY FOR ME, HE FEELS THE EXACT SAME WAY.
HURRY BACK, BABY.
BE RIGHT WITH YOU, DEAR...
...I JUST HAVE TO...
WAK
UMFF
...TAKE OUT THE CA
FIRST!
SHE-HULK?! WHAT ARE YOU DOING? I ALMOST HAD HER!
SORRY, PATSY. BUT I CAN'T LET YOU DO THAT.
WHY ON EARTH NOT?
BECAUSE...
...YOU'RE NOT LICENSED TO BE A SUPER HERO.
BUT IF YOU'D LET ME WALK YOU THROUGH THESE REGISTRATION FORMS...

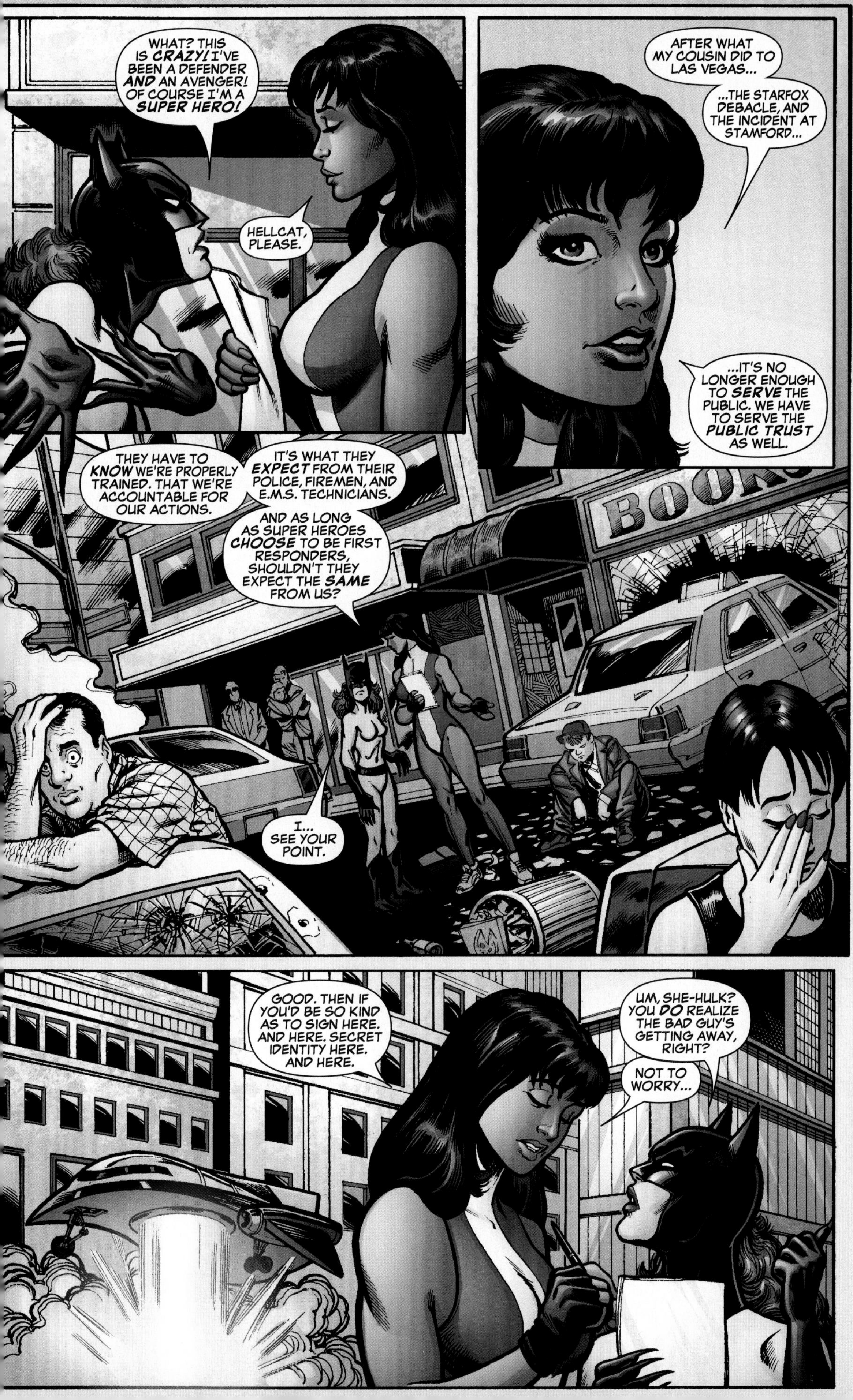
WHAT? THIS IS CRAZY! I'VE BEEN A DEFENDER AND AN AVENGER! OF COURSE I'M A SUPER HERO!
HELLCAT, PLEASE.
AFTER WHAT MY COUSIN DID TO LAS VEGAS...
...THE STARFOX DEBACLE, AND THE INCIDENT AT STAMFORD...
...IT'S NO LONGER ENOUGH TO SERVE THE PUBLIC. WE HAVE TO SERVE THE PUBLIC TRUST AS WELL.
THEY HAVE TO KNOW WE'RE PROPERLY TRAINED. THAT WE'RE ACCOUNTABLE FOR OUR ACTIONS.
IT'S WHAT THEY EXPECT FROM THEIR POLICE, FIREMEN, AND E.M.S. TECHNICIANS.
AND AS LONG AS SUPER HEROES CHOOSE TO BE FIRST RESPONDERS, SHOULDN'T THEY EXPECT THE SAME FROM US?
I... SEE YOUR POINT.
GOOD. THEN IF YOU'D BE SO KIND AS TO SIGN HERE. AND HERE. SECRET IDENTITY HERE. AND HERE.
UM, SHE-HULK? YOU DO REALIZE THE BAD GUY'S GETTING AWAY, RIGHT?
NOT TO WORRY...

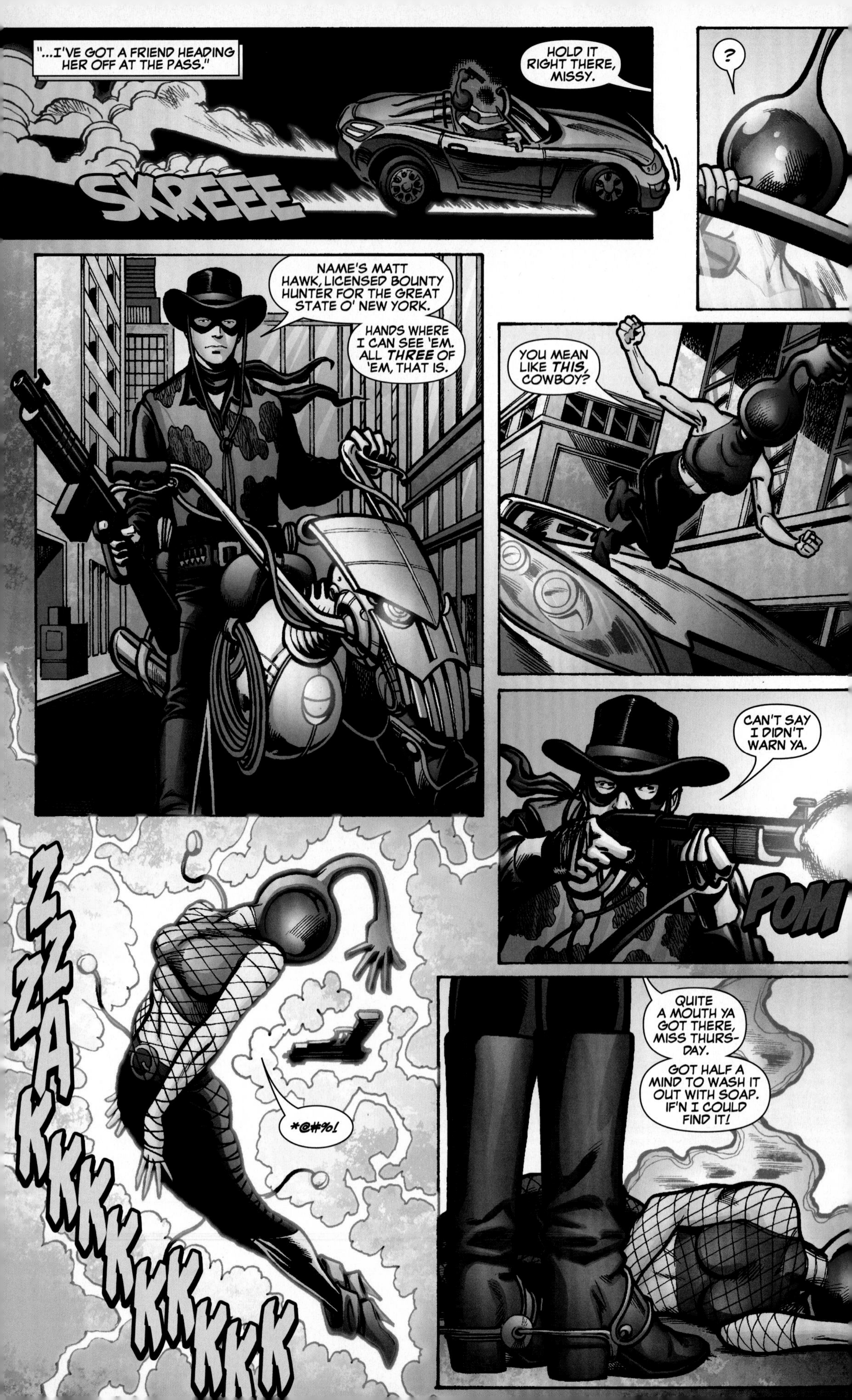
"...I'VE GOT A FRIEND HEADING HER OFF AT THE PASS."
HOLD IT RIGHT THERE, MISSY.
SKREEE
?
NAME'S MATT HAWK, LICENSED BOUNTY HUNTER FOR THE GREAT STATE O' NEW YORK.
HANDS WHERE I CAN SEE 'EM. ALL THREE OF 'EM, THAT IS.
YOU MEAN LIKE THIS, COWBOY?
CAN'T SAY I DIDN'T WARN YA.
POM
ZZZAKKKKKKKKKK
*@#%!
QUITE A MOUTH YA GOT THERE, MISS THURS-DAY.
GOT HALF A MIND TO WASH IT OUT WITH SOAP. IF'N I COULD FIND IT!

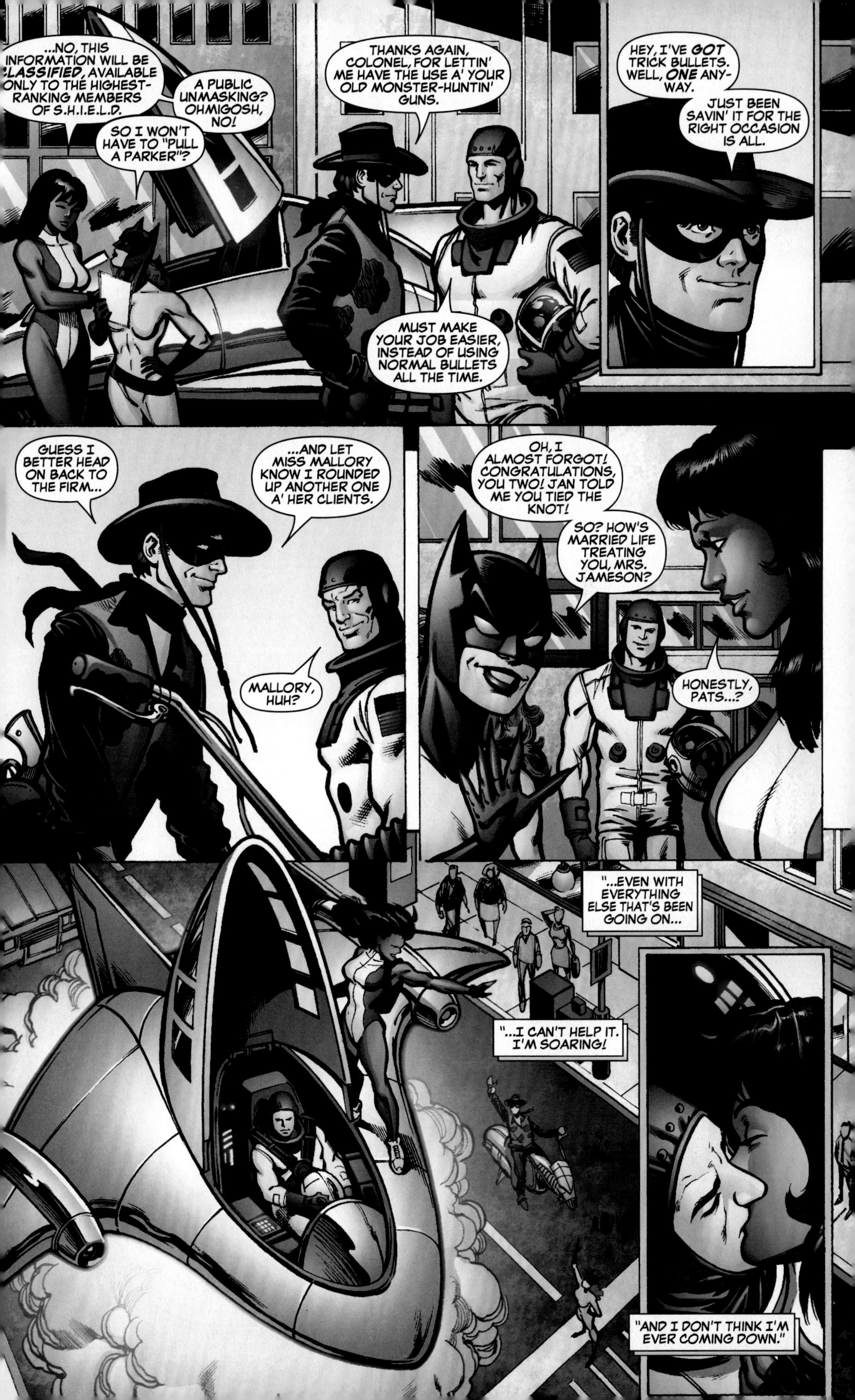
...NO, THIS INFORMATION WILL BE CLASSIFIED, AVAILABLE ONLY TO THE HIGHEST-RANKING MEMBERS OF S.H.I.E.L.D.
A PUBLIC UNMASKING? OHMIGOSH, NO!
SO I WON'T HAVE TO "PULL A PARKER"?
THANKS AGAIN, COLONEL, FOR LETTIN' ME HAVE THE USE A' YOUR OLD MONSTER-HUNTIN' GUNS.
MUST MAKE YOUR JOB EASIER, INSTEAD OF USING NORMAL BULLETS ALL THE TIME.
HEY, I'VE GOT TRICK BULLETS. WELL, ONE ANYWAY.
JUST BEEN SAVIN' IT FOR THE RIGHT OCCASION IS ALL.
GUESS I BETTER HEAD ON BACK TO THE FIRM...
...AND LET MISS MALLORY KNOW I ROUNDED UP ANOTHER ONE A' HER CLIENTS.
MALLORY, HUH?
OH, I ALMOST FORGOT! CONGRATULATIONS, YOU TWO! JAN TOLD ME YOU TIED THE KNOT!
SO? HOW'S MARRIED LIFE TREATING YOU, MRS. JAMESON?
HONESTLY, PATS...?
"...EVEN WITH EVERYTHING ELSE THAT'S BEEN GOING ON...
"...I CAN'T HELP IT. I'M SOARING!
"AND I DON'T THINK I'M EVER COMING DOWN."

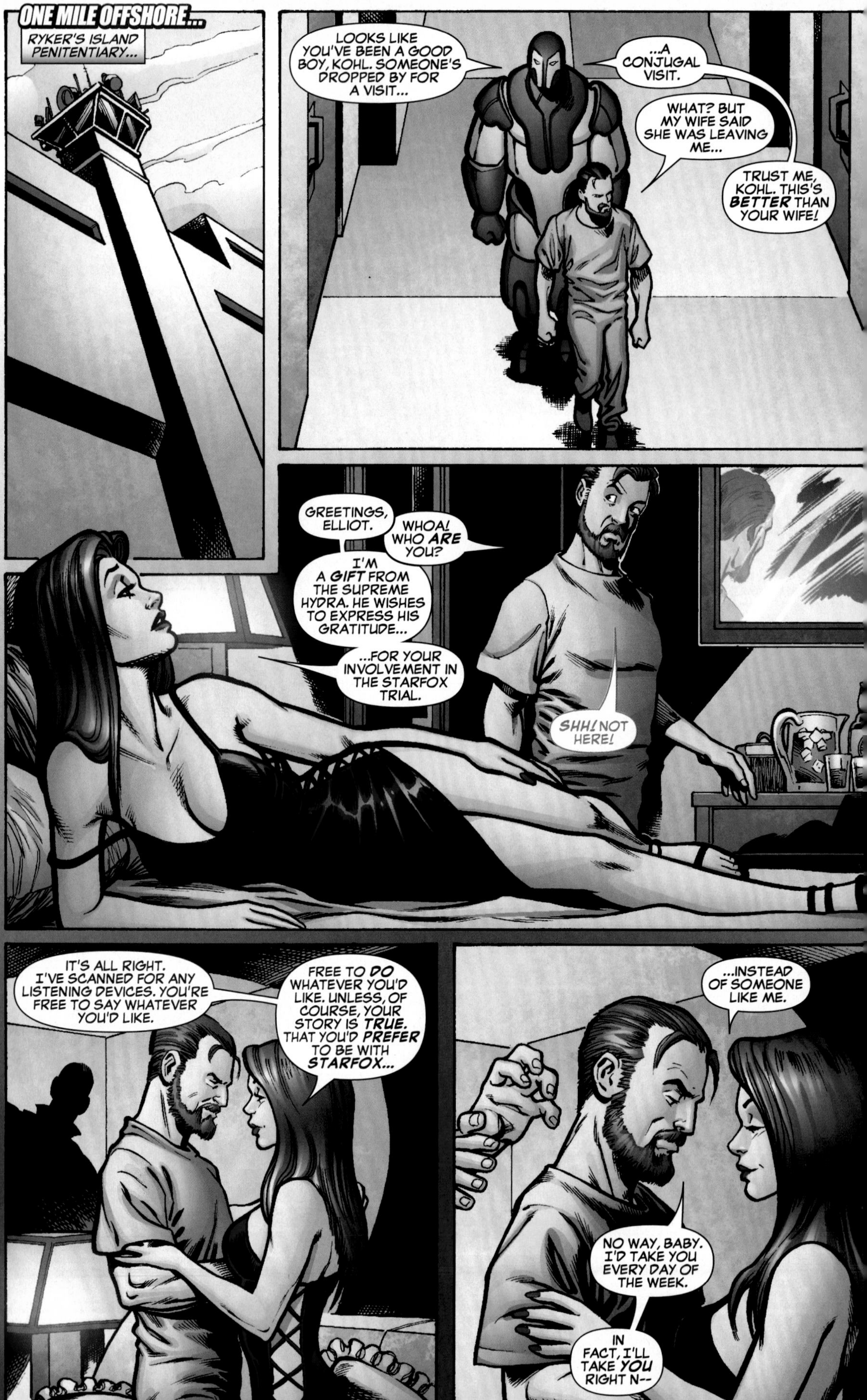
ONE MILE OFFSHORE...
RYKER'S ISLAND PENITENTIARY...
LOOKS LIKE YOU'VE BEEN A GOOD BOY, KOHL. SOMEONE'S DROPPED BY FOR A VISIT...
...A CONJUGAL VISIT.
WHAT? BUT MY WIFE SAID SHE WAS LEAVING ME...
TRUST ME, KOHL. THIS'S BETTER THAN YOUR WIFE!
GREETINGS, ELLIOT.
WHOA! WHO ARE YOU?
I'M A GIFT FROM THE SUPREME HYDRA. HE WISHES TO EXPRESS HIS GRATITUDE...
...FOR YOUR INVOLVEMENT IN THE STARFOX TRIAL.
SHH! NOT HERE!
IT'S ALL RIGHT. I'VE SCANNED FOR ANY LISTENING DEVICES. YOU'RE FREE TO SAY WHATEVER YOU'D LIKE.
FREE TO DO WHATEVER YOU'D LIKE. UNLESS, OF COURSE, YOUR STORY IS TRUE. THAT YOU'D PREFER TO BE WITH STARFOX...
...INSTEAD OF SOMEONE LIKE ME.
NO WAY, BABY. I'D TAKE YOU EVERY DAY OF THE WEEK.
IN FACT, I'LL TAKE YOU RIGHT N--

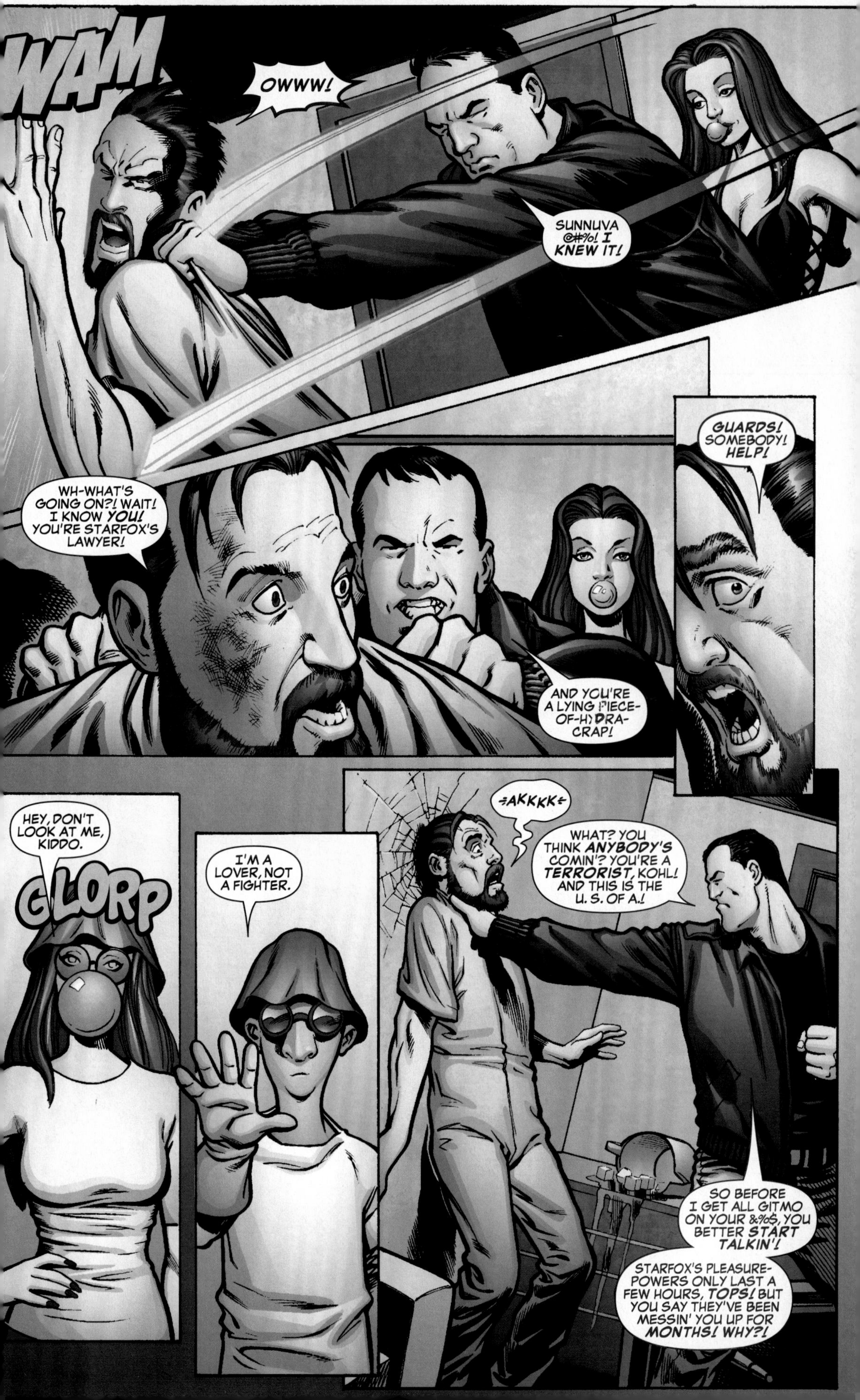
WAM
OWWW!
SUNNUVA @#%! I KNEW IT!
WH-WHAT'S GOING ON?! WAIT! I KNOW YOU! YOU'RE STARFOX'S LAWYER!
AND YOU'RE A LYING PIECE-OF-HYDRA-CRAP!
GUARDS! SOMEBODY! HELP!
HEY, DON'T LOOK AT ME, KIDDO.
GLORP
I'M A LOVER, NOT A FIGHTER.
AKKKK
WHAT? YOU THINK ANYBODY'S COMIN'? YOU'RE A TERRORIST, KOHL! AND THIS IS THE U. S. OF A.!
SO BEFORE I GET ALL GITMO ON YOUR &%$, YOU BETTER START TALKIN'!
STARFOX'S PLEASURE-POWERS ONLY LAST A FEW HOURS, TOPS! BUT YOU SAY THEY'VE BEEN MESSIN' YOU UP FOR MONTHS! WHY?!

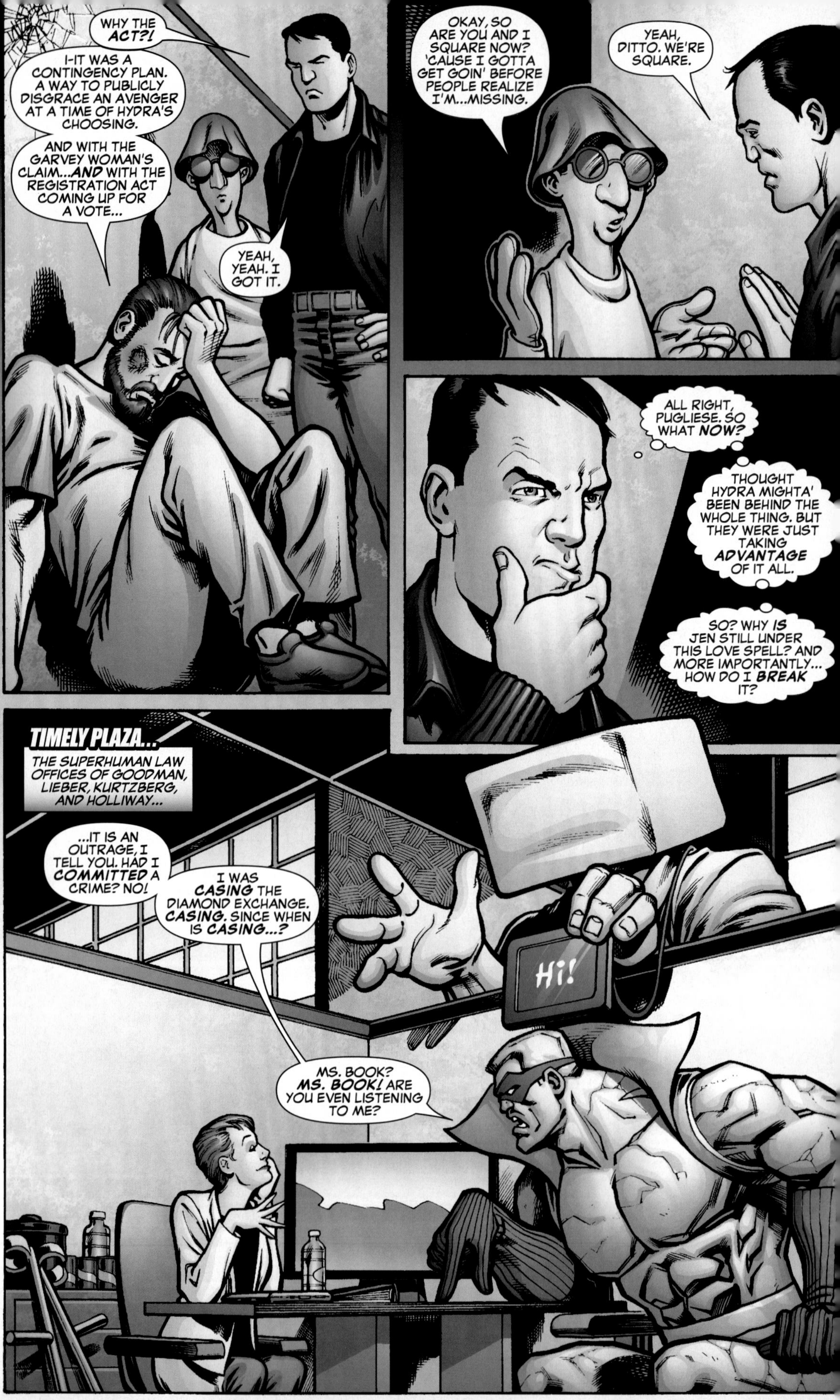
WHY THE ACT?!
I-IT WAS A CONTINGENCY PLAN. A WAY TO PUBLICLY DISGRACE AN AVENGER AT A TIME OF HYDRA'S CHOOSING.
AND WITH THE GARVEY WOMAN'S CLAIM...AND WITH THE REGISTRATION ACT COMING UP FOR A VOTE...
YEAH, YEAH. I GOT IT.
OKAY, SO ARE YOU AND I SQUARE NOW? 'CAUSE I GOTTA GET GOIN' BEFORE PEOPLE REALIZE I'M...MISSING.
YEAH, DITTO. WE'RE SQUARE.
ALL RIGHT, PUGLIESE. SO WHAT NOW?
THOUGHT HYDRA MIGHTA' BEEN BEHIND THE WHOLE THING. BUT THEY WERE JUST TAKING ADVANTAGE OF IT ALL.
SO? WHY IS JEN STILL UNDER THIS LOVE SPELL? AND MORE IMPORTANTLY... HOW DO I BREAK IT?
TIMELY PLAZA...
THE SUPERHUMAN LAW OFFICES OF GOODMAN, LIEBER, KURTZBERG, AND HOLLIWAY...
...IT IS AN OUTRAGE, I TELL YOU. HAD I COMMITTED A CRIME? NO!
I WAS CASING THE DIAMOND EXCHANGE. CASING. SINCE WHEN IS CASING...?
Hi!
MS. BOOK? MS. BOOK! ARE YOU EVEN LISTENING TO ME?

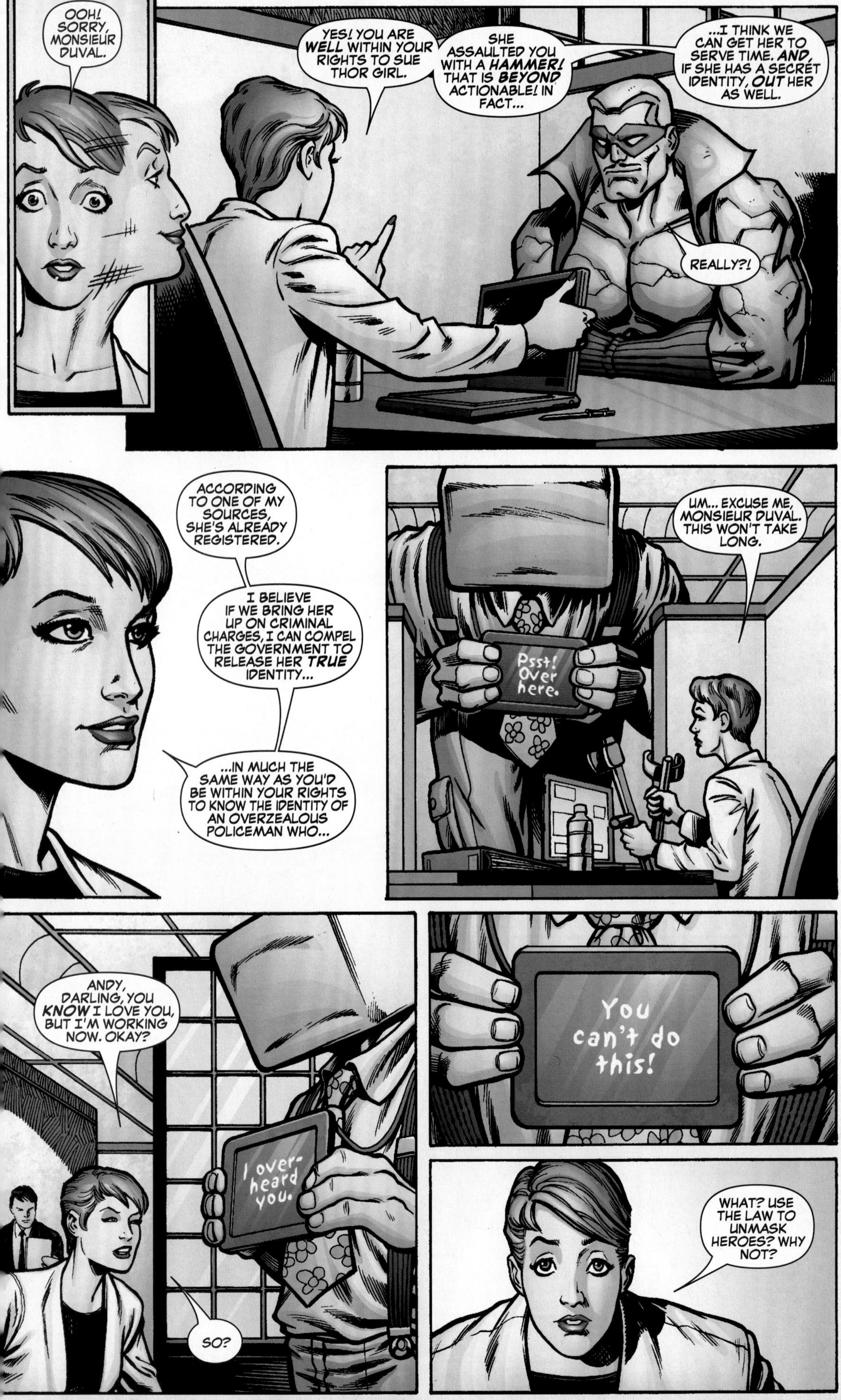

OOH! SORRY, MONSIEUR DUVAL.
YES! YOU ARE WELL WITHIN YOUR RIGHTS TO SUE THOR GIRL.
SHE ASSAULTED YOU WITH A HAMMER! THAT IS BEYOND ACTIONABLE! IN FACT...
...I THINK WE CAN GET HER TO SERVE TIME. AND, IF SHE HAS A SECRET IDENTITY, OUT HER AS WELL.
REALLY?!
ACCORDING TO ONE OF MY SOURCES, SHE'S ALREADY REGISTERED.
I BELIEVE IF WE BRING HER UP ON CRIMINAL CHARGES, I CAN COMPEL THE GOVERNMENT TO RELEASE HER TRUE IDENTITY...
...IN MUCH THE SAME WAY AS YOU'D BE WITHIN YOUR RIGHTS TO KNOW THE IDENTITY OF AN OVERZEALOUS POLICEMAN WHO...
UM... EXCUSE ME, MONSIEUR DUVAL. THIS WON'T TAKE LONG.
Psst! Over here.
ANDY, DARLING, YOU KNOW I LOVE YOU, BUT I'M WORKING NOW. OKAY?
I over-heard you.
SO?
You can't do this!
WHAT? USE THE LAW TO UNMASK HEROES? WHY NOT?

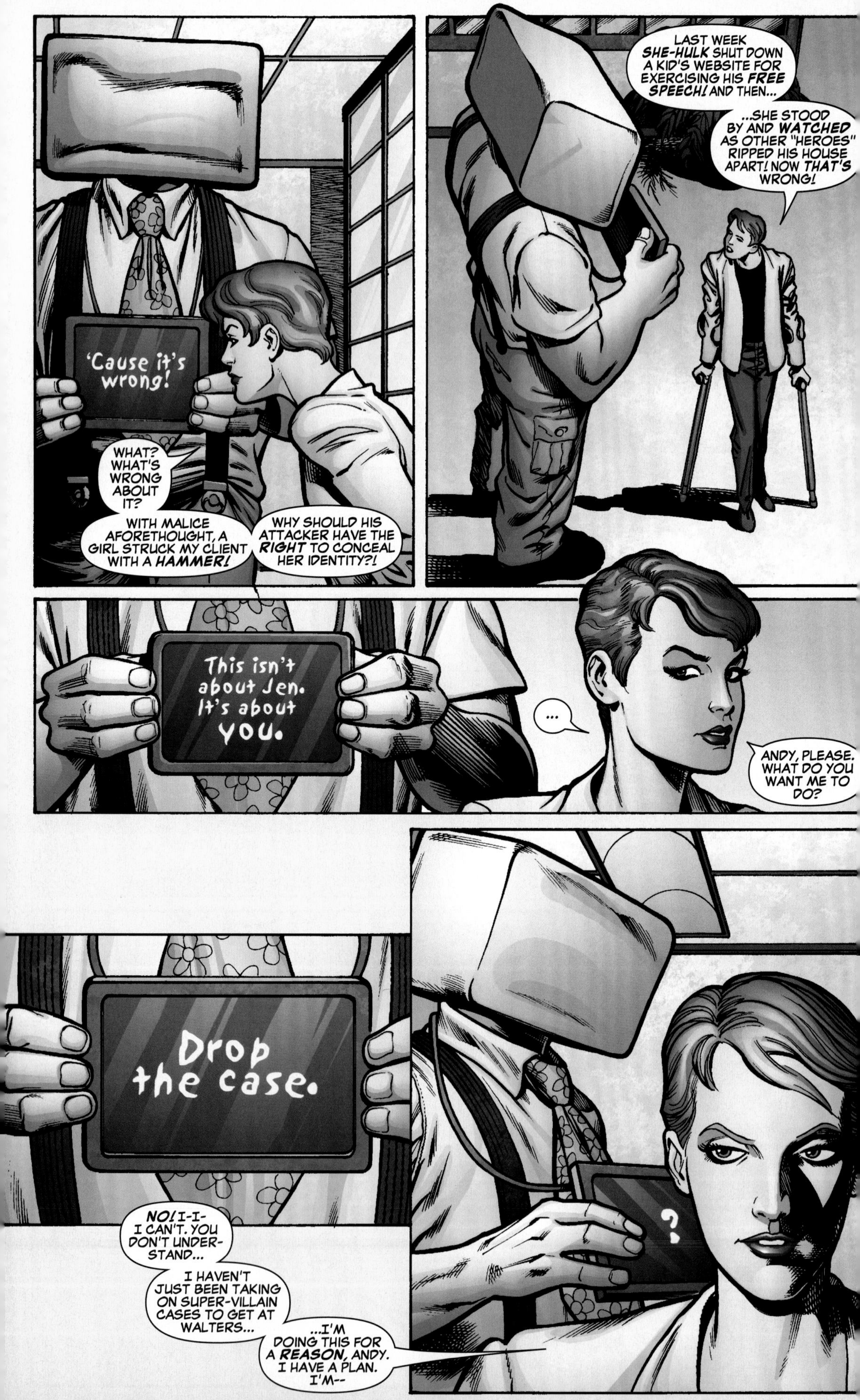
'Cause it's wrong!
WHAT? WHAT'S WRONG ABOUT IT?
WITH MALICE AFORETHOUGHT, A GIRL STRUCK MY CLIENT WITH A HAMMER!
WHY SHOULD HIS ATTACKER HAVE THE RIGHT TO CONCEAL HER IDENTITY?!
LAST WEEK SHE-HULK SHUT DOWN A KID'S WEBSITE FOR EXERCISING HIS FREE SPEECH! AND THEN...
...SHE STOOD BY AND WATCHED AS OTHER "HEROES" RIPPED HIS HOUSE APART! NOW THAT'S WRONG!
This isn't about Jen. It's about you.
...
ANDY, PLEASE. WHAT DO YOU WANT ME TO DO?
Drop the case.
?
NO! I-I-I CAN'T. YOU DON'T UNDER-STAND...
I HAVEN'T JUST BEEN TAKING ON SUPER-VILLAIN CASES TO GET AT WALTERS...
...I'M DOING THIS FOR A REASON, ANDY. I HAVE A PLAN. I'M--

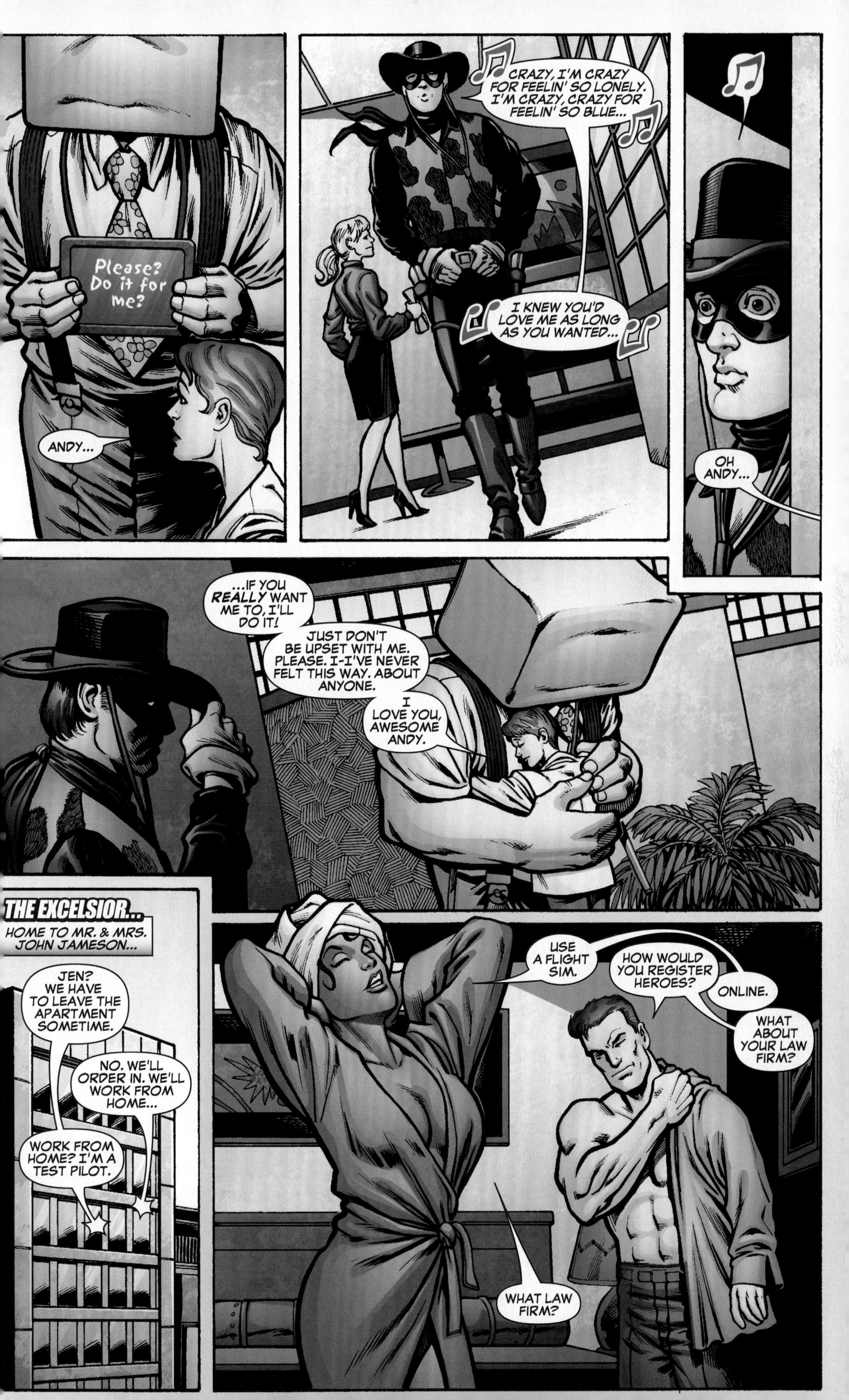
Please? Do it for me?
ANDY...
CRAZY, I'M CRAZY FOR FEELIN' SO LONELY. I'M CRAZY, CRAZY FOR FEELIN' SO BLUE...
I KNEW YOU'D LOVE ME AS LONG AS YOU WANTED...
OH ANDY...
...IF YOU REALLY WANT ME TO, I'LL DO IT!
JUST DON'T BE UPSET WITH ME. PLEASE. I-I'VE NEVER FELT THIS WAY. ABOUT ANYONE.
I LOVE YOU, AWESOME ANDY.
THE EXCELSIOR...
HOME TO MR. & MRS. JOHN JAMESON...
JEN? WE HAVE TO LEAVE THE APARTMENT SOMETIME.
NO. WE'LL ORDER IN. WE'LL WORK FROM HOME...
WORK FROM HOME? I'M A TEST PILOT.
USE A FLIGHT SIM.
HOW WOULD YOU REGISTER HEROES?
ONLINE.
WHAT ABOUT YOUR LAW FIRM?
WHAT LAW FIRM?

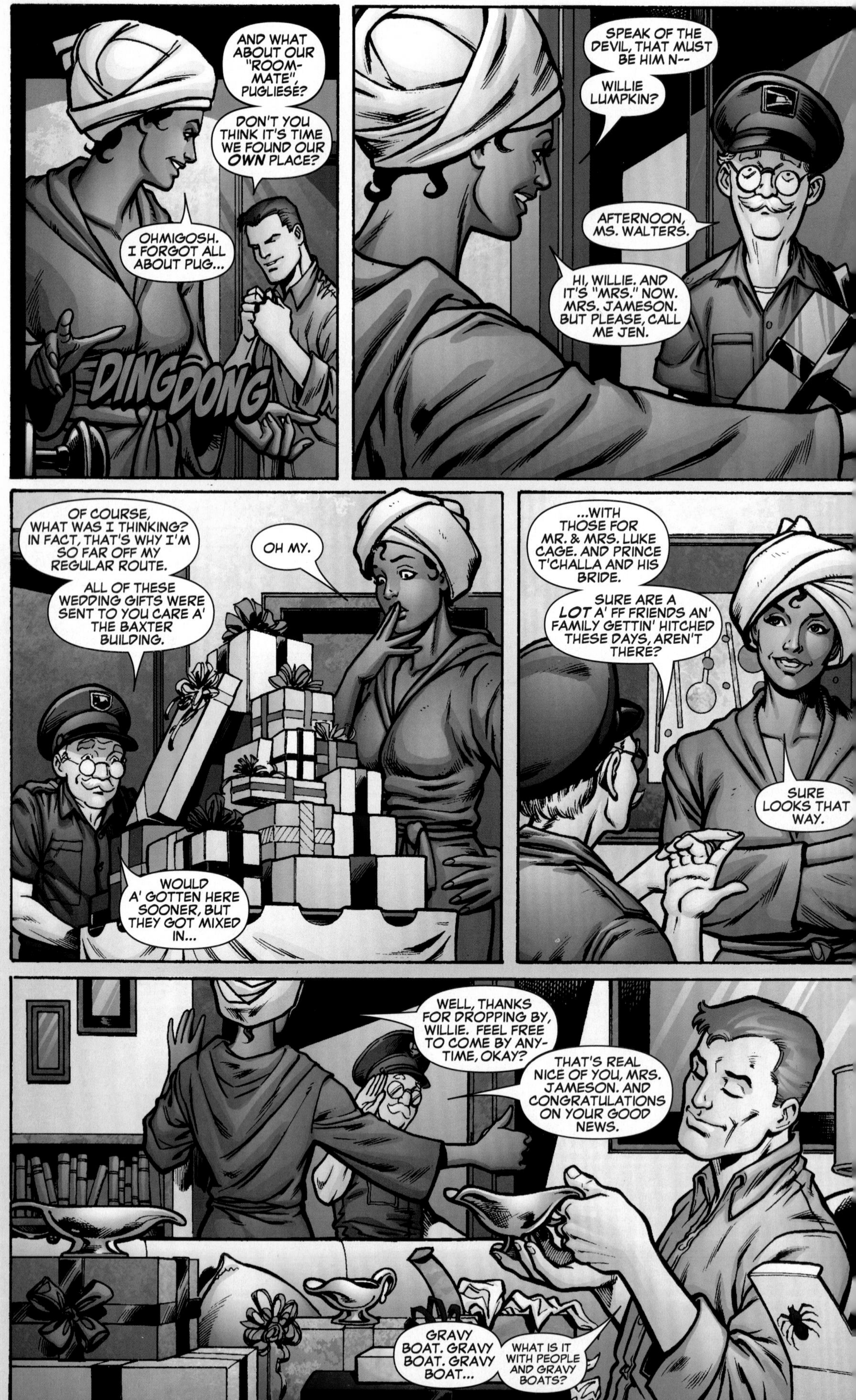
AND WHAT ABOUT OUR "ROOM-MATE" PUGLIESE?
DON'T YOU THINK IT'S TIME WE FOUND OUR OWN PLACE?
OHMIGOSH. I FORGOT ALL ABOUT PUG...
DINGDONG
SPEAK OF THE DEVIL, THAT MUST BE HIM N--
WILLIE LUMPKIN?
AFTERNOON, MS. WALTERS.
HI, WILLIE. AND IT'S "MRS." NOW. MRS. JAMESON. BUT PLEASE, CALL ME JEN.
OF COURSE, WHAT WAS I THINKING? IN FACT, THAT'S WHY I'M SO FAR OFF MY REGULAR ROUTE.
ALL OF THESE WEDDING GIFTS WERE SENT TO YOU CARE A' THE BAXTER BUILDING.
OH MY.
WOULD A' GOTTEN HERE SOONER, BUT THEY GOT MIXED IN...
...WITH THOSE FOR MR. & MRS. LUKE CAGE. AND PRINCE T'CHALLA AND HIS BRIDE.
SURE ARE A LOT A' FF FRIENDS AN' FAMILY GETTIN' HITCHED THESE DAYS, AREN'T THERE?
SURE LOOKS THAT WAY.
WELL, THANKS FOR DROPPING BY, WILLIE. FEEL FREE TO COME BY ANY-TIME, OKAY?
THAT'S REAL NICE OF YOU, MRS. JAMESON. AND CONGRATULATIONS ON YOUR GOOD NEWS.
GRAVY BOAT. GRAVY BOAT. GRAVY BOAT...
WHAT IS IT WITH PEOPLE AND GRAVY BOATS?

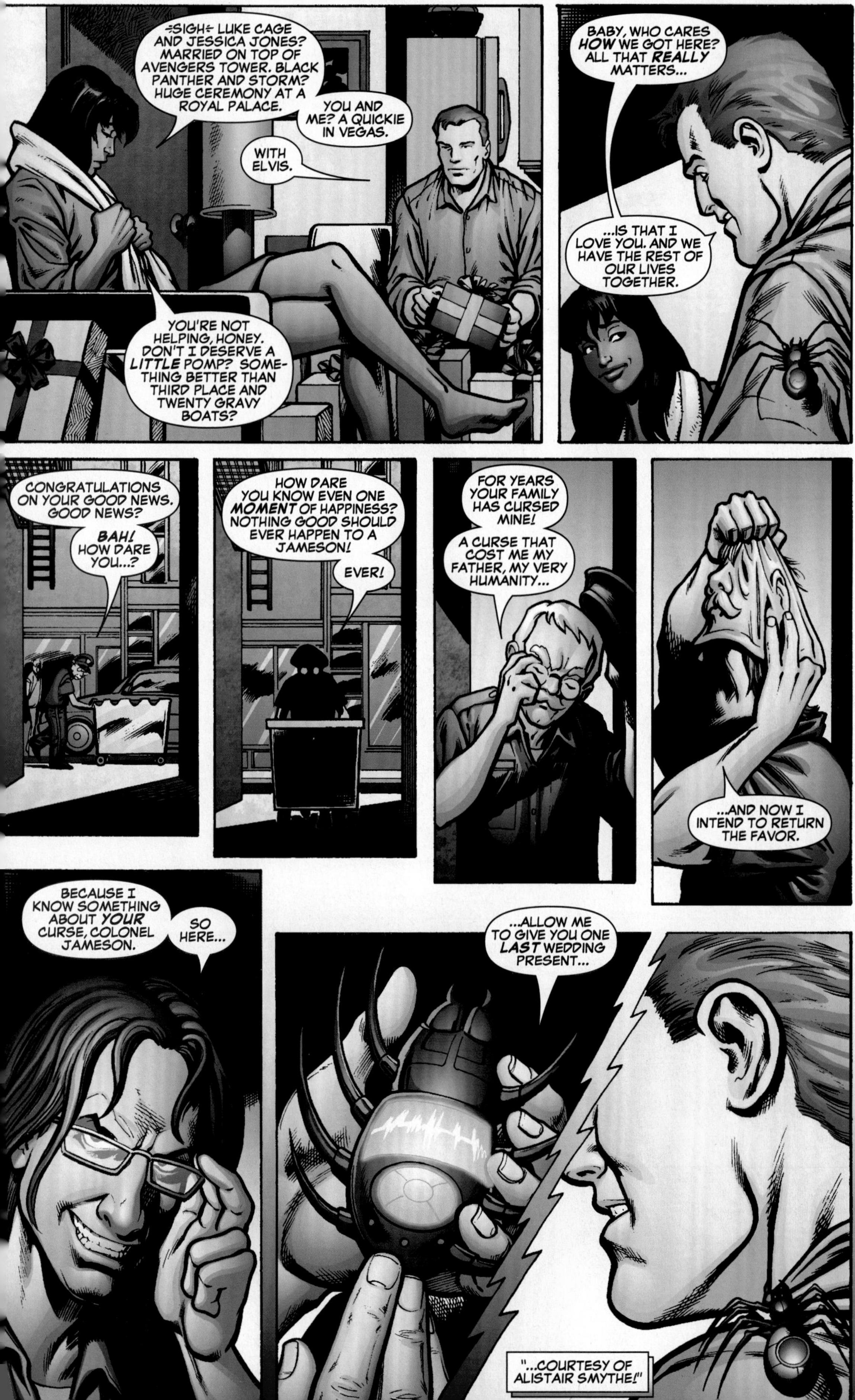

=SIGH= LUKE CAGE AND JESSICA JONES? MARRIED ON TOP OF AVENGERS TOWER. BLACK PANTHER AND STORM? HUGE CEREMONY AT A ROYAL PALACE.
YOU AND ME? A QUICKIE IN VEGAS.
WITH ELVIS.
YOU'RE NOT HELPING, HONEY. DON'T I DESERVE A LITTLE POMP? SOMETHING BETTER THAN THIRD PLACE AND TWENTY GRAVY BOATS?
BABY, WHO CARES HOW WE GOT HERE? ALL THAT REALLY MATTERS...
...IS THAT I LOVE YOU. AND WE HAVE THE REST OF OUR LIVES TOGETHER.
CONGRATULATIONS ON YOUR GOOD NEWS. GOOD NEWS?
BAH! HOW DARE YOU...?
HOW DARE YOU KNOW EVEN ONE MOMENT OF HAPPINESS? NOTHING GOOD SHOULD EVER HAPPEN TO A JAMESON!
EVER!
FOR YEARS YOUR FAMILY HAS CURSED MINE!
A CURSE THAT COST ME MY FATHER, MY VERY HUMANITY...
...AND NOW I INTEND TO RETURN THE FAVOR.
BECAUSE I KNOW SOMETHING ABOUT YOUR CURSE, COLONEL JAMESON.
SO HERE...
...ALLOW ME TO GIVE YOU ONE LAST WEDDING PRESENT...
"...COURTESY OF ALISTAIR SMYTHE!"

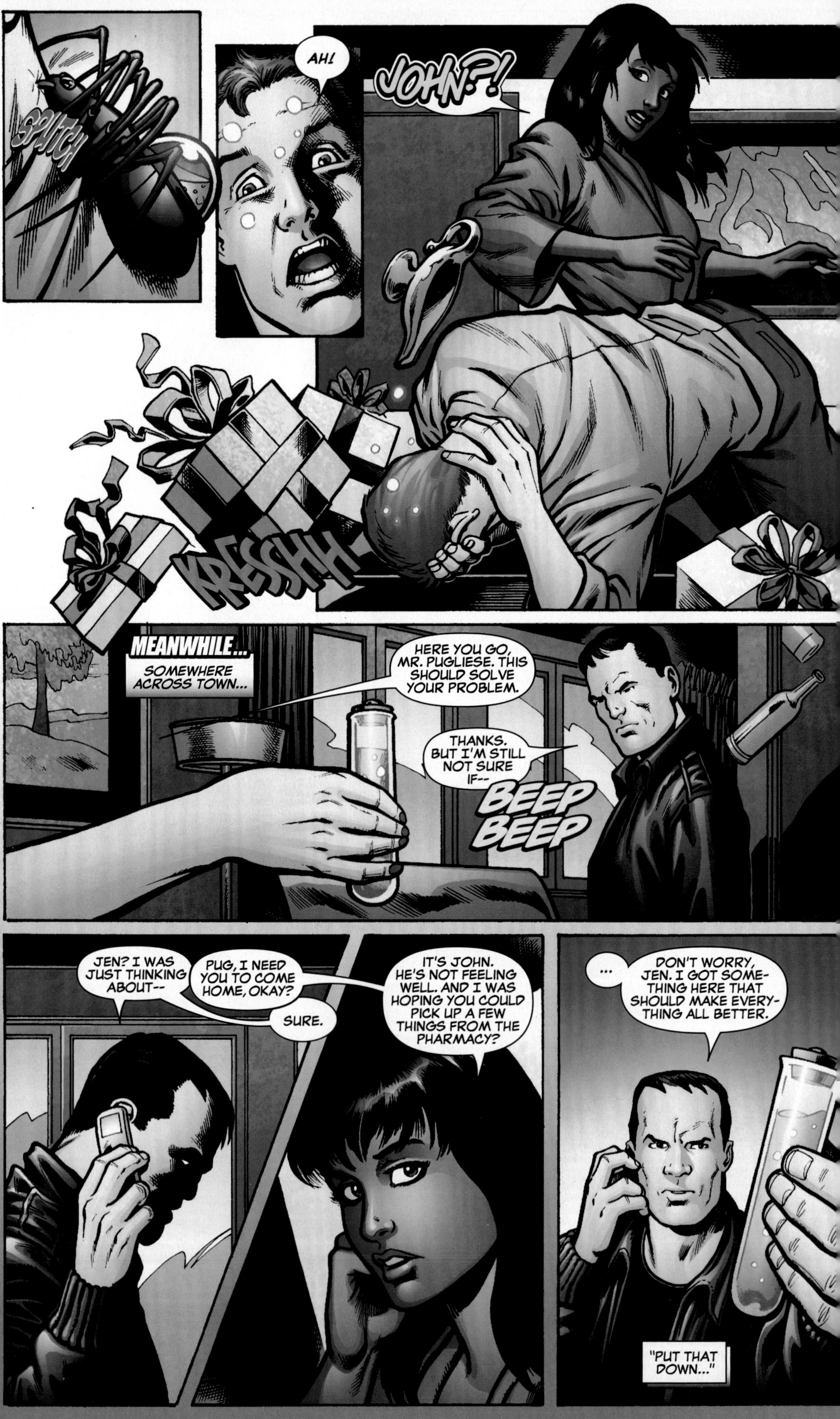
SPLITCH
AH!
JOHN?!
KRESSHH
MEANWHILE... SOMEWHERE ACROSS TOWN...
HERE YOU GO, MR. PUGLIESE. THIS SHOULD SOLVE YOUR PROBLEM.
THANKS. BUT I'M STILL NOT SURE IF--
BEEP BEEP
JEN? I WAS JUST THINKING ABOUT--
PUG, I NEED YOU TO COME HOME, OKAY?
SURE.
IT'S JOHN. HE'S NOT FEELING WELL. AND I WAS HOPING YOU COULD PICK UP A FEW THINGS FROM THE PHARMACY?
...
DON'T WORRY, JEN. I GOT SOMETHING HERE THAT SHOULD MAKE EVERYTHING ALL BETTER.
"PUT THAT DOWN..."

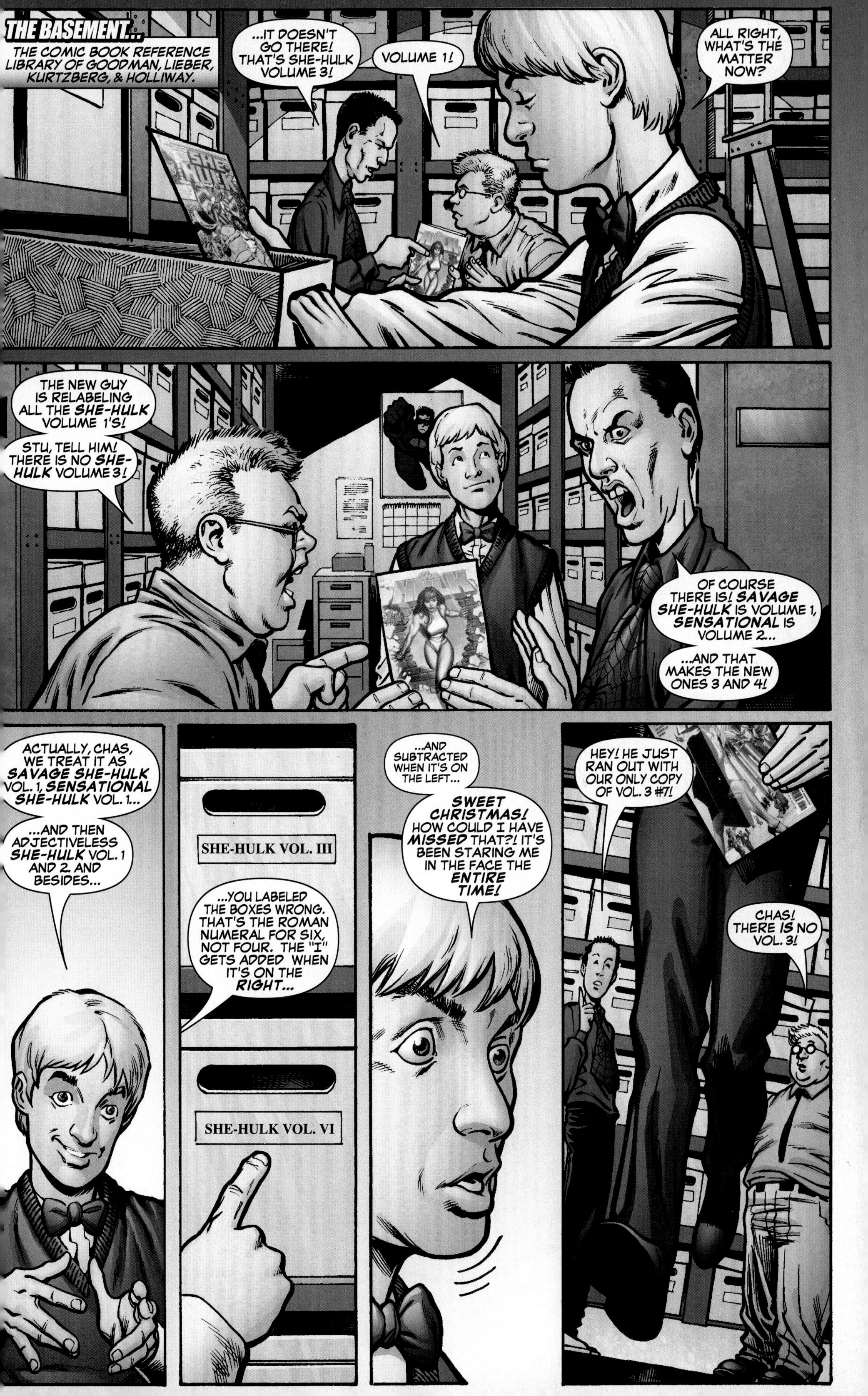
THE BASEMENT...
THE COMIC BOOK REFERENCE LIBRARY OF GOODMAN, LIEBER, KURTZBERG, & HOLLIWAY.
...IT DOESN'T GO THERE! THAT'S SHE-HULK VOLUME 3!
VOLUME 1!
ALL RIGHT, WHAT'S THE MATTER NOW?
THE NEW GUY IS RELABELING ALL THE SHE-HULK VOLUME 1'S!
STU, TELL HIM! THERE IS NO SHE-HULK VOLUME 3!
OF COURSE THERE IS! SAVAGE SHE-HULK IS VOLUME 1, SENSATIONAL IS VOLUME 2...
...AND THAT MAKES THE NEW ONES 3 AND 4!
ACTUALLY, CHAS, WE TREAT IT AS SAVAGE SHE-HULK VOL. 1, SENSATIONAL SHE-HULK VOL. 1...
...AND THEN ADJECTIVELESS SHE-HULK VOL. 1 AND 2. AND BESIDES...
SHE-HULK VOL. III
...YOU LABELED THE BOXES WRONG. THAT'S THE ROMAN NUMERAL FOR SIX, NOT FOUR. THE "I" GETS ADDED WHEN IT'S ON THE RIGHT...
SHE-HULK VOL. VI
...AND SUBTRACTED WHEN IT'S ON THE LEFT...
SWEET CHRISTMAS! HOW COULD I HAVE MISSED THAT?! IT'S BEEN STARING ME IN THE FACE THE ENTIRE TIME!
HEY! HE JUST RAN OUT WITH OUR ONLY COPY OF VOL. 3 #7!
CHAS! THERE IS NO VOL. 3!

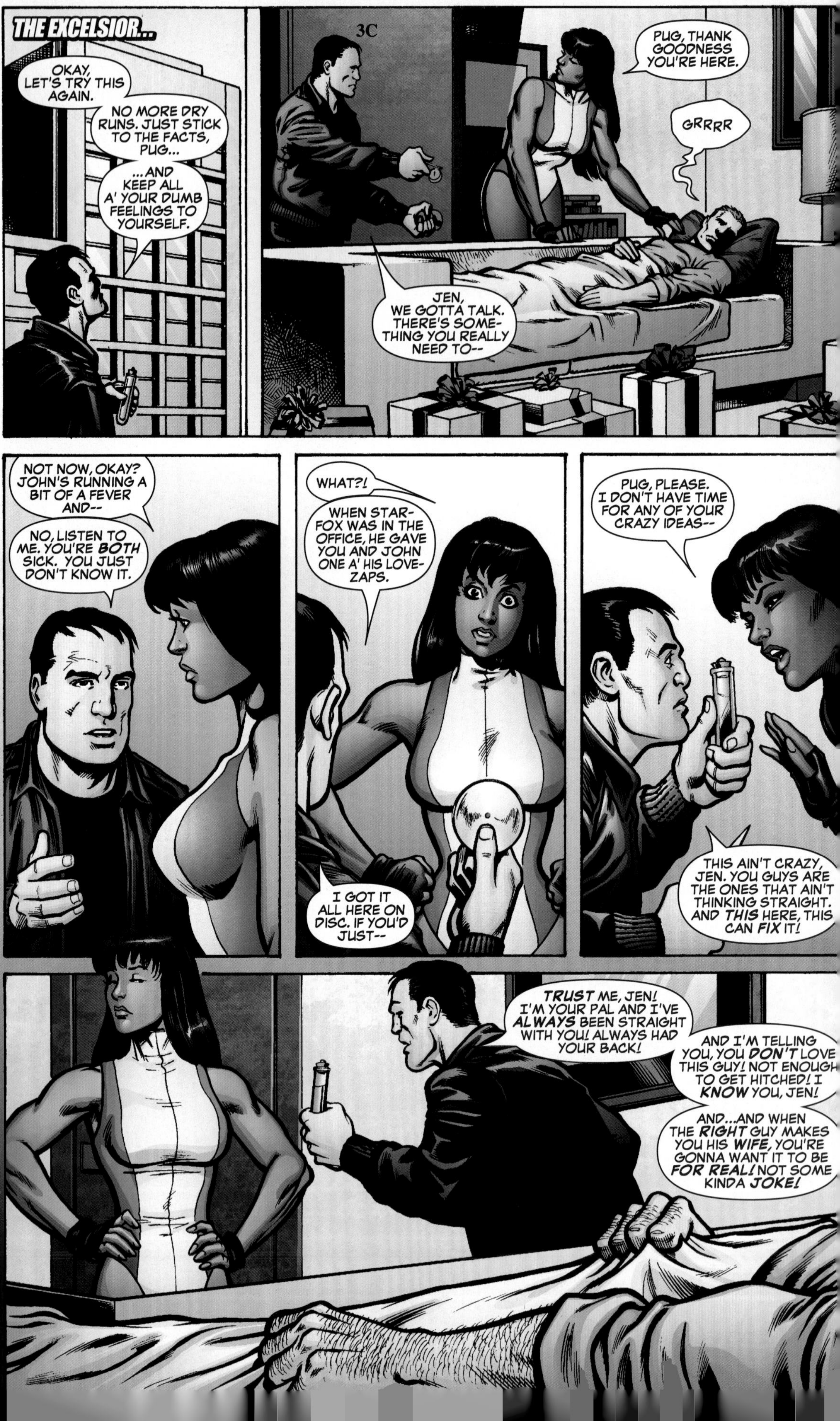
THE EXCELSIOR...
OKAY, LET'S TRY THIS AGAIN.
NO MORE DRY RUNS. JUST STICK TO THE FACTS, PUG...
...AND KEEP ALL A' YOUR DUMB FEELINGS TO YOURSELF.
3C
PUG, THANK GOODNESS YOU'RE HERE.
GRRRR
JEN, WE GOTTA TALK. THERE'S SOMETHING YOU REALLY NEED TO--
NOT NOW, OKAY? JOHN'S RUNNING A BIT OF A FEVER AND--
NO, LISTEN TO ME. YOU'RE BOTH SICK. YOU JUST DON'T KNOW IT.
WHAT?!
WHEN STARFOX WAS IN THE OFFICE, HE GAVE YOU AND JOHN ONE A' HIS LOVE-ZAPS.
I GOT IT ALL HERE ON DISC. IF YOU'D JUST--
PUG, PLEASE. I DON'T HAVE TIME FOR ANY OF YOUR CRAZY IDEAS--
THIS AIN'T CRAZY, JEN. YOU GUYS ARE THE ONES THAT AIN'T THINKING STRAIGHT. AND THIS HERE, THIS CAN FIX IT!
TRUST ME, JEN! I'M YOUR PAL AND I'VE ALWAYS BEEN STRAIGHT WITH YOU! ALWAYS HAD YOUR BACK!
AND I'M TELLING YOU, YOU DON'T LOVE THIS GUY! NOT ENOUGH TO GET HITCHED! I KNOW YOU, JEN!
AND...AND WHEN THE RIGHT GUY MAKES YOU HIS WIFE, YOU'RE GONNA WANT IT TO BE FOR REAL! NOT SOME KINDA JOKE!

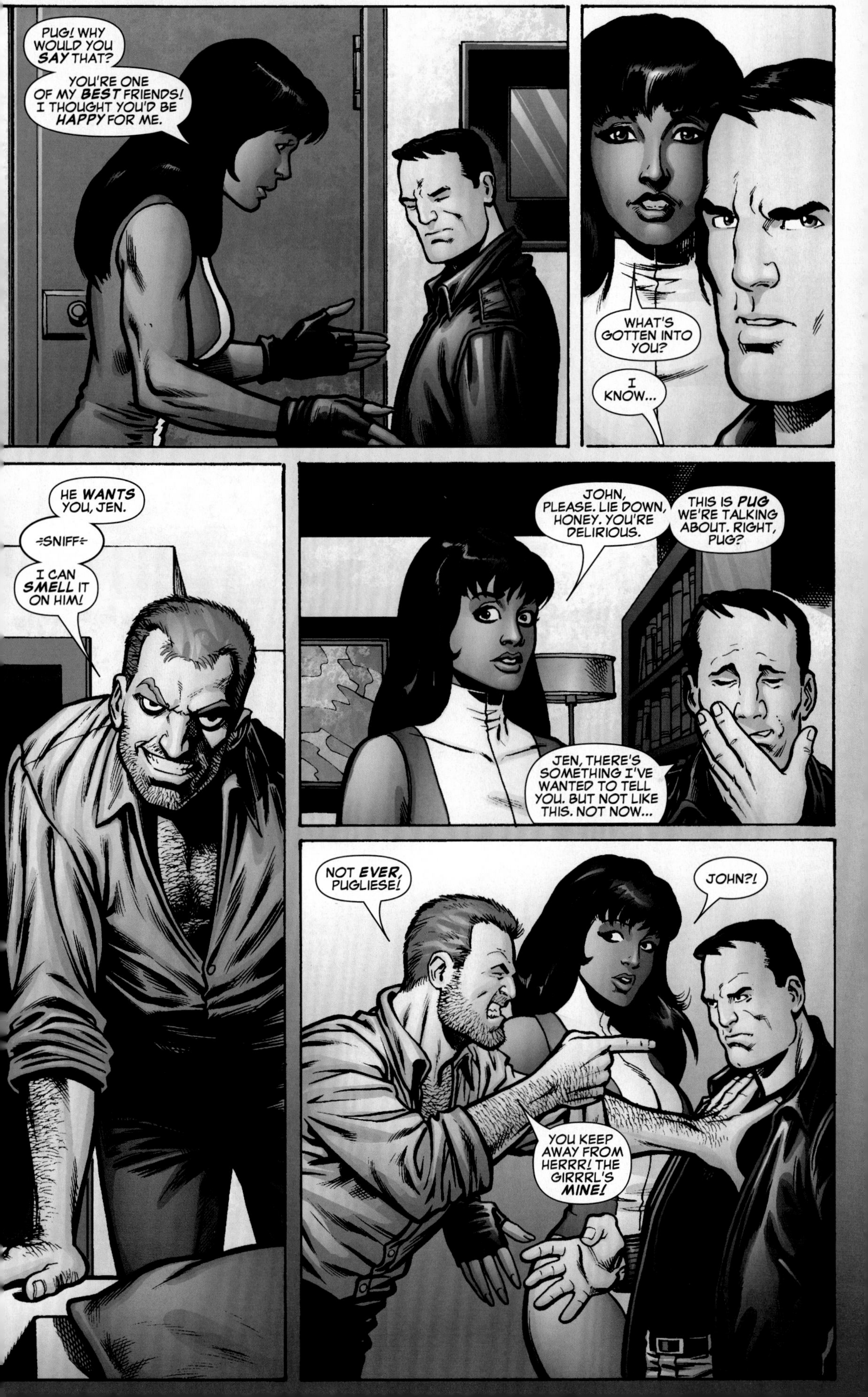
PUG! WHY WOULD YOU SAY THAT?
YOU'RE ONE OF MY BEST FRIENDS! I THOUGHT YOU'D BE HAPPY FOR ME.
WHAT'S GOTTEN INTO YOU?
I KNOW...
HE WANTS YOU, JEN.
=SNIFF=
I CAN SMELL IT ON HIM!
JOHN, PLEASE. LIE DOWN, HONEY. YOU'RE DELIRIOUS.
THIS IS PUG WE'RE TALKING ABOUT. RIGHT, PUG?
JEN, THERE'S SOMETHING I'VE WANTED TO TELL YOU. BUT NOT LIKE THIS. NOT NOW...
NOT EVER, PUGLIESE!
JOHN?!
YOU KEEP AWAY FROM HERRR! THE GIRRRL'S MINE!

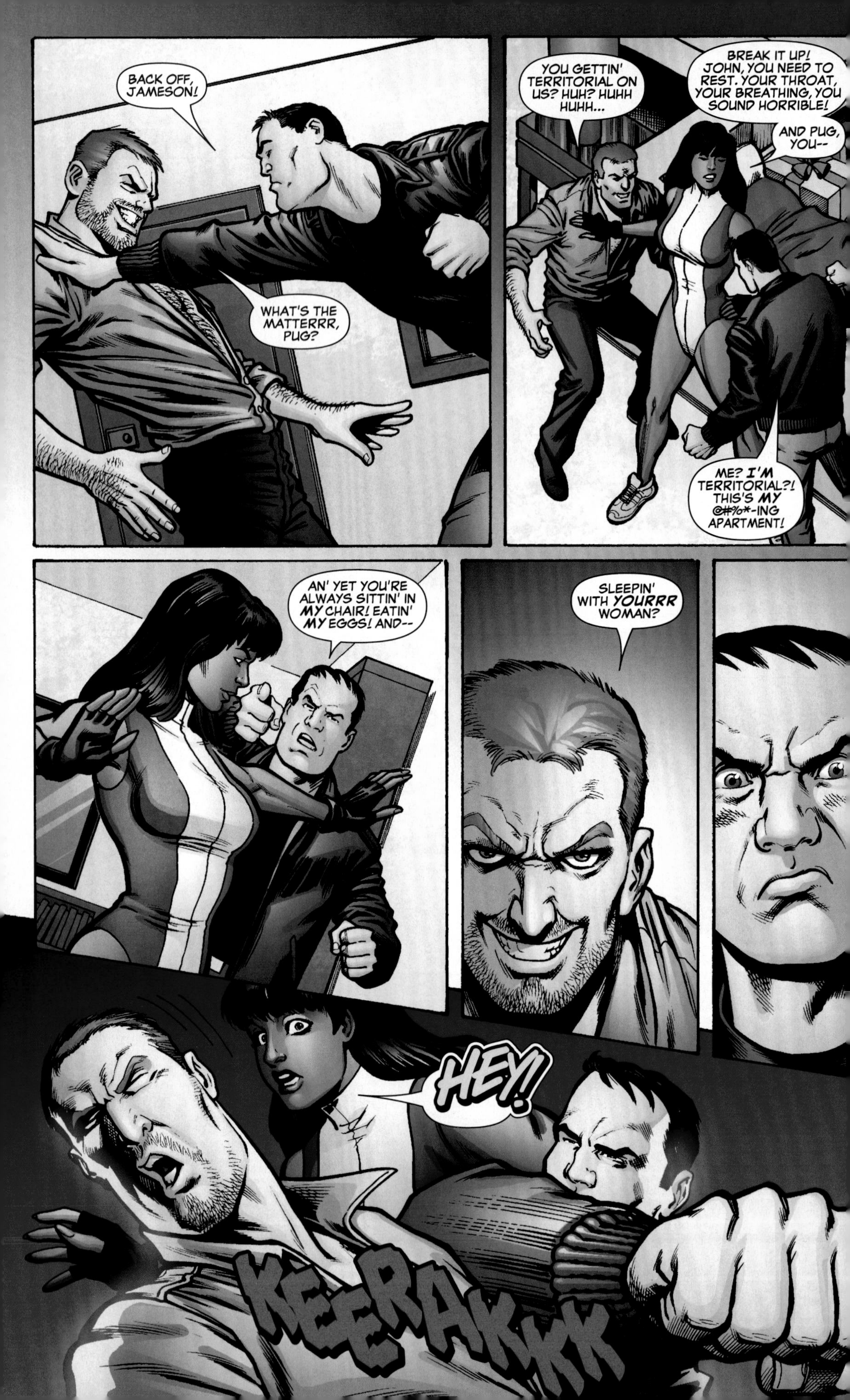
BACK OFF, JAMESON!
WHAT'S THE MATTERRR, PUG?
YOU GETTIN' TERRITORIAL ON US? HUH? HUHH HUHH...
BREAK IT UP! JOHN, YOU NEED TO REST. YOUR THROAT, YOUR BREATHING, YOU SOUND HORRIBLE!
AND PUG, YOU--
ME? I'M TERRITORIAL?! THIS'S MY @#%*-ING APARTMENT!
AN' YET YOU'RE ALWAYS SITTIN' IN MY CHAIR! EATIN' MY EGGS! AND--
SLEEPIN' WITH YOURRR WOMAN?
HEY!
KEERAKKKK

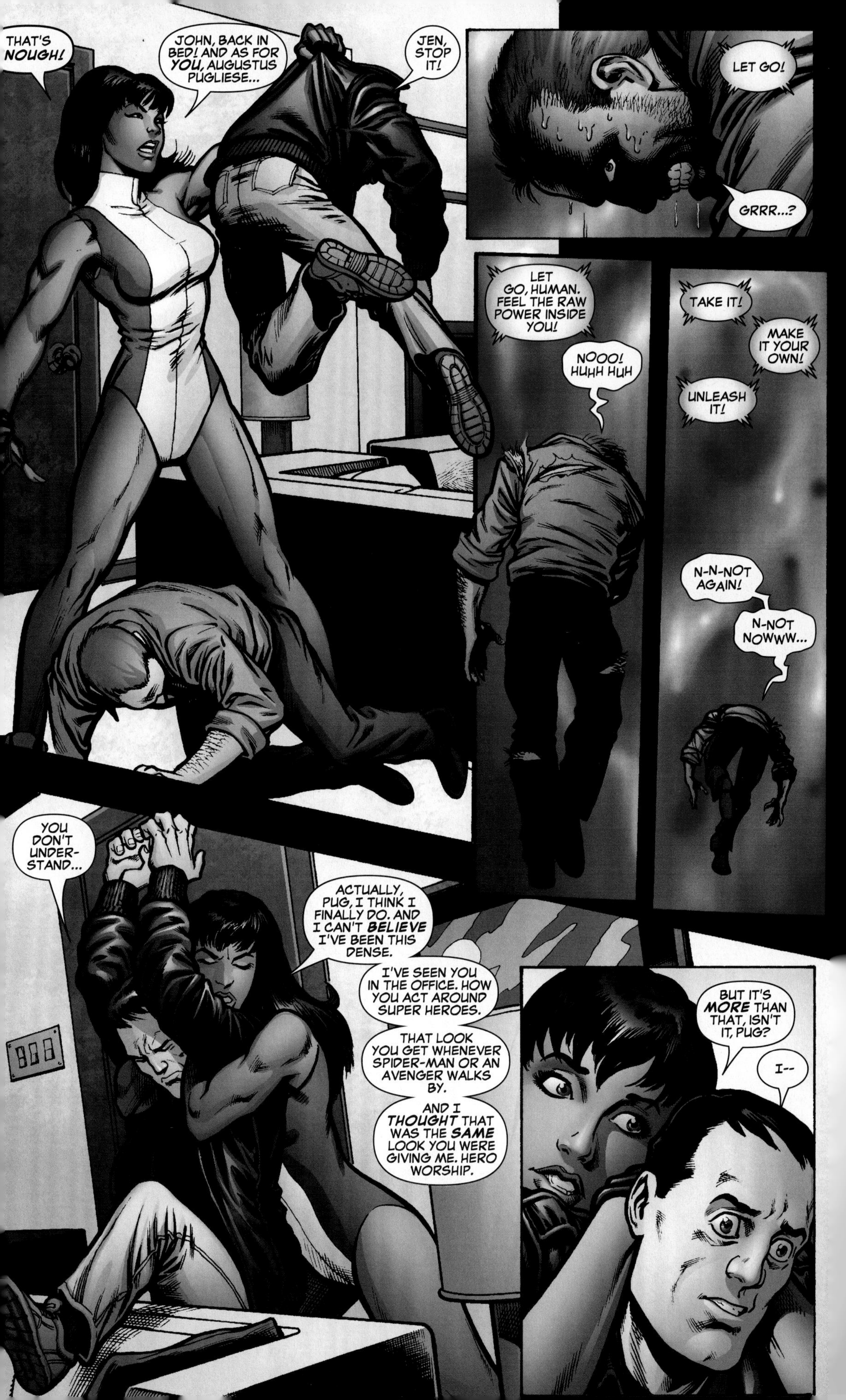
THAT'S NOUGH!
JOHN, BACK IN BED! AND AS FOR YOU, AUGUSTUS PUGLIESE...
JEN, STOP IT!
LET GO!
GRRR...?
LET GO, HUMAN. FEEL THE RAW POWER INSIDE YOU!
NOOO! HUHH HUH
TAKE IT!
MAKE IT YOUR OWN!
UNLEASH IT!
N-N-NOT AGAIN!
N-NOT NOWWW...
YOU DON'T UNDER-STAND...
ACTUALLY, PUG, I THINK I FINALLY DO. AND I CAN'T BELIEVE I'VE BEEN THIS DENSE.
I'VE SEEN YOU IN THE OFFICE. HOW YOU ACT AROUND SUPER HEROES.
THAT LOOK YOU GET WHENEVER SPIDER-MAN OR AN AVENGER WALKS BY.
AND I THOUGHT THAT WAS THE SAME LOOK YOU WERE GIVING ME. HERO WORSHIP.
BUT IT'S MORE THAN THAT, ISN'T IT, PUG?
I--

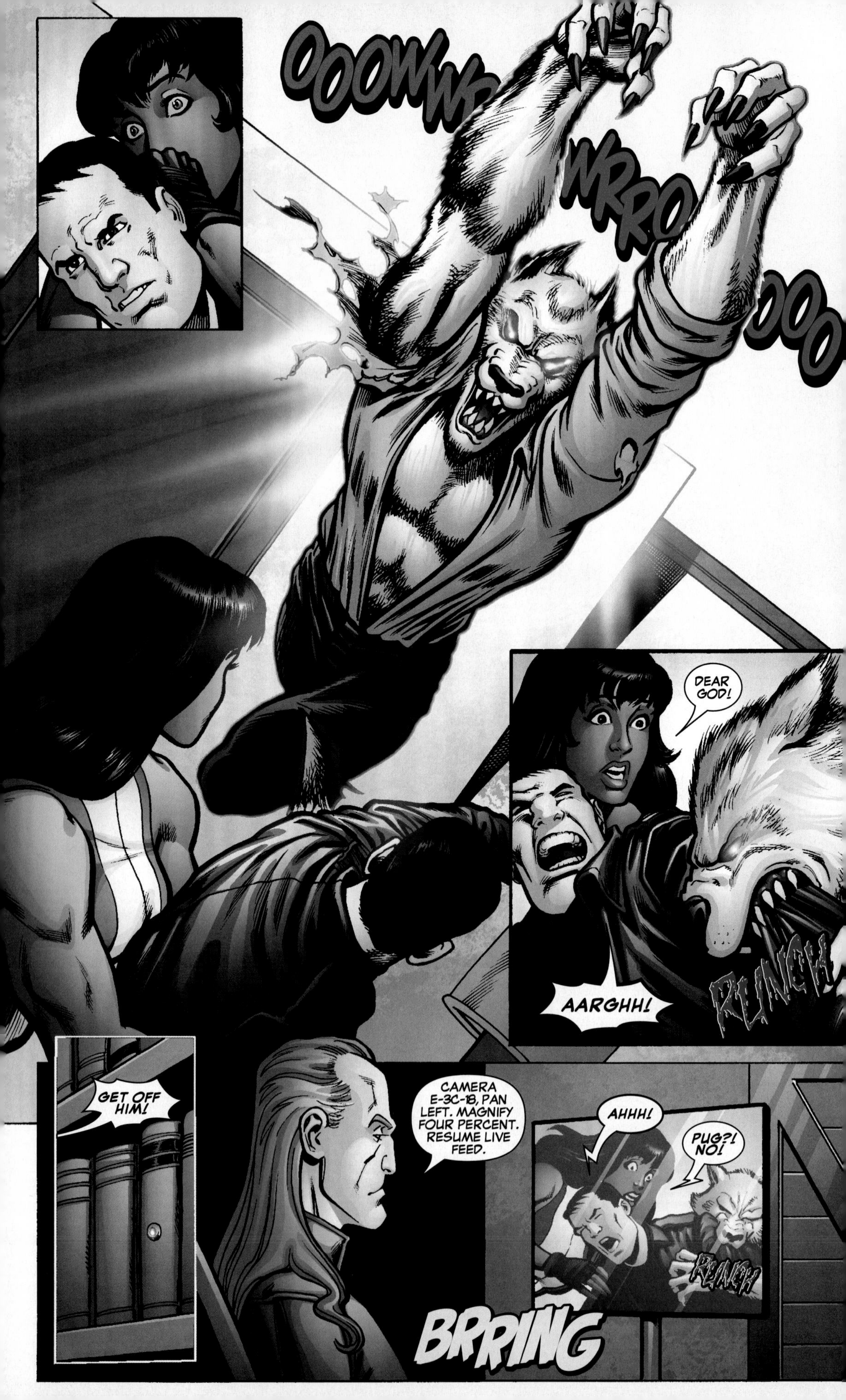
OOOWWRRRROOOO
DEAR GOD!
AARGHH!
RUNCH
GET OFF HIM!
CAMERA E-3C-18, PAN LEFT. MAGNIFY FOUR PERCENT. RESUME LIVE FEED.
AHHH!
PUG?! NO!
RUNCH
BRRING

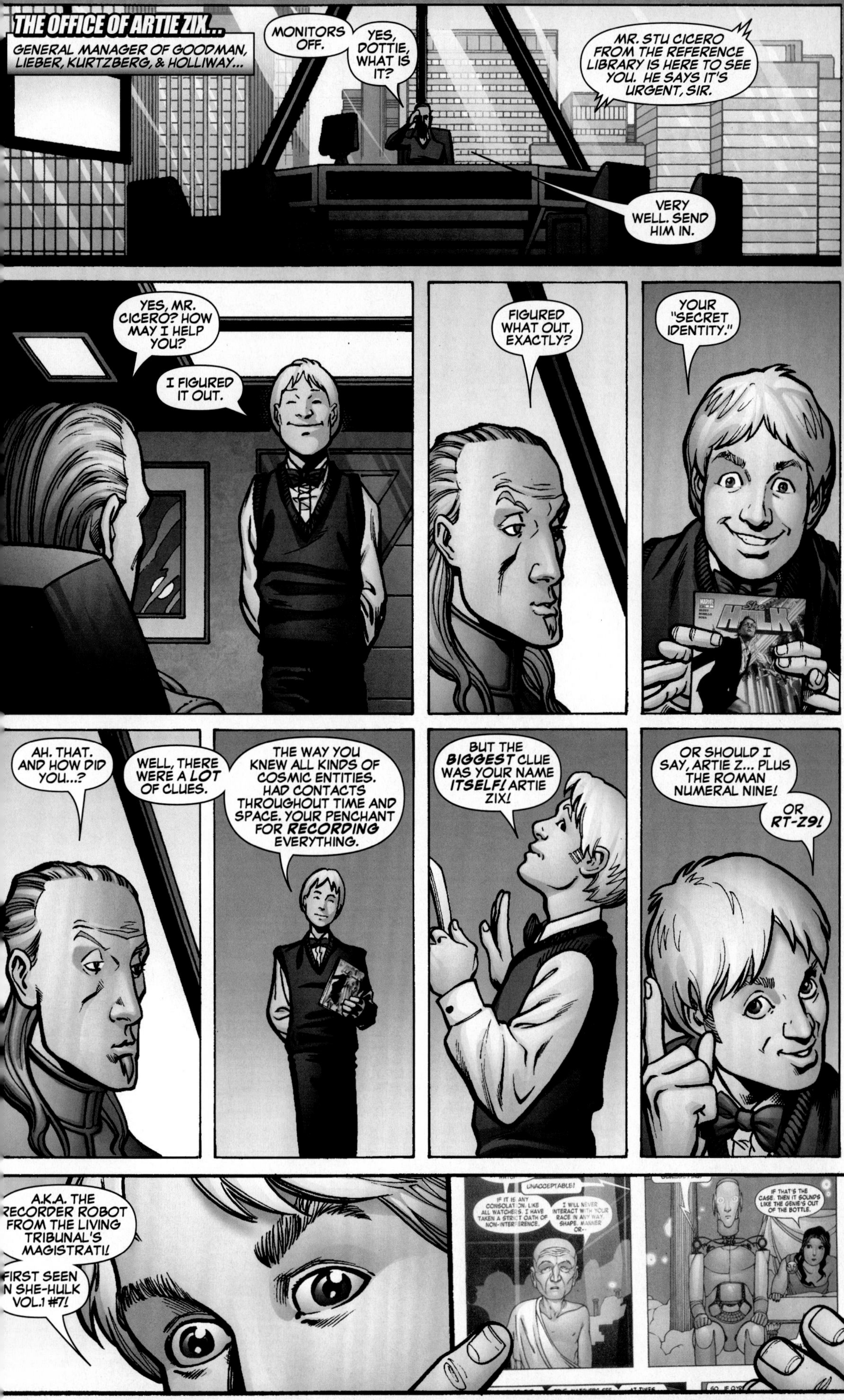
THE OFFICE OF ARTIE ZIX...
GENERAL MANAGER OF GOODMAN, LIEBER, KURTZBERG, & HOLLIWAY...
MONITORS OFF.
YES, DOTTIE, WHAT IS IT?
MR. STU CICERO FROM THE REFERENCE LIBRARY IS HERE TO SEE YOU. HE SAYS IT'S URGENT, SIR.
VERY WELL. SEND HIM IN.
YES, MR. CICERO? HOW MAY I HELP YOU?
I FIGURED IT OUT.
FIGURED WHAT OUT, EXACTLY?
YOUR "SECRET IDENTITY."
AH. THAT. AND HOW DID YOU...?
WELL, THERE WERE A LOT OF CLUES.
THE WAY YOU KNEW ALL KINDS OF COSMIC ENTITIES. HAD CONTACTS THROUGHOUT TIME AND SPACE. YOUR PENCHANT FOR RECORDING EVERYTHING.
BUT THE BIGGEST CLUE WAS YOUR NAME ITSELF! ARTIE ZIX!
OR SHOULD I SAY, ARTIE Z... PLUS THE ROMAN NUMERAL NINE!
OR RT-Z9!
A.K.A. THE RECORDER ROBOT FROM THE LIVING TRIBUNAL'S MAGISTRATI!
FIRST SEEN IN SHE-HULK VOL.1 #7!
UNACCEPTABLE!
IF IT IS ANY CONSOLATION, LIKE ALL WATCHERS, I HAVE TAKEN A STRICT OATH OF NON-INTERFERENCE.
I WILL NEVER INTERACT WITH YOUR RACE IN ANY WAY, SHAPE, MANNER OR--
IF THAT'S THE CASE, THEN IT SOUNDS LIKE THE GENIE'S OUT OF THE BOTTLE.

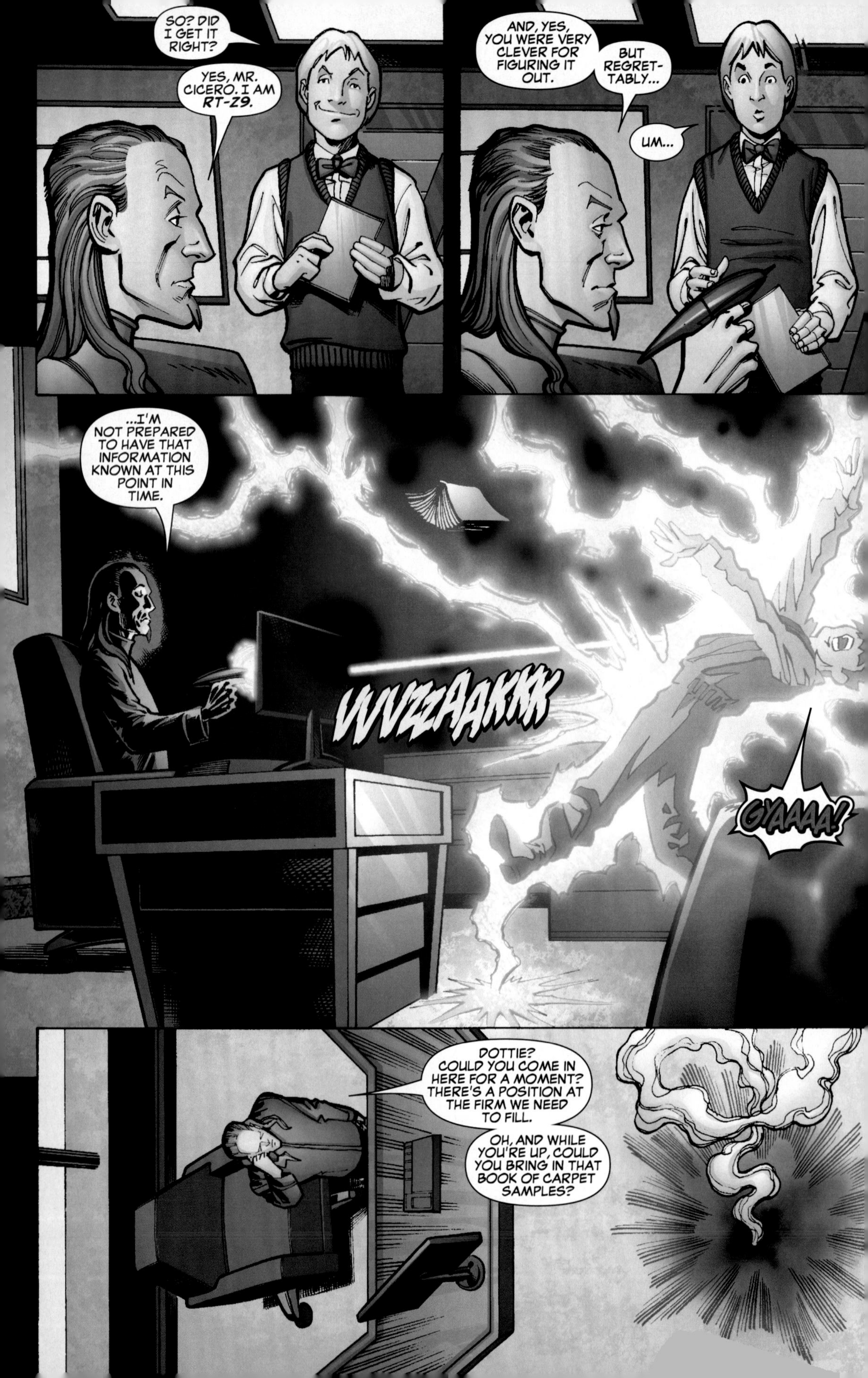

SO? DID I GET IT RIGHT?
YES, MR. CICERO. I AM RT-Z9.
AND, YES, YOU WERE VERY CLEVER FOR FIGURING IT OUT.
BUT REGRET-TABLY...
UM...
...I'M NOT PREPARED TO HAVE THAT INFORMATION KNOWN AT THIS POINT IN TIME.
VVVZZAAKKK
GYAAAA!
DOTTIE? COULD YOU COME IN HERE FOR A MOMENT? THERE'S A POSITION AT THE FIRM WE NEED TO FILL.
OH, AND WHILE YOU'RE UP, COULD YOU BRING IN THAT BOOK OF CARPET SAMPLES?

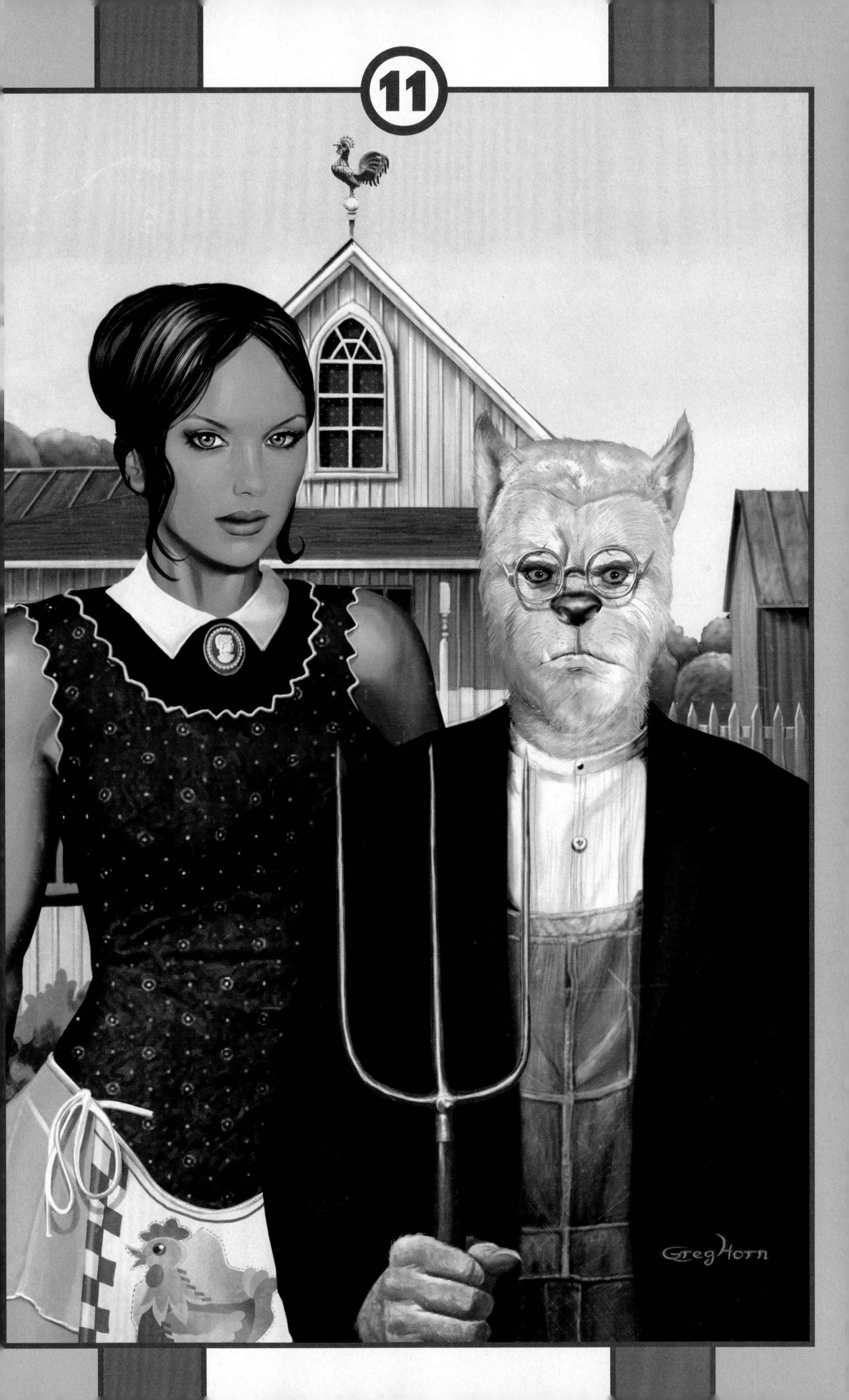
11
Greg Horn

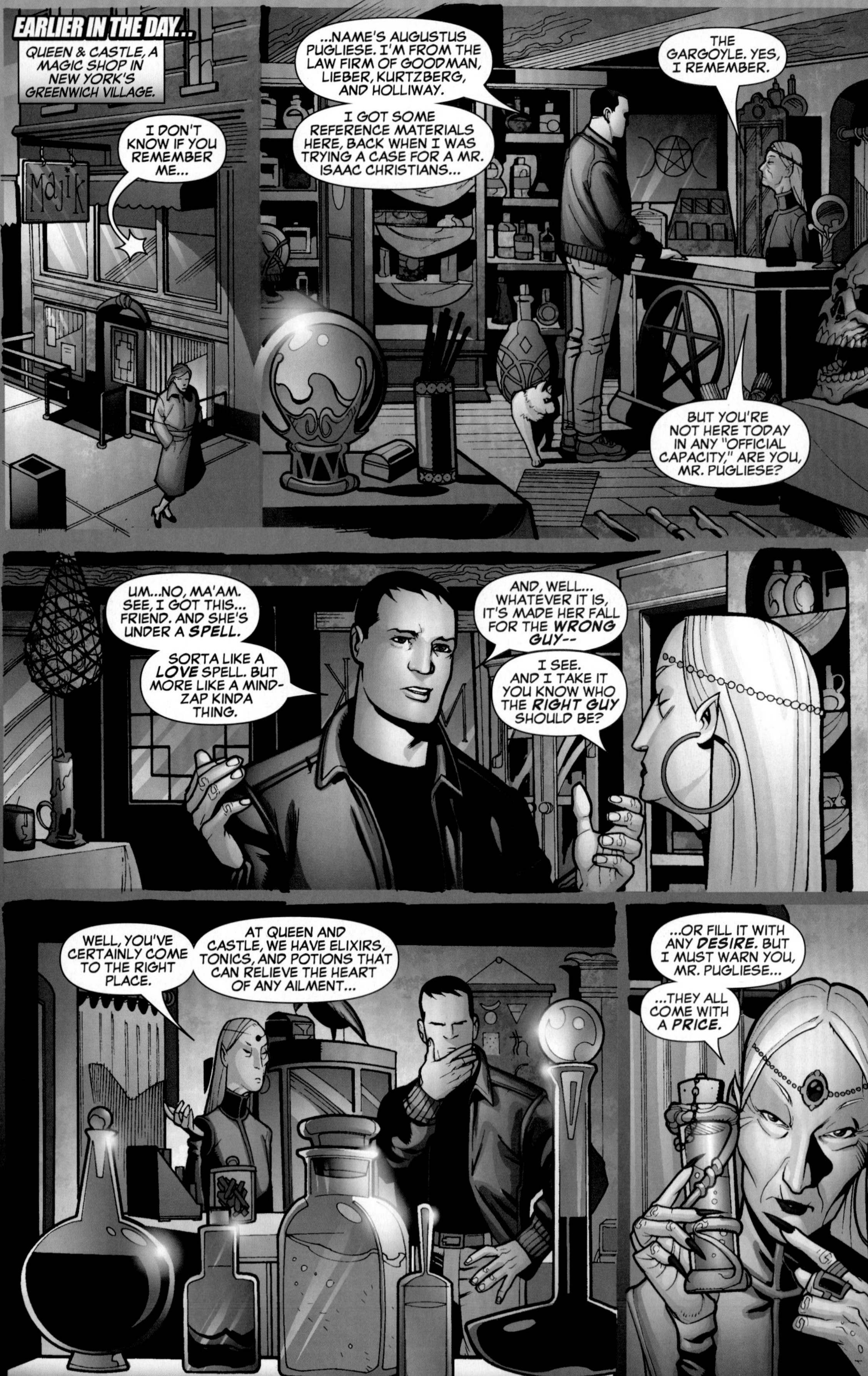
EARLIER IN THE DAY...
QUEEN & CASTLE, A MAGIC SHOP IN NEW YORK'S GREENWICH VILLAGE.
Majik
I DON'T KNOW IF YOU REMEMBER ME...
...NAME'S AUGUSTUS PUGLIESE. I'M FROM THE LAW FIRM OF GOODMAN, LIEBER, KURTZBERG, AND HOLLIWAY.
I GOT SOME REFERENCE MATERIALS HERE, BACK WHEN I WAS TRYING A CASE FOR A MR. ISAAC CHRISTIANS...
THE GARGOYLE. YES, I REMEMBER.
BUT YOU'RE NOT HERE TODAY IN ANY "OFFICIAL CAPACITY," ARE YOU, MR. PUGLIESE?
UM...NO, MA'AM. SEE, I GOT THIS... FRIEND. AND SHE'S UNDER A SPELL.
SORTA LIKE A LOVE SPELL. BUT MORE LIKE A MIND-ZAP KINDA THING.
AND, WELL... WHATEVER IT IS, IT'S MADE HER FALL FOR THE WRONG GUY--
I SEE. AND I TAKE IT YOU KNOW WHO THE RIGHT GUY SHOULD BE?
WELL, YOU'VE CERTAINLY COME TO THE RIGHT PLACE.
AT QUEEN AND CASTLE, WE HAVE ELIXIRS, TONICS, AND POTIONS THAT CAN RELIEVE THE HEART OF ANY AILMENT...
...OR FILL IT WITH ANY DESIRE. BUT I MUST WARN YOU, MR. PUGLIESE...
...THEY ALL COME WITH A PRICE.

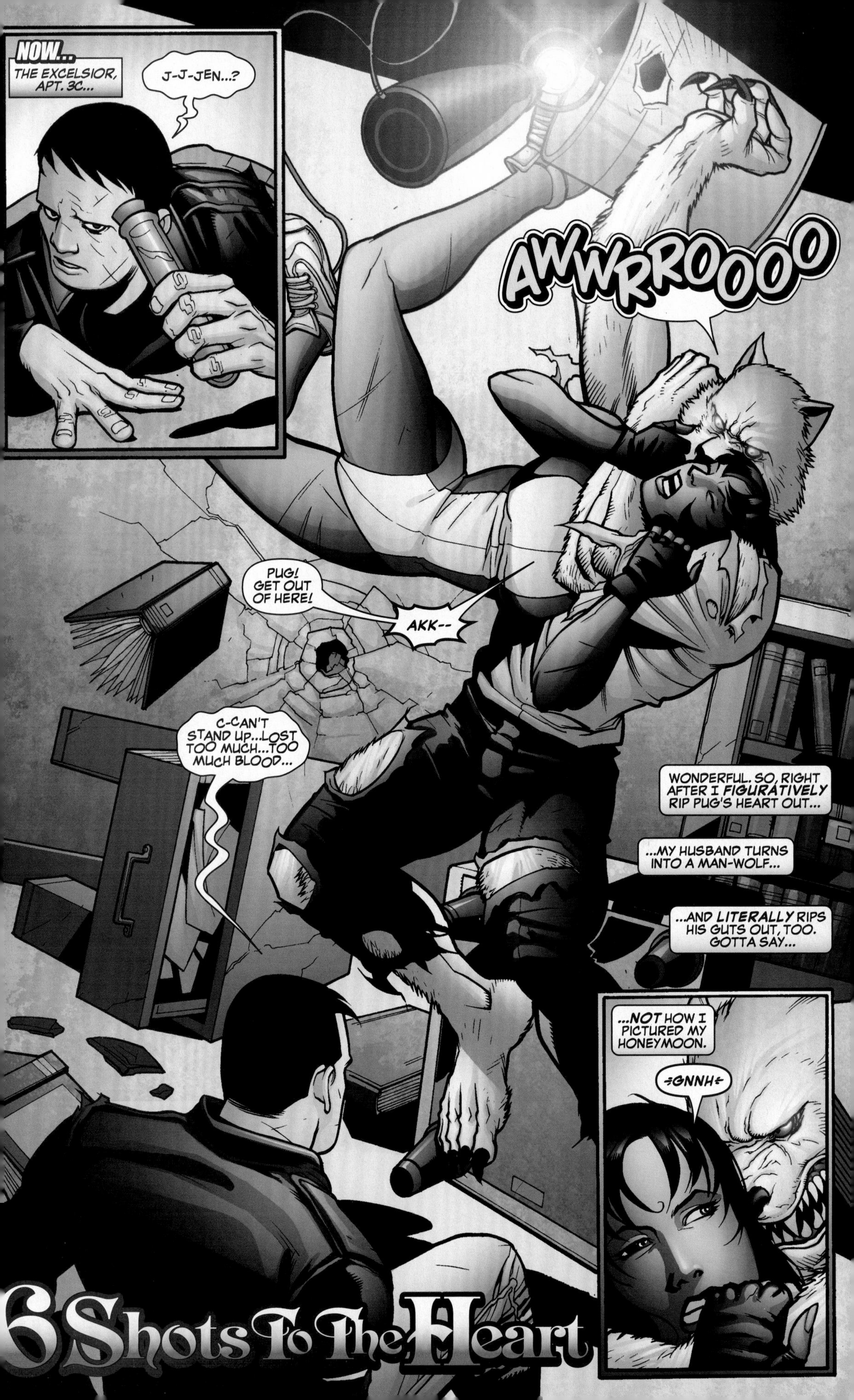
NOW...
THE EXCELSIOR, APT. 3C...
J-J-JEN...?
AWWRROOOO
PUG! GET OUT OF HERE!
AKK--
C-CAN'T STAND UP...LOST TOO MUCH...TOO MUCH BLOOD...
WONDERFUL. SO, RIGHT AFTER I FIGURATIVELY RIP PUG'S HEART OUT...
...MY HUSBAND TURNS INTO A MAN-WOLF...
...AND LITERALLY RIPS HIS GUTS OUT, TOO. GOTTA SAY...
...NOT HOW I PICTURED MY HONEYMOON.
=GNNH=
6 Shots To The Heart

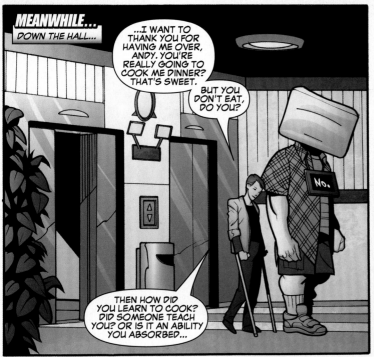

MEANWHILE...
DOWN THE HALL...

...I WANT TO THANK YOU FOR HAVING ME OVER, ANDY. YOU'RE REALLY GOING TO COOK ME DINNER? THAT'S SWEET.

BUT YOU DON'T EAT, DO YOU?

THEN HOW DID YOU LEARN TO COOK? DID SOMEONE TEACH YOU? OR IS IT AN ABILITY YOU ABSORBED...

NO.

...LIKE HOW YOU ABSORB SUPER POW--

3C

BAMMM

HUH?

What was that?

KRASH

AWROO

WUMP

JOHN!

SHE-HULK AND HER NEW HUBBY, HUH? DON'T WORRY, ANDY. THAT'S WHAT... NEWLYWEDS DO.

C'MON, WHY DON'T YOU TAKE ME TO YOUR PLACE. IF YOU'RE LUCKY, I'LL SHOW YOU HOW IT'S...

MATT?

MISS MALLORY.

OH! IT TOTALLY SLIPPED MY MIND. YOU'RE STILL STAYING AT ANDY'S.

NOT ANYMORE, MA'AM. THINK IT'S TIME I MOVED ON.

YOU FINALLY FOUND YOUR OWN PLACE?

NO. I AIM TO HEAD OUT WEST. I MAY NOT BE ABLE TO GO BACK TO MY OWN TIME...

...BUT THIS BIG CITY LIFE? IT'S TOO...COMPLICATED FOR A FELLA LIKE ME.

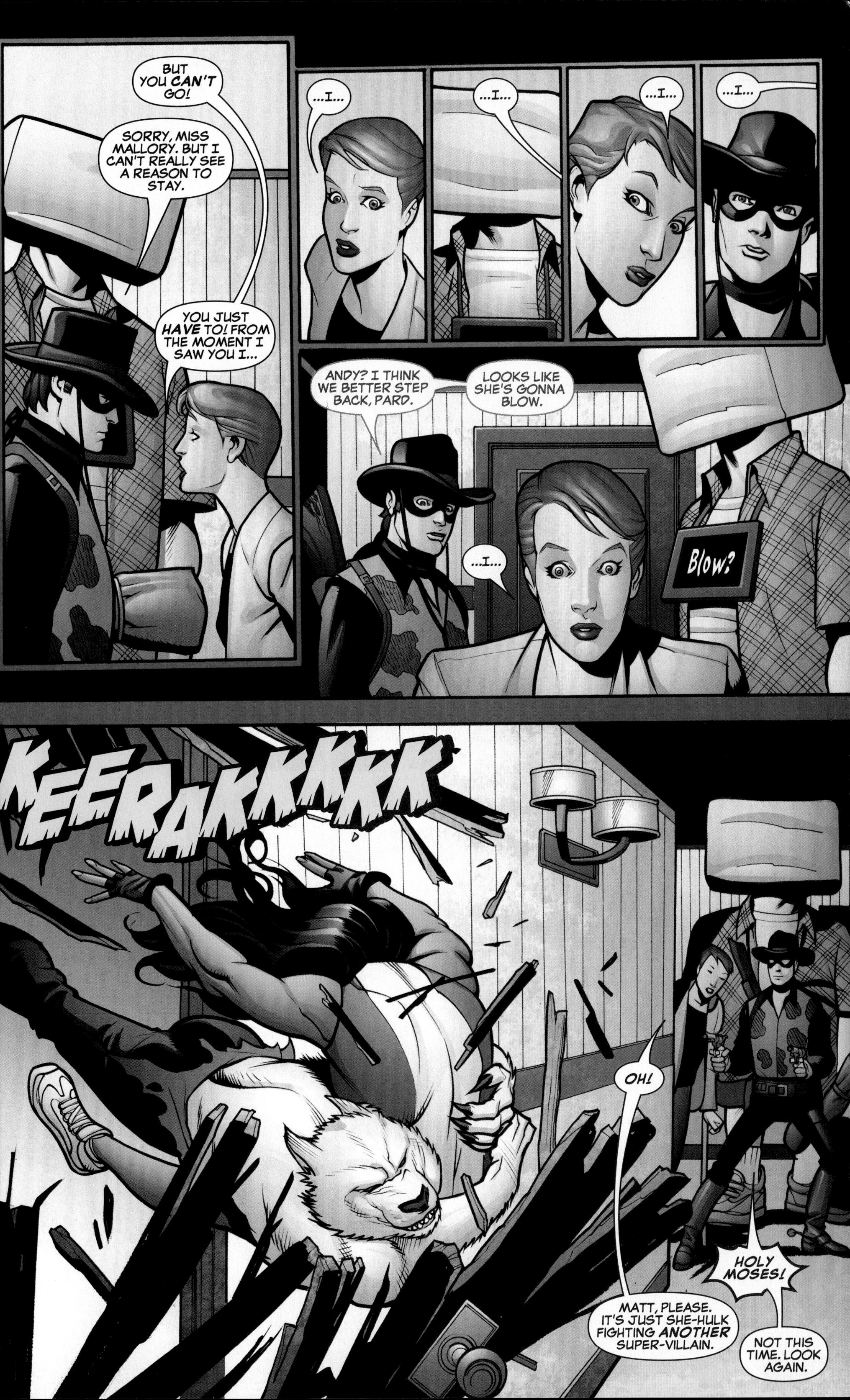
BUT YOU CAN'T GO!
SORRY, MISS MALLORY. BUT I CAN'T REALLY SEE A REASON TO STAY.
YOU JUST HAVE TO! FROM THE MOMENT I SAW YOU I...
...I...
...I...
...I...
...I...
ANDY? I THINK WE BETTER STEP BACK, PARD.
LOOKS LIKE SHE'S GONNA BLOW.
...I...
BLOW?
KEERAKKKKK
OH!
MATT, PLEASE. IT'S JUST SHE-HULK FIGHTING ANOTHER SUPER-VILLAIN.
HOLY MOSES!
NOT THIS TIME. LOOK AGAIN.

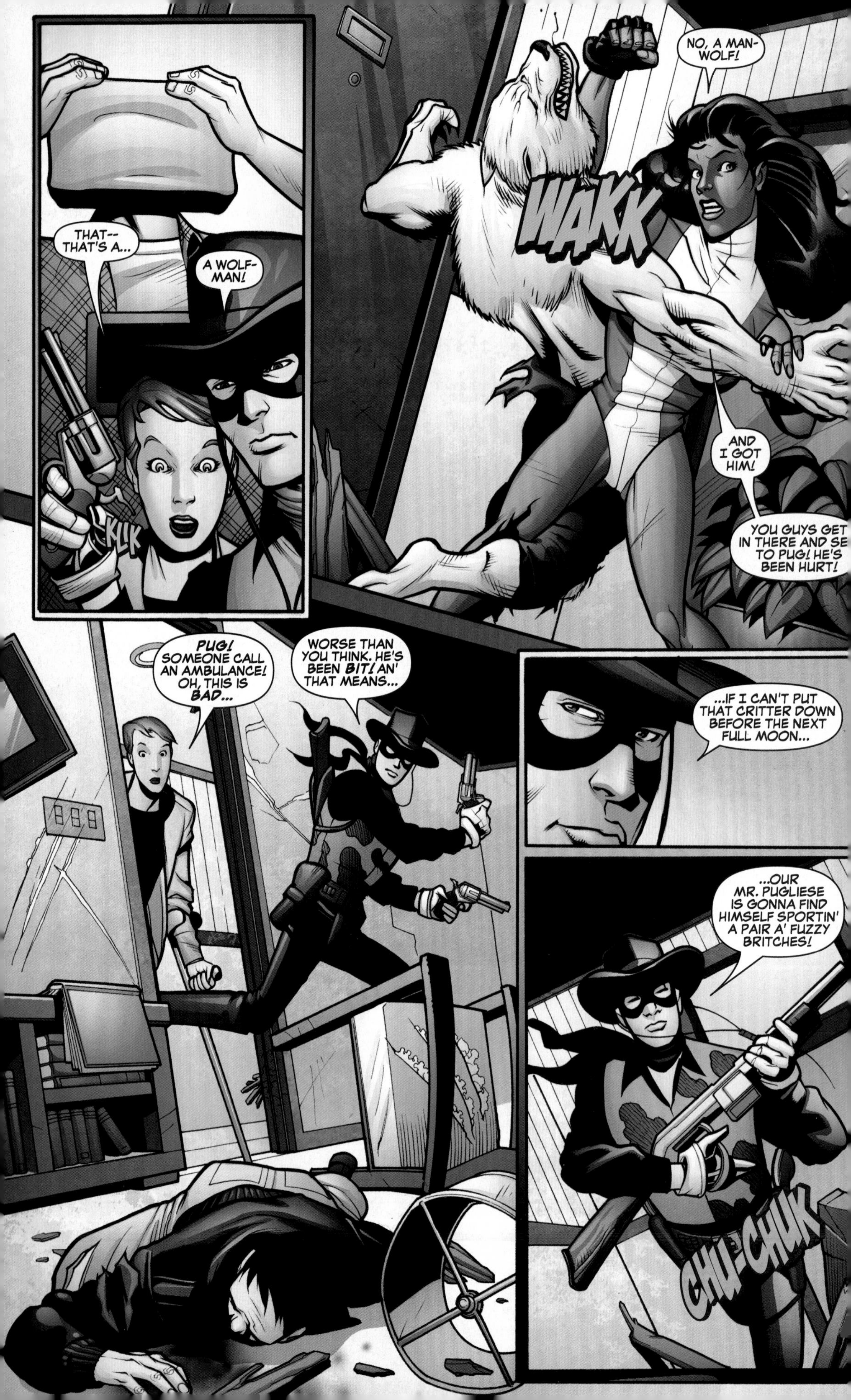
THAT-- THAT'S A...
A WOLF-MAN!
KLIK
NO, A MAN-WOLF!
WAKK
AND I GOT HIM!
YOU GUYS GET IN THERE AND SE TO PUG! HE'S BEEN HURT!
PUG! SOMEONE CALL AN AMBULANCE! OH, THIS IS BAD...
WORSE THAN YOU THINK. HE'S BEEN BIT! AN' THAT MEANS...
...IF I CAN'T PUT THAT CRITTER DOWN BEFORE THE NEXT FULL MOON...
...OUR MR. PUGLIESE IS GONNA FIND HIMSELF SPORTIN' A PAIR A' FUZZY BRITCHES!
CHU-CHUK

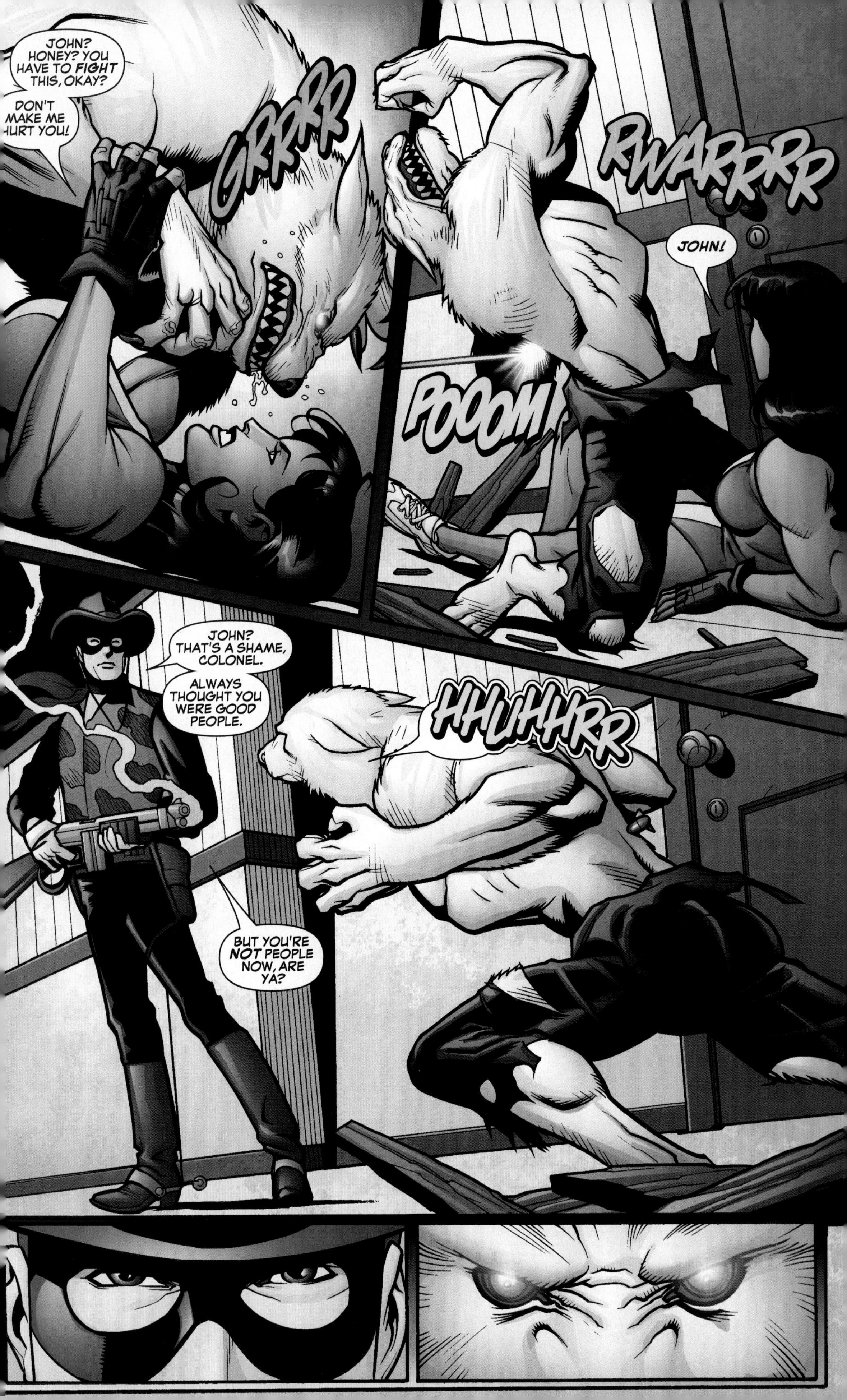
JOHN? HONEY? YOU HAVE TO **FIGHT** THIS, OKAY?
DON'T MAKE ME HURT YOU!
GRRRR
RWARRRR
JOHN!
POOOM!
JOHN? THAT'S A SHAME, COLONEL.
ALWAYS THOUGHT YOU WERE GOOD PEOPLE.
HHUHHRR
BUT YOU'RE **NOT** PEOPLE NOW, ARE YA?

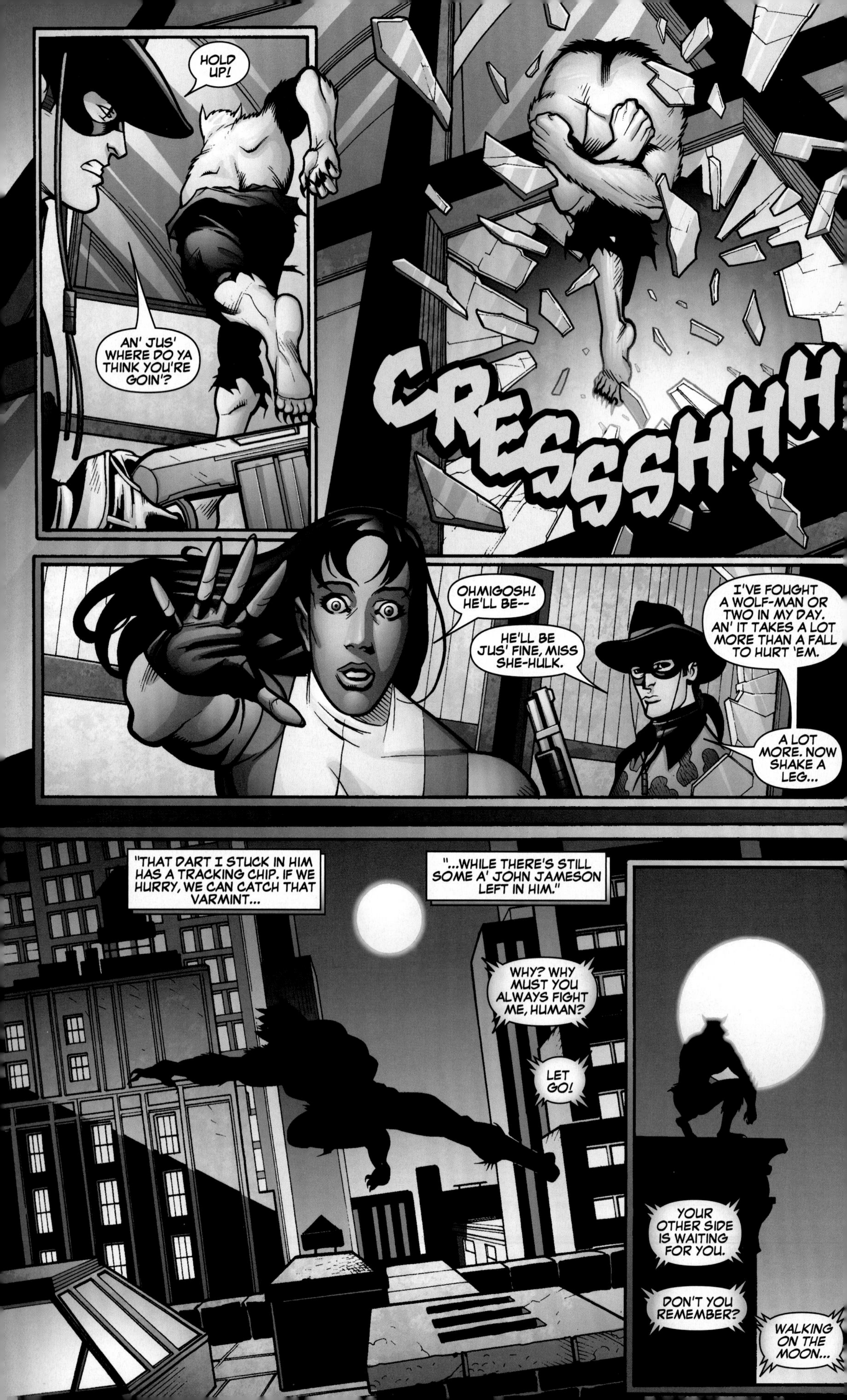
HOLD UP!
AN' JUS' WHERE DO YA THINK YOU'RE GOIN'?
CRESSSHHH
OHMIGOSH! HE'LL BE--
HE'LL BE JUS' FINE, MISS SHE-HULK.
I'VE FOUGHT A WOLF-MAN OR TWO IN MY DAY. AN' IT TAKES A LOT MORE THAN A FALL TO HURT 'EM.
A LOT MORE. NOW SHAKE A LEG...
"THAT DART I STUCK IN HIM HAS A TRACKING CHIP. IF WE HURRY, WE CAN CATCH THAT VARMINT...
"...WHILE THERE'S STILL SOME A' JOHN JAMESON LEFT IN HIM."
WHY? WHY MUST YOU ALWAYS FIGHT ME, HUMAN?
LET GO!
YOUR OTHER SIDE IS WAITING FOR YOU.
DON'T YOU REMEMBER?
WALKING ON THE MOON...

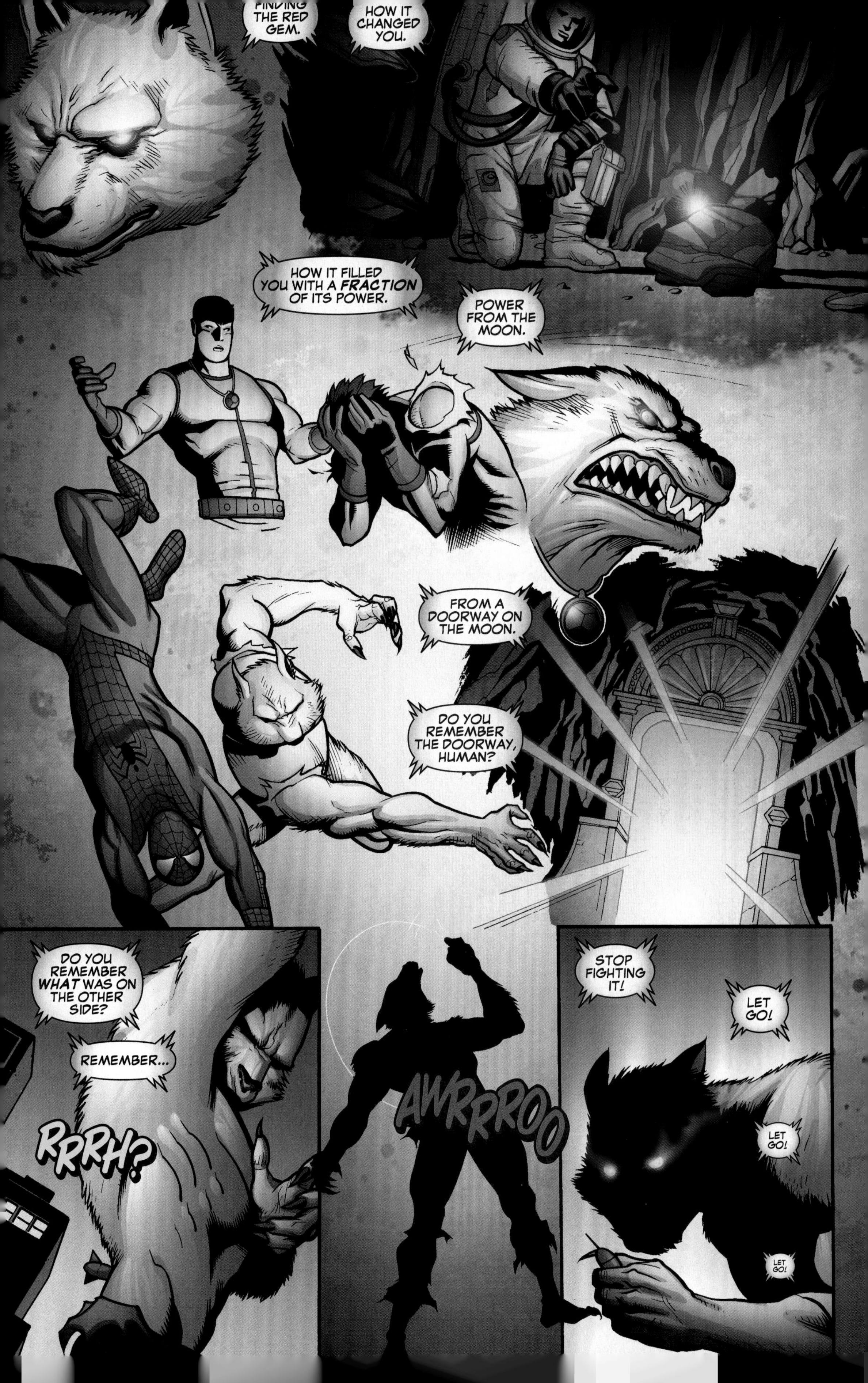
FINDING THE RED GEM.
HOW IT CHANGED YOU.
HOW IT FILLED YOU WITH A FRACTION OF ITS POWER.
POWER FROM THE MOON.
FROM A DOORWAY ON THE MOON.
DO YOU REMEMBER THE DOORWAY, HUMAN?
DO YOU REMEMBER WHAT WAS ON THE OTHER SIDE?
REMEMBER...
RRRH?
AWRRROO
STOP FIGHTING IT!
LET GO!
LET GO!
LET GO!

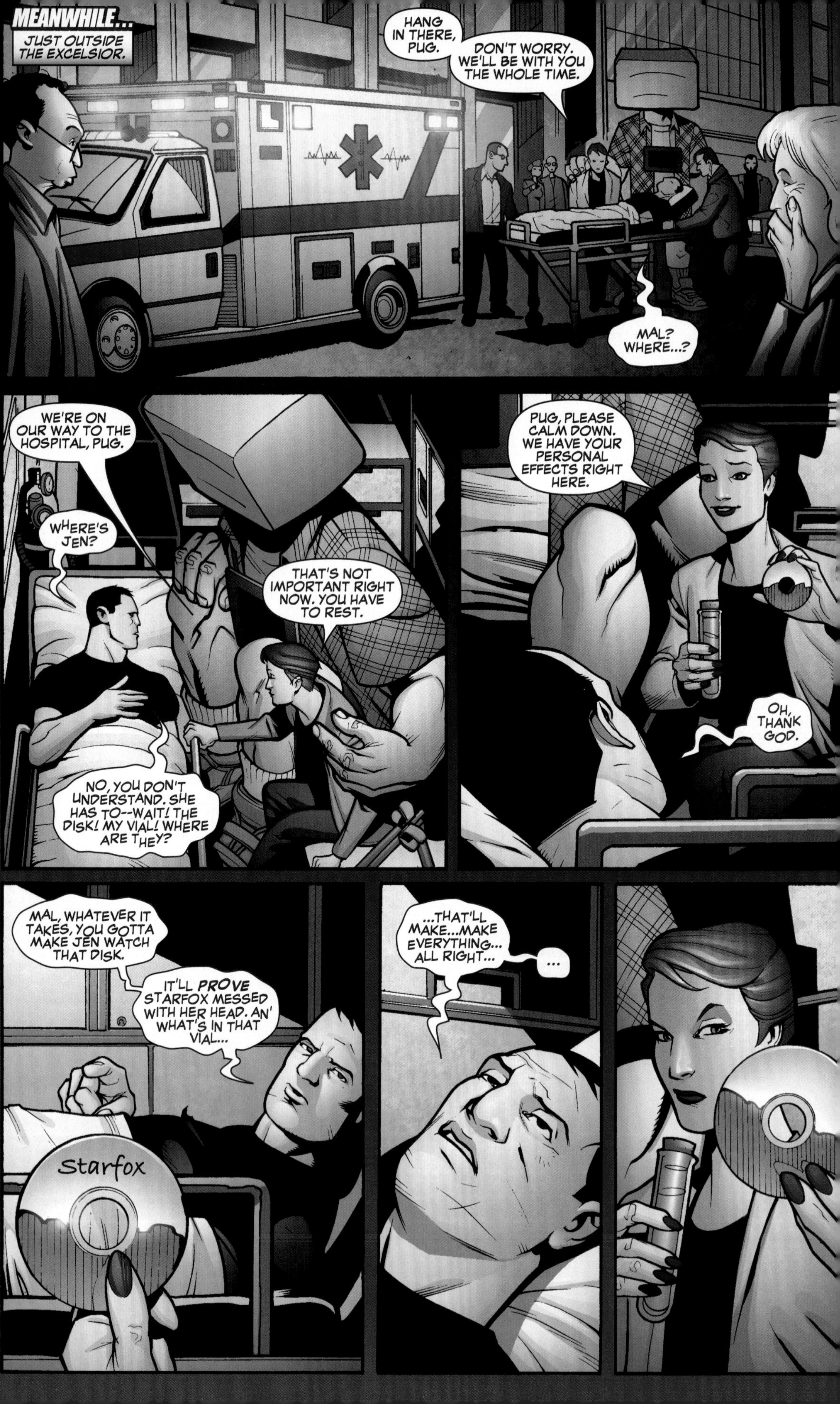
MEANWHILE...
JUST OUTSIDE THE EXCELSIOR.
HANG IN THERE, PUG.
DON'T WORRY. WE'LL BE WITH YOU THE WHOLE TIME.
MAL? WHERE...?
WE'RE ON OUR WAY TO THE HOSPITAL, PUG.
WHERE'S JEN?
THAT'S NOT IMPORTANT RIGHT NOW. YOU HAVE TO REST.
NO, YOU DON'T UNDERSTAND. SHE HAS TO--WAIT! THE DISK! MY VIAL! WHERE ARE THEY?
PUG, PLEASE CALM DOWN. WE HAVE YOUR PERSONAL EFFECTS RIGHT HERE.
OH, THANK GOD.
MAL, WHATEVER IT TAKES, YOU GOTTA MAKE JEN WATCH THAT DISK.
IT'LL PROVE STARFOX MESSED WITH HER HEAD. AN' WHAT'S IN THAT VIAL...
Starfox
...THAT'LL MAKE...MAKE EVERYTHING... ALL RIGHT...
...

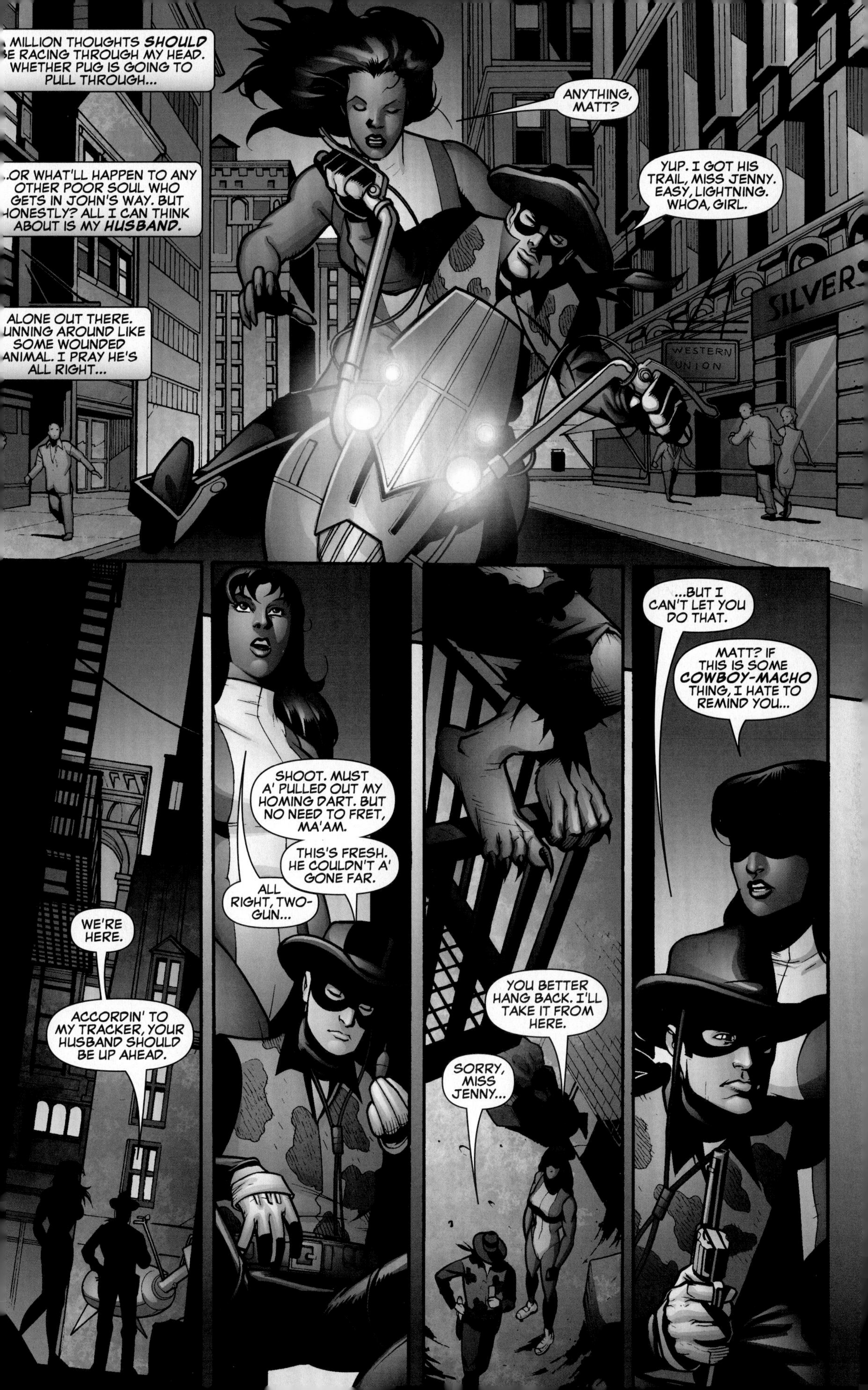
A MILLION THOUGHTS SHOULD BE RACING THROUGH MY HEAD. WHETHER PUG IS GOING TO PULL THROUGH...
ANYTHING, MATT?
...OR WHAT'LL HAPPEN TO ANY OTHER POOR SOUL WHO GETS IN JOHN'S WAY. BUT HONESTLY? ALL I CAN THINK ABOUT IS MY HUSBAND.
YUP. I GOT HIS TRAIL, MISS JENNY. EASY, LIGHTNING. WHOA, GIRL.
ALONE OUT THERE. RUNNING AROUND LIKE SOME WOUNDED ANIMAL. I PRAY HE'S ALL RIGHT...
SILVERS
WESTERN UNION
WE'RE HERE.
ACCORDIN' TO MY TRACKER, YOUR HUSBAND SHOULD BE UP AHEAD.
SHOOT. MUST A' PULLED OUT MY HOMING DART. BUT NO NEED TO FRET, MA'AM.
THIS'S FRESH. HE COULDN'T A' GONE FAR.
ALL RIGHT, TWO-GUN...
YOU BETTER HANG BACK. I'LL TAKE IT FROM HERE.
SORRY, MISS JENNY...
...BUT I CAN'T LET YOU DO THAT.
MATT? IF THIS IS SOME COWBOY-MACHO THING, I HATE TO REMIND YOU...

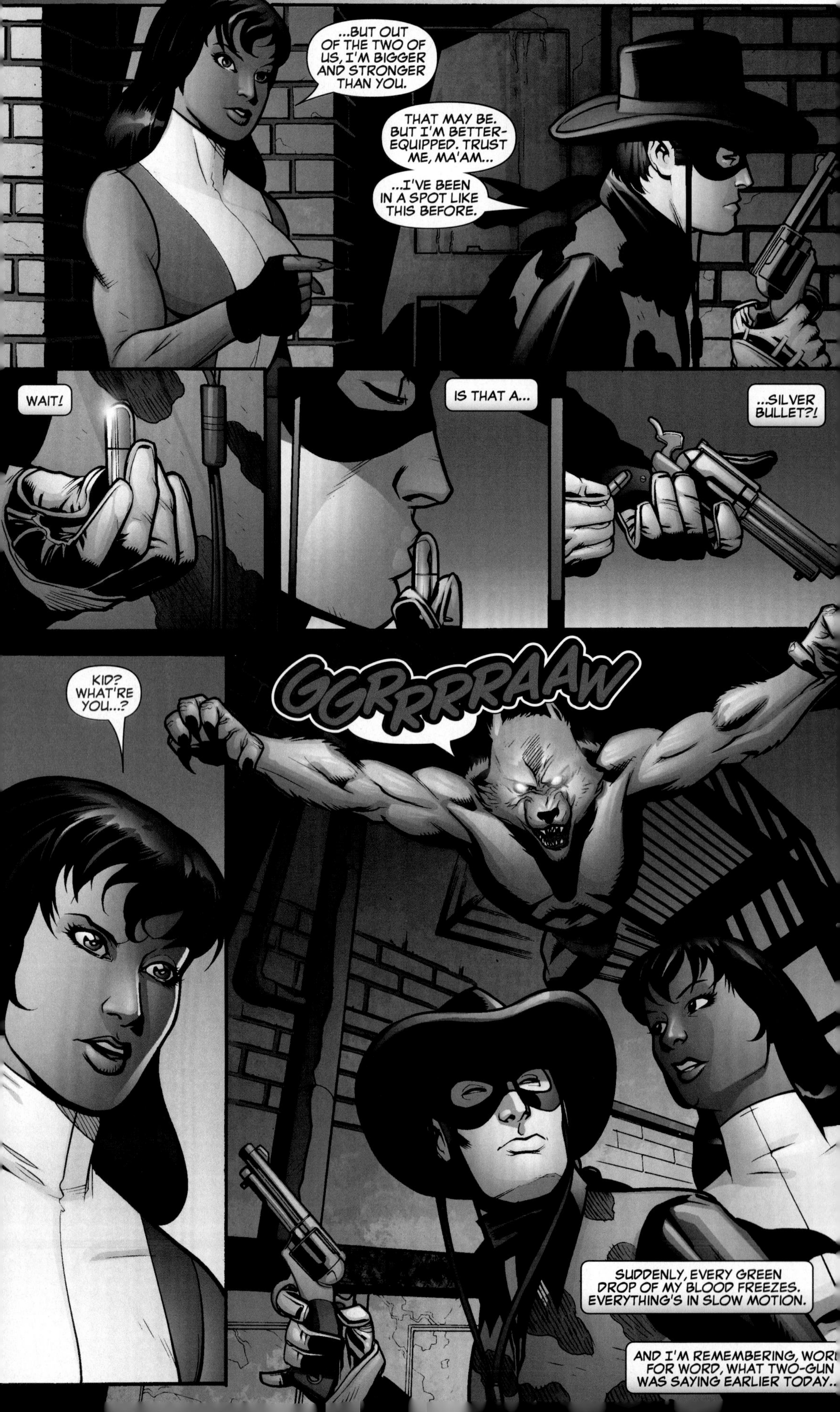
...BUT OUT OF THE TWO OF US, I'M BIGGER AND STRONGER THAN YOU.
THAT MAY BE. BUT I'M BETTER-EQUIPPED. TRUST ME, MA'AM...
...I'VE BEEN IN A SPOT LIKE THIS BEFORE.
WAIT!
IS THAT A...
...SILVER BULLET?!
KID? WHAT'RE YOU...?
GGRRRRRAAW
SUDDENLY, EVERY GREEN DROP OF MY BLOOD FREEZES. EVERYTHING'S IN SLOW MOTION.
AND I'M REMEMBERING, WORD FOR WORD, WHAT TWO-GUN WAS SAYING EARLIER TODAY...

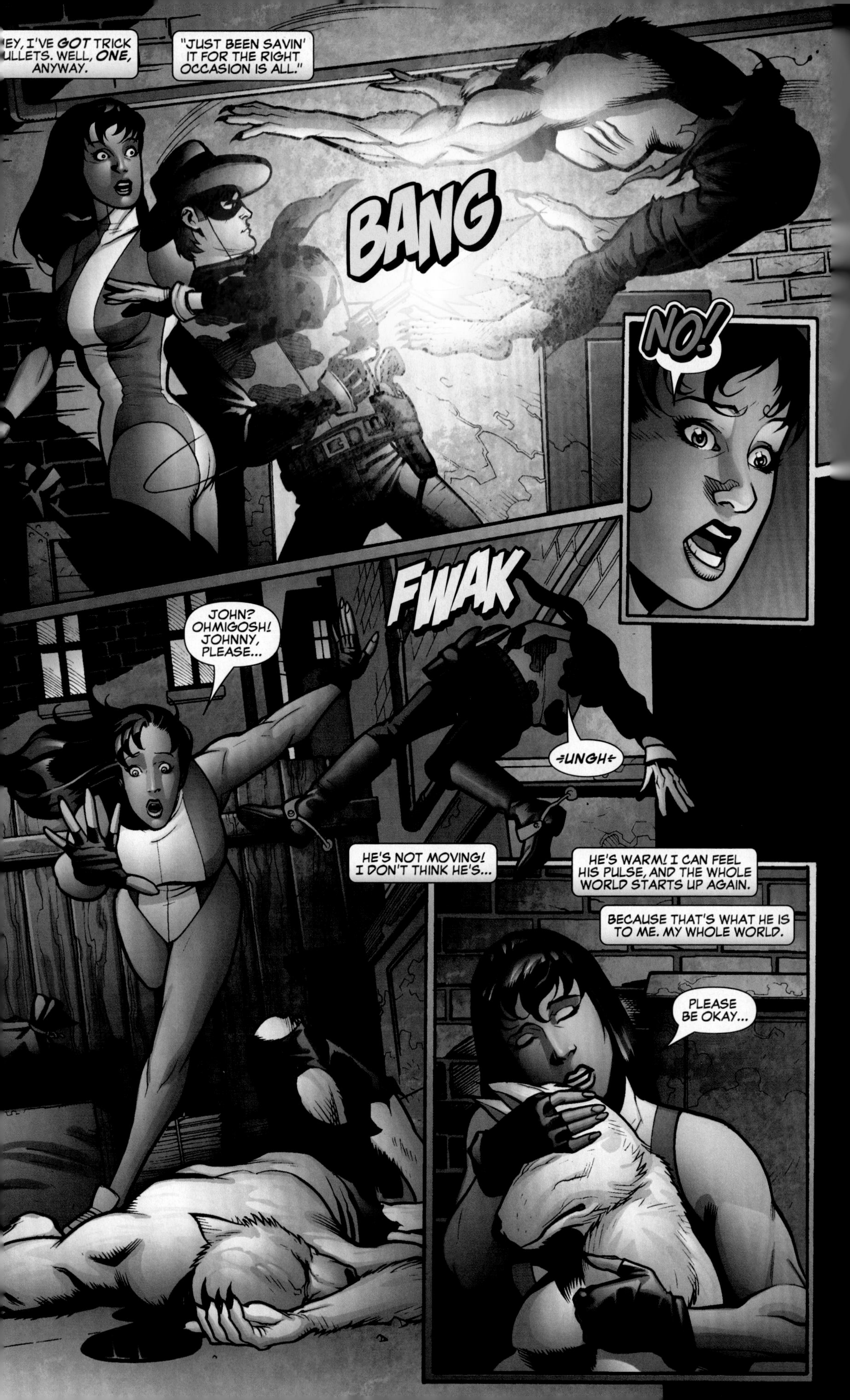
EY, I'VE GOT TRICK ULLETS. WELL, ONE, ANYWAY.
"JUST BEEN SAVIN' IT FOR THE RIGHT OCCASION IS ALL."
BANG
NO!
FWAK
JOHN? OHMIGOSH! JOHNNY, PLEASE...
UNGH
HE'S NOT MOVING! I DON'T THINK HE'S...
HE'S WARM! I CAN FEEL HIS PULSE, AND THE WHOLE WORLD STARTS UP AGAIN.
BECAUSE THAT'S WHAT HE IS TO ME. MY WHOLE WORLD.
PLEASE BE OKAY...

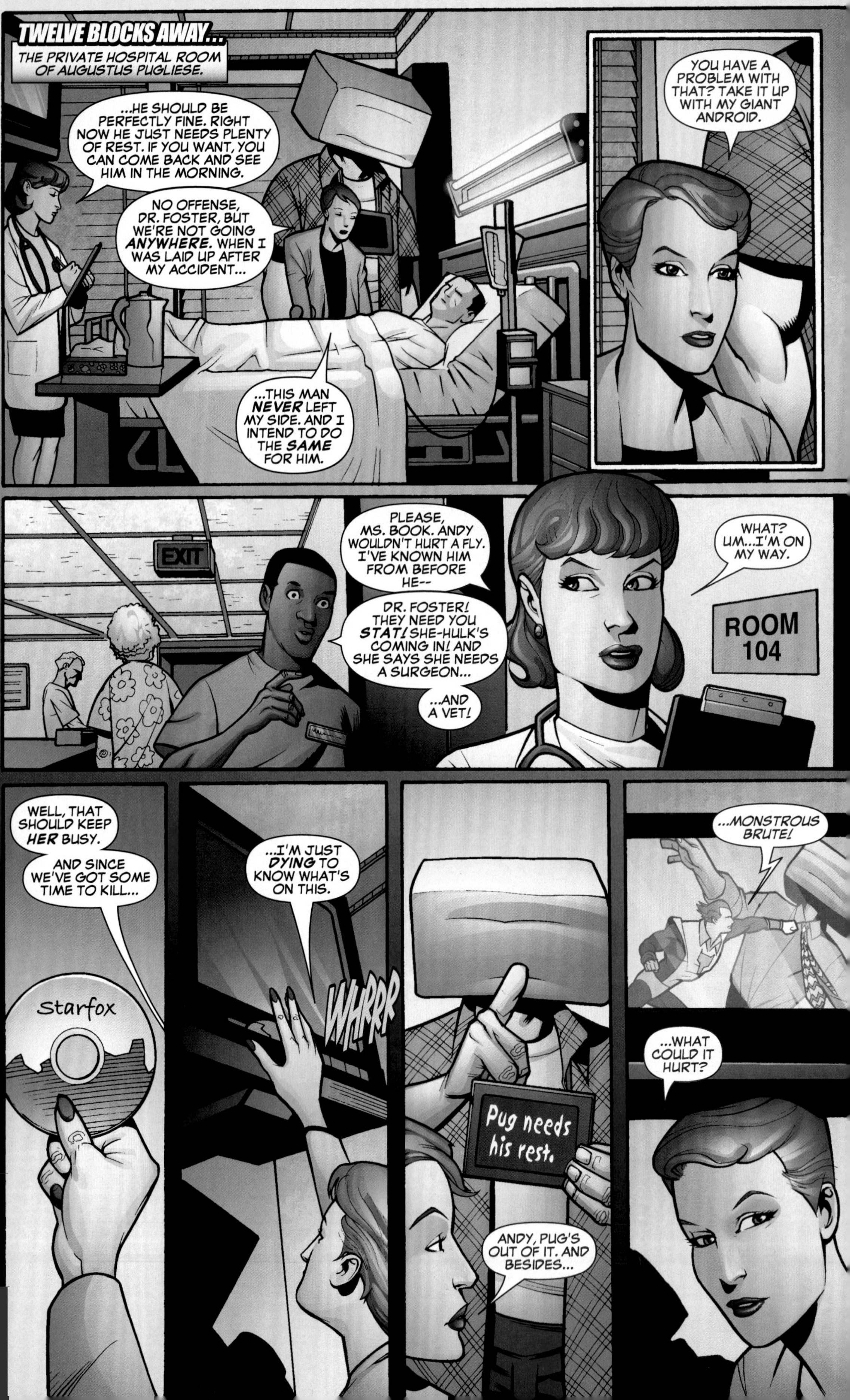
TWELVE BLOCKS AWAY...
THE PRIVATE HOSPITAL ROOM OF AUGUSTUS PUGLIESE.
...HE SHOULD BE PERFECTLY FINE. RIGHT NOW HE JUST NEEDS PLENTY OF REST. IF YOU WANT, YOU CAN COME BACK AND SEE HIM IN THE MORNING.
NO OFFENSE, DR. FOSTER, BUT WE'RE NOT GOING ANYWHERE. WHEN I WAS LAID UP AFTER MY ACCIDENT...
...THIS MAN NEVER LEFT MY SIDE. AND I INTEND TO DO THE SAME FOR HIM.
YOU HAVE A PROBLEM WITH THAT? TAKE IT UP WITH MY GIANT ANDROID.
EXIT
PLEASE, MS. BOOK. ANDY WOULDN'T HURT A FLY. I'VE KNOWN HIM FROM BEFORE HE--
DR. FOSTER! THEY NEED YOU STAT! SHE-HULK'S COMING IN! AND SHE SAYS SHE NEEDS A SURGEON...
...AND A VET!
WHAT? UM...I'M ON MY WAY.
ROOM 104
WELL, THAT SHOULD KEEP HER BUSY.
AND SINCE WE'VE GOT SOME TIME TO KILL...
Starfox
...I'M JUST DYING TO KNOW WHAT'S ON THIS.
WHRRR
Pug needs his rest.
ANDY, PUG'S OUT OF IT. AND BESIDES...
...MONSTROUS BRUTE!
...WHAT COULD IT HURT?

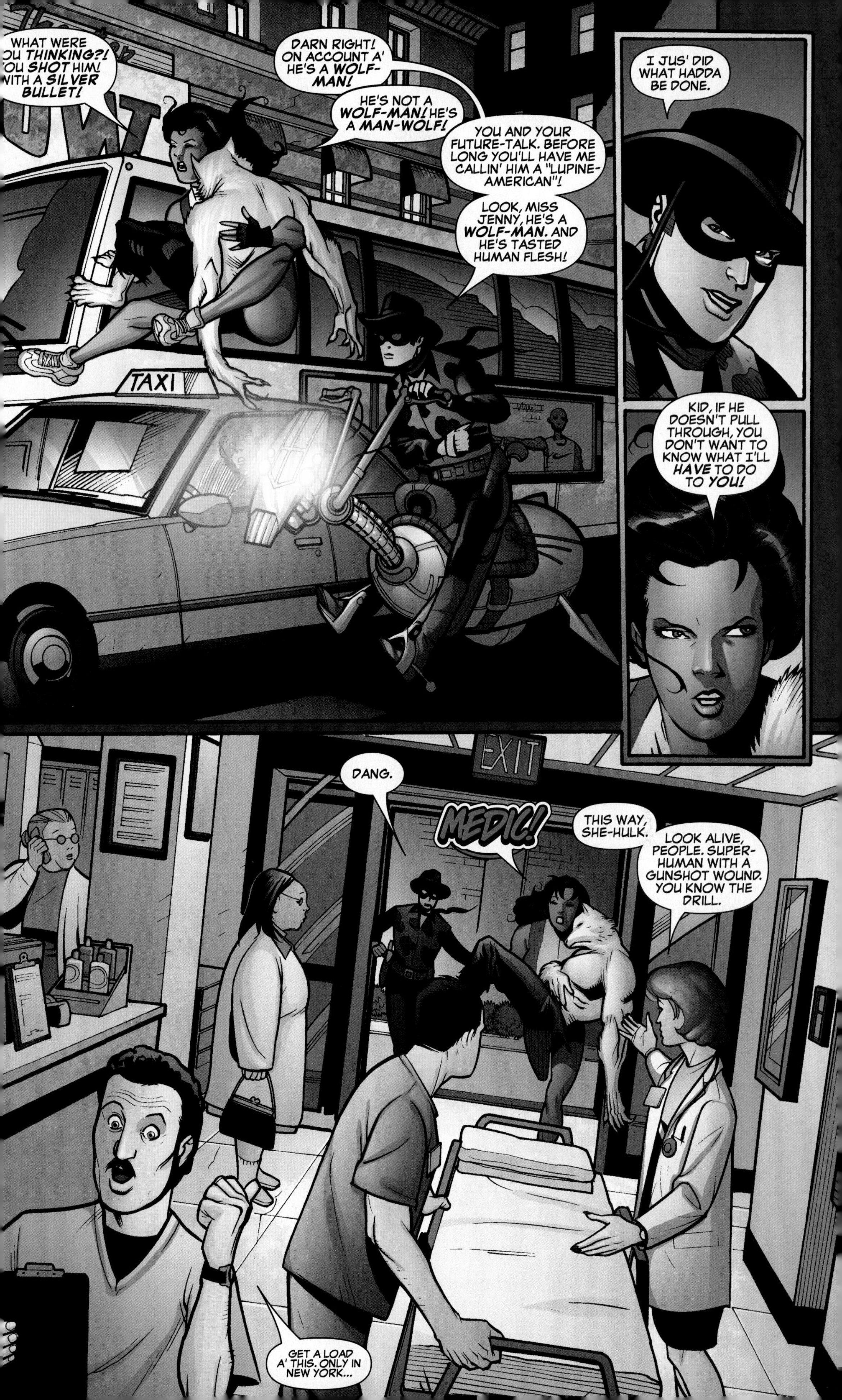
WHAT WERE YOU THINKING?! YOU SHOT HIM! WITH A SILVER BULLET!
DARN RIGHT! ON ACCOUNT A' HE'S A WOLF-MAN!
HE'S NOT A WOLF-MAN! HE'S A MAN-WOLF!
YOU AND YOUR FUTURE-TALK. BEFORE LONG YOU'LL HAVE ME CALLIN' HIM A "LUPINE-AMERICAN"!
LOOK, MISS JENNY, HE'S A WOLF-MAN. AND HE'S TASTED HUMAN FLESH!
TAXI
I JUS' DID WHAT HADDA BE DONE.
KID, IF HE DOESN'T PULL THROUGH, YOU DON'T WANT TO KNOW WHAT I'LL HAVE TO DO TO YOU!
EXIT
DANG.
MEDIC!
THIS WAY, SHE-HULK.
LOOK ALIVE, PEOPLE. SUPER-HUMAN WITH A GUNSHOT WOUND. YOU KNOW THE DRILL.
GET A LOAD A' THIS. ONLY IN NEW YORK...

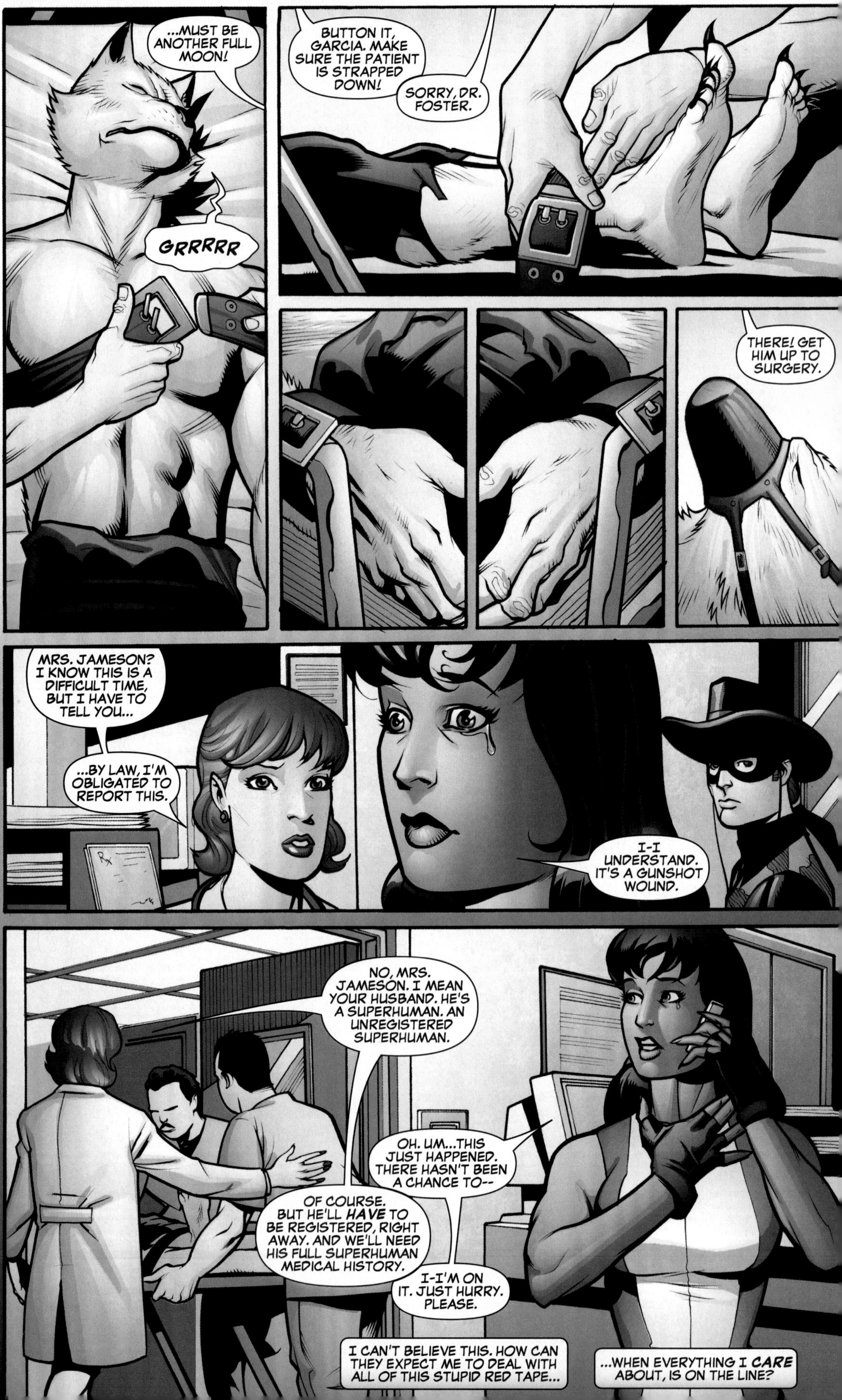
...MUST BE ANOTHER FULL MOON!
GRRRRR
BUTTON IT, GARCIA. MAKE SURE THE PATIENT IS STRAPPED DOWN!
SORRY, DR. FOSTER.
THERE! GET HIM UP TO SURGERY.
MRS. JAMESON? I KNOW THIS IS A DIFFICULT TIME, BUT I HAVE TO TELL YOU...
...BY LAW, I'M OBLIGATED TO REPORT THIS.
I-I UNDERSTAND. IT'S A GUNSHOT WOUND.
NO, MRS. JAMESON. I MEAN YOUR HUSBAND. HE'S A SUPERHUMAN. AN UNREGISTERED SUPERHUMAN.
OH. UM...THIS JUST HAPPENED. THERE HASN'T BEEN A CHANCE TO--
OF COURSE. BUT HE'LL HAVE TO BE REGISTERED, RIGHT AWAY. AND WE'LL NEED HIS FULL SUPERHUMAN MEDICAL HISTORY.
I-I'M ON IT. JUST HURRY. PLEASE.
I CAN'T BELIEVE THIS. HOW CAN THEY EXPECT ME TO DEAL WITH ALL OF THIS STUPID RED TAPE...
...WHEN EVERYTHING I CARE ABOUT, IS ON THE LINE?

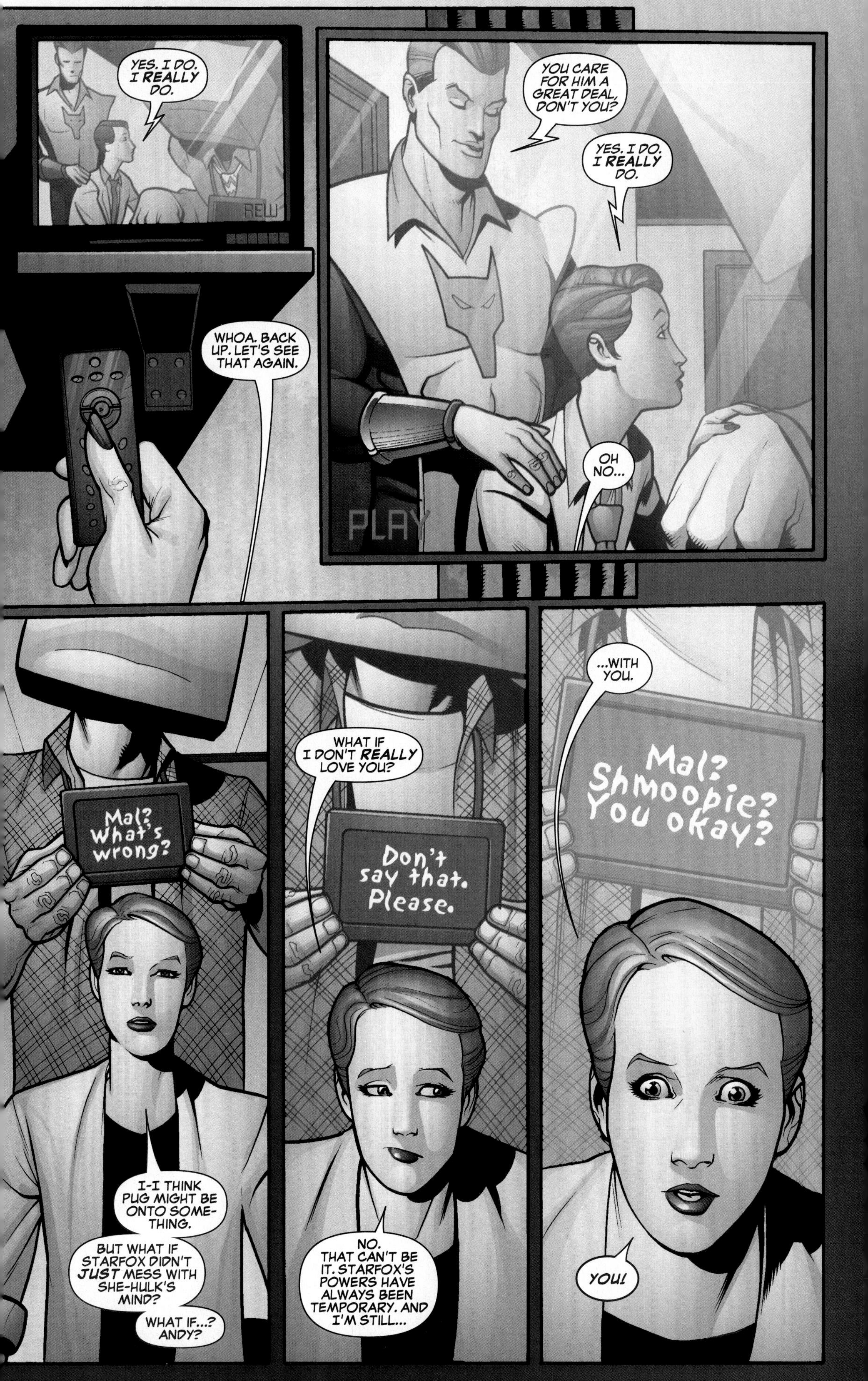
YES. I DO. I REALLY DO.
REW
YOU CARE FOR HIM A GREAT DEAL, DON'T YOU?
YES. I DO. I REALLY DO.
WHOA. BACK UP. LET'S SEE THAT AGAIN.
OH NO...
PLAY
Mal? What's wrong?
I-I THINK PUG MIGHT BE ONTO SOME-THING.
BUT WHAT IF STARFOX DIDN'T JUST MESS WITH SHE-HULK'S MIND?
WHAT IF...? ANDY?
WHAT IF I DON'T REALLY LOVE YOU?
Don't say that. Please.
NO. THAT CAN'T BE IT. STARFOX'S POWERS HAVE ALWAYS BEEN TEMPORARY. AND I'M STILL...
...WITH YOU.
Mal? Shmoopie? You okay?
YOU!

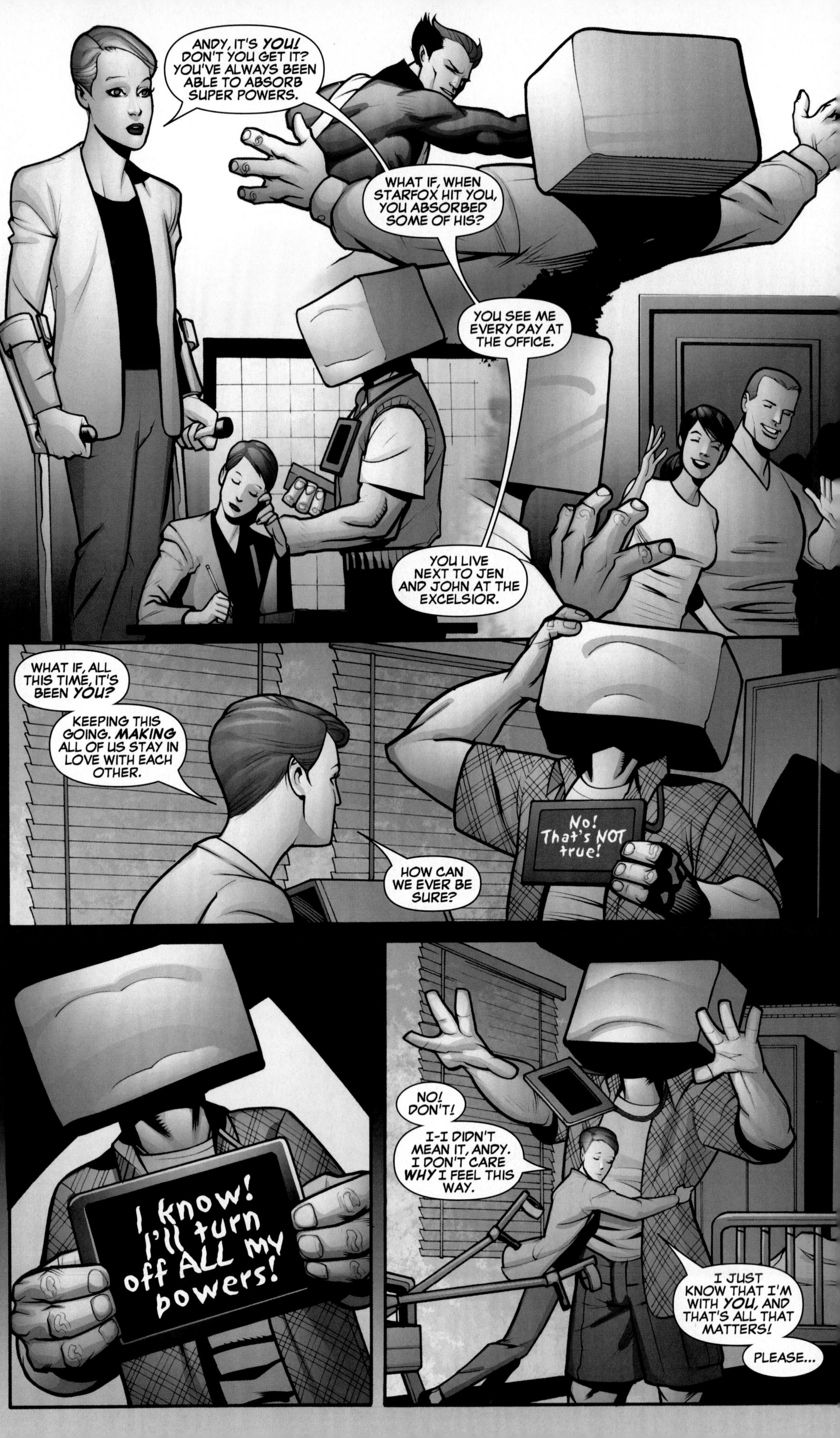

ANDY, IT'S YOU! DON'T YOU GET IT? YOU'VE ALWAYS BEEN ABLE TO ABSORB SUPER POWERS.
WHAT IF, WHEN STARFOX HIT YOU, YOU ABSORBED SOME OF HIS?
YOU SEE ME EVERY DAY AT THE OFFICE.
YOU LIVE NEXT TO JEN AND JOHN AT THE EXCELSIOR.
WHAT IF, ALL THIS TIME, IT'S BEEN YOU?
KEEPING THIS GOING. MAKING ALL OF US STAY IN LOVE WITH EACH OTHER.
HOW CAN WE EVER BE SURE?
No! That's NOT true!
I know! I'll turn off ALL my powers!
NO! DON'T!
I-I DIDN'T MEAN IT, ANDY. I DON'T CARE WHY I FEEL THIS WAY.
I JUST KNOW THAT I'M WITH YOU, AND THAT'S ALL THAT MATTERS!
PLEASE...

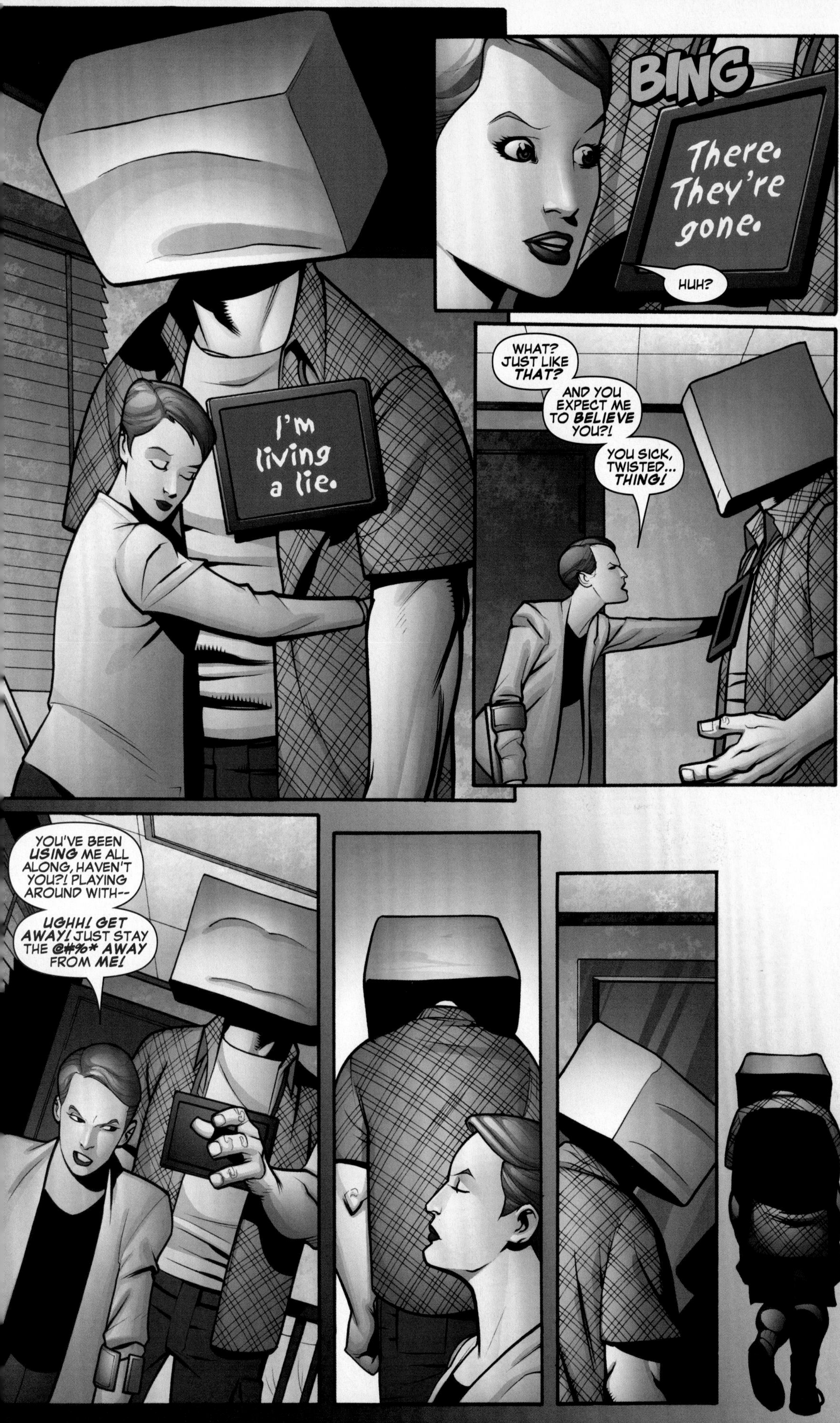
I'm living a lie.
BING
There. They're gone.
HUH?
WHAT? JUST LIKE THAT?
AND YOU EXPECT ME TO BELIEVE YOU?!
YOU SICK, TWISTED... THING!
YOU'VE BEEN USING ME ALL ALONG, HAVEN'T YOU?! PLAYING AROUND WITH--
UGHH! GET AWAY! JUST STAY THE @#%* AWAY FROM ME!

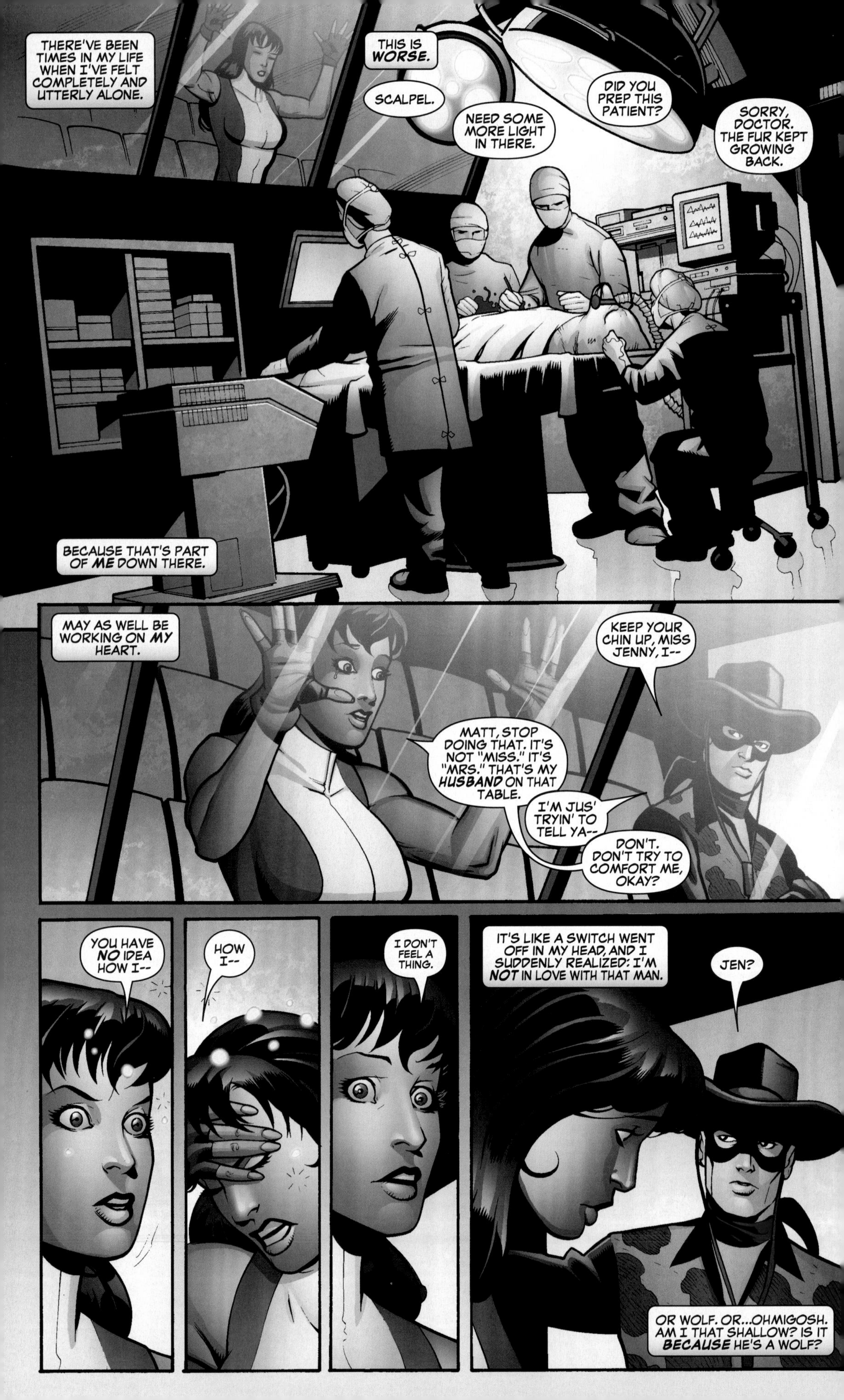

THERE'VE BEEN TIMES IN MY LIFE WHEN I'VE FELT COMPLETELY AND UTTERLY ALONE.
THIS IS *WORSE.*
SCALPEL.
NEED SOME MORE LIGHT IN THERE.
DID YOU PREP THIS PATIENT?
SORRY, DOCTOR. THE FUR KEPT GROWING BACK.
BECAUSE THAT'S PART OF *ME* DOWN THERE.
MAY AS WELL BE WORKING ON *MY* HEART.
KEEP YOUR CHIN UP, MISS JENNY, I--
MATT, STOP DOING THAT. IT'S NOT "MISS." IT'S "MRS." THAT'S MY *HUSBAND* ON THAT TABLE.
I'M JUS' TRYIN' TO TELL YA--
DON'T. DON'T TRY TO COMFORT ME, OKAY?
YOU HAVE *NO* IDEA HOW I--
HOW I--
I DON'T FEEL A THING.
IT'S LIKE A SWITCH WENT OFF IN MY HEAD, AND I SUDDENLY REALIZED: I'M *NOT* IN LOVE WITH THAT MAN.
JEN?
OR WOLF. OR...OHMIGOSH. AM I THAT SHALLOW? IS IT *BECAUSE* HE'S A WOLF?

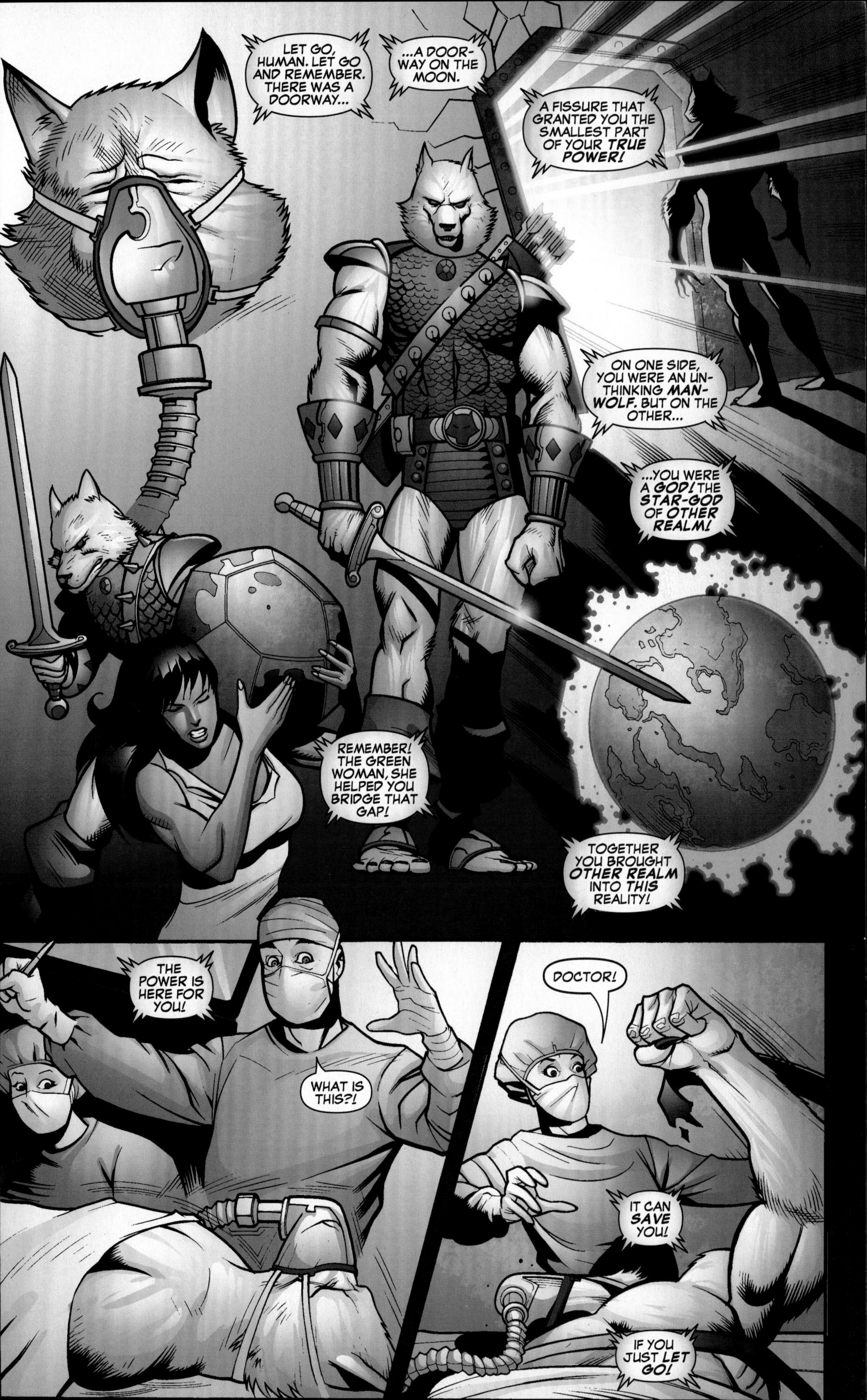
LET GO, HUMAN. LET GO AND REMEMBER. THERE WAS A DOORWAY...
...A DOORWAY ON THE MOON.
A FISSURE THAT GRANTED YOU THE SMALLEST PART OF YOUR TRUE POWER!
ON ONE SIDE, YOU WERE AN UN-THINKING MAN-WOLF. BUT ON THE OTHER...
...YOU WERE A GOD! THE STAR-GOD OF OTHER REALM!
REMEMBER! THE GREEN WOMAN, SHE HELPED YOU BRIDGE THAT GAP!
TOGETHER YOU BROUGHT OTHER REALM INTO THIS REALITY!
THE POWER IS HERE FOR YOU!
WHAT IS THIS?!
DOCTOR!
IT CAN SAVE YOU!
IF YOU JUST LET GO!

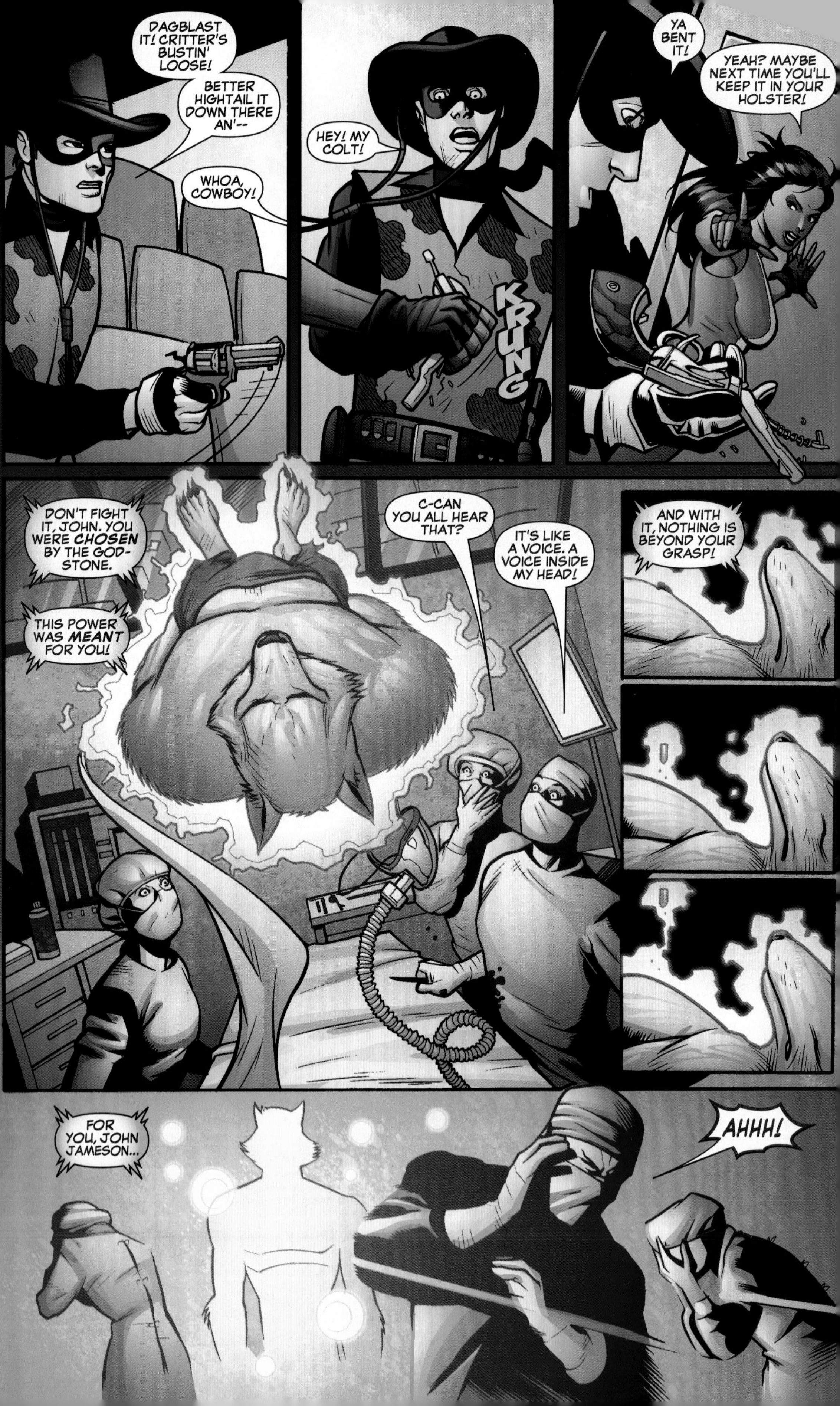
DAGBLAST IT! CRITTER'S BUSTIN' LOOSE!
BETTER HIGHTAIL IT DOWN THERE AN'--
WHOA, COWBOY!
HEY! MY COLT!
KRUNG
YA BENT IT!
YEAH? MAYBE NEXT TIME YOU'LL KEEP IT IN YOUR HOLSTER!
DON'T FIGHT IT, JOHN. YOU WERE CHOSEN BY THE GOD-STONE.
THIS POWER WAS MEANT FOR YOU!
C-CAN YOU ALL HEAR THAT?
IT'S LIKE A VOICE. A VOICE INSIDE MY HEAD!
AND WITH IT, NOTHING IS BEYOND YOUR GRASP!
FOR YOU, JOHN JAMESON...
AHHH!

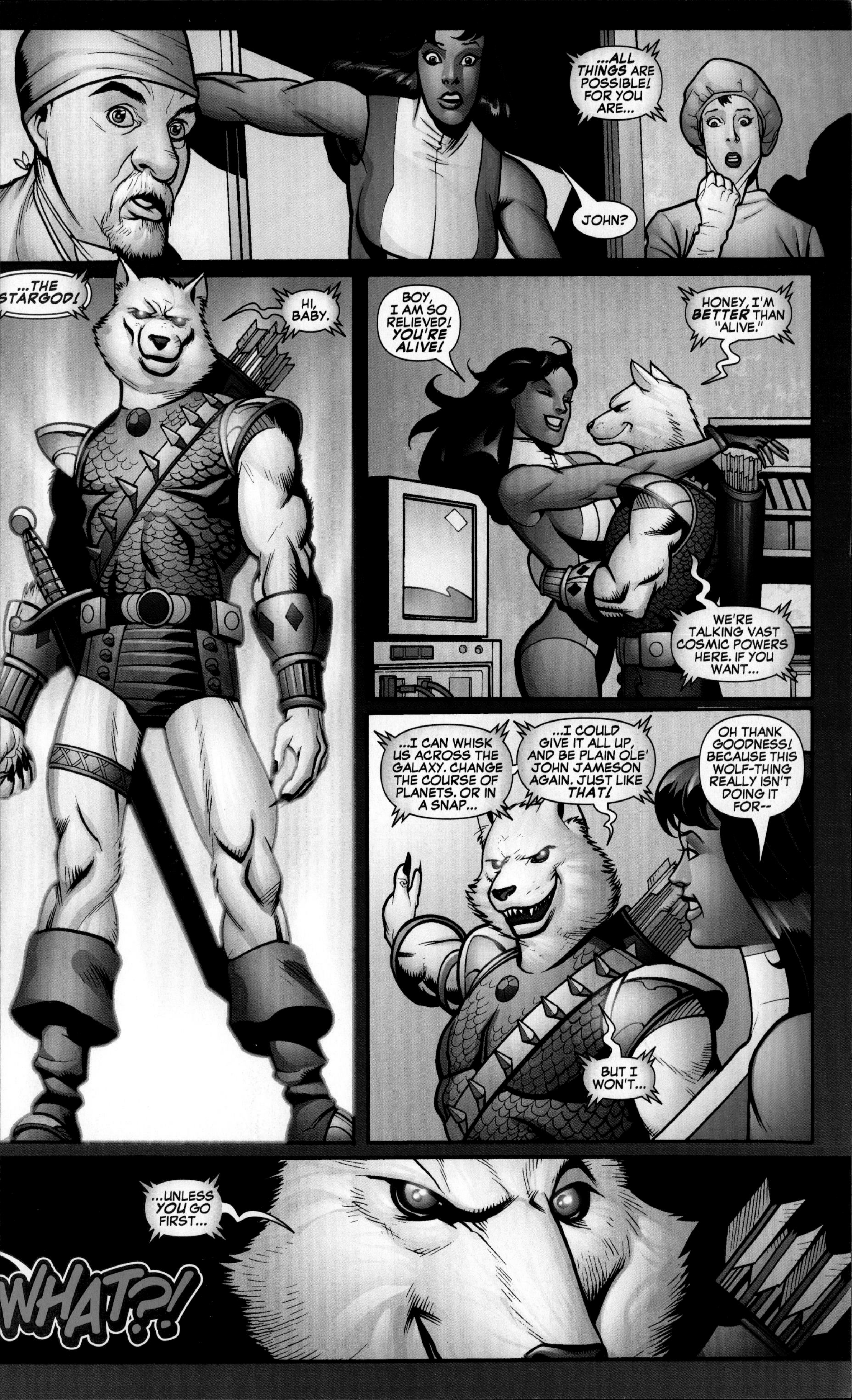
...ALL THINGS ARE POSSIBLE! FOR YOU ARE...
JOHN?
...THE STARGOD!
HI, BABY.
BOY, I AM SO RELIEVED! YOU'RE ALIVE!
HONEY, I'M BETTER THAN "ALIVE."
WE'RE TALKING VAST COSMIC POWERS HERE. IF YOU WANT...
...I CAN WHISK US ACROSS THE GALAXY. CHANGE THE COURSE OF PLANETS. OR IN A SNAP...
...I COULD GIVE IT ALL UP, AND BE PLAIN OLE' JOHN JAMESON AGAIN. JUST LIKE THAT!
OH THANK GOODNESS! BECAUSE THIS WOLF-THING REALLY ISN'T DOING IT FOR--
BUT I WON'T...
...UNLESS YOU GO FIRST...
WHAT?!

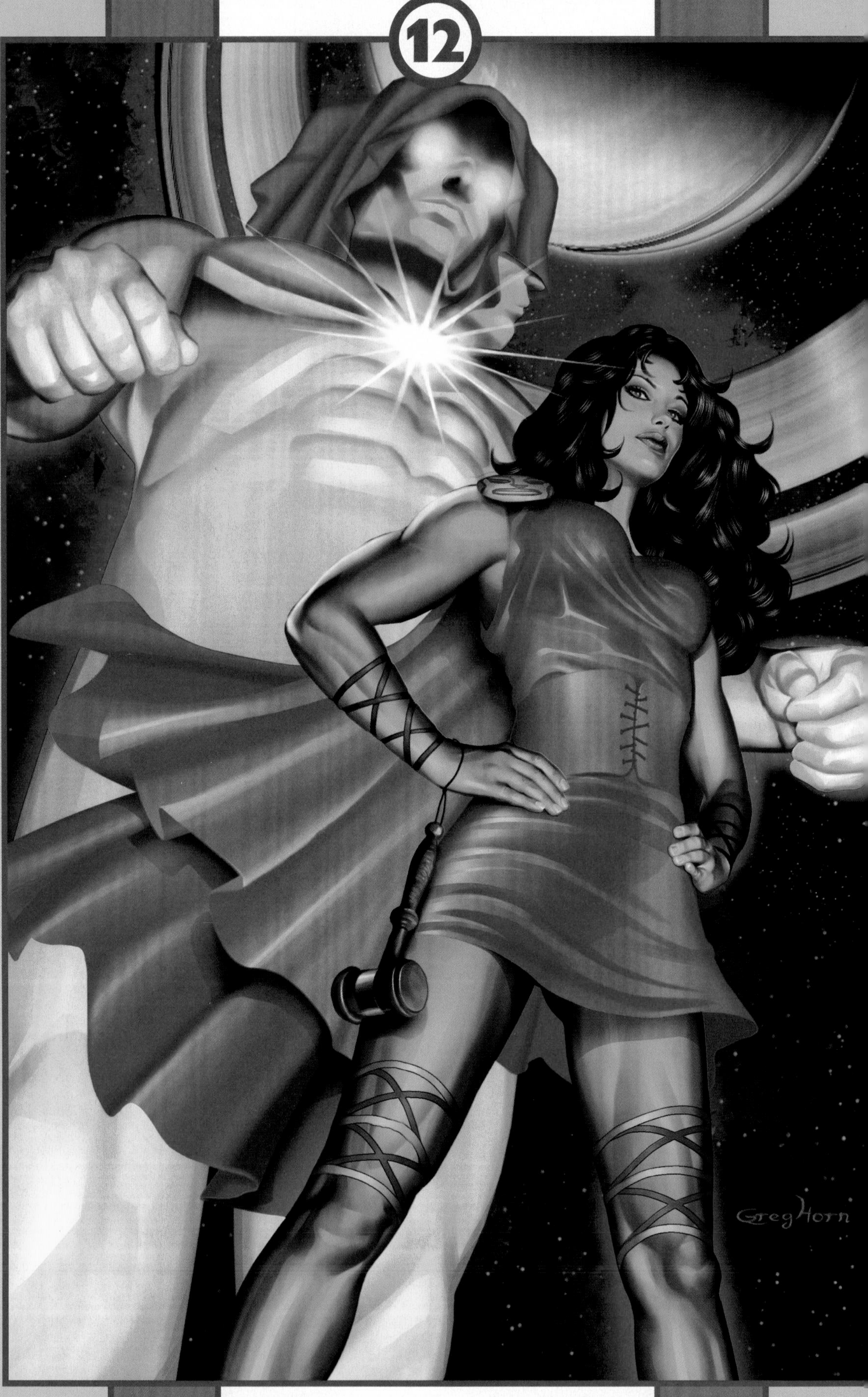
12
Greg Horn

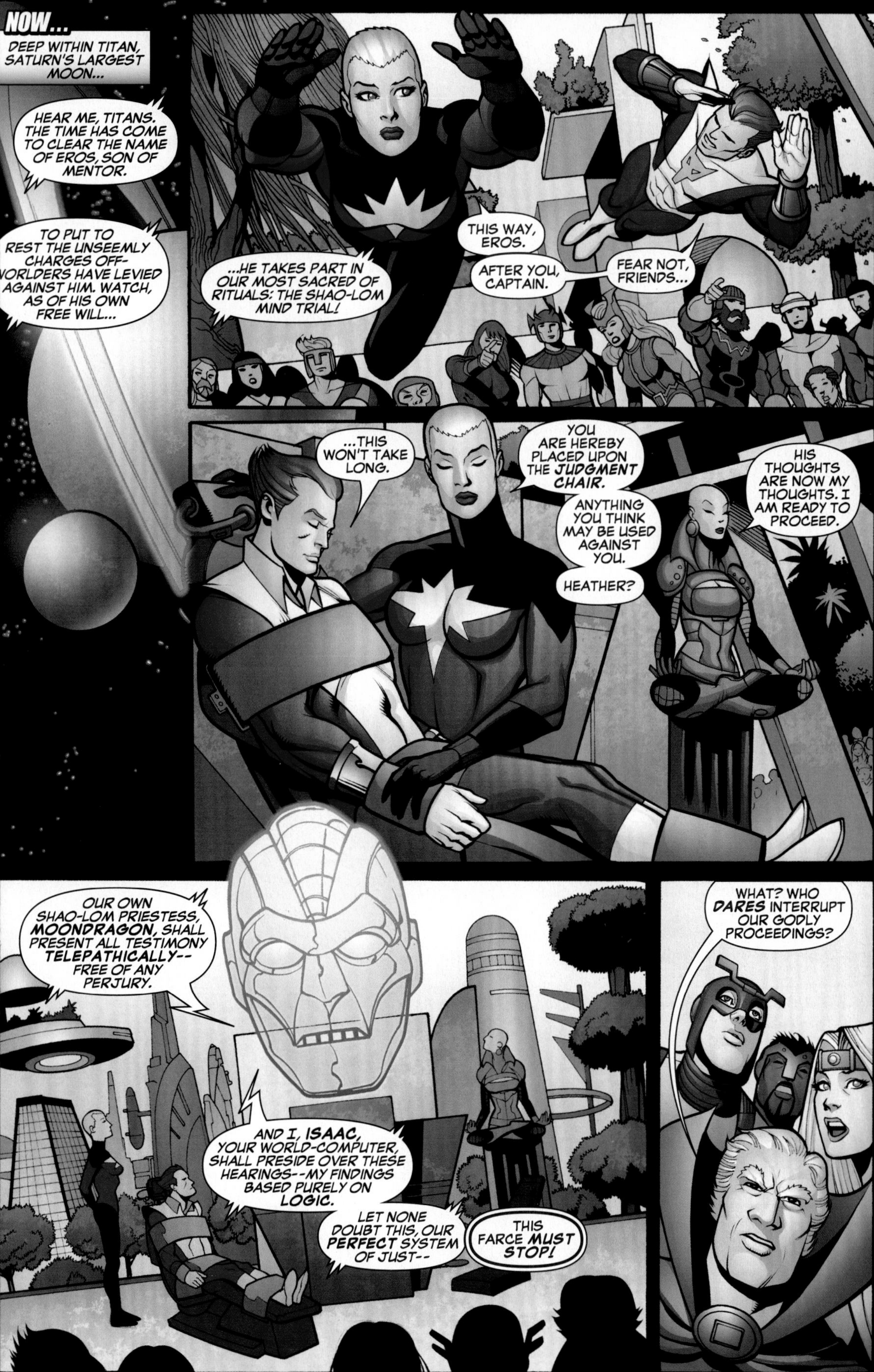
NOW...
DEEP WITHIN TITAN, SATURN'S LARGEST MOON...
HEAR ME, TITANS. THE TIME HAS COME TO CLEAR THE NAME OF EROS, SON OF MENTOR.
TO PUT TO REST THE UNSEEMLY CHARGES OFF-WORLDERS HAVE LEVIED AGAINST HIM. WATCH, AS OF HIS OWN FREE WILL...
...HE TAKES PART IN OUR MOST SACRED OF RITUALS: THE SHAO-LOM MIND TRIAL!
THIS WAY, EROS.
AFTER YOU, CAPTAIN.
FEAR NOT, FRIENDS...
...THIS WON'T TAKE LONG.
YOU ARE HEREBY PLACED UPON THE JUDGMENT CHAIR.
ANYTHING YOU THINK MAY BE USED AGAINST YOU.
HEATHER?
HIS THOUGHTS ARE NOW MY THOUGHTS. I AM READY TO PROCEED.
OUR OWN SHAO-LOM PRIESTESS, MOONDRAGON, SHALL PRESENT ALL TESTIMONY TELEPATHICALLY-- FREE OF ANY PERJURY.
AND I, ISAAC, YOUR WORLD-COMPUTER, SHALL PRESIDE OVER THESE HEARINGS--MY FINDINGS BASED PURELY ON LOGIC.
LET NONE DOUBT THIS, OUR PERFECT SYSTEM OF JUST--
THIS FARCE MUST STOP!
WHAT? WHO DARES INTERRUPT OUR GODLY PROCEEDINGS?

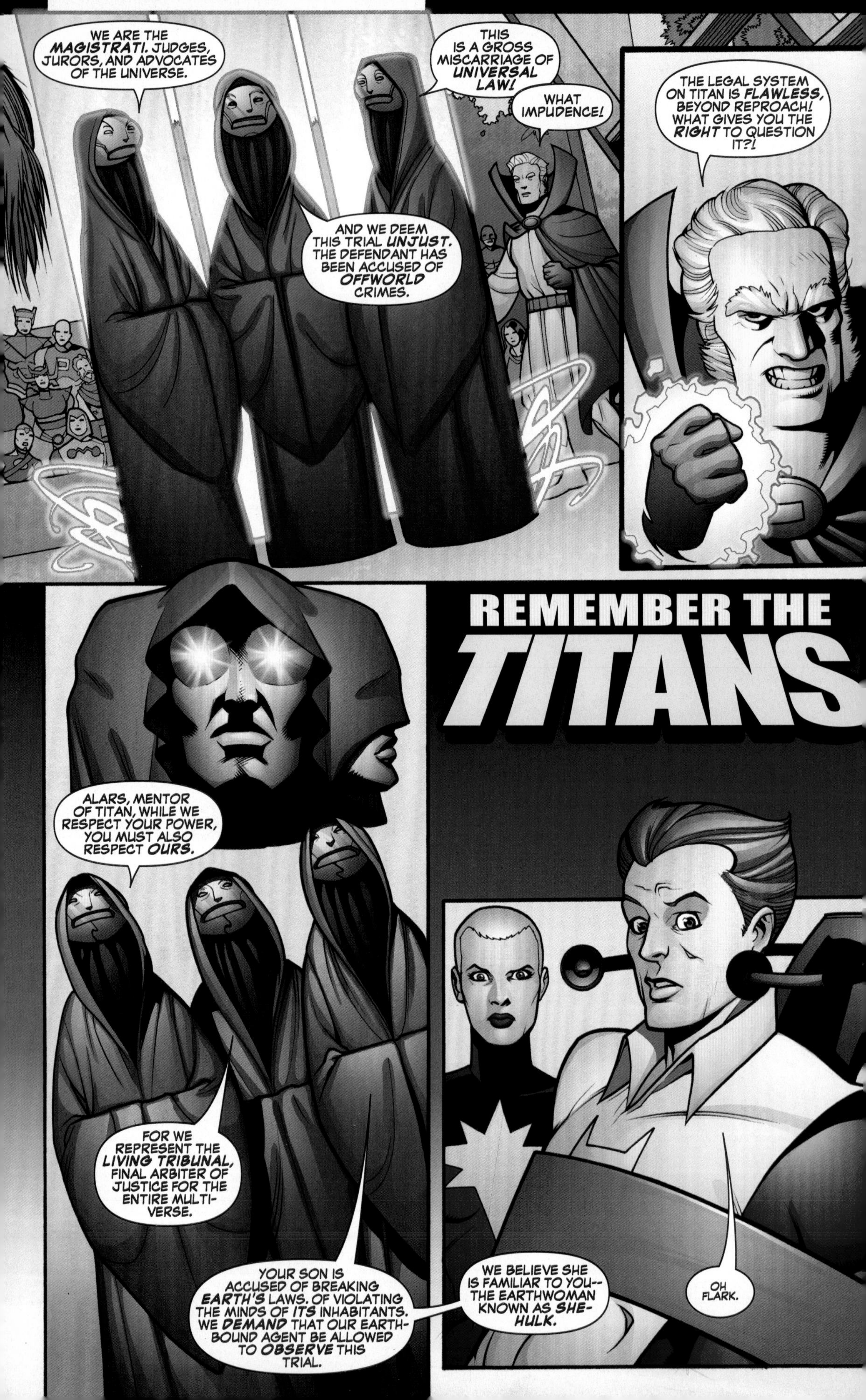
WE ARE THE MAGISTRATI. JUDGES, JURORS, AND ADVOCATES OF THE UNIVERSE.
THIS IS A GROSS MISCARRIAGE OF UNIVERSAL LAW!
WHAT IMPUDENCE!
AND WE DEEM THIS TRIAL UNJUST. THE DEFENDANT HAS BEEN ACCUSED OF OFFWORLD CRIMES.
THE LEGAL SYSTEM ON TITAN IS FLAWLESS, BEYOND REPROACH! WHAT GIVES YOU THE RIGHT TO QUESTION IT?!
REMEMBER THE TITANS
ALARS, MENTOR OF TITAN, WHILE WE RESPECT YOUR POWER, YOU MUST ALSO RESPECT OURS.
FOR WE REPRESENT THE LIVING TRIBUNAL, FINAL ARBITER OF JUSTICE FOR THE ENTIRE MULTI-VERSE.
YOUR SON IS ACCUSED OF BREAKING EARTH'S LAWS. OF VIOLATING THE MINDS OF ITS INHABITANTS. WE DEMAND THAT OUR EARTH-BOUND AGENT BE ALLOWED TO OBSERVE THIS TRIAL.
WE BELIEVE SHE IS FAMILIAR TO YOU-- THE EARTHWOMAN KNOWN AS SHE-HULK.
OH FLARK.

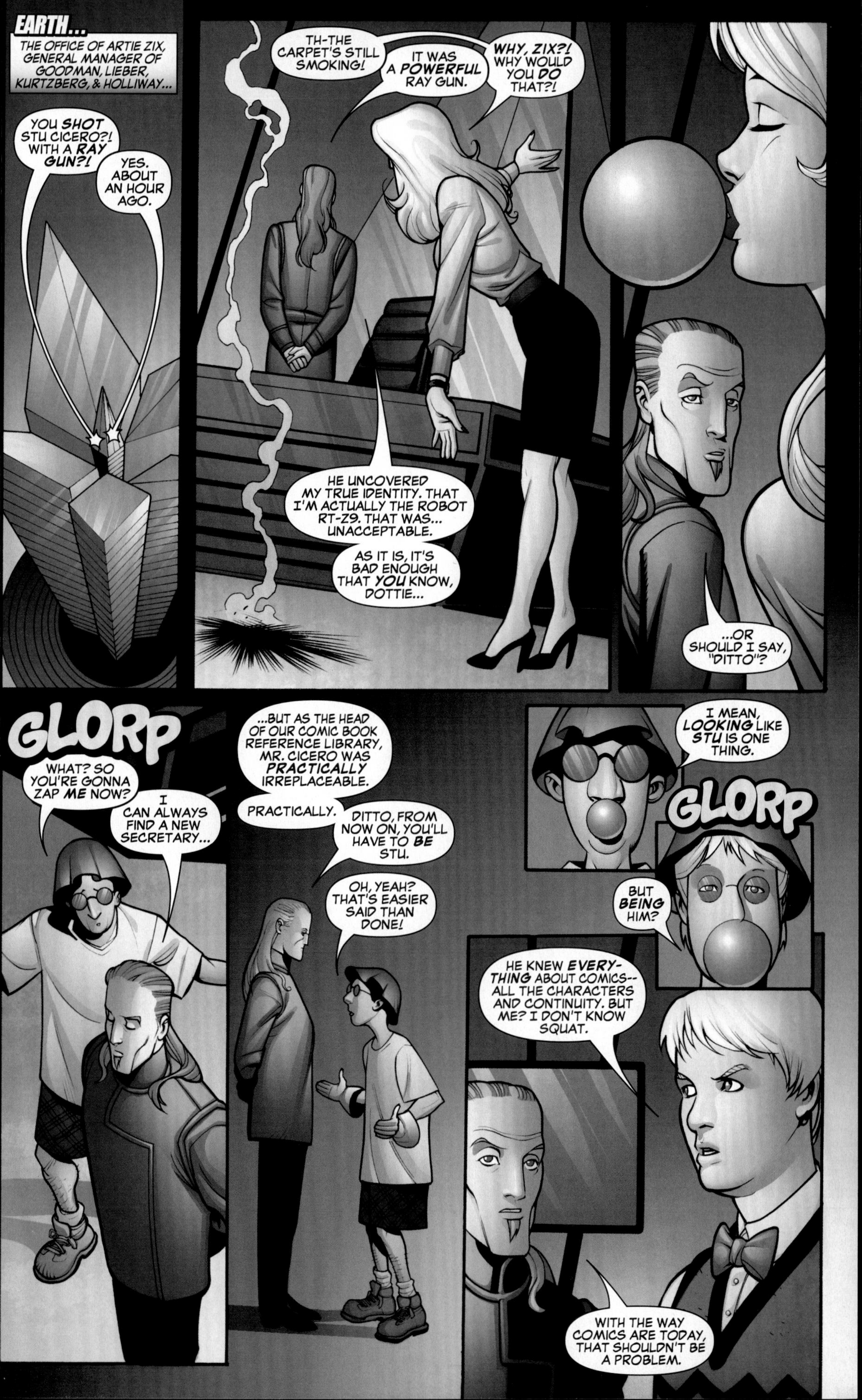
EARTH...
THE OFFICE OF ARTIE ZIX, GENERAL MANAGER OF GOODMAN, LIEBER, KURTZBERG, & HOLLIWAY...
YOU SHOT STU CICERO?! WITH A RAY GUN?!
YES. ABOUT AN HOUR AGO.
TH-THE CARPET'S STILL SMOKING!
IT WAS A POWERFUL RAY GUN.
WHY, ZIX?! WHY WOULD YOU DO THAT?!
HE UNCOVERED MY TRUE IDENTITY. THAT I'M ACTUALLY THE ROBOT RT-Z9. THAT WAS... UNACCEPTABLE.
AS IT IS, IT'S BAD ENOUGH THAT YOU KNOW, DOTTIE...
...OR SHOULD I SAY, "DITTO"?
GLORP
WHAT? SO YOU'RE GONNA ZAP ME NOW?
I CAN ALWAYS FIND A NEW SECRETARY...
...BUT AS THE HEAD OF OUR COMIC BOOK REFERENCE LIBRARY, MR. CICERO WAS PRACTICALLY IRREPLACEABLE.
PRACTICALLY.
DITTO, FROM NOW ON, YOU'LL HAVE TO BE STU.
OH, YEAH? THAT'S EASIER SAID THAN DONE!
I MEAN, LOOKING LIKE STU IS ONE THING.
GLORP
BUT BEING HIM?
HE KNEW EVERY-THING ABOUT COMICS-- ALL THE CHARACTERS AND CONTINUITY. BUT ME? I DON'T KNOW SQUAT.
WITH THE WAY COMICS ARE TODAY, THAT SHOULDN'T BE A PROBLEM.

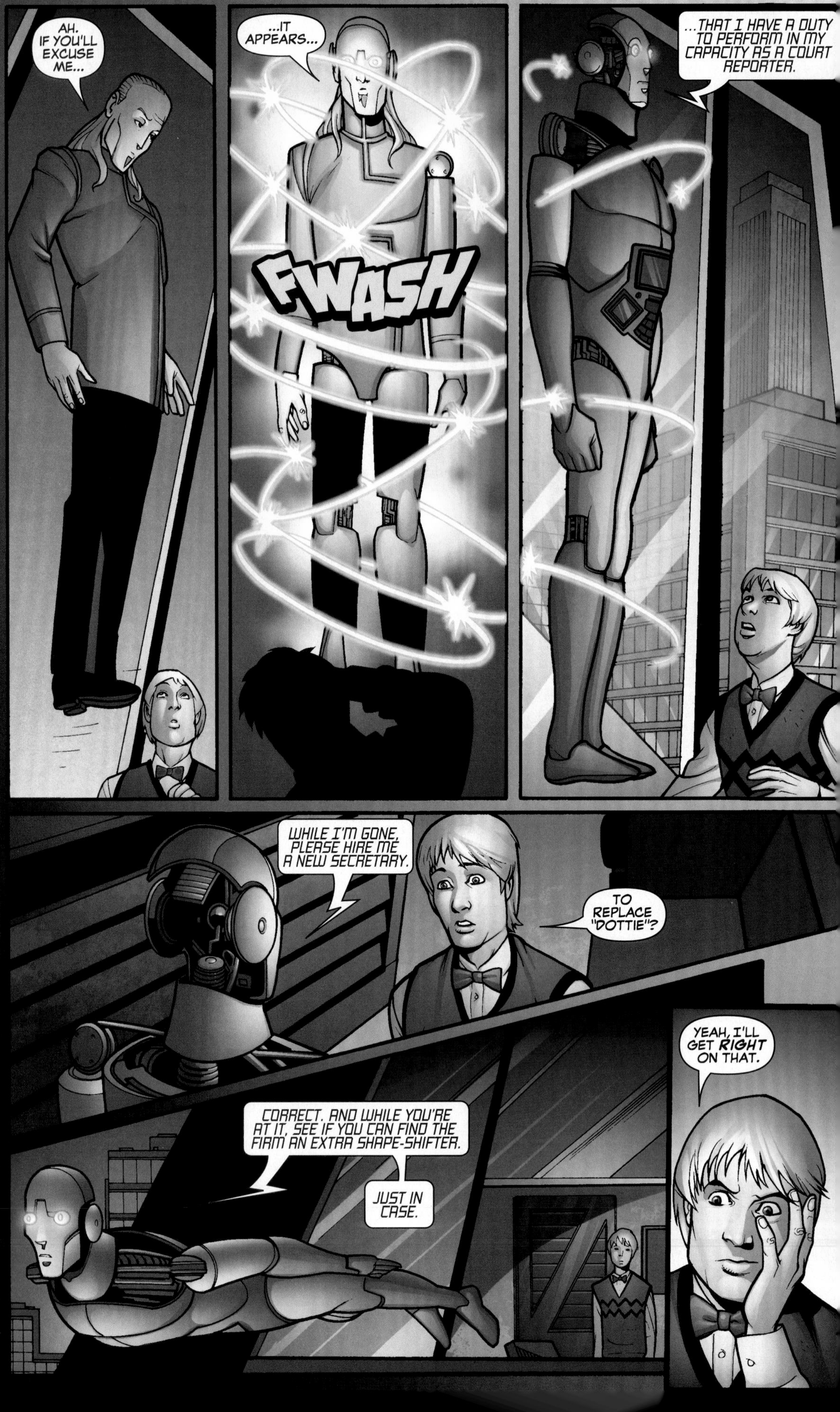
AH. IF YOU'LL EXCUSE ME...
...IT APPEARS...
FWASH
...THAT I HAVE A DUTY TO PERFORM IN MY CAPACITY AS A COURT REPORTER.
WHILE I'M GONE, PLEASE HIRE ME A NEW SECRETARY.
TO REPLACE "DOTTIE"?
CORRECT. AND WHILE YOU'RE AT IT, SEE IF YOU CAN FIND THE FIRM AN EXTRA SHAPE-SHIFTER.
JUST IN CASE.
YEAH, I'LL GET RIGHT ON THAT.

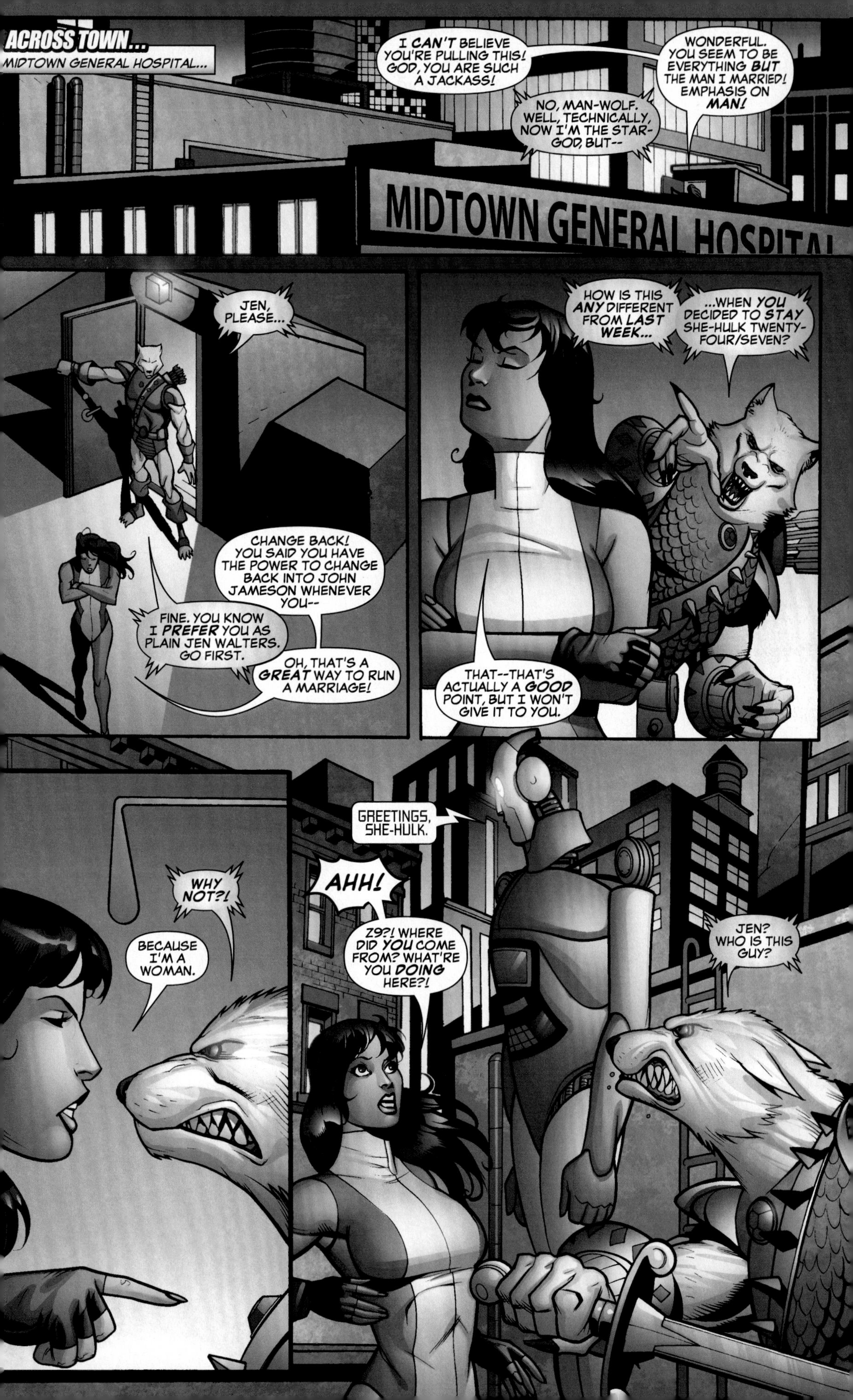
ACROSS TOWN...
MIDTOWN GENERAL HOSPITAL...
I CAN'T BELIEVE YOU'RE PULLING THIS! GOD, YOU ARE SUCH A JACKASS!
NO, MAN-WOLF. WELL, TECHNICALLY, NOW I'M THE STAR-GOD, BUT--
WONDERFUL. YOU SEEM TO BE EVERYTHING BUT THE MAN I MARRIED! EMPHASIS ON MAN!
MIDTOWN GENERAL HOSPITAL
JEN, PLEASE...
CHANGE BACK! YOU SAID YOU HAVE THE POWER TO CHANGE BACK INTO JOHN JAMESON WHENEVER YOU--
FINE. YOU KNOW I PREFER YOU AS PLAIN JEN WALTERS. GO FIRST.
OH, THAT'S A GREAT WAY TO RUN A MARRIAGE!
HOW IS THIS ANY DIFFERENT FROM LAST WEEK...
...WHEN YOU DECIDED TO STAY SHE-HULK TWENTY-FOUR/SEVEN?
THAT--THAT'S ACTUALLY A GOOD POINT, BUT I WON'T GIVE IT TO YOU.
WHY NOT?!
BECAUSE I'M A WOMAN.
GREETINGS, SHE-HULK.
AHH!
Z9?! WHERE DID YOU COME FROM? WHAT'RE YOU DOING HERE?!
JEN? WHO IS THIS GUY?

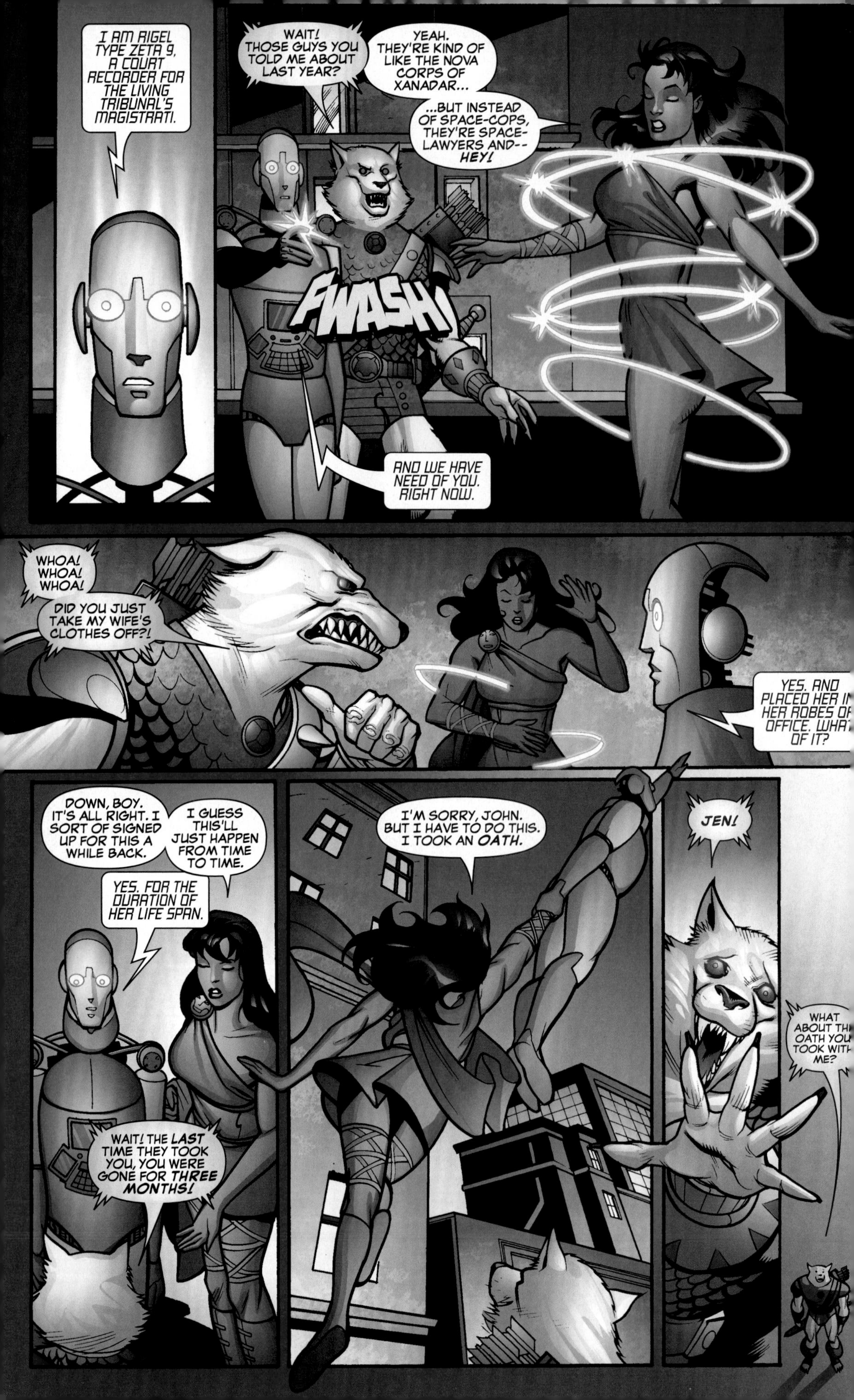
I AM RIGEL TYPE ZETA 9, A COURT RECORDER FOR THE LIVING TRIBUNAL'S MAGISTRATI.
WAIT! THOSE GUYS YOU TOLD ME ABOUT LAST YEAR?
YEAH. THEY'RE KIND OF LIKE THE NOVA CORPS OF XANADAR...
...BUT INSTEAD OF SPACE-COPS, THEY'RE SPACE-LAWYERS AND-- HEY!
FWASH!
AND WE HAVE NEED OF YOU. RIGHT NOW.
WHOA! WHOA! WHOA!
DID YOU JUST TAKE MY WIFE'S CLOTHES OFF?!
YES. AND PLACED HER IN HER ROBES OF OFFICE. WHAT OF IT?
DOWN, BOY. IT'S ALL RIGHT. I SORT OF SIGNED UP FOR THIS A WHILE BACK.
I GUESS THIS'LL JUST HAPPEN FROM TIME TO TIME.
YES. FOR THE DURATION OF HER LIFE SPAN.
WAIT! THE LAST TIME THEY TOOK YOU, YOU WERE GONE FOR THREE MONTHS!
I'M SORRY, JOHN. BUT I HAVE TO DO THIS. I TOOK AN OATH.
JEN!
WHAT ABOUT THE OATH YOU TOOK WITH ME?

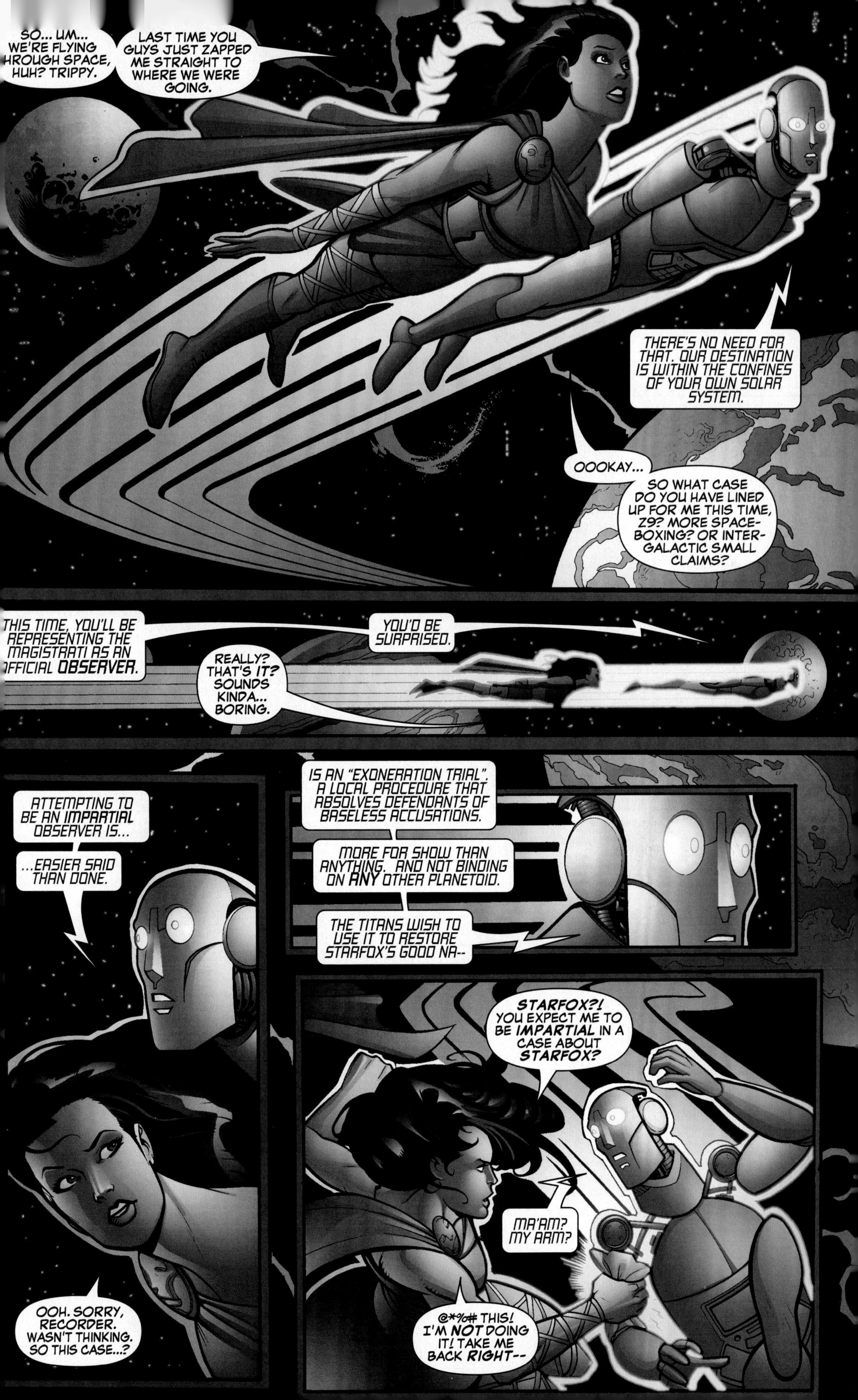
SO... UM... WE'RE FLYING HROUGH SPACE, HUH? TRIPPY.
LAST TIME YOU GUYS JUST ZAPPED ME STRAIGHT TO WHERE WE WERE GOING.
THERE'S NO NEED FOR THAT. OUR DESTINATION IS WITHIN THE CONFINES OF YOUR OWN SOLAR SYSTEM.
OOOKAY...
SO WHAT CASE DO YOU HAVE LINED UP FOR ME THIS TIME, Z9? MORE SPACE-BOXING? OR INTER-GALACTIC SMALL CLAIMS?
THIS TIME, YOU'LL BE REPRESENTING THE MAGISTRATI AS AN FFICIAL OBSERVER.
REALLY? THAT'S IT? SOUNDS KINDA... BORING.
YOU'D BE SURPRISED.
ATTEMPTING TO BE AN IMPARTIAL OBSERVER IS...
...EASIER SAID THAN DONE.
OOH. SORRY, RECORDER. WASN'T THINKING. SO THIS CASE...?
IS AN "EXONERATION TRIAL". A LOCAL PROCEDURE THAT ABSOLVES DEFENDANTS OF BASELESS ACCUSATIONS.
MORE FOR SHOW THAN ANYTHING. AND NOT BINDING ON ANY OTHER PLANETOID.
THE TITANS WISH TO USE IT TO RESTORE STARFOX'S GOOD NA--
STARFOX?! YOU EXPECT ME TO BE IMPARTIAL IN A CASE ABOUT STARFOX?
MA'AM? MY ARM?
@*%# THIS! I'M NOT DOING IT! TAKE ME BACK RIGHT--

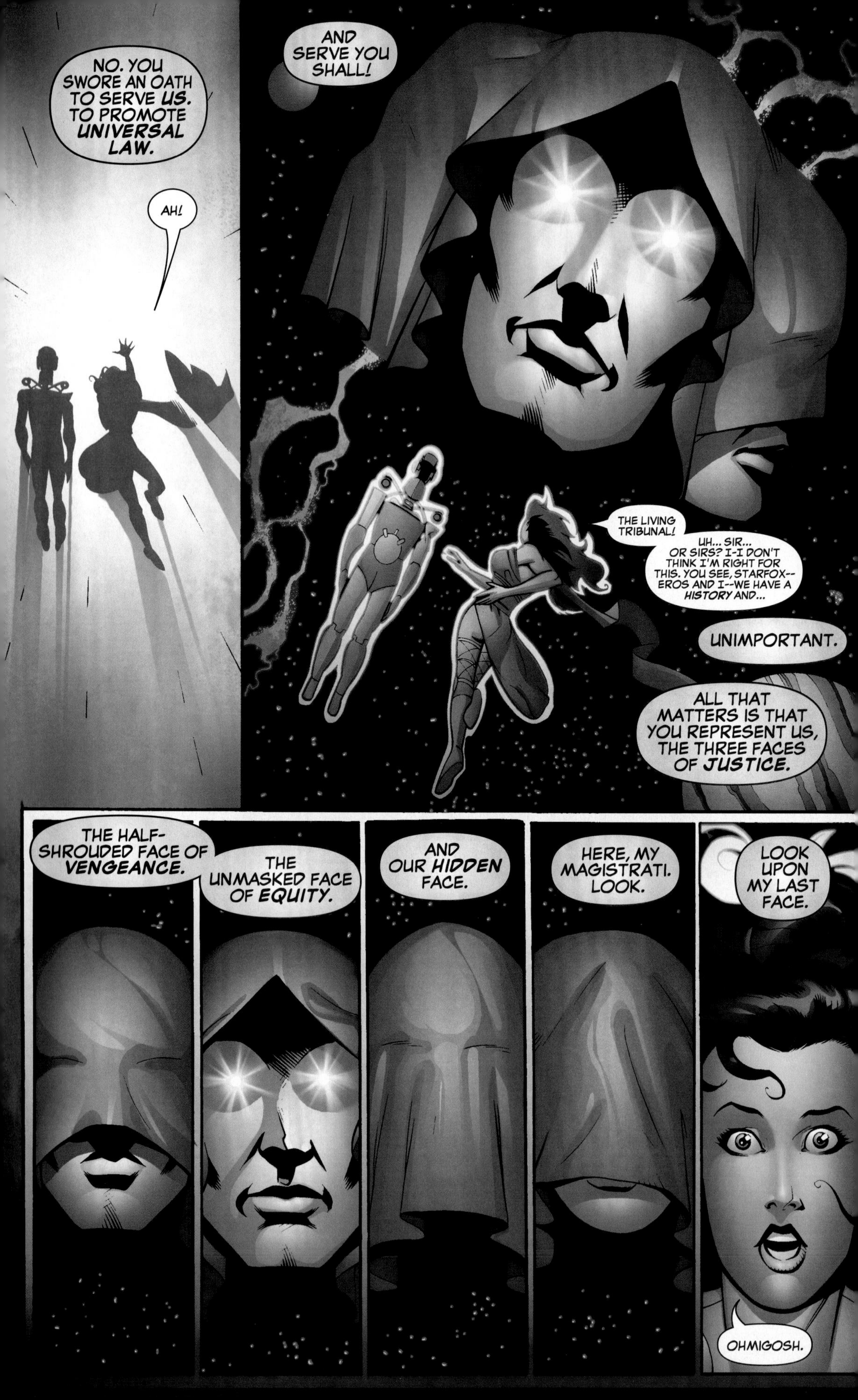
NO. YOU SWORE AN OATH TO SERVE US. TO PROMOTE UNIVERSAL LAW.
AH!
AND SERVE YOU SHALL!
THE LIVING TRIBUNAL!
UH... SIR... OR SIRS? I-I DON'T THINK I'M RIGHT FOR THIS. YOU SEE, STARFOX--EROS AND I--WE HAVE A HISTORY AND...
UNIMPORTANT.
ALL THAT MATTERS IS THAT YOU REPRESENT US, THE THREE FACES OF JUSTICE.
THE HALF-SHROUDED FACE OF VENGEANCE.
THE UNMASKED FACE OF EQUITY.
AND OUR HIDDEN FACE.
HERE, MY MAGISTRATI. LOOK.
LOOK UPON MY LAST FACE.
OHMIGOSH.

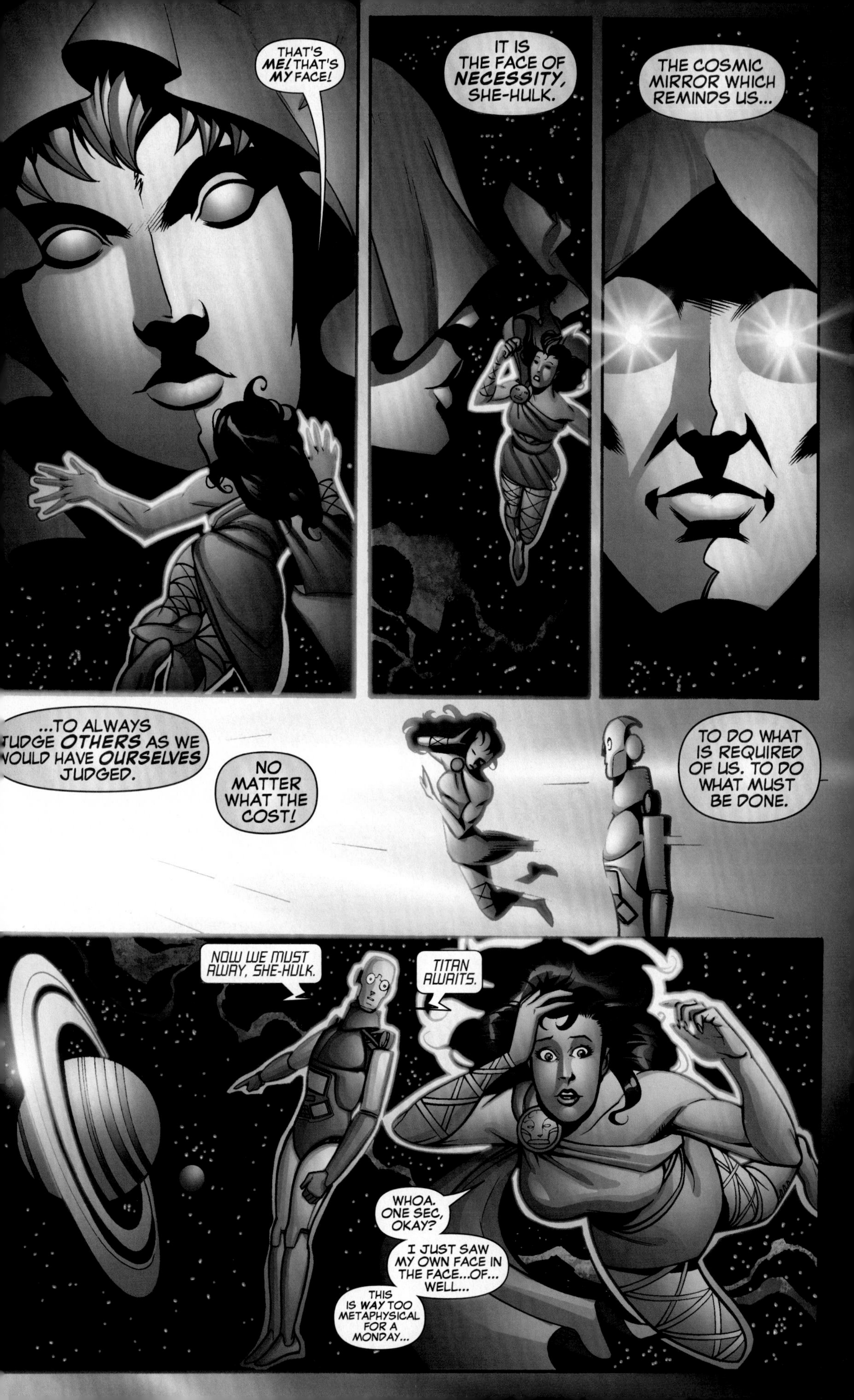
THAT'S ME! THAT'S MY FACE!
IT IS THE FACE OF NECESSITY, SHE-HULK.
THE COSMIC MIRROR WHICH REMINDS US...
...TO ALWAYS JUDGE OTHERS AS WE WOULD HAVE OURSELVES JUDGED.
NO MATTER WHAT THE COST!
TO DO WHAT IS REQUIRED OF US. TO DO WHAT MUST BE DONE.
NOW WE MUST AWAY, SHE-HULK.
TITAN AWAITS.
WHOA. ONE SEC, OKAY?
I JUST SAW MY OWN FACE IN THE FACE...OF... WELL...
THIS IS WAY TOO METAPHYSICAL FOR A MONDAY...

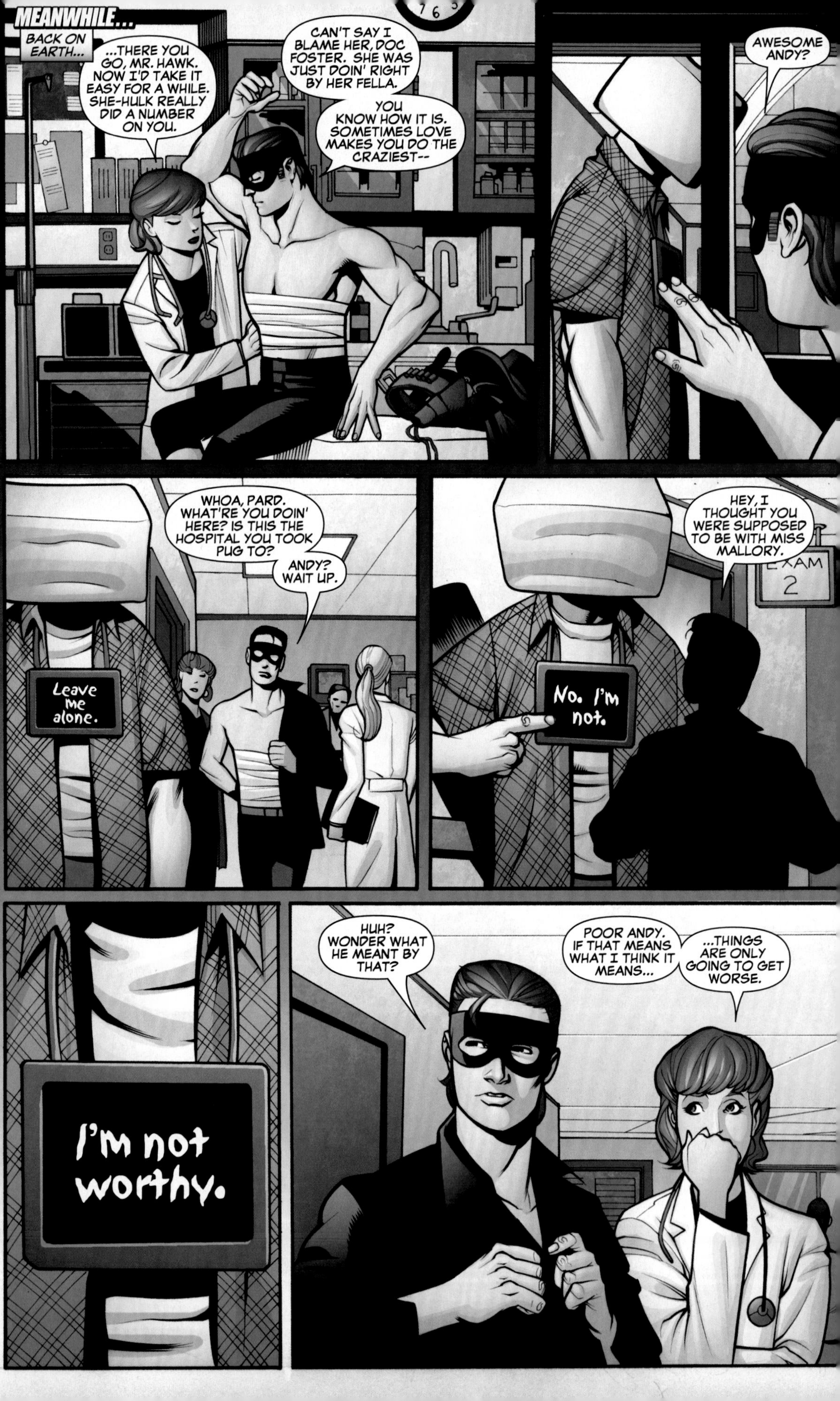
MEANWHILE...
BACK ON EARTH...
...THERE YOU GO, MR. HAWK. NOW I'D TAKE IT EASY FOR A WHILE. SHE-HULK REALLY DID A NUMBER ON YOU.
CAN'T SAY I BLAME HER, DOC FOSTER. SHE WAS JUST DOIN' RIGHT BY HER FELLA.
YOU KNOW HOW IT IS. SOMETIMES LOVE MAKES YOU DO THE CRAZIEST--
AWESOME ANDY?
WHOA, PARD. WHAT'RE YOU DOIN' HERE? IS THIS THE HOSPITAL YOU TOOK PUG TO?
ANDY? WAIT UP.
Leave me alone.
HEY, I THOUGHT YOU WERE SUPPOSED TO BE WITH MISS MALLORY.
EXAM 2
No. I'm not.
I'm not worthy.
HUH? WONDER WHAT HE MEANT BY THAT?
POOR ANDY. IF THAT MEANS WHAT I THINK IT MEANS...
...THINGS ARE ONLY GOING TO GET WORSE.

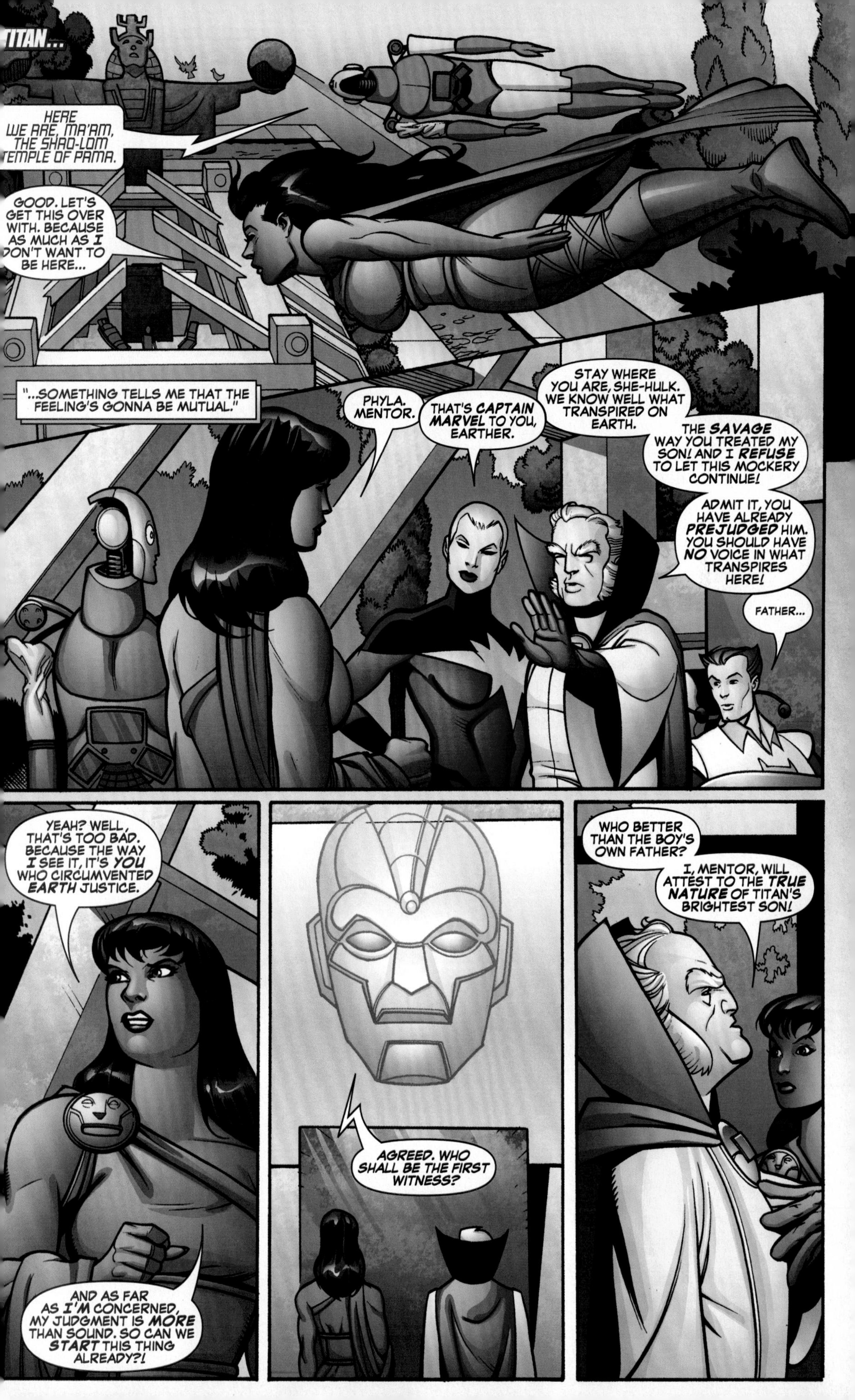
TITAN...
HERE WE ARE, MA'AM, THE SHAO-LOM TEMPLE OF PAMA.
GOOD. LET'S GET THIS OVER WITH. BECAUSE AS MUCH AS I DON'T WANT TO BE HERE...
"...SOMETHING TELLS ME THAT THE FEELING'S GONNA BE MUTUAL."
PHYLA. MENTOR.
THAT'S CAPTAIN MARVEL TO YOU, EARTHER.
STAY WHERE YOU ARE, SHE-HULK. WE KNOW WELL WHAT TRANSPIRED ON EARTH.
THE SAVAGE WAY YOU TREATED MY SON! AND I REFUSE TO LET THIS MOCKERY CONTINUE!
ADMIT IT, YOU HAVE ALREADY PREJUDGED HIM. YOU SHOULD HAVE NO VOICE IN WHAT TRANSPIRES HERE!
FATHER...
YEAH? WELL, THAT'S TOO BAD. BECAUSE THE WAY I SEE IT, IT'S YOU WHO CIRCUMVENTED EARTH JUSTICE.
AND AS FAR AS I'M CONCERNED, MY JUDGMENT IS MORE THAN SOUND. SO CAN WE START THIS THING ALREADY?!
AGREED. WHO SHALL BE THE FIRST WITNESS?
WHO BETTER THAN THE BOY'S OWN FATHER?
I, MENTOR, WILL ATTEST TO THE TRUE NATURE OF TITAN'S BRIGHTEST SON!

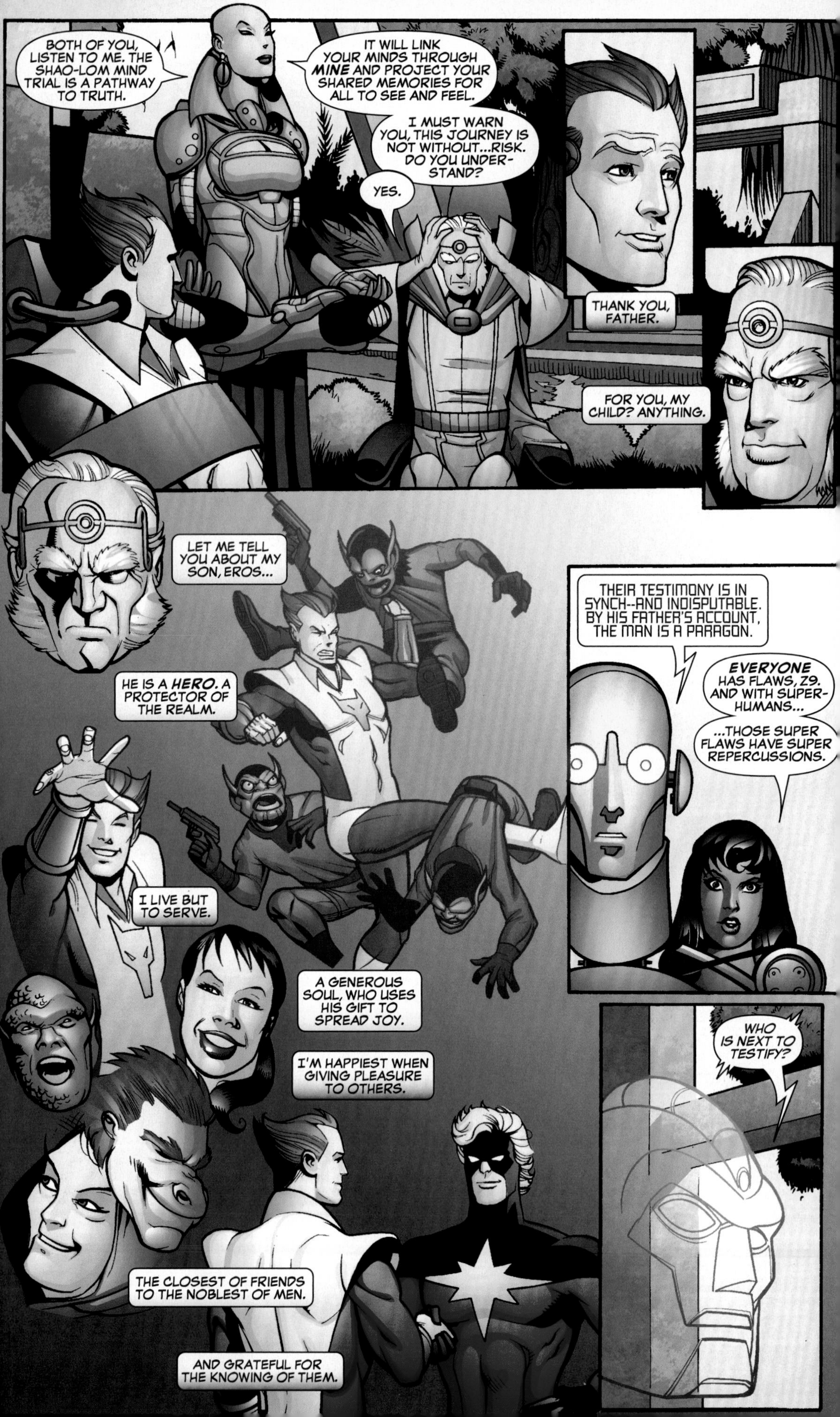
BOTH OF YOU, LISTEN TO ME. THE SHAO-LOM MIND TRIAL IS A PATHWAY TO TRUTH.
IT WILL LINK YOUR MINDS THROUGH *MINE* AND PROJECT YOUR SHARED MEMORIES FOR ALL TO SEE AND FEEL.
I MUST WARN YOU, THIS JOURNEY IS NOT WITHOUT...RISK. DO YOU UNDERSTAND?
YES.
THANK YOU, FATHER.
FOR YOU, MY CHILD? ANYTHING.
LET ME TELL YOU ABOUT MY SON, EROS...
HE IS A ***HERO.*** A PROTECTOR OF THE REALM.
I LIVE BUT TO SERVE.
A GENEROUS SOUL, WHO USES HIS GIFT TO SPREAD JOY.
I'M HAPPIEST WHEN GIVING PLEASURE TO OTHERS.
THE CLOSEST OF FRIENDS TO THE NOBLEST OF MEN.
AND GRATEFUL FOR THE KNOWING OF THEM.
THEIR TESTIMONY IS IN SYNCH--AND INDISPUTABLE. BY HIS FATHER'S ACCOUNT, THE MAN IS A PARAGON.
EVERYONE HAS FLAWS, Z9. AND WITH SUPER-HUMANS...
...THOSE SUPER FLAWS HAVE SUPER REPERCUSSIONS.
WHO IS NEXT TO TESTIFY?

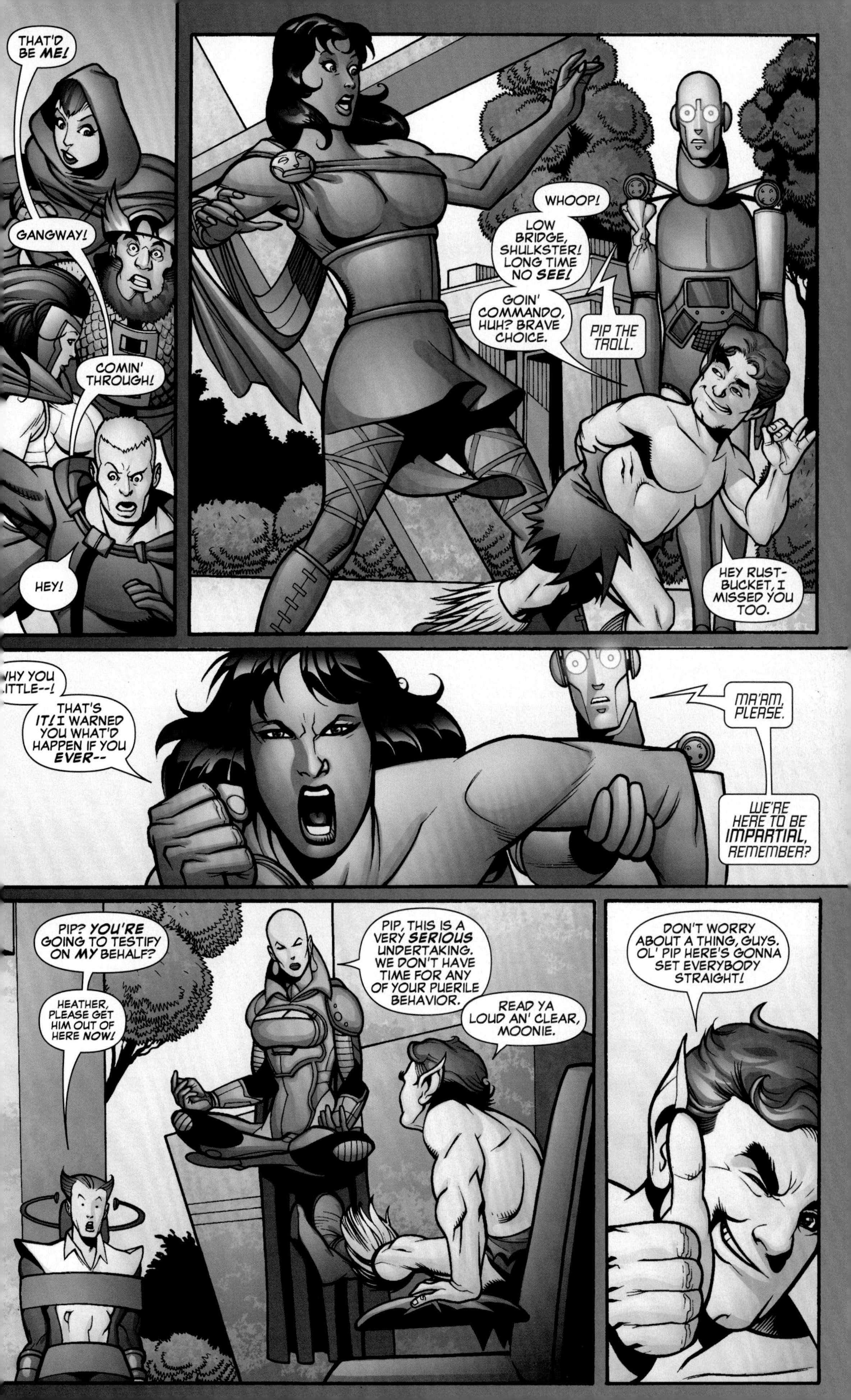
THAT'D BE ME!
GANGWAY!
COMIN' THROUGH!
HEY!
WHOOP!
LOW BRIDGE, SHULKSTER! LONG TIME NO SEE!
GOIN' COMMANDO, HUH? BRAVE CHOICE.
PIP THE TROLL.
HEY RUST-BUCKET, I MISSED YOU TOO.
WHY YOU LITTLE--!
THAT'S IT! I WARNED YOU WHAT'D HAPPEN IF YOU EVER--
MA'AM, PLEASE.
WE'RE HERE TO BE IMPARTIAL, REMEMBER?
PIP? YOU'RE GOING TO TESTIFY ON MY BEHALF?
HEATHER, PLEASE GET HIM OUT OF HERE NOW!
PIP, THIS IS A VERY SERIOUS UNDERTAKING. WE DON'T HAVE TIME FOR ANY OF YOUR PUERILE BEHAVIOR.
READ YA LOUD AN' CLEAR, MOONIE.
DON'T WORRY ABOUT A THING, GUYS. OL' PIP HERE'S GONNA SET EVERYBODY STRAIGHT!

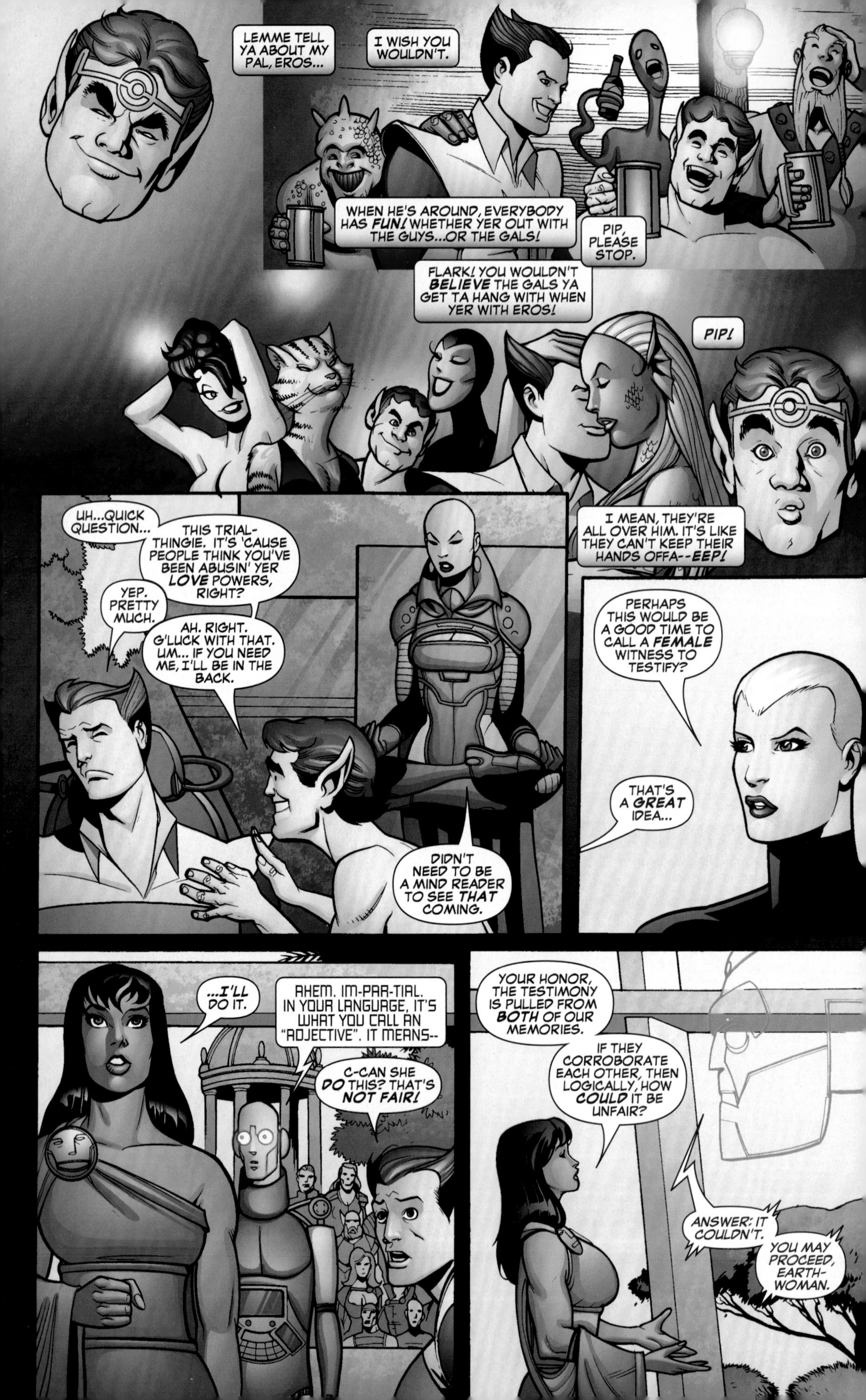
LEMME TELL YA ABOUT MY PAL, EROS...
I WISH YOU WOULDN'T.
WHEN HE'S AROUND, EVERYBODY HAS FUN! WHETHER YER OUT WITH THE GUYS...OR THE GALS!
PIP, PLEASE STOP.
FLARK! YOU WOULDN'T BELIEVE THE GALS YA GET TA HANG WITH WHEN YER WITH EROS!
PIP!
I MEAN, THEY'RE ALL OVER HIM. IT'S LIKE THEY CAN'T KEEP THEIR HANDS OFFA--EEP!
UH...QUICK QUESTION...
THIS TRIAL-THINGIE. IT'S 'CAUSE PEOPLE THINK YOU'VE BEEN ABUSIN' YER LOVE POWERS, RIGHT?
YEP. PRETTY MUCH.
AH. RIGHT. G'LUCK WITH THAT. UM... IF YOU NEED ME, I'LL BE IN THE BACK.
DIDN'T NEED TO BE A MIND READER TO SEE THAT COMING.
PERHAPS THIS WOULD BE A GOOD TIME TO CALL A FEMALE WITNESS TO TESTIFY?
THAT'S A GREAT IDEA...
...I'LL DO IT.
AHEM. IM-PAR-TIAL. IN YOUR LANGUAGE, IT'S WHAT YOU CALL AN "ADJECTIVE". IT MEANS--
C-CAN SHE DO THIS? THAT'S NOT FAIR!
YOUR HONOR, THE TESTIMONY IS PULLED FROM BOTH OF OUR MEMORIES.
IF THEY CORROBORATE EACH OTHER, THEN LOGICALLY, HOW COULD IT BE UNFAIR?
ANSWER: IT COULDN'T.
YOU MAY PROCEED, EARTH-WOMAN.

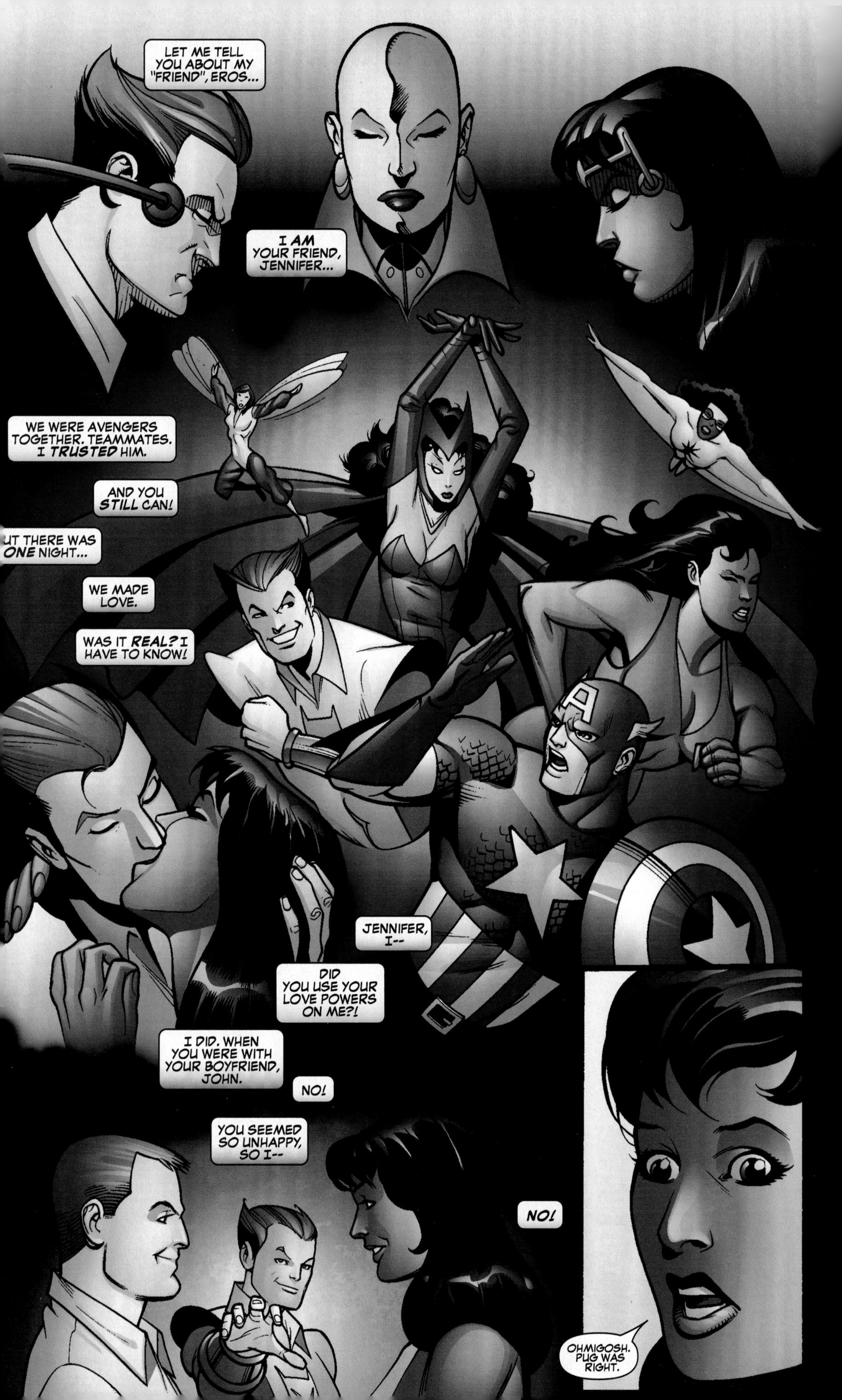
LET ME TELL YOU ABOUT MY "FRIEND", EROS...
I AM YOUR FRIEND, JENNIFER...
WE WERE AVENGERS TOGETHER. TEAMMATES. I TRUSTED HIM.
AND YOU STILL CAN!
UT THERE WAS ONE NIGHT...
WE MADE LOVE.
WAS IT REAL? I HAVE TO KNOW!
JENNIFER, I--
DID YOU USE YOUR LOVE POWERS ON ME?!
I DID. WHEN YOU WERE WITH YOUR BOYFRIEND, JOHN.
NO!
YOU SEEMED SO UNHAPPY, SO I--
NO!
OHMIGOSH. PUG WAS RIGHT.

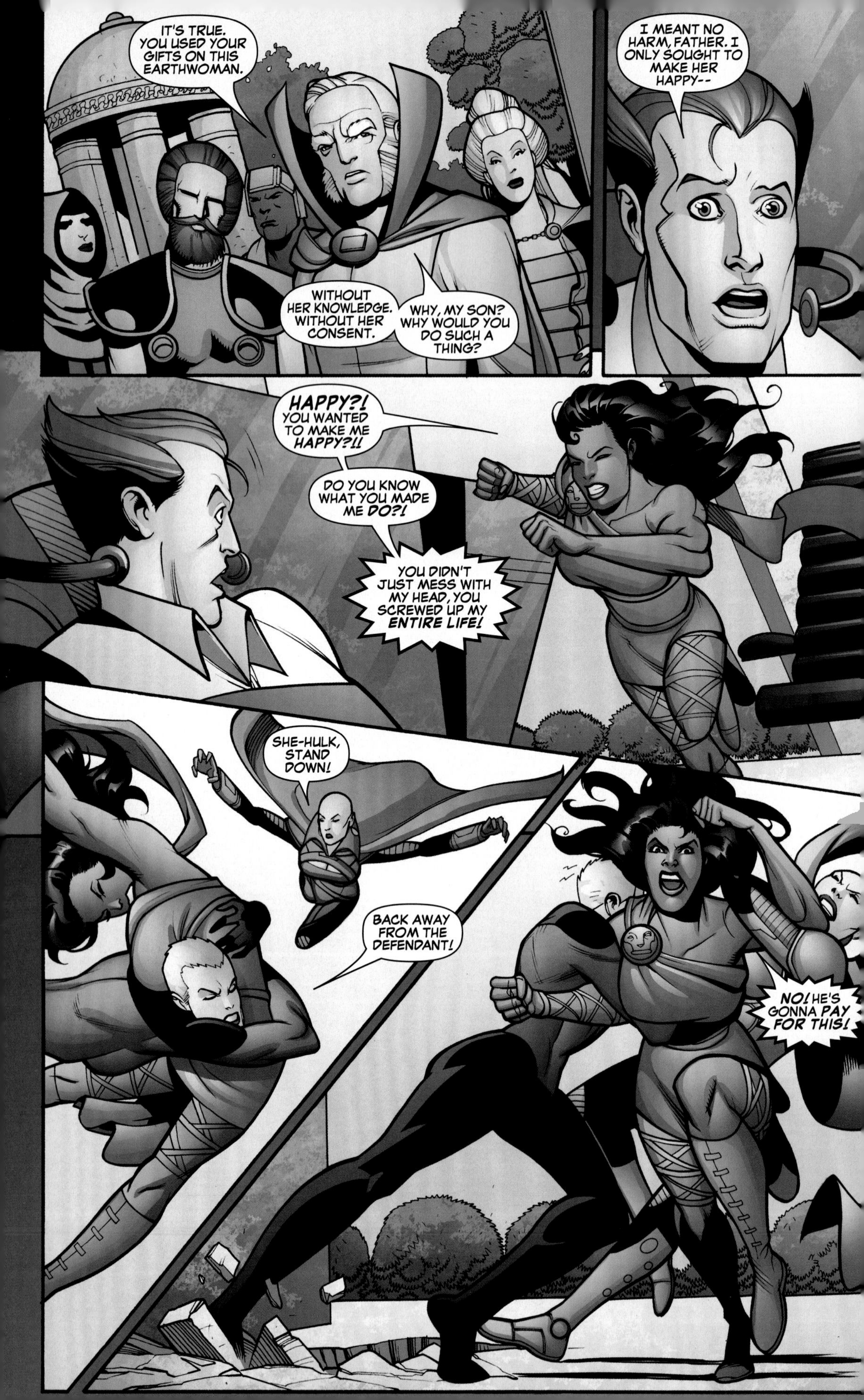
IT'S TRUE. YOU USED YOUR GIFTS ON THIS EARTHWOMAN.
WITHOUT HER KNOWLEDGE. WITHOUT HER CONSENT.
WHY, MY SON? WHY WOULD YOU DO SUCH A THING?
I MEANT NO HARM, FATHER. I ONLY SOUGHT TO MAKE HER HAPPY--
HAPPY?! YOU WANTED TO MAKE ME HAPPY?!!
DO YOU KNOW WHAT YOU MADE ME DO?!
YOU DIDN'T JUST MESS WITH MY HEAD, YOU SCREWED UP MY ENTIRE LIFE!
SHE-HULK, STAND DOWN!
BACK AWAY FROM THE DEFENDANT!
NO! HE'S GONNA PAY FOR THIS!

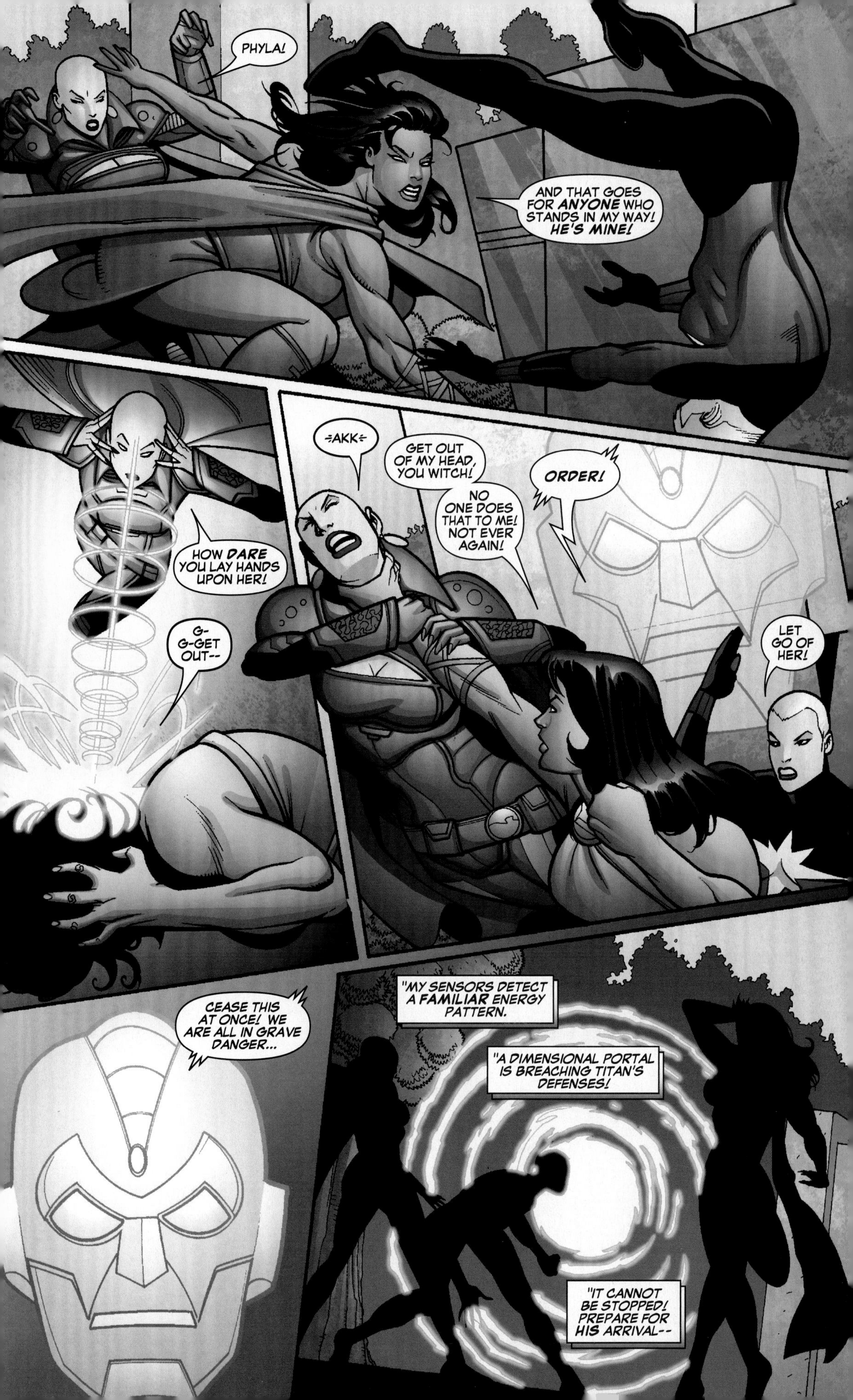
PHYLA!
AND THAT GOES FOR ANYONE WHO STANDS IN MY WAY! HE'S MINE!
HOW DARE YOU LAY HANDS UPON HER!
G-G-GET OUT--
AKK
GET OUT OF MY HEAD, YOU WITCH!
NO ONE DOES THAT TO ME! NOT EVER AGAIN!
ORDER!
LET GO OF HER!
CEASE THIS AT ONCE! WE ARE ALL IN GRAVE DANGER...
"MY SENSORS DETECT A FAMILIAR ENERGY PATTERN.
"A DIMENSIONAL PORTAL IS BREACHING TITAN'S DEFENSES!
"IT CANNOT BE STOPPED! PREPARE FOR HIS ARRIVAL--

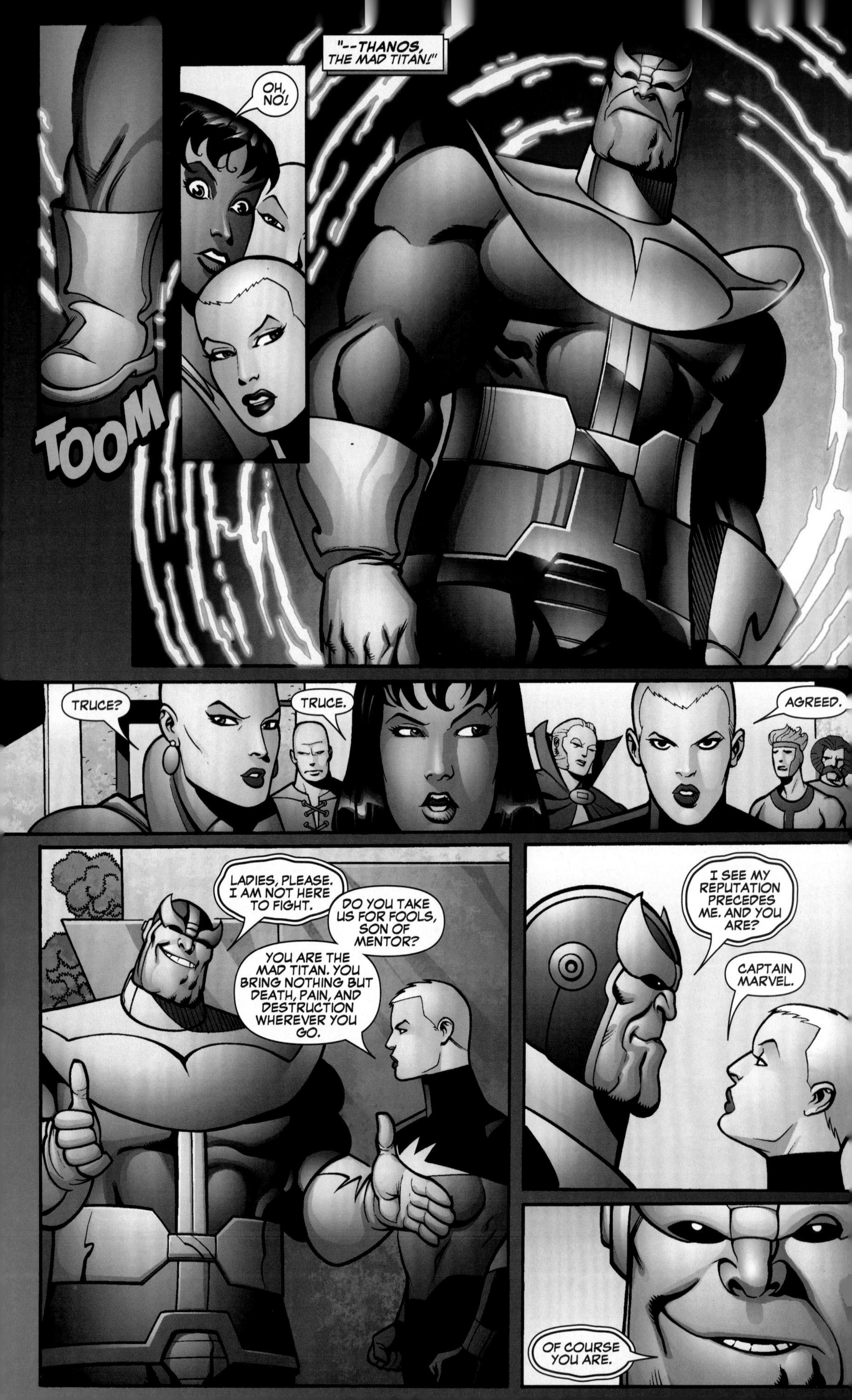
"--THANOS, THE MAD TITAN!"
OH, NO!
TOOM
TRUCE?
TRUCE.
AGREED.
LADIES, PLEASE. I AM NOT HERE TO FIGHT.
DO YOU TAKE US FOR FOOLS, SON OF MENTOR?
YOU ARE THE MAD TITAN. YOU BRING NOTHING BUT DEATH, PAIN, AND DESTRUCTION WHEREVER YOU GO.
I SEE MY REPUTATION PRECEDES ME. AND YOU ARE?
CAPTAIN MARVEL.
OF COURSE YOU ARE.

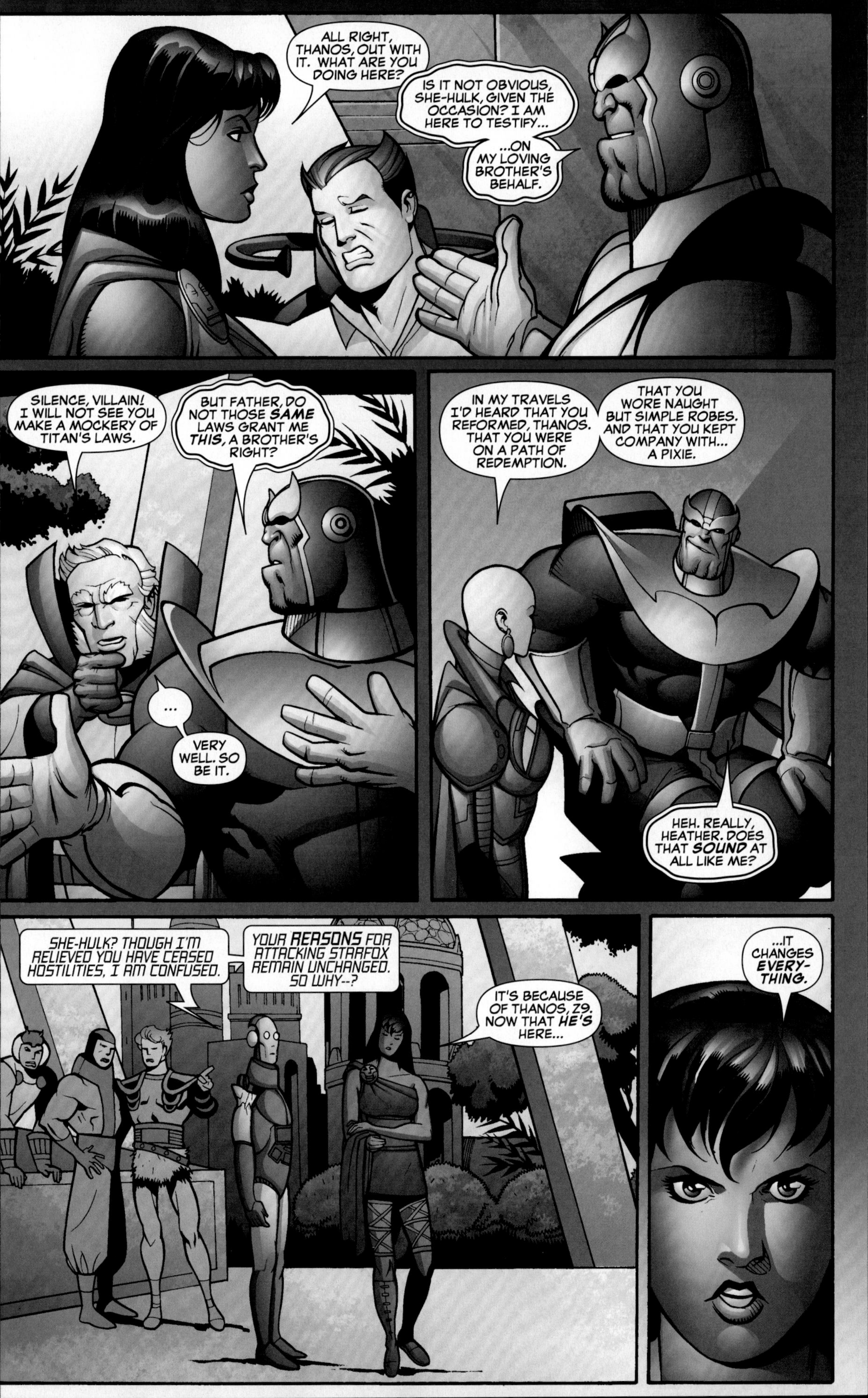
ALL RIGHT, THANOS, OUT WITH IT. WHAT ARE YOU DOING HERE?
IS IT NOT OBVIOUS, SHE-HULK, GIVEN THE OCCASION? I AM HERE TO TESTIFY...
...ON MY LOVING BROTHER'S BEHALF.
SILENCE, VILLAIN! I WILL NOT SEE YOU MAKE A MOCKERY OF TITAN'S LAWS.
BUT FATHER, DO NOT THOSE SAME LAWS GRANT ME THIS, A BROTHER'S RIGHT?
...
VERY WELL. SO BE IT.
IN MY TRAVELS I'D HEARD THAT YOU REFORMED, THANOS. THAT YOU WERE ON A PATH OF REDEMPTION.
THAT YOU WORE NAUGHT BUT SIMPLE ROBES. AND THAT YOU KEPT COMPANY WITH... A PIXIE.
HEH. REALLY, HEATHER. DOES THAT SOUND AT ALL LIKE ME?
SHE-HULK? THOUGH I'M RELIEVED YOU HAVE CEASED HOSTILITIES, I AM CONFUSED.
YOUR REASONS FOR ATTACKING STARFOX REMAIN UNCHANGED. SO WHY--?
IT'S BECAUSE OF THANOS, Z9. NOW THAT HE'S HERE...
...IT CHANGES EVERYTHING.

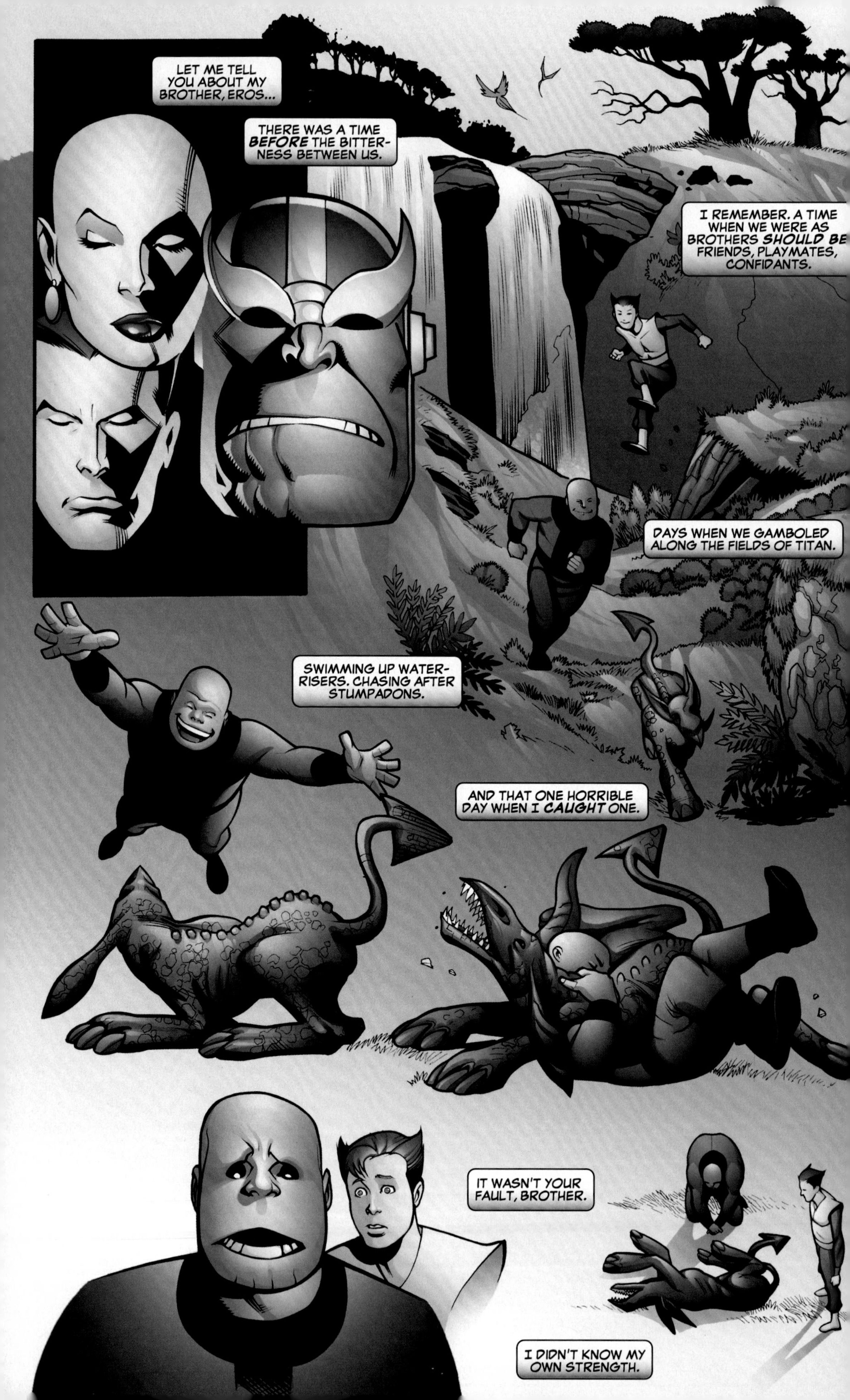
LET ME TELL YOU ABOUT MY BROTHER, EROS...
THERE WAS A TIME BEFORE THE BITTERNESS BETWEEN US.
I REMEMBER. A TIME WHEN WE WERE AS BROTHERS SHOULD BE FRIENDS, PLAYMATES, CONFIDANTS.
DAYS WHEN WE GAMBOLED ALONG THE FIELDS OF TITAN.
SWIMMING UP WATER-RISERS. CHASING AFTER STUMPADONS.
AND THAT ONE HORRIBLE DAY WHEN I CAUGHT ONE.
IT WASN'T YOUR FAULT, BROTHER.
I DIDN'T KNOW MY OWN STRENGTH.

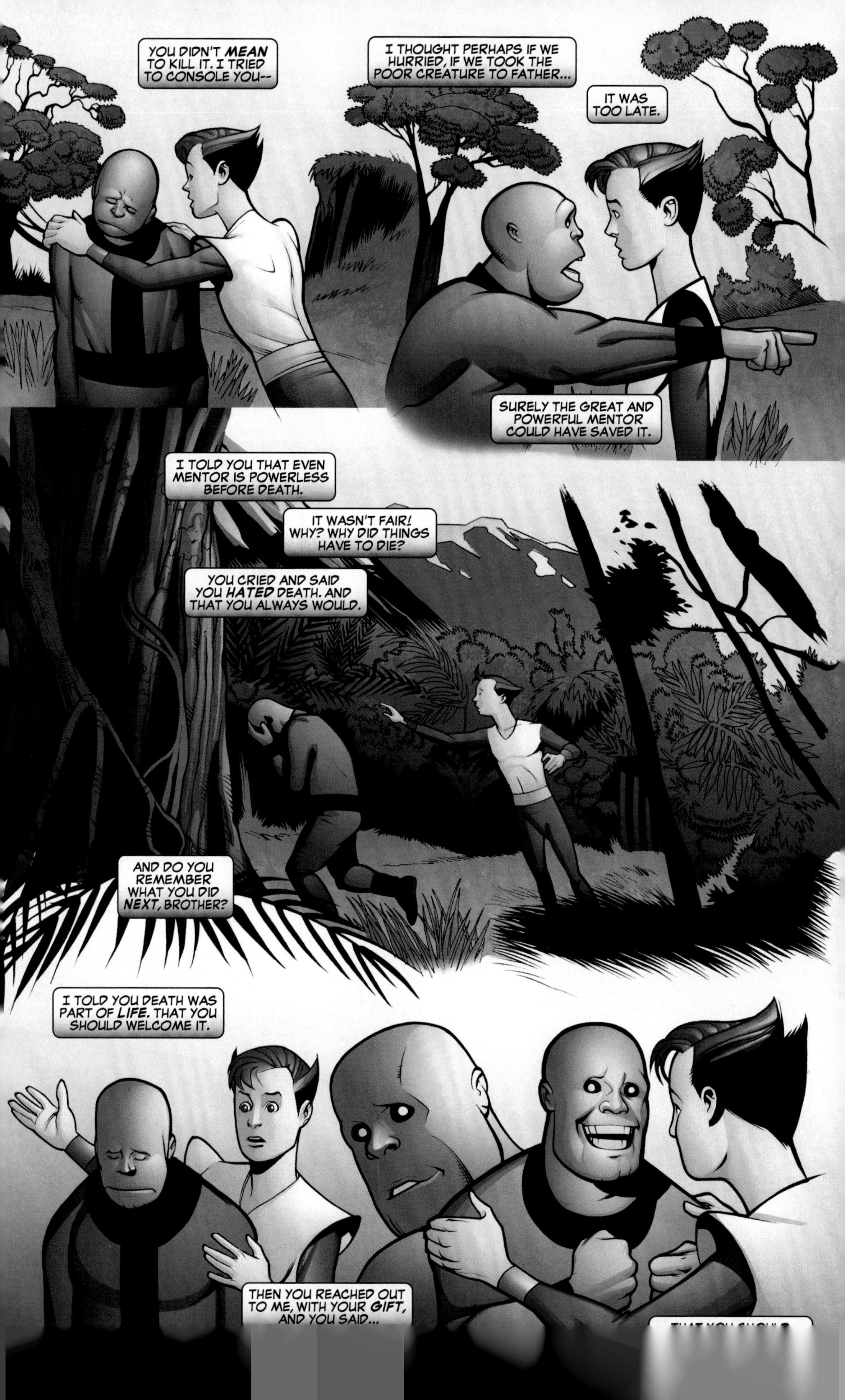
YOU DIDN'T MEAN TO KILL IT. I TRIED TO CONSOLE YOU--
I THOUGHT PERHAPS IF WE HURRIED, IF WE TOOK THE POOR CREATURE TO FATHER...
IT WAS TOO LATE.
SURELY THE GREAT AND POWERFUL MENTOR COULD HAVE SAVED IT.
I TOLD YOU THAT EVEN MENTOR IS POWERLESS BEFORE DEATH.
IT WASN'T FAIR! WHY? WHY DID THINGS HAVE TO DIE?
YOU CRIED AND SAID YOU HATED DEATH. AND THAT YOU ALWAYS WOULD.
AND DO YOU REMEMBER WHAT YOU DID NEXT, BROTHER?
I TOLD YOU DEATH WAS PART OF LIFE. THAT YOU SHOULD WELCOME IT.
THEN YOU REACHED OUT TO ME, WITH YOUR GIFT, AND YOU SAID...

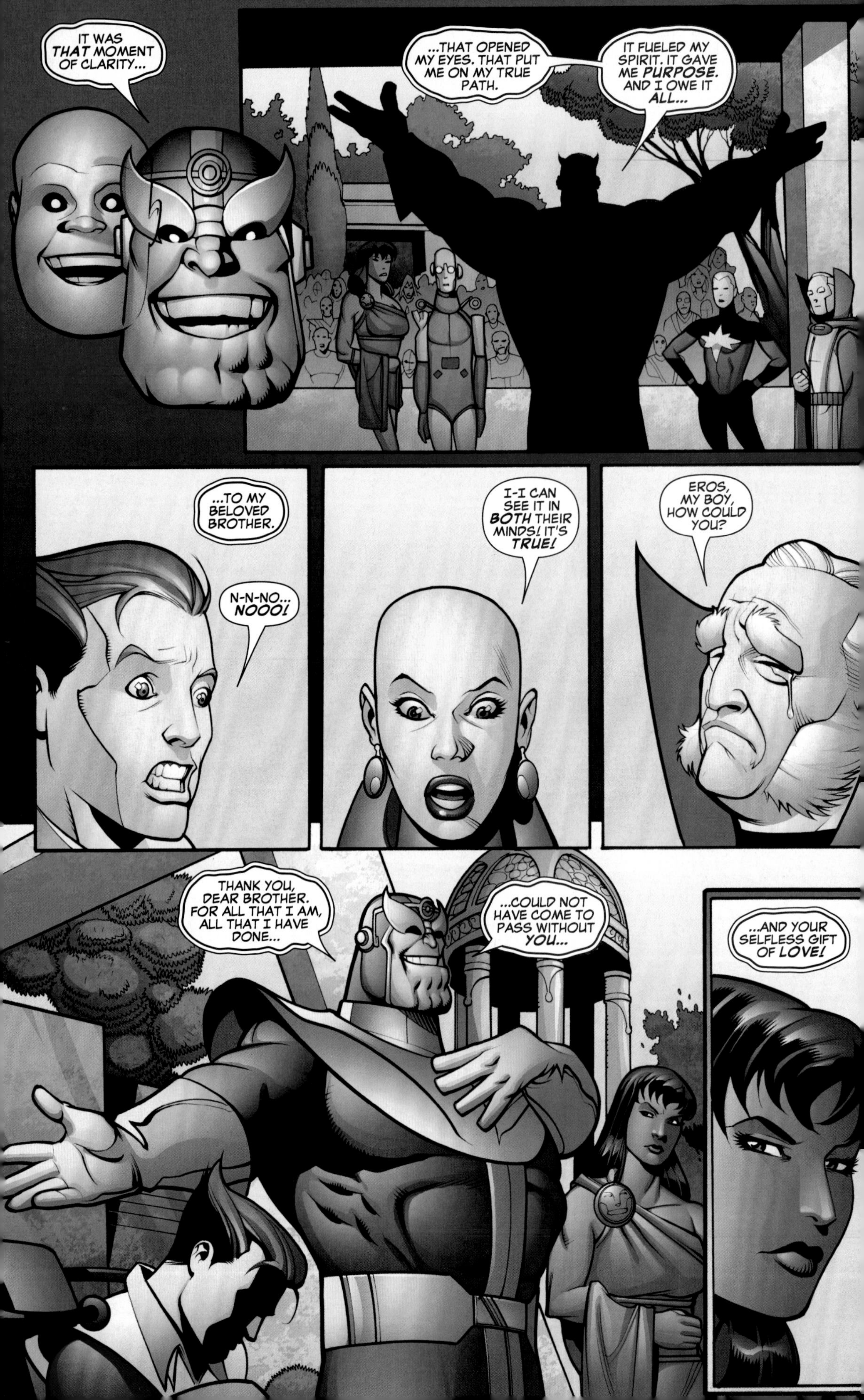
IT WAS THAT MOMENT OF CLARITY...
...THAT OPENED MY EYES. THAT PUT ME ON MY TRUE PATH.
IT FUELED MY SPIRIT. IT GAVE ME PURPOSE. AND I OWE IT ALL...
...TO MY BELOVED BROTHER.
N-N-NO... NOOO!
I-I CAN SEE IT IN BOTH THEIR MINDS! IT'S TRUE!
EROS, MY BOY, HOW COULD YOU?
THANK YOU, DEAR BROTHER. FOR ALL THAT I AM, ALL THAT I HAVE DONE...
...COULD NOT HAVE COME TO PASS WITHOUT YOU...
...AND YOUR SELFLESS GIFT OF LOVE!

13

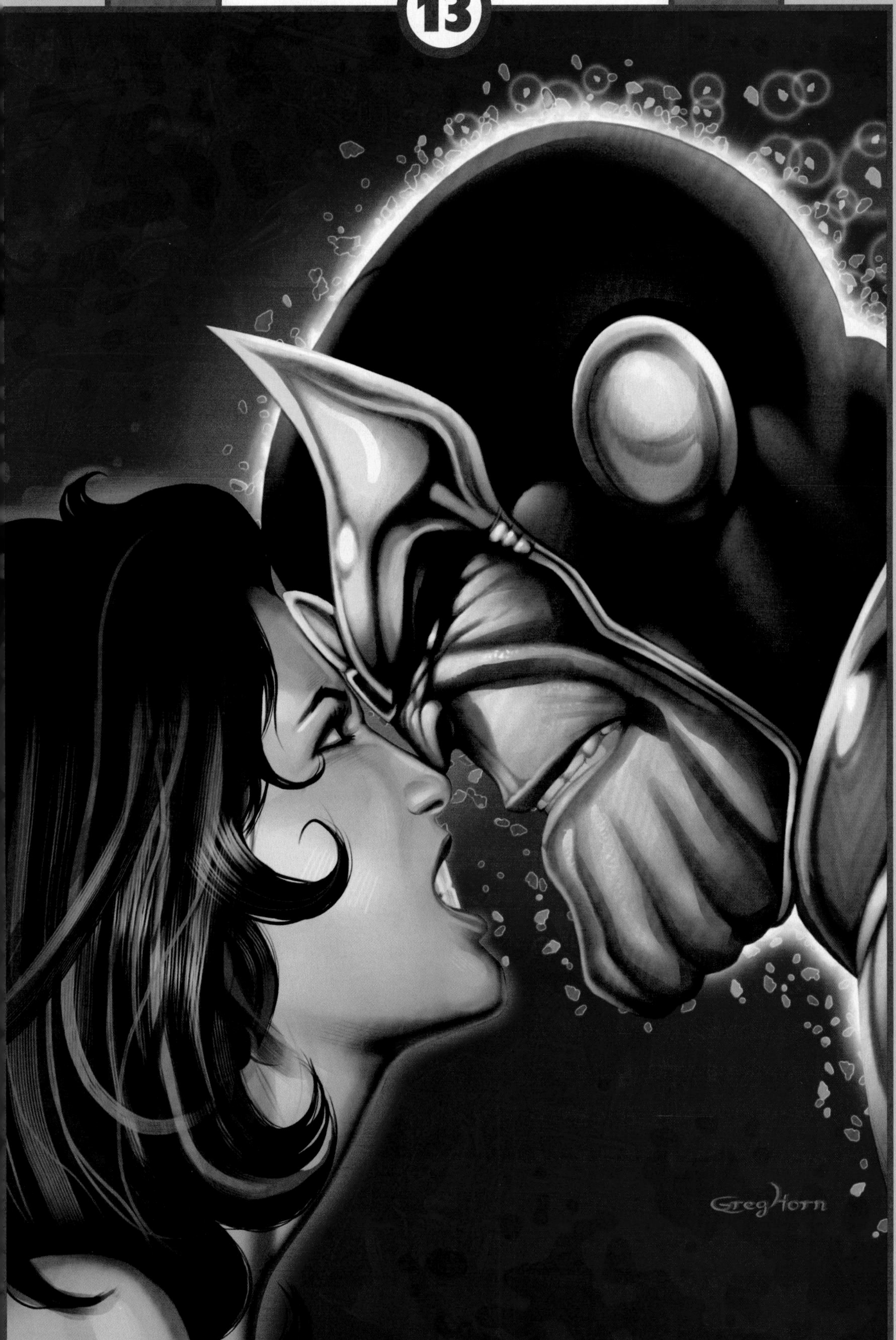
Greg Horn

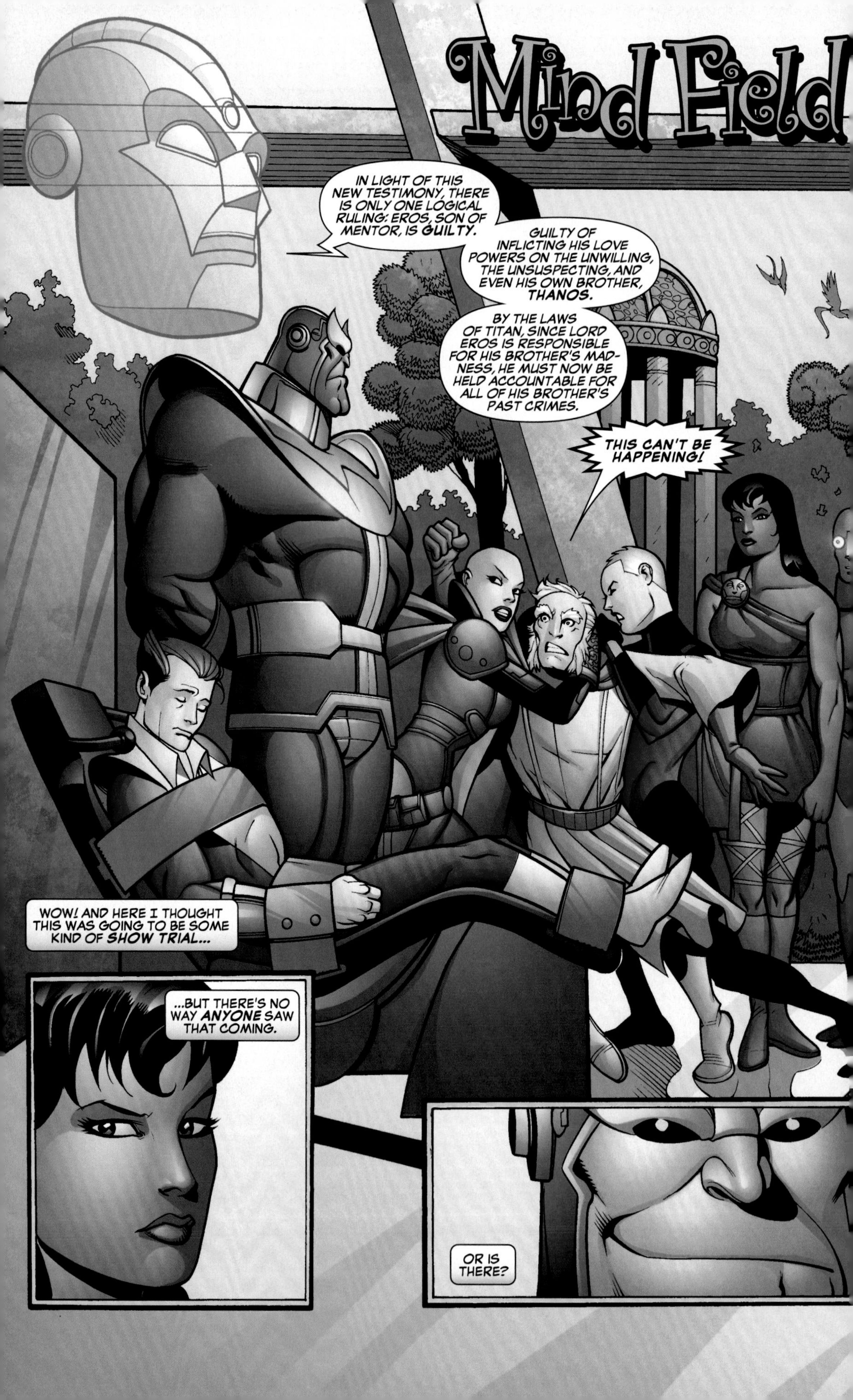
Mind Field
IN LIGHT OF THIS NEW TESTIMONY, THERE IS ONLY ONE LOGICAL RULING: EROS, SON OF MENTOR, IS GUILTY.
GUILTY OF INFLICTING HIS LOVE POWERS ON THE UNWILLING, THE UNSUSPECTING, AND EVEN HIS OWN BROTHER, THANOS.
BY THE LAWS OF TITAN, SINCE LORD EROS IS RESPONSIBLE FOR HIS BROTHER'S MADNESS, HE MUST NOW BE HELD ACCOUNTABLE FOR ALL OF HIS BROTHER'S PAST CRIMES.
THIS CAN'T BE HAPPENING!
WOW! AND HERE I THOUGHT THIS WAS GOING TO BE SOME KIND OF SHOW TRIAL...
...BUT THERE'S NO WAY ANYONE SAW THAT COMING.
OR IS THERE?

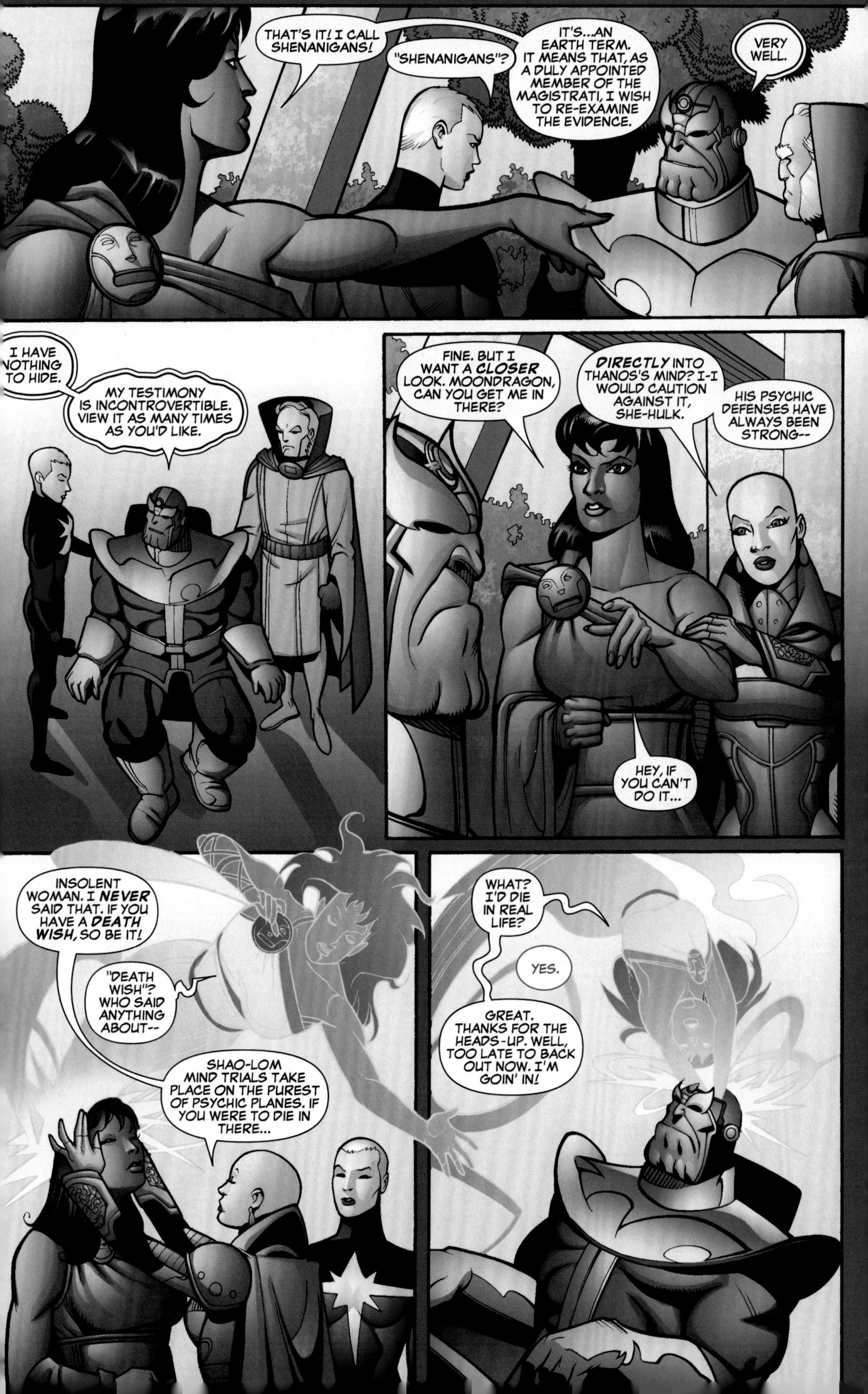
THAT'S IT! I CALL SHENANIGANS!
"SHENANIGANS"?
IT'S...AN EARTH TERM. IT MEANS THAT, AS A DULY APPOINTED MEMBER OF THE MAGISTRATI, I WISH TO RE-EXAMINE THE EVIDENCE.
VERY WELL.
I HAVE NOTHING TO HIDE.
MY TESTIMONY IS INCONTROVERTIBLE. VIEW IT AS MANY TIMES AS YOU'D LIKE.
FINE. BUT I WANT A CLOSER LOOK. MOONDRAGON, CAN YOU GET ME IN THERE?
DIRECTLY INTO THANOS'S MIND? I-I WOULD CAUTION AGAINST IT, SHE-HULK.
HIS PSYCHIC DEFENSES HAVE ALWAYS BEEN STRONG--
HEY, IF YOU CAN'T DO IT...
INSOLENT WOMAN. I NEVER SAID THAT. IF YOU HAVE A DEATH WISH, SO BE IT!
"DEATH WISH"? WHO SAID ANYTHING ABOUT--
SHAO-LOM MIND TRIALS TAKE PLACE ON THE PUREST OF PSYCHIC PLANES. IF YOU WERE TO DIE IN THERE...
WHAT? I'D DIE IN REAL LIFE?
YES.
GREAT. THANKS FOR THE HEADS-UP. WELL, TOO LATE TO BACK OUT NOW. I'M GOIN' IN!

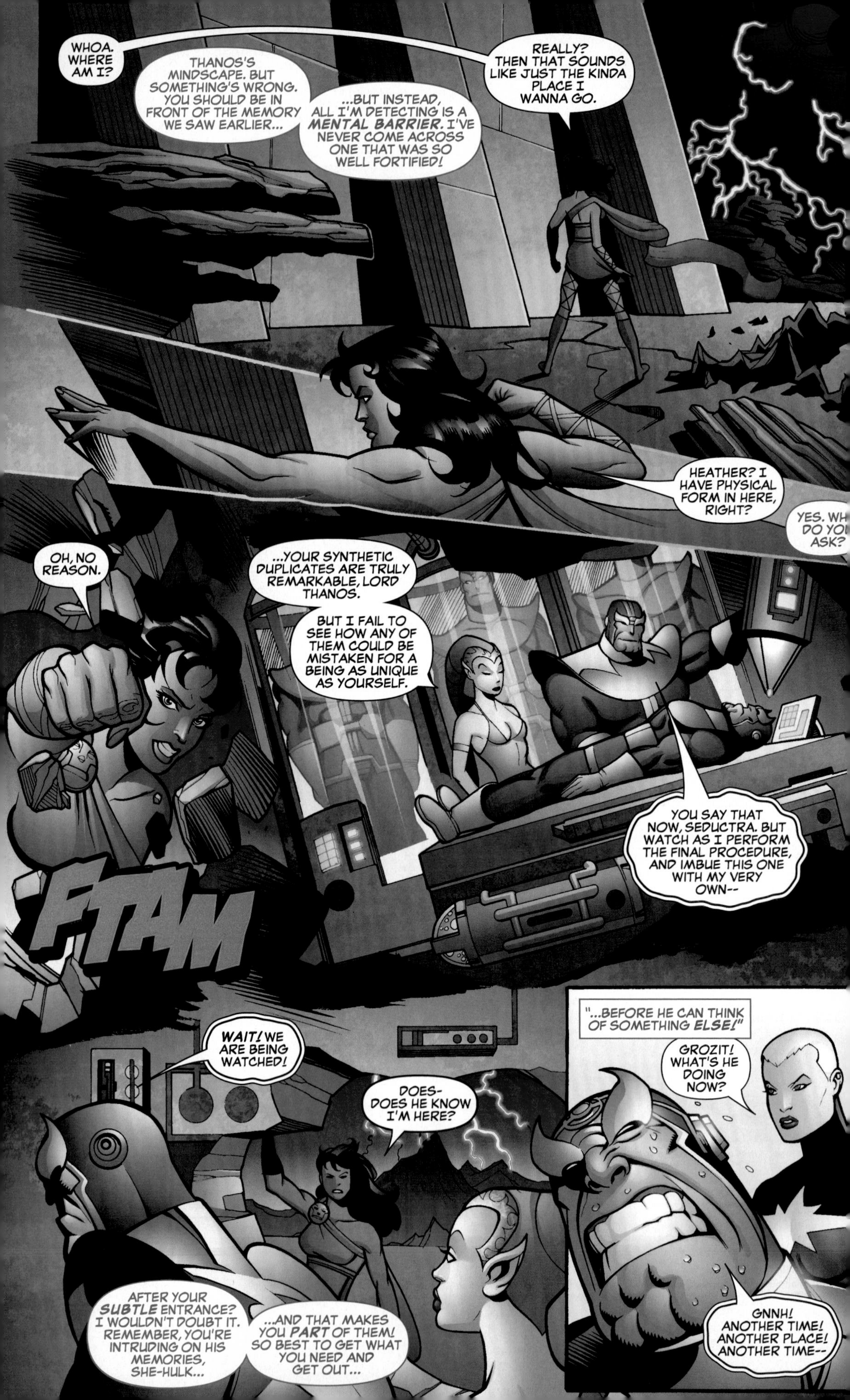
WHOA. WHERE AM I?
THANOS'S MINDSCAPE. BUT SOMETHING'S WRONG. YOU SHOULD BE IN FRONT OF THE MEMORY WE SAW EARLIER...
...BUT INSTEAD, ALL I'M DETECTING IS A MENTAL BARRIER. I'VE NEVER COME ACROSS ONE THAT WAS SO WELL FORTIFIED!
REALLY? THEN THAT SOUNDS LIKE JUST THE KINDA PLACE I WANNA GO.
HEATHER? I HAVE PHYSICAL FORM IN HERE, RIGHT?
YES. WH DO YO ASK?
OH, NO REASON.
FTAM
...YOUR SYNTHETIC DUPLICATES ARE TRULY REMARKABLE, LORD THANOS.
BUT I FAIL TO SEE HOW ANY OF THEM COULD BE MISTAKEN FOR A BEING AS UNIQUE AS YOURSELF.
YOU SAY THAT NOW, SEDUCTRA. BUT WATCH AS I PERFORM THE FINAL PROCEDURE, AND IMBUE THIS ONE WITH MY VERY OWN--
WAIT! WE ARE BEING WATCHED!
DOES-DOES HE KNOW I'M HERE?
AFTER YOUR SUBTLE ENTRANCE? I WOULDN'T DOUBT IT. REMEMBER, YOU'RE INTRUDING ON HIS MEMORIES, SHE-HULK...
...AND THAT MAKES YOU PART OF THEM! SO BEST TO GET WHAT YOU NEED AND GET OUT...
"...BEFORE HE CAN THINK OF SOMETHING ELSE!"
GROZIT! WHAT'S HE DOING NOW?
GNNH! ANOTHER TIME! ANOTHER PLACE! ANOTHER TIME--

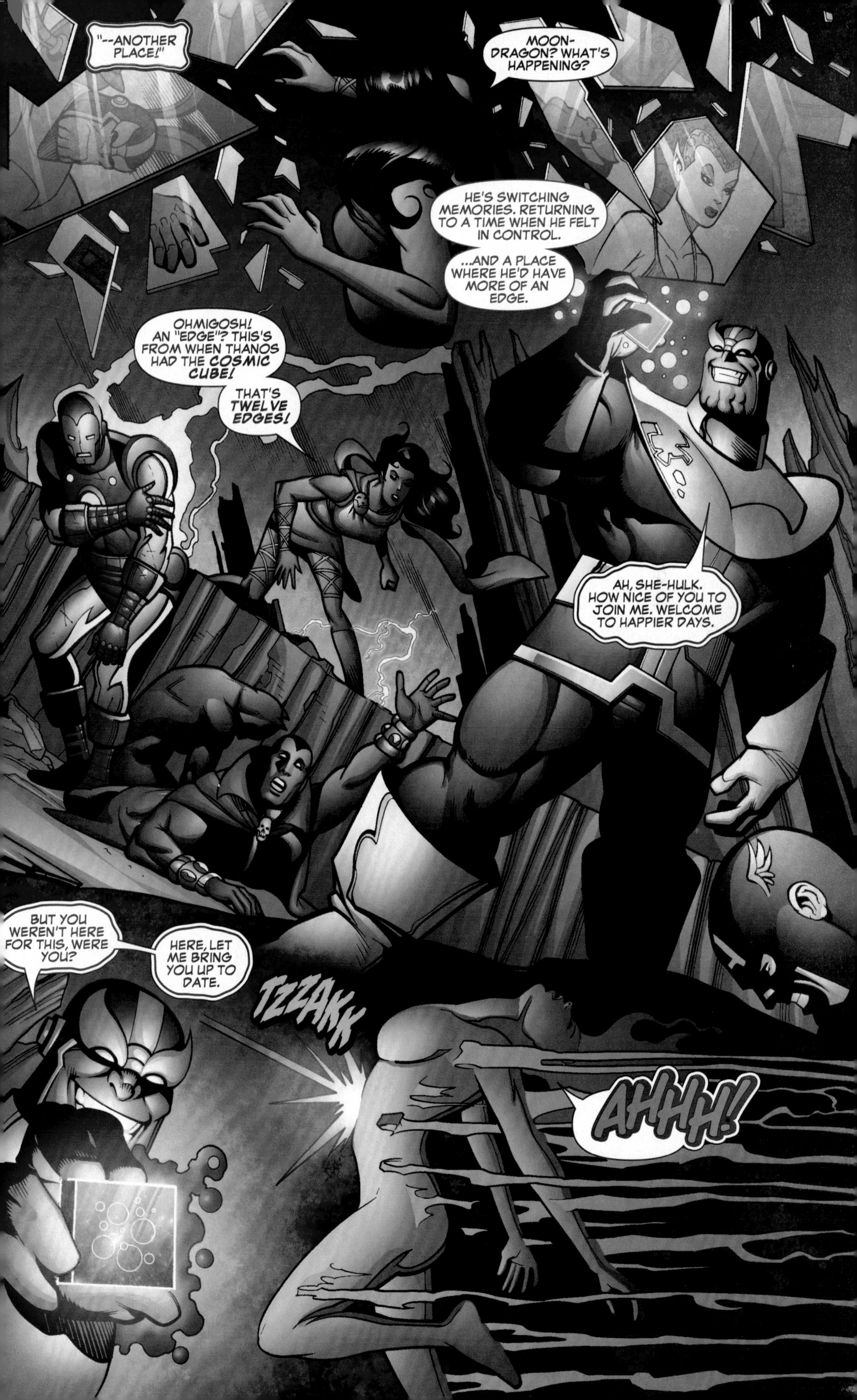
"--ANOTHER PLACE!"
MOON-DRAGON? WHAT'S HAPPENING?
HE'S SWITCHING MEMORIES. RETURNING TO A TIME WHEN HE FELT IN CONTROL.
...AND A PLACE WHERE HE'D HAVE MORE OF AN EDGE.
OHMIGOSH! AN "EDGE"? THIS'S FROM WHEN THANOS HAD THE COSMIC CUBE!
THAT'S TWELVE EDGES!
AH, SHE-HULK. HOW NICE OF YOU TO JOIN ME. WELCOME TO HAPPIER DAYS.
BUT YOU WEREN'T HERE FOR THIS, WERE YOU?
HERE, LET ME BRING YOU UP TO DATE.
TZZAKK
AHHHH!

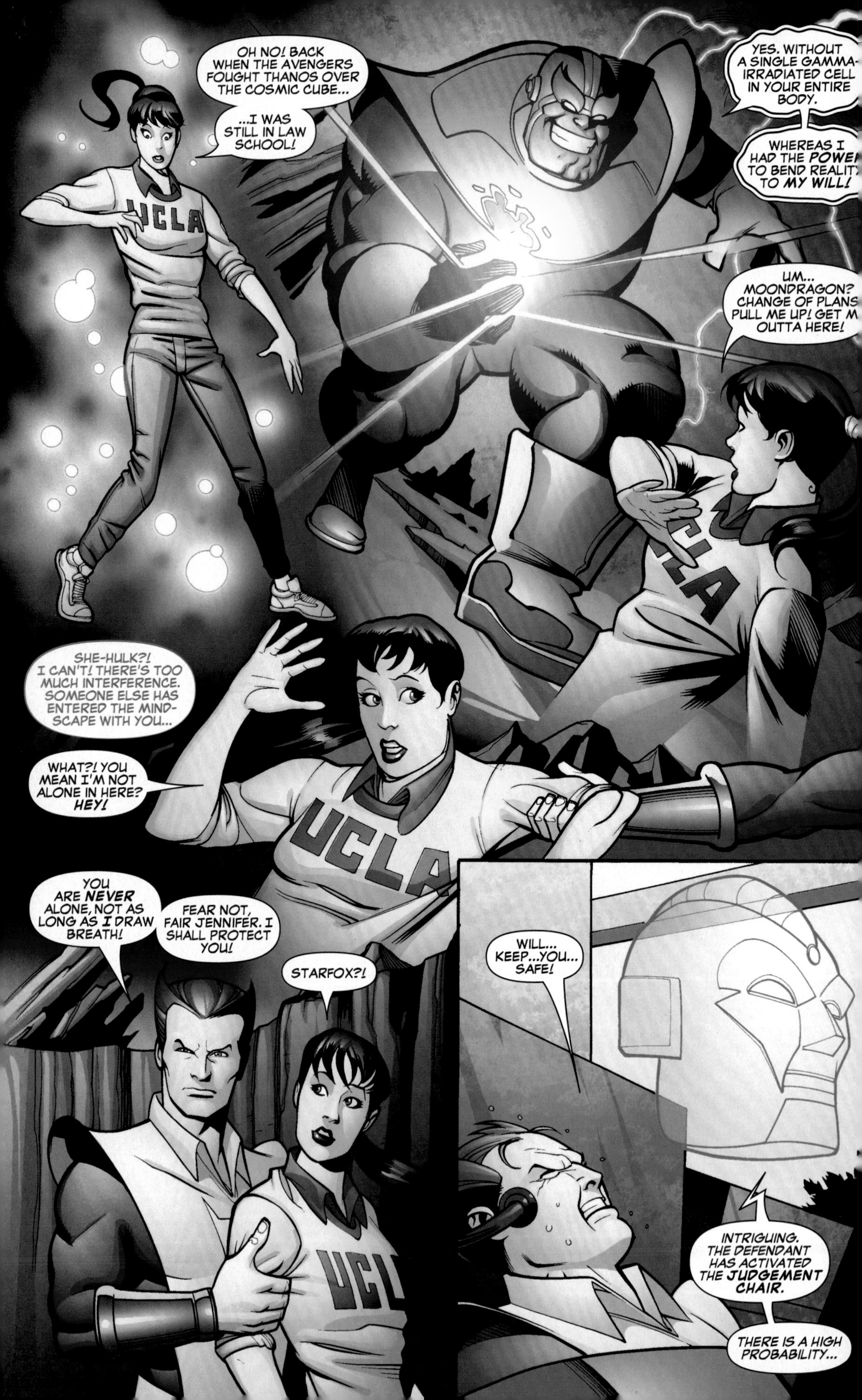
OH NO! BACK WHEN THE AVENGERS FOUGHT THANOS OVER THE COSMIC CUBE...
...I WAS STILL IN LAW SCHOOL!
YES. WITHOUT A SINGLE GAMMA-IRRADIATED CELL IN YOUR ENTIRE BODY.
WHEREAS I HAD THE POWER TO BEND REALITY TO MY WILL!
UM... MOONDRAGON? CHANGE OF PLANS PULL ME UP! GET ME OUTTA HERE!
SHE-HULK?! I CAN'T! THERE'S TOO MUCH INTERFERENCE. SOMEONE ELSE HAS ENTERED THE MIND-SCAPE WITH YOU...
WHAT?! YOU MEAN I'M NOT ALONE IN HERE? HEY!
YOU ARE NEVER ALONE, NOT AS LONG AS I DRAW BREATH!
FEAR NOT, FAIR JENNIFER. I SHALL PROTECT YOU!
STARFOX?!
WILL... KEEP...YOU... SAFE!
INTRIGUING. THE DEFENDANT HAS ACTIVATED THE JUDGEMENT CHAIR.
THERE IS A HIGH PROBABILITY...

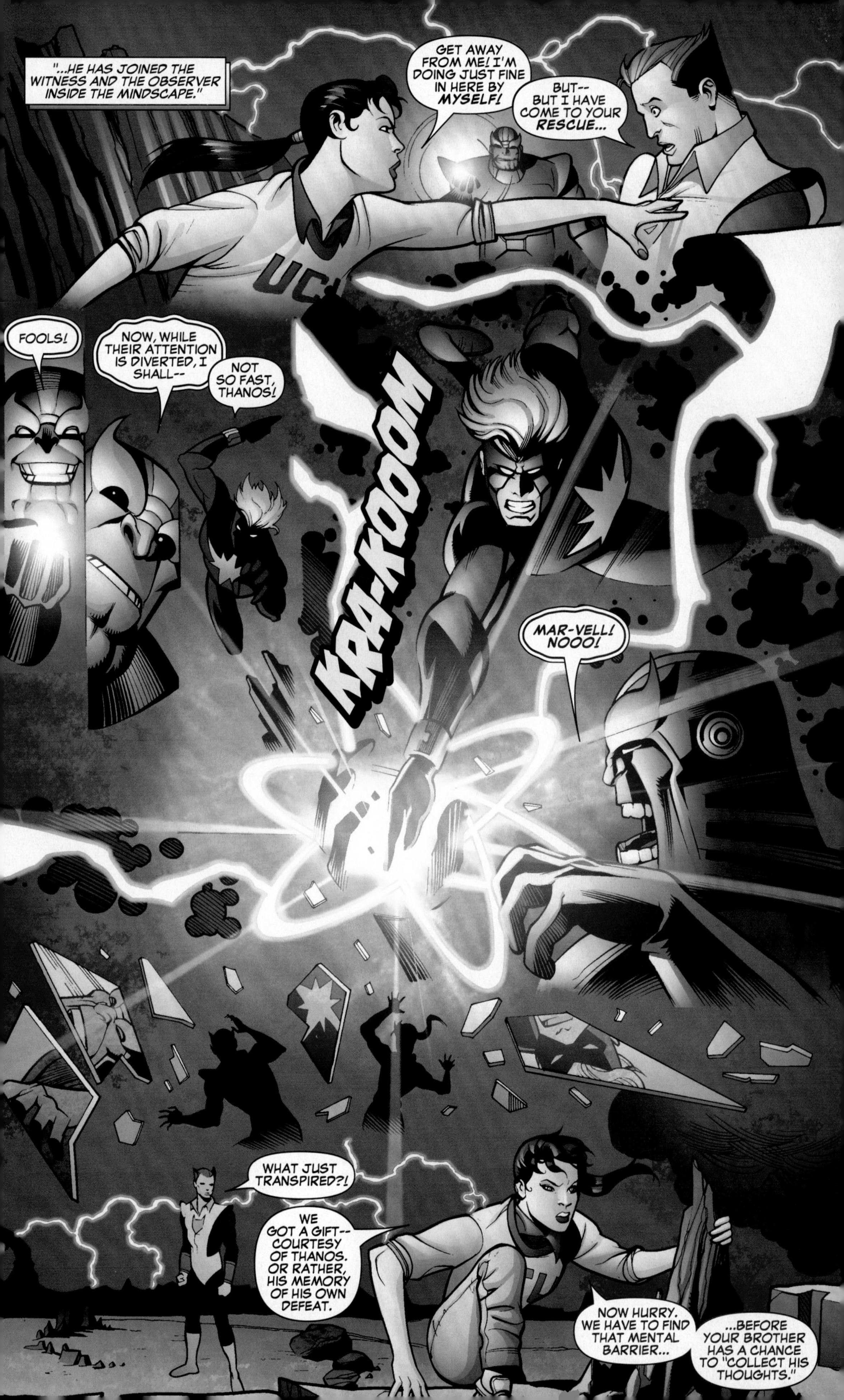
"...HE HAS JOINED THE WITNESS AND THE OBSERVER INSIDE THE MINDSCAPE."
GET AWAY FROM ME! I'M DOING JUST FINE IN HERE BY MYSELF!
BUT-- BUT I HAVE COME TO YOUR RESCUE...
FOOLS!
NOW, WHILE THEIR ATTENTION IS DIVERTED, I SHALL--
NOT SO FAST, THANOS!
KRA-KOOOM
MAR-VELL! NOOO!
WHAT JUST TRANSPIRED?!
WE GOT A GIFT-- COURTESY OF THANOS. OR RATHER, HIS MEMORY OF HIS OWN DEFEAT.
NOW HURRY. WE HAVE TO FIND THAT MENTAL BARRIER...
...BEFORE YOUR BROTHER HAS A CHANCE TO "COLLECT HIS THOUGHTS."

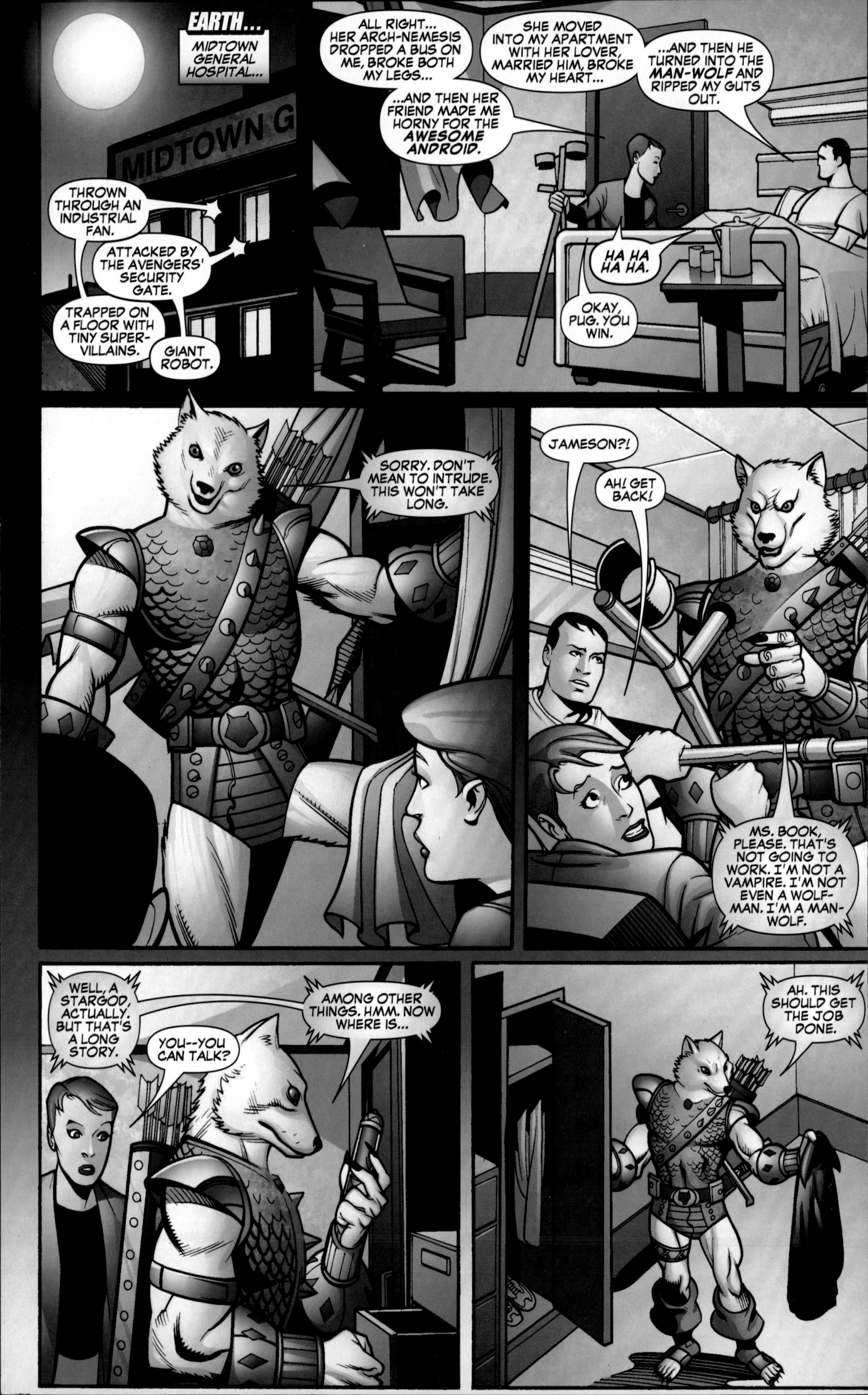
EARTH...
MIDTOWN GENERAL HOSPITAL...
MIDTOWN G
THROWN THROUGH AN INDUSTRIAL FAN.
ATTACKED BY THE AVENGERS' SECURITY GATE.
TRAPPED ON A FLOOR WITH TINY SUPER-VILLAINS.
GIANT ROBOT.
ALL RIGHT... HER ARCH-NEMESIS DROPPED A BUS ON ME, BROKE BOTH MY LEGS...
...AND THEN HER FRIEND MADE ME HORNY FOR THE AWESOME ANDROID.
SHE MOVED INTO MY APARTMENT WITH HER LOVER, MARRIED HIM, BROKE MY HEART...
...AND THEN HE TURNED INTO THE MAN-WOLF AND RIPPED MY GUTS OUT.
HA HA HA HA.
OKAY, PUG. YOU WIN.
SORRY. DON'T MEAN TO INTRUDE. THIS WON'T TAKE LONG.
JAMESON?!
AH! GET BACK!
MS. BOOK, PLEASE. THAT'S NOT GOING TO WORK. I'M NOT A VAMPIRE. I'M NOT EVEN A WOLF-MAN. I'M A MAN-WOLF.
YOU--YOU CAN TALK?
WELL, A STARGOD, ACTUALLY. BUT THAT'S A LONG STORY.
AMONG OTHER THINGS. HMM. NOW WHERE IS...
AH. THIS SHOULD GET THE JOB DONE.

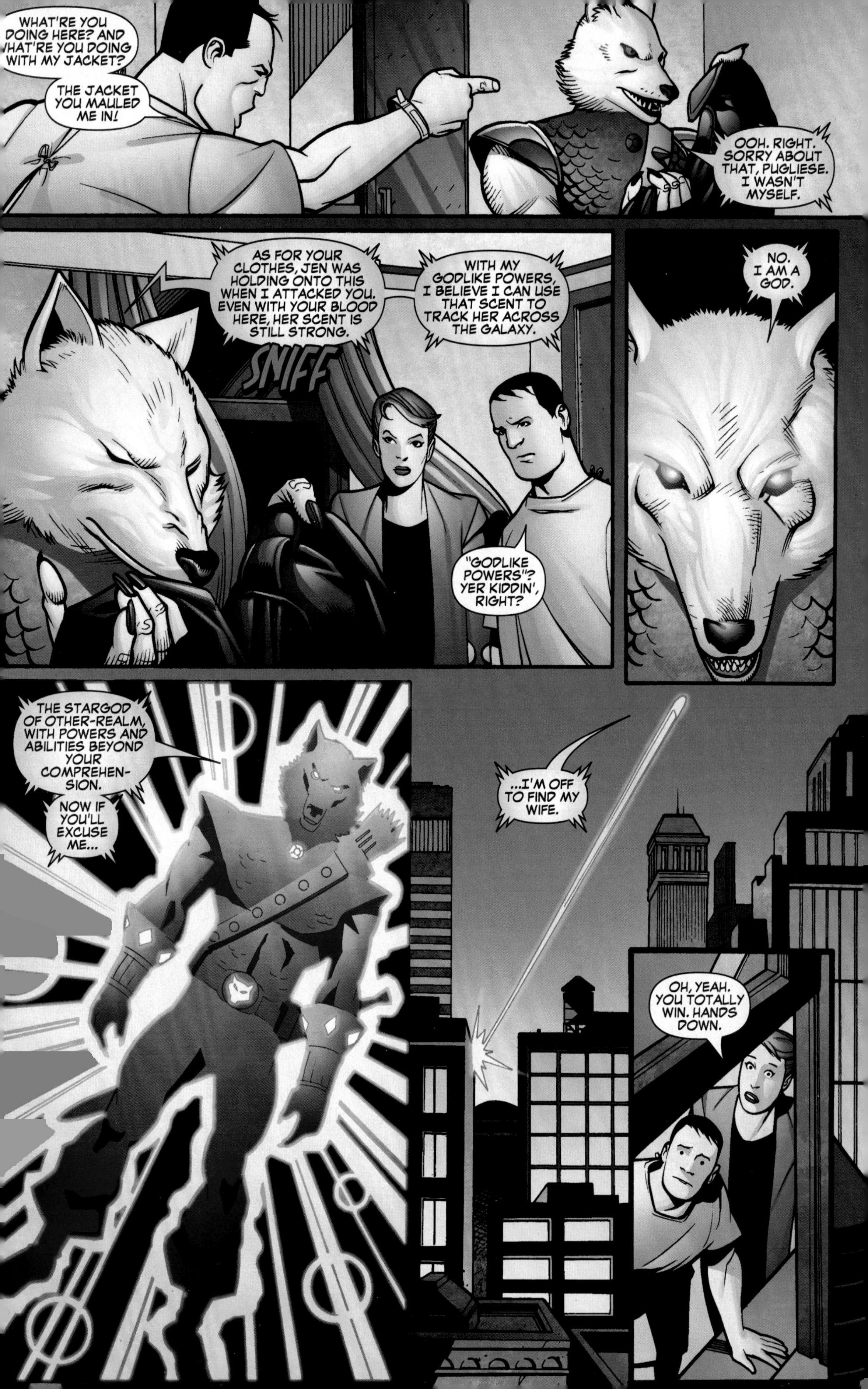
WHAT'RE YOU DOING HERE? AND WHAT'RE YOU DOING WITH MY JACKET?
THE JACKET YOU MAULED ME IN!
OOH. RIGHT. SORRY ABOUT THAT, PUGLIESE. I WASN'T MYSELF.
AS FOR YOUR CLOTHES, JEN WAS HOLDING ONTO THIS WHEN I ATTACKED YOU. EVEN WITH YOUR BLOOD HERE, HER SCENT IS STILL STRONG.
SNIFF
WITH MY GODLIKE POWERS, I BELIEVE I CAN USE THAT SCENT TO TRACK HER ACROSS THE GALAXY.
"GODLIKE POWERS"? YER KIDDIN', RIGHT?
NO. I AM A GOD.
THE STARGOD OF OTHER-REALM, WITH POWERS AND ABILITIES BEYOND YOUR COMPREHEN-SION.
NOW IF YOU'LL EXCUSE ME...
...I'M OFF TO FIND MY WIFE.
OH, YEAH. YOU TOTALLY WIN. HANDS DOWN.

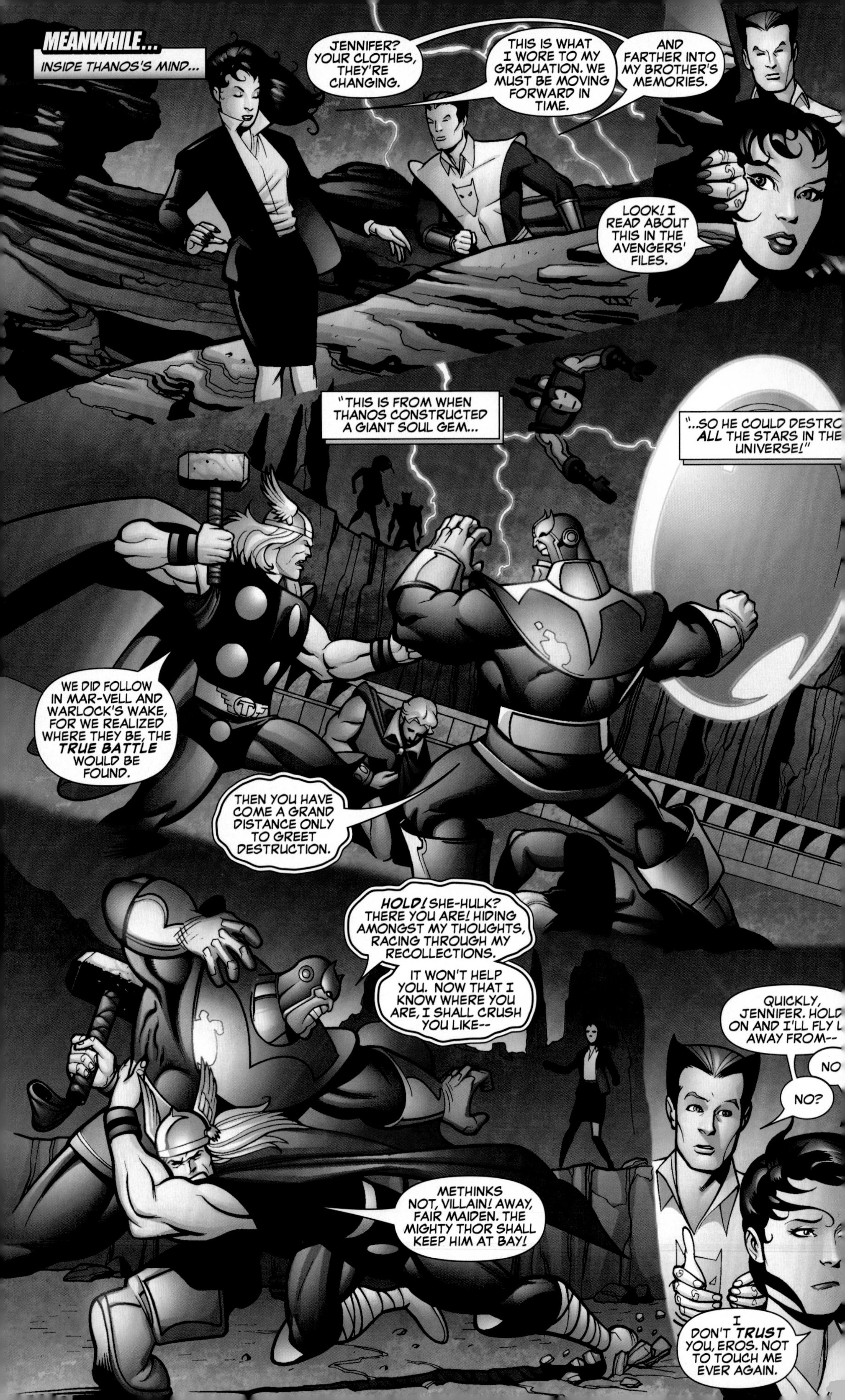
MEANWHILE...
INSIDE THANOS'S MIND...
JENNIFER? YOUR CLOTHES, THEY'RE CHANGING.
THIS IS WHAT I WORE TO MY GRADUATION. WE MUST BE MOVING FORWARD IN TIME.
AND FARTHER INTO MY BROTHER'S MEMORIES.
LOOK! I READ ABOUT THIS IN THE AVENGERS' FILES.
"THIS IS FROM WHEN THANOS CONSTRUCTED A GIANT SOUL GEM...
"...SO HE COULD DESTRO ALL THE STARS IN THE UNIVERSE!"
WE DID FOLLOW IN MAR-VELL AND WARLOCK'S WAKE, FOR WE REALIZED WHERE THEY BE, THE TRUE BATTLE WOULD BE FOUND.
THEN YOU HAVE COME A GRAND DISTANCE ONLY TO GREET DESTRUCTION.
HOLD! SHE-HULK? THERE YOU ARE! HIDING AMONGST MY THOUGHTS, RACING THROUGH MY RECOLLECTIONS.
IT WON'T HELP YOU. NOW THAT I KNOW WHERE YOU ARE, I SHALL CRUSH YOU LIKE--
QUICKLY, JENNIFER. HOLD ON AND I'LL FLY AWAY FROM--
NO
NO?
METHINKS NOT, VILLAIN! AWAY, FAIR MAIDEN. THE MIGHTY THOR SHALL KEEP HIM AT BAY!
I DON'T TRUST YOU, EROS. NOT TO TOUCH ME EVER AGAIN.

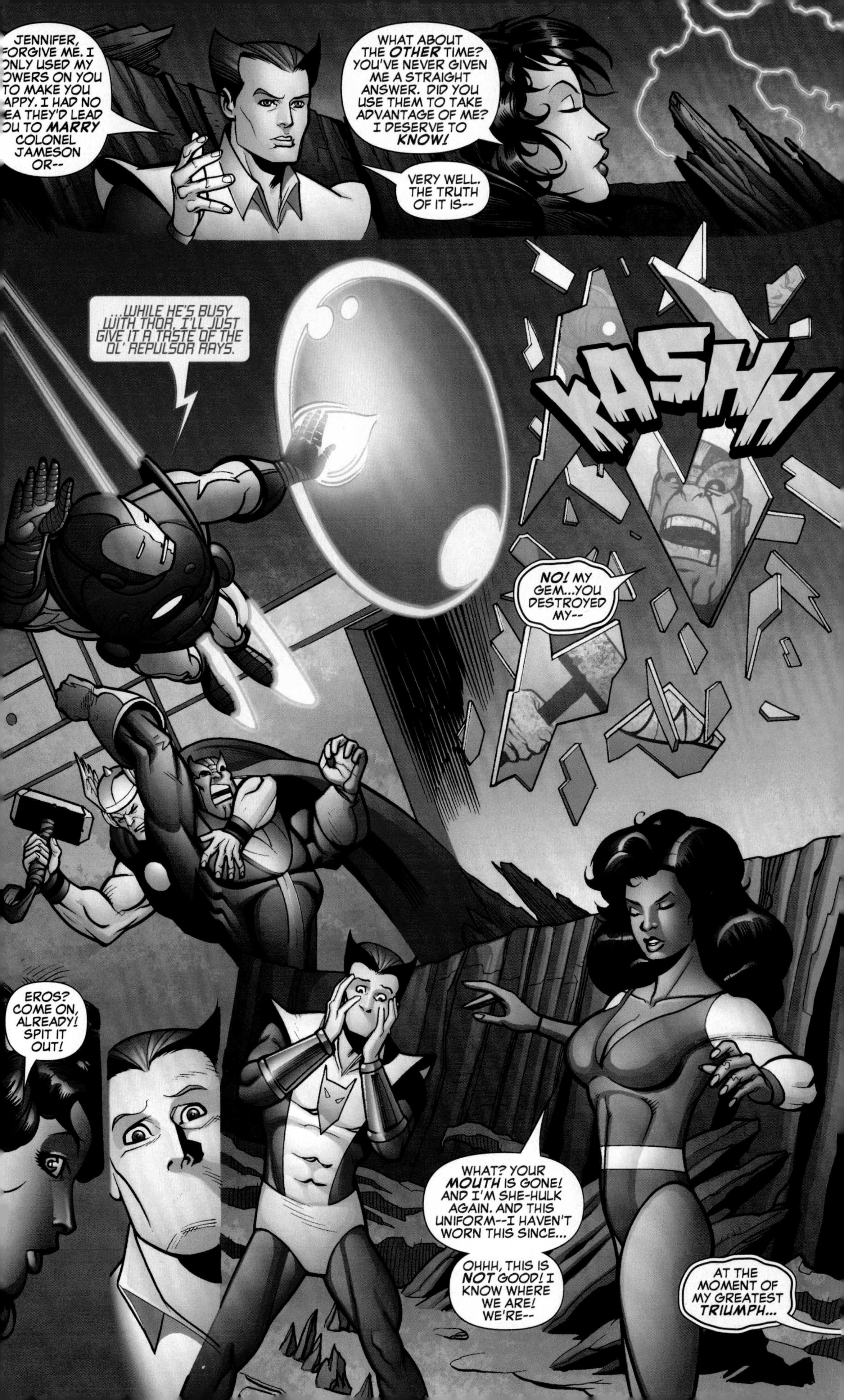
JENNIFER, FORGIVE ME. I ONLY USED MY POWERS ON YOU TO MAKE YOU HAPPY. I HAD NO IDEA THEY'D LEAD YOU TO MARRY COLONEL JAMESON OR--
WHAT ABOUT THE OTHER TIME? YOU'VE NEVER GIVEN ME A STRAIGHT ANSWER. DID YOU USE THEM TO TAKE ADVANTAGE OF ME? I DESERVE TO KNOW!
VERY WELL. THE TRUTH OF IT IS--
...WHILE HE'S BUSY WITH THOR, I'LL JUST GIVE IT A TASTE OF THE OL' REPULSOR RAYS.
KASHH
NO! MY GEM...YOU DESTROYED MY--
EROS? COME ON, ALREADY! SPIT IT OUT!
WHAT? YOUR MOUTH IS GONE! AND I'M SHE-HULK AGAIN. AND THIS UNIFORM--I HAVEN'T WORN THIS SINCE...
OHHH, THIS IS NOT GOOD! I KNOW WHERE WE ARE! WE'RE--
AT THE MOMENT OF MY GREATEST TRIUMPH...

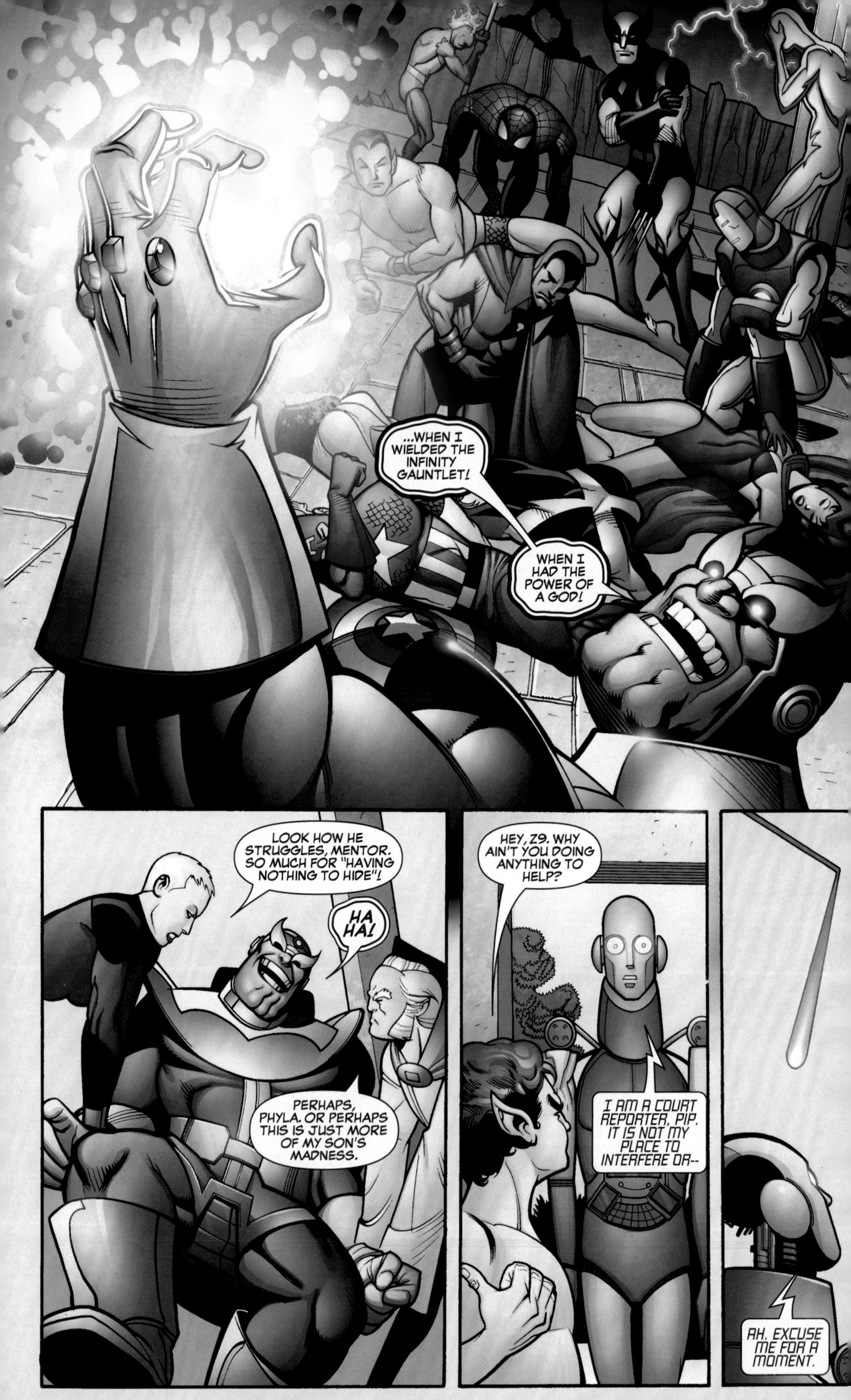
...WHEN I WIELDED THE INFINITY GAUNTLET!
WHEN I HAD THE POWER OF A GOD!
LOOK HOW HE STRUGGLES, MENTOR. SO MUCH FOR "HAVING NOTHING TO HIDE"!
HA HA!
PERHAPS, PHYLA. OR PERHAPS THIS IS JUST MORE OF MY SON'S MADNESS.
HEY, Z9. WHY AIN'T YOU DOING ANYTHING TO HELP?
I AM A COURT REPORTER, PIP. IT IS NOT MY PLACE TO INTERFERE OR--
AH. EXCUSE ME FOR A MOMENT.

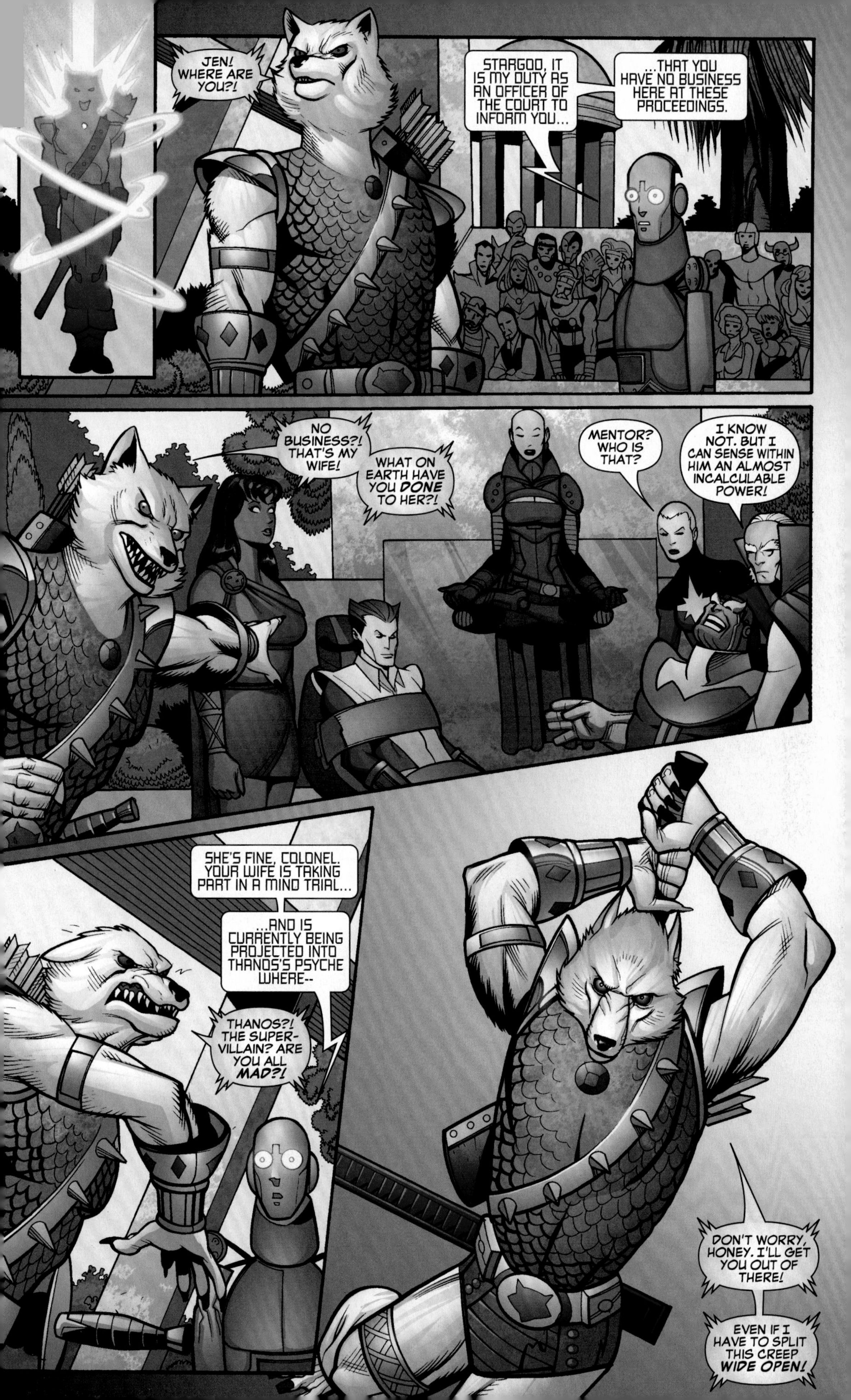
JEN! WHERE ARE YOU?!
STARGOD, IT IS MY DUTY AS AN OFFICER OF THE COURT TO INFORM YOU...
...THAT YOU HAVE NO BUSINESS HERE AT THESE PROCEEDINGS.
NO BUSINESS?! THAT'S MY WIFE!
WHAT ON EARTH HAVE YOU **DONE** TO HER?!
MENTOR? WHO IS THAT?
I KNOW NOT. BUT I CAN SENSE WITHIN HIM AN ALMOST INCALCULABLE POWER!
SHE'S FINE, COLONEL. YOUR WIFE IS TAKING PART IN A MIND TRIAL...
...AND IS CURRENTLY BEING PROJECTED INTO THANOS'S PSYCHE WHERE--
THANOS?! THE SUPER-VILLAIN? ARE YOU ALL **MAD?!**
DON'T WORRY, HONEY. I'LL GET YOU OUT OF THERE!
EVEN IF I HAVE TO SPLIT THIS CREEP **WIDE OPEN!**

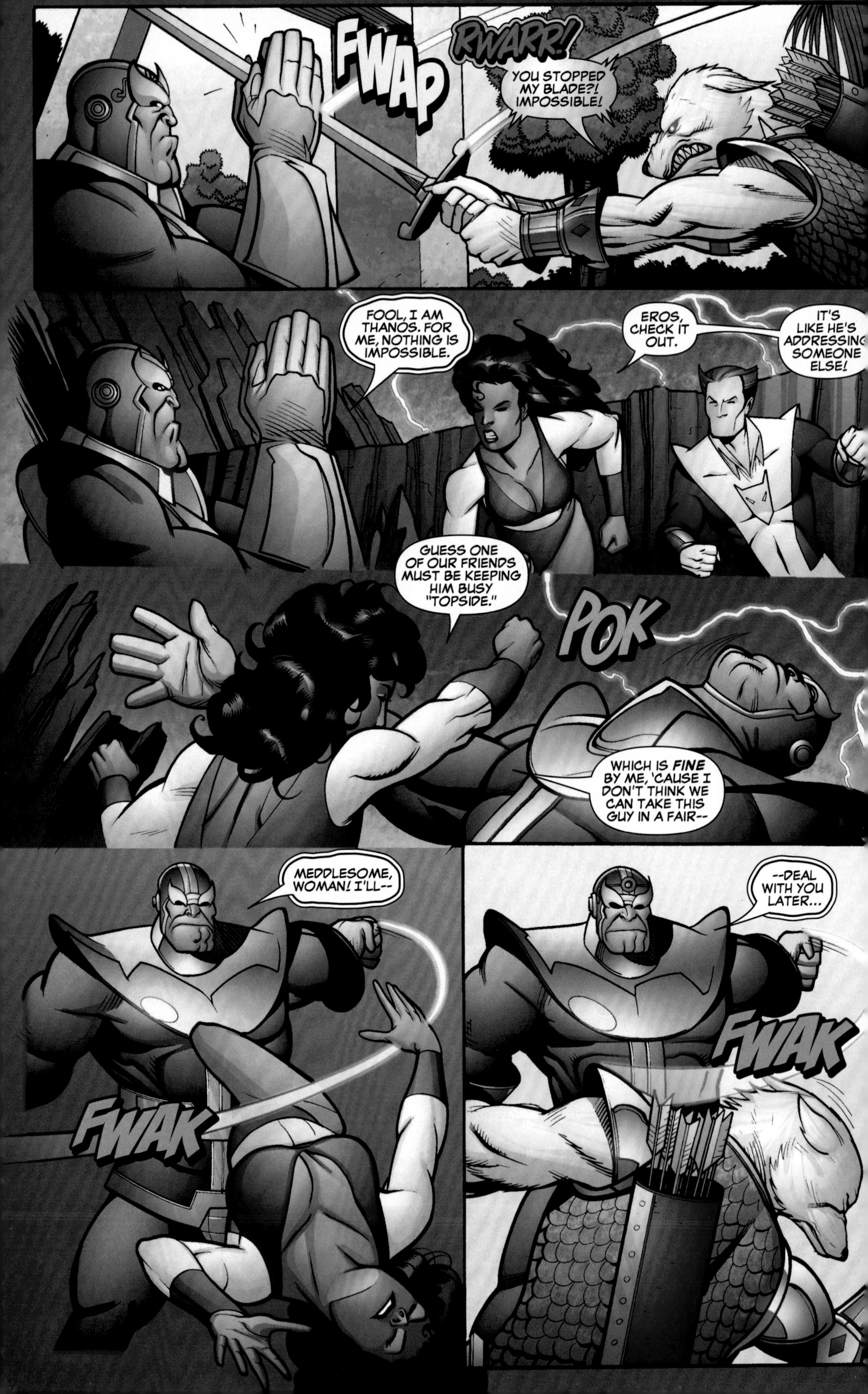
FWAP
RWARR!
YOU STOPPED MY BLADE?! IMPOSSIBLE!
FOOL, I AM THANOS. FOR ME, NOTHING IS IMPOSSIBLE.
EROS, CHECK IT OUT.
IT'S LIKE HE'S ADDRESSING SOMEONE ELSE!
GUESS ONE OF OUR FRIENDS MUST BE KEEPING HIM BUSY "TOPSIDE."
POK
WHICH IS FINE BY ME, 'CAUSE I DON'T THINK WE CAN TAKE THIS GUY IN A FAIR--
MEDDLESOME, WOMAN! I'LL--
FWAK
--DEAL WITH YOU LATER...
FWAK

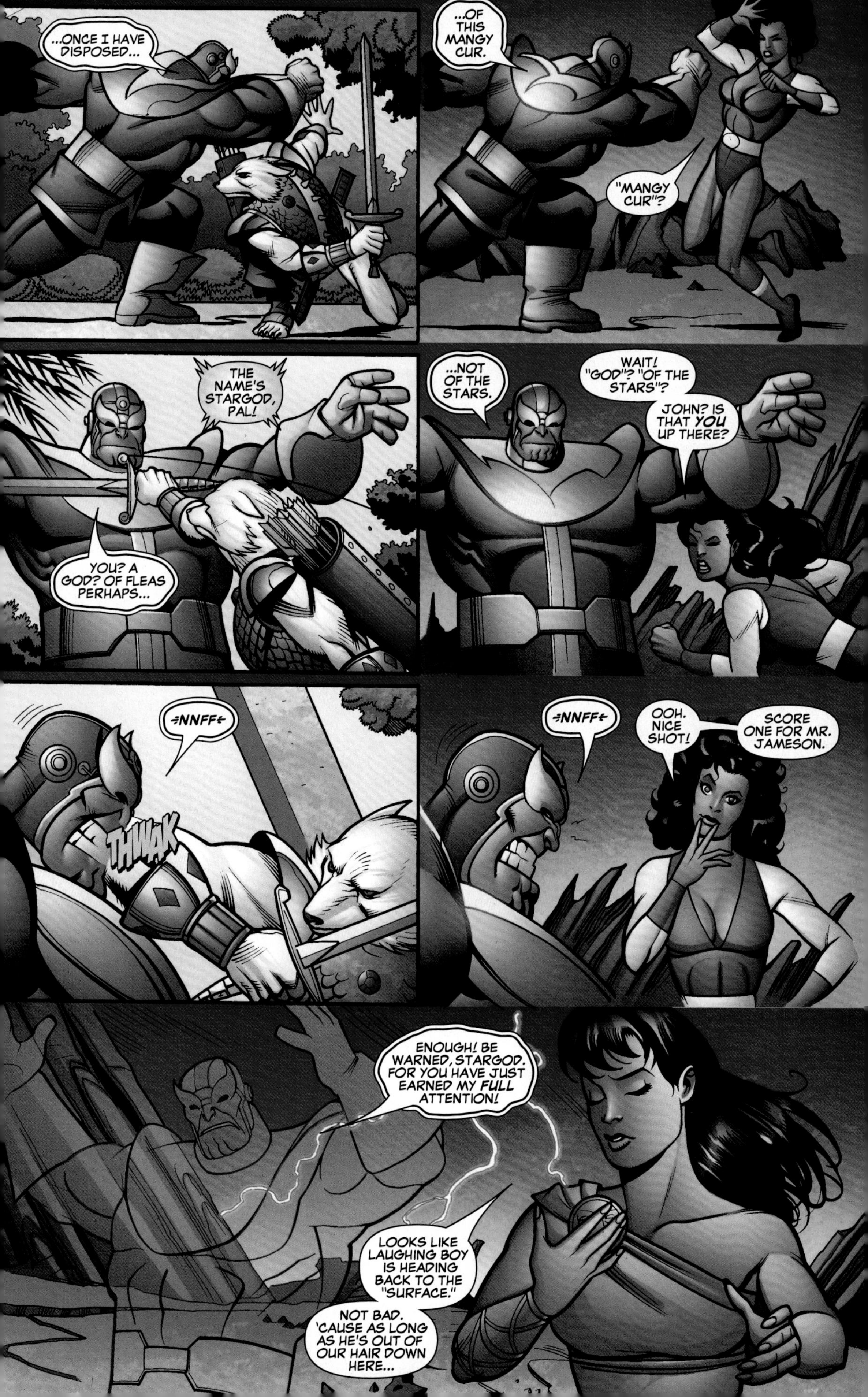
...ONCE I HAVE DISPOSED...
...OF THIS MANGY CUR.
"MANGY CUR"?
THE NAME'S STARGOD, PAL!
YOU? A GOD? OF FLEAS PERHAPS...
...NOT OF THE STARS.
WAIT! "GOD"? "OF THE STARS"?
JOHN? IS THAT *YOU* UP THERE?
NNFF
THWAK
NNFF
OOH. NICE SHOT!
SCORE ONE FOR MR. JAMESON.
ENOUGH! BE WARNED, STARGOD. FOR YOU HAVE JUST EARNED MY *FULL* ATTENTION!
LOOKS LIKE LAUGHING BOY IS HEADING BACK TO THE "SURFACE."
NOT BAD. 'CAUSE AS LONG AS HE'S OUT OF OUR HAIR DOWN HERE...

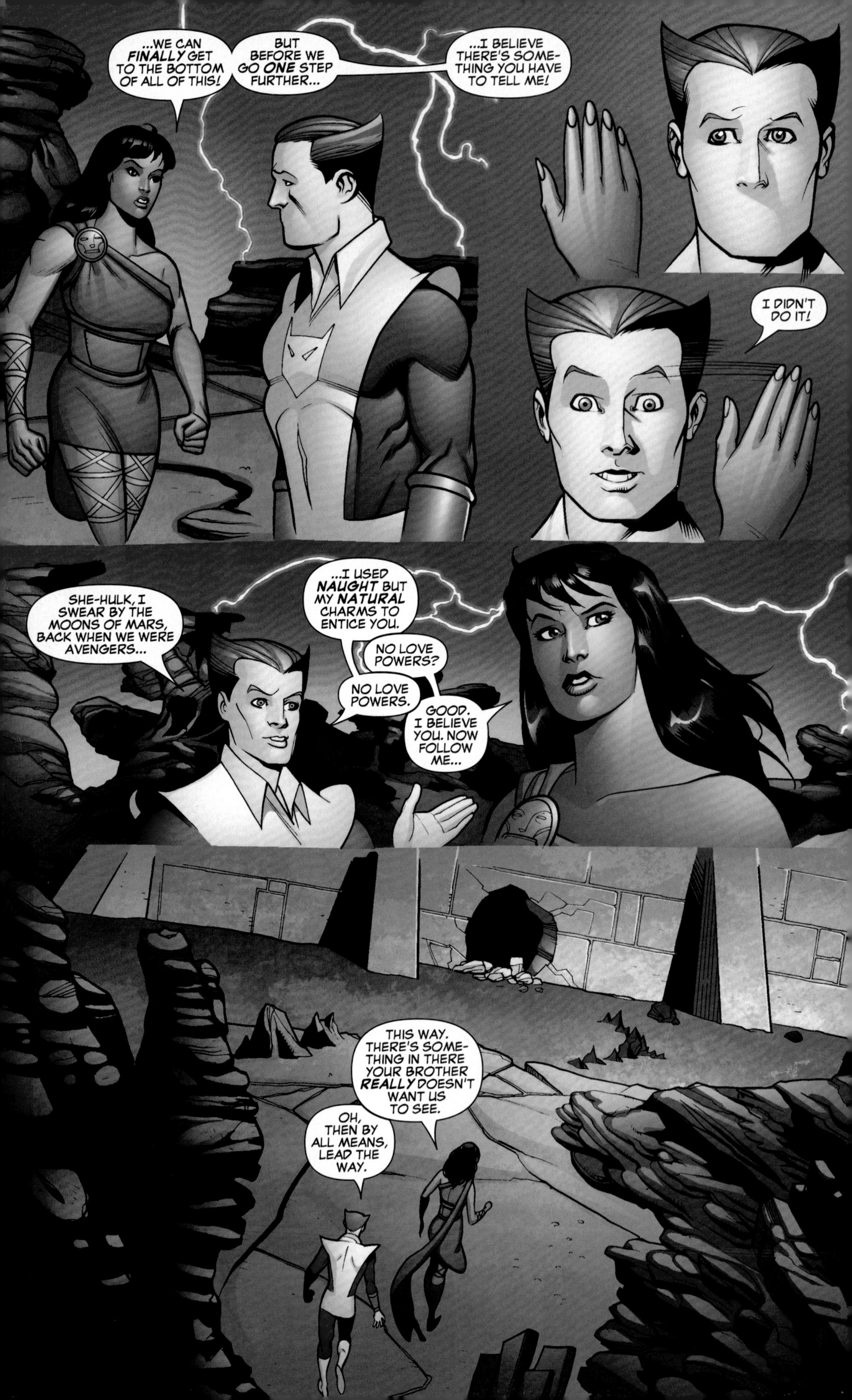
...WE CAN FINALLY GET TO THE BOTTOM OF ALL OF THIS!
BUT BEFORE WE GO ONE STEP FURTHER...
...I BELIEVE THERE'S SOME-THING YOU HAVE TO TELL ME!
I DIDN'T DO IT!
SHE-HULK, I SWEAR BY THE MOONS OF MARS, BACK WHEN WE WERE AVENGERS...
...I USED NAUGHT BUT MY NATURAL CHARMS TO ENTICE YOU.
NO LOVE POWERS?
NO LOVE POWERS.
GOOD. I BELIEVE YOU. NOW FOLLOW ME...
THIS WAY. THERE'S SOME-THING IN THERE YOUR BROTHER REALLY DOESN'T WANT US TO SEE.
OH, THEN BY ALL MEANS, LEAD THE WAY.

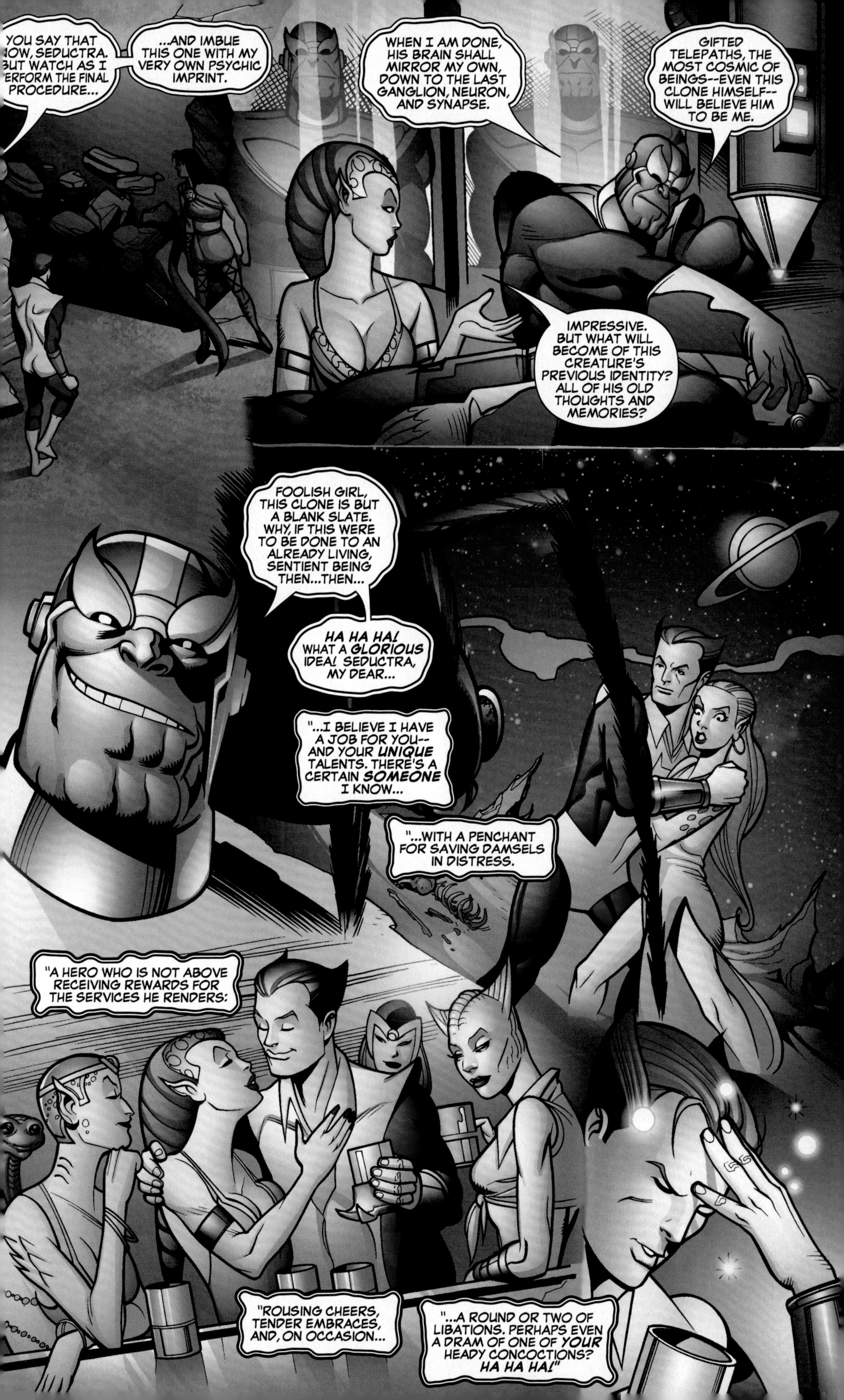
YOU SAY THAT NOW, SEDUCTRA. BUT WATCH AS I PERFORM THE FINAL PROCEDURE...
...AND IMBUE THIS ONE WITH MY VERY OWN PSYCHIC IMPRINT.
WHEN I AM DONE, HIS BRAIN SHALL MIRROR MY OWN, DOWN TO THE LAST GANGLION, NEURON, AND SYNAPSE.
GIFTED TELEPATHS, THE MOST COSMIC OF BEINGS--EVEN THIS CLONE HIMSELF--WILL BELIEVE HIM TO BE ME.
IMPRESSIVE. BUT WHAT WILL BECOME OF THIS CREATURE'S PREVIOUS IDENTITY? ALL OF HIS OLD THOUGHTS AND MEMORIES?
FOOLISH GIRL, THIS CLONE IS BUT A BLANK SLATE. WHY, IF THIS WERE TO BE DONE TO AN ALREADY LIVING, SENTIENT BEING THEN...THEN...
HA HA HA! WHAT A GLORIOUS IDEA! SEDUCTRA, MY DEAR...
"...I BELIEVE I HAVE A JOB FOR YOU--AND YOUR UNIQUE TALENTS. THERE'S A CERTAIN SOMEONE I KNOW...
"...WITH A PENCHANT FOR SAVING DAMSELS IN DISTRESS.
"A HERO WHO IS NOT ABOVE RECEIVING REWARDS FOR THE SERVICES HE RENDERS:
"ROUSING CHEERS, TENDER EMBRACES, AND, ON OCCASION...
"...A ROUND OR TWO OF LIBATIONS. PERHAPS EVEN A DRAM OF ONE OF YOUR HEADY CONCOCTIONS? HA HA HA!"

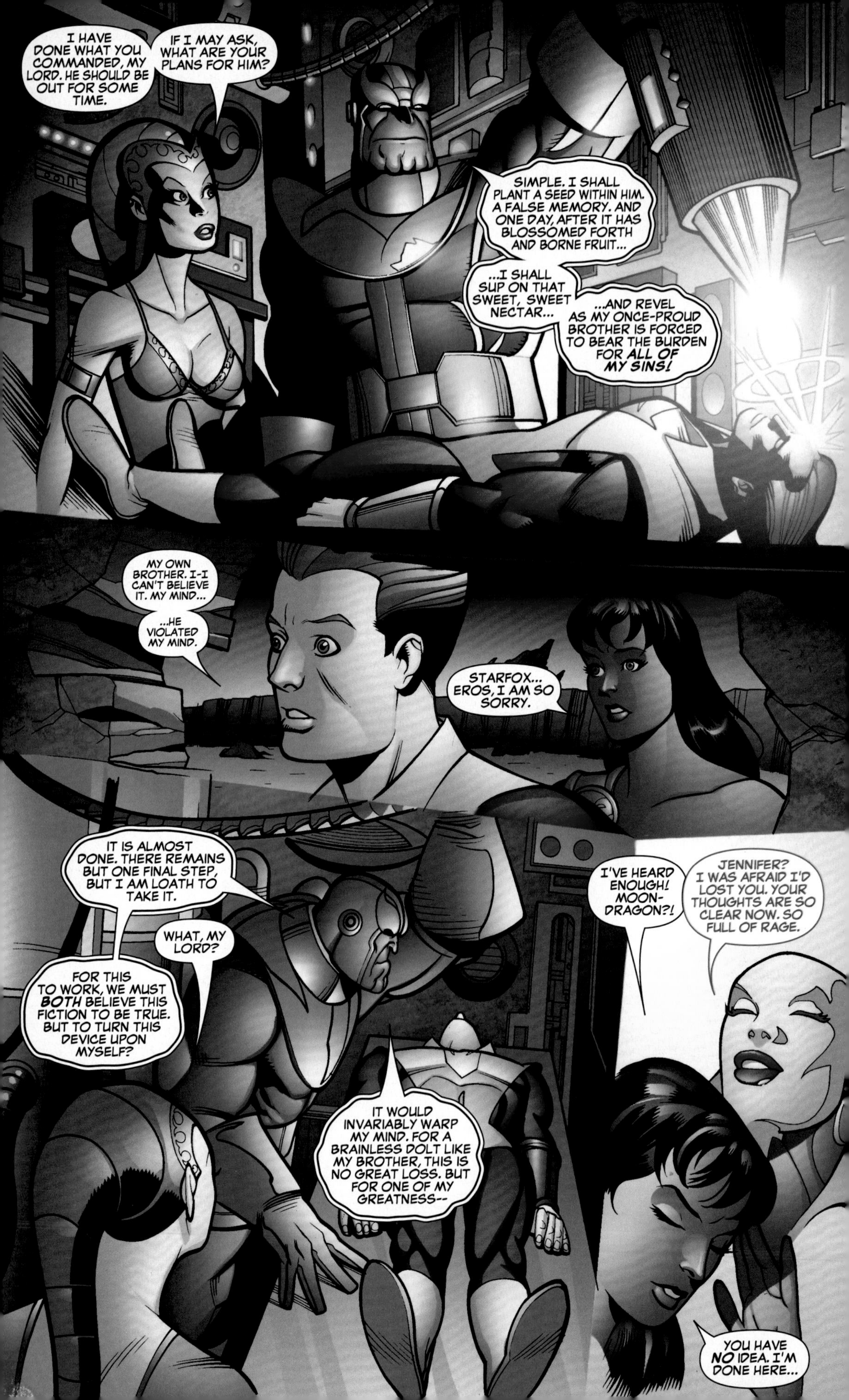
I HAVE DONE WHAT YOU COMMANDED, MY LORD. HE SHOULD BE OUT FOR SOME TIME.
IF I MAY ASK, WHAT ARE YOUR PLANS FOR HIM?
SIMPLE. I SHALL PLANT A SEED WITHIN HIM. A FALSE MEMORY. AND ONE DAY, AFTER IT HAS BLOSSOMED FORTH AND BORNE FRUIT...
...I SHALL SUP ON THAT SWEET, SWEET NECTAR...
...AND REVEL AS MY ONCE-PROUD BROTHER IS FORCED TO BEAR THE BURDEN FOR ALL OF MY SINS!
MY OWN BROTHER. I-I CAN'T BELIEVE IT. MY MIND...
...HE VIOLATED MY MIND.
STARFOX... EROS, I AM SO SORRY.
IT IS ALMOST DONE. THERE REMAINS BUT ONE FINAL STEP, BUT I AM LOATH TO TAKE IT.
WHAT, MY LORD?
FOR THIS TO WORK, WE MUST BOTH BELIEVE THIS FICTION TO BE TRUE. BUT TO TURN THIS DEVICE UPON MYSELF?
IT WOULD INVARIABLY WARP MY MIND. FOR A BRAINLESS DOLT LIKE MY BROTHER, THIS IS NO GREAT LOSS. BUT FOR ONE OF MY GREATNESS--
I'VE HEARD ENOUGH! MOON-DRAGON?!
JENNIFER? I WAS AFRAID I'D LOST YOU. YOUR THOUGHTS ARE SO CLEAR NOW. SO FULL OF RAGE.
YOU HAVE NO IDEA. I'M DONE HERE...

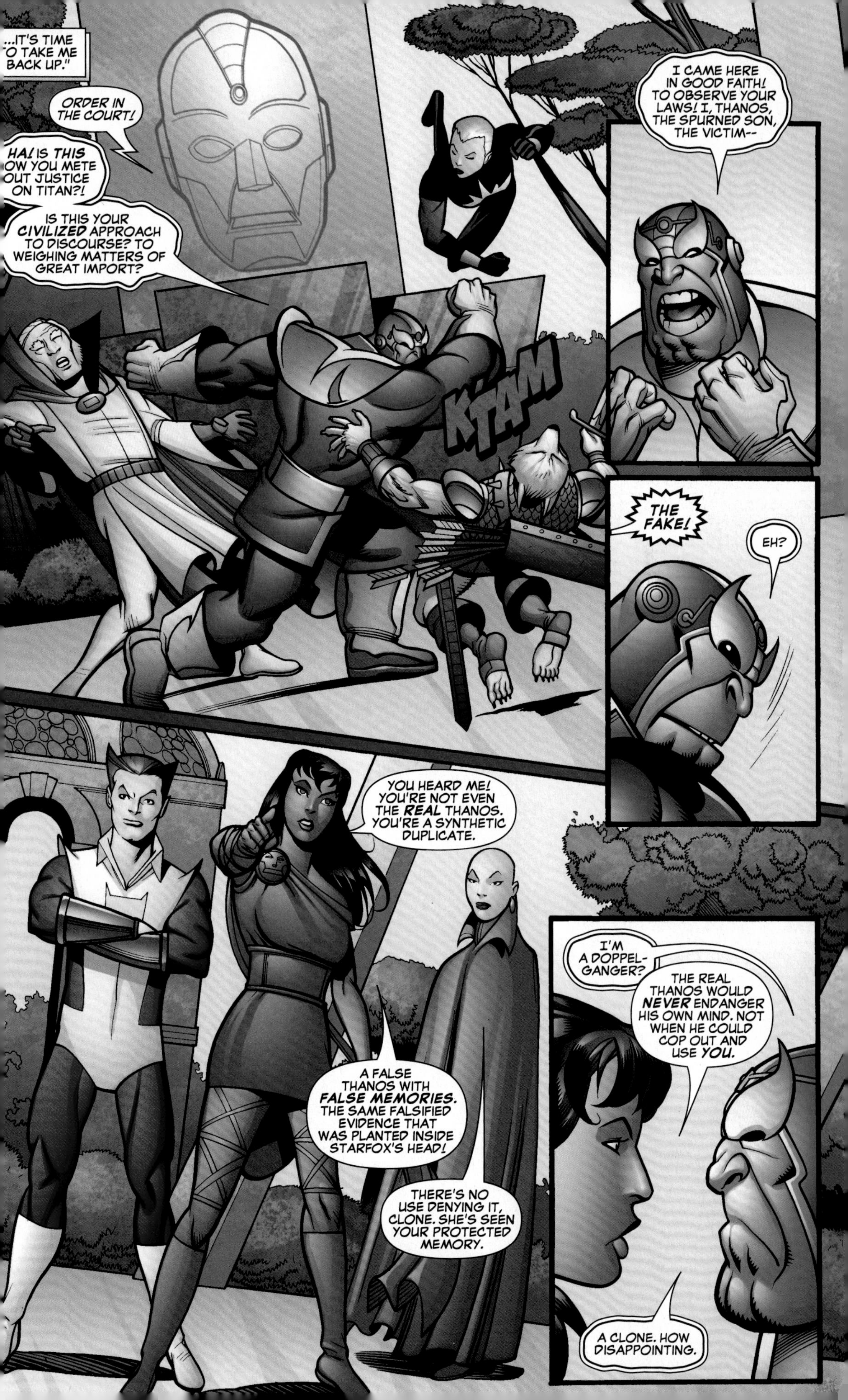
...IT'S TIME TO TAKE ME BACK UP."
ORDER IN THE COURT!
HA! IS THIS HOW YOU METE OUT JUSTICE ON TITAN?!
IS THIS YOUR CIVILIZED APPROACH TO DISCOURSE? TO WEIGHING MATTERS OF GREAT IMPORT?
I CAME HERE IN GOOD FAITH! TO OBSERVE YOUR LAWS! I, THANOS, THE SPURNED SON, THE VICTIM--
K'TAM
THE FAKE!
EH?
YOU HEARD ME! YOU'RE NOT EVEN THE REAL THANOS. YOU'RE A SYNTHETIC DUPLICATE.
A FALSE THANOS WITH FALSE MEMORIES. THE SAME FALSIFIED EVIDENCE THAT WAS PLANTED INSIDE STARFOX'S HEAD!
THERE'S NO USE DENYING IT, CLONE. SHE'S SEEN YOUR PROTECTED MEMORY.
I'M A DOPPEL-GANGER?
THE REAL THANOS WOULD NEVER ENDANGER HIS OWN MIND. NOT WHEN HE COULD COP OUT AND USE YOU.
A CLONE. HOW DISAPPOINTING.

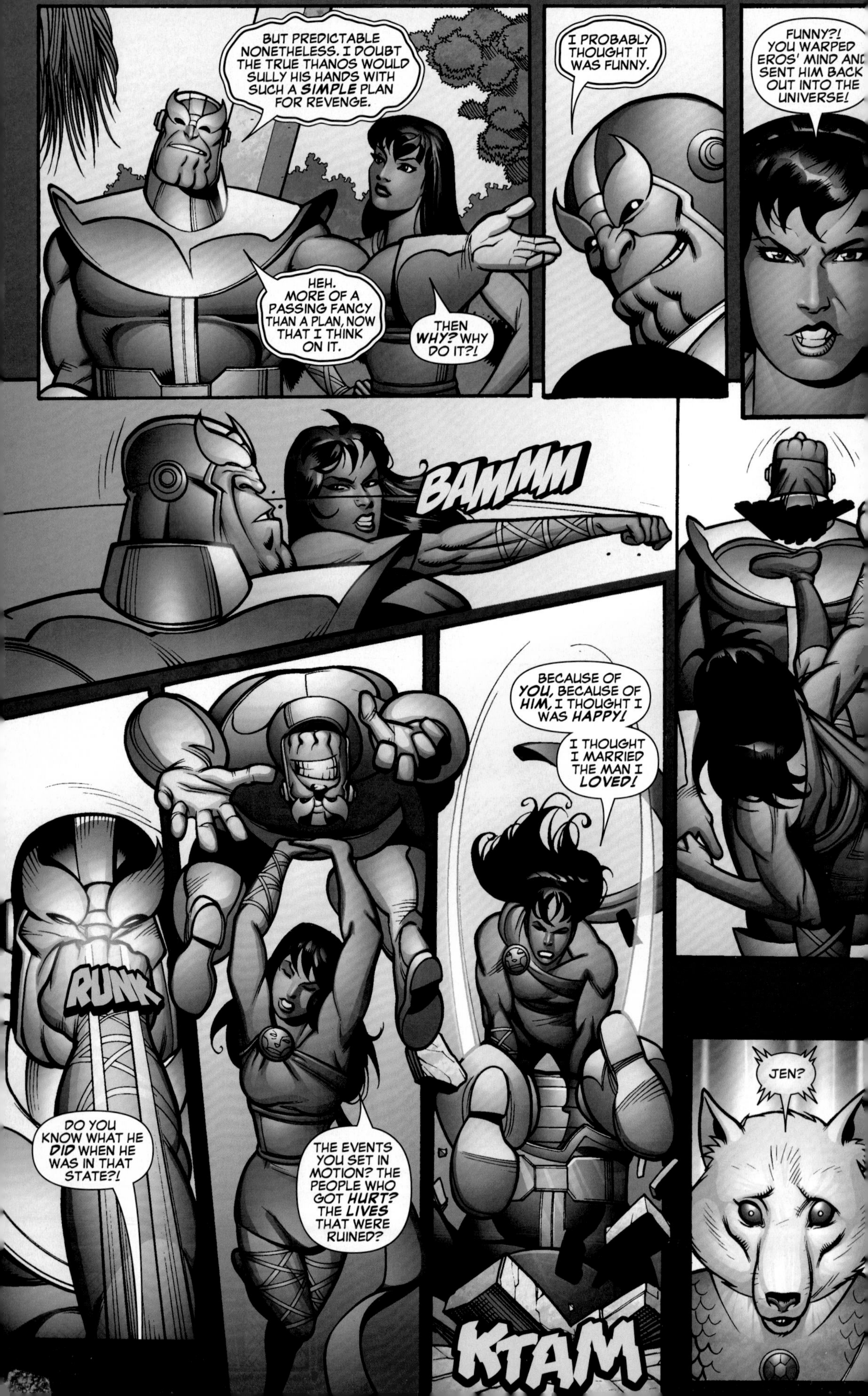

BUT PREDICTABLE NONETHELESS. I DOUBT THE TRUE THANOS WOULD SULLY HIS HANDS WITH SUCH A SIMPLE PLAN FOR REVENGE.
HEH. MORE OF A PASSING FANCY THAN A PLAN, NOW THAT I THINK ON IT.
THEN WHY? WHY DO IT?!
I PROBABLY THOUGHT IT WAS FUNNY.
FUNNY?! YOU WARPED EROS' MIND AND SENT HIM BACK OUT INTO THE UNIVERSE!
BAMMM
RUNK
DO YOU KNOW WHAT HE DID WHEN HE WAS IN THAT STATE?!
THE EVENTS YOU SET IN MOTION? THE PEOPLE WHO GOT HURT? THE LIVES THAT WERE RUINED?
BECAUSE OF YOU, BECAUSE OF HIM, I THOUGHT I WAS HAPPY!
I THOUGHT I MARRIED THE MAN I LOVED!
KTAM
JEN?

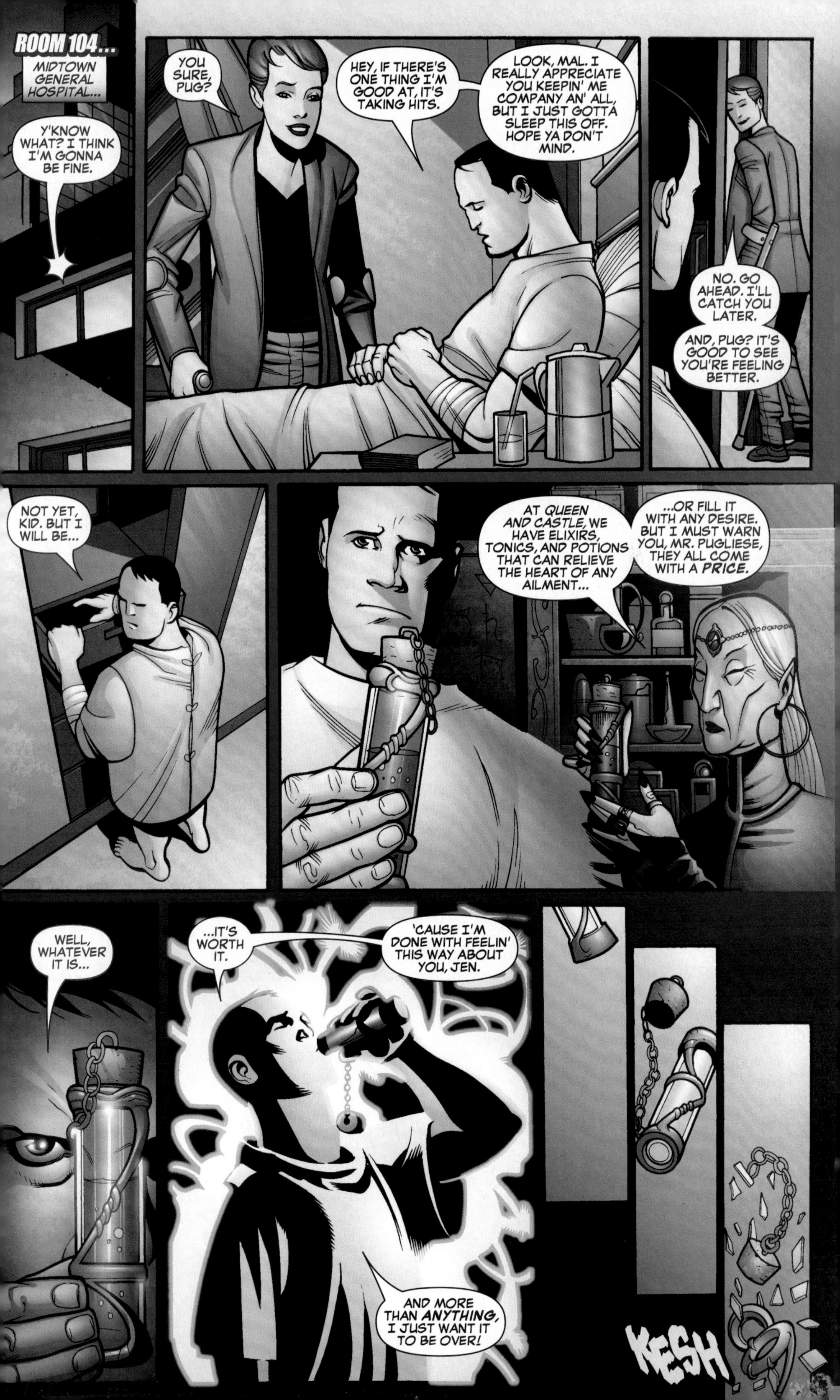

ROOM 104...
MIDTOWN GENERAL HOSPITAL...
Y'KNOW WHAT? I THINK I'M GONNA BE FINE.
YOU SURE, PUG?
HEY, IF THERE'S ONE THING I'M GOOD AT, IT'S TAKING HITS.
LOOK, MAL. I REALLY APPRECIATE YOU KEEPIN' ME COMPANY AN' ALL, BUT I JUST GOTTA SLEEP THIS OFF. HOPE YA DON'T MIND.
NO. GO AHEAD. I'LL CATCH YOU LATER.
AND, PUG? IT'S GOOD TO SEE YOU'RE FEELING BETTER.
NOT YET, KID. BUT I WILL BE...
AT QUEEN AND CASTLE, WE HAVE ELIXIRS, TONICS, AND POTIONS THAT CAN RELIEVE THE HEART OF ANY AILMENT...
...OR FILL IT WITH ANY DESIRE. BUT I MUST WARN YOU, MR. PUGLIESE, THEY ALL COME WITH A PRICE.
WELL, WHATEVER IT IS...
...IT'S WORTH IT.
'CAUSE I'M DONE WITH FEELIN' THIS WAY ABOUT YOU, JEN.
AND MORE THAN ANYTHING, I JUST WANT IT TO BE OVER!
KESH

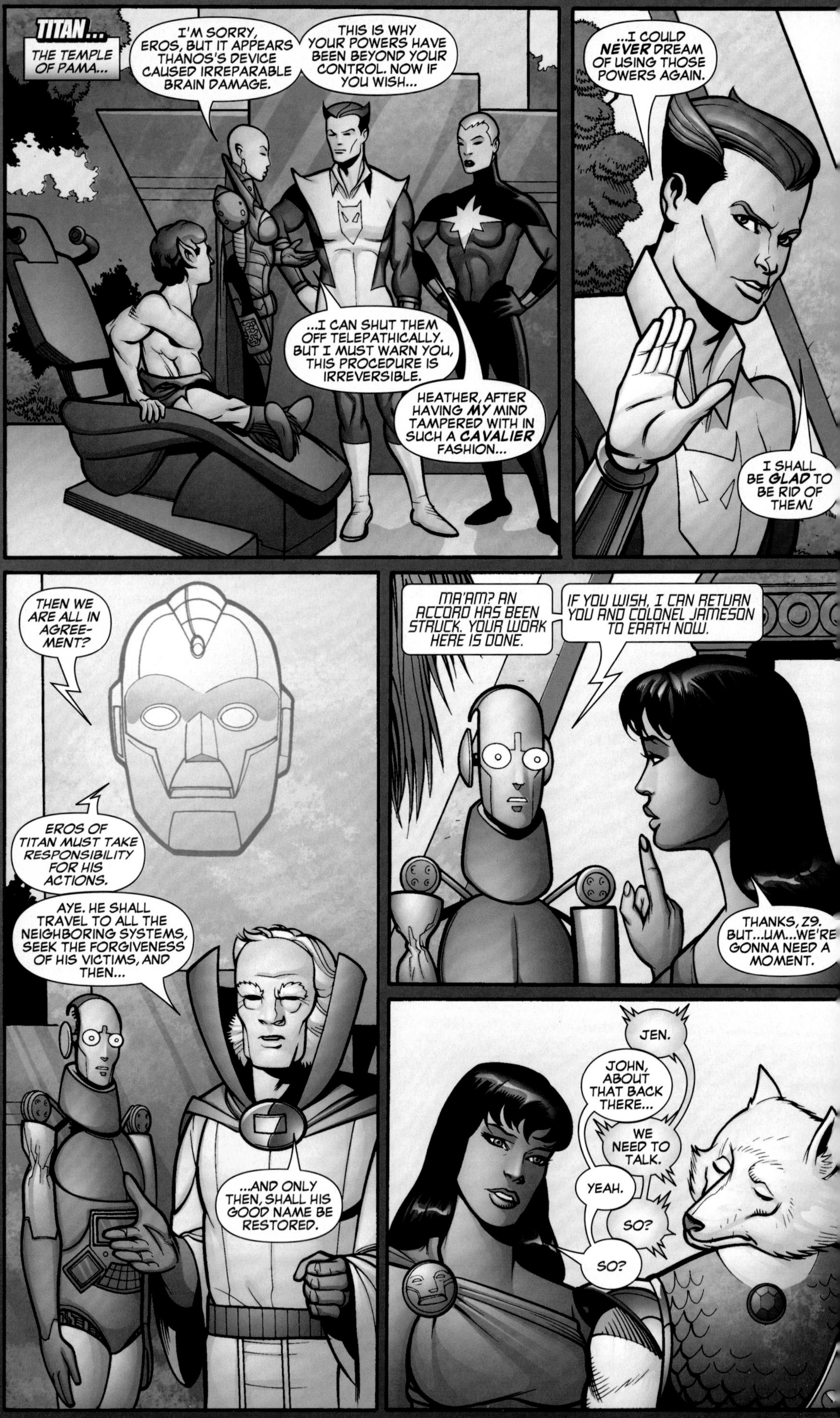
TITAN...
THE TEMPLE OF PAMA...
I'M SORRY, EROS, BUT IT APPEARS THANOS'S DEVICE CAUSED IRREPARABLE BRAIN DAMAGE.
THIS IS WHY YOUR POWERS HAVE BEEN BEYOND YOUR CONTROL. NOW IF YOU WISH...
...I CAN SHUT THEM OFF TELEPATHICALLY. BUT I MUST WARN YOU, THIS PROCEDURE IS IRREVERSIBLE.
HEATHER, AFTER HAVING MY MIND TAMPERED WITH IN SUCH A CAVALIER FASHION...
...I COULD NEVER DREAM OF USING THOSE POWERS AGAIN.
I SHALL BE GLAD TO BE RID OF THEM!
THEN WE ARE ALL IN AGREE-MENT?
EROS OF TITAN MUST TAKE RESPONSIBILITY FOR HIS ACTIONS.
AYE. HE SHALL TRAVEL TO ALL THE NEIGHBORING SYSTEMS, SEEK THE FORGIVENESS OF HIS VICTIMS, AND THEN...
...AND ONLY THEN, SHALL HIS GOOD NAME BE RESTORED.
MA'AM? AN ACCORD HAS BEEN STRUCK. YOUR WORK HERE IS DONE.
IF YOU WISH, I CAN RETURN YOU AND COLONEL JAMESON TO EARTH NOW.
THANKS, Z9. BUT...UM...WE'RE GONNA NEED A MOMENT.
JEN.
JOHN, ABOUT THAT BACK THERE...
WE NEED TO TALK.
YEAH.
SO?
SO?

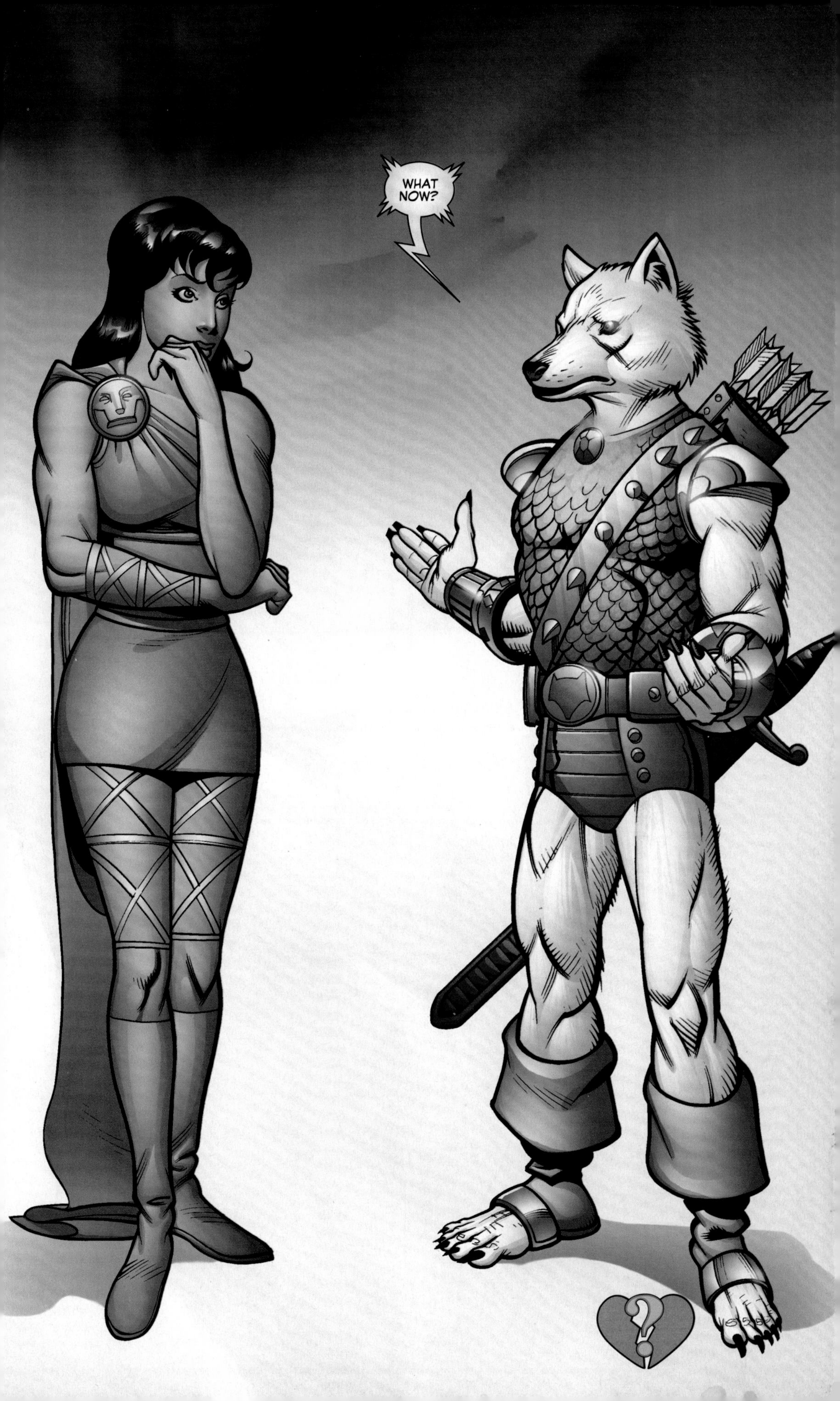
WHAT NOW?

SHE-HULK SKETCHES BY
Paul Smith

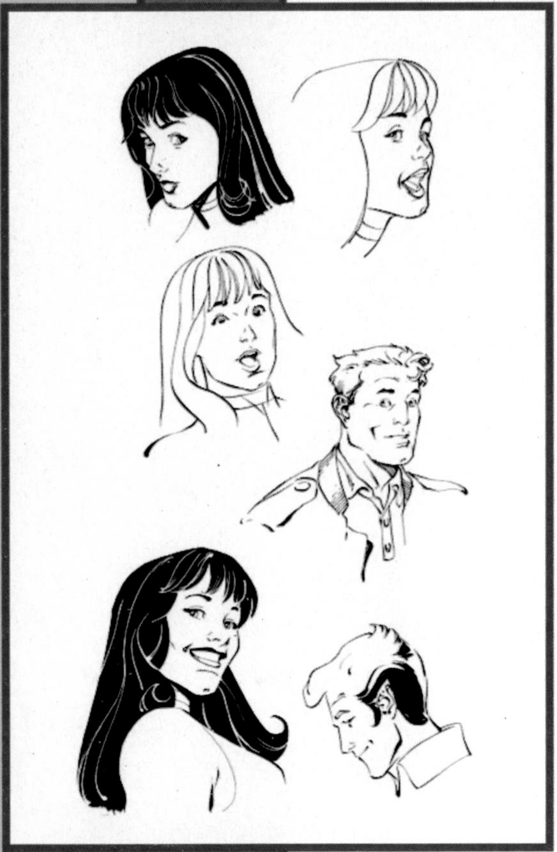

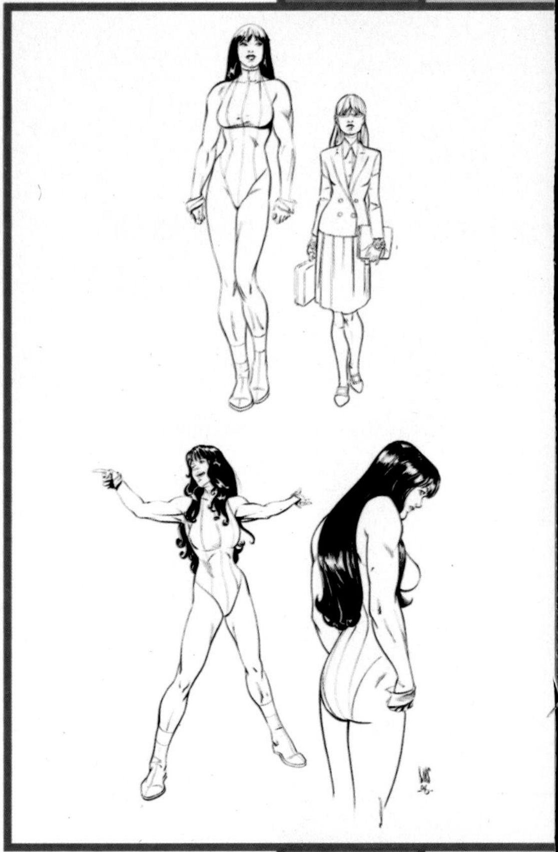

SHE-HULK BY
Paul Smith

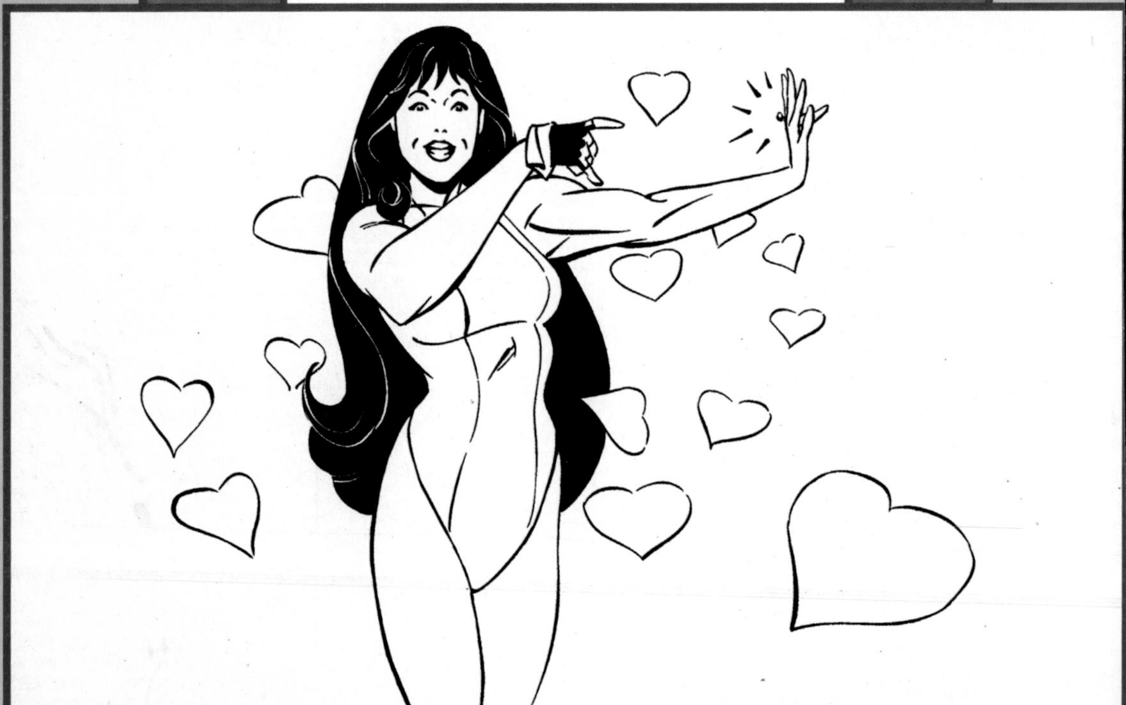